The Tomorrow Country

Gail Hamilton

High Shore Books

High Shore Books
www.ghamiltonwriter.com
Library and Archives Canada Cataloguing in Publication
Title: The tomorrow country / Gail Hamilton. Names: Hamilton, Gail, author. Description: Previously published: Demorestville, Ontario: Hamilton House, 2010. Identifiers: Canadiana (print) 20240404262 | Canadiana (ebook) 20240404319 | ISBN 9781988676029 (softcover) | ISBN 9781988676036 (EPUB) Subjects: LCGFT: Historical fiction. | LCGFT: Novels. Classification: LCC PS8565.A5354 T65 2024 | DDC C813/.54—dc23

This novel is a work of fiction. Any references to historical events, to real people, living or dead; or to real locales are intended only to give the fiction a sense of reality and authenticity. Other names, characters, places and incidents either are a product of the author's imagination or are used fictiously, and their resemblance, if any, to real-life counterparts is entirely coincidental.

Cover design by John Kicksee
Author photo by Paula Martin
Interior design by Nicolas Beron

ISBN 978-1-988676-03-6 E-book Version
ISBN 978-1-988676-02-9 Print Version

Second Edition 2024

To Margaret, Muriel, Madeleine, Rosalind, Rosemary,
Polly and Barb whose encouragement never failed.
And Bill and Peggy who made it all possible

Cast of Characters

Amelia Radmore Corman	A sheltered reformer determined to rescue abandoned children and send them to new lives in Canada.
Strawberry Rose	Dazzling musical sensation bent on adventure. Catching the eye of a royal rake she gets more adventure than she bargained for
Red Nell	Irish tinker transformed into a bizarre underworld force. Her weakness is fierce ambition for her daughter, Strawberry Rose
Adam Crisp	After ten years of exile in Canada he seeks revenge for the wrongs that sent him packing. He gives his heart unwisely and that is his undoing
Henry Crisp	Adam's wealthy, scheming younger brother. Obsessed by Rose, he lies in wait to spring his trap.
Louisa Crisp	Their mother desperately trying to social climb in a London society with no patience for clumsy provincial *nouveau riche*
Morton Jenks	Mean, larcenous overseer of the Infant's Asylum who suffers torments trying to force his nerve to match his greed
Mary	Slow-witted, much abused Asylum servant who protects Katie with her life.

The Children

Katie Abandoned newborn in a gutter, Katie is now a street child trying to survive in warrens where few reach their 20th birthday. Her only hope is Amelia.

Laura Pampered but illegitimate darling of an Elizabethan manor tossed upon charity by unscrupulous relatives.

Cully Rickety, abused survivor of a basket-making sweatshop. Eternally optimistic, passionately loyal.

Will Soot-stained climbing boy whose simple, honest devotion struggles to save Katie in her darkest hour.

ARE YOU PART OF THIS STORY?

You may have a secret history you don't suspect.

Between 1869 and the 1940s thousands of destitute, orphaned or abandoned youngsters in Britain were plucked from appalling conditions and sent overseas as Home Children. They toiled on lonely farms, battled ridicule and exploitation to become a precious part of their new land. Too often, they hid their difficult origins even from their own families. Yet Canada, alone, has almost four million descendants from these brave little immigrants.

Perhaps you are one of them. Find out more from the British Home Children groups working to restore hidden pasts.

The
Tomorrow
Country

CHAPTER ONE

"God in heaven, the child's...alive!"

The curate stood to his toe tops in London filth. His face turned grey. He wanted to faint.

He was only twenty-two and never before away from his sheep-raising village of Ayleham, Surrey. His round brown eyes were mild as a sheep's. Gusts jerked at his hopelessly old fashioned coat and tried snatch his hat, a hand down from the vicar. Only his cravat held firm, for the vicar's wife had tied it herself in the predawn rush to catch his train for Victoria Station.

His business had taken only an hour to conclude. Then how his innocent heart bounded. He was footloose for a day at the very core of the Empire. Widowed Queen Victoria owned a palace not a mile away. Soldiers with sunburnt, tropical faces talked of India and whistled through the streets. The Thames was jammed with ships disgorging mahogany and nutmeg and aromatic chests of Ceylon tea.

Such crowds! Such a din!

Vast stone porticoes yawned at him, guarded by doormen magnificent as pashas. Jewelled snuff boxes, ornate soup tureens, painted China mandarins winked gorgeously from shop windows His pulse stopped altogether when a street conjurer breathed a tongue of flame at the sky.

He had been afloat, bobbing and spinning on the glorious tide of London. It's heart-tide, the tide of the City, that ancient, unimaginably opulent square mile under the dome of St. Paul's where the spoils of an empire had been poured into white-fronted mansions, immense public buildings and the splendour of its bridges.

Then Great Ben struck noon.

The curate halted, cold inside. He'd been agog, credulous as a boy while Old Scratch laughed to see one more fool slide into the glittering trap.

He mustn't let the vicar find out how he'd squandered the morning!

God, in the form of the vicar, would grill him on his return. In the familiar, moss-grown church of Ayleham, farmers and good housewives learned that life was a constant skirmish with Satan. They might jerk from a fireside nap to battle for their souls. The vicar lived on this drama, growing gaunt and beetle-browed. When he discovered his stumbling curate must go to London, he had reared up from behind the vestry coat rack.

"Fleshpots jingling in golden harnesses! Pits of sin blacker than the Serpent's maw! You look and you take heed, my lad. Tis Babylon you're going to!"

With all Ayleham breathless for the tale, the curate could hardly say he'd gorged on treacle tarts and gaped at tumblers on the Strand.

Reluctantly, he turned from the lacquered carriages, the flags streaming in the smoky golden sunshine and set out to see for himself the foulness and misery gnawing the city's underbelly.

He hurried east past the Tower and, in his innocence, hired a half-crazed hag to guide him into districts tough sailors dared not go. She brought him down sweating alleys, past broken doors breathing excrement to this, a festering garbage heap oozing toward the Thames.

"Aye, it be!" she cackled contemptuously.

She had a draggle of dirt coloured hair, a verminous dress held together by pieces of twine and knobby bare feet hard as goat hoofs. A goaty smell permeated the air around her and she clutched the curate's coins under a ragged shawl.

Gin for a month if she didn't get knocked for it.

With her toe, she kicked at the lump of naked flesh still glistening with blood and mucus.

The lump flipped over, exhibiting limbs, frail as frog's legs, wavering close to a blue-tinged stomach sticking with horse dung. The stomach was attached to matchstick ribs, tiny shoulders and the disproportionately large head of the newborn.

The head flopped, pinched and death-like. Yet inside even so unpromising a dwelling, a human spirit rallied. Out belted a squall so indignant the curate jumped like a horse from a firecracker.

"A...baby," he sputtered as if he had never seen one before. "Who would leave a baby here!"

The colour drained from his lips and his neck and even from his fingers protruding from under his cuffs. He felt a whirling inside and knew the Devil had played him a horrid joke. How very far he felt from Ayleham, Surrey, where the height of depravity was knocking down gate posts on a drunken holiday night!

"Them as can't feed it. Pah!"

The crone aimed her toe at the wretched scrap again.

The curate slumped to the wall, noisily, violently ill.

For some moments, it looked as though he were going to continue his slide down the bricks as he clawed for some handhold in this twisted nether universe into which he had been flung. With a mighty effort, he forced himself erect, mild eyes blinking rapidly.

"It has to be...rescued! I...there must be somewhere for... surely..."

He looked from the woman to the infant and back again, whiskers aquiver.

His guide stepped on into the alley, anxious to show her charge the gin cellars and the gals packed on street corners hoping to make a few pennies for a roll. Smashing bit of luck, a gent like this. None came down this far for fear of getting their gizzards cut out and roasted on a stick!

The curate grasped at her shawl. The rotten fabric gave way. The woman's stick flew halfway to clouting him senseless. Every rag was precious. Cough yourself dead, you would, without some scrap to keep off the fog.

The curate fumbled out another coin. As a pie-faced boy, he had learned apology early and edged to his current station in life through an earnest desire to please. The woman snapped up the money. The curate's pockets and their contents were of consuming interest to her but she was too feeble to do other than take what he gave her and steer him clear of those who would empty his pockets by force.

The baby tried again to cry but succeeded only in a faint mewling sound. Its body had turned bluer with the cold. Its tongue protruded from dehydration.

"We must help this child at once!"

Scraps of his mission as God's servant, hitherto unreal, fluttered through his dismay. A fearful thrill clutched him. Why here, literally, was a lost lamb abandoned to the blast.

A lamb that he must save!

His companion shuffled toward the next corner. The curate grew more agitated.

"You must take this babe to a...a foundling home. I can't...I won't budge until it's done!"

He dared exert his rank, meagre as it was, over this degraded creature. Surely the infant should have been long dead. Yet here it was, hitching its froggy limbs, trying to suck nourishment from the very air, its frown unnervingly direct, its fierce grasping at life demanding a response.

"Come by t'river, sir. There be mud larks there, up to their hanks in t'mud, lookin' fer bits o'coal."

She promised to show where Bunty Dave got crushed between the barges, the bloodstains still on the decks. The curate only looked greener. Her lips curled in on toothless gums. Oh, oh, it was over! The miraculous luck of the curate's purse stolen by a worm squirming underfoot!

She scooped up the child.

"Take it then!" She jammed it into crook of the churchman's arm.

Curate Banning staggered, not from the weight, which was nothing, but from the shock of supporting another human life. His bachelor frame went rigid. His hands, which had never touched a baby before, fumbled and fluttered.

Then the reek of the gutter assaulted his nose. The small body began to slide from his grasp. His scalp tightened. A length of umbilical cord, chill and limp, had slapped across his wrist.

"Oh, no no! I didn't mean... I thought you would..."

Rising gorge choked him. He wanted to fling the thing and run. He shut his eyes and jerked his hand to the bare bottom to keep the child from plunging to the ground.

"Yourn tis," his guide rasped, shaking her matted locks.

All the bitterness of a life spent grubbing for crusts blazed into the woman's one good eye. She had got shut of half a dozen brats like this. Wished them dead and dead they were as this one ought to be.

The curate started to tremble in earnest.

"Please, I beg you, take the child."

The rescue of souls had heretofore been a spiritual matter. He was gagging, certain he could not hold his burden one moment longer. The whites of his eyes threw a fright into the woman.

"Oh, no. Not with them officers!"

She was having no dealings with officers. Not her. They'd steal her coin and her shawl. Put her in the workhouse where there was no drink and she'd die of the shakes.

"Then pray return some money."

Even her bad eye widened. In a ragged blur, she bolted from sight.

"Wait," bleated the curate. "Oh, please...wait!"

Alone in the wilderness of stained brick, overhanging roofs, and glistening, revolting footways, the young man panicked. His guide had vanished like a rat down its sewer. He slammed up against a broken wall, his feet deep in sodden ash.

He was forced to grab the infant's leg to keep it from falling. The leg was as horrid as its bottom yet also firm and slightly warm under his grip. Renewed astonishment struck him.

This flicker of life really would exist or perish at his whim!

Satan smoked at his elbow, sulphurous and wily.

"No one will ever know," whispered the Tempter. "Go away and never think of this again."

The gaunt little abdomen quivered trying to cry, presenting Banning with the first raw fact of life he had ever encountered. It threw into livid reality the religious pap of a lifetime. The umbilical cord had been raggedly slashed. Below it flowered tiny female genitals.

When the curate realized what he was looking at, a wave of scalding heat engulfed him. He had been brought up to believe ladies scarcely had legs, never mind...private parts. Pulling off his coat, he rolled the child into its folds and sped off in search of help.

The area, like nearly all the East End, had been thrown up hastily and meanly to house the burgeoning poor of the Industrial Revolution. The population of London had reached a million by eighteen hundred. Then, even as the city fathers were crying out was there no end to starving Irish, displaced weavers, ambitious pedlars and runaway farm wenches, the number doubled and tripled and quadrupled. The tide inundated a city whose rudimentary government could not cope with the dizzying, unimaginable change to a modern world. Amidst the conflicting and jealous multitude of autonomous districts and civil parishes, no one had responsibility for the regulation of housing, drains, disease control, labour practices or even provision of drinkable water.

Consequently, its houses of bad brick and ersatz plaster needed only the London dampness, grime and clogged gutters to crumble at once into the worst of slums. The curate stood surrounded by blackened courts, sinister dead-ends and tortuous lanes, some hardly more than a yard wide. The barred, decaying windows were shuttered yet there was to it all a sense of universal breathing, of eyes peering out of slits in doors and of underlying danger.

Banning bumped off sudden walls, backed out of exitless courts until he stumbled onto a wider thoroughfare. A few low shops broke the monotony.

The first adults the curate saw lounged about an open door spilling drunken song. Gratefully, he panted up.

"Please," he begged between breaths, "could any of you gentlemen kindly direct me to a...a charity institution?"

Gentleman was about the last description that applied to the gathered rag tag. Some were boys, with bare shins exposed and streaked faces. Some were men hulking under badly fitted shirts, some had the sunken, blue-veined faces that indicated the depredations of drink. All were pinched and filthy, including the scattering of mat-haired women who fixed the curate with sharp, widened eyes.

Silence fell. The group had been struck dumb by civility of speech coupled with the appearance of a respectable waistcoat and white shirt amidst the surrounding dirt. The spectacle of the noxious infant wrapped in an unpatched coat capped their astonishment.

The curate found himself encircled by wolfish faces showing up scars and ruined eyes and sagging flesh. Feet shifted in the gutters, softly squinching.

The curate, at last, sensed menace, perceived dimly in terms of certain big boys who had tormented his childhood rather than in the more definite possibility of being knocked senseless and stripped in the alleyway for the money in his pocket and the wealth his clothes represented pawned and transformed into gin.

Oh, dear me, he thought, putting his predicament into the strongest terms he was able. A quarrel he couldn't see was going on in the gin cellar and he had interrupted the amusement of the watchers. Something crashed, followed by a high female squalling. Banning jumped, unaware that women could make such a sound.

"Please, a foundling home. The poor child must have help straightaway."

Though he had heard much of foundling homes, he had never actually seen one. In his village, all children, no matter how questionable of origin, had hearths to take them in.

Perhaps it was the shining trust on his face. Perhaps it was the novel sight of a man holding a newborn child as though it were exceedingly precious and also hot as a clinker. Perhaps it was his own air of poverty, clean and careful, but poverty nevertheless. Whatever caused his luck, the curate failed to spark the savage instincts just under the surface.

The largest man began to grin.

"A foundlin' 'ome! Ha ha, lads. If I knowed a foundlin' 'ome, I'd get into it meself."

His companions guffawed. The faces came closer, exhaling oniony breath.

"Please, surely...."

A shriek from the gin cellar brought the big man round.

Let 'im 'ave it, Moll," he bellowed encouragingly. "Bash 'is noggin. We'll stand you a pint!"

The rest feinted with their fists as though cheering a dogfight though their eyes were still on the curate. A boy began waving a white linen handkerchief which Banning realized had been picked from his own pocket.

His mouth flew open but a few grains of sense squelched his protest. He backed away, as from a pack of mastiffs, then took to his heels in dread lest the men hound after him.

They preferred the gin cellar, perhaps because the gin cellar was their only spot of gaiety in that sea of desolation, crime and disease. Belatedly, hair-raising tales of footpads and murderers galloped into the curate's head.

Sacred Jehosepat! They could find him dead against a rain barrel with his liver sliced out!

As he tried to decide between the terrors of the crooked lane he was in and those of the populated thoroughfare, a female shape glided to his elbow and spoke a proposition so irregular it took some moments before the curate could make sense of it. Fiery embarrassment consumed the roots of his hair.

He tried to flee, but another woman was clamped to his sleeve.

"Ere," scolded the first, "'e's mine. I sees 'im first. Such a nice gintleman. 'E'll give me money for me lodgin'."

"NO!" gasped the clergyman, shuddering to his heels. "Oh, no, no, NO!"

Mrs. Warren would swoon onto her tea tray. And the vicar... oh, if the vicar found out he had fallen into the grip of fleshpots and wantons...

"See, 'e don't want you. It's me. I'm ever so much more fun. Come over 'ere with me, luv."

The creature was actually bridling and prancing before him, thin as a broom, rudely contradicting the curate's conviction that fleshpots were voluptuous as parlour cushions and glittering all over with vain ornament. He broke free. Unbelievingly, he saw the two women shove each other for the right to drag him into a doorway.

"Wait," he cried. "Take me to a foundling home and I'll give a shilling to each of you!"

The fight stopped as though a pistol had been fired.

"A bob!" croaked the small one, suspicious and incredulous.

"Yes, yes, for each," he promised dizzily. "Just take me to shelter for this child."

The women exchanged a silent communication. The news that the curate had at least two shillings on him put him in danger of physical attack. Only fears that the uproar would bring the men to snatch the booty kept the women from executing the scheme. Together, they turned and tramped off down the alley, the curate trotting urgently behind.

Whether the streets improved or not, the curate couldn't tell, so preoccupied was he with keeping up to his guides. He splashed through fetid puddles and twice stubbed his toe on prostrate hulks that uttered human cries. Finally, they stopped before a sooty brick building with barred windows and a stout, forbidding doorway.

"What is it?"

Silently, the women pointed to a small, neatly painted sign that read, Infants' Asylum. Banning made for the knocker. The females blocked his way. He saw with surprise that they could not yet be fifteen. They closely resembled the undernourished alley cats foraging feverishly while trying to avoid being eaten themselves by the hungry human population.

"Our bob!"

"First let me make sure...."

"Now!"

Awkwardly, the curate fished out the exorbitant amount and had it snatched before he could open his fingers. Two pairs of eyes ran over him avidly but again had to abandon outright robbery.

Before he could speak, they were gone.

CHAPTER TWO

Banning pounded on the door of a building that appeared fortified against the streets around it. The infant had not uttered a sound or perhaps breathed for some time. When the door opened a crack, revealing a rough-boned face, he thrust the coat forward.

"I've a child for shelter. Poor creature. I found it in a muck heap by the river."

Morton Jenks, the warden, squinted downward.

"We want no such here. It's not alive."

"It is, it is. Look!"

Banning poked a flaccid little shoulder. The child obliged with a hiccough that hitched its bosom.

"We're full!"

Mr. Jenks wanted no puling brat that would die on his hands and have to be disposed of out of Asylum funds. No percentage in that any more. Not since do-gooding Miss Amelia Radmore had got her embroidered gloves on the place.

Curate Banning was so astonished his inborn timidity fled.

"You can't refuse a babe in need! You dare not. In the name of the Lord," he added, invoking the deity whose attention he had spent his life trying to avoid.

Mr. Jenks let out a rusty laugh, showing the cavernous back of his mouth and several large teeth. He was a big man and filled the doorway like a wall.

"I've turned away crowds, my lad. We'd have hundreds here if we let in free entry. We take only what Miss Radmore chooses worthy. So get away!"

He started to swing the door shut. Banning thrust himself frantically into the opening.

"In the name of charity, man! In the name of..."

Blindly, he grasped at every stiff-necked moral platitude the vicar had droned out. Their dryness vanished, their glowing hearts began to shine like beacons amidst the fearful blackness all around.

For the first time, the curate's callow face burned with conviction. Unknowingly, he pushed himself to the brink of private heroism.

A bulwark against the tide of misery washing at the door, Mr. Jenks stood unmoved. His lips closed like a sealed purse. His brushy brows lifted in ridicule. His pride, the great moustache that stood out under his nose, twitched rudely while his balding head seemed to symbolize the scant succour here.

This was a neighbourhood where four out of five did not survive their infancy. Those who did often dearly regretted their luck. This was the first time the curate had met the hardened face of professional charity and saw there was there was only one way.

"Well, I'll pay!"

He pulled from his pocket the reason for this one and only visit to wicked London, the several pounds inheritance willed to him by his great uncle Matthew. Had the people of an hour earlier caught an inkling of its existence, his body would already have been floating face down in the Thames.

The warden's jaw dropped open like a hungry mutt sighting a roast. Brass! A regular sodding windfall! Imagine, a church mouse with that sort of cash!

Mr. Jenks' manner changed abruptly. His freckled eyelids lowered, hiding his excitement. A box for the brat would only cost a pittance. He would keep the rest for himself.

"Well, that's different. We takes good care of infants that come supported, like."

He released the door and held out his arms for the baby. The curate was, with immense relief, about to hand it over when a cold gleam in the man's eye stopped him. In the last few hours he had received a short, rude education about the underside of human nature. He stood, irresolute.

"Now, now, what's the matter here?"

A voice abrim with soothing cheer chimed out from behind Mr. Jenks. A woman rolled into sight, beaming with round ruddy cheeks and small, twinkling, very black eyes. She resembled nothing so much as a collection of warm muffins all bound together by an apron string. Her calico dress majestically draped the various independently moving mounds of her. For one so large, her step was peculiarly soft, stealthy. Mr. Jenks swung round. With a pained, half furious expression, he made room for his wife.

"A gentleman with an infant for us, my dear. That's willing to give us something toward its support."

A questioning, significant glance passed between the couple then flicked to the notes clutched in the curate's fist. An avid frisson rippled Ida's flesh. She burst into the sunniest of smiles, her arms thrust out.

Well, well, give us the little darlin' then."

Banning hesitated but the woman emitted such a storm of motherliness that the money and the child were in her embrace before he knew what had happened. Stoutly resisting Mr. Jenks' attempts to close the door on him, he followed the child inside.

"I want to see it dressed and...fed," he declared stubbornly.

A nagging uneasiness drove him to stay. An uneasiness well justified. This same Ida Jenks was a notorious baby farmer. That is, she discreetly undertook the care of children whose existence embarrassed their progenitors. Transactions took place late at night with muffled figures who alighted from cabs. Furtively, a wailing bundle would be handed over along with a sum of money related in size to the social position of the transactor and their desperation to jettison damning evidence of adultery, seduction, rape or idiot genes in the family. The radiant maternal warmth of Ida Jenks salved tortured consciences. Within its first month, the child could be relied upon to die of whooping cough, fever or failure to breathe in the cradle.

Ida was an artist at her trade.

Unfortunately, Ida had no head for business even though she proved an invaluable resource for certain well-connected gentlemen of the criminal persuasion. Each region of London had its underworld force. These self-made despots struggled for power and territory as savagely as any congregation of sharks at a kill. Ida had worked under the sway of one Teapot, a sallow ruffian with the face and instincts of a moray eel. He demanded endless "tea" for his pot and broke the fingers, then the necks of those who failed to contribute.

Deciding that Ida needed close supervision, Teapot settled upon Morton Jenks, a discontented, meanly ambitious Southwark verger who had exhibited a talent for numbers by trying to cheat at Teapot's betting games. Morton was brought to heel by two bully boys in an alley, then offered a position as Ida's loving husband. Since the other choice was the Thames, Morton and Ida were married forthwith. Too late, Jenks realized what he had been saddled with.

Ida was addicted to infanticide and also quite mad.

"Oh, look at its sweetums wee face," cooed Ida. "Just look."

Her eyes took on the dreaminess Jenks knew well. Thank bloody Christ here was one brat whose demise no one would question. That would get the need out of Ida's system for months of peace to come.

The curate stood waiting for action. Mr. Jenks carefully pocketed the money, then bellowed over his shoulder.

"Mary! Get out here at once!"

The shadow that scurried out of the back appeared to be an old woman until the curate was astonished to see a fresh face of about fourteen attached to the bent, humped shape. The features, vigorously scrubbed, were plain and heavy as half risen dough with the thickened brow that proclaimed slow wits. Brown hair was pulled into a scanty knot at the back of her head. A full fronted apron was tied about her, so close under the chin because of her hump as to give the impression of a vast bib meant to shroud her deficiencies.

"Take this infant and clean it and feed it," Mr. Jenks commanded. "And look smart about it."

Mary opened her eyes very wide. Blue eyes, they were, the only pretty, lively part of her.

"Oh, has Miss Radmore...."

"Ask no questions! We're taking this one in. You, my girl, are charged with its care. If there's trouble, the trouble will be all yours, I guarantee!"

This was for the curate's benefit. Mary flinched slightly, as if from habit, then hurried, with her curious gait, to take charge of the coat.

"Oh," she breathed when she caught sight of its contents, "Oh, oh my!"

Mr. Jenks gestured toward the door, expecting the curate to leave, but the young man insinuated himself fully into the room. He felt much braver now that the child was out of his arms.

He found himself in a large low chamber lit mostly by a parsimonious fire burning in a large grate. The floor was stone, scrubbed to its grain, grey and clammy. The walls were white washed. A few pieces of heavy furniture sat about, their bulk contrasting oddly with a row of tiny chairs at the far end, rigidly aligned as conscript soldiers. The cleanliness and order was so welcome after the reeking streets that the curate drank it in gratefully before he noticed that it was of the carbolic, threatening kind surpassing anything even the vicar's wife could produce.

The building was, in fact, an old converted soap works and the fireplace one of those formerly used to boil cauldrons of fat and lye. Upstairs, some thirty infants and toddlers were asleep in rows. All were dosed with Godfrey's cordial, an opium mixture heavily used among the poor to keep their children unconscious in unattended rooms until the parents could struggle home at night. The downstairs, besides this main room, contained the quarters of the Jenks. In the cellar was a cramped steaming kitchen. Mary slept on a bench under the stairs.

Mary retrieved a basin from the passageway and filled it from a water jug. As she did so, sudden chimes sounded the hour. Curate Banning was startled to see, against the rough plaster, an incongruously ornate clock of carved walnut with a filigreed face and a free standing skeletal figure, presumably Father Time, swing a scythe at the room.

"Ah, that's our timepiece," supplied Mr. Jenks piously. "Given here from a fine house, it is, to make the little children think upon their souls."

Mary unwrapped the infant. With surprising skill, she washed off the dried mucus of birth and the ashy street filth which floated free in the water.

The curate watched her with half appalled fascination. Her entire back curved as if a giant hand had squeezed it. In the middle, the tortured vertebrae showed through the fabric of her dress in a row of blunt, erratic knobs. Her walk was a curious shuffle and her chest a concave shadow between her forward pointing shoulders, one of which dropped lower than the other, looking viciously dragged down.

Jenks nodded towards her.

"Out of the mines up north, she is. Hauled carts of coal up the tunnels till her back got turned down like that. Ain't supposed to be girls in the pits these days but lots are made to go down on the sly. Especially the old pits, back of the hills, as can't afford machinery. Ran away, finally, and found her way here to work. Miss Radmore takes particular interest in her. How's that for luck!"

"Who is Miss Radmore," the curate inquired, not taking his eye from the baby.

"Why, our benefactress," Mr. Jenks bobbed his head automatically. "Miss Radmore sent the clock down special as well as a good many of the other bits and pieces you see about. She oversees the money to support the little ones. I'll make the child right with her," he added, dropping a confidential wink.

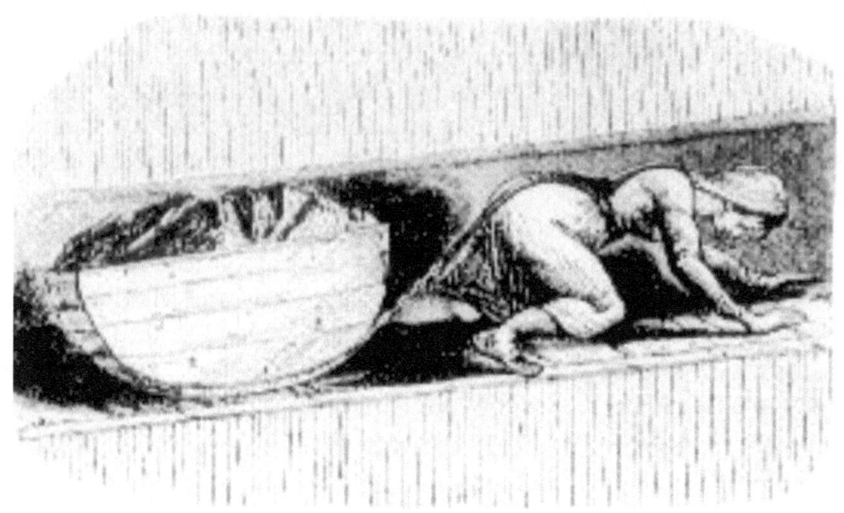

Dragging carts of coal to the surface.

Though Jenks detested Amelia Radmore heartily, he was tied to her like a blind pig for as long as she deigned to keep her hand in. It was either work with the charity lady or take a cutthroat's chance with the gallows. The very idea drowned Mr. Jenks in oily rivulets of sweat.

He had neglected Ida, that's what did it.

In his own devious way, he revolted against the yoke Teapot clapped on him. Morton Jenks yearned for a quick fortune without recourse to hard honest toil. Hard honest toil was for fools. Hard honest toil got a fellow nothing but starvation and an early grave as any glance at the labouring class made plain. A sly, quick hand in the pocket of another, that was how one got one's brass as far as Jenks could see. So he writhed with a continual torment of greed, constantly frustrated by his own limited imagination and a chronic weakness of nerve.

His job had been to handle the money, arrange the transfer of children, keep Ida discreet and see the little corpses respectably buried with nary a hint of their real fate. All this for a pittance while pounds and pounds flowed through his hands to Teapot.

He began extracting small sums, thinking they'd never be missed. This led to accepting babies Teapot didn't refer, including one from a well-to-do lady who had actually thought Ida a reputable nurse. When that child died, the woman had roared in, coppers in tow, shrieking at the top of her lungs. The coppers tore the place apart. Jenks escaped charges by a margin so fine his knees still turned to barley water thinking about it.

Teapot did not take kindly to this lapse, especially since the trail led directly to him. Teapot's toughs were in the very act of slashing up Jenks' ears and kicking in his ribs when they were put to flight by new toughs swarming over the neighbourhood. Jenks scuttled home and cowered there. He was tacking his own ears back together with sticking plasters when a new bully shouldered through the door.

"You needn't turn such a shade of mushroom, Mr. Jenks," the fellow informed him cheerily. "I just come to tell you this here turf is now owned by Red Nell."

"A..."

Jenks almost gasped out "woman" in spite of his terror of this man's great shoulders and blunt, muscular hands. A different species from the brutes employed by Teapot. Sharper looking, with much too purposeful eyes.

The fellow grinned. "Aye, a woman. And one you'll have no wish to cross. She grinds up those that cross her into farthing pieces and tosses 'em down drains to feed the rats."

Jenks turned even greyer. His visitor flexed his powerful fingers.

"Red Nell knows what you've been up to, Mr. Jenks, and thinks you right proper bait for the gallows. But if you is willing to do something for little orphans, well, Red Nell might overlook your shortcomings. Seeing as you have orphans ready at hand, that is. Red Nell might hatch you a jolly surprise."

That was how Jenks learned that Red Nell and her henchmen had snatched the territory around the Asylum from Teapot in a swift, warlike coup. Instantly, Red Nell imposed her own regime, well organized and subtle but iron nevertheless. She remained mysterious and frightening. Jenks only glimpsed her looking out through the blinds of the hansom cab in which she made her rounds. Irish, she was, with a broad, flat face under screaming masses of henna red hair and the fantastic hats that were her trademark.

To meet her hooded green eyes directly was to feel the hairs the back of the neck stand up in cold alarm.

With tentacles that must have extended into the most un-expected places, Red Nell produced Amelia Radmore, a wealthy and earnest young lady determined to aid the "deserving poor". Jenks found himself set up as warden of a foundling home, with Miss Radmore as patron. His work was to bilk this unsuspecting do-gooder of a suitable sum each month.

"And remember," Red Nell's deputy rapped out, "if you falls short, why Red Nell has certain connections with the constabulary that could make it uncomfortable for you, especially about the neck."

Trapped once again, and by a woman, no less. Jenks had seethed. Blackmail it was, to be stuck with a houseful of drooling brats, to actually have to protect them and raise them. Oh, a humiliation scarcely to be tolerated.

He'd almost prefer the blows of Teapot's thugs.

Without recourse, Mr. and Mrs. Jenks settled in as proprietors of the Infant's Asylum. It became one more penny-pinching charity with each infant to be accounted for to the troublesomely officious Miss Radmore. Every month she appeared in a heavy family coach to look wisely at the books and make up new rules for the benefit of the children.

Fearful economies and deceits had to be resorted to in order to scrape up the regular tribute. Red Nell's idea of a joke, Jenks supposed. Restraint had worked until Curate Banning showed up at the door. Now here was a rural puppy with money in his hand and an unowned foundling about to die of it's own accord.

Temptation was simply too alluring to withstand.

Mr. Jenks thought of the tiny hoard of skimmings he had already begun. He licked his lips while the curate watched Mary produce a bottle to which was attached a thick, much-gnawed nipple. The bottle was filled with a weak-looking mixture of water and milk to which sugar was added. Mr. Jenks shifted from foot to foot in fear that the baby would expire before their eyes and the visitor demand his money back.

To the amazement of all, the infant emerged from the bath faintly rosy.

Forgetting that the baby was naked, the curate leaned forward as Mary dribbled liquid into the child's throat. Instead of choking, the throat worked and the chest began to heave in a renewed tumult for survival. When the nipple was tried, the small mouth clamped around it, struggling after the milk with an almost disconcerting ferocity of spirit.

In the firelight, a delicate fringe of hair fluffed as it dried over the round little skull. The lumpy face of the newborn had smoothed into an expression of intense concentration. After some erratic suckling, the tiny fists waved as if in jubilation.

The thread of life, shredded down to its last strand, had been miraculously knit up again.

The curate so far forgot modesty as to assume the tiny fists waved gratefully to him. Exultant warmth bloomed inside. Recklessly, he imagined himself and the Good Samaritan colleagues in the matter.

He had given the child its life.

In return, the child had granted him a gift beyond his own humble powers of estimation.

The gift of simple courage.

Looking from Mrs. Jenks, the very picture of maternal solicitude, to Mary, her misshapen outlines softened by the baby in her lap, the curate released a breath full of trusting happiness and took his leave.

Instantly, civility vanished. Mr. Jenks bolted the door and turned back to Mary.

"That's enough coddling. Put the brat down and get on with your jobs."

Rousing a little out of her stolidity, Mary pulled the baby closer to her breast. "It ain't had enough ter eat yet. It 's got ter have more or t'won't live."

She spoke slowly, with an awkwardness that always irritated Mr. Jenks. They employed her because she would work twenty-four hours out of the day and was considered too dim-witted to notice Ida's tricks.

Now, contrarily, she dropped her head and kept on feeding the baby.

"Put it down!"

Mary's blue eyes flew wide at the menace in Mr. Jenks' voice. She could feel the baby moving against her, wanting to butt the bottle like a hungry lamb.

Oh shame! And the tyke such a fighter too!

Stubbornly, her head sank lower yet over her concave chest. Mr. Jenks pulled his jaws together, took a single step and clouted Mary on the side of the head.

The blow knocked the girl off the stool onto the floor. She slid sideways, flinging out one arm to save herself, barely managing to keep hold of the child with the other. The bottle clattered across the flagstones. The baby set up a wail. Ida twitched musingly, her eye fixed on the child.

"Get along with you, I said," growled Mr. Jenks, looming up.

For a moment, Mary cowered then lifted herself half up. She was a plodding creature who had borne much in life. Her childhood had been crushed and her mind narrowed but inside her resided a spirit that the trials of her existence had not been able to extinguish.

To be sure, it was a slow spirit, and blind. It had taken the ruin of her body and near death from maltreatment in the mines to finally rouse it and prompt Mary to plunge away over the dark moors in search of respite.

Yet once quickened, it could never forget the lesson. It lay like a clumsy beast, no longer unconscious, but only asleep.

This blow, as so many others had not, jarred it awake. Instantly, it fastened itself upon the child.

"I seen the money that gintlemun give you! I seen how much!" Mary declared, in her thick North Country accent. "For this tyke tis and not yer own pockets. Soon's Miss Radmore comes, I'm agoin' ter tell so's she can put it down in the book."

Mr. Jenks halted as though the doorpost had threatened him. It was the longest speech he had ever heard from Mary. He was astounded at how much she understood.

And, damn it, how had she seen the cash!

"I'll see you out on the streets where you belong, Miss Humpback. You'd starve in a week!"

Mary tucked the baby tighter against her side. The tiny warm thing felt as if it were burrowing into her. Her head drew in against the expected blow but her eyes didn't waver.

"Miss Radmore'd see me by the door," she answered, taking his threat literally and announcing her own equally literal plan. She would, indeed, sit by the door until Miss Radmore visited, even if it took three months and Jenks knew it.

Jenks let out a choking exclamation and swung his big fist. Mary drew swiftly back and curled herself into a ball about the baby. It was clear no physical violence could budge her. She'd known all there was to know of that down in the mine.

Jenks stood over her, breathing heavily.

Oh, to flatten this misshapen toad. Kick her into the gutter to beg and starve! But then he'd have to explain her absence to Miss

Radmore who had fixed upon Mary as her especial pet. Amelia Radmore would not take quietly to Mary's disappearance.

Damnation!

Greed and fear fought out a gritty battle in his breast. The curate's money lay in his hand, enough, with what he was laying by, to make his escape in two or three year's time. A pub! That's what he dreamed of. A nice dark pub where he could fix bets and skim the wages of working men. In Birmingham or even Glasgow. Some northern city where Red Nell's clutches surely didn't stretch. He'd make a run for it, jettisoning Ida and the brats like chaff in the wind.

However, he was not fool enough to run without money. Weren't there enough broken down tramps and famished labourers to prove the pitfalls of that. He had to hang onto the money. But if Red Nell found him holding out on a nice plum like this...

Cold droplets started up on Jenks' forehead. Red Nell made iron bargains and was terrible when crossed. The most feared punishment was Red Nell's embrace, a piece of ship's hawser twisted until the ribs collapsed, making the victim appear to have died from a crushing hug. No one could say Red Nell lacked a sense of humour.

Jenks' eyes bulged as he felt the rope already tightening. Now that this moon calf had noticed the money, how could it be kept secret! There were always the constables, ready to take an interest in Ida's past if Red Nell egged them on.

No, no! Better to virtuously pass the money to Amelia Radmore. At least, he'd have a chance to cheat a good deal of it back. He ran a violent hand over his skull and glowered at Mary.

"I'll see to you later! Come along Ida!"

He was perspiring again under his collar. Ida had fixed herself on the brat and, blast it, how was he going to keep the woman from her games!

They left Mary sprawled in the firelight, frozen with astonishment. For the first time in her life, she had scored a victory. Stunned, she retrieved the bottle, hoisted herself back onto the stool and commenced feeding the baby again.

A girl-of-all-work, Mary laboured as a matter of course from before dawn to far into the night, receiving only her meagre keep and a kindly pat from this new Miss Radmore. Mary worked without expression, for the pit had hammered all emotion out of her save what it took to keep on living. Mary's face, like her rigid body, never changed. She hoarded only two things to her bosom; those light, smiling touches of Amelia and the memory that once, long ago before the mines, she'd had a mother of her own.

Perhaps these humble treasures had worked more life back into her than she knew. The stinging welt on the side of her face burned all the way through her body. Her inner self, stirred with such difficulty, showed no inclination to subside. Never had Mary seen a baby so frail and weak and yet so ravenous for life. It suckled noisily, often losing the nipple, often pausing to gather strength for its next onslaught where many a stronger infant simply shut its eyes and died. If there was anything Mary admired, it was tenacity.

And I saved yer, she thought in a rush. *Me!*

The wonderment bloomed through her slow mind, like a brilliant flower unfurling on previously dark and sterile ground. Her eyebrows lifted higher and wider apart as if the idea were physically forcing itself between them that she, humpbacked Mary, had done this thing. The bruise on her cheek rang like a battle scar.

For several minutes, she sat just looking down at the fluff of hair and the eyes shut tight while it fed. After a moment, a new, unheard-of sound issued from her.

Mary began to hum.

To hum very softly over the small head cradled against her an old North Country lullaby, shaky at first, and in fragments, but growing stronger as the dim, nearly lost notes crept back. Out of her hard, unloved life, the first seeking tendril of devotion curled toward the child, a tendril that promised to grow into a protecting vine so tough that only grim death would be strong enough to tear it away again.

Far away and a great many hours later, Curate Banning beheld the sunset from the jouncing back of a turnip cart. His impulsive gift had not even left him the price of a railway ticket, forcing him to hitch rides on passing wagons and to walk in between. His feet were blistered inside his ruined footwear and his young body fearfully jolted from the rude conveyances he had flagged down. He was exhausted and disheveled almost beyond recognition. At the village, the wrath of his vicar awaited him, for Banning's inheritance, so impetuously given away, had been pledged to the missionary fund.

Another time the young man would have quaked with trepidation and despair. Today, fear of the vicar strangely failed to move him. When rain began at the crossroads and he was again put down to walk, he turned to gaze at the sooty haze of London staining the horizon.

His breast puffed out. Striding homeward, he began to grin.

"Onward to Jerusalem," he belted out, bursting into a joyful hymn.

At long, long last, he felt a worthy soldier in the armies of the Lord!

CHAPTER THREE

"Ask him again, nice and slow, what did he do with the bairn!"

The gravelly lilting Irish was so strong any casual listener would have been hard put to make out the words. Everyone in the room understood it well, especially the unfortunate suspended by his elbows between the two men just inside the door. The prisoner, in contrast to the brawn holding him, was of the nervous, weedy type whose legs had windmilled as he was carried up the stairs. Wicky was his name, for he was thin as a candlewick and just as flexible when it came to hire for a furtive, nasty job.

Wicky, snatched from his regular business of robbing drunks, ran his mind frantically over all his recent peccadilloes. This could be just a novel way of procuring his services, meagre as they were, though the thunderous faces of his companions boded otherwise. One was a heavy-shouldered, black-haired man barely able to restrain himself from crushing Wicky's arm. The other, slimmer and handsomer, was just as tenacious for all his affected curls and flash coat of mustard stripes.

Lifted bodily up the stairs, Wicky thrashed in earnest, prudently fearing narrow places and scowling blokes he wasn't acquainted with. When they emerged into the chamber above, he stopped kicking, struck into immobility.

Mirrors was his first thought. Gor blimey! Like a Haymarket bawdy house."

There were only two pier glasses, mismatched and facing each other. Wicky saw himself multiplied into a swarm of struggling captives in a low, wide room full of dusky, fearful corners and a strange earthen smell that unsettled his London-born nostrils.

Over the battered floor a gaudy burgundy carpet was flung, splotched with yellow cabbage roses. A gas chandelier with ornate peach globes hung grandly but unlit from the pitted ceiling. The single window was sealed by green velvet drapery weighed down by shredded gold fringe. A picture, framed in chipped gilt, of a craggy seashore, leaned against the drape. From atop an empty mahogany whatnot, a large china Toby jug grinned jovially at the bright fire in the hearth. These furnishings, kept with pride of possession and not much awareness of their use, betrayed not only a love of rioting colour but added, against the cracked plaster and unpainted board, a carnival gaiety to the room.

Then Wicky made out the seated figure in front of the firelight. His legs sagged altogether. He wasn't wanted for his services here. Oh no! Not a fellow who picked up his brass doing odd jobs for Teapot, mortal enemy of the woman before him, Red Nell.

Despite the jumbled opulence of the room, there was only one chair. He stood at a disadvantage before Nell. Her seat, with thrusting arms and looming back, gave the impression of a throne.

Nell had not been looking at Wicky. She leaned toward a pot suspended by a hook over the fire, stirring it meditatively. The soft, homey burbling of the contents was wildly incongruous with the raw force emanating from the nearly motionless figure. Without moving, she seemed to pounce. A sense of claws and rending shook Wicky as his captors set him down on his own two feet.

Nell's body was an imposing pyramid of solid, muscular flesh that had never known a corset. Stout boots, ready for a country road, peeped out from series of coloured petticoats under a skirt of green and yellow plaid. From the waist up, Nell wore a loose scarlet jacket with frogging inherited from a military gentleman who had got the worst of some long forgotten fight.

The stiff masses of Nell's hair were once the carrot red that had given her her name. Now their vividness was thanks to raw henna imparting a frightening purple-orange shade never seen on natural tresses.

The hair was crowned by a hat, emphatic as a battle flag. Today canary straw quivering with bunches of red and white artificial cherries.

Nell craved and coveted hats, a legacy of the days when, newly arrived and starving, she had been abused in the streets, not knowing hatlessness, in London, was the certain sign of prostitution. Now she owned dozens. The way to preface a plea, propose a deal, or just plain fawn, was to send Red Nell a hat.

Some were pitiful home made scoops with nary a ribbon. Some were lavish turrets of satin and peacock feathers, otter tails and lacquered birds' nests no mortal head could support. Nell displayed them on a row of pegs in a rainbow band about the walls, adding the fantastic air of a pedlar's wagon loaded to go. The hats were emblems of the growing numbers suing for her favour.

Yet no petitioner was foolish enough to think Nell distracted by a gewgaw. A bargain made, was a bargain kept, or the transgressor was apt to be found against an alley wall, dead of the rope's embrace.

"I ain't never seen no baby," Wicky cried, so fogged by fear that he truly believed he hadn't. He tried not to look at the pier glasses where Red Nell's image was repeated, a madly helmeted Amazon troop poised to strike.

Red Nell gave the pot another stir. She was well aware of the effect of the mirrors. She had learned a great many tricks during her slashing conquest of the neighbourhood.

Power, only power, was what counted.

"Try to remember," she grated, her voice so loaded with menace that Wicky's bladder flinched.

Nell's wide jaw, beaky nose and high pale brow attested that she had not been beautiful in her youth. She had never given beauty a thought for she possessed something more potent: a vital, compelling force that drew people naturally to her and bent them to her will. In those careless, far off days, she'd spun her magnetism laughingly about the campfire to snap up Big Flann as a husband and have her babies, one a year, in the snugness of her wagon while Flann traded horses, lifted rabbits and worked sporadically at the harvest.

They had been wandering Irish tinkers then, not worrying about tomorrow's breakfast. That was before hunger, death and treachery had shown her where her real gifts lay and concentrated them into a terrifying force. All her formidable intensity looked out at Wicky in her unblinking gaze.

"I never seen no baby! I never!" he protested again, even as his memory flared luridly with the night, weeks ago. Gaffer Stury, in Teapot's employ, had whistled him into a dark doorway and handed over an incredible ten shillings.

"Got a bit o' trash 'ere, Wicky. Toss it where it won't trouble us no more. In the drink, if you know wot I mean."

He'd been handed a woman's shawl with a brat inside it, newborn and proper sickening with slime.

Oh ho, thought Wicky, old Gaff's fancy woman's got herself into a mess then. He's chucking the evidence.

Wicky asked no questions. Gaff was touchy with a blade. Besides, this sort of job was common enough with thousands trying to rid themselves of mouths they couldn't feed. The Thames regularly washed out to sea its dross of infant corpses. Many's the poor, exhausted drudge that breathed the lighter for it.

Wicky had hurried through the night, as familiar with the byways as any scavenger rat. His fingers tested the shawl, surprised to find it heavy embossed silk, far beyond anything Gaff's woman might be expected to own. Prigged from a real toff it must have been. Not a hole in it that Wicky could make out.

Greedily calculating its worth, he stopped short of the Thames. Why risk tossing the brat in the water when the cold would kill it in a minute anyway. Unrolling the infant into the muck, he skittered off to a woman who paid cash for flash shawls and wasn't queasy about the stains. Wicky had supposed himself a clever lad and thought no more about the incident.

Until today.

Nell's broad bosom heaved once. Never give anything away, never rely on any but your own. Only her own were there in the room. Joe Varden, and Sparley Dan, her sons both.

Lying! Lying! Lying! she thought furiously. He's murdered Gwyn's baby, plain as the warts on his face.

Aye, and Teapot murdered Gwyn, let her die in childbed and left her stiff for me to find. Gwyn, straight as a moorland rush, the very one I was training up, the only one with wits enough to take her place by me.

And wits to be contrary too.

Nell pushed the thought of their struggles away. Compact, self-willed Gwyn, her favourite daughter, dead in a coal cellar, with an old, cracked teapot propped jeering by her side.

The two men growled in their throats, the larger sinking his fingers savagely into Wicky's stringy arm. Joe Varden, that's who he was. Wicky cursed himself for not recognizing Nell's bulldog and bolting while he had the chance.

Nell squelched the howl of grief inside her bosom. I'll rip your turf from under you, Teapot, she resolved. House by house, street by street, till you're hanging from a boathook over the river tide.

Nell meant to rule here, as much as anyone could in London's treacherous, eternally shifting underworld. She thought of the warrens already torn from Teapot and a savage satisfaction shivered through her. Take my Gwyn, bash my Flann, leave him dead! Hey, Teapot! I'll grind your testicles for dog meat yet.

Red Nell's hand slid to her lap. Wicky suddenly spotted the silk shawl.

"Bring him closer."

Wicky saw his own reflection twist and gape as he was dragged forward.

She's nothin' but Irish, dirty Irish. No business here pushin' Brits around. Why ain't she beggin' with the rest of them where she belongs!

Why Red Nell wasn't among her destitute country folk was a question Wicky would never be bright enough to answer. Wicky would have been astonished had he seen her years before, disgorged from the bowels of a pig boat at the London docks, a living skeleton fleeing the potato famine with an equally skeletal husband and wraiths of children wailing to be fed.

That Nell reached London at all attested to remarkable powers of survival. We might have been in our wagon yet, she thought, except for cursed blight. Every potato in Ireland turned putrid before the folk could set a tooth in it.

The blight upon the potatoes was doubly a blight upon the tinkers with nothing stored and only their shrewdness to live upon.

Within weeks all trade, all work dried up. There were no fairs, no crowded pubs, no money to be had. Nell and her family were stoned from villages for fear they carried the dreaded cholera ravaging the countryside. Flann parked them in a valley where they might live off game, berries and petty theft while he shouldered his way north to look for work alone.

Nell saw the land stripped by those as famished as she. The plague-struck village housed bloated dead that the half-dead were too weak to bury. Driven to the seashore, Nell found it scoured clean of every mussel, winkle and chance dead fish. Mad with hunger, she struggled with those feebler than herself for handfuls of kelp to feed her young.

They'd devoured the kelp raw, its crust of salt washed off in the peaty spring the few surviving rabbits were too harried to come near. Nell had lain in the wagon, hallucinating about roast potatoes and sizzling haunches of beef. A jumble of campfire tales, passed down as the topsy turvy fortunes of Ireland buffeted her people from century to century, swept through her.

Corma the hunter with her belt of hammered gold and seashells braided in her hair, shot the king's red stag and roasted it whole. Oh Nell could hear the fat crackling.

An abbess rose out of the fog and clubbed one of Cromwell's generals dead with a crucifix as she skipped the convent wall. She and her eight tall children raided afterward out of the green

Mountains of Morne and Nell could see the mutton stew bubbling in the pot.

Bandits and drovers and fast-fingered fairground sharps danced through her head. They kept rough-coated nags that could clear a six-foot wall by moonlight and they fattened themselves on soda bread and mulberry pie and sausage in the pan.

Every third generation or so threw up a Celtic beauty who drew trouble the way the Shannon drew fish to spawn. If she drank buttermilk her skin would shame the lilies. If she laughed the very monks in the cloister would fight each other with fists just for her glance. And if she glanced, well then, such mayhem would follow that the family would be lucky to flee with wagons intact and nobody's neck stretched on a rope in the town behind them.

Flann had left behind a breezy woman, full of roaring, boisterous humour and swathed in a crimson cloak. When he returned, tottering on his feet, he found a hollow-eyed abstraction, all thought and feeling forged into an awesome determination to live no matter what the cost.

When they managed to get aboard a pig boat for London, Nell took two things with her. One was an abiding hatred of charities for no charity had fed her and hers while she swayed by the road watching cattle and grain and turnips flowing past to England for those who had money to pay. The other was the distilled ferocity of all the generations behind her, come to her aid in this extremity.

Wicky's feet sank into the carpet. He felt the suck of quicksand from which he would never rise.

"Don't lie to me, boyo. We know you're one of Teapot's rats. Teapot snatched the girl while she was struck with the pains o' childbirth. Fair dead she is. Teapot left the body where we'd be sure to stumble on it."

"What girl? I don't know nothin' about no girl," Wicky groaned, twisting fruitlessly this way and that. "For the love 'o God, I'm beggin' you, let me go!"

Red Nell let out a low laugh, the sort to make the scales rise on the back of a snake.

"I think you do know, Wicky. Oh, I think you do." Her hands tightened into fists around the shawl. "I want that baby!"

When Nell and Flann arrived in London, they could barely walk. Nell stole a loaf of bread and from it gained strength to work cleaning the chamber pots of a low lodging house in return for shelter inside the cellar way. Good enough for Irish, the landlord said. Country bred Nell never forgot the stench or the sneer. To this day, she burned peat in her fireplace, instead of coal, for the memories of open hills it brought.

The place turned out to be a robbers' lurk and the landlord one of Teapot's fences. Soon he used Flann, and then Nell to smuggle stolen goods through the streets, for who would suspect such wretched, ragged bundles. In London, Flann had never recovered his spark of life and languished in the soot. Teapot himself picked out Flann that night for the trip down Cobber Lane.

Nell hadn't comprehended Teapot's ratty, nasal laugh until she met Flann, as instructed, and handed over the gunny sack. Half a block on, she saw him set upon by toughs who beat him dead when the captured sack spewed out useless garbage.

Even as Flann fell, Nell felt the lightning pierce.

Set up, they were! Flann sent out with a sack of trash while the real loot sped away in a cab under the very noses of the thugs.

Nell had choked her screams back in her throat. Nor did she fall on Teapot in a useless fury. Heart torn, she gave not the slightest sign she knew, even with her last child quickening in her womb.

But the final piece of iron had pierced through. Red Nell the underworld force was born. Time to stop struggling for crusts. Time to snatch the banquet, loaf, table and all.

With terrible patience, Nell bided her time and discovered she had one enormous, unsuspected asset. Though illiterate, her memory absorbed everything, lost nothing, and calculated figures faster than a bank full of clerks. By watching, Nell came to know the value of each piece that passed through the fence's hands, where he bought, how he sold, who, in the Peelers, were paid off, and how much was made in a month.

Each week, she worked her way further into the fence's trust, even after the birth of her baby. The fence, thinking her ignorant, treated her eagerness as a tremendous joke and sent her on ever more hazardous errands.

When, at last, he sent her out as knife bait, she calmly stabbed the fence with his own bread carver and buried him in the cellar. Taking his hoard, she installed herself in his stead, announcing she now owned the business. Her youngest child she hid away. From that moment on, she engaged in mortal combat with Teapot.

That she survived Teapot's enmity was testament to her staggering perseverance. Red Nell's cunning and relentlessness drove Teapot back, house by house, street by street even as he reeled with incredulity at what this bog-trotter, this...this woman, was doing to him.

Nell's secret was organization beyond anything Teapot's low criminal mind could conceive. She amassed money, for money was power, missing no tiny source of revenue in her domains. Without scruple, she collected protection money, ran the betting in dog and rat fighting contests, fixed boxing matches and pigeon races, financed cracksmen and fenced what they stole, bought shares in pubs, took over houses of prostitution and even extracted money from vendors and beggars in return for seeing they kept their profitable street corners. She especially liked to milk charities, developing so deft a touch, they had no idea what was happening to their funds.

Red Nell was simply more intelligent than Teapot, drawing followers because, even in that criminal world, she was fair. Savage when crossed, but fair. In the fragmented, ever-changing jumble of expanding London, Red Nell's anachronistic clannishness had great appeal. When you were one of hers, you belonged somewhere. When trouble came, Nell's cohorts were deployed, a tactic that made her seem much stronger than she was and helped to bring street after street under her sway.

But it's hard, she thought, keeping watch all the time, never knowing when Teapot's going to strike. Slippery, devious, unpredictable, he eluded her grasp. Now that he had dealt a devastating blow, the thirst for retribution burned hotly in Nell's heart. He yet might destroy them all.

Nell shifted slightly in her chair, full of troubled thoughts.

The older she became, the more possibilities tumbled upon her, causing determination, excitement and a kind of weariness to war inside her. When she'd begun by squeezing pennies from beggars she'd never dreamed vast sums could be made fooling with properties where the next road cut might be. Down at the docks, dozens of things could be done with the cargoes of ships or with the ships themselves, Nell supposed, frustrated and teased by shifting possibilities far beyond her reach. Why merely the few things she did in the streets around her involved manipulations that would have boggled poor Flann's head. "Nell, Nell," he would have laughed, "'tis a regular mogul empress you've become. You'll never take to living in a wagon now."

No never! Such fools we were, breaking our backs at harvest to profit a bloated squire asleep by the fire. Or poaching a scrawny rabbit, scared of the goal while the landlord in London stuffed himself with Stilton cheese and drove about in carriages paid for by rents and fines. Wake up and look about, or they'd have you swabbing their chamber pots till the workhouse rolled you into your grave.

Yes, so many possibilities, Nell thought, such an addle to a tinker woman with no scrap of learning from a book. Help was what she needed, the sort of help that came only from one's own.

From earliest days, Nell scanned her children for the qualities she needed. Brought up separately, instructed never to acknowledge Nell as mother, they didn't question that they'd work by her side as soon as they could. Though her ideas of education were dim, she'd seen they learned to read and write, by God, so they'd never have to stare blankly at a written paper the way their mother did. Mostly, they were made proof against Teapot's skullduggery and taught all the many businesses of the street under Nell's keen eye. Nell wasn't without her own desire to found a dynasty.

Grow strong or die. And someday, someone must take over.

For a while she thought her second son, Sparley Dan, would be the one, the same Sparley Dan of the gaudy waistcoat holding Wicky's arm. Sparley had been so clever that at eleven he was already raking in a lively income as a gagsman, selling fresh tales to beggars and tramps who needed them for cadging on their rounds. He could play with numbers as easily as Nell and think up schemes that would make a magsman gape. Schemes he never examined for flaws, schemes he acted upon so recklessly that Nell had to bail him out of scrape after scrape until she finally realized Sparely Dan must have a tight rein all his life to be the faintest use at all.

Joe Varden, Nell's eldest, had never been considered. A fearsome, ox-shouldered man with Flann's black Irish hair and unwavering eyes, he was perfectly suited to be Nell's chief enforcer on the street. He was direct, hot-tempered and utterly loyal but he hadn't a subtlety in him. Left on his own, Teapot would gobble him up in a week.

Of Rose, her last child, she could not judge at all. Rose, born in an attic, with young Joe guarding the door, eight long months after Flann was dead. A pink baby, like the wild roses that blooming on the shores of Lough Neagh and named in memory. A baby hidden in corners and dragged from lurk to lurk as Nell and Teapot warred. A toddler overlooked by merest chance, crouching under a washstand, while Teapot's ruffians used axes on a room.

The heart in Nell heaved as she saw she could not keep so small a child out of the path of Teapot's ravening. With Rose shrouded in her arms, she'd slipped through the dark streets to the one place she could deposit her trust, the knot of gypsy wagons parked on Rowhythe Common for the Rowhythe Fair.

Like had long recognized like. Nell had handed Rose into the lead wagon and whispered into Old Anna's ear. Old Anna had looked at the child such a long time Nell shivered with superstition.

"There's folk," Old Anna had said at last, "down the coast."

Nell put it about that the child had died. Rose was safe out Teapot's clutch. Gold crossed palms yearly. Old Anna looked in when the caravan passed and said Rose thrived like a seabird on those windswept rocks. Tumbling with a brood of young like herself, Rose lived a hardy existence amongst folk who fished when they could, smuggled by choice and rollicked in the face of storms. The girl was like money in the bank to Nell, an unknown sum. When she would be called in, Nell hadn't a notion.

Wicky twisted again, bringing Nell's mind back to Gwyn. Precious Gwyn, with a mind like a lightning strike and nerve to match. Stubborn, difficult Gwyn who loved her mother and battled her and turned even the smallest co-operation into a mortal match of wills. Gwyn, so full of spirit and animation, whose queer, compelling loveliness was not the lush rose of her young sister, but the tough, wild briar, bringing forth in the wilderness its spare, exquisite bloom.

She had her own way, even when it came to the man, Nell thought bitterly. Silent as a post, shielding him. Was it that strutting pirate from the China clipper, Nell asked herself. Oh, I'd hound him over the seven seas and drown him in the deepest!

Grief boiled up in Nell's entombed heart. Red Nell fought it fiercely. The fool girl had got herself murdered and that's what happened when you got careless. Death was too familiar to Nell. She had no room for mourning. Only revenge!

Her gaze, the basilisk's gaze, returned to Wicky.

"Tell us," she said.

The shawl in her lap slithered like a live thing. Wicky shrank away.

"T'wasn't me. Somebody else took it and threw it away."

Oh gor, oh gor, why didn't he bite off his tongue!

"Where?"

Red Nell's eyes looked like demon's eyes, knowing perfectly it had been him. Wicky was shaking all over now, too terrified even to struggle. Words stuck in his throat were torn out of him by a will more powerful than his.

"Down by...down by the...river. In the muck. By the...K-Katherine Dock."

It wouldn't last a wink there. Not with all the starving dogs.

Red Nell heaved her bulk to her feet. Wicky reading his fate in her scowl, collapsed sightlessly.

"The babe is dead, but we'll look for it nevertheless. Just ourselves, for if the bairn by chance survived and Teapot got his paws on it again..."

She left the rest unsaid. Sparley Dan grimaced but Joe Varden took immediate action. His great paws found Wicky's neck. Wicky jerked once and his eyes bulged out in surprise.

The blind, permanent surprise of death.

CHAPTER FOUR

"Storm ain't done yet. You can't go home."

No less than four village lads clattered after Rose as she skipped up the track from the low grey houses spilling to the shore. Waves smashed against the jetty from the wild sou'westerly blow that had kept the fishermen imprisoned for days. The cliffs above showed jagged glimpses through the driving mists.

The coast of Cornwall was a hard, rugged place at the best of times. Nevertheless, Rose, who lived with the Mabbins over at Two Spar Cove, was bent on getting home. Things were very thin with the Mabbins at the moment. The mainsail on Jack's fishing lugger had finally blown out, taking the mast with it. The boat had money against it already after Jack and the whole village had been caught by a drop in fish prices, a drop engineered by Pynder Company agents, trying to slip their greedy fingers into everything profitable they could reach.

Jack had had to borrow against the earnings of his two older sons to get replacements. No sooner had the bargain been set than those very lads, Dave and Mawky, stumbled in, broke as hedgehogs and black and blue all over besides. They'd gone tinning in Pynder's mine, for hadn't the men of Cornwall been digging tin since before old Caesar and his Romans. Cheaper tin arrived from the Americas. The mine shut without warning, owing gobs of back wages. The boys jumped into a riot over it and got split heads from Pynder's bully boys.

"Well," said Maeve as she stuck plasters on her sons, "the cow's gone dry and we're staring at the last turnip in the bin. "I guess we're down to baking fresh sail pie."

Maeve had come from Cork so her Irish brogue added a dry humour. Pynder's meant to seize the boat if they could, but Jack had laughed from his net mending and the boys had stopped looking so desolate. They even revived enough to tell of the riot in the epic terms natural to a Mabbin while the wind howled down the chimney.

Rose had sat among all the little Mabbins like the blossom of her name flaming incongruously in the midst of a dark gorse thicket. If the gypsies had chosen a family with a horde of children to absorb her, they hadn't be able to pick one into which she would disappear.

Jack and his family were wiry, lantern-jawed, narrow-boned and agile. In contrast to Rose's strawberry mop, the Mabbins were topped with black thatches straight as a mare's tail and just as coarse. Rose tanned to toasted gold in the summer sun. The Mabbins turned swarthy as rooks with only their impudent grins to break their bushy-browed duskiness.

The Mabbins displayed all the characteristics of people who lived by hard, dangerous endeavours. They were reckless, merry, full of pranks and rude irreverence. Their bluster turned now and then into spectacular flares of temper. Once embarked upon a venture, they plunged in with all the bloody-minded purpose necessary to snatch their boat from the Three Sisters Reef or battle out of a strange pub with earnings intact.

When spirits began to flag again and even sail pie looked out of the question, Jack and Maeve exchanged a glance. Things were so bad that Jack lifted from the mantel the chipped, high-backed mother-of-pearl comb that had lain there ever since Rose could remember. "Straight off a Spanisher," Jack told Rise with his customary wink, "blown out of the water for tryin' to sneak up with cannons on crafty old Queen Bess."

"Its time the Spanishers stood us to a dinner. Hetty Goss has always had her eye on this. Rose, you run round and trade it for some top black ale and two of those struttin' hens she treats like her near relations."

So Rose had fought her way along the track to the village. Food wasn't abundant there either, but Hetty Goss had a dozen prize chickens which lived mostly in her kitchen. Hetty had long coveted the Spanish comb which had carving in its crest and winking bits of colour she was convinced were real jewels. Rose set out home with trussed up hens in her sling and a lidded jug of ale. There would be a feast under the rafters tonight.

"I'm going home," Rose told her followers with a sidelong glance of her grey-green eyes. At eleven, Rose was already used to people trying to divert her from her path.

"Can't, can't!" the boys chanted, darting after her.

Claiming to scorn girls mightily, they cavorted like half-grown cart horses the minute one hove into sight. When Rose was in sight, they crashed into barrows and hung from branches and swaggered in boat sterns in hopes of her attention. They meant to tease her all the way home and, if they were lucky, get a sliver of good soda bread from Maeve Mabbin. Even boys in love could not leave off thinking of their stomachs.

Their capering filled Rose with the impulse to devilment.

"I'm going by the Nose!"

"You're not," they hooted. "You'll be hided alive if Jack finds out you've gone by the Nose. Serve you right if you get blown into the sea like an old eggshell."

That fixed it.

Rose headed for the hulking cliff called the Pirate's Nose that cut off the village from the cove. There was a path of sorts along its face, but since a rock fall had taken the middle out of it, it was now only used by stoats after gull eggs or children driven on the fiercest of dares.

Today, such a traverse seemed unthinkable.

Rose, feeling heroic, didn't see why she should struggle round the muddy cart track when there a short cut.

The boys hadn't believed Rose even when she began to scramble upwards. Hooting and jostling, they climbed behind her, every moment expecting her to lose her nerve.

When the flank of the cliff suddenly steepened and gravel began to slide from under their feet, the teasing died away. Not looking at each other, and not looking down, the boys kept behind Rose doggedly, still determined not to be outdone.

At the broken part, they were high above the sea. The crashing waves below sent up spume to mix with the swirling mists. All that was left of the path ahead was a ledge scarcely wide enough for a goat never mind huge-footed boys. Rose stepped onto it, holding on tightly with her fingers in the crevices.

"Rose, don't be daft!"

Rose laughed through a haze of strawberry curls. Her skirt whipped in the wind. "Why, I thought you were all coming up with me. To tell on me to Jack."

She inched along further. The boys stopped, bunched on the last of the wide part. The first lad gamely put his foot out but felt his heel in space.

Rose's look said, either come or don't come. A worse torment than a taunt. She set her jug down and reached out a hand.

"Come on, I'll help you."

Not even for that would any boy budge. With a shrug, Rose hopped over a spine of rock to another ledge a few feet on. With a groan, the boys gave up their pursuit as Rose vanished round a corner like the warmth of a bonfire going away. Poor sorts, they felt. Rose might never look at them the same again. A tragedy in their boyish hearts.

Rose was not as cool as she appeared but would not turn round. "Once begun, it's all sail hoist," Jack used to say to her, "and tell the rocks to catch you if they can!"

Luckily, the wind was off the water so it stuck her to the rocks like a burr on a sheep.

"The wind is your friend," Jack often said, "so long as you don't fight with it. Seize the wind, run before it, make it take you where you want to go."

Clinging from rock to rock, she at last leaped down into Two Spar Cove, the chickens and the jug intact, enormously pleased with herself. The tide was out, leaving a crescent of soaking sand over which she could scamper to another steep thread of a path led right up to the house door.

Rose scooted along, fizzing with elation. Contrary to what the boys had said, Jack wouldn't hide her if he found out. He'd grumble and bluster, then cancel it all with a vast, admiring wink. Risk was the wine of life in the boisterous house where Rose lived.

The rolling wind-torn mist filling the narrow cove didn't bother Rose. She had played there since earliest childhood and knew every inch whether she could see it or not. She nimbly dodged the rocks that thrust up here and there like rough black fangs. Consequently, she was astonished to bang her knees not on a rock but a keg lying on open sand. From its splintered side trickled a darkly golden stream.

Rose smelled it, touched it to her lips and with a surge of amazement, recognized it. Brandy! And not just brandy but cognac, which Jack had taught her, as he had taught all his children, to tell from all less valuable imitators no matter what sort of stamp they might be masquerading under.

Jack was a man in mourning for the great age of smuggling which had passed abruptly not a dozen years before when the Admiralty had taken over the patrols, making the exercise too dangerous to be worth the candle. Jack's youth had been spent sliding boats from coves on moonless nights and rowing silently up to foreign ships standing to with all lights darkened. He had lugged cases of wine and tobacco, salt and French damask up steep cliff paths and into dripping caves. A shifting web of connections had spread from the village outward through gypsies, traders and close-mouthed middlemen for the profitable disposal of the goods.

Jack, a famous man with a yarn, filled Rose's head with smuggler's tales from the moment she could understand. According to Jack, the Mabbins had followed the trade when they could for the past two hundred years and been privateers before that, the envy of the coast for their daring. If Jack were to be believed, Excise men turned into blundering buffoons within ten miles of a Mabbin and the Duke of Cornwall himself would wear nothing else but silk breeches smuggled in through Two Spar Cove.

Rose knew all about the Mabbin who had spirited the entire imprisoned crew of the Happy Moon out of Pendennis castle under the noses of the guards. And the Mabbin who'd fired six-pounders at the naval sloop-of-war, Fairy, which had ventured too close for his liking. And Black Barney Blake who never made a one of his hundred runs without advice from one of Jack's family. Why even kings and queens, bless their royal foolishness, only existed so they could be outwitted by a Mabbin.

Jack trained his children the way he himself had been trained. By the age of eight, they not only knew cognac but could tell Jamaica rum from Puerto Rico light and identify any other liquor that might pass across the Channel. The smoke from the best Latakia tobaccos was perfume in their noses. They could list the seals on French champagne and pick out silk by the feel in the murkiest dark. You never knew, Jack ruminated mournfully, when the Navy might take itself off to chase the Moors and leave the folk at home to get their livings the best way their wits would allow.

Because of a long, concealing head, Two Spar Cove had once been a favourite smuggler's landing. Heart beating fast, Rose peered into the driving mist about her and saw another keg. And another! Out of the mist the bowsprit of a ship pierced the greyness, careening out of the leaping breakers straight toward the sand.

Rose actually gasped, then realized it was the swirling of the mist that gave the impression that the ship was moving, for the vessel was caught fast in the rocks. It would never sail anywhere again.

A wreck!

For all the legends and all the salvage scattered through the houses along the coast, Rose had only seen two wrecks and they had been but a grounded coaler and an old fishing boat sinking on distant rocks, not spilling bounty from their punctured sides like this.

The storm jib snapped in tatters and the ship vanished again. Not a dozen yards from Rose, another gap opened in the mist, revealing a dark figure staggering along. Other shapes loomed up, stumbling about, soaked and cursing, as they felt their way frantically this way and that along the sheer cliff wall that rose at the back of the cove.

Men from the ship, Rose thought in a flash, knowing they'd drown like rats if they couldn't find a way out of there before the tide rolled in.

For one long moment, Rose remained motionless, breath coming fast. Then, she pulled the lid from her jug, dumped the dearly bought ale into the sand and filled the container as best she could from the breached brandy keg. Agile as a wraith, she slipped wide around the lurching men and up the hidden path to the house as fast as she could go.

"A wreck, a wreck!" she cried in a fearful state of excitement as she burst through the sturdy old door.

When she had finally made the Mabbins understand, her news had the effect of a stick poked into a sleeping anthill. Jack and Dave and Mawky jumped up from attempting, uselessly, to mend the old mainsail so they might sell off the new. Maeve spun round from the fireplace, her broad face and arms ruddy from heat. All the little Mabbins tumbled out of the corners where they had been nesting. They were people of action unwillingly mewed up by the weather. Rose's words shot life into their veins and put the old daring back in their eye.

Jack tipped Rose's jug to his lip and came away with his swarthy face alight.

"By God! If there's enough of this we'll never have to grub another rock for Pynder as long as we breathe."

Maeve had her taste from the jug and licked her lips with thoughtful relish.

"And who," she asked significantly, "would carry the like o' this close along the coast?"

Jack whacked his fist gleefully upon the table.

"A Pynder boat! Oh lads, kiss your wages welcome. T'was very kind of 'em to come right into our own cove to pay."

Rose never forgot the heady joy of being in on the adventure, a reward for daring the Nose. In short, the village was to be roused, just as in the old days. It would take the lot of them if the ship were to be stripped before the tide washed in. When young Nick asked where all the booty was to be hidden, Jack gave him a tousle on top of his head.

"We'll open up the pit, of course!"

An awed murmur ran through the room. The Mabbin house itself was built over the mouth of an old tin mine run out centuries before. In the glory days, half the village hid their prizes there and never been detected. The pit had been sealed up for years, a place of fearful legend for the children. Its tunnels ran back into places where human feet had not trod since Charles II had been king. They'd surely swallow any little Mabbin who got in by accident and wandered in the dark.

The final obstacle was the stumbling crew sure to drown if nobody showed them how to escape the tide flooded cove.

"We'll have to have them here," decided Maeve, for the men couldn't be got out of the cove without blundering into the house, "and keep them where we can watch them. We'll dry them out and entertain them kindly, Rose and me. With luck, they'll be dead asleep as soon as the chicken is in their bellies and the fire warms their bones. The ship will break up by morning anyway, with not a one of them the wiser."

Jack, Dave and Mawky vanished into the mist, deeming it best that Maeve say her menfolk were off tinning. Maeve dispatched the chicken in the shed while the younger Mabbins chafed bitterly at being made to stay behind. Rose and young Nick were charged with scouring the cove for the sailors and herding them, every last one, up to the kitchen before the villagers showed themselves. They returned with a trail of bedraggled shapes blindly grateful to stumble into a humble Cornish fireside ministered by a kindly housewife with her brood about her knees.

The Mabbin home was rough and random, built at odd whims out of the ruin over the old tin mine. Nestled steeply into the hill, it was finished, as a great many Cornish dwellings were, with timbers from wrecks, giving the interior the strange, cosy, nomadic feel of living inside an overturned boat that might, someday, take to the sea again with its inhabitants inside.

Around the hearth, the roof soared away on the curving ribs of an old ship-of-the-line, piled up one night, not so long after the Battle of Trafalgar, on the Corrith Rocks. A handsome fragment of poop carving formed the lintel over the low seaward window. Sawn blocks of mainmast made stools for the children close to the fire. Assorted ship's furnishings, including a brass clock, a captain's chair and several water-stained seaman's trunks, added their use to the plain, sturdy furnishings of local manufacture.

The house also contained scattered relics from smuggling days, proof to Rose of events in Jack's extravagant tales. The children slept under a tattered billow of blue and gold velvet that had once been a lady's court cloak. Rose drank from a goblet of fine Austrian crystal which had half its foot broken off. A crouching idol of ebony wood and heathen make had served all the little Mabbins as a doll, staring back at them amiably with the cowrie shell making up its one remaining eye. Jack's wedding gift to Maeve had been a necklace of whalebone, fantastically ornamented with scrimshaw by the harpooner who must have whiled away a month of idle shipboard evenings carving it.

The bedraggled crew turned out to be a clutch of seamen who said they'd all got off onto the rocks save a character named Snooks, sucked over the stern in their attempts to tack away from shore. When they got a hot drink in them, Maeve saw with worry that they were hard men reviving enough to think of what they might be losing with the ship.

The hardest of the lot was the captain. "Mackle", he growled, when asked his name. He confirmed Maeve's suspicions of a valuable cargo by a clamp-jawed silence about what the ship carried and where it was heading. He was a large bald man with massive wrists, a livid cut on his forehead and cheekbones rough as cliff rock. He began to pace restlessly, folding and refolding his arms as though reliving the wreck. Captains and crew were paid with a percentage of the profits and were held responsible. Mackle listened to the wind moaning wildly and driving in sheets of rain. Time and again, he tried to peer into the gathering blackness, though any view of the cove from the house was quite impossible.

"Where's that husband of yours," Mackle demanded again.

"Gone to the mines, Lord bless him," Maeve said as she tended the simmering black pot.

When this didn't calm Mackle's darting eyes, Maeve told Rose to get down the bowls, for there was stew on the hob and a roomful of famished sailors perishing just for the smell.

The whole great kettleful, swimming with the precious chickens and the last turnips, vanished down the men's gullets with never a glance at the little Mabbins who followed each spoonful with yearning eyes.

It seemed as though the stew would do the trick. The crew began nod with weariness. Yet Mackle, though he now sat on a bench by the fire, did not stop his darting glances. Maeve's two youngest sons, not even eight, were eaten with restlessness at not being allowed out with the men. Mackle frowned with undefined but palpable suspicion.

Maeve was on tenterhooks and Rose could feel it, for the entry to the pit was not far from the house through a concealed opening behind some rocks. Jack and the boys were risking their necks just to reach the wreck through the deadly, storm driven breakers. They would be tramping, at that very moment, along with most of the village, back and forth into the pit with their booty balanced on their shoulders.

As her sharp ears seemed to pick up distant thumps and shuffles, Rose felt her pulses jump. When something, probably one of the shutters, made a muffled bang, Mackle turned his head. He could not be a captain along the Cornish coast and not know the reputation of the region.

The wind carried a second thud. The captain rose slowly to his feet, clearly meaning to step outside, even though the whole house rattled with the pelting downpour. The other men stirred themselves alert at the captain's movement. Rose saw Maeve stand frozen and remembered, with tearing clarity, the tales of prison and hangings and transportation for those so foolish as to be caught. What if the captain found his way to the path round back and stumbled upon the furtive procession.

With a swoop of daring, Rose glided between the captain and the door

"Shall I sing," she asked Maeve brightly, "to cheer up the men?"

"Oh yes, give us a song, darlin'," Maeve cried hastily. "Captain Mackle, just wait till you hear our Rose!"

Without moving from the captain's path, Rose launched at once into a chorus of "Betsy Bailey's Old Black Cow".

Mackle took two more steps toward the door before being arrested by a voice as sweet and merry as the linnets flying over the heather. His hard, bruised face, which looked about as sensitive as a boulder, registered involuntarily surprise.

Rose felt a touch of fearful power. To save them all, she threw herself into the song as she had never thrown herself into a song before. They'd never catch a Mabbin, she resolved. Not while she was there to turn them from their way.

"Betsy Bailey's old black cow
Wore baggy knickers when she took a bow.
Betsy Bailey sold the milk
And danced a jig all dressed in silk..."

Listen to me, Rose willed tremulously, to keep the captain's hard eyes from the door. She breathed fiercely against the fear in her throat. Then the fear passed and the thing that always came to her when she sang unfolded, like the happy petals of a flower. She slipped entrancingly from "Betsy Bailey" to "Hoist the Topsail, Lads," then to the lilting "Heather on the Moors,"

She watched the captain stand undecided, then shift back toward the hearth and sink down upon the settle, his head against the high, curved back. The crew were watching her, absorbed. The children had forgotten about the chicken and Maeve had let herself relax.

Something in her bones told Rose this was only right, proof of her specialness, the way she had known since that long ago dim memory of when she had been dropped into Maeve's arms. It wasn't just that her fairness that made her stand out among the offspring of swarthy Jack. It was Old Anna and the gypsies who came every year to look at her and after they left there was money in the jar and a roast on the spit and booms of good humour around the crackling hearth.

"Why, ye must have a mother rich as a duchess and twice as handsome," Jack told her, short of the facts himself, "up in London town."

But then, he'd also told her he'd traded the pixies two sea chests of heathen Islamer gold for her and still got the best of the bargain. Other times, he'd insist he plucked her up off the shore, all tangled in seaweed and singing in a foreign tongue. There'd been a crown embroidered on her stocking too, unfortunately stolen away by magpies the first time Maeve hung it on the line to dry.

The sense of difference was a secret, puzzling, cherished shield against the terrors that come to children who do not know where they really belong.

Why had her mother, rich as a duchess, sent her away? Why had she not been wanted even though she had been named for that most beautiful of flowers?

What was wrong with her that she was living with the Mabbins and not in a home of her own!

When pointed out for her hair or teased as a changeling, Rose made of her very a burden a virtue and gloried in it. Someday her real parents would come for her, sailing in a ship with flags streaming, or driving in a coach with red silk cushions and a trumpeter riding behind. Her high-flown notions came partly from her own fancy and partly from sitting with the Mabbins in the village pub drinking in the most improbable seafaring tales, embellished obligingly because the child was so interested and such a fetching little thing.

It seemed only right to Rose that her magic worked upon the sailors. She beguiled them until the hollow roar of the incoming tide told them that no living thing could get near their ship till the following day. One by one, they nodded off until even the terrifying Captain Mackle was snoring harmlessly against the settle, grey with fatigue and dreaming of cream from Betsy's accommodating cow.

CHAPTER FIVE

"Oh, darlin,' like the old days, it was. Better than the old days, for when did we ever find such a stuck pig of a ship stuffed with French brandy and French wines and crates of fancy goods you haven't seen the like of all your livin' days. Why we even found Dutch lace, handmade by cloistered nuns, worth a fortune by the inch, wet or dry."

Jack, so battered and exhausted he could barely stand, jigged round the hearth with Maeve. He had already tossed Rose up to the ceiling for finding the wreck, and he'd tousled all the little Mabbins and made them giddy on visions of roast goose and plum cakes big as rowboats and a pony apiece to race across the hills.

"We'll eat this winter and the village too and leave off cursin' Pynder and his mines."

Jack was just kissing Maeve on her laughing cheek when the door flew open with such force it sent Maeve's prized Stafford bowl crashing to the floor. Captain Mackle filled the space with a thundering scowl and a sodden coat. All of his hard sailors crowded behind him.

"My ship is stripped to the keel and you're the scoundrels that's done it. Yield up the goods before we rip the heads off the lot of you!"

Only after the rescued crew had been sent on to the village dock for quick passage out had Jack dared slip gleefully home. The men from the village, and the women too, had worked through the night, risking the tide, the rocks, the treacherous, sucking breakers. Through rain and wind they'd humped the windfall up the cliff into Mabbin's pit where it would lay secure until it could be quietly sold, bit by bit, cash warming pockets rubbed thin from Pynder's greed.

Everyone counted on the ship breaking up by morning. Yet the sturdy vessel had ridden out the night, its looted holds yawning. Mackle had only to look at the trampled marram grass and the weary, sea-lashed villagers to know what had happened. He guessed the ringleader at once.

"Go!" Jack hissed to Maeve, who gathered her children with one fluid movement and bolted for the side door.

"Hey!" Mackle shouted.

But Maeve and the children were gone before he got halfway across the floor. All save Rose, whom Mackle snatched hard by her hair and jerked backward. Maeve and the children scattered like quail over the brow of the hill toward the village.

For Jack and Rose, escape was cut off.

Mackle planted himself in the middle of the room, flanked by a barrel-chested mate and a bald seaman who looked a relative of the captain. Mackle flung Rose to the floor with a bone-jolting crash.

"Miserable brat! That'll teach you to sing a different tune."

Rose scrambled behind Jack where she stared at Mackle, her scalp hurting hideously. Mackle fixed Jack with a cold, aggressive gaze.

"Well," he growled, "are you going to tell me where the cargo is or not!"

Jack tensed, expecting to be rushed by the sailors. Mackle wrinkled his lip.

"I won't try to beat it out of you, knowing I'd probably break your thick skull first. There's faster ways to find out!"

Two sailors came in carrying kegs on their shoulders.

"You and your thieves missed the fo'csle where we had a tidy bit o' blasting powder. Put 'em in that pantry, boys, and nail the door up so this rat can't reach 'em."

They flung out Maeve's precious stoneware crocks from the larder and put the kegs inside. A long fuse trailed out under the door.

"Now," gritted Mackle, "I'm lighting the fuse. Tell me where the cargo is and I'll put it out. Don't tell me, and you and the chit here can be blasted to the Hebrides for all I care. When it goes under the door, we'll leave you to it!"

Mackle struck a match and touched it to the fuse. Rose watched, riveted, as it began to hiss and sparkle across the planks of the floor. With all the hungry village depending on him, Jack could not, would not tell.

Time stretched into a frayed band. Mackle followed the fuse, ready to stamp it out with his huge seaboot, smirking his evil smirk.

The tendons along Jack's stubbly jaw twitched and tightened. His black eyes glittered fiercely.

"You can be damned," Jack exploded finally, just as the burning fuse reached the pantry door. "I wish to bloody Christ we'd left you all in the cove to drown!"

When the burning end disappeared into the larder, out of reach of Mackle's foot, the captain's face twisted with surprise, then fury.

"Out, lads, out! Shut the rotters in with their choice."

Mackle and his sailors tumbled out the two doors, dropping the bolts as they went. They were stout doors and not to be burst through. Jack grabbed Rose.

"The pit!" he panted, flinging her down the ladder with him to the cellar and then wrestling with all his strength at the old Welsh cupboard that concealed an entrance.

No sooner had he pried it aside than the whole world burst apart with one tremendous roar. Shock waves blew Jack and Rose through the opening behind the cupboard into the blackness of the pit. Walls splintered, timbers fell, and a huge cascade of earthen rubble filled up the way they had just come. The two lay, stunned in a rain of fragments from the ceiling, thinking they were killed.

Eventually, the pelting stopped and the pressure lifted from their skulls. Through the ringing in her ears, Rose heard Jack try to move. All light had vanished. In a frightening rasp of a voice, Jack told her to find the lantern that used to hang by the door.

Rose stumbled to her feet and fell down again over the debris around her. She crawled on, inching and scraping her legs until she bumped into the wall. The peg was there but the lantern was half buried below, most of its glass broken. Mercifully, the matches were still tied to it. It's feeble light revealed a heavy earth fall, obliterating the entry. In the other direction, lay the ship's cargo jammed to the ceiling and the smuggler's entrance gone.

Jack tried to get up but collapsed with a groan. A dark stain blotched his thigh. He looked into Rose's staring eyes and summoned his old humour.

"Well, we surely put the joke to Mackle."

"But...our house..."

"Now surely you wouldn't have wanted me to spill out the news about our treasure just because of a house!"

Jack levered himself up onto his elbow, giving Rose a broad, bracing wink through his grimace. His hand swept round the kegs and crates walling them in.

"What's a house against all this! It's us and the whole village struttin' like earls and livin' all year on fresh gooseberries and cream. We're out of Pynder's clutches if we've got the nerve to keep what we've grabbed."

"But how are we going to get out?" Rose asked plaintively.

The lantern made only a tiny yellow ring of light in the oppressive blackness. Even Rose knew that besides the remains of the house, a good part of the hillside probably sealed them in.

Jack hesitated a long while, then jerked his head toward the blackness beyond the stacked kegs.

"The old tunnels, girl," he murmured through pain-gritted teeth. "You'll have to go down yourself and get me some help."

Rose shivered all over at the twisting passages where no one had been for two hundred years.

"But...the knackers..."

Everybody knew old tunnels were where the knackers lived, hideous, huge-headed creatures said to be the ghosts of miners killed in the pits. They tapped at the rock with their sharp little picks and caused horrible accidents. They took out their spite on any of the living to get within their reach.

Jack saw the results of his story telling coming back upon him and stifled a groan. Clutching at his leg, he fought to keep his chin from sinking on his chest.

"Why... all you have to do is sing. Knackers hate music. They crouch down at the back of their holes with their hands clapped over their hairy ears. Nothing can touch you if you've the company of a song."

Rose swallowed hard. She could see Jack depending on her, so blasted with dirt only the whites of his eyes showed up in his face. Behind him towered the precious treasures from the wreck she had found. Jack was right. A poor sort she'd be if she didn't have the nerve to help keep what they'd won.

She faced the murky tunnel mouth. There could be rockfalls in there and flooded passages, and floors that might collapse underfoot, plunging her down into whole nests of knackers...

"Betsy Bailey ate her bread,
While she stood upon her head..."

Putting one foot ahead of the other Rose edged forward, the yellow circle of light running over stone heaps, gaping cavities, smooth bits of gravel that gleamed like malevolent eyes. Behind her, Jack sank down, contorted around the searing in his thigh.

During the interminable journey, Rose crawled over rotted timbers, squeezed through holes with barely enough space for her body

between the debris and roof of the tunnel, slid forward down drops
she knew she could never back out of again. She skirted rubble perhaps just left by a knacker at work and froze each time the wavering
lantern flame threatened to gutter in the stagnant air.

All the while, she felt her song, like a blessing, carrying her
along.

Then she turned a corner and fell down a long slope, skinning
her knees and losing the lantern as it tumbled ahead of her. She
stopped, with sickening thud, against another rock wall and blackness closed in.

The lantern flame had finally gone out. She was trapped!

Rose lay petrified for she saw a gleam ahead that could only be
the demonic eyes of a knacker. A scream rose, but she swallowed
it, blood pushing wildly through her veins.

"The old black cow she...she slept in a bed
With a s-s-sack of cod fish under her head...."

Rose felt as if she were shrieking at the knackers, "Come and
get me! Come and get me! I dare you to try!"

The gleams flared, and suddenly became simple bits of rock
again, for the lantern flame revived. Not only had it revived, it
leaped up, vigorous and bright, as though drinking up some new
draught of life. The dead, stony smell had given way to an earthy
gust that spoke of roots and soil newly soaked with rain.

Fresh air!

Frantically, Rose clawed ahead until she came upon a tangle
that was the tips of the roots that clogged what must once have
been an ancient horizontal ventilation shaft. It was so overgrown
that it was all Rose could do to thrust her thin little body through
madly toward the daylight glimmering at the other end. Her dress
in tatters, all of her bleeding from scrapes, she burst out onto the far
side of the hill. Fleet as a fawn, she sped away down to the village
to get help and find the boys.

Many hours later, in the cove hidden beyond the village, Rose
sat on a bundle next to Maeve and the younger Mabbins. Dave and
Mawky were visible in the dusk, working the Mabbin lugger round
toward the shore. Jack lay on an improvised litter, his face ashy
and his leg bound up tightly in makeshift bandages. The family had
hidden out all day from Pynder's men and scurried to this deserted
bit of beach when evening set in.

Maeve had been sheltering Rose inside her woollen cloak. As
the lugger worked closer, Maeve took Rose over to where Jack

rested. Jack was a sorry sight from the explosion and his rough rescue from the mine. Rose herself, scratched up all over and ornamented with blooming purple bruises, didn't look much better.

"We're going to Cork," Maeve said to Rose, smoothing back the mass of curls she spent an hour brushing the dirt out of, "to my folk. We have to lie low till the hue and cry is done."

Maeve slipped her strong arm around the child and was silent for a moment.

"We can't take you with us," she told Rose softly. "There's too many of us for the boat already and we don't know where we'll be staying. Anyway...it's time for you to go back to with your own."

At Rose's blinking incomprehension, Jack heaved himself painfully to his elbow.

"You couldn't stay in the village either, not with that hair of yours and Mackle knowing you. There'll be no end of Pynder toughs nosing round. I'll not leave you anywhere in their reach. Besides, look who's come for you."

He pointed and a lean gypsy lad stepped from behind the rocks, leading a brown horse.

"Old Anna knew and sent him," Jack told Rose. "He's been nearly two days in the saddle."

"Where will I be then?"

Rose looked from one to the other of the only family she had ever known. Cold dread plucked at her stomach.

"Why, you'll go home, of course."

Home? It took a full minute for Rose to disentangle the word from the ruin upon the hill.

"To see my mother, the duchess?" Rose suddenly asked, her breath stopping in her bosom.

"To be sure, to be sure," Jack boomed though he had no idea where the gypsy would take her. "And she wouldn't want you dragging your heels about getting away."

Jack needn't have screwed himself up bolster Rose on. Her swiftly welling fears sank away, replaced by galloping anticipation. It was true! It had happened at last, the magical thing. All the fancies she had built over the years flashed brightly in her imagination. She was wanted after all. Her wonderful mother had called for her. She was going home where she really belonged!

Rose hugged Jack and hugged Maeve and then hugged all the young Mabbins who crowded around her in a tumbling chorus of rough squeezes and, finally, bursts of tears. When the family lifted

Jack into he boat and clambered in behind him, Rose watched them go. She saw the lugger slide swiftly out through the chop and heel, with a Mabbin flourish, round to the west, Maeve in the bow, still waving. Then she found herself hoisted up behind the gypsy. The horse turned from the sea, carrying Rose away, light as thistledown, along the roads to where the gypsies camped.

The gypsies finally arrived in London.

Nell hurried anxiously through the streets in response to the message the Romany girl had brought, then remembered to calm herself as she approached Old Anna's wagon. Dignities had to be preserved. When she and Anna met, it was a grave gavotte between two heads of state.

As always when Nell stepped into the dim, crowded, country-smelling interior of the wagon, she was overcome with a rakingly familiar sense of home. After the necessary mouthfuls of thick, sweet tea had been swallowed, Old Anna lowered her wrinkled lids.

"I've brought her back," Anna informed her astonished guest. "She's over watching the horses getting shod."

Old Anna told Nell about the wreck and the flight of the Mabbins. But when Nell asked about Rose herself, Anna only pursed up her lips. Her eyes flickered with that same tantalizing, troubling gleam that had filled then when Nell had first presented Rose as a toddler. She dispatched her granddaughter to summon their charge.

The gypsies had made their way slowly, trading and bargaining and sometimes pilfering along the way. Rose had swiftly emerged from mourning the loss of the Mabbins and the bewilderment of sudden change. The shocks were soon buried under the delight of riding on tailgates through strange towns and trotting barefoot through different dew each morning. The countryside changed constantly around her. The campfires at night were jolly gatherings with music and more tall tales. She gave up asking where they were taking her. She received no answer save that it was to London town.

News Rose hoarded to herself. Despite the wrench of dislocation, Rose knew in her bones events were moving as they ought. Something momentous was happening. Her destiny was now coming true. She had never been one of the Mabbins. Not truly. Any day now, she was going to meet her splendid mother, the duchess with crowns on her stockings who kept trumpeter in her employ. And then...

Rose could not quite envision what came next except that it must happy fanfare for her arrival. She made herself believe it so strongly that her old fears were almost stuffed down out of sight.

Their arrival, finally, at the great city, only confirmed that the magic was about to happen. What else but magic, Rose thought in awe, could possibly take place in this unimaginably complicated, thrilling place so crammed with people and buildings and boys turning somersaults in the streets.

When Old Anna sent for her, she dashed lightly up the steps into Anna's wagon. Inside, she stopped cold and recoiled at broad, gargoyle-like female before her with the tilting flowery hat and shrieking purple-red hair. A female who seemed to give off waves of forbidding intensity. Even before Old Anna opened her mouth, the gypsy's darting glance gave Rose a horrible premonition.

"This," Old Anna announced, into the midst of Rose's welling horror, "is your mother."

No! No! Rose shrieked inwardly, knowing in her core that this was wrong, wrong, wrong!

As for Nell, she was speechless for staring at the strawberry curls, the sun-kissed skin, the mesmerizing eyes full of shattering alarm. If she'd had a scrap of religion, she might have crossed herself.

Oh, wasn't it her troublesome luck to spawn one of the legendary, trouble-making Celtic beauties who left nothing but mayhem behind them. And wasn't Rose, girl that she still was, the very image of Nell's own grandmother, tormented up and down the coast of Sligo, Mayo and Donegal by every lust-ridden pup they stumbled into and finally the cause of a riot on the shores of Lough Erne.

What in creation, Nell asked herself despairingly, am I going to do with such a creature!

CHAPTER SIX

"You've been traipsing into the Whitechapel rookeries every month!" James Radmore shouted, aghast. "Nine years! Nine years you've supported this...this nest of cast-off bastards!"

That James said "bastards" in front of his only sister testified how much he was beside himself. He flung up and down the drawing room of their London townhouse. Amelia stood caught against the window, cheeks aflame.

"Yes, I have!"

She grappled for courage, remarkably upright for one whose life was bursting in her face. She'd known for years that James might find out. Now that he had, he was taking it with far more violence than she had anticipated

"Behind my back!"

"Well, you'd never have let me do it if I told you."

"I certainly wouldn't! For God's sake, Amelia, if you wanted to do charity work, there are church bazaars and missionary societies. We're overrun with missionary societies. Couldn't you collect bibles to save the Ponga Wongas or some such like that!"

"No!"

Typhoid had taken their parents. James had been responsible for Amelia since she was twelve and he nineteen. Most of those years, he alternated between jailer and divine oracle in her eyes. At twenty-seven, his frown still made her heart thump rapidly.

Now he was scowling like thunderclouds. He was a neat, erect, precise man with a very straight mouth and a noble brow that had always been his secret vanity. His suit and waistcoat were dark and restrained, since James was in banking. Or rather, he was associated with a bank. The Radmores had plenty of money from old, gentlemanly investments which young man might use very comfortably so long as he didn't appear to be enjoying himself. James, to his mortification, found himself lacking the ability to follow in the footsteps of their father who had been a famous doctor. His noble brow was flushed to the roots of hair and his waistcoat heaved furiously.

"Why! In heaven's name, Amelia, why?"

Even in anger, he was beginning to look wounded. When James looked wounded, Amelia suffered agonies of self-reproach for days. Desperate resolution made her face her brother grimly.

"Because I wanted to really help someone. I wanted something useful to do."

That was not strictly true. Left behind in the house, expected to go to teas and prayer meetings and the better sort of shops, a seething, inchoate frustration had welled in her breast. She could put no name to it save that she longed for adventure.

Adventure, however, was hard to come by for a genteel unmarried young woman trapped in the quicksands of propriety. How frustrating it was to hear of sunburnt parties slogging toward the source of the Nile, to read of tea clippers racing each other round the Cape to London with the first cargo of the season, yet know she had only to cross her legs while sitting to scandalize a room. A woman, Florence Nightingale, had marched off to Crimea and nursed a whole army back to health. And hadn't her own father been the celebrated Sir Lionel Radmore, lionized about the greatest houses in London for his advances in the treatment of marsh fever.

The world is expanding every which way before my very eyes, Amelia had thought. I'm stuck tapping my toes upon the fender.

Bouts of frenzied embroidery and church bazaar work failed to absorb the restless energy inside her. Despite her denial, Amelia had investigated the missionary societies, even, for a mad moment, considered giving her all to teach hymns to Hottentots in Africa. Then she'd chatted to Mrs. Cole who was setting up ragged schools to educate the very poor. Mrs. Cole had understood at once.

"I'll keep my eye open for something, my dear. Lord knows there's misery enough for all the help in London."

Amelia's restless energy warred with a terrible shyness, the result of her cloistered upbringing by James. Behind her dignity, she battled to conquer this frailty. She flung herself onward when the weakness came over her or the words grew paralyzed upon her tongue. Innocently, she drove herself to challenges that would have sunk many a braver soul.

A small private orphan's home had seemed a lot to take on, but there had been no one else to shoulder the responsibility, even with Mrs. Cole promising help with the funds. James would have had apoplexy if he'd known! Amelia's trepidation had been so thrilling she'd accepted before embattled reason could stop her! After Mrs. Cole had left, Amelia, only eighteen at the time, had whirled before the mirror and pressed a hand to her bosom. "You mad, reckless, headlong creature!" she had cried to her reflection, so giddy she had to resort to scripture to steady herself.

Oddly enough, it was the coachman who presented the worst obstacle. A large, grizzled family retainer, he had strict ideas about womanly behaviour.

"Beggin' your pardon, miss, but that ain't a fittin' neighbourhood for a lady. I wouldn't be doin' my duty if I drove you there."

In the end, it had been the desire for a bit of a stir up that had induced him to go. Griggs had learned his calling in the country, wrestling a heavy coach and four through mire and storms. He harboured contempt for London's easy, respectable streets.

But Whitechapel, now that was something a driver could get his teeth into. If Miss Amelia were hell bent on going, why he would get her there and back with nary a hair disturbed. He made her keep the blinds down, though, no matter how many beggars clamoured at the wheels. And outside the Infant's Asylum, he stood guard, a neddy stuffed with lead hidden in his greatcoat pocket.

Once a month Amelia made her visit, feeling very practical as she scanned the accounts that Mr. and Mrs. Jenks obligingly kept in such good order. She tasted the heady power of making up rules to do the children good.

Financing has been the hard part. Though her allowance was generous, the Asylum gulped astounding sums. She had to inveigle more out of James and quietly sell her mother's emeralds to augment the money collected from fundraising efforts Amelia organized with Mrs. Cole. James had teased her about extravagance, then lectured her, all the more puzzled because she was not mad for fashion and could make the same dress last longer than any other lady that he knew.

"Gad, Amy, you'd think I was keeping a duchess. What do you do with all that money?"

For a shameful moment, Amelia had been tempted to invent a tribe of heathen pygmies needing reclamation. Concealment by omission she had committed for the sake of the children. She could not bring herself to lie.

"I am giving to charity," she declared, looking him squarely in the eye. James couldn't very well question his sister's word. His acquiescence had been quite intoxicating but now the jig was up.

Never mind! I'm proud of what I've accomplished!

Patiently, she seated herself on the sofa and tried to make James see. She spoke passionately, for the experience had changed her more than she knew. Despite the closed carriage blinds, the trips to the Asylum had revealed a London she would never, in their gracious square, have imagined existed. The wide streets and dignified, white-fronted houses, had turned to twisting roads where ragged women clutched at the wheels. Stenches rose and pinched faces peered from broken windows. She knew now that the rich and the poor were carefully separated so the sight of starving bone grubbers need never disturb a barrister's evening meal.

"You should see the children at the Asylum now, James. So clean and industrious. Why even when they were toddling they wanted to help with their own support. Mr. Jenks kindly finds piecework for them to do."

They were nearly all eight or nine now. Amelia thought of them as her own children though she only saw them lined up for her visits. The one she remembered most was Katie, a queer, wiry little thing whose questing green eyes always caught Amelia somewhere in the throat. A curate had found her in a trash heap, Mr. Jenks said, and left a sum for her keep. Curiously, this child always made Mrs. Jenks' lower lip stick out.

"Fractious, Miss Radmore. She's been in fights. Them as get born with tempers always come to no good no matter how we try."

Of course Amelia had seen only a neat curtsy and a face overwhelmed with admiration at Amelia's maroon polonaise dress or her Leghorn straw bonnet with real stuffed humming birds perched on the side. Such fascinated interest was hard to resist. Amelia felt there was a brightness in the child. A brightness obscured, but which nevertheless shone out, for those with eyes to see it, like a light from under a locked door.

Yes, Katie and humpbacked, slow-witted Mary, the servant-of-all-work, were her favourites. Amelia always asked after these two, making sure the world knew whose protection they were under.

"She's just a child," Amelia would say to Mr. Jenks of Katie. "Once she's apprenticed she'll do us proud."

Mr. Jenks would look even more gloomy.

"Well ma'am, I hope so. But if she gets out of hand she won't be fit to be apprenticed. We'll have no choice but the workhouse."

At this, Amelia shuddered but made no comment. Mr. Jenks ran the place. She must take his opinion seriously.

"Industrious my foot!" James exploded. "Living off a simple-minded fool is more like it. Genuine ladies do not go to

Whitechapel. Good lord, if the fellows at my club ever find out, I'll never have courage to set foot inside again."

"James!"

"You're only encouraging vice," he cried. "Where do you think those children come from! And why should...street women stop having them if idiots like you take them off their hands and bring them up!"

He was more enraged than Amelia had ever seen him, mainly, so far as she could see, because she had dared to do something on her own. Nevertheless a sickened, guilty churning started up inside her. Ladies did not know about nasty things. It was ill-bred, degrading to even think of vice. James, speaking openly to her of... of street women, showed how much she had fallen in his estimation.

Argument was useless while they were both in such a state. Amelia stood up abruptly and found her gloves.

"We'll speak of this tomorrow when your head has cooled. I have an appointment."

James planted his feet like a challenged bull.

"I forbid you to go!"

"It's only a lecture."

"Then you won't mind if you miss it!"

Amelia's heart began to thud unsteadily.

I will mind! I will mind! cried the racing thing inside her. She felt the crumple of silk in her fist.

"I promised Mabel Corman to go with her. She'll be here within the hour."

The name turned James a violent red.

"I also forbid you to associate with Mabel Corman!" he declared grimly. "She is...frivolous."

He spat out the final word, meaning all the worse words he was too much the gentleman to utter. Guiltily, Amelia thought of Mabel's massed corkscrew curls and the startling pink panels in her skirts from the new aniline dyes. How, Amelia wondered, can other women think I'm fortunate for having only a brother to deal with!

Amelia herself was of the earnest, handsome variety who would truthfully stick to only bread at Lent and stand with face alight at evensong. Her hair lay in smooth dark coils and she favoured dresses of dusky lilac bound by yards of intricate black cording. Lavender enveloped her rather than Mabel's flamboyant jasmine. She had even overlooked Mabel's ringing laugh and too many dimples in the certainty that under the daring flounces lurked a spirit as passionate and serious as her own.

Friend, her heart whispered thrillingly. And someday, perhaps, sister!

For a moment, just a moment, Edwin Corman's flushed face swam before her, his lips parted urgently, his big hand squeezing hers as the press of admirers at his last lecture swept them together.

"Come Thursday, Miss Amelia, if you have a stout heart. Afterward, we'll speak."

She had thought she would faint from the promise in his words. She could only cast him a single feverish look. It was happening, oh it was happening. In spite of all James' watchfulness, a man wanted her.

She faced her brother, trying to keep the hunger form her voice.

"Mabel has been working her heart out for the rescue schemes. What's the harm of a speech about taking children to Canada where farmers are crying out for help? Children who are dying in the gutters. Orphans like my very own at the Asylum. Why there are thousands of people without homes, children who sleep in doorways, under packing boxes in Convent Gardens, who'll have no recourse but to turn to crime..."

A choking sound cut her off.

"Do I hear my own sister talking familiarly of the gutters? And you wonder why I forbid you to go with Mabel Corman! A person without introductions, an acquaintance taken up at a...a lecture hall!"

James' nostrils flared. Amelia felt a horrible thud inside her.

He knows, she thought, biting the inside of her lip to prevent her panic from showing.

"We...we can't ignore reality," she began again gamely. She would have had to be headless not to guess how the people around the Asylum lived. "Children are abandoned in the...the gutters."

"Children of depravity," James shot back so coldly Amelia shivered. "If their parents would stop being drunken sots and get honest work none of this would happen."

"Honest work is one thing but honest pay is another," Amelia retorted, her blood getting up. "What's a woman to do if she sews and sews for twenty hours of the day then can't make enough to buy her food. How much can a woman stand before she tries to get money any way she can. I've...I've seen them on the street corners sometimes. They look like scarecrows. Their eyes, James. Oh...their eyes! There's supposed to be a hundred thousand fallen women in London alone, driven to it by..."

Aghast, James crashed into a side table.

"That's enough!" he yelped as if he feared people in the street might overhear. "That's what you've been hearing at these lectures, haven't you. Not one thing fit for a decent woman's ears! No more of it, I say. You will disassociate yourself from this...this infant's home at once!"

His eyes were actually bulging! She was twenty-seven! Twenty-seven! And James still dared speak to her with such command as that!

Wild protest surged up. In the last year these rushes had been coming out of nowhere, like hot liquid pouring through Amelia then draining out, leaving a steaming after-heat. Secretly, she had wondered whether something was going wrong with her insides, her fluids thrown out of balance by too much pacing, too much thinking. Oh, couldn't James see they were going on and on, just the two of them, older, stodgier with each passing year.

She must, absolutely must, get to the lecture.

"Mabel will be here any moment. I can't send her away. I must at least go today."

"No!"

A dark angry colour was working up James' neck exactly as if he were being filled with red ink. The moment Amelia had always dreaded was here. She must fight now. She must fight and win or be forever at his beck. She took firm hold of her gloves and drew herself up in the slanting light falling through the drapes.

"I'm going to go with Mabel," she got out in a voice reduced to a scratchy thread. When it came right down to it, she was cut from the same stubborn cloth as James.

Her brother stilled. Then his eyes narrowed and his fingers gripped his lapels. Just like an outraged rooster, Amelia thought.

"You defy me?"

It was almost a whisper. James moved a step closer.

"Do you?"

Still Amelia did not speak. The dark colour now suffused James' entire face. Vehement fury leaped into his eyes.

"You do defy me! And I know why. You have conceived an infatuation! For that...that charlatan, Edwin Corman!

The cameo brooch at Amelia's breast jumped. Then a damning flood of scarlet streamed across her cheeks, bringing James within a foot of her, breathing loudly.

"I forbid it! He has no home and certainly no money. He is nothing but a damned mountebank, a...a carnival barker raising money for one ridiculous scheme after another. Why that's what he lives on—charitable donations. A leech lying in wait for trusting women. The man is a..a Methodist, by Judas! I forbid..."

Amelia whirled upon him.

"Forbid, forbid, forbid! Is that all you can think of, James! That and this vile attack. How do you know he is not as good and sincere as any man alive!"

"Oh, I know all right. I knew the moment I heard you were associating with this Mabel creature. Why do you think I got the wind up right away and asked around. I've been entirely too lax with you. Corman last spoke in Greenwich and there was a furor there over how much of the funds..."

"That was perfectly innocent. Edwin explained everything. Edwin..."

James' hand sent a china shepherdess flying to her doom.

"Oh, it's Edwin is it! I see!"

Amelia had been caught. Tears of rage worked at the back of her eyes. She had been goaded into a disastrous outburst. Now she stood her ground in unyielding silence. James stared back, his eyes ablaze. They bored into Amelia and finally struck home. He wants to keep me forever, she realized in a rush. Keeping his house, being his hostess. He wants to keep me, not just from Edwin, but from every man. I shall never get away. I shall never have a life of my own!

The thought was like a trap clanging shut around her ears. The money belonged to James, the house belonged to James, the very dress on her back belonged to James. She had nothing at all and no way to escape.

James stood motionless until she was sure his sister could not answer back. Then he swung on his heel, shoulders straightened in an unmistakable hitch of victory.

"I'll leave you to come to your senses while I go to my club. I'll be taking the carriage."

Without the carriage, Amelia was stranded as effectively as a pebble on the beach. A lady could travel no other way.

As James opened the front door, Amelia ran out into the passage, skirts streaming behind her.

"Prig!" she shrieked, flinging away a lifetime of propriety and setting the canary squawking in its cage.

James forgot to instruct the butler to bar Mabel Corman's entrance. Mabel found Amelia immobile on the sofa, skirts huddled around her knees, her expression that of a condemned prisoner watching life slide away. She rushed to Amelia's side.

"My dear, whatever is the matter?"

"The carriage isn't here. James had forbidden me to go."

"Oh!" Mable breathed, understanding immediately for that was Mabel's chief and inestimable talent.

They sat in silence for some moments before Mabel's pitying eyes drove Amelia to her feet. She wanted to fling herself against the window glass.

"I must go, I must!" she murmured, leaning her forehead against the frame. Why had she never noticed before how much the wood between the panes looked like bars.

Mabel knit her brow under the absurdity of egret feathers she wore as a hat. She was short, deliciously round and almost lost in a mass of magenta ruffles. The clock behind her chimed delicately.

"I doubt we'd catch them still at the hall. Edwin has something very daring planned."

Amelia's drooping shoulders were more eloquent than any tears. Mabel wished James in the room so she could fling a fire iron at his head. Lightly, she laid a hand on Amelia's sleeve.

"Edwin's going to take the party, those that dare go, into the clefts to see a room where they keep children locked up making baskets. He means to show exactly what the emigration schemes will save the little ones from."

Edwin's words rang in Amelia's ears. Come Thursday if you have a stout heart. Afterward, we will speak.

Her breath escaped as though she had been struck.

If you have a stout heart!

So that's what he meant, she thought exultantly. To see if I have the stuff to stand beside him in his work. To see if I am stout and brave.

Edwin's face came to her, earnest and questioning, his voice alive with promise. Yes, she must see Edwin today. Today was the test. If she were absent, Edwin would think her faint hearted, rejecting him. Tomorrow, he moved on to Liverpool. Without a declaration it was impossible that she write to him or try to contact him in any way. Propriety would bar her. Edwin would be lost forever. She turned to Mabel.

"Do you have the address?"

Every one of Mabel's flounces jerked.

"It's only the men he's taking. They've promised to bring a full account."

"Do you have the address!"

"Well, I know which lane, but it's in the most awful section of... oh, it's impossible."

Though Mabel thought of herself as daring and worldly wise, Edwin was a good brother who also kept her to the tea and lecture circuit. She began to be afraid of the fearful determination growing on Amelia's face. It was unthinkable that two women without a carriage, never mind a protecting chaperone, could venture alone into those deep slums. There'd be drunken men in the roadway and horrid reeks. Anything might happen. Anything!

"We must go ourselves," Amelia cried, "to show we can face the worst!"

She must act or die.

"We couldn't possibly...."

"We could! You're not afraid, are you?"

Mabel, too, always hated it when Edwin made her stay behind. She gathered herself staunchly. Who knew what Amelia might do if left here on her own.

"I shouldn't be afraid if you weren't," she lied stoutly.

"All right, then. We'll go!"

Before they could think, they sped toward the front door, then halted.

"We shall...have to take a cab," Amelia said in a hushed voice. "And we must order it ourselves. Parker would be too scandalized."

Sobered by such an immediate encounter with impropriety, the two women crept through the entrance lobby, almost escaping unnoticed into the street. The surprised butler spotted the tail of their skirts and rushed to inquire just in time to see them climb into a hansom cab across the square. When he heard the address, disbelief paralyzed him. Then he leapt up as if a spring had been released.

"Bethnal Green! Miss Amelia can't go there. I must get Mr. James at once!"

The cab's interior smelt of horsehair, old sweat and unsavoury assignations. Mabel and Amelia clung together as the vehicle lurched abruptly into streets that teemed with hungry faces and drunken shouts from doorways the women feared to glance into. A swearing beggar stumbled against the side of the cab and fell. Mabel began to talk swiftly about Canada to take their minds off their contraband expedition.

Amelia knew that Canada was full of snow and bears and loyal subjects harvesting masts for ships. The Audleys had sent their youngest son there on remittance after that scandal in the army, so it was a place the desperate could resort to. Oh, if only she and Edwin could be there, clear and free, instead of in these dingy streets with beggars clutching at the wheels.

"Courage," Amelia whispered as the driver shouldered the horse through the crowds and finally halted before a ruinous doorway that gaped on its hinges. Two cats squalled on a ledge. Amelia's hand flew to her throat.

Be brave, be brave! Edwin will be there.

"Is...is this it?" Mabel asked the driver faintly, praying it could not be. The prospect of visiting the clefts, had been exciting. She had dared this journey with Amelia rather than miss it. And...and Edwin would be there to shield them.

"Down there. Can't get the 'orse no closer." The driver pointed down an alley with a door at the end. His hard, up and down look that wondered why two such flash prostitutes, for that's what he took them to be, would visit this dismal hole.

"'Ey, move on. Ain't no bloody cab yard!"

A barrow man thumped his fist into the back panel, causing the horse to bridle.

"We must...get down," Amelia said, determined to step out even at the mouth of the Inferno.

They alighted into a lane running with slop and cried out when the cab immediately abandoned them. The coster gaped openly and wiped his face in a smear of fish scales for his barrow was full of dull-eyed mackerel.

"Ooooh, I say! What fancy bits 'o tickle. Yer won't earn nothin' 'ere, lassies. Ain't two farthin' t' rub together in the 'ole blinkin' lane."

Mabel turned violent scarlet stt the same moment she realized entire hem of her skirt was soaked and glistening with filth.

"Edwin, oh where is Edwin!"

Frantically, she scanned the crooked byways and the blind court across from them. The court was heaped with refuse. When one of the piles reared up, both women almost screamed. A naked, hairless child of about three rooted in the filth that covered it. It pulled a potato peeling from the heap and stuffed it hungrily into its mouth. Amelia's stomach heaved and blood sank away from her head.

"We....must go inside. Now, please!"

Two rough men began leering. Mabel tore her eyes from the ghastly child. Whatever had possessed her to allow herself and Amelia to come here on their own! They stumbled through the door into a dank hall also piled with garbage. Something bolted, squeaking from their footsteps. Mabel stifled another shriek.

"Oh, Amelia, I had no idea! This is dreadful!"

A large figure lurched into the doorway, grunted and fell insensible to the floor. The odour of cheap gin momentarily overcame the other stenches.

"He's...he's drunk," gasped Mabel, wringing her hands.

They could not now get out without stepping over that fearful body. Amelia felt for the comfort of Mabel's arm. In the gloom at the end of the corridor, they picked out gleams through the cracks of what had to be a door.

We're to give no warning," Mabel whispered, "or they'll run away. Edwin wants to actually save some children if he can. It'll mean a big boost in attendance."

"Then we shall do it!"

They picked their way along holding tightly to each other.

"Edwin said it was in...in a cellar. We must simply lift up a door and peer in."

The door was more like the top of a bin than an entrance to anywhere. Amelia felt her fervour returning. Her breast swelled at the thought of Edwin finding her here, already confronting the evil.

"Now!" she whispered. And pried open the crooked door.

A blast of air, fetid from lamp smoke, unwashed bodies, mould and decay rushed at their faces. They stared into a cavern which had slimy puddles in the corners, mildew coating the walls and blackened cobwebs drooping overhead.

When their eyes got used to the dimness, they saw seated about, in every nook and cranny, a child. Or rather, a raggedy, skeletal excuse for a child. Six steps led down for the cellar was very shallow. All around were heaps of thin wood, handles and bottoms which the children were assembling into rude little baskets with wood strips woven on the sides.

Amelia, who thought she had seen rough sights on the way to the Asylum, now realized what Griggs had shielded her from.

Some of the children peered up as the door opened, looking as though they could barely lift their heads. Yet their small hands never ceased moving, black with dirt and some showing raw fingers and sores along their scrawny arms.

"They…they get paid by the dozen baskets," Mabel whispered shakily. "And that loaf there…when they fall over, they get a slice. They…have to pay for it out of their wages. Some of them can't keep up and…and starve."

On a crate in the centre sat a crumbling lump of bread next to the lamp by which all the children were supposed to work. On a second crate, his back to the door, sat a man with a switch in his hands. His coat, missing one sleeve, shone greasily with dirt. Though scarcely bigger than the children, his baldness and grey elflocks gave away his age. He watched his charges with the intensity of something cornered. When one of them began to cough, the dry, gritty cough of the truly ill, he automatically thrashed it across the face, adding fresh welts to those already criss-crossed there, a number festering. The child, an emaciated girl, shut her mouth and sat convulsed with inner spasms, but made no more sound.

Amelia reeled. The Asylum took in the children of destitute widows or the offspring of respectable workmen laid low by sickness or accident. But these! These were scarcely recognizable as human beings, let alone children!

Her choked breath caused the man to swing round. A toothless mouth, around which the rest of his face caved like a shrunken apple, flapped open. One eyelid drooped slackly. The other flew up over the wide wet eye of a subterranean creature suddenly exposed.

"'Ey, get away!" he hissed in a cracked, furious voice.

Accustomed to defending his lair from drunks, tramps and the desperately homeless, he rushed at the door, stick in one hand, lamp in the other. When the light revealed two finely dressed ladies, he skidded to a halt on the bottom step.

In all his life of cellars, garrets and malodorous alleys, he had never seen anyone like these up close. Their smooth faces radiated health and beauty like light shed from angels. Mabel's egret plumes waved in cloudy grandeur in the dimness of the hall. The watered silk moiré of Amelia's dress shimmered from its complicated folds.

The sight was so alarming, so inexplicable, that it quite unhinged the man. Something was wrong, so dreadfully wrong that he could not even pause to think what it was. Survival depended on knowing when to fight and when to bolt

"Out!" he bellowed at the children, backing up. "Out! Move! Scarper!"

The signal was well known, no doubt because such an operation had to shift quickly to avoid thugs and street gangs. The lethargic children heaved to their feet and stumbled about, grabbing as many of the baskets to their breasts as they could hold. One of the larger worked at the bar blocking a door at the other side of the cellar which, no doubt, led to an alley. From under the crate, where he had been sitting, the man snatched a grubby cloth bag that clinked of coins. Stuffing it inside his shirt, he backed toward the other exit, lamp held above his head like a puny weapon against avenging seraphim.

Amelia had forgotten all about Edwin Corman. She only saw starving young ones left to lice and festering sores while the beast responsible was about to get away.

He shan't escape. I won't let him!

As the bar gave way, Amelia launched herself down the steps and clutched the man by the elbow. He yelped from fright and jerked away to where the children had all piled up against the door jamb like terrified mice. Undaunted, Amelia began to claw at the man again, the back seams of her bodice ripping from the effort.

For all his bandy body the fellow was strong. Seeing he could not get past the children, he flung Amelia to one side, dropped the lamp, and made for the door up into the hall. The frenzied creature ploughed into Mabel and swept her ahead of him out into the lane. As she fell into the mud, he kicked free of her flounces and fled.

Mabel righted herself barely in time to avoid being trampled by a lathered carriage horse. James hauled her precipitously to her feet, his face chalk.

"Where is my sister?"

Numbly, Mabel pointed toward the interior, then froze. A lurid orange light flared in the gloom, outlining the cellar doorway like one of the mouths of Hell.

"Oh, my God!"

James flung himself inside to see Amelia staring in disbelief at the flames from the broken lamp leaping into the tindery heap of basket wood and crawling up her skirt. The children, finally yanking open the alley door, streamed out like singed cockroaches. The blast of air sent the flames spurting into the cobwebs overhead.

When the shrieks began, Mabel clapped her hands over her ears and twisted madly this way and that. Then a volley of children bursting past would have trampled her had any of the pallid things possessed the substance to do so. Their frail bodies bounced and stumbled , spilling the baskets as they bolted. Through the roaring in her head, Mabel remembered why she had come here.

"I must save something! I must! I must!"

Reaching into the melee, Mabel grasped the wrist of waif. It was the girl who had coughed and been switched. Immediately, the child to howl, flinging her tatted hair from side to side. When Edwin Corman came running up, he found Mabel with her eyes shut tight, leaning into the screams of the basket child to drown out the horror going on inside.

CHAPTER SEVEN

"Here we are." The chimney sweep halted outside the same door Curate Banning had entered years before. "Full 'o young 'uns. Just the place to see if you've the makin's of a climbin' lad."

The Infants' Asylum was as fortified as in Banning's time, a bare, dark-bricked building holding itself apart from the unsavoury streets twisting around it. The sweep, Joshua Croom of Mawton Alley, rapped deferentially with one sooty hand. With the other, he gripped the wrist of a small, straw-haired boy whose face was streaked with tears.

"And if any o' them nosy officers bothers us, you say you're my son. Hear?"

"I ain't your son!" the boy answered back with more stubbornness than his reddened eyes warranted.

He was a raw-boned child, desperately skinny, but with a gangling solidity nevertheless. If he had been a colt, he would have been a very young Clydesdale, scrawny limbs already promising the thickness and strength of the breed. In the boy's case, the breed ran back through a thousand years of yeoman farmers, hardy shepherds and obstinately loyal pikemen before the cotton mills had arrived to suck up the labour from the land. He held his head up straight despite the storm of crying which had left him, wrung out and hiccoughing, in the grip of this stranger who certainly wasn't the father he had been pried away from in the tavern scarcely an hour before.

"Of course you ain't," the sweep replied matter-of-factly. "But if you wants something in your belly, you'll lie like Jack Tar's parrot when I tells you. What's your name anyway?"

"Will."

"Will. That's a good 'un. You better be willin' to work, that's all I say!"

Fancying his own wit, the sweep chuckled. Involuntarily, Will started, his throat closing up with fear. Back when he was a wee tad, and couldn't help himself wetting the mattress they all slept upon, old Emma used to jerk him from his sleep and fling him to the floor. "The Black Man will get ye, ye sopping little stink! And chaw ye up for matchsticks! Och, how're we ever going to dry this mess with no coals for the fire and the damp growing on the walls like fur on a frog!"

Two more tears squeezed out. Trying valiantly to blink them away, Will looked down to where the sweep's hand darkened the sleeve of the unmended shirt he wore. More black marks showed on his neck, jaws and forehead, as if he had been examined like a calf before sale, which he had. Men's trousers, cut off at the knees, ballooned comically about his waist where they were tied with a knot of twine. The frayed ends hung down as far as his ankles and bare feet horny and stained from the road.

Pa's pants. He gave 'em to me yesterday. He knowed he was goin' to shuck me off!

His dad had got them off a rag and bone cart and chopped at the legs, squinting with the intense concentration of the stupendously hung over.

The door opened sharply. The bristling moustache of Mr. Jenks advanced. The sweep pressed his hat to his chest. A top hat proper to a gentleman of the chimney pots in a world which, due to the unfortunate odor and blackness of the trade, shunned him as a leper.

"Afternoon, Mr. Jenks. Time to do your chimney again. Ain't it a corker how the soot do build up."

One eye winked, for he was one of the men Jenks had an arrangement with. The chimney got cleaned more often than it needed and Croom set his mark beside a generous fee of which he collected half. The rest slid quietly into Jenks' voluminous pockets. Amelia Radmore was bilked, easy as a baby, as long as everything got written up, nice and neat, in the book. The years had made Jenks craftier. After Red Nell inexorably took her cut each month and enough food was bought to keep the brats alive, Jenks found dozens of ways to lay hands on the remainder.

Mr. Jenks' face bore a high flush for the knock had distracted him just as he reached for the pliable cane that hung by the jamb.

"You're late, Croom. Tain't the children's exercise period."

Croom was only slightly late. It was Jenks who had furiously ordered the children back inside. Like any canny sea captain, he knew that when you scotched a mutiny, you made sure the entire crew was lined up to watch.

Damned idiocy, these Radmore notions about "taking the air" in the yard every day when the brats might better stick to their work tables earning their keep. Jenks kept to the rule only out of fear that, if he omitted it, someone might blab to Miss Amelia, most likely that ugly hunchback Mary who blurted the truth to any question asked. Jenks had never decided whether Mary as sly as a greased stoat or merely simple in the head. After her astonishing revolt regarding the curate's money, she had relapsed into her expressionless stupidity so thoroughly that Jenks found it harder and harder to credit what she had done. But he hadn't forgotten. Oh no! And if it hadn't been for Miss Radmore, he'd have booted the creature down a cocked alley years ago.

"Sorry, Mr. Jenks. I be getting myself this lad to help. We hiked it over here as if our tails was afire."

Croom had hurried, but not too briskly to lose the pleasure of the ale sloshing inside him and his triumph as the lumbering, drunken out-of-work cotton spinner had lost the boy to him. And at nut covey! A game you couldn't put over on a crossing sweeper any more. The boy had bleated, "Pa, Pa," in a high, stunned voice until he and Croom were outside in the street. Then how the little blighter had howled. Oh well, Croom had seen plenty of howling boys, been one himself, for it was a rum thing, breaking them in to the job. Give it a week, though, and this here Will would jump right snappy. And learn the trade. After all, wasn't the city all soot from arse-hole to breakfast time and who but the sweeps kept it from choking up entirely?

Jenks jerked his head toward the interior. He wanted Croom's fee in this month's account. Immediately, Croom began taking one item after another from his handcart which bristled with brushes and brooms and buckets and a ladder in sections.

"All right, lad, take these sheets and spread 'em round the chimney, tidy like. To keep the soot from getting about."

Placing two heavy, folded cloths in the boy's arms, he shoved him through the door towards the yawning fireplace.

The room, lit by weak sunlight beating at the panes, was now furnished with three long work tables and was frightfully, formidably neat. At the tables sat a number of girls, mostly ages eight or nine, but with some younger interspersed. They were dressed identically in plain brown dresses with coarse white pinafores over them, so that they resembled premature autumn leaves, each with a dab of snow to smother her. Each had a straight braid hanging down her back into which all varieties of hair, dark or pale, thin, thick, curly or straight, had been alike subdued. Each had a wary face bleached out from the diet of bread pudding and the mewed up indoor existence.

If the devil made work for idle hands, then the devil was out of luck here. Life had brightened when Jenks discovered that little orphans, once allowed to reach the age of three or four, were admirably suited to sweatshop labour. Where previously he had only been able to cheat Miss Amelia out of expense money, now his natural enterprise sprang to the fore. From the moment each child could hold thread and needle she was put to the labour of stitching plain caps, plaiting straw, edging linen handkerchiefs, constructing silk flowers, doing whatever other small work Mr. Jenks could obtain. Amelia imagined industrious youngsters contributing joyfully to the maintenance of their home. The reality was a drove of red-eyed miniature serfs toiling from before dawn while the profits nimbly vanished the way of Mr. Jenks' other skimmings.

Jenks ran his eye proprietarily over all the bent heads, his expression something between disgust at still being the warder of brats and smugness at having worked the unpromising vein so well. Enough now, he told himself gleefully, to make his bolt for Manchester or Glasgow, forever out of the clutches of Red Nell. Ten times a day his gaze flew to the hiding place of his treasure. So clever. No snooping fingers would pry it out of there. By spring he would plan his escape and be gone.

Surreptitiously, the children gaped, for the sweep was an extraordinary sight. A short, rubbery man, he was as black as if he had been dipped in pitch and left to dry. Soot was ingrained in every pore of his skin, every thread of his clothes and the odor that rose from him was that of a house just burnt with all of the inhabitants inside. His legs came together in the middle in a curious knock-kneed way, adding a comic note to the cocky swagger with which he carried his top hat down one street and up another, crying "'Weep, 'Weep, 'Weep!" until someone dashed out wanting him to attend to the hearth.

Knowing the effect of his blackness, the sweep rolled the whites of his eyes at the little girls and showed them the red inside of his mouth. They stared all the harder. They so rarely got to see the sweep or anyone else for that matter. Other than brief activity in the bit of yard, the door kept them resolutely sealed away from the turbulent world just outside. They had never seen a tree, skipped on grass, or guessed there was a great river with boats not a half dozen streets away.

Will was ten steps into the room before he realized he was being stared at.

Girls! And him with his gob all sopping tears!

His ears blossomed into scarlet beacons. With a mighty effort, he turned his rigid back to the worktables. That's when his gaze locked into a pair of green eyes burning with such indignation that he could not at first grasp that they belonged only to a small, red-haired girl scarcely as old as himself.

Then he felt her look, like tangible heat, sizzle past him to Mr. Jenks. A wonder she don't fry up! Will thought. The girl's mouth was a taut white line scraped into a whiter face. Her eyes tilted upward, giving her the appearance of half-grown cat just dragged, spitting, from a tree. She was suspended by her elbow from the grip of a huge, florid woman who looked benignly pleased with her catch.

Unlike all the other children behind their tables, the girl was not spotless. Mud, like war paint, decorated her cheeks in diagonal smears and her pinafore was so filthy she must have dived, belly first, at the ground. A gaping hole at her shoulder revealed a chemise, also shredded, and a flash of skin so white it could not have been told from the chemise except that it seemed to be quivering. Wild tendrils, jerked from her braid, stood out around her head electrified by an outrage all their own.

"The sheets, lad. Don't stand yawpin' like a moon dolt at the gals."

Croom prodded Will in the back. A tiny ripple passed through the children, the closest they dared come to a titter. They were stitching gloves today. Jenks got the cut-out pieces by the gross from a jobber in Rimley Street who altered the invoices. The children, surrounded by mountains of white hands clutching at their labour, sewed up the fingers. The youngest, three and a half, still drunkenly emerging from the opiate fog of Godfrey's Cordial, was tied to her chair and briskly whacked whenever she started to keel sideways. To wake up in Mr. Jenks' sweatshop after the stupefied docility of the nursery was sometimes more of a surprise than a growing child could handle.

Awkwardly, Will laid his bundle on the floor and tried to tug a corner loose. He could hear the girl breathing fiercely.

She's in the soup about something. Is she ever!

The tension crackling around her was so strong he forgot for a few moments the tugging grief in his own breast. Jenks waited until Croom had brought in buckets and a broom and had spread the sheets carefully over the open mouth of the hearth. Now, indignation rolling high in him, he returned to the matter at hand.

"You, Katie Mucker! Get ready for what's coming to you!"

As Ida Jenks let go, her husband aimed a cuff, but the girl staggered adroitly, righting herself just out of range. Thin-boned and erect in her ruined dress, she planted her feet and braced for the storm. She had grown up bracing for storms right from the moment Banning had rescued her, in such an alarming state, from the gutter.

Mr. Jenks never let her forget where she came from. Even her name had been maliciously concocted to keep her humble. Lady Muck he called her when he had her cornered and her head came up in an unconscious but utterly telling imitation of her heroine in all the world, the regal Amelia Radmore.

Slowly Jenks approached, flicking the cane in his hand. It flexed like the tail of an angry beast and represented the condition of Mr. Jenks' mind. His slatey eyes raked Katie's green ones. There was no mistaking the state between them. War! War ever since the windfall of the curate's money had slipped from his grasp into Miss Radmore's dainty, do-gooding paws.

Mr. Jenks had been gravely disappointed when the baby hadn't immediately died, a profitable, uncounted little corpse disposed of with no one any the wiser. Once Miss Amelia spotted the whelp he was forced to be responsible. And the child proved tough as a yard weed whose roots can be churned into the mud, parched in the blast, trodden to shreds, yet will pop up again, saucier than ever at the first respite of rain or sunshine. She had thrived on the half indigestible infant pap. Measles, whooping cough, even scarlet fever failed to carry her off. Months and months of Godfrey's Cordial had not turned her into an idiot as it did many another child. No indeed, it hadn't so much as dimmed the whirring little brain so bent on mischief. Undaunted, she had scrubbed acres of flagstones, lugging a pail of water almost a big as herself. She emerged from punishing fasts of water and bread cubes thin as a broomstick but apparently no weaker.

Ida Jenks was also disappointed. Badly so. One last indulgence, that's what her husband's eyes had promised her at the door. Disappointment made her bustle and beam and over Katie as never over any child before. Half a dozen times during Katie's first year, Mr. Jenks had found his wife bending over the infant's cot, that smiling, deadly trance in her eyes. Breaking into icy perspiration, he'd jerked her violently away, cursing the chains of matrimony that made him keeper to this infanticidal lunatic. The more Jenks had to protect Katie, the more her survival became an affront. Especially since he knew that sneaking Mary had a hand in it, though damned if he could catch her.

Cursed burr under his tail the brat was. Why, as soon as she'd got enough pap into her to keep her alive, she'd turned into a compound of hot pepper and strong lungs, yowling lustily amidst a roomful of other babies staring pallidly at the ceiling. Oh, Godfrey's Cordial would knock her out all right should anybody manage to get enough down her but you couldn't trust it to keep her that way. Unless she was actually tied to the cot, she'd be crawling into the fireplace, crowing after the pigeons on the windowsills, working at the handle of the door to get down to the kitchen where Mary sweated like a heavy ghost amidst the clouds of steam.

Shouts, cuffs and thumps could stop her but never break her. Her mouth would draw down at the corners in what, in other children, would be a prelude to a howl. In Katie it was a look of such mute, bull-headed defiance that Mr. Jenks longed to snatch her up bodily and...

Jenks bit down hard on his back teeth.

When put to the worktable, how readily the brat had snapped from her nursery daze and gaped about with avid, wonderstruck green eyes. She had taken to the work, too, quick and light-fingered, before baulking at its tedium.

Well, baulking is cured pretty quick with a cane. The cane whispered now, but Katie was too full of inner raging to flinch. She saw Jenks lower his lids in anticipation, his large ears laid permanently back along his skull. Just like old Pinny's cart horse, Katie thought, when Pinny gave it a prod in the rump. His moustache, twitched dangerously.

"Explain your disgusting, soiled condition!"

Hot coals flared in Katie. Resolutely, she stared at Mr. Jenks' black waistcoat which had shiny spots and a cheap watch chain hanging across it.

Old Piss-face. Crap Gizzard. Stinky Fart! Green Dog Turd!

Words from over the yard wall which no bricks could keep out. Messages from the rattling, shouting, turbulent, maddeningly tantalizing world of outside. It had gripped her since she had first found footholds in the mortar, where Old Jenksy couldn't see, and hung over the yard wall's forbidden top gazing avidly at the carters, the raggedy women, the tempting cobbled street twisting round a corner out of sight.

Katie felt everyone staring at her, waiting. Everyone except the boy with ears the colour of radishes who kept his back to her and struggled with the end of a sheet. Mr. Jenks leaned back on his heels, expert at whacking small dawdlers on the back of the head and blackening doorways so suddenly that childish knees turned to whey.

Jenks no longer minded the presence of Croom. Deep in his creaky works, he harboured a theatrical streak warming to an audience. A miserable sweep would tell no tales to their benefactor.

"I said, explain yourself!"

Tension was already high. For three days now, it had been in peak readiness for Miss Radmore's monthly visit and Miss Radmore, for the first time in memory, had not appeared. This had thrown everyone into a turmoil, fraying nerves, causing heads to lift at each rattle of wheels in the street.

The secret of hoodwinking Amelia Radmore, Jenks had early discovered, was to have everything squeakily, shinily, rigorously clean. A week before her visit, preparations began. Walls, floors, tables were scrubbed. The sheets were dragged off the cots, the children's dresses slapped through the wash and hung out to dry. The day before the visit, regardless of wind, rain or snow, each child was hustled into the yard, plunged, yelping, into a tub of icy water and also scrubbed. The morning of the visit, their hair was combed, their ironed pinafores put on and the fear of the devil put into them lest their tongues let anything untoward slip to the lady. Amelia would duly arrive and inspect the drawn up children. When she commented that they looked rather pale, Mr. Jenks would assume a lugubrious expression.

"Little orphans always looks pale, ma'am. They's thinking on their mamas up in heaven. My Ida does her best to make it up."

"Did you feed them that crate of pippins I had sent down last week?"

"Oh yes, ma'am, but with orphans it don't make a deal of difference in their health."

The apples had brought good coin from the greengrocer and the children had never suspected their existence.

Katie stood out because of her hair. Not red exactly, but a vivid coppery auburn, like beech leaves on the turn. When you looked at it, it seemed the only colour in the room. Her pale skin took a flush from it and dared to hint at freckles. Beneath its mettlesome splash even her orphan scrawniness failed to look undernourished. Rather, she seemed constructed instead of wires and springs, ready to jump into trouble with the least provocation.

Katie lived for Miss Radmore's visits. If a goddess of the air had descended each month on a golden cloud, she could not have made a greater impression on the child. Miss Radmore was an emissary from the outside, a glimpse of the wonders that must exist just where the street twisted from sight. Katie drank in the scent of lavender as if it were a heavenly elixir and shivered deliciously at the rustle of Miss Radmore's vast, majestic skirts, their flounces edged with unimaginable yards of cording. Brooches winked at Miss Radmore's throat, the only jewelry Katie had ever seen, and tiny stuffed birds perched on her hat. Amelia Radmore was another species altogether from the people jostling past the Asylum every day. Miss Radmore's face was kind and lovely and her eyes danced with excitement just at being there.

There was always enough to eat the day Miss Radmore came though she was never shown the children having a meal lest their ravenous wolfing rouse suspicions. After Amelia had seen the children, she would take tea in the private parlour, doing her best to look wise as Morton Jenks went over the books. When she climbed back into her carriage, aglow with altruistic satisfaction, the Jenks would heave a sigh of relief. For the next three weeks the Asylum would slide back into its everyday disorder. Ida sat rocking by the fireside, her husband skimmed money and Mary did all the work. In the corners, grime built up, rations were cut and the children slaved without respite, growing grubbier and grubbier. In the fourth week the great purge began all over again.

Now the tension of holding the virtuous pose along with anxiety about Miss Radmore's whereabouts was telling on them all, and had certainly caused the scrap in the yard. The cane gesticulated sharply. A narrow-faced girl by the window dropped her needle. Katie didn't budge. Her gaze dared rise to the hard black knot of Mr. Jenks' cravat.

Ask Prue Furlip, Donkey-bum! She started everything!

A glance at Prue brought the light of battle to Katie's eye. Prue was sitting primly at her work; her face wiped clean, the mud on the back of her skirt neatly concealed by the chair. Prue was let come in. Prue was let sit down. Nothing was going to happen to her.

Prue was the oldest, largest girl there, with hair the colour of eggshells and bullying eyes. She was a "temporary", taken in for extra cash while her mother and father—words Prue trailed over Katie's consciousness like cutting tools—got their butcher shop set up and could come get her. She had pushed in like a lumbering cuckoo among frailer nestlings and immediately attacked the one who seemed most precariously tolerated in the place, Katie Mucker. With the instinct of her kind, she had sensed at once that Jenks was an ally. If there was a chance to get Katie, he would let Prue try.

"You! What happened?"

Jenks slammed the cane down on the table in front of the girl who had dropped the needle. The crack made Will drop his sheet, Croom jump, and the unfortunate girl, Sally Miles, scatter unstitched glove pieces in a blizzard around her.

"Muh..muh...mud g-got thrown, s-sir!" Sally stammered, instantly white as the gloves. She had nothing to do with the incident outside but that did no lessen her fear. Punishment had little to do with justice here and a great deal to do with whomever Mr. Jenks felt like tormenting.

Katie felt again Prue's fingers rubbing slime into her hair, trying to thrust her face into the puddle and turned her heated look on Sally for knuckling under. Didn't Sally know it was no use saying anything to Old Jenksy. He just got you for it no matter what.

The pleasurable flood inside Jenks was growing hotter. He had broken every child to his will sooner or later. Every child but Katie.

He turned back to Katie whose mouth was turned down in veriest stubbornness. As always, he remembered the curate's crisp notes sliding from his grasp.

"And why was it thrown?" he demanded, twirling the cane till it hissed in the air.

Katie's hands balled into fists. Her righteous anger fought with a familiar knot tightening in the pit of her stomach. Valiantly, she struggled not to feel small, not to shrink as was so easy to do when old Jenksy yanked at his lapels like that and licked his lips as if he were about to have a meal. She had known since babyhood, that if she let herself start shrinking, she'd shrink and shrink away to a little dot, and then she'd disappear. Ever since Katie could remember, Jenks had hated her and it did no good to hotly wonder why.

Because you're a...a you-know-what. Bad!

But she didn't feel bad. She felt like herself. And furious!

Croom, normally banished to empty rooms, liked his bit of entertainment too. Right borin', he supposed, stuck here with all those bleached bits 'o girls. Need to prod one of 'em and make her jump!

Will stood by helplessly, confused about what he was expected to do. Work! That much he knew even through the churning inside him. Young as he was, he'd picked stones, cleaned fish, sweated on treadmills, lugged bags when his dad hired out to as porter. He didn't remember his mother or a home even, except the hovel where they'd all been jammed in with wrinkled Emma after the mill stopped. It was the towns he'd never forget and dragging his feet on the long, long roads between them, sleeping in sheds, under hedges, his father, hangdog, begging for work.

The worst was the taverns with their stink of gin and drunken shouts. Sometimes he could hide. Other times he was grabbed from behind his stuporous father and slammed up on the table. "Drink up, lad!" they'd roar, pouring raw spirits down his throat until he was reeling. Then they pushed him from one to the other while he staggered about, madly trying to escape, laughter smashing at his ears.

Oh yes, he knew how it felt to be trapped in front of a sea of jeering faces. When he saw Croom tilting his blackened head in Katie's direction, stiffness climbed his spine. Racked by storms though he was, his sturdy little spirit raced over and planted itself by the embattled girl. Croom's glance swerved and caught the boy's open sympathy.

Well, well, he thought, surprised at what the pup had in him. And over a whey-faced by-blow that's naught to nobody!

The cane slammed the table again. The children jumped like beans in a box. Katie drew her body together under her pinafore. Willful, passionate child, they called her. Wicked, wicked child. Full of bad blood, born in a gutter. Shouldn't be put with nice children at all! If a bowl were dropped or a spoon lost or food gobbled, Katie got the blame. Clumsy! Careless! Baaaad! Her breathing speeded up, queerly shallow. A fearful exhilaration touched her as she saw the battle drawing nigh.

On Katie's side there was only Mary. Silent, despised, lowly Mary, slipping Katie bits of her own dinner when Katie was banished, fasting. Secretly scrubbing her bit of floor for her. Sometimes clumping upstairs late, after a weary deal of work was done, to tuck her in.

Oh Mary...

Katie longed to turn, to see whether Mary were in the hallway watching. Though Mary could do nothing, she always hovered, granite-faced, through the slaps, the tirades, the days of bread and water for this or that imagined sin. If her admiration fixed on Miss Radmore, her heart belonged to Mary. Mary was the bulwark on which Katie built her life, her protection, the nourishment on which she fed her hungry little soul. And that, could Jenks have known it, was the secret of the child's survival. She had something to live for. Unlike the other children of the Asylum, Katie was passionately loved.

"Why was mud thrown?" Jenks demanded again. He could feel the rage pulsing in Katie. He wished he could break her obstinate little neck!

The hardening mud on Katie's cheeks pinched like tiny rude fingers.

He wants me to be scared! He wants me to be scared!

Dozens of times she had been scared, staring down at his great splayed boots, trying to keep her knees from shaking. The other children knew to keep their heads down and start howling the moment they were luckless enough to attract old Jenksy's wrath. Katie knew she should do this too, that it might get her out of the caning sure to come. But she couldn't. She never had. Clenching her teeth hard, she lifted her gaze from Jenks' cravat to his narrow eyes and stared at him full on.

Stick a turd up your nose and sneeze, Jenksy!

Never before had the red-headed brat dared look at Jenks like that. The revolt must be put down at once.

Katie had straightened up like a young gamecock in a barnyard scrap. Though she couldn't know it, the constant struggle with Mr. Jenks was as bracing as a dash of icy water, a gulp of bitter tonic burning down the throat. Other children might lose themselves in a fog of drowsy vacancy. Against the stupefying numbness of Asylum life, Katie snatched at the thing that would send blood speeding through her, the dart and flash of the mongoose and the cobra. She was an infant warrior shooting childish arrows at the tiger with no real knowledge of the tiger's devouring power. Despite the dire consequences, the stir of it fizzed up inside her like the contents of a bottle with the neck broken off.

Father Time on the clock leaned forward as though he contemplated jumping into the fray. All the seated children, even Sally

Miles, gazed transfixed, glad of anything at all that broke the ever-lasting dullness of stitching gloves all day.

I don't care about them! Katie told herself fiercely, I don't, I don't!

But she did, oh she did. And because she did, she sensed that the only person in the room who wasn't one of them was the red-faced boy in baggy trousers who was staring, not at her, but at Jenks in open dismay.

Jenks longed to have at Katie with the cane but he knew he could get no answer when her face was set like that. He could not afford such a defeat. So he turned on helpless Sally again.

"Why!" Jenks roared at her.

Sally's jaw flapped uselessly, emitting small, squawky sound .

This bullying of hapless, pop-eyed Sally was too much for Katie. The molten stone in her breast swelled into a volcanic bubble and burst.

"Because," she yelled at her tormentor, "I was called a...a bastard!"

CHAPTER EIGHT

The minute it was out, unconsciously enunciated in the pear-shaped tones of Miss Amelia, Katie almost clapped both hands over her mouth. "Bastard" was the word no child raised under the rule of Amelia Radmore was ever supposed to utter, though Prue had no trouble at all. Old Jenksy grinned and rocked on his heels. Katie had fallen into his trap.

"But you are a bastard," he pronounced silkily. Though the word probably described many of them, they rigorously maintained the fiction of respectable parentage. With satisfaction, Jenks saw Katie blanch.

"And we'll report your language to Miss Radmore, my little gutter mouth. She'll think you're a positive infection. She'll say off to the workhouse with you!"

Mr. Jenks' goal, so far unachieved, was to get Katie shipped to the workhouse, that place of horror to all poor. Let her try her chances among the crammed in, lice ridden castoffs there. The moustache twitched again.

"Thank Prue Furlip!"

Prue's jaw dropped in scandalized delight. Frantically, Katie looked about the room, but the only face that did not thirst for the spectacle belonged to the boy. He looked as aghast as she felt though he couldn't possibly know that Prue was the most...the most...spiteful, mean, tormenting girl in all of London.

And he had blue eyes, just like Mary!

The quality she had caught in the boy had to come bred in the bone or not at all—common decency. For an instant she stared at Will, taking an impression that would remain the rest of her life. Jenks grasped her braid, wrenching her head round to face Prue.

"Thank her!" Jenks commanded. Katie fought for her dignity the way a climber fights whose fingers give way, one by one, on the crumbling side of a cliff. Then she couldn't breathe.

"Th...th...thank you,...P...Prue!"

The words were forced out. The pricks of a million molten tears swarmed at the back of her eyelids. The tears, at least, would not get out. Never, never would old Jenksy make her cry!

"Now," Jenks continued, "what do we do with children who are full up with nastiness?" He answered for her. "We clean them out!"

Ida clutched a long-necked bottle, eyes shiny with anticipation. Though Ida had been thwarted of her murderous intentions during Katie's infancy, she continued to circle round and round the child, fascinated with that unnamed, undefined thing that made Katie so different from the others.

"Noooooo!"

The protest choked as Ida pried Katie's jaws open and jammed in the neck of the bottle. Castor oil, thick and vile, blurped in oily gouts down the back of Katie's writhing tongue. As Katie convulsed to expel the revolting laxative, Ida whipped away the bottle and clamped the small mouth shut.

"Now there's a dear," the woman cooed until the child had ceased to jerk and struggle. "Works on the bowels, this does. Purges out the badness. Oh, it'll do you ever so much good!"

When Ida released her, Katie's breath erupted in hacking gasps but the castor oil stayed down. White, oily finger marks fanned across her mottled cheeks.

Loathsome, loathsome castor oil! Tasting of rotted metal and worms crushed under stones, making Katie want to screech and howl and fling herself against a wall. Only sight of Prue, self-important and sneering, kept Katie from vomiting outrageously in front of everybody.

Jenks who had been waiting for her to cry, now recoiled from the seething hatred in Katie's eyes. Croom was watching him fail to break this defiant scrap of a girl.

"On your knees! We shall ask the Lord for forgiveness."

Burning from her many unequal battles, Katie did not feel the flagstones cutting at her kneecaps when Jenks forced her down. She only saw Prue puffing up like a pigeon, staring contemptuously.

She's going to go after me in the yard again. Old Jenks wants her to. So he can get at me!

Bad stock, Jenks thought. Born to bolt the traces no matter how the whip was laid on. Well, the sooner you bolt, the sooner I'll be shut of you, my young mucksnipe!

But unless she revolted, and revolted spectacularly, he couldn't get rid of her, any more than she could get rid of that eyesore, Mary.

Amelia Radmore always asked after her misfits, making sure they were alive and well to pester him.

Croom, in the midst of shoving a bucket under the chimney, immediately bowed his head and shot out one black paw to bend Will's too. Damned little gaping baboon. You'd think he was the one who was going to get it, not the girl.

Over the sickening ooze of castor oil, Katie became conscious of the presence in the passageway. A shadow that was Mary. Mary frowning with all her dumb ferocity at Jenks. Oh Mary, Mary...help!

"Oh Lord, witness the grievous faults of this wicked, wicked child, who is willful and ungrateful in her heart, a contemptible sinner...."

Katie knew what her own grievous faults were, for they were often pointed out. First, she had been thrown her away on a dung heap when she was a baby because she wasn't good enough to keep. Second, she had no father and, third, she had no mother who wanted her at all.

Katie had little idea what a father was though she was made severely to feel the lack. About the function of a mother she was much less vague. A mother was someone like Mary. Someone who slipped her an extra vest when it was so cold the frost stood up on the inside of the windows. Someone who dried her as quickly as she could on the fearful day they were given baths. Someone who dared to squeeze her shoulder on the stairs. Someone who was simply...there!

Really lucky children, she supposed, got someone like Mary all to themselves.

Jenks replenished his lungs.

"Oh Lord, the fires of hell are ravenous for this child. Disgusted by her sins, You hold her over the pit like a detestable insect. Born in sin, cast out from Your flock, her flesh will burn for all eternity unless..."

Prayer always threw the children into petrified immobility. Their knowledge of Christianity was sketchy in the extreme, but terrifying. Assuring Amelia that religious instruction was not neglected. Jenks had Mr. Willoughby of nearby St. Witold's in once a month to rant and thunder. Mr. Willoughby was a gnarly specimen with tufts of yellow hair sticking out of his ears and a voice like grape shot loose in the bottom of a barrel. Without a thought of imparting basics, Willoughby bellowed out his finest brimstone sermons, working himself up into a wonderfully pleasurable lather before his captive audience of round-eyed, quaking girls.

Consequently, the children thought of Jesuschrist as a strange monster, part carpenter, part sheep, who got nailed to a tree and killed because they, the very girls at the Infant's Asylum, were full to the neck with sin, a substance very much like the stinky backyard mud after a rain. Sin made them slow and bad so that they ate too much and didn't finish their gloves on time.

Jesuschrist had bled a mighty washtub full of blood in which they'd one day have to plunge themselves to prevent the devils who lived just below the cellar from smelling the sin and roasting them like sausages in fireplaces bigger than mail coaches. This dreadful scheme had been thought up by somebody invisible called God, who was always jealous. God squatted in the roof beams, like a never-sleeping Mr. Jenks, watching everything people did so He could get them for it after they were dead.

Mr. Willoughby was given to graphic illustration of his points. His favourite was to catch a large moth and hold it over a candle until it had writhed itself to a crisp in imitation of what awaited disobedient orphans in the crackling fires of Hell. He stared hard until each child felt she, too, had a hairy body ready to ignite at the slightest spark. Sally Miles had fainted clean away. The children were more scared of Jesuschrist than any tribe of cannibals fearing demons crouched inside the volcano's rim.

Momentarily, the smell of singeing moth filled Katie's nostrils. She lowered her head, trying to see Mary.

Now a young woman, Mary had changed little since Katie's arrival save to acquire added heaviness about the jaw and forehead. Her hands were red, as always, from the work, her speech more taciturn than ever, but the blue eyes had become infinitely brighter, full of life and purpose from keeping watch on Katie through the day.

Mary gave off love for Katie silently, the way a furnace gives off shimmering heat. Only Katie could feel it. Jenks, Ida, the rest of the children, as though they all lacked some essential sense, could no more notice the radiant, sustaining power of the emotion flung out by Mary than they could have noticed had the battered chair in the chimney corner fixed its affections on one of them and sat four square on the flagstones, loving with all its might.

Even as she stolidly scrubbed the stairs and lugged up pots of porridge from the steaming nether region of the kitchen, Mary cared. This caring fell as warm rain upon a vital, hungry seed. Without even knowing it, Katie loved Mary back with all the fervent affection natural to her, the love of a child for its mother who had no other mother to direct it to.

Prue stuck out her tongue. Before Katie knew what she was doing, she curled her lips back and stuck out her tongue rudely back.

"Amen."

Mr. Jenks caught Katie with her face contorted and naked wrath in her eye. He allowed a slow unpleasant hitch at the corners of his mouth. She was growing taller, he realized with surprise. And her perversity was growing with her like a noxious weed. Crookeder and ruder by the day, he'd tell Miss Radmore. As could only be expected in a red-haired bastard from a Thames-side ditch.

Indeed, Katie's hair, now pulled into untidy clumps, was of the springy, intractable type that had to be daily wrestled into a braid like a savage's topknot. Only Mary noticed, with enormous secret pride, how it caught sunlight in a mass of gold and copper threads out in the yard. To Jenks, Katie's hair only produced certainty as to her parentage.

"An Irish by blow!" he said often to Ida. "Some papist slut dropped her pup in the muck and left it. Afraid of the priest, no doubt!"

"Aye," Ida would agree, watching while Mary stirred yet another greyish pudding. "Them Irish, all over the city like fleas ever since the potato blight. Ought to ship 'em home in barges."

Speaking of Irish always made Jenks think of Red Nell and how he was still impaled on her hook. Impotent fury alternated with a furtive and fearful satisfaction in his growing horde. Soon, oh very soon, he was going to bolt the traces himself.

Drawing out the silence, Jenks examined Katie with more attention than he had in months. To match her hair, she had impertinently cut features in a long oval of a face, though whether they would turn out pretty or odd would depend on the whim of the next few years. If they turned out pretty, and if the lads didn't get to her first, she could be turned over for a tidy sum to certain old gentlemen who had a taste for them young. But Mr. Jenks, along with a great many other things that would have petrified Amelia, knew well the unlikelihood of Katie escaping the street boys once she was among them.

The thought of Katie's future pleased Jenks all the more since, in some obscure way, he thought Red Nell had an interest in her. Nell's thug had come, four months after Katie's arrival, and demanded to look at the babies. Fuming, Jenks had had to let him, but he was damned if he were going to give Red Nell one scrap he didn't have to.

"Oh that one, " he'd said over Katie who was still scrawny as a plucked chicken. "Widow from Greenwich brought it in. Going to Australia, she was. Didn't think the young 'un would last the trip."

"You swear!"

Jenks found himself, pinned by his lapels, against the wall. This was Joe Varden, Red Nell's chief bully boy, knotted up with some dark longing to smash a head.

"I s-swear," Jenks had stammered.

Joe had let him down and gone to look at the baby again, but there were six more like her, all with their own stories. Finally Joe left, cursing under his breath.

For weeks, Jenks had thought of going to Red Nell with the truth, in case there should be money in it. The memory of Joe's contorted face stopped him, along with the suspicion that payment might just as easily be a quick knife thrust if Joe found out Jenks had lied.

So to hell with the bloodsuckers! Jenks told himself with bluster. What could such a gutter rat be to them anyway?

Still, whenever Jenks was suffering particularly under Red Nell's yoke, it was satisfying to take it out on Katie.The worst of it was her eyes, Jenks thought. Too damned green, too damned interested. No pauper brat had business peering out at the world as keenly as that. How dare she look as if she guessed every time he was straining not to pass wind in front of Miss Radmore. Katie could scowl like a magistrate and had been caught skipping in the yard despite constant meals of boiled potatoes and watery broth.

"Sly," muttered Jenks. "If she were ten years older, I wouldn't trust her behind my back with a knife."

As usual, it was Mary who who didn't tell when she found Katie giving way to indignant midnight tears. The comfort of warm arms would have been too much for the rules. However, Katie felt almost as comforted knowing Mary was hunched on a stool glowering with all her might in Mr. Jenks direction.

Mr. Jenks pushed back his coat cuffs.

"Katie Mucker, take your punishment."

The castor oil rolled in a turgid wave. Automatically Katie stretched out upturned palms and shut her eyes, screwed up against the coming assault on her sensitive, defenceless fingertips. Jenks felt Croom watching him and saw Katie steeling herself. She wouldn't howl no matter how he beat her. Damn her obstinate hide!

Catching Katie suddenly by the scruff, he tipped her face forward over a chair. She felt, rather than heard, the ripple of cloth and, unbelievingly, realized her skirt and petticoat had been hiked up, leaving her thin drawers exposed to the whole gaping room.

In the Radmore world, bodies were muffled from neck to toe lest one turn to stone at the sight of unclothed flesh. A scorching sweat broke out over Katie's forehead. The cane slashed across her buttocks, raising thin lines of blood, lines Miss Radmore was guaranteed not to see.

Rockets of pain shot down Katie's thighs and up her spine. Mr. Jenks' breath whistled through his nostrils as Katie twitched like a hooked fish and clutched blindly at the rungs of the chair. He'd make her beg and howl...

The cane stopped in mid-air. Jenks let out a dry croak filled with disgust and swift, gloating triumph.

"Ugh! Filthy, filthy animal!"

For an instant, Katie couldn't comprehend. Then she felt a hot, wet gush in her drawers and...oh, crumb, oh dogface, knew the oil had made her bowels give way. Unable to move, she felt the hotness spilling downward, along the backs of her legs for all to see.

Iron fingers dug into the back of her neck.

"Stay there, you odious beast. Let everyone see what an abomination you are! You'll scrub the room from corner to corner. And work till you've made up for clothing you've so willfully ruined! And," Jenks delivered the final, crushing blow, "Miss Radmore will be informed about every disgusting bit of your behaviour!"

Jenks could hardly contain the glee. He knew how much Katie would writhe and shrivel while all the brats gawked at the dark blotch spreading across Katie's rear.

Miss Radmore is going to come any minute, thought Katie in a panic, forgetting the whole room and even Prue. Miss Radmore is going to see me! Old Jenksy WANTS her to see me like this! Churning outrage made her so rigid she felt she'd never move again.

Croom became aware of how uncomfortably silent everything had become. Jenks stood still as a gatepost, the children were riveted at seeing another of their number brought so low.

"Hey, boy, look alive here!"

Blood burned in Will's face as if it were himself sprawled across the chair. No one noticed Mary who was crushing the folds of her skirt in her fists as though they were tender sections of Mr. Jenks' neck.

"Take the grate out and set them buckets in to catch the soot."

Jenks turned. A connoisseur of children, he now looked Will up and down with a critical eye.

"He's going to be a big one," he commented with the implication that Will wasn't quite suited to be a climbing boy.

"Aye sir, that he will," Croom agreed, disconcerted by this new joviality.

"See the wrists on him and the feet. Better think about your larder."

Will shrank, fearing with good reason rough men in search of amusement.

"There must be plenty of small boys about if you want a climbing lad," continued Jenks expansively.

"Aye, but I won this one free and clear at the pub."

Croom had found a nice, obedient country lad, not one of those London eels who would be gone the moment his back was turned.

"Really," prompted Jenks, interested now.

Croom rose further to the bait.

"Regular swill pot, Will's dad. Got soused and signed up for a sailor, then remembered boys can't go on ships so I played him and won. Bloke was too splashed to hang onto a brass ha'penny, never mind this here cub. Cursed like twenty when he lost. Then told the boy he'd be better off with me and good riddance. His own son!"

Will threw up his young head.

"My pa's alright when he's sober! He's a good pa, he is. He just... he was all cut up about no work and havin' to go on the sea..."

The outburst died as Croom's cheeks puffed out.

"Well, you won't be seeing him any more, will you lad, so don't matter what kind of pa he was. You're on your own knock for good!"

The sweep let that sink in then shook himself to business.

"I'm goin' up on the roof to do what I can. You shove these here buckets underneath to catch the soot. And mind you see so none gets about and soils the work of all these busy lasses."

He shoved Will, along with two pails and a whisk, under the sheet spread protectively from the mantle. Minutes later, he was heard on the tiles, his circular brush, attached to section after section of handle, sending cascades of grit rattling downward.

Jenks tapped the cane against his knee. The children began stitching hurriedly. Katie remained like a stone, the splotch on her drawers growing larger and larger while Ida put the castor oil bottle regretfully back on its shelf. Mary backed further into the shadows, still crushing the folds of her skirt.

Presently Croom returned, a grim anticipation on his face.

"Now, lad, time for you to do your part."

Drawing back the sheet, he revealed Will, now blackened head and shoulders from the shower of soot. He was holding two full pails, and coughing. Between the pails was a sooty pile where he had tried to sweep up the excess. Croom banded him a stiff hand brush and scraper.

"Get up inside there and scrap the twisty part I couldn't get at. I'll give you a boost up."

Will peered incredulously into the dimness above his head.

"I can't get up there. It's only big enough for a rabbit."

"Aye, it is. And you're my rabbit, so earn your keep."

Will pushed himself back inside the fireplace mouth and cautiously stood up. The chimney narrowed so there seemed scarcely room for his shoulders. A trickle of soot stung his eyes and the acrid smell of the winter's fires came at him. His heart thudded once as something buried deep in his mind hitched spasmodically. Hesitantly, Will extended a hand and found the flue narrowed only inches higher.

"Up you get."

Croom seized his leg and forced him upward.

Will cried in alarm, heart now rattling against his ribs. Croom kept shoving him upward relentlessly. Will flailed with his free leg to finally get a toehold on the rough brick at the back of the fireplace. Croom let go. Will came crashing back onto the hearthstone. When this happened twice more, Croom lost his good temper.

"Don't be so clumsy. Take a hold, I say. There's chinks to stick your toes."

"It's...it's too narrow," Will's voice shook with panic as the dread thing convulsed at the bottom of his mind.

"Phsaw! When I was a lad we was up 'em like monkeys."

Aye, and felt the bones of his young legs twisting into today's knock knees as he stood for hours in the blackness, scraping and brushing. Saw his brother get the sore between his legs and die of the sweep's disease, testicles swollen horribly. Prayed the spot he had down there right now was just an another pimple and not... and not...that!

He grasped Will's leg again.

"Get up there!" he growled, but Will only tumbled down again. Croom was too large to get fully under the opening and give Will the shove that would put him up the chimney once and for all.

Fresh inspiration dawned for Jenks. He could feel the intransigence in Katie growing back the way it always did. Jenks jerked her upright.

"Since you are the filthiest creature in London, miss, you can help the chimney sweep!"

Croom was taken aback.

"Oh now, Mr. Jenks, I don't need the aid of any nice little orphan girls. Ain't I got me a lad to do the rough stuff."

"Katie is not a nice little orphan girl," Jenks said with relish. "She is a misbegotten whelp and her devilish pride must be brought low. Get over to the chimney, girl!"

Katie's skirt fluttered down to hide her drawers. But the wetness soaked her stockings. Indignation and shame rushed up her body in a scarlet tide.

"Get on your hands and knees. The boy can stand on your back!"

As Jenks propelled her across the room, she was horribly aware of the drips on the flagstones behind her. Prue stuffed her fist against her mouth. And Miss Radmore would be...disgusted. Miss Radmore would hate her forever! Miss Radmore whose carriage could even now be drawing to a halt!

Will, crouched on the hearthstone, his eyes full of a terrible understanding. As Jenks pushed Katie down, Will scrambled hastily aside so that all of him, except his shins, was hidden in the chimney. Croom dared not interfere with the game.

"All right boy, get on her back."

"Oh no, please sir, not on a..a girl..."

This was worse than the time they had tried to make him torment the shoe black boy who had limped on a twisted leg. Katie felt his calves tremble against her. Their bond of mutual misery tightened.

"Get up there, or I'll cane your legs. Look smart!"

Whimpering softly, Will did as he was told. Hoisting himself part way into the black space above, he set his feet onto Katie's back.

But for her set teeth, Katie would have crumpled. Because the girl felt so full of springy fragile bones, Will hurriedly got one leg up, then a second, bare toes clinging to an uneven ledge just above the fire level. Up in the chimney hole and he felt it squeezing his upper arms. Inside him, the old, shrouded memory was heaving itself to its knees.

"I can't go up here. I can't. It's all dark and I'll get stuck."

Mary moved restlessly in the hall, not liking the mention of dark. The pits had been dark and rife with beetles and agony.

Croom sighed. Purposefully, he whipped a wadded newspaper from his pocket, touched match to it, and thrust the whole blazing thing under the chimney hole. Will was warned only by one inexplicable whiff of smoke before the flame singed the soles of his feet. Yelping, he tore at the firebricks with toes and fingers and didn't stop until he found himself far up the chimney, the soot of his passage swirling round his head.

Will had one arm twisted above his head against the crooked bricks. The other was squashed into his side. The soot was clogging his nostrils, spilling bitterly into his throat. He would never get out. He'd choke to death. He'd die!

He began to wrench his body violently inside the tiny space, trying to claw up, claw down, claw anywhere but this Stygian trap where he was smothering. His lungs sucked in sharp flakes, expelled them out, coughed and rasped.

The buried memory burst its seals, and engulfed him. The mill! He had been at the mill when it had been burned. She was working there and he just toddling. The flames ate up the sky! The screams! His mother trying to get to him, her gaping mouth vanishing into the flames as the wooden wall came crashing down...

Will began to shriek, thinly, hysterically. He was tearing the flesh of his shoulders on the ridges of mortar, smashing his shins against the bricks, but the angle of the flue held him tight.

The flaming paper left an angry scorch on Katie's cheek as she flung herself out of the way. The screams of the boy, horribly magnified by the black cave of the fireplace, felt as if they were coming from her own lungs. She caught a nightmarish glimpse of Croom bobbing his head, apologizing for the noise. And Jenks nodding back, one thumb stuck into his vest, familiar nasty enjoyment lighting his face.

Katie began to shake. The shrieks became truly her own, all the cries she had ever kept inside her, the rage choked back because she was only a wicked bastard, so small, afraid of the cane. The boy was shrieking to her, to anybody, crying for help.

She twisted to her knees, then to her feet, a besmirched, clench-jawed apparition. As Mr. Jenks predicted, she bolted the traces at last. Not caring if old Satan himself stuck her on his toasting fork, she grabbed up a bucket of soot and flung it, with all her might, straight into Jenks' astounded face.

CHAPTER NINE

The street door opened. For one split second there was glimpsed an excruciatingly fashionable morning coat, a moss plaid waistcoat with glistening watch chain, tight fawn trousers, starched collar and the vastest of yellow silk cravats, all beneath the face of one just discovering toads in his soup.

Before the eyes of all, the tongue of soot billowed upward and outward, so lovingly enveloping this elegance that one would have thought the doorway suddenly furnished with a large black paper silhouette. A second gentleman, two steps behind, took soot on the cheek and shoulder. The brass work of the brougham and the hindquarters of a pair of thoroughbreds escaped altogether.

All motion, all sound died, even Will's shrieks, for he had fainted in the chimney. The rows of girls were caught with hands upraised, trying to bat the flakes from their pinafores which it was fatal to soil. Croom was grabbing for a sheet in a horrified, futile attempt to contain the disaster. Jenks was strangling on a huge lungful of inhaled grit. Katie hung in the air, arms and bucket out thrust, vengeful, unholy glee blazing from every line of her quivering form.

Only the particles of soot continued to float, whirling up to the ceiling, spinning back upon themselves, settling down in drifts across the dozens of snowy gloves now representing three days' work utterly ruined.

The gentleman at the door emitted two high pitched, shuddering sneezes, then a bellow of fury.

"Thunderation!"

Slamming down his silver-headed walking stick, he began brushing furiously at his face and his coat. The man behind him, much older and not nearly so extravagantly dressed, just stood, brows climbing his forehead, staring into the room.

The natural command in the first gentleman's voice jolted Jenks to attention. Even as he pawed at his eyes and coughed in gasping snatches, he scrambled to scrape and bow in the presence of the ruling class.

"Oh, begging your pardon sirs. Begging your pardon. Most unfortunate. An accident sir, all an accident. This wicked monstrous child..."

His voice died weakly as the one stinging eye he managed to open showed him how expensively the gentleman was turned out and how shiny the brougham behind him. Right on a day when it was Miss Amelia who should be visiting.

"Be quiet!" the stranger roared in outrage. Then, contradicting himself, he demanded, "What is the meaning of this!"

He was foppish and swaggering for all that he looked barely twenty. Panic shot through Jenks. Without knowing it, he tried to tug at his forelock. Soot showered down from his hair, turning the white of his eye into a vivid ring. One lid watered copiously from the soot lodged under it.

"A thousand apologies, sir. You've caught us at a bad moment, a very bad moment. One of the orphans has just gone mad. Stark raving. She picked up a bucket of soot and threw it. Bad blood she has, devilish bad. Oh, how can I help you, sir?"

The fellow's handkerchief was now as black as the rest of him and completely useless. He flung it down and slapped at his clothes as if they had filled with vermin. He already felt contaminated just from riding through these wretched streets. Streets he had never dreamed existed. Streets to make a decent chap retch. And now to be attacked merely for opening a door! He puffed up even more outrageously.

"You can help me by holding your tongue and standing out of my way. If you're responsible here, this place is disgusting!"

"But sir, I can explain..."

"BE QUIET!"

The young man was so livid even Jenks shrank back. The cloud of soot was almost settled now. Father Time on the clock had acquired a dark cap. Snowy pinafores were hopelessly smudged. Black crescents settled on noses and cheeks giving the children a grubby, rodent look.

For an endless moment, the visitor surveyed the scene, breathing heavily. Jenks and the seated children flinched as he turned snappily to his companion.

"Do you see, Parkinson! Do you see this...this degenerate mess and still expect that I shall let them go on bleeding money from the Radmore estate!"

At the mention of the Radmore name, Jenks blanched beneath his inky coating. His jaws flew open to begin renewed apologies but could not get the words out. The other man was Mr. Parkinson, the parish commissioner for the district.

Mr. Parkinson, despite the soot dusting his neck and shoulder, presented the sober, substantial appearance of the middle-class. Silver mingled in his side-whiskers. Gravity sat on his brow. Lines around his mouth hinted at a rather heavy knowledge of the woes within his jurisdiction.

"I admit, Mr. Radmore, that the disorder is unpardonable. However, the Asylum has a fine reputation and is much needed when there are so many unfortunate waifs and orphans..."

"Pah! Waifs and orphans! What would happen to waifs and orphans if this were the African jungle? Tell me that?"

Though he'd already had a disconcerting ride with this fellow in the carriage, Mr. Parkinson looked startled. His mouth remained shut as he remembered being routed from his luncheon to play guide. His companion branished his ornate walking stick emphatically.

"They'd die out, that's what they'd do. A young animal without parents to fend for it simply perishes. And good riddance too. If the parent didn't have the stuff to survive, why should the cub. Let them grow up and breed and what happens, Mr.Parkinson? What?"

The commissioner jerked back a half step, more speechless still.

"Weakens the stock, that's what happens," the young dandy supplied, beginning to pace on his plump, superbly outlined legs. "Just look at these children. How old are they? Seven? Eight? Nine! Do they look like good strong healthy children to you, Mr. Parkinson? The kind of children Britain wants?"

Mr. Parkinson was about to say that Britain had them whether she wanted them or not. A sharp gesticulation cut him off.

"No, they are not," the orator answered himself, swinging his walking stick like a pointer along the rows of petrified girls. "They're undersized. Bad colour. Dirty. And look at them crouched like rabbits staring at us. Poor show of spirit, if you ask me. Mentally deficient if you put them to the test!"

"I have to disagree," put in Mr. Parkinson, finally finding his tongue. "Many intelligent people spring from most disadvantageous..."

"Impossible! If they were intelligent, they wouldn't be in this fix. Why look at this one," he pointed directly into Katie's contorted face. "You heard the fellow here. This one has actually gone mad!

If a horse or a dog goes mad, Mr. Parkinson, there's no cure except a bullet through the head!"

Bullet through the head!

Mary gasped and shuffled into the room, eyes dark with alarm. Mr. Parkinson drew the full dignity of the Church of England between himself and this devil-spawned persuasion.

"Mr. Radmore, there is hunger aplenty in the streets and those that don't get fed look pale and thin. However, the kindness of Miss Radmore to this institution has been something that God in his mercy..."

"Pah! God in his mercy! Fairy tales! Read Darwin, read Spencer and you will find out about God in his mercy! Nature runs the universe, not some bearded ninny in a bedsheet. Survival of the fittest! That's the ticket! If there isn't enough to go round here, why let them scramble for the food supply. Then we'll soon find out who's fit to have it."

The stiffened face of the commissioner gratified the young man so much he twirled his stick in a silver arc. Mr. Jenks felt his collar become very tight. Radmore, Radmore, he thought frantically, which one is he?

"I'll admit I had heard things were bad," their visitor went on, "but I never imagined how bad until today. Do you know what I've seen in these streets?" He fixed his eye upon Katie as if she might tell him. "I've seen the dregs. Cripples hauling themselves about like half-squashed insects. Blind people. Waxy men and women not the size of a twelve-year-old. Scabrous children scampering down alleys, arms no bigger than pencils. Packs of them. Why there must be thousands in this city. By Jove, Parkinson, doesn't that fact give you a shock?"

The commissioner remained silent. Privately, he felt he had seen too much ever to be shocked again, but his companion seemed to be cooling down.

The disdainful features turned back to the children and examined them again, up and down. At Oxford, at the Galapagos Club, they had striven to outdo each other in atheistic, scientific pragmatism, but it had been all theory. Now, by gad, he was seeing the real thing right in front of his nose.

"Well, I'm shocked, if you're not," he declared, making another flourish with his stick, "And do you know what's keeping their half brains and sickly bodies clogging up the streets, Mr. Parkinson?" He whirled on that embattled gentleman. "Charity, that's what! Charity like this establishment. Charity interferes with the laws of nature. You don't see bears giving charity, or hawks, do you?"

Mr. Parkinson was forced to admit that he had never seen bears giving charity. Still, he tried to rally.

"To relieve the suffering of the poor is blessed work."

"Suffering of the poor! Damn it man, have you no eyes! Disease, depravity, idiocy! When pups are born like that, you don't feed them, you wring their necks. If these people are kept alive and allowed to breed, why, in two generations the country will be drowned in runts and idiots. That wasn't who built the Empire—runts and idiots! Our British stock is the finest, the noblest in the world. Do you want to see it trampled under by a horde of knock-kneed half-wits like this!"

With Parkinson rendered speechless, the indignant visitor turned his attention to Jenks who resembled a blackened fence post.

"You are in charge here?"

Jenks began bobbing despite the fiery pain in his right eye.

"That I am, that I am. My apologies again, sir, for this..."

"Bloody hell, stop groveling and listen. Last Tuesday week, Miss Radmore was severely burned and Mr. James, her brother, managed to get himself killed altogether trying to dispense charity. Murdered, I say, by a bunch of ingrates who took to their heels like cockroaches. Only managed to get our hands on one of the little brutes. I'm Julius Radmore, cousin and heir to Mr. James Radmore's estate."

He paused, allowing the news to penetrate. Jenks knew, dimly, that Miss Amelia had a brother who provided a generous allowance for his sister to spend. The pale ring of flesh just above Jenks collar turned the colour of chalk.

Julius Radmore, who did sport a mourning band on his arm, beat more dust from his sleeves and studied his ruined spats. One of the girls dared to sneeze, a thin dry sound compounded of soot and fright. Julius glanced at her sharply. His lip curled.

"Miss Amelia might pour aid into this ridiculous charitable scheme, but I, sir, am made of different stuff. I came into town today, I endured the wretched crowds and appalling stinks to look for myself and give you the benefit of the doubt. Smart orderly children, even orphans, might be worth their keep." His eye swept the room, proving that smartness and orderliness had fled along the Thames to Greenwich. "But this..."

"Begging your pardon sir," beads of sweat, like large black warts, were popping out on Jenks' forehead, "begging your pardon, but..."

"My good man, you may beg my pardon as much as you want, but it won't change the fact that I was assaulted the moment I opened the door by one of your insane charges. Hey, what's that?"

Renewed moaning issued from the flue where Will was beginning to revive.

"Oh, there's a lad up the chimney, sir. Climbing boy. Just learning his trade, he is."

"Lad up the chimney! Howling!" Julius Radmore snorted. "Oh, that corks it! Bad investment all round, this place. Only proves my theories if all you've got to show for it is a mad girl and...that!" The point of the stick jabbed at Mary, hunched and misshapen. Julius stared coldly before returning to Jenks. "You've heard my opinion of charity. I'm closing up this institution at once. All of you are to be out by next Friday afternoon as I'm giving the lease to a warehousing concern. My man of business will see to the details. Good day!"

In a silence more thunderous than an earthquake, Julius Radmore stepped toward the street. As he went, the clock chimed through its soot in doleful alarm. Julius turned back, picking out where it hung high upon the wall.

"So that's where the clock went. Part of a pair from the drawing room. A Williams, actually. Damned valuable. Don't know why Amelia brought it here, silly woman, when she knew I collect the things. Martin, put it in the box and take it back to the house this minute."

Martin, evidently the coachman, dragged up a chair, lifted the clock from the wall, and marched out with it. As it passed, Mr. Jenks' eyes bulged and his throat worked as if he were being garroted on the spot. Inside the clock, in a secret drawer built to hide Georgian billet doux, lay all his painfully thieved, carefully hidden hoard!

As the rattle of the carriage faded, Mr. Jenks tried to breathe. He couldn't. His lungs were useless, flapping sacs. An enormous pounding set up in his head.

His money! All his money! The years of sweatingly altering the books, of cheating hole-in-corner shops that sold finished gloves and handkerchiefs, of nursemaiding brats, of grinning and scraping before the sanctimonious Amelia Radmore and waking up with nightmares about Red Nell. All carried away under the coachman's arm. All for naught!

His much planned escape, which had been so near, evaporated. Nor could he even begin again. Julius Radmore was closing the place like a book!

Silence, punctuated only by Will's faint moans, smothered the room. The children sat in round-eyed incomprehension but Ida came to life. The motherly smile was wiped, at last, from her face.

"It is true? We're all to be turned out on the streets?"

Her eyes whitened like a beast recoiling from a gunshot. It was poverty, after all, that had driven her to baby farming and she had a healthy fear of having to seek employment. Mary hung by the hall door, her face a knot of frowns as she tried to digest the bewildering events. She was making sure the man who threatened Katie was gone. The knowledge had not yet reached her brain that, for such as her, humpbacked and slow, there would be no employment at all.

Paralysis still gripped Jenks. So many times had he gloated over his tavern that now he actually felt it tumbling down about him, its glasses shattering at his feet, the pay packets of mill workers slipping from his palms.

Oh, all the years of petty dealings, all the sly furtive conniving, all the cold quivers in the small of his back when Amelia Radmore walked about with that sober proprietary look. All wasted, come to naught because one gutter-whelped bastard chose today to go berserk.

He began to shake. Rage rushed in, this time a genuine killing rage, only to be assuaged by the tender neck bones crushed beneath his fingers. Maddened, he turned on Katie.

"Yes, it's true," he spat at Ida viciously. "Out on our arses without a crust, both of us! And the brats dumped in the workhouse!"

At word "workhouse", Mary jerked from an inner convulsion. She'd never seen a workhouse but she knew people would cough their last in an alley rather than go there. Little children were torn from their mothers. "Kept in a cellar and gnawed at by rats!" the fishmonger told her, goggling. Rats! Mary felt the pit rats, big as cats, scuttling over her legs as she strained in the harness.

"No," cried her mouth soundlessly. "No!"

Katie stood frozen in her posture of defiance, her legs braced apart, fists still knotted around the empty bucket. Because the soot had come down the chimney on her back, her hair and shoulders were black, but her face remained white. Her eyes blazed molten emerald at Mr. Jenks. Then the soot bucket dropped to the floor with a nerve-jarring clatter. Jenks flung out his great forefinger.

"This filthy little bastard here, throwing soot about, made us all look so bad Mr. Radmore wouldn't keep the place on a bet! She's the one that's put us on the street!"

The violence in Jenks' voice, totally devoid of his previous tormenting relish, pierced through. Katie's looked frantically around for Mary. When she saw that Mary's face was the colour of putty, a racing panic seized her breast. Something awful, far more awful than the tossing of a bucket of soot, had happened. And it had to do with her.

Katie felt disaster coalesce around her. As every eye in the room burned into her, the last of the rebellion fled from of her brain. Her childish instincts quailed before this terrifying adult thing. She sensed the same fury that sent lynch mobs ravening for blood.

Croom began swiftly tossing his gear into the sheet he was holding and rolled it into a lumpy bundle. With a single vigorous jerk, he pulled Will, almost insensible, from the chimney. Ida had lifted herself away from the castor oil shelf and stood with her bulk trembling.

"She deserves a beating," Ida cried in sudden force. She saw herself as she had been in her youth, turned out from her post as a lady's maid, swollen with the master's bastard. A bastard she'd got rid of as soon as it was born.

The violence burning in Jenks' fingertips began shooting up his arms. Damn it to Hell! If only he'd had a row of clean, industrious orphans he would have been able to talk Mr. Julius round. Katie had put paid to that! Now he was out on the streets again, worse than when he'd started years ago. Before he went, by God, he meant to wring her miserable neck!

Forgetting even the pain under his lid, he advanced, flanked by Ida. In a second, he had Katie by the front of her dress, the pinafore wadded in his fist, the seams cutting sharply under Katie's arms. Helplessly, Katie felt herself lifted up. Flecks of spittle wet Jenks' moustache. Murder, bloody murder flared up in his eye. Oh the joy of snapping those scrawny, insolent bones.

For one interminable second, his breath quivered in his nostrils. Then he flung Katie backwards at the fireplace where she slammed against the bricks just under the mantle.

Blindly, Katie twisted as she fell and scrambled to her knees as she crashed on the floor. As her head came up, she was faced by Ida's advancing bulk. The faces of all the other children froze grotesquely. Ida's grimace, her naked, lunatic self revealed in full, was terrible to see. Mr. Jenks, blackened and hulking, looked so much like one of Mr. Willoughby's demons that Katie's heart jammed in her throat. Escape was cut off from every direction. Unable to find other protection, she flung herself back into the small cave of the fireplace itself where she rolled up into a ball.

Wrathfully, Jenks kicked over the second bucket of soot. The pail careened sideways, the dust filled the hearth with a whirl so dark that Katie could scarcely be seen.

Mary stared as Katie became a dim and ghostly shadow like the dozens of shadows that sweated and groaned around her in the mine.

The pit! The pit! They're trying t'put my Katie in the pit!

The dull beast within Mary leaped from its torpid slumber and reared up in shrieking ferocity. Before anyone could reach Katie, a flailing whirlwind had knocked Ida off her feet and sent Jenks reeling from the force of her passage. Plunging into the cloud of soot, Mary dragged Katie out of the fireplace and stood at bay, the child clutched to her concave breast.

Mary's assault stunned the room. Jenks had stumbled against a table, clutching it for balance. The creature had torn open his waistcoat so badly all the buttons bounced on the floor. Ignoring sprawled Ida, Jenks spun on the two figures flattened against the mantel. His every fibre longed to smash them, yet he could not. Mary looked altogether too terrifying and strange—much-kicked kitchen cat transformed into a hissing panther.

"Get out!" he roared instead. "Get out of here now. Both of you. Don't ever let me see your faces again."

When they didn't move, he snatched up a wooden work box and hurled it forcefully. It splintered on the chimney, raining glove fingers on Katie's head. Mary staggered in confusion. Jenks picked up another one.

"There! There's more of Mr. Julius' property! And more!"

The second workbox slammed into Mary's knees. The third smashed against the mouth of the fireplace and bounced back out, splitting in half. When Jenks grabbed a fourth, Mary yanked Katie after her and raced toward the door. As they passed, Jenks drew back his big fist. With a deliberate viciousness Katie would never forget, he clouted Mary hard on the side of the head.

Mary staggered but did not fall. Mary could have hovered in the air if necessary to save Katie. She hauled the child outside and they ran, accompanied by Jenks' maniac bellowing, Mary with her heaving, limping step, Katie stumbling and swaying as Mary dragged her on and on.

They ran until their knees gave out from under them and Mary's face was mottled as a piece of mouldy cheese. Katie was dazed by the open air and sunshine.

"W...where are we going, Mary?"

"Anywhere. Anywhere ter get away!"

And she started up again, plunging down street after unknown street as if fearing Jenks had sent out slavering hounds to drag them down. As Katie's feet banged along the rough cobblestones, a mighty fear welled up. Her wrist was pulled alarmingly in Mary's horny hand. They pushed their way through crowds at street crossings, and walked and walked until Katie, exhausted, could go on no more.

They stopped by a low stone wall and leaned over it, panting. Katie's legs shook and her hip throbbed badly where she had been flung against the fireplace bricks. Only then, when their breath came back, did they realize, from the stares, that they were as blackened and torn as if they had been dragged from under a coal slide. Mary pulled Katie down an alley where an ancient rain barrel stood. Wetting her hem, she began wiping Katie's face and her own. Katie saw that Mary's mouth was red, as if she had been eating cherries. Mary put her fingers to her lips and they came away dabbed with colour.

"Oh, Mary, you're bleeding. Did old Jenksy hurt you? Did he?"

Mary wiped her lips hastily.

"He did give me a proper bang, didn't he!" She wiped her mouth again and then grinned suddenly into Katie's distressed face. "It all right lass. He couldn't harm me if he tried. Me and thee, we won't be parted. No workhouse for us. We'll make our own way, we will."

"But what will we do?"

Mary pulled Katie into a doorway and bent down awkwardly until she was at eye level. Her loosened hair lent a wildness to her thrusting jaw and quivering lips. The lumpen immobility was gone and Mary's whole soul stood trembling in her face.

The spark that had kindled with Katie's arrival had grown into the towering blaze that fed and illumined Mary's heart. Dumbfounded at being loved for herself alone, she returned the child's affection with passionate vehemence, for Katie was the only creature in her put-upon, loveless life, save her own dead mother, that her feelings had been able to stir for. Katie and Mary were kindred. Mary had felt it the moment the dying baby had clamped onto the nipple and seized life again. Dull Mary, who recognized in this bright child the same rushing spirit that long ago had driven her maddened self out of the mine to freedom. She looked about her swiftly. Her eye settled on an old fruit seller holding her tray against the traffic.

"Katie, my lass, we're agoin' ter start all new. Just thee and me. We can...why, we can sell things just like that there woman. But we got ter stick tergether and we got ter be hard and able to stand it. Can tha do that?"

For a moment, Katie was paralyzed by the sight of Mary's eyes, enormous and feverish with a light Katie had never seen in them before. Her fear rose again as her young being began to sense the shambles of her known life about her. Yet mixed with the fear grew a thrill she had, as yet, no power to understand.

Why, they were on the street, free and alone for the first time in Katie's life. No Mr. Jenks! No more everlasting gloves to sew! They had escaped into the great outside!

She didn't know how to be hard or what Mary expected her to stand. She didn't care. Mary was asking her, equal to equal. A speeding excitement brought two spots of colour to her cheeks and turned her eyes green as wind-tossed leaves.

What she felt was the restless blood in her stirring fully for the first time. Her tight face broke suddenly into a laugh. Without thinking, she launched herself at Mary and flung her arms about Mary's neck in gesture so bold, so unprecedented as to render Mary speechless with surprise.

Katie pressed her face against Mary's hair and inhaled the scent of lye soap as familiar to her as the soft, sweet humming that had soothed her baby eyes. Her volatile spirit rushed from the depth of shock and fright to a dizzying high.

"Yes," she promised recklessly. "Oh yes!"

CHAPTER TEN

"Do you want to be the Queen of Denmark today or the Queen of Spain?"

Laura tossed back her chestnut curls to consider the question seriously. She could be the Tsarina of Russia if the fancy took her, or the Empress of Austria or even the Maharani of Jaipur. However, she was feeling quite daintily regal just now.

"Denmark," she said decisively. Denmark was nice and close and not big enough to scare anybody, certainly not her grandmother whose role at tea was unquestioned. She was always the Queen of England, the most powerful person in the world.

Very well, we'll ask Lucy to bring the Royal Copenhagen teapot," Lady Atworth beamed. "Bollo can be your page in case any pastries do not meet your approval."

Bollo, a pug-nosed King Charles spaniel, wagged her silken tail expectantly. Her girth indicated she had disposed of a great many tidbits passed up by discriminating royal palates. As this was the first tea of the year in the garden, prospects looked promising indeed.

"What is it today, Lucy?" asked Pindling, the butler, when the maid stepped through the doors opening onto the terrace.

"Guess."

"Ah....Denmark!"

"Right!" exclaimed Lucy, impressed. "However did you know?"

"Miss Laura tilts her head like that and folds her hands in her lap when she's feeling like Denmark. Regular picture, isn't she?"

The two faithful retainers paused to admire the darling of the house seated at the table with its quilted undercloth and damask overcloth awaiting the fine china set. Laura might be only nine, but already she had absorbed the bearing and inborn assurance of her imperious grandmother, echoing that wayward lady in delicious miniature as she perched on her wicker chair.

"Miss Tate has her nose of joint again," Lucy murmured, not without satisfaction. Lucy had been with Lady Atworth since hiring on as a petrified tweeny at fourteen. With the other servants, she joined in a solid phalanx against brash newcomers such as this governess not in residence a fortnight. "Got ideas about bringing up young ladies. Thinks ma'am is spoiling our Miss Laura dreadfully."

"Well, she'll change her mind or she'll leave like the others, I guarantee."

You couldn't help but pamper Miss Laura, Pindling thought, having Mr. Charles' beautiful brown eyes and that splendid shade of chestnut hair that had been in the Atworths right back to Lady Marguerite Atworth that was old Queen Elizabeth's third favourite lady-in-waiting. Besides, it wasn't possible to spoil Miss Laura. No matter how much she was given, she never threw tantrums or acted horrible. She proved she was a true Atworth by smiling graciously, taking it all as her due.

The butler hoped Miss Laura would never have to really prove she was a true Atworth. There was some funny business there though he well knew it wasn't his place to speculate. He himself had seen young Mr. Charles turn white that time he got the letter and cry out, "I must go to her!" just as if some ghost had clutched him by this neck. There was all the upset when Mr. Charles went charging off, then got thrown from that roan devil he was riding not five miles from home. After the funeral, Lady Atworth herself, mourning streamers flying behind her, had rattled away in the carriage and returned three days later with Miss Laura all wrapped up like a rosebud in fine Brussels lace.

"My granddaughter," she had announced in that commanding voice that brooked no inquiry. "Mr. Charles married while up at university. The mother, poor thing, is as dead as he. Open up the nursery, Pindling, and see if you can find his late lordship's cradle."

"Were nothing but a cottage we stopped at," grumbled Tom, the coachman, after he had rubbed down the weary horses and swallowed two of Cook's excellent kidney pies. "No proper place at all to nurse out any daughter of Mr. Charles."

Intense curiosity on the part of the staff and then of the rather scattered country neighbours met only Lady Atworth's intimidating stare. Lack of information eventually relegated the mystery to the back of people's minds though the questions remained. Who had Mr. Charles married so precipitously and why had he not brought her back after the wedding to surround her with the consequence of Atworth House? The Atworths were not ones to stand down to public opinion. Had the bride been even from one of those new families rich through trade, Lady Atworth was quite capable of welcoming her to the house.

"I hope there's cherry jam today. It's my favourite."

"Of course there"ll be cherry jam," smiled the older woman, her formidable features softening as they always did at this miracle who had come so unexpectedly, out of ruin, to breathe life once again into the Elizabethan halls of Atworth House. "Cook knows better than to have no cherry jam when the Queen of Denmark comes to call."

Lady Atworth was that stalwart, competent variety of woman who had kept the English country gentry vigorous for the last five hundred years. She was square-boned, but not fat, long in the face with a strong jaw and forthright eyes looking out from under a wiry mass of iron grey hair tamed into a chignon surrounded by side ringlets. She wore plain lilac, having gotten out of mourning in a scandalously short time. Dearly as she had loved Charles, she declared she had no intention of frightening the child by sailing into the nursery like a raven looking for its dinner. The servants, accustomed to her legion eccentricities, secretly agreed. A widow for the last fifteen years, Lady Atworth was quite accustomed to getting her own way.

"What did Miss Tate teach Your Majesty this morning?"

"Geography," replied Laura, brightening at the sight of Dundee cake and fresh scones approaching. She had impeccable manners. She would not eye the goodies in detail until after Gran said grace, unfolded her napkin and poured tea into the delicate china cups. Lucy, curtsying with a grave drollery, saw the two queens well supplied with dainties, then retired as they fell back into their everyday selves.

"What sort of geography?"

"We learned about the trees of North America. And where the trees stop there is only grass, hundreds and hundreds of miles of it. Why, you could put a dozen Englands in there and never even see them. Buffalo herds live in the grass and have funny curved horns. The red men make robes out of the skins and sleep in them even if they get full of fleas. Miss Tate says I should be learning to embroider."

"Nonsense!" sputtered Lady Atworth who was terrible at embroidery. "Wouldn't you rather see a buffalo?"

Laura cut daintily into the piece of cake on her plate.

"I don't see how I could unless it was in a zoo. They're so far away we could never get there and there wouldn't be any nice places to sleep if we tried. No, Gran, I'd rather stay home and make the most thrilling piece of stitching. Miss Tate says I could start with gillyflowers right away."

"Harumph!" muttered Lady Atworth, sounding very much like Queen Victoria indeed.

And she made up her mind on the spot to do the unheard of and travel as soon as Laura was older. The child was clever and obedient but getting far too preoccupied with the pretty details of life. Only to be expected, of course, spending her time locked up by herself behind the gates of Atworth House.

Lady Atworth had chosen this retiring life deliberately though she was social at heart and missed the goings and comings of country life. Company had been small sacrifice beside the well being of her infant granddaughter. She and Laura must live in splendid isolation until all speculation about Laura's origin had faded. Then, in seven or eight years, when the two of them returned from a sojourn abroad, Laura would burst upon the neighbourhood, a gleaming new star in that small firmament. She would be such a beauty and such a lady that no one would ever guess that Charles had involved himself with a tea shop waitress and made no marriage at all.

What a defiant confession Charles had made before storming off on that horse. He loved Maisie, he shouted, and he didn't give a damn who objected. "Why didn't she tell me!" he stormed while he paced up and down looking so painfully young and yet so fierce. "Why did she wait to fall ill in lodgings! I'm fetching her and the child this instant!"

He never found out that Maisie was dead and the baby almost to the workhouse for lack of a relation to take it in. A sad business, a very sad business all round, Lady Atworth sighed, but just the sort of folly Charles would fall into. He had been a good boy, Charles. Not a rake, only an innocent lad up from the country who harboured a sentimental streak. A soft-cheeked working girl, struggling against the world, was just the sort to take his heart entirely. Good families had dealt with these entanglements for centuries. Lady Atworth was different only in that she had boldly salvaged her grandchild instead of, as was the custom, letting the evidence sink forever out of sight.

"Don't you think the new yellow tea cloth would be better with a flounce around the bottom? I could embroider it myself," Laura said, biting into a scone.

"What?"

Laura repeated her question. Lady Atworth came back to the present abruptly. The tea cloth seemed perfectly adequate.

"All right, all right, if you want to embroider, tell Miss Tate you can begin, though it's a waste of time, if you ask me. The house is chock full of embroidery already."

"Oh Gran, I mean, Your Majesty, that's not the point. All ladies embroider. Miss Tate says they look soooo graceful stitching before the fire and it gives a lady something to do with her hands while a gentleman talks."

Lady Atworth swallowed a mouthful of tea to squelch her rejoinder. After all, hadn't she hired Miss Tate to bestow just this sort of refinement. In her own youth, embroidery had been the last thing on her mind. She'd been horse crazy, wanting only to grow up to hunt with the best. She had, too. And a good toss in the mud only improved her appetite.

Oh well, ladies seemed more delicate these days and Lady Atworth was determined that Laura should be properly trained even if it involved miles of embroidery.

What mattered, Lady Atworth thought, examining with satisfaction Laura's large-eyed, delicate-lipped loveliness, was that the girl make an excellent marriage. A marriage so splendid and so secure no whiff of scandal would ever touch it. When Laura was ready to come out, the shroud of solitude would be tossed aside. Then the county would see what balls, what parties Atworth House was capable of. Suitors would come scrambling, even those high-nosed Whynchleys and Scolmans and Hales who all had more land than they knew what to do with and crops of growing boys to settle it on. Oh, thought Lady Atworth delightedly, there was so much a determined grandmother could do.

"Why are you smiling, Gran?"

"I'm thinking of your wedding. What a grand reception we shall have, right out here on the lawns."

"Shall we open the gallery too?" asked Laura who was vastly fond of the linenfold paneling and grim-looking ancestral portraits hanging rather haphazardly along its walls.

"The whole house. They'll come from miles and miles around. We'll have to double them up in the bedrooms we'll have so many overnight guests."

"Who shall I marry?"

"You shall have your pick of the county. Anyone you fancy."

By this she meant the substantial landed gentry to whom the Atworths belonged. The great nobility was not to be thought of. Anything from a squire down was out of the question.

The two spent a pleasant fifteen minutes at this game which Lady Atworth considered as essential as schooling young hunters over bars before they took the stone walls and ditches of the countryside. Ah yes, and Laura was such a thoroughbred, the Atworth blood in her proclaiming itself even as a fine Arabian could never conceal its lines even if hitched to a plow.

"No matter who I marry, I shall always live at Atworth House," Laura declared for she was deeply attached to the rambling old structure with its Tudor rose brick and small-paned leaded windows set into frames of mellow golden stone. From earliest childhood she had listened to the vast holm oaks that splotched their shade on the patterned slate of the roof and whispered about the tall chimneys. She had played behind the great stone urn from the time of Queen Anne. She had peeped through the ancient boxwood hedges which protected the kitchen garden where two gnarled pear trees were trained against the wall. She had spotted rooks' nests in the massive limes which made the approach to Atworth House a shady avenue. She had curled in the window seats where the very pegs in the wood were almost four hundred years old.

Pride of blood had been instilled with such care that Laura knew the history of the Atworths right back to Sir Geoffrey Atworth who, in the Wars of the Roses, had held Stanway Bridge against repeated attacks for thirty-four days and received this very ground she sat upon for his reward. Laura's lack of human playmates had made her turn for companionship to the romantic stories of the past which peopled her imagination in exciting panoply. When bored, she could always join, in her mind, the wild ride up the valley by her Royalist ancestor, Sir Francis Atworth, who outwitted two Roundhead regiments and arrived in time to warn the family off to safety. She could wait in the fragrance of the herb garden for Lady Edith whose pleasant ghost was said to collect fresh lavender and distill it into an essence that could be scented in the halls if you tiptoed out just when the moon was high. She especially liked Sir Ranald who had kept hounds in the library and Lady Joan who had climbed down the ivy one night and galloped her horse to the top of Dimble Hill to meet a highwayman. They were all like cousins and sisters to Laura, her own family, almost visible, waiting just around the corner to wink at her, make her one of their exclusive company.

Lady Atworth pursed her lips. At the back of her mind, always, was the delicate matter of succession. Atworth House must always go to the next of kin. After Laura, the next in line was that objectionable Faxon Atworth of Durbury. Lady Atworth had made her will, of course, naming Laura. But if Faxon ever did any researches...

He wouldn't have the presumption, she decided, and he'd probably be dead before the problem came up. Lady Atworth, barely fifty and hale as an up-country hunting horse, intended to last at least another thirty years and by then Laura would be queening it over this very spot and have a crop of sons to squelch all invaders. Thank heaven the Durbury Atworths lived seventy miles away and never visited because old Lord Atworth had dearly loved a feud.

"You shall live where you wish," Lady Atworth answered generously, yet thinking that Laura fit in at Atworth House as she would fit in nowhere else in the world. "And you may have the last scone on the plate."

Laura reached for it, then paused.

"There's some for the poor box, isn't there?"

"Certainly. You know Cook always makes extra," Lady Atworth replied, pleased Laura had not forgotten her duty to the unfortunate. One couldn't have privilege without its attendant obligations.

Laura put butter and jam on the scone and nibbled on it speculatively.

"Gran, why are there poor people?"

Lady Atworth hesitated, about to say the reasons she was familiar with—sickness, drunkenness or a drop in harvest work. Yet lately there were so many strange, threatening tramps on the road and ragged workers begging between towns, with equally ragged families dragging behind. A body couldn't help but wonder what had become of all the jobs that honest country labourers had swarmed off in such numbers to grab up. The population had been so shaken around into cities that England actually had to import food from as far away as Australia, to self-sufficient Lady Atworth an atrocious state of affairs.

Certainly England was supposed to be in the grip of the most astounding expansion the world had ever seen if one could believe the huffings and puffings of the Bedfordshire Mail and Messenger. Every day someone was inventing bigger looms, noisier engines, more whirling belts to catch befuddled workers unaware and chomp them up. London was being torn down and built up again with such dreadful fake Gothic monstrosities that Lady Atworth refused to visit the place any more. And in Bedford, her own Bedford, they had a string of dye works that turned the water in their fine trout river orange!

Personally, she blamed everything on the railways. Why they just punched them straight through a person's land with so much as a by-your-leave and flung up such heaps of earth that in a thousand years it would be plain where the trains chuffed by, scaring the milk from the cows. Within her own living memory, they had spread all over the country, bringing the wrong people in, carrying the wrong goods out and deliberately, yes quite deliberately, she believed, upsetting good British order that had taken hundreds of years to achieve. If they didn't have railways, they wouldn't be able to build those smoking factories in the Midlands and then haul their ridiculous products down to the sea. They couldn't lure those poor men, good farm labourers all, down into the mines to work like moles and die of rockfalls all for the sake of some metal nature never intended to see the light of day. And they wouldn't have those despicable land agents eying fine pasture land for subdivisions to house the workers the coach cars carried in.

Lady Atworth felt herself growing agitated lest a railway threaten her estate. She took a calming sip of tea, wishing mightily that she could have a fine old grumble with like-minded neighbours. Laura's eyes were still fixed on her questioningly.

"People are poor because they believe a lot of bosh about going to work in factories. If they'd stay in their villages where they belong, they could each have a garden and grow cabbages to eat. And there'd be no need to build railways," Lady Atworth added with finality.

Laura agreed wholeheartedly. She, too, was on the side of order. When she grew up, she wouldn't have a single thing about Atworth House changed. Unselfishly, she shared her scone with Bollo and let out a sigh of utter satisfaction. Indulged full of jammy cake by her grandmother, promised a fine lord for a husband, and seeing Atworth House her private fief, how could life be any more complete!

CHAPTER ELEVEN

"Oh look, " Katie whispered in a fever, "Here's a lady coming. She'll buy. I know she will!"

Her single braid bounced excitedly as a stout woman hauling a market basket walked toward them. The woman would stop in front of Mary. She just had to!

There, in the unforgiving streets, Katie and Mary were launching themselves into their new life of self-employment. In a world where the poor were bound like ants to their neighbourhood and practically everything had to be bought at the house door, hawkers abounded on the doorsteps.

"Thicker'n mice in a pantry," Mary said about at all the vendors lugging their trays and baskets. "Guess we can do that too."

From the depths of her bodice she had drawn out all the gift coins Amelia Radmore had given her over the years. Enough for some stock. Even enough to rent cheap lodging for a week. A veritable horde in Mary's estimation.

Not being city bred, Mary's blundering inquiry informed her she must start at the bottom as a vendor of perishables. She and Katie rented a heavy tray and filled it, according to the season, with strawberries.

"Oh!" was all Katie could say, overcome at the sight of the glistening redness. In her whole life, she had hardly ever tasted fresh fruit.

Mary, whose tongue was as blunted as the rest of her, inhaled a great breath.

"Strawberries, ma'am, fresh red strawberries!" she grated out, drawing her heavy boots back underneath her skirt.

The words were lost in the crash of iron-rimmed wheels on cobblestone. A dust cart rumbled by. When it had gone, the woman had passed by with it on the other side.

In passionate disappointment Katie watched the sturdy backside vanish.

"Be 'nother in a minute," Mary affirmed patiently, hitching the tray to give her shoulders some relief. "Can't expect ta sell ter the first one yer tries, now can yer!"

They had taken a post in Wheeble Lane, just off a main thoroughfare, not so very far from the great old Tower of London, though the Tower might have been on the moon for all Katie or Mary knew of its existence or its history. They had first tried the larger street but it was impossible to stand still in the dangerous moving crush of horses, vehicles and pedestrians. Omnibuses had their striped-trousered "cads" or conductors shouting beside them, almost kidnapping unwilling passengers aboard. Wretched men encased in sandwich boards bumped the walls dragging about advertising for competing companies. Vendors of turnips and crockery and fish shouldered their barrows through. Rattling wagon loads of barrels and crates battled hansom cabs and delivery vans and coffee sellers' carts. Streams of people struggled along the narrow pavements, stumbling over protruding doorsteps as they went.

All niches where a seller could possibly hold out were already defended by tenacious occupants. Mary and Katie, struggling with the unaccustomed awkwardness of the tray, were winnowed into Wheeble Lane near the door of their own lodging house. The Lane proved a shortcut to the next main thoroughfare and, to their inexperienced eyes, promised business enough.

"It'll do," Mary announced. Any place would do. The tray strap was cutting into her bent spine and she had to start lightening the load.

Scarcely two days has passed since their headlong flight from the Asylum. Two dizzying days which shattered the order of Katie's former life and made it seem an unbelievable dream. For all its harshness, the Asylum had sheltered her from the city around it, closing the shutters against street brawls, walling out the intense struggle for survival. Now noise and confusion assaulted Katie until she felt like buttermilk shaken up in a jar. Her tender senses reeled, her amazed eyes could not open wide enough to drink everything in.

She knew there were hundreds of streets in London, for she had tramped them until her legs were numb. Her toes had been bruised by a gentleman's cob sweating its way around a poulterer's van. Wheels taller than herself shook her with their deafening rattle as they cut in front of her, maneuvered by big men standing up in the wagon boxes, shouting and hauling the reins.

Feet and legs and bodies were everywhere. On one street, she'd stumbled into a lady's bustle and started back at all the hard metal ribs under the cascade of taffeta. In narrow byways, grubby children, younger than herself, jumped like monkeys over wooden boxes piled into doorways. Smells of coal smoke, horses, coffee, hot grease, damp wool, stagnant puddles tingled in her nostrils. Shop windows flashed a wondrous blur of feathered hats, iced cakes, painted rocking horses, haunches of mutton as she sped by. Once, there had been a boy turning handsprings in the dust but Mary wouldn't stop. The great metropolis was alive around them, roaring and clattering and throbbing. The unending mob that was its life-pulse drove them before it, jostling and pushing. Mary clung onto Katie's wrist so tightly that the joint grew red and swollen under her grip.

"If yer gets lost here," Mary warned starkly, "I'll never find her again, ever!"

Katie only wove her fingers more tightly into Mary's.

"Sure you'd find me, Mary. You'd always know where I was," she said with the perfect childish certainty that made the street tumult intoxicating instead of terrifying. Mary clucked brusquely, but her blue eyes flared. She would indeed find Katie if it were a dozen Londons she were lost in.

They had spent forever in the alley where they had first taken refuge while Mary patiently scrubbed at their hands and faces with her damp handkerchief until their skin shone pale and clean again in the midst of the rest of their sooty selves. As Mary had her comb in her pocket, they shook out their hair, combed it carefully and braided it up again so that it's darkened tint seemed almost a natural colour and not the contribution of the chimney. Their clothes presented a harder problem, though Mary discovered that a great deal of the soot could be shaken out if they beat their skirts vigorously. They went on a brief search for a vendor of needles and Katie stood patiently while Mary stitched up the tears. Mary rinsed out Katie's disgustingly soiled petticoat at the rain barrel and rolled it into a bundle to be dried later. She despaired over Katie's soot smeared pinafore until Katie got the bright idea of turning it inside out.

So Katie stood now with the seams of her pinafore showing but otherwise tidy. Happiness kindled inside her. Hadn't she and Mary made a bargain that would keep them together for always doing what they liked, just the two of them! Katie would do anything for Mary. Anything! And they would be the most tremendous success in the world!

Katie said as much that very morning as she hopped up from the pallet in the cheap lodging house Mary had to them into. Just finding the room had been an adventure. The narrow stairway, twisting twice to the second floor had assumed the fascination of a voyage to the Indies. The tough inspection of the potentate in residence, Mrs. Gossidge, had seemed a testing of merit only right that they must pass.

"All right, I'll take you," Mrs. Gossidge declared tartly, after a narrow-eyed examination of both Mary's hump and her money. "At least there'll be no goings on with the men!"

Why Mary should flinch like a horse taking a smack on its nose, Katie couldn't tell. In the gloomy, airless space they were given, they found two other women sleeping heavily, hollow faces turned from the candle flame. A third pallet, empty, they found belonged to a girl who made her living singing ballads in the he street.

"Phew, it smells so dusty. And those ladies snore!"

At the first seep of dawn, Katie bounded up to find their fellows gone and Mary wide awake. Mary gave a chuckle.

"Well, I say one thing, lass, yer game. That tha are!"

"I'm going to be the gamest girl in London! And so are you!"

Astonishingly, Mary laughed, a light, youthful sound few guessed could live inside her twisted body. With a little shake, she tossed off fears too adult for Katie to see.

"Let's hope, lass. And let's be off ter the market or there'll be nothing left."

The two allowed themselves a moment of stainless, singing hope. Surely nothing but luck could come to two such fast friends and jolly companions sallying forth on a bright summer morning to conquer London Town.

Wheeble Lane was a dog-leg passage wide enough for two horses abreast and a wide-wheeled cart. Rough cobbles slanted to a central gutter running with slops. Mrs. O'Rielly from their lodging house, who sold the pig's trotters and who had directed them to the market, nodded to them from over her basket. A ruddy man sold pickled whelks, fried fish and stewed eels from a table in his doorway. At the far end, behind a low pub called The Bird, a bloated fellow in a military jacket swayed on crutches, offering bootlaces for sale. "Veteran of Crimea," he intoned over and over, the laces his excuse to beg. These accorded Katie and Mary a flat, assessing glance but Katie, alight with sunny faith, was too inexperienced to understand the principle of economic competition and too enthralled by the odours drifting through the shutters of a pie seller baking stock on the premises.

Mary and Katie ensconced themselves in the crook where one of the drab houses fell back a step. For the next hour they vainly offered their wares to passing women who either ignored them or cast frowns. Undaunted, Katie hummed with the slice of bread and jam she'd had for breakfast. Hope for a sale straightened her spine when a rough looking fellow, not out of his teens, sauntered up to the tray.

He wore fustian breeches tied at the waist with a cord and a shirt grimy from cuff to collar. Over it, he sported a waistcoat of eye boggling red and yellow tartan so new as it suggest being very recently stolen. A shovel cap tilted over his eyes. The hobnails in his boots scraped the cobbles in teeth-jarring squeals.

"New 'ere, ain't you?"

Casually, he picked up a strawberry, inspected it, then flicked it against the wall behind them where it smashed redly against the brick. Katie let out a soundless gasp. Mary stilled, squinting at the wall opposite as if the fellow wasn't there.

"This 'ere's Red Nell's lane, you know. Wheeble Lane. She charges rent."

How could anyone own a lane, Katie wondered indignantly, waiting for Mary to ask exactly that. Mary's face remained as immobile as hardened dough with only her fingers twitching slightly on the edges of the tray. Eyes narrow and impudent, the fellow walked to one side of them, then the other, surveying Mary's deformity as if it were some display for his private amusement.

Hunchy like that, you'll never sell nothing. You're so ugly you'd make a hog throw up!"

Bert, for that was his name, said this with deliberate easy malice. Katie was too stunned to wonder why Mary didn't retort hotly back. Bert's yellow-toothed grin waited for a reaction. Katie began to breathe faster and faster, but only when Bert ran his fingers contemptuously over Mary's hump did disbelief give way to snapping anger.

"You get away from here," Katie spluttered. "Keep your dirty hands to yourself!"

Grrinning, Bert reached over and rudely jerked her nose!

The passionate nature so grimly warned against erupted to the surface. Katie flew at Bert, arms flailing, face white with fury. Before she reached the gaudy vest, she was painfully yanked to a halt in mid-air and slammed down upon the cobbles. Incredibly, it was not Bert, but Mary who had grabbed her from behind. Katie staggered into the tray, sending scarlet berries to ruin at their feet.

"Leave him be!"

"But...."

"Leave him be, I said!"

Mary's voice was hard as flint and totally without inflection. Bert kept grinning.

"That's what I likes to see. Manners. I'll let you off light today, seein' as you is just startin' up. But if you want this spot, nice and safe, it's tuppence every tray you sell. And don't think you can cheat. Red Nell knows everything that happens on her turf."

He scooped up a handful of berries and strolled off, stuffing them into triumphant jaws. Katie shook all over with fury, Only after Bert was completely out of sight did Mary release her.

"Why'd you let him do that!" Katie demanded. "Didn't you hear what he said about you!"

Mary's face only grew stonier. Katie's chest heaved under her pinafore. Her nose hurt, her memory burned with the picture of his hands running scornfully over Mary's hump and the red juice of their precious strawberries staining his lips. Berries she hadn't been allowed to taste.

"I was going to kick him. I was going to make him go away. He's awful!"

"Aye, he's awful," Mary agreed, her eyes dark and her breath scraping rapidly, as if she had just run a race.

"Then why didn't you let me..."

"He'd flatten thee, lass. And me too. Tha'd better learn right now never to mix with such as him. What's a few berries if it makes him go away. Worth it, ain't it!"

Katie said nothing and suddenly Mary was shaking her by the shoulder, shaking her so violently the girl's head flopped back and forth and her teeth bit the tender insides of her cheeks.

"Ain't it?"

No! No it isn't! Katie wanted to shout, but Mary's face loomed so close it blotted out the lane. In the merciless heat of Mary's gaze burned all the horrors of the Yorkshire coat pits, knowledge no child should ever have to know. Chill fear snaked into Katie's stomach just as Mary meant it to, momentarily extinguishing rebellion.

"Y..yes, it is," Katie stammered. "Oh, Mary..let me go!"

Mary released her grip and Katie stood here, rubbing the finger marks. The tumult within her had not subdued.

"Let's go away, then. Go and find another lane."

Mary shook her head. With a large sigh, she hunkered down to retrieve their fallen stock.

"There's a Bert in every lane, lass. We'd best stay here ter deal with the devil we know. He ain't harmed us and maybe he'll leave us be if we pay up our coin fer this Red Nell, whoever she might be."

Katie had a quite different opinion though she didn't dare voice it. The bruised, wounded sides of the berries made her seethe all over again. She opened her mouth, then shut it tightly again. Mary's first lesson in street survival had sunk in.

The mysterious bully, Red Nell, had also made a deep impression on Katie. Red Nell was responsible for Bert's nastiness. Red Nell was responsible for making Mary shake Katie as she had never been shaken by Mary before. From that moment, Katie saw Red Nell as a tyrannical adversary whose despotism was a blight on the small universe of street sellers.

Mary chose a large strawberry, only slightly battered.

"Here," she murmured, as if the sweet, tart, glorious taste bursting inside Katie's mouth could take away the outrage of it all.

The rest of the day did not go well. The spill had reduced their stock and the berries rescued from the cobbles swiftly took on a brown, shrunken appearance. Katie hovered close to Mary, every moment expecting Bert to reappear.

"I hope he gets boils. I hope Red Nell gets boils!" Katie grumbled vehemently and felt a little better.

Though Mary knew little of street selling, she applied herself doggedly, her approach as simple and direct as her mind. She waited for women with baskets and, with a hitch of her apron, she stepped directly in front of them.

"Strawberries, luvely strawberries! Buy some fer yer tea!"

Invariably, the woman would be taken aback back, for Mary was startling even a city teeming with hawkers. Her North Country accent, without intention, was harsh and blunt and Mary had none of the ingratiating patter of the other vendors, even the old woman selling pigs' trotters. This, along with the forward thrust of Mary's grotesque shape, which, by rights, ought to have belonged to a whining beggar, combined to give some undefined offence. With a sniff or a glare, the prospective customer would step around Mary and hurry on her way. Late in the afternoon, passersby took to glancing critically into the tray.

"Imagine tryin' to hawk them banged up berries."

Mary bore these rebuffs with the same blank face with which she had borne Mr. Jenks rages. Katie, however, was first astounded by these constant refusals and then began to bristle like a fighting pup. Mary's grip held her in place.

"Termorrow, lass. We'll do better termorrow."

Their fortunes did not improve. Two days of pacing the cobbles reduced their feet to aching pads and their stock to reddish mush from which the few whole berries had to be carefully extracted. By the third day, it was fit only for the gutter.

Defeated, Katie and Mary trudged back toward their lodgings. When they reached the cart from which they bought their ration of bread and tea Mary propelled her past.

"Yer'll have ter pull in yer belly, lass. There'll be nothing from the cart ternight."

Mary trudged up the lodging house stairs, damp hems slapping at her heels. From the lower regions, laughter and the smell of frying mackerel rose to torment their thwarted appetites. Though meals at the Asylum had been scanty and monotonous, they had been regular. Driven by her hollow stomach, Katie dared to protest. Mary shook her head, impenetrable as a brick when she wished to be. Katie plopped down on the straw-filled mattress.

"But why?"

This question had provoked endless trouble at the Asylum. Mary pulled her brows together.

"Because we ain't got money ter buy any dinner with. We got ter buy new stock and rent the tray again for termorrow."

Katie digested this while rubbing at her ankle bruised on a doorstep. She had little experience of money, having hardly ever seen any.

"Why haven't we got any money?" she inquired, wanting really to know since it seemed to have so much to do with whether she got a big slice of bread or not.

"Because we didn't sell enough today, that's why! It takes brass ter pay for our bed and brass ter fill our bellies! Them as don't have brass ends up in the workhouse, and then God help 'em, I say!"

Mary's chin now rested completely on her chest, the lids of her eyes half closed as if she lacked the strength to hold them up. Katie could not yet conceive of being homeless, foodless in the streets, but the world "workhouse" stirred a racing fear. The workhouse was where Mr. Jenks meant to put them. She imagined it as a set of jaws slavering to gulp them up. More questions died on her lips. Her keen child's intelligence told her suddenly that Mary was suffering from a wound.

Poor Mary, she thought, forgetting her stomach altogether. Poor, poor Mary.

And right there, in the dimming light, Mary changed from an all knowing, all protecting figure to something not so powerful.

I've got to think of something to help. Yes, I do.

The idea that she could somehow look after Mary was so unsettling that Katie could not, at first, speak. Yet even as she struggled, her memory threw up a little fellow she had seen following his father's vegetable barrow. "Coly-flower, coly-flower, penny apiece!" he piped, his high, childish voice carrying over the din of the streets.

In a flash, she clutched Mary's hand.

"Mary, I'll help you sell, tomorrow. I'll say the words. And I'm not so hungry. Really, I'm not."

Mary, to whom this idea had never occurred, peered at Katie in some surprise. Slowly, her head lifted from between her shoulders. She, too, remembered all the small children selling watercress and fuzees and nuts and cotton braces.

"Why, lass, tha's got summat there. Folks is always partial ter a tidy lookin' wee lass. Aye, sell tha will!"

Despite her gnawing stomach, Katie slept with her head nestled against Mary's shoulder and a brave smile on her lips. Mary's nearness more than made up for the cracking plaster, the barren floorboards, the musty reek of unwashed clothes that had replaced the scent of carbolic and flagstones of the Asylum. Oh, she'd work like sixty just to make Mary smile her crooked smile once more.

On a deeper level, Katie had learned a terrible equation. Money equals food. Food equals survival. To her had come that day a first ghostly glimpse of destitution, the spectre that haunted the merchant prince as much as the corner beggar and explained the national mania for turning everything conceivable into solid, comforting cash.

CHAPTER TWELVE

"Hold still, lad. I got to do it again. Hardens you to the work, it does."

Croom gripped Will by the scruff with one hand. With the other, he doused strong brine from a bottle onto Will's bleeding elbows and knees. The more salt one got onto skin torn up by chimney mortar, the sooner the callouses formed and the easier the boy would scamper up flues without being driven. His elbows would stop bleeding and his kneecaps looking half torn off.

Will uttered a deep groan but stood still. Have to give the little blighter that, Croom thought as salt bit into the abraded flesh. He can take it when he has to.

Otherwise, he'd have chucked Will after the fiasco at the Asylum for the lad wasn't a natural climber, that was certain. Some masters lit actual fires in the grate to get a new boy to climb, but more than once, they'd suffocated halfway up. A sweep couldn't leave a dead boy up the flue, could he!

Will shut his eyes against the bitter searing. Chimneys! Dark unspeakable black tunnels full of soot that clogged his lungs and ground itself into his scrabbling palms like crystals of black glass.

He and Croom had been out before dawn, crying "'Weep! 'Weep! 'Weep!" through the streets to get business before the morning fires were lit. Some of the chimneys were still hot. Will suffered a nauseating fear that the smoke would again come behind him, smothering him in a cramped hole from which frantic struggles could not get him free. Oh how he hated chimneys!

Yet it never occurred to him to hate Croom for putting him up there, just as it he never thought of taking to his heels down the street. He simply stood, stoically waiting for the pain to pass, then he opened his lashes again, a small, grubby climbing boy ready for more work.

"Good chap!" Croom exclaimed admiringly. Used to savage hatred or wild snivelling from new climbing boys, the sweep decided that Will was a rare one after all. A lad who would stick to the job and do what he was told with no nonsense out of him. Previously unknown urges stirred in the sooty bosom, the inchoate longing of a man to hand on something of himself even if it were only a sweep's brush and knowledge of how to scrape a dog leg flue.

By gum, the lad's bone honest, he thought, suddenly putting his finger on the idea that had been eluding him for days. Comes by it natural too, Ain't that precious! He rooted in his back pocket for his handkerchief, black as the rest of him, and blew his nose.

"I'm just going to wet my whistle here at The Bird. You keep your eye on the brushes. You've earned a rest."

Pleasure lit Will's face in the form of a swift, unexpectedly sweet smile completely without enmity. A smile that turned the anxious lines of his face childlike again, the way Will might have looked had he ever been hugged or known what it was to play. It was the first time Croom had seen the look.

I must be gettin' old, Croom thought. And he stamped into The Bird calling for straight gin to drown the tightness in his chest.

Katie and Mary had bought their second stock of strawberries from a wagon still wet with country dew. If Katie was thinner, the open air had given her colour, revealing a skin that struggled toward freckles at the faintest excuse for sun. Her hair picked up flecks of morning light, her mouth was gloriously red from the two strawberries she and Mary had each eaten to brace their spirits.

"Now, lass, let them hear what yer made of," Mary encouraged back in Wheeble Lane.

Katie opened her mouth and found herself speechless. Everyone was taller than herself. Nobody was looking at her, everyone as looking at her, including the pickled whelk man and Mrs. O'Rielly beside her basket of pigs' trotters. She took a second breath and a gang of street urchins shrilled by swinging a rat they had killed.

Go on," Mary urged. "Talk nice ter the ladies, smile nice as yer can. Make 'em buy."

With rough affection, she pushed back tendrils from the girl's forehead. Katie pursed her lips together for they were both trembling. To openly accost an adult, never mind a stranger, bucked every precept drilled in at the Asylum. And who should come strolling around the corner but Bert, waistcoat enriched by coffee stains, cap tilted jauntily.

"Tryin' it again, are you? Daft as coots!"

He propped himself against the opposite wall to witness their second commercial defeat, from time to time popping a nut into his mouth to improve the show. Katie saw the sneer sliding across his lips.

Old Jenks! Old Jenks! Old Jenks!

The thin half-healed lines on her buttocks stung, hatred of all bullying curled heatedly within her. Any minute Bert was going to stuff another handful of their berries down his insatiable throat!

Katie glared balefully. Bert's grin widened seeing the young snip defying him. Bert couldn't know her boots had turned to lead and her tongue lay paralyzed in her jaws. Mary gripped Katie by the shoulder.

"Come, we'll step around the corner."

Katie shook her head vigorously. Instinct learned in the Asylum told her not to back away. Show fear to Bert and he'd eat their berries till doomsday.

Around the corner, Croom emerged from The Bird considerably more jovial. Though never a hard drinking man, he enjoyed company and found, lately, that he needed more and more ale to make him forget the painful soot-wart between his legs that refused to go away. What's more, the lad hadn't whined to come inside like most lads did, following the mug with dog's eyes, silently begging for his own tot of gin. Lots of lads were sots by the age of ten if they could get the brass for it, but young Will had drawn up sharply, only too glad to squat with the brushes outside the door.

"Here's a penny to buy a bite with," rumbled Croom, thinking of the brine. "Hurry up about it now!" And he went off to relieve himself in an alley corner.

In wonder, Will felt the coin pressing his palm. He could not remember when he had had a penny all his own to spend, if ever. The salt sting in his flesh vanished as he edged down Wheeble Lane in search of something marvelous to buy.

Like any child with limited funds, he suffered agonies of indecision. Down the larger street there was a shop laden with sweets and plum duff, but it was too far away. He considered the pig's trotters of the old Irishwoman, inhaled the heady aroma of fried fish mixed with the lingering intoxication issuing from the back of the pieman's premises. He could not afford a lovely pork pie crackling with thick brown pastry...

A hunched form shifted, a mound of brilliant scarlet burst upon him. Strawberries! Once he and his father had found strawberries on the other side of a hedge they slept under. Oh the muffled laughter as they gorged, wiping away the juice with the backs of their sleeves.

Yes, strawberries!

Will made his way toward them, eyes fixed on the tantalizing tray. Clutching his penny tighter, Will found himself in front of a small girl staring past him at a yellow waistcoat, lips sealed as if she never intended to open them again.

"Please, miss, how many berries for a penny...."

Will broke off as the green eyes caught him, hitting with the same impact they had had at the Asylum.

"You!" he exclaimed from sheer surprise. "It's you!"

Jerked from her duel with Bert, Katie could not, for an instant, tell who this stranger was, for Will was now smeared with black and splotched with brine. His eager gladness tipped her. Why, it's the climbing boy, she realized, and felt a corresponding uprush of spirit. They gazed at each other shyly.

"How many for a penny, then?" Will asked, recklessly investing the whole amount in one item. Katie, still tongueless, indicated a pottle. Will's eyes lit as he took the treasure in his hand.

"Come along, boy! Don't you know there's work!"

Croom's shout helped Will find his voice.

"Me 'n the guv', we live in Mawton Alley and do chimneys all about here. If you're selling, I'll see you lots of times."

Katie nodded. Will hurried off, trying to eat the berries as quickly yet as slowly as he could. He didn't remember much after he was put up the chimney at the Asylum but he was glad to see the girl out making it on her own knock. Unconsciously, he'd already put her into the empty category labelled "friend".

I just sold something, Katie thought. Almost forgetting Bert, she took heart.

"F...fresh strawberries," she sang out bravely. "Fresh rrrred strawberries."

Her voice carried over the clatters of the Lane with a sweet, musical lilt. To her amazement, a woman actually turned back from entering the pie shop, bought a tuppence worth of strawberries and patted Katie on the head besides. Bert's sneer shrank. Katie and Mary exchanged an excited glance. Success! Success!

This scene was repeated three times within the hour until even Bert gave up. By noon, the two realized Katie was the engine that would drive their fledgling enterprise. Her decent dress and pinafore, smirched and mended as they were, set her off from the other street children clad in conglomerates of adult clothes chopped down to size and tied together with twine. Her straightforward green eyes, as yet innocent of the shrewdness imbibed at birth by street urchins, compelled attention. The simple manners and clear speech inculcated by the Radmore regime contrasted with the loudness and impudence all around her. Even Mary, behind her, did not repel. The sight of the hunchback woman, somehow protected by this appealing child moved a smile on the lips of those who stopped and bought.

"By gum, lass," declared Mary, grinning one of her rare grins, "yer can sell, yer can. We're going ter eat ternight!"

And eat they did, a regular feast of bread, ginger beer and boiled meat pudding, sinking them into sleep with visions of sixpences dancing in their heads.

CHAPTER THIRTEEN

They must make Radmores out of pig iron and old boot leather, Mabel thought as she opened the door softly to look at her friend. Amelia lay in the bed that used to be Mabel's, eyes closed, mouth firm against the tug of pain. Amelia had suffered everything, even James' death, with scarcely a whimper. I'd have shrieked fit to wake a city block, Mabel decided. Just let them try cutting stay laces and picking charred bits of petticoat out of me!

Amelia had lost almost a quarter of her glossy hair, burned or ruthlessly hacked away so her poor neck and cheek could be open to the air. For days she hadn't been allowed to move while her ravaged flesh knit up again. Amelia had drawn into herself for the fight, forbidding everyone the room save Mabel, Aggie the maid, and Dr. Brough.

Mabel shifted the tray she carried. Immediately Amelia opened her eyes and banished the grimace. Gliding forward, Mabel rested her fingers lightly on the coverlet. She could not, as she wished to, take one of Amelia's hands in hers for they were both still swathed in bandages and supposed to remain at rest.

"How are you, my dear?"

"Better," murmured Amelia, giving her usual answer. Her mask was second nature now, but Mabel had seen the early days, when Amelia had no shield for the frightened, pain-racked being whose known world had just been torched away.

"You'd say that if your legs were being gnawed off by badgers. Have a good howl, why don't you. Store things up and get a ruined liver for your trouble."

"I'm afraid my liver is the least of my troubles," Amelia replied, mustering a ghost of her old dryness.

Angry red scar tissue, new and forming, snaked up the side of her neck, reached thin fingers across her cheek and into the shorn side of her head. Mabel meant to jar Amelia out of her heroic fortitude today. If she did not, Edwin would surely drive her to raving distraction.

"You do look better," Mabel replied, as she did each day when she came in. It wasn't always strictly true. A number of times it had been a patent lie.

"Do I?"

A faint, gallant smile touched Amelia's lips. Jagged bristles stood up at her right temple. The scars stabbed each time she moved on the pillow.

"Well, you'll have an ear like a tomcat after a fight and you can forget about side curls till your hair grows back. Otherwise you're coming along smashingly. Look, I've brought you some raspberry cordial."

Amelia, who thought she had had rather too much of sickroom tact, was taken aback by this frankness. Before she could comment, Mabel was helping her sip the ruby drink. When Amelia started to look broodingly pensive again, Mabel set the cup down with a clunk. Oh no, you don't, she thought. It's time this ivory tower came tumbling down.

"I think I'll go out this afternoon and buy you a false ear."

"What!"

Mabel laughed at Amelia's expression.

"There's a shop in Lesser George Street with a whole section for false ears. Gutta percha, you know, for ladies whose own ears are not satisfactorily placed. They're the most delicious pink and they come with choice of ear bobs...."

"Mabel, stop it. I know when you are trying to fool me."

"I'm not. Honestly, I swear," declared Mabel leaning closer. "And do you know what else I can get you? A false bosom. Guaranteed to follow movements of the respiration. You'll need one if you don't start eating more of Aggie's stew."

Amelia blinked with scandalized eyes. Never been teased in her life, Mabel thought, and sorely in lack. Even in the early days, Amelia's imposing dignity and James' sheer pompousness had tried Mabel's nerves. Well, James would never be pompous again, poor fellow. The iron courage of the Radmores he had shown in the end, smothering the flames around Amelia with his own body. He had died, not from burns, but from striking his head on the jagged cellar wall while flinging them both toward the open door.

"Are there really false bosoms?" Amelia asked, unable to help herself.

"Certainly. French, of course. Who else would invent such a thing!"

Amelia struggled with curiosity for several long moments.

"And how do you...how are they attached?"

She had lifted her head from the pillow despite the scars on her neck. Surviving locks of her hair fell across her forehead, bringing back the promise of her former handsomeness.

"With straps, I should think. And buttons at the back. Firm little buttons that wouldn't come loose at a pinch."

"A pinch?"

"Well, yes, I suppose, even a good strong pinch."

Shock warred in Amelia's face with a sudden, startled humour. Go ahead, go ahead, Mabel breathed, laugh. James isn't here to scold you any more. Mabel grinned and Amelia gave way to the sort of giggle one couldn't take back.

"Dear, dear, I wonder how you know such things," she chided, trying to control the corners of her mouth.

"Part of the perks of working for charity. You can inquire into the most interesting subjects and no one suspects it isn't for noble reasons. Such fun to study frivolity, all to mount a campaign against it, naturally."

"You mean you actually went into the shop and..."

"Certainly!"

Amelia, blushing, hadn't guessed the devilment in Mabel's eyes. Yet her weeks in Mabel's small house, free of James' custodial presence, had been like being carried out to sea on some frightening, freeing crest of foam that could not be escaped or stopped.

"Mabel, you haven't been completely devoted...."

"I have!" Mabel exclaimed with perfect truth. "But I don't have to be a sobersides night and day. Goodness, how tiresome."

Amelia's bandaged wrists gave a spasmodic hitch.

"Oh, don't make me want to hug you. Dr. Brough will have a fit if I lift my arms. Is he coming in to see me today?"

"At four o'clock," said Mabel, seizing the moment. "Right now you have another visitor. Edwin is here. You must take pity and let him in."

Blood rushed violently to Amelia's face as it always did when Edwin was mentioned. He was the one who had lifted Amelia in his arms from among the blackened baskets and carried her straightaway to the small house he rented with his sister so that Mabel could care for her friend with her own hands. He had postponed his Birmingham speaking tour until he knew she was out of danger then stomped off in a whirlwind, thundering fearfully at his unsuspecting audiences. When he returned, he laid siege to the room but Amelia always refused to admit him.

"I can't see him. Not...today."

"Bosh! You've been perfectly able to see him for days. I can't stand him underfoot a moment longer. He's worse than a pack of hounds."

Mabel would never forget how her brother had gone deathly white when he discovered it was Amelia he was carrying from the cellar. Edwin, who did nothing by halves, had fallen in love like a boulder toppling off a cliff. Now, whatever the outcome, Mabel was determined to put an end to his suspense.

"No!" Amelia cried in alarm. "Please. I just...I can't!"

"You'll have to sometime. You'll be out of bed soon. Julius has inquired regularly about your welfare and offered to send a big trunk of your clothes."

This was a mistake. Amelia tore her eyes from the door behind which Edwin paced.

"I want nothing from that strutting, godless, interfering toad! Not even my own dresses! Oh, how could he have done that to the Asylum the very minute he inherited. Mr. and Mrs. Jenks, the children scattered in a single day and me too ill even to know about it. I'd rather starve than go back and live with that...that poisonous rot he picked up at university!"

Julius Radmore was the reason Amelia was with the Cormans, not in her own home—because it wasn't her home any more. Cousin Julius, all of twenty-one, foppish and puffed up with shocking, atheistic ideas imbibed from the Oxford Galapagos Club, was heir to the Radmore fortune, being the nearest male. Rushing to take possession, he had discovered Amelia's support of the Infant's Asylum. Unlike Amelia, he firmly believed, prompted by Spencer and Darwin, that charity only degraded the noble British stock by keeping nature's mistakes alive.

When Amelia grew well enough to find out what he had done, she raged and swore she would never take a scrap from horrid Julius even though he never questioned his duty to support a spinster relative who came with the house, the carriage and the cash.

"Edwin went out and looked for the children as soon as he heard," Mabel said soothingly. "Most of them are at the workhouse until some other provision can be made."

"But Katie and Mary..."

"I'm sure they'll turn up. You mustn't get agitated."

Amelia subsided while Mabel tucked the coverlet about her.

"I wish Mr. and Mrs. Jenks were able to look after them. They worked so hard at the Asylum and were so conscientious. Too bad Edwin never found the couple."

"Well, actually he did," put in Mabel, deciding that now Amelia could be told. "At least he found Mrs. Jenks. She was in sort of a daze, without a penny to her name."

"Oh no! How could Julius!"

"I'm afraid it was her husband. According to the lady, Mr. Jenks took all the money they'd got from selling their bits and pieces and just...disappeared."

She explained the garbled story, as much as Edwin had been able to get out of the woman, and told how Edwin got her a job in a chop house kitchen, so she would at least to able to eat. "She had eyes blank as bits of china. 'Morty, I won't stand for this, Morty,' she kept saying. 'I'll find you, see if I don't!' Edwin thinks she a little...um, mad."

Amelia would not believe ill of Mr. Jenks and flew to Ida's defence.

"Poor, poor woman. Oh, I'll have to find some decent position for her as soon as I'm up and around."

"Good. That'll certainly be in a week or two. Edwin's been sitting out there all afternoon. I shan't say you refuse him today."

Amelia's eyes grew large and dark.

"Perhaps in a week...please, Mabel."

Every time she even thought of Edwin Corman, confusion tumbled through her. The memory of his arms bearing her up, the sound of his feet running on the cobbles, his voice rasping, "Oh God, Oh God," with every step shook her and swayed her. Yet though he made this wild emotion storm in her breast, she scarcely knew the man. She was also imposing herself on his house, penniless and grotesque, oh so grotesque! She would die if she had to speak to him today.

"Oh, you're just one big chicken. Goodness, even Edwin is bright enough to guess that hair grows back. If that's what's bothering you, look what I brought."

From her pocket, Mabel produced a bedcap absurd with ruffles.

"I shall look like a pillowcase in that."

"A very charming pillowcase too."

Mabel deftly tucked the cap over the bristles and pulled the collar of the nightgown up to cover most of the angry scars. A lacy frill drooped fetchingly over Amelia's left eye.

"There! Now I'm going to let the poor fellow in!"

Mabel swept out and left the door open. Edwin appeared as if conjured from a bottle.

"May I please come in?" he requested softly.

Amelia would have forbidden him had her tongue not cleaved to the roof of her mouth. Without waiting, Edwin came quickly to the side of the bed. His hair was standing straight up, as though he'd been raking his fingers through it for days.

"I couldn't have lasted a minute longer without seeing you."

He was a square, solid, forceful looking man with an impetuously florid complexion and a dense fringe beard that gave him a sea-going appearance. His sturdy tweeds had seen so much activity they had given up being gentlemanly and bagged out into comfort at elbows and knees. The pulse at his temple gave away that his heart was thumping furiously.

"I...I want to thank you for you hospitality," Amelia began, overcome with a paroxysm of self-consciousness. "I should never have got through except for Mabel's care."

"Our house is your house. We hope you will regard it so from now on."

Amelia swallowed, feeling the scars burn trails anew up her cheek. Oh, why had she imagined beauty nothing but vanity and never guessed the inconvenience when it was gone.

"Please, I couldn't impose. I shall soon be well..."

"Impose!" Edwin cried, all his resolutions about a circumspect approach forgotten. "Impose! How could you impose! If I had a hundred houses I should want you sitting like a queen in every one of them!"

Edwin had a booming, headlong manner of speech that sent words ricocheting to all corners of the room. His tweeds and his energy overwhelmed the pale order of the sickroom. Amelia felt her breath die away to the bottom of her lungs.

"That would...keep me rather busy, wouldn't it?" she heard herself reply idiotically.

"Yes...no, oh how silly of me!" Edwin raked his fingers through his hair for the thousand-and-first time that day. "I mean, I don't even have one house. Mabel and I rent this one. In fact, I live on charity. My income comes out of collected funds and changes every week according to cash on hand and whatever crisis happens to be going. I've no right to make you an offer of any kind."

He's not going to propose!

The thought hurtled into Amelia's mind and told her that this was the fear she had been wrestling with since her first conscious moment after the fire.

"But I'm asking you to marry me anyway. Drat it...I beg your pardon, blast...I mean, I'm no good at flowery talk. I had a whole bag of it lined up in my head and it just spilled away the minute I saw you. What's the use of mumbling round a bush? Nothing but a torture to both of us. Straight to the point, I say. Always straight to the point."

Edwin stopped short and looked astounded at the words that had just tumbled out of his mouth. He'd had so many conversations with Amelia in his imagination that it was as if he had been talking intimately with her for weeks, even though he had scarcely exchanged a word with her the whole time. She'd think him a lunatic.

Amelia could not move under the coverlet. Her eyes grew huge with the surprise of it and saw Edwin half obscured by the lace of the bedcap.

He is proposing! He is! He is!

This man who had spoken to her only at lectures and over tea with Mabel. This man who was glowering at her with such spike-haired intensity as if what he really meant was to throw her over his shoulder and stomp out. A clamour set up inside her, a drunken, giddy clamour that seemed to have nothing to do with joy or fear but be some new emotion altogether on its own.

Then her mouth went horribly parched.

"Oh Edwin, it's..it's not your fault this happened to me. You don't' have to offer...ohhhh!"

He had snatched up her hand, but her involuntary yelp made him drop it again. He towered over the bed looking down in frustration at all the whiteness enveloping Amelia. His waistcoat buttons trembled with the force of feeling inside.

"Miss Amelia, never think that," he cried. "I want you because I'm a selfish beast. You've courage and you've strength and I want it at my side. All I can offer you is a share in work that's hard and damned distressing. But it's work that makes a difference. Just to see one of those urchins cleaned up and fed, why it fills a fellow up with a whacking satisfaction, right up to here!" His palm slammed his collarbone emphatically though he meant to indicate his heart. "I can't provide even a fraction of what's you're used to, but we won't starve either. What do you say?"

Edwin couldn't have hit it better. The panic and confusion that had gripped Amelia since the fire, found order, something to clutch onto. It not only clutched hard, but the rugged Puritan inside Amelia roused as at a clarion challenge. She looked up at the gold-rimmed spectacles that sat so foolishly amidst all that agitated masculinity and thought suddenly how softly and vigorously his beard curled. Amelia wanted to touch it, touch a man's beard, an idea that had, in her whole life, never before crossed her mind. She began to feel washed toward Edwin on a swirling, inevitable tide.

"I might never have full use of my right hand," she warned, over a galloping pulse.

Starts of joy shook Edwin, making his spectacles quiver.

"Doctor Brough says you'll be able to write. Thumping good appeals for money, I hope. I'm no good with paper myself."

"You mean like, 'For every waif you save, God saves a patch of heaven just for you,'?"

"Yes!"

Amelia felt the stir of a new freedom, a new power. Edwin, dear Edwin, would never try to forbid.

"And, 'Disciples of Mammon, redeem yourselves. Rescue the homeless babes!'"

Inside her rose an indefatigable desire to work, to organize, to fling herself into the furnace of Edwin's look.

"Yes!" His spectacles were going to fall off his nose if he didn't stop nodding.

"And, 'The helpless orphan today is a sinew of the Empire tomorrow.'"

"Oh yes, yes! Capital! You'll do!"

"So will you!"

Into the cataclysmic silence that fell, Amelia and Edwin just stared at each other. There should be fanfare, Amelia thought through her daze or...or singing birds or....violets!

"Oh, capital!" Edwin cried again. He circled the bed in his excitement, but because Amelia was swathed to the chin and forbidden to move, he was forced to turn his bear hug into an awkward, smacking kiss planted in the middle of her bedcap.

Outside the door, Mabel stopped listening and tiptoed off, grinning to herself. She had known Edwin would go charging in all directions the moment the barrier was down and there'd been no telling what Amelia might do. Mabel had taken care of the problem handily. Ardent temperance supporter that she was, she'd spiked the raspberry cordial generously with gin.

CHAPTER FOURTEEN

The lives of Katie and Mary took on a pattern. Up before first light to buy stock then the trudge to their patch of pavement to face a long day of crying their wares. In the evening there would be a meal of bread and drippings and tea. Or, if they were "in luck", they could celebrate with a baked potato from the cart or a helping of fried fish, since all those who lived in lodgings had to eat from outside.

High summer came to London, trying to dispense sunshine and cheering warmth through the perpetual pall of coal smoke that gave the finest days a yellow cast. Warmth penetrated the twisting streets making the poorest inhabitants push back their caps to squint at a blithe sky. Caged birds offered for sale found heart to twitter and sing. Petunias with sooty petals bloomed bravely in window boxes. The very bricks, smoky as they were, seemed suffused with a ruddiness kindly to the passing eye.

Despite the wearing hours, Katie vibrated with life. If she missed the regular meals of the Asylum, her tough little spirit frolicked free of its grinding routine. Each day was a fresh adventure. On days when the rain sheeted down unbroken or fog had made it impossible even to grope their way from their lodging, they had only tea for supper. Katie barely thought of hunger in the luxury of having Mary all to herself, just the two of them, sitting cross legged on the thin pallet, perfect companions, while the rest of the world clattered by outside. On days when sunshine or brisk breezes hinting of the sea whet people's appetites and the tray sold out two or three times over, Katie would gambol like a foal let out in a pasture, her braid flying.

"I guess we showed them, didn't we, Mary!"

"Aye, that we did!" Mary always assented, her visible pride making Katie want to leap the chimney pots.

And they'd spend recklessly on a treat of plum duff or a muffin from the muffin man which they ate with gusto while Tonio, the

Italian accordion lad, pumped out *Santa Lucia*, rolling his dark eyes at them.

Katie grew to love the whole brawl of London, the scrape of clogs on the streets, the wares in the windows of pawnshops, the quarrels, the cries of women in childbirth, the tipsy singing from pubs. She knew the name of the dustman's old dun mare. She grinned at the "high hip" ladies who would trade used clothes for a potted germanium or a shiny milk jug. She treasured a bit of blue ribbon given her by a shop girl who had just spent the last of her wages on a handful of pretty things.

Especially dazzling to her were the street entertainers, the juggler, the German family with musical instruments and the clown who worked the Lane once a week, his hoary jokes a wonder to Katie.

"Why is the city of Athens like a candle wick?" he had asked her.

Having never heard of Athens, she stared at the creases of his face glistening under the crude clown paint.

"Because it is in the midst of Greece," he answered himself, and strode off slapping his thigh.

Katie laughed uproariously though she had never heard of Greece either and hadn't the least idea of the point of the joke.

Once in a while, two Peelers would stroll down the Lane, buttoned into blue uniforms and swinging short black sticks. The inhabitants would go still in their places like mice near a cat, for the poor were honest haters of the police. When the two turned the corner, a whoosh of relief filled the air. Yet the policemen never stopped, never complained about barrows or beggars or tried to make hawkers move on. That, Mary knew, was a benefit of the sum she handed over to Bert each week no matter how much Katie seethed against this tribute to Red Nell.

Nell herself was occasionally sighted, though only glimpsed dimly through the shaded windows of the closed hansom cab in which she always travelled. No one knew much about Red Nell except that she had once been an Irish tinker woman fleeing the great potato famine, and that she had fearsome sons to enforce her orders. The protection she provided when you paid her tribute, was balanced by equally swift retribution for straying. Any traffic with her mortal enemy, Teapot, was a quick way to end up a corpse in the Thames.

From her tinker days, Nell retained her comfort in wheeled vehicles and her love of horseflesh. Hitched to cab was always a rawboned, muscular, carefully fed horse that could probably outrun a Cup winner if required. Nell's driver, Nips, was a man of broad but dwarfish proportions, his brawny bundles of shoulders, completely overtopping his unnaturally short, bowed legs which barely reached the front of the driver's box. Nips was thought to be mute, from the way he never issued a spoken command to the horse but controlled the cab expertly by means of mysterious jerks of the reins. No matter what the commotion, Nips always stared straight ahead out of his dour, lumpy face while giving the eerie impression of not missing a thing. Once or twice, Katie had glimpsed the fierce eyes and shockingly hennaed red hair that gave Nell her name. Mary kept a heavy hand upon Katie when Nell's cab was near.

Harry, the pickled whelk man, decided he liked Katie and Mary, fruit not being in competition with whelks. He was a broad-bellied soul gravitating to fishy things since he had been born by the sea, not too far from Portsmouth. At a look from Harry, Bert gave up serious harassment, satisfying himself with insulting asides and stolen berries as he ambled by.

And, best of all, Katie saw Will at least once a week as he and Croom took a short cut through Wheeble Lane. They talked a great deal very quickly, making the most of the time Croom spent in The Bird. Even when they could only wave, the day seemed cheerier for both.

Mary and Katie became part of the intricate, precarious world radiating from the local market. A world where one could buy practically anything in the streets. The poor, working brutal hours and clustered densely about their jobs, had neither time, money nor strength to search farther afield for the necessities of life.

So an old woman, trudging back from selling cakes of blacking, could pick up a nice bit of plaice, already filleted, to fry for her son and daughter-in-law when they got out of the boot-making plant. A dockman in a rush might buy a dozen oysters for his pockets, to pry open with his knife while the ship's hatches were being uncovered. The barrow man pushed his barrow heaped with turnips, cabbages, carrots, onions or cauliflowers, often with the dealing done by his wife. There were curds and whey, shrimp and mussels, geese, ducks and chickens, live or dressed. For those hungry on the spot, there were hot eels, pea soup, penny pies, baked potatoes, spice cakes, crumpets and sweetmeats. For the weak of chest, brandy balls and cough drops helped combat the effects of the polluted air. For the thirsty, there was tea, coffee, ginger beer, lemonade, new milk from a cow led on a rope, and, occasionally, even water.

A gentleman, out for a stroll, was besieged by flower girls offering him bunches of violets or yellow primroses for the lady on his arm. A coster lass, dashing to meet her sweetheart, could buy a frilled cap to wear indoors while they had a drink at the pub. If a boot lace broke, there were laces at hand or pin cushions, combs and bonnets. There were Lucifer matches, grease-removing compounds, rat poison, pen knives, tea trays, bird cages, herring toasters, fire screens, shirt buttons, spectacles, paper hangings and dolls. In other stalls, puppies, squirrels, goldfish and even tortoises languished patiently waiting for a buyer.

Young flower seller in the street.

For those without money for new, there were the dealers aplenty in second hand articles. A good china bowl with only a chip out of it could be got for a fraction of the price of a whole one. Thin towels, cut from old sheeting, did a passable job for that minority interested in washing. Cheap boots, not too broken, had saved many a foot from the cruel cobblestones. Katie and Mary took desperate care of their boots. If they ruined them, where would they ever get more?

There were people who made livings scouring the sewers for useful debris, sifting London's tons of ashes, catching rats for rat killing contests in the backs of pubs. Everything, even cigar butts picked up from the streets and cut open for the scraps of tobacco to be sold to the poor, was turned into money. Money was everything. Without money there loomed the workhouse, starvation, sickness and swift, inexorable death.

As the weeks slipped by, Katie's flute-like voice managed enough sales so that they could pay for their lodging and usually eat. Yet, for all their initial optimism, they never seemed to get a penny ahead. Though Katie could stop customers, Mary had not been raised to the streets and her slow brain did not grasp the niceties of bargaining or the sleight of hand by which the experienced costers kept what small advantage they had on their own side. She did not see juice pricked from oranges, old figs brushed and sold as new, cotton braces sworn to be silk, rice ground among the pepper, short weight and short count given with the skill of the magician's hand.

After the strawberries were gone, they sold cherries, then nuts, then as fall nipped in, apples. They wished they could afford to go into small wares but barely managed to keep in what stock they had. Sales struggled along like an awkward bird, flapping its wings but never managing to actually fly.

Mary's intense but inarticulate love for Katie was apparent in every hour she supported the heavy tray, every drop of rain she bore, every rude insult to her hump she could not reply to. Katie reciprocated with a feeling so deep and secure she wasn't even aware of it. As long as Mary was beside her, everything could not be other than all right.

Though their struggles might loom large to themselves, Mary and Katie were but two more particles in the enormous ocean of poor that made up Queen Victoria's London. The invention of the steam engine had forever altered England. Traditional society broke up before its impact like pack ice before a tidal wave. "Labour!" cried the cities, starting up their factories and their foundries. "Labour, we must have labour!" And the people, needing to eat, left their farms and their villages, their hand looms and their smithies and poured in.

London staggered under their weight and turned into a "great wen" gobbling up the countryside, spreading at a rate of two thousand houses a year, outstripping in size and population any other city on earth. It remained appallingly backward. Mid century, the Medical Officer of Health described the subsoil of the City as "seventeen million cubic feet of decaying residuum." Fashionable Belgrave Square and Hyde Park Gardens abounded in foul deposits and blocked drains which spread purulent throats, typhus, febrile influenza and a myriad other diseases. If even the Queen's apartments at Buckingham Palace were ventilated through the malodorous common sewer, what was happening among the dwellings of the poor did not bear thinking of. When the city built sewers emptying into the Thames, the result was a river so polluted the Houses of Parliament had to hold sessions behind curtains soaked in chloride of lime and in the Tooley Street Fire of eighteen sixty-one, the river itself went ablaze on account of its coating of tallow.

As the new city grew from the muck of the old, the deeply entrenched philosophy of laissez-faire allowed it to spread as wildly and as crookedly as it pleased. "Mustn't interfere with the labour reserve," harumphed the industrialists from their comfortable villas built out of range of the smoke. Left to itself, the labour reserve starved obligingly when not wanted and crowded the gates with yet another generation of hungry youth when there was rumour of jobs.

East End London sprang up to house this reserve, stretching from the Tower of London east to the River Lea, miles of mean and squalid streets whose area alone was greater than any city on the Continent. It's names, Wapping, Shadwell, Limehouse, Mile End and so on were a litany of misery. Its factories, sweatshops and tenements only added to this sea of desolation and the only spots of cheer were the sing song caves packed shoulder to shoulder where chronic drunkenness ate up meagre wages, spawned brawls and left men and women alike insensible in the gutters.

Laissez-faire, held sway here too. If a master wished to plunge an exhausted child into a tub of ice water or hit her violently on the side of the head to keep her awake, he was perfectly free to do so. A woman was encouraged to get her living by sixteen hours in a sweltering garret constructing artificial flowers for the millinery trade. Afterward, a weary act of prostitution in the alley behind would raise her earnings to the point where she could afford a bit of pudding for supper and perhaps even a bed. Cholera and typhoid walked about selecting whom they fancied. Mothers weakened by tuberculosis were favourites as well as scrawny babies already bitten by cesspool rats. Rental accommodation was strictly pay-as-you-go. The lucky ones got a two-room house with a kitchen in the basement and a dank rain barrel behind. Inhabitants of less desirable rooms sat up all night in their clothes, knowing the free enterprising lice and bedbugs would make sleep impossible. Those poor with no homes at all could compete for piles of ashes to soften the cobblestones or huddle, as any citizen had the right to huddle, on the benches of London Bridge, oblivious to the rain.

Yet the poor by their scant hearths warmed their innards with tea imported on the great China clippers and stomped their clogs to the tune of Rule Britannia from the sheer joy of belonging to the mightiest, cleverest, most just nation on earth. Let a British merchant find a source of teak or mahogany, let him poke his nose up some African River in search of copper or ground nuts and, presto, the Royal Navy was right there behind him inviting the new territory into the Empire and unloading a crop of lads spawned, like young bull pups, from the floggings of the public schools. Short on feeling they might be, but they were long on tenacity, vigorously equipped to take over and rule the sprawling British territories.

"And what is the reason for our supremacy?" a schoolmaster might ask, rapping a desk globe girdled in Imperial Red. In his heart he probably shared his students' opinion that it was because God was an Englishman and His people the only nation fit to bring shoes, croquet and parliamentary procedure to the heathen multitudes burdening the rest of the world.

For the real reason, the schoolmaster had but to look out of the window at the towering smokestacks, and whirring machinery that throbbed like a giant heartbeat sending pulses to the furthest scarlet splash on the globe. No other nation on earth could weave wool so, build railway cars or produce such flashing acres of Sheffield cutlery. The raw materials of Africa, India, the Americas and the East flowed into British ports and British factories for Britain alone could produce the manufactured goods the world was clamouring for.

So the poor ran the looms and the rich prospered mightily, secure in the unassailability of private property, acquiring Oriental screens and grand pianos to prove it. About the time Katie was born, England was in the grip of the most terrifying surge of energy and expansion the country had ever seen.

Into this turbulent flood of change, Katie and Mary had flung themselves, joining a feverish horde of tumblers, laundresses, crossing sweepers, horse holders, flower sellers, shop clerks, dustmen, gamblers, beggars, thieves and prostitutes, all struggling madly to stay alive. It was up to them alone to survive in the ruthless, uncaring rush. That they were there at all was a testament to their luck and the toughness of their constitutions. Whether they would continue to make their way was daily growing more questionable.

CHAPTER FIFTEEN

"Oh Edwin, it's...lovely!"

Amelia stood with her husband before a narrow, vacant building dripping soot from its windowsills and sure to be a torment of stairs inside. The street was equally dismaying for it twisted down an incline on which horses slipped and pedestrians cursed. A few shabby shops punctuated the drab facades. Equally drab people shuffled along, frayed and grimy. Mud clogged the gutters, poverty and despondence tainted the air. It seemed the last place a pair such as Edwin and Amelia should choose to establish themselves.

Edwin let out an uncomfortable laugh.

"Lovely is hardly the word, my dear, but it's what we can afford, I'm afraid."

Edwin had fully expected Amelia to recoil at first sight but here she was, advancing without demur toward the door. She clasped her hands in front of her, avoiding the grubby door handle. Her right hand was seamed with scars under its protective glove, but Amelia had regained the use of it quite tolerably.

"Well, aren't you going give me the tour?" she asked with determined holiday lightness.

"Amy...we really don't have to take it. Not this one. It really is rather lamentable inside. Some kind of cabinet-making concern went belly up, I believe."

Money! If they just had more money, they could have got something decent. But even after giving up the small rented house and counting everything Edwin saved from his lectures, this was the sum total of accommodation possible.

Amelia looked at Edwin out of wide, direct eyes. If optimism were edible they could have fed an army for a year.

"We do have to take it. Oh, Edwin, I wouldn't care if it were barrels stacked in an alley, we simply must have a place to put the children. How can we leave a single one in that workhouse any longer!"

The moment she'd been able to totter onto her feet, Amelia had gone off to the workhouse to see the remnants of the Asylum children. They had rushed to her like chicks in a rainstorm. She could not, would not, leave them in that atrocious place.

Edwin looked even more uncomfortable. It was one thing to make gallant promises in the heat of a marriage proposal. It was quite another for a man to bring his wife to such a place. But Amelia was so resolute. Seeing Edwin's doubts, she smiled up with perfect confidence.

"It's our start, darling. We've got enough for the first rent. After that you'll be bringing in plenty of money from your lectures, especially now that you don't have to share with anybody. Oh it was so brave of you to strike out on your own."

Edwin flushed warmly in the vicinity of his cravat and not entirely from her praise. He'd been congratulated on his marriage at the organization he worked with, but the congratulations were mixed with frowns. Edwin was an enthusiastic lecturer, but a man with a wife became an expensive commodity to support. When he'd announced that he and his wife planned to start a small, independent refuge of their own, the frowns had turned into scowls.

"Mr. Corman, we can't allow funds to be used outside of our agency. Share and share alike, as you well know."

There'd been no place inside the agency for what Amelia had in mind, nowhere for the children to go. And Edwin just didn't have the heart to tell her no. He had to either give up the idea of a private venture or resign. In a burst of headlong brashness, he had chosen to resign. Amelia never guessed the impasse he had been put to.

Yet now, seeing himself reflected, surrounded by stars, in Amelia's eyes, Edwin felt strength flowing through him anew. How could he doubt that substantial sums would soon be rolling in, attracted by the lure of his golden tongue? The first moment they could, they'd move to a decent street and expand.

Amelia tore her mind from budget problems and allowed herself visions of a well-run children's home. Rows of snowy pinafores danced before her eyes. Oh, how exciting to be free at last and starting out on her own!

"Do you think it will hold all the children?"

"We'll use a shoehorn if we have to," Edwin promised, dimly but powerfully aware of the compulsion driving Amelia, a compulsion born in that blazing cellar where James lay, already dead, and the basket children, fleeing on their stick legs, rent the heart with their screams. The one they had captured, Cully, waited at the workhouse with the Asylum children, hair cropped down to her skull to get the vermin out.

"And Ida Jenks must be the housekeeper," Amelia asserted, for Ida was still slaving at the chop house, stained with pork grease, quivering like the last survivor on an earthquake's lip. "Let's look inside.

Edwin opened to door with the rusty borrowed key and escorted Amelia tenderly inside. Then he was off again, tramping through the ground floor and down to the basement and back up again before Amelia had a chance to dust off her hems.

The dress she wore tried for a bustle and caught up enough fabric from the overskirt to drape it, but it was only a plain echo of the complicated creations she had worn without a thought before her marriage. Her wardrobe now had all been supplied by Edwin, and Amelia had seen it made up in the most modest manner possible, dark, plain, serviceable serges and ribbonless bodices replacing the opulence of old. Far from being disappointed at the necessary economies, Amelia was delighted. She was a simple labourer now in the endless fields of charitable endeavour and proudly wore the unadorned armour of her calling. Shining raiment, she felt, wouldn't have suited her more.

After the initial terror, Amelia could not believe how well she liked austerity. The soul of one of Cromwell's puritans might have been reborn in her for the way she took to the challenge of keeping herself and Edwin respectable on as little as possible from the collected funds. Cabs were a novelty, sharing a servant was a novelty and now that she managed real money, she knew that Mr. Jenks had been most prodigal in his use of the funds at the Asylum.

"Phew, needs a good scrub up here." Edwin said, dusting his hands. "Are you game for stairs, top floor and all?"

"Need you ask?"

With a half sigh, she watched him gallop up to the landing and out of sight, then set out after him. She knew his head was already buzzing with a dozen schemes that he would burst out with the next moment she saw him.

After her ordered, sheltered life, Edwin Corman had certainly been a shock. Reckless declarations from a sick bed were one thing, but after she'd married him, Amelia had been frightened to death to find out he really didn't have any money just as he had told her. On top of that, he was a man who knocked things off shelves with his elbows and gave orations at three in the morning if she were so foolish as to question his pet opinions.

Recovery from her newlywed dismay had come the moment Amelia realized that here was a man who needed organizing. He might be a rushing torrent, leaping high into the air, refusing to admit of rocks or obstacles in his path, but Amelia had no intention of being drowned. Rousing to a lively battle of wills, she immediately set out to impose order on the fascinating chaos she had wed.

And he, in turn, was supporting her in founding the refuge, a haven for urchins living like outcast animals in the streets. Oh yes, what a world Edwin had introduced her to! Despite her private experience with the Infant's Asylum, she'd had no idea how much of London was sunk in ghastly, hopeless poverty.

The worst was the children. Helpless creatures spawned by drunken prostitutes, turned out maids, abused factory workers ravished by their own bosses. Families who could not get work tramped the streets, spindly youngsters stumbling after them. Widows locked their babies alone in a room sixteen hours at a time while they tried to scrape up a crust doing washing or stitching hat linings. Left to the mercies of the slums, infants were smothered when intoxicated parents fell on top of them. Those older might be worked until they dropped or sold outright into prostitution. Many ran away from cruel taskmasters. Others were simply abandoned. The workhouse took what it could, of course, but the scandals there were almost as bad—children mixing with hardened vagrants, living in packs amid rats, disease and squalor.

Unlike James, who was shocked that his sister knew babies weren't left under cabbage leaves, Edwin respected her enough to let her take in much of the unspeakable horror. Time and time again she found it hard to credit that in this, the eighteen seventies, in the finest country on the face of the earth, such conditions were allowed to exist.

But they won't exist for long, she told herself, lifting her head. Not when the British public knows the whole truth. Something will be done!

A great deal had already been done. There were laws to prevent child labour in factories and mines. There were laws limiting young shop assistants' hours to fourteen a day. There was a new law suggesting, in theory, at least, that children should attend school, though it didn't specify who was to pay. There were ragged schools for the poor run by a variety of organizations. There were the intrepid reporters, such as Henry Mayhew, who had looked into the lives of the poor, and published the unvarnished results. There was the great Lord Shaftsbury, that tireless reformer and the myriad charities hard at work on the scene.

"Come here, Amelia. There's a capital window at the back."

Heaps of decaying debris from the woodworking enterprise lay about to the extent that it would take a shovel to clear the place. Several planks in the floor were broken where workmen's benches had been ripped out. Swirls of dust motes rose up into the weak light falling through the window which looked out over a depressing alley. The panes of glass, some of them broken, were obscured by clots of cobwebs. In the corner, a whole section of plaster had fallen down from damp and never been swept up.

Edwin slowed in the face of the cobwebs and turned.

"Amy, we really don't have to take this one. I had no idea...about the plaster and the rubbish..."

"Nonsense," Amelia shot back, a refusing to admit dismay. So much of her changed state held jolts like these that she felt she was inured. "We need this kind of room. We can get the children in here, all if we squeeze the cots. And downstairs we can have our own little parlour."

Edwin stared at her through his spectacles.

"In this neighbourhood? It's full of slop workers and the indigent and...heaven knows what else..."

"Yes, here! Besides, with Mabel going off to Scotland with the Improvement Society, we don't need to rent a separate place."

"Oh Amy..."

"No, Edwin. I want to live here. We have to be near the children, don't we? How else can we supervise?"

And anyway, there was no money for them to live anywhere else. She took Edwin's big hands in her own.

"Plenty of others, like the ones who teach the ragged schools, live in much worse and thrive. I should feel like a perfect bloated leech set up in fine lodgings eating up our capital. I want to get on as fast as possible with our plan."

Since she knew already not to let Edwin get too worked up over an idea, her appealing face hid the tremor of anticipation underneath. No matter how poor their refuge, she meant to join, just as soon as she could, one of the noblest charitable efforts in London— the child emigration scheme.

It had caught her imagination the first time she had heard about it in Edwin's lecture. Why less than ten years ago, Miss Maria Rye had taken a boatload of children to Canada. Children gathered from the streets, the workhouses, and the Kirkland Industrial School. These children, abused and unwanted in Britain, were snapped up by grateful Canadian farmers who needed labour and swore to treat them like their own.

The idea was catching like wildfire. Miss Annie Macpherson was already making a voyage, sometimes two, every year with distribution homes in Canada and eager applicants for children waiting for her train. Dr. Barnardo, had a boys' home in Stepney and lived by the words, "No destitute child refused admission". He sent children with Miss Macpheron's party as well as did others engaged in the same work. Dr. Barnardo meant to handle emigration himself, he said, as soon as he could set up his own distribution homes.

These people were already legends in Amelia's mind—the quiet, ascetic Miss Macpherson, the peppery, dramatic Barnardo, the somewhat haughty, dark-eyed Miss Rye. All of them dedicated to a cause Amelia intended to make her own.

Yes, the motto was, "Save the children, help the Empire." The vast lands of Canada cried out for population while children here had to turn to crime because there were no jobs. In Canada, they could engage in healthful, outdoor labour far from corrupting cities. They would grow into sturdy, honest citizens, British citizens, Amelia thought with satisfaction, a bulwark against those other European hordes trying to get in.

Before even the emigration scheme, Amelia had discovered that girls could be sent out for domestic training and boys to certain houses of industry to learn a useful trade. What practical little citizens she intended to deposit on the soil of that land across the sea. The more children who came through the front door, the more must go out through the back to newly minted Canada to make room.

"Are you sure?"

"Positively! Now let's go and take the lease. I want to see about the cleaning before the day is out."

Amelia envisioned neat rows of cots, a kitchen, wash up corner, an alcove for Ida Jenks to sleep. She would take the place in hand no matter how unpromising it looked. Oh, if only Mary and Katie could be here!

She wrenched her mind from that. No amount of inquiries had turned them up. Ida Jenks had got the queerest look when asked.

All the other children had been able to say was that Katie and Mary run away through the streets. Nobody could imagine where they might have stopped.

"The Everlea Infirmary is closing up and there's a dozen cots we can have." Amelia informed her husband decisively. "We can be in full operation inside of a week."

Edwin looked vastly impressed.

"Our pocketbook…"

"What with your lecturing and my passionate appeals how could we go wrong?"

A large arm gave Amelia a squeeze.

"That's why I married you, Amy. You're absolutely magic at winkling money out of waistcoat pockets. No one stands a chance once you get a pen in your hand."

Yes, she was rather good at it, she had to admit. But she'd have to winkle an awful lot of money out of an awful lot of waistcoat pockets to make up for the sources she'd lost when she'd married. Those sources had been staunchly Anglican. They were hardly likely to look kindly on a woman who abandoned the true and official faith for Nonconformism the minute she reached the altar.

For Amelia, the biggest wrench accompanying her marriage had been that of turning Methodist. She'd overcome her crisis of conscience with the conviction that it was a wife's duty to accept her husband's religion just as much as she accepted his name. Swallowing her qualms in one gargantuan gulp, Amelia had plunged in. Now, cut off from all that was familiar, Amelia cleaved bravely to Edwin, fitting herself into the alarming beliefs of his chapel the way a person might force herself into some new and unfamiliar skin.

As Amelia tilted the cap hiding her chopped hair, Edwin suddenly laughed and kissed her neck beside the scars twisting the lobe of her damaged ear. Amelia sucked in her breath and closed her eyes. The kissing still took getting used to. A dangerous, dizzying practice that led to things Amelia could scarcely acknowledge, save that they were so tumbled and so sweet. Oh, how she pitied all other women who could not make such a thoroughly headlong, utterly wonderful marriage as her own, Methodist or no.

She sighed happily and pressed her forehead against Edwin's own, committing herself again to the torrent that carried her on.

"If only we are steadfast," she repeated, with utter British certainty, "Providence will provide exactly what we need.

CHAPTER SIXTEEN

"Who's that?"

Katie and Mary sighted a raven-haired woman leaning into Harry's doorway. A lithe, jaunty woman wearing the vigor of her prime for all that her skirt was carelessly ragged at the bottom and her head bonnetless. The woman's face was startlingly sun-browned, her stance easy as any gypsy on a stroll.

By now, Katie and Mary knew the regulars for several streets around and could spot strangers coming through to beg or sell. This newcomer was laughing familiarly with Harry as she gulped whelks with gusto. Harry, thumbs in his braces, grinned back. What was worse, the woman's free hand rested on a tray of shining apples!

"Do you think she's going to sell in our Lane?"

Mary's brow drew into a knot, worried about the delicate balance of the apple business. Competition could knock her and Katie out altogether.

"Don't know, lass."

They walked by Harry after his customer had gone.

"Fine appetite that lady had," Mary commented with some asperity. Harry was still grinning.

"Appetite! Why that's Flashin' Maud. Big appetites she has all round. Surely you remember..," he paused, shaking his jowls. "No, you wouldn't. You weren't here till summer. Flashin' Maud's been walking out of London, working in the hop fields and haying and such like. Used to do it myself when I were younger. Hordes of 'em go. They'll be back soon's the cold sets in."

Flashin' Maud did not openly compete with Katie and Mary. She simply sauntered where she pleased, flashing at everyone that half bemused, half impudent smile that had given her the name. Everyone grinned back, even Bert who turned foolishly pink and took a friendly cuff on the ear.

That day sales for Katie and Mary dropped alarmingly. Yes, Flashin' Maud was back!

The autumnal wind turned nippy. Mary and Katie had only black tea for supper as an economic precaution. They lived at same bare lodging house. The second floor, rented only to females, gave a whiff of respectability. Mrs. Gossidge, with her infirm husband, watched everything from a room by the front door. The back was occupied by her son Peter who dragged his barrow inside each night and quarrelled spectacularly with his wife.

The already small rooms had been divided into cubby holes. That was how housing was increased among the poor who could not pay for improvements. The demand and the overcrowding had grown ever worse as the new railways gobbled huge bites out of poor districts where land was cheapest. Two of the females who shared the space with Mary and Katie were almost never seen. They rose the earliest and straggled in latest, stuffing bread into their mouths, dropping to the mattresses with their clothes on. They were employed by a hat maker, Katie learned. Since this was the busy season, they had to work whatever hours were asked or lose their jobs. One of them coughed ominously, choking to keep silent as she passed Mrs. Gossidge's door.

The third occupant, a gaunt girl of about fourteen, they sometimes noticed in the streets, for she made her living as a ballad singer, strolling about or haunting theatre doors late at night. Her sweet, thin voice enchanted Katie since music of any sort had been completely unknown to the child before she went into the streets. That Jane always sang the same song scarcely mattered. Katie stood rooted to the spot, the melody of Annie Laurie swelling in her breast.

"Her brow is like the snawdrift,
Her throat is like the swan,
Her face it is the fairest
That e'er the sun shone on."

Someday, Katie vowed, she was going to see a snawdrift, and maybe even a swan which she pictured as a kind of giant pigeon with a neck like a girl.

Yet when Katie and Mary arrived home one night, they found Jane sitting on the steps, her bundle on her knees, crying bitterly. Mary's policy was to ignore steadfastly the sucking mire of misery all about them. Katie stopped, jarred by Jane's glistening tears.

"What's the matter?" she asked in a small voice.

Jane burst into sobs again.

"I got to leave 'ere. I can't pay for tonight. I...I got to go to those awful places down on the Rye!"

This was disaster. Everyone, even Katie knew that if you couldn't pay for a decent place, you had to go down where they had lice and all the dirty people, men and women together, slept in one smelly room.

Mary uttered a heavy grunt indicating they could do nothing for poor Jane. Katie didn't budge.

"Didn't you make enough today?"

Surely, surely the whole world would pay to hear of Annie Laurie. Jane shook her head miserably.

"People's tired of my old song. I got to learn a new one. I...I found this paper blowing in the street, but I can't learn it. I can't read. I don't know what it says."

She extended a page of sheet music which bore the clear imprint of a boot and had been so long in Jane's pocket it was almost falling apart along its creases.

Katie remembered lavender-scented Miss Radmore reading to them sometimes in her stately voice. A wave of longing passed over her. Katie bent over the paper in the last grey daylight. The alphabet danced maddeningly, hedging its secrets about with pointy black legs. Jane watched in hope that quickly seeped away.

"Oh give it back to me. You can't read it either."

"And you can't stay. Get along wi' you now. Come back when you've got brass!"

Mrs. Gossidge had appeared, thinking Jane was trying to slip undetected back into the house. Again crumbling into tears, Jane backed into the street. Katie and Mary stood motionless, aware of a sudden icy breath on their necks. When they got to their room, protest gushed up inside Katie.

"It isn't fair!"

At which Mary laughed a harsh, frightening laugh that caused Katie to recoil involuntarily.

"Why tha should be a justice 'o the peace. Then we'd all have cakes for supper and fine feather pillows for our heads!"

The winds blew colder after Jane had gone, gusting with rain under lowering skies. Within the week they found four other strange vendors in the neighbourhood. Two sold gloves, the third, candles, and the fourth, hot chestnuts, indicating that winter was prowling in.

On the Wednesday, there was a great to-do in the lodging house. Mrs. O'Rielly had had some sort of fit in the night. When she didn't appear at her station, Katie and Mary waited anxiously. They had come to know her as one long separated from her family and homeland by the 'thrubbles". The money she made daily was all that supported her.

Mrs. O'Rielly remained on her pallet in the room across from Katie and Mary. "Useless, she is," fretted Mrs. Gossidge, patrolling the hall. "Can't hardly walk and one of 'er arms is all bent up to 'er ribs like a claw."

Katie longed to ask what a fit was and how it could bend an arm like a claw. Mary stopped her. Better never to ask anything of Mrs. Gossidge.

Four days later, Mrs. Gossidge's son, who ought to have been on his rounds, wheeled his empty barrow up to the door. Curiously, they saw him place a cloth bundle in the barrow and then a pail.

"Why, that's Mrs. O'Rielly's pail, that she keeps the pig's trotters in. I wonder..."

Katie's words died at the reappearance of Peter, this time with Mrs. O'Rielly in his arms. Her grey hair, always tidy beneath her chip bonnet, straggled loose across her face. What was worse, she was twisting and moaning. When she saw the barrow, she began to screech.

"Dinna take me to the worrukhouse," she wailed. "Oh please, please no. Let me die in me own bed!"

Peter was red and sweating but the house could not be stuck with a helpless old woman no longer able to pay her pittance of rent. Inexorably, he laid Mrs. O'Rielly in the barrow, pillowed on her bundle, and grasped the handles. The last sight the Lane had was of the old woman thrashing and crying, her stricken body making it impossible for her to twist over the barrow side and drop to the cobbles.

Only when the cries faded did Katie realize Mary had been holding her by the shoulder, fingers sunk in so deeply they bruised the bone. And eerie, frightened stillness hung over the Lane reminding everyone how tenuous was their own hold on food and shelter. Then normal sounds started up. Mary let Katie go.

Katie rubbed her shoulder, unable to tell whether the pain came from the inside of her or the outside. Her skin felt as if it were crawling all over. The workhouse! Oh, the workhouse! That's what happened when you couldn't sell any more!

"We'll have a Chelsea bun for our supper," Mary said, her voice suspiciously toneless.

"I don't want a Chelsea bun!"

"We'll have it anyway. Now let's walk about for a bit."

Despite Katie's best efforts, sales continued to drop off. In October and November the number of street sellers swelled alarmingly as those who had been off harvesting, working the village fairs or just tramping the country, flooded back, upsetting the fragile summer equilibrium of Wheeble Lane. Katie measured sales intimately via the number of missed meals and the amount of leftover stock weighing down Mary as they struggled home at night. Mrs. Gossidge began to eye them the way a carter eyes a limping horse earmarked for the knackers.

The day came when they pawned Mary's chemise, then Katie's much-abused pinafore. In November, hollow from three days of foodlessness the unthinkable happened. Katie and Mary could not advance the night's rent.

The two hovered before Mrs. Gossidge's open door, feeling the very chill of desolation blowing out of it. Katie held herself stiffly, her heart slowing and speeding by turns. Mary simply stood, face immobile, looking more than ever like a rock in the rain.

Impatient with Mary's stillness, Katie opened her mouth to say indignantly that there would be a profit tomorrow! She was pushed aside by a heavily breathing woman in a blue linsey-woolsey dress and rouge.

"'Ere's for the bed, Missus. I'm agoin' to flop down now, that worn out I am!"

Mrs. Gossidge took the coins and pointed the woman up the stairs. She turned to Katie and Mary standing there.

"Your bed's gone. Nothing I can do about it."

For one awful moment, Katie expected Mary to beg, but Mary only pulled her shawl in a knot around her. Her features remained motionless, yet they were not a mask. Every lineament informed the world that she never begged, never pleaded. Her darkly burning eyes met Katie's. For one instant, the child felt to the bottom of her being the deep, blind pride that held Mary together underneath her racked exterior.

Anyway, pleading would have no effect on Mrs. Gossidge who had heard plenty in her time. The economic structure of the lodging house was as rickety as any other on that poor street. A few profitless nights and it might all came tumbling down.

Slowly, like Jane before them, Katie and Mary had to step into the street and turn their faces toward the Rye. Katie hurried along, fear and guilt swirling in her breast. Your fault, your fault, taunted a voice. You didn't sell enough today. She couldn't shake the notion that she was responsible for the two of them. Oh, if only she weren't a helpless child!

Katie clung to Mary as they passed dark, stifling lanes encrusted with human exhalations, hovels lit by a single candle flickering over the pale faces huddled inside. The least frightening lodging house leaned tipsily toward an alley and was propped up by rough characters about the door picking their teeth with straws. They jeered at Mary as she shouldered through.

The proprietor was called simply Mump who hulked inside the open door like an old, stale animal guarding a squalid den. His greasy shirt and greasier breeches recorded every meal he had eaten in a year. He had no hair, little neck and warts on his eyelids which made him seem scarcely able to open his eyes. Evincing no interest whatever in the character or suitability of prospective lodgers, he only jerked a thumb over his shoulder.

"Tuppence a doss," he growled, his deceptive, warty gaze quick to spot from whence Mary was digging out the coins from the pawnshop. Deep in her bosom Mary kept the stock money. Always, no matter what happened to them, they must have stock money or they might as well forget about living altogether.

They were herded into a low-ceilinged room in which bundles of rags were scattered about. True to rumor, men, women and children mixed indiscriminately, some boisterous, some roasting their flesh as closely as possible to the fire in the gate, most laying like dead things, snoring heavily, not wanting to miss a moment of sleep time in this sheltered place.

Mary stopped warily inside.

"Huh! Just like a sheep pen."

Kate pressed close. A thick scent of gin permeated the air.

"Oh Mary, do sheep...drink?"

"No, lass, but if they had ter sleep here, they'd soon take ter it, I'm sure!"

They stepped over an old man with bare feet cracked as neglected hooves and sought a corner to remove themselves from the mob as far as possible which was not very far. No one paid them any mind, for the lame, the one-eyed, the grotesque were here in numbers. So were the lewd, for there was giggling and squealing going on in the opposite corner. Mary tried to spread the rag bundle wide enough for two. Katie caught a movement.

"Mary that woman is scratching!

Indeed, the woman was—not the casual scratches but digging, almost unconscious gouges that indicated well established vermin. Katie, still ingrained with Miss Radmore's insistence on cleanliness, looked on with indignation.

"I dare say, t'won't be long afore we're scratchin' too," Mary replied dryly.

Surely Mary was making a joke. The muffled giggles changed. Katie began to push herself up to see. Mary grasped her shoulder and thudded her flat.

"Don't look a' the dirty creatures! Don't yer dare!"

Katie could only add one more puzzle to the many puzzles stored up in her active mind as she drowsed off. Drifting into her dreams came homeless Jane, singing plaintively:

"... for bonnie Annie Laurie,

I'd lay me doon and dee."

Winter swooped down upon the city. Bursts of icy drizzle and the stinging smoky pall sent everyone speeding about their business. Appetites for fresh fruit waned and it was the hot pie sellers who benefited. People had little patience for shivering hawkers thrusting apples under their noses.

Too much changed figures haunted the crook of Wheeble Lane. Mary was so thin her shoulder blades pressed sharply, like amputated wings, through the old plaid shawl she tied about her. The knobs of her vertebrae now resembled a row of blunt fasteners precariously holding her crooked body together. In the concave hollow of her chest, her woman's breasts had shrunken almost flat, though her muscles were tough as ship's ropes from carrying the tray. Her face had grown, if possible, more impassive, emptied of all clues to her thoughts save that flicker of blurred pride when someone inspected her wares condescendingly then walked away. The stubborn animal devotion she harboured for Katie only grew more intense.

In Katie herself, no one would have recognized the well-scrubbed orphan trained to curtsy to adults and clasp her hands before her when spoken to. Her chemise was gone too now. Her dress hung slackly about her frame, torn from street incidents and lack of needles to mend it. Strawberry stains spotted one side of Katie's skirt and a brisk trade in cherries one day had permanently stained the sleeves. What's more, since the move to the Rye lodging house, it had grown dirtier and dirtier for Katie had no other to wear while it was washed, much less a place to wash and dry it. Her hair was still plaited tightly but mats Mary could not untangle stuck out frowsily around the child's head.

For all Mary's efforts at outdoor standpipes, using the dampened hem of her own skirt as a washcloth, the general grime of London settled upon Katie. Her skin greyed. Dark colorations ringed her neck. Sudden showers left streaks on her cheeks. Her fingernails were blackened crescents she couldn't hide while handling the apples. A harder, hungrier look lit her eyes. Her pleas to buy lost a good deal of the polite, appealing edge from the Asylum. The more she resembled the ragtag urchins about her, the less people were inclined to buy, for it had been the novelty of her clear diction and unpatched pinafore that had drawn them.

"Never mind," whispered Mary as people hurried by. "They didn't see our tray."

Katie drank in this reassurance. Despite the cold and hunger Katie had already endured, despite the loss of their chemises and the rough places they now had to live, she still knew in her heart that nothing really awful could happen as long as Mary was there.

The weeks progressed. Raw wet winds from the Hebrides raced down the streets, driving before them whirling flakes of snow. Mary and Katie soon shivered so constantly they didn't even think about it. They pressed themselves into doorways and rushed to soak up the erratic sunshine like hopeful plants abandoned to the blast. They had moved from the upstairs room of Mump's lodging house to the kitchen floor where the night charge was only a penny. Of course, no bundle of rags went with that, causing many of the kitchen lodgers to stagger in pragmatically dead drunk in order to get any sleep at all on the cold flagstones.

The lodging place, mean and dangerous as it was, became precious for the shelter it afforded. They went without food regularly to secure it. Warmth and rest they needed, more even than bread and a scrap of bacon. If they were in luck someone might come in selling, at give-away prices, cakes or vegetables stolen from the market.

Each night was the same, with old Mump at the door, sharp as a prison warder, his hand out for the penny. Flashin' Maud was never found at such places. She went into small wares for the winter and did even better than with apples. Who could resist buying when they also got a saucy joke and a laugh to warm them as they passed? Profits became smaller and smaller for Katie and Mary until twice Mary almost couldn't hand Mump his coin. Finally, at the end of a long grey Sunday, when the pall of religion settled on top of the smoke, Mary didn't turn her steps toward Mump's at all.

"Mary...?"

Katie's question foundered at Mary's stony look.

"Ain't got but enough fer half a tray termorrer," she said curtly. "We have to find another place ter sleep."

"If we hadn't been giving that Red Nell our money, we'd be all right, wouldn't we, Mary?" Katie demanded, returning to the constant bugaboo in their lives.

Mary sighed, Red Nell got precious little these days, with them hardly ever selling a full tray any more. Stubborn Katie would not understand that, in a world where coppers or thugs could harass a hawker into starvation, it was Red Nell's protection that allowed them to sell at all. Red Nell grew, in Katie's mind, into a fiend of mythic proportions

They now sheltered at night in a shed once housing livery vehicles to which a farthing gave them entry. Other bodies were packed in though with scant warmth since one side was open to the weather. Each day, prospects for Katie and Mary grew more precarious.

CHAPTER SEVENTEEN

The front door slammed, causing Amelia to sink weakly into the parlour chair she and Edwin had so recklessly treated themselves to on moving in. Barlow, who owned the dilapidated building and didn't seem to have a mister to his name, had been trying to collect his rent. Cheeks drowned in humiliation, Amelia had had to make excuses for the second month in a row.

"My husband returns from lecturing tomorrow. We'll have it then, I'm sure. It's so...unpredictable when income arrives from tours."

I'm stammering, she thought as her eyes appealed in vain. Barlow was a lean, sallow man well hardened in the vicissitudes of East End property management. He pursed his lips and took on a stony, belligerent look. The only thing he understood was that he had got himself stuck with a useless set of gentry on the skids. They were one month behind. They weren't going to get away with two.

"End of the month, Mrs. Corman. I don't see my brass by then, I'll ask you to vacate. And I'll have to hold onto your bits and pieces toward what is already owed."

He'd been gone ten whole minutes before Amelia translated "bits and pieces" to mean their furniture and, horrors, maybe even their clothes!

Her earlobes began to scorch. This couldn't be happening. It was inconceivable that she, daughter of the celebrated Dr. Radmore, raised with a personal maid and a houseful of tutors, should face eviction into the street without so much as a change of petticoat!

That's what you get for turning Methodist cried the voice of residual Anglicanism. Amelia pressed her nails into her palm. Not only might they be on the street at the end of the month, there wasn't even enough money to see that everyone in the household, including young Cully and the Asylum children she and Edwin had managed to rescue from the workhouse, could have regular meals until then.

"I will not panic, I will not panic," she repeated against the rising gorge in her throat.

Nevertheless, she did panic, staring, for the first time, straight into the pit that gaped beneath the precarious lives all around her. The same fear shook her as gripped the beggar when his legs would no longer drag him to the corner to beg, or the bankrupt slop merchant, or the desperate lace-maker struck with another pregnancy just when her eyes gave out from strain. Running the Refuge had ceased to be an adventure. It had become a clawing battle to stay alive.

How will we ever pay these bills!

The children, Amelia thought, with a sudden chill. They'll have to go back to the workhouse. And just after she and Edwin had pried them out of there, the pathetic remnants of Mr. Jenks' brave little band. Such respectable, deserving youngsters they were too, with their pinched, white faces and scrambling eagerness to obey. The skin on her nape shrank at condemning anyone to that place again.

What a shock to discover what happened when the world guessed one was short on funds. The deference, kindness and consideration Amelia had taken for granted all her life quite evaporated when it was found the lady and gentleman did not have the wherewithal to support their genteel appearance. Mouths tightened, brows furrowed and tradespeople shifted from foot to foot uneasily.

"Beggin' yer pardon, ma'am, but I only works for me brass in advance, like. Got young 'uns meself to feed."

In this part of London, far from the circles where Radmores had been known and respected, Amelia discovered the awfulness of being regarded as a failed toff sliding into ruin. Her elegant speech, her spare, straight grace of movement could not help but stand out among the scurrying poor even had she been clad in rags herself. It was all she could do not to flinch before the assessing looks and cynical smirks as she hurried about her business. Her air of brisk authority was all she had to cover the fact that nothing could be paid for till Edwin returned from his lectures with the money he had earned.

Amelia had seen dreadful sights in the region. A pitiful creature haunting a corner selling stationery who had once been a lady and traveled in France. A cab driver, hunched stolidly in the rain, who had owned three haberdashery stores. A woman of the streets who cursed drunkenly from the gutter in accents as fine as Amelia's own. What could be ahead for these people, Amelia wondered, except a losing struggle with cold and hunger, then a wretched workhouse death.

Black terror welled up. What if they lost all the children? What if they couldn't pay, ever again? What if she and Edwin...

With a faint choking sound, Amelia forced herself upright. Her stout puritan heart struggled to rally.

Stop this! Stop at once! Providence takes care of its own. I know Edwin will come back with the money.

Clutching these shreds of wifely faith, Amelia brushed away all thought of the Radmore fortune even then being squandered by Julius on a life of dandyism, dissipation and disgusting atheistical heresies. Julius had washed his hands of Amelia the moment she wed.

"You've chosen a man with no money," Julius had written, acknowledging her swift, defiant marriage to Edwin, "and I wish you the joy of him. From the vehemence of your leave-taking, I confidently trust you will not apply to me for assistance when your husband's lack of practical enterprise becomes all too apparent.

P.S. Since you refuse to receive them, I have donated your personal effects to the annual Galapagos Club Scholarship Bazaar."

As she flung the letter away, Amelia hoped Julius enjoyed his retaliation for her rage about the Asylum. She hoped he was pleased at shedding a troublesome female relative who might have burdened his newfound riches. She hoped he would remember every detail when he finally roasted in some blazing nether region of Hell!

Amelia refused to regret abandoning her dresses, though she now knew, in painful detail, just how much all that silk and fine corded wool would have brought pawned or even sold outright in the second hand clothing markets. She had never returned to the Radmore house after her accident and was proud to wear garments provided by her husband. Sturdy, honest, serviceable garments, just like her marriage, and certainly suited to the work she now dedicated herself to.

If only she could keep up that work.

The monstrous clutching sent Amelia sliding to her knees in prayer.

"Oh dear Lord, please, please bring Edwin soon with the rent, and please let Mrs. Jenks find a decent meaty stew bone tonight for the pot. The children...."

The crash of the knocker caught Amelia with her hands clenched, skirts pooled around her. Frozen, she listened for Ida Jenks to answer the door before remembering that Ida was out haggling for the very stew bone Amelia had been praying about.

Fearing a return of Barlow, Amelia rose apprehensively. Or, worse than Barlow, it might be some desperate woman trailing a string of famished waifs at her heels. I can't turn away any more children, I just can't, Amelia groaned, dreading yet another rending appeal. Once word had got round, a tide of children had flooded to the door. No wonder Mr. Jenks had kept the Asylum bolted and fortified. How else could one defend against the blows to the soul any poor neighbourhood constantly provided?

Bracing herself, Amelia drew back the bolt. The door creaked open upon a female figure of such extraordinary aspect Amelia momentarily lost her powers of speech.

What Amelia saw first was hair of a colour no earthly human head ever sported. This glaring red mass was tortured into curls and stuffed under a turret of a hat mercilessly lacquered with ebony, crested with dyed rooster feathers and planted aggressively forward on its wearer's skull. The hat, in turn, dropped swathes of veiling down past a square set of jowls and a black jet collar brooch big as a monkey's fist. Below the jowls, the stout anatomy was poured into an astonishing hourglass shape pinched in the middle by a corset that had surely taken two longshoremen to lace. This whole was encased in black bombazine complete with ruching, cording and triple flounce. A reticule, parasol and bead-fringed shoulder cape finished the picture. A closed hansom cab waited obediently at the kerb.

"Mrs. Fitzroy, ma'am," the apparition announced, making what appeared to be a humble bow. "Excuse me for coming spur o' the moment, like, but would ye be sparing a moment for a poor old mither that's thrubbled in her mind about her young?"

Oh no! Not Irish! The cab was probably crammed to the roof with homeless babes!

"I'm so sorry, but there's no room here. The Refuge is so terribly short of funds we don't know how we're going to feed the ones we have."

The apparition looked surprised.

"Ah, it's not refuge I'm asking. Nor draining o' your pocketbook. No fear 'o that!"

Waving her hands against the very idea, the caller advanced onto the door sill, causing Amelia to fall back before the massed dark skirts. Before she knew it, Amelia found herself swept into the tiny office where she had previously been begging divine intervention in the matter of rent and dinner.

"Oh, well, please sit down then, "Amelia managed, trying not to gawk. "How may I help you?"

She hoped the woman wasn't going to ask for a job. Surely someone who could hire a hansom cab wouldn't want to scrub and cook after orphans.

The caller settled into the parlour chair as by natural right and heaved a lingering sigh cut short by the ferocious pressure of her corset.

"Clara Fitzroy is me name. Mrs. Clara Fitzroy. And it's perhaps somethin' to our mutual satisfaction I'd be providin'."

The thick Irish accent rolled softly through the room, making Amelia lean forward to make out the meaning. She wished she could see more clearly through the veil, but supposed some bereavement was keeping her visitor modest. So little did Amelia know about the workings of the neighbourhood that she would not have had the sense to be astounded if someone had told her

her guest was none other than the real power behind all the local comings and goings, Red Nell herself.

Yet Red Nell it was, squeezed into a corset for the first time in her life and rigged out in a getup that was her conception of respectable widow's attire. Only a mission of monumental significance could have caused her to mount such a tortuous masquerade.

Nell watched Amelia, picking up the unmistakable thrum of anxiety. She knew all about Amelia's plight and all about her habits, too. It was no accident that Nell had arrived when Ida Jenks was out, Barlow had laid on the frighteners, and the orphans were occupied upstairs. She had chosen her moment with the greatest of care.

She was taking an enormous risk, she knew, but it had to be done. No one else could possibly be trusted with such a task. So much, so very much, hinged upon it. And it wasn't often that Nell wanted something that she couldn't squeeze out, threaten out or just plain snatch.

"I'm afraid I don't understand..," Amelia began, still trying not to stare at her bizarre guest.

Behind the veil, Nell fixed her dimly seen features into lugubrious lines.

"Ah...begging yer pardon, ma'am, but I'm a simple widow woman that wants to help the dear wee ones of London Town. So many of the bairns, so poor and hungry. Why, t'would break your heart just thinkin' on 'em."

Red Nell heaved her bosom, making the jet brooch wink in the watery light. Amelia's heart picked up a couple of beats. Was it possible, possible at all!

Oh yes, it was possible, for the woman's dress was new fabric and her hat, for all its preposterous construction, sported ribbons of genuine silk.

The Lord does provide, Amelia thought in a burst of wondering jubilation. Providence does look out for its own! Even Methodists! This queer female has come to make a donation!

Hard put to keep from leaping in her seat, Amelia mustered a beatific smile.

"The need is enormous," she began, instantly falling into the language of appeal she and Edwin had repeated so many a time. "And right here we're in danger of having to close and send our dear children back to the workhouse. Anything at all would help."

Amelia tried to keep from looking too desperate. Nell's eyes gleamed. She laid her finger along the side of her chin, embarking on a delicate approach.

"Me dear departed husband was a bit of a business man in these parts. Bought a buildin', he did and left me with the lease of it sitting idle on me hands. A lovely place for wee orphans to snuggle into I was thinkin'."

Red Nell paused to let the fish leap for the bait. Amelia's mouth gaped open as widely as Red Nell could wish.

"You...you wish to donate the use of a building?" Amelia whispered, barely able to believe her ears.

Shifting her behind on the chair, Nell gritted her teeth against the corset. What an infernal contraption! No wonder toff ladies were always keeling over into their soup.

"Of course, the building isn't in such a nice part 'o town," Nell murmured, "but it could be made a tidy place. My heart is fair wrung out, it is, over the wee orphans."

"To the homeless, any building is suitable," Amelia returned piously, keeping her bosom from visibly leaping. "Would you honour me by having a cup of tea?"

A short time later, with her little finger stuck out from the handle of the teacup, Nell sipped at the last of Amelia's precious tea horde and almost smacked her lips. She let Amelia sit in bright-eyed suspense as she described the building she possessed. Through the Irish brogue, Amelia made out a substantial basement kitchen, three solid floors that could be packed with children, and a place where she and Edwin could live while supervising the whole. A palace, a virtual palace if it were true what this woman was hinting. The prize seemed suddenly so large, and so desperately needed, that Amelia began to quiver, afraid it couldn't be true.

"Ah, yes," sighed Nell, watching Amelia slavering at the lure. "I'm that well-fixed I don't need rent from the property. Happy I'd be to give you the use of it. Indeed, full 'o joy. All for a small consideration of me own."

"Yes?" Amelia was unable to imagine anything she wouldn't do. She should have turned Methodist years ago if this sort of bounty ensued.

A suspenseful moment ticked by as Nell adjusted her face soulfully under the veil and fluttered a hand to her heart. Fluttering did not come easily to Red Nell but the corset would not let her lean confidentially.

"Well, I'm a simple widow woman as got no connections and knowing little enough 'o what's beyond these streets," she began, "but I've a great love in me heart for me child. Aye, me one dear child, bless her heart. A wonderful child, a gift from the fairies if I didn't know better. Fair stunnin' she is and sings like twenty nightingales when they're full up 'o gin."

Amelia generously ignored the reference to strong drink.

"You would like your daughter to work for me?"

A job would be nothing at all if the Refuge could find a rent-free home.

Nell made a broad, fanning motion with her fingers.

"Oh, fair and I thank you for the offer, but me lovely Rose, she has a great gift and a great ambition to go with it. And so she ought after me spending pocketfuls on lessons for her and feeling the joy spring up in me heart each time I hear her sing. Tis an artist she wants to be. And make her way where people can hear her who've got ears to appreciate."

"You mean," Amelia frowned, hoping she had got it wrong, "that she wants to go upon the...the stage?"

Only the most dreadful sort of women went on the stage. Sure enough, Nell pulled her mouth into a moue.

"Faith, yes, the stage," Nell said with distress. "That's what's got me poor mither's heart in a dither. A gem, she is, my Rose, a jewel just winkin' in the darkness when the whole world was meant to see. If I do nothin', why she'll pine away to a wisp for lack of her heart's desire. But if I let her go in front of all the staring eyes with just this poor old widow woman beside her as can't protect her from a fly...well, you see I mean."

Nell willed herself to look sorrowful as the twelve Dierdres of Donegal and helpless to boot. In spite of herself, Amelia was deeply touched by delicacy manifesting itself from such an unexpected source.

"Oh, I do, I do," she murmured sympathetically, enveloped in the spell cast by the woman. "But I don't see what this has to do with me."

Nell pulled an even more lugubrious expression.

"Oh, ma'am, my Rose could have her wish if she had more protection than I could give. Your protection, ma'am."

"But I have no protection to give!" Amelia exclaimed incredulously. "And I know nothing about the stage."

"Ah, you've more protection than you can imagine, a fine lady such as yerself as is the daughter of a famous doctor and can walk around like you was one among all them West End quality. And it's fine, respectable West End establishments I want my Rose to perform in. No one could think ill of her if she came introduced on the arm of one such as you and your good man."

"Me! Introduce a singer to a music hall!"

Amelia suffered a sudden, fearfully coloured speculation as to the sort of daughter this woman might have. Her visitor raised her hands in alarm.

"Oh, wait now, ma'am, begging yer indulgence. Not a music hall so to speak but some elegint, refined sort of place where ladies can decently go."

Nell's idea of such places was a jumbled composite extracted from hearing her son, Dan, read the newspapers, but she was determined Rose should have her chance. And have it on the best basis possible, which meant belonging to a clan. Amelia sat in puzzlement, wondering where on earth she could introduce a thick-brogued Irish singer.

"What I'm askin' for me daughter," Nell said slowly, "is that you give her all of your protection, for I'll be havin' nobody at her because she wasn't born in a basket of silver. You must claim her as a Radmore, like yerself. Only as a blood relative will I let her go out beside you. I'll leave it to you to spin a proper tale."

When this sank in, Amelia was horrified. The woman actually wanted her to lie! Wanted her to enter respectable establishments, trailing some unspeakable younger version of this female before her, and lie!

Providence was playing wicked pranks. Amelia swept to her feet.

"What you are proposing is unthinkable, Mrs. Fitzroy. A fraud. Impossible! I don't know how you imagined I could be drawn in to such impertinence. Let me see you to the door!"

Behind a jerk of the widow's veil, Nell swiftly concealed her reaction and let her face crumple into lines of bitter disappointment. She'd jumped too soon in the tricky negotiation. Yet her terms were her terms and how was she to guess fine ladies were such a touchy lot. At the door she fished in her reticule for the pasteboard card on which she'd got Dan to write an address.

"Ah, truly sorry I am, ma'am, especially for the wee little orphans. I'll just be leaving this with ye, ma'am, should ye care to see the buildin' I'm proposin'."

Undeterred by Amelia's indignation, Nell gave a final bob and hoisted herself into the waiting cab. She had expected Amelia to baulk at first, though not quite so vehemently. As the cab drove off, Amelia had no inkling of the mother's ambition bubbling up in Nell's breast nor the hooded eyes that knew the game was far from over.

CHAPTER EIGHTEEN

"Not for three more months?"

Despite the money Edwin had put in her hands, enough, almost, to pay the rent owing and feed them for a few more weeks, Amelia heard her husband's news with a clanging in her ears. The five lectures she had been counting on to save them had been postponed. They were all likely to starve before Edwin got near a podium again.

"Why didn't you write me?" Amelia ground out through set teeth. If Edwin had only written, perhaps something could have been done. Edwin tugged at the points of his waistcoat and stared tensely out of the cracked window beside him.

"Well, I...there didn't seem any reason in worrying you..."

Worrying me! Amelia wanted to scream. What do you think you're doing now, coming home with such a tale!

The words, so very nearly exploded from her that she pressed her fingers hard to her lips to stop them. She was enraged with Edwin. So enraged she'd barely prevented herself from shrieking like a cat.

How could this happen?

Not half an hour before, she had rushed to the door and into Edwin's arms, filled with leaping joy at his return. Oh, how she had buried her face in his neck, drinking in the beloved, familiar scent of his woollen jacket, adoring the scrape of his beard against her cheek, seeking hungrily for comfort of his broad, solid chest.

Now here she was ready to fly at her husband in a passion, to ask—no, demand—how he could have been so blind as to not understand the spot the postponement had put them in.

So this was how women became shrill wives. This was how tender marriages dissolved into bitter quarrelling and the coldnesses that she herself had felt across a room.

Oh, Edwin!

Amelia bowed her head, swallowing hard against this unsettling tide of knowledge. In that one catastrophic instant she understood every shrewish woman, every hot-faced pair trading barbs in the streets.

And she, so recently a bride, stood on the brink of joining the wretched crew!

A door, long and carefully concealed, abruptly opened, thrusting Amelia rudely into the land of the truly married. A land she didn't recognize yet a place that all must come to sooner or later after taking the sacred vows. A fate no warnings could ever make a laughing bride believe.

She couldn't look at Edwin, but she could see him reflected in the narrow window panes. She could pick out his bulk, his hair betraying how he had dragged his fingers through it.

As she gazed, a new vision flooded in as though she were seeing her husband clearly for the first time. Gone was Edwin the bulwark who could protect her from all harm. Before her glimmered only another struggling soul, standing just as she did now, frightened and not knowing what to do.

When he bent his noble, bear-like head, she saw it wasn't because he hadn't understood what the postponement meant. It was because he did and hadn't dared to write her. Oh, how could she even think of flying at him now!

Fondness rushed back, all mixed up with that other black emotion that swirled like ink in a bowl of milk. The towering fury sank away, extinguished by the devotion Amelia had granted Edwin that one momentous day from her sickbed.

"Mr. Wilkes says I might be asked to fill in for Brodger," Edwin said with uncharacteristic hesitance, "if the man's gout flares up from the damp."

Amelia saw how useless it would be to rant. Edwin might beg her pardon, or rage back, or berate them both for their mutual foolishness. His seamless armour had fallen away. Whatever he did, he could not remedy the fix the Refuge found itself in now.

Fear snaked through Amelia, followed by a sudden, blindly magnificent surge of idealism, the same that had impelled her to take on the Infant's Asylum and, later, throw herself into marriage with Edwin. She felt the unbreakable marriage bond holding her tightly to her course. Well, she would not let it choke her. She would glory in it. She would, she must, keep it sweet.

When so many would have torn into battle, Amelia kept her calmness. Exhaling very slowly, she stepped forward, as women have done from time immemorial, to staunch Edwin's invisibly bleeding wounds.

"We'll be fine," she murmured lightly, touching him on the arm. She began to plan how they would skimp on the meals and keep something back from Barlow, jollying him shamelessly if they had to. "We'll all just tighten our belts until you get another lecture. I'm sure something will turn up."

Edwin's expression of grateful relief was interrupted by an enormous crash below the stairs, followed by a high-pitched shriek from Ida Jenks. Edwin and Amelia rushed to the basement door just in time to collide with Ida lurching up out of clouds of belching, sooty smoke.

"The stove...it's all tumbled down. And every spud we have is rollin' in the dirt. Oh....oh..."

Edwin, closely followed by Amelia, plunged past the howling figure and fought, coughing, down to the basement kitchen. The old iron range on which the refuge's food was cooked, had indeed collapsed in pieces, dropping its load of burning coals on the floor.

Luckily, the floor was earthen, the coals no threat to the building. Yet by the time Edwin had fumbled open the cellar hatch and Amelia had flung all the water from the drinking buckets at the hissing heap, a large enough disaster emerged. The ancient contraption, exhausted by years of hard use and supported precariously by columns of bricks, had simply broken apart in the middle, rendering itself useless for anything except scrap iron. The sopping floor was now churned to mud underneath it. Worst of all, the great cooking pot lay on its side in a corner, its load of partially cooked potatoes trodden into the muck.

Amelia wiped back strands of hair with a grimy hand and looked up. At the open cellar hatch the passersby from the street crowded about gaping in. Opposite them, at the top of the stairs, all the children stood jammed together staring down. They were staring not at Amelia or Edwin, but at the ruined potatoes strewn about their feet.

They're hungry! Amelia realized sickly. They're afraid there won't be anything more to eat with the potatoes gone! And....I'm afraid of it too!

The pale, steaming potato halves protruding from the sludge produced, to Amelia's horror, a hunger pang in her stomach, a loosening of saliva in her mouth. All her high purpose of a few minutes before drained away.

Oh, oh, it was all too much. Too much that she, Amelia Radmore, should be standing here as a common spectacle, with sopping feet and soot smeared face, hungering after trampled potatoes on a cellar floor!

Only barely did Amelia prevent herself from burying her face in her hands and bursting into howling sobs.

Instead, she was torn instead by that clarity that sometimes visits those pushed to the edge of their endurance. A stark, apocryphal vision of the future. This wasn't just a temporary hole they were in. The stove might be propped up again and Edwin get a lecture soon, but there would be another time just like this and another, making them always dependent upon the fickle whims of luck just to have potatoes to eat and a place to lay their heads. If they survived at all, they'd never be more than a tiny, pathetic, grime-edged charity, their work haphazard, their dreams in tatters, their weariest struggles resulting in only the rescue of a pitiable few.

She could resign herself or she could refuse to let their lives dribble away into that futile hole. Gulping air, Amelia straightened bravely. The long white scars up the side of her neck gleamed in the greyish light.

"Well, well, children," she called out, "hurry up and lend a hand to get this water mopped up. "We'll have the stove mended as soon as it's cool enough to touch. In the meantime, two of you go with Mrs. Jenks to the cook shop and buy enough roast beef and turnips for everyone tonight."

At this wild extravagance, Ida gaped and the children lit up with incredulous anticipation. Amelia extracted enough from the precious horde in her pocket to pay for the purchase, then turned to Edwin. He had a throbbing red burn on the back of his hand and one trouser leg soaked to the knees. The smoke swept Amelia back to another cellar and the unspeakable slavery within which Edwin had tried to put right.

He shall keep his pride, Amelia resolved fervently. And so will I! Now where did I leave that widow's wretched card!

CHAPTER NINETEEN

"Tis a tidy nook would suit ye grand," Nell commented, finally breaking the humble silence she had maintained while Amelia had poked under stairs, craned into the attic, and ranged through room after room of the building Nell had brought her to.

At Amelia's note, Nell had barely had time to squeeze into her widow's garb, eyes gleaming. The trout had responded to the bait, oh yes. Now for a fine hand indeed to land such a troublesome prize as Amelia Radmore.

Playing Amelia meant standing back in an attitude of meek offering while Amelia carried out her inspection of the plain, substantial brick structure Nell had chosen as tempting for an orphans' home. Scoured and swept, it stood on the quietest street in Nell's domain.

Amelia had not looked at Nell the whole time. Her face was tight, her stomach rigid but no spasm of humiliation could stop the feverish calculations galloping through her head. The building proved beyond anything Amelia had expected. Already, she saw it full of cots, rows of cots, each with a small, scrubbed, recently fed waif sitting on it. A busy kitchen in the basement with a massive new stove. And there, in front of those tall windows, a workshop just like Mr. Jenks had had where children helped to earn their keep. She and Edwin could have their own parlour with the green chair by the fire. There'd be an office with a vast writing desk full of pigeonholes where all the business of the Refuge would be organized. Edwin would write his lectures there and agents from the shipping lines would explain the details of group passage across the ocean. Outside, a freshly painted sign...

Amelia quelled this rush of hungry plans and slowly turned.

"I see it meets yer approval," Nell murmured. "Now the best thing is to come meet me darlin' Rose."

Whatever notions Amelia had nursed of appealing to Mrs. Fitzroy's finer nature to drop her demands about her daughter vanished away. Rock hard resolution bristled beneath the soft Irish words.

Amelia remembered how she had driven Mrs. Fitzroy from her door. Once again, her stomach rolled at silently begging for this woman's charity. The part of her that was still privileged Amelia Radmore longed to flee, prevented only by those small, hungry faces crowded at the top of the cellar stairs.

Steeling herself, Amelia stepped toward the cab. Apparently, there was no such thing as something for nothing in this world, not even from Providence. Whatever radish-nosed, spot-faced, squawk-voiced, appalling child this woman might have, Amelia resolved, at least she would go and look at her.

The cab took them to a flat-fronted building mainly distinguished by the iron grilles on its windows and a fading signboard announcing Mrs. Gresham's Superior Ladies' Academy.

Amelia's relief at discovering the girl was in such an institution vanished the moment she stepped inside. She recognized it at once as the sort of garish pretence usually established to part the ignorant from their money or raise embarrassing by-blows grudging progenitors paid to half educate and wholly hide away. Mrs. Gresham herself only increased Amelia's fears about the unseen Rose. A gaunt, pointy-shouldered woman who sucked her teeth and eyed all comers with habitual suspicion, she seemed more suitable to be a prison warder than the proprietor of a ladies' academy.

"Rose's cousin, Mrs. Amelia Corman, favourin' us with her comp'ny," Amelia heard Nell saying. Before Amelia's jaws could open Mrs. Gresham was shaking her hand with dampish, bony fingers. Nell was pleased to see Mrs. Gresham straighten hastily at Amelia's genuinely silver-plated tones.

"Where's me darlin' Rose?" Nell asked, secretly enjoying Amelia's discomfiture at being turned into an instant relative. Begin as you mean to go on, Nell thought. No use Gresham getting any ideas she shouldn't. Nell had seen that Mrs. Gresham, like Amelia, had no idea who she really was. Their dealings had always been brief, Mrs. Gresham's eye mainly on the money changing hands. Her principal asset, for Nell, had been her ability to guard like a tigress such domain as her precarious enterprise afforded her. Once Nell impressed Mrs. Gresham with the importance and the lucrativeness of the charge entrusted to her care, their relations had been quite satisfactory.

Satisfactory, that is, until a month ago when Rose had so spectacularly bolted the Academy.

"In the drawing room. I'll order some tea."

Mrs. Gresham jerked an ostentatiously embroidered bell pull then hurried out, Amelia suspected, to oversee the kettle herself. After the blast Gresham had received about Rose's escapade, Nell expected her daughter to be ready and presentable to Amelia's eye. She also expected the skylight Rose had climbed out of to be nailed tightly shut, inside and out.

The room so grandly termed the drawing room was a long, narrow apartment overcrowded with pieces of furniture chosen for their ability to impress the tasteless rather any relation to each other. All of it gave off a smell of must, mothballs and young ladies who hadn't had quite enough baths.

"Rose, me dear," Nell called out, pushing on in. "Come and meet the lady I've been talkin' of."

Amelia had failed to notice the single occupant of the room. A soft swish of skirts caused Amelia to turn and find herself reduced to immobility.

One thing Amelia instantly knew—the name was perfect. For if one of the lush, dew-petaled tea roses for which the country was famous had managed to change itself into human form, it would be this presence before her.

Rose Fitzroy drifted up from the sofa as fetchingly as mist rising from a summer bank. She impressed Amelia with a bewilderingly curly mass of strawberry blonde hair heaped atop her head, tilting grey-green eyes and a ripe mouth that would have thrown any man alive into an instant hallucination of a kiss.

"Oh," was all Amelia could say as she was introduced. The spot-faced, appalling creature evaporated out of Amelia's head.

This inner disorientation did not abate as Amelia was seated in one of the stuffed armchairs and allowed to continue her gaze. She had expected a girl, not this fully blooming young woman surely beyond the age of ladies' academies. Even encased as Rose was in that terrible juvenile, choke-necked brownish dress, an impression of yearning came through, of compressed vitality desperate to burst into rampant life.

Trouble, shouted a sudden voice inside Amelia. That girl is trouble!

Amelia squelched the voice, not knowing she was already responding to the secret warmth Rose engendered in almost everyone she met.

How can she live here, Amelia wondered in spite of herself. How can she and that beady Mrs. Gresham manage inside these same four walls every day?

That Rose was at Mrs. Gresham's and not labouring with her brothers at Nell's elbow was a result of chance, timing and the growing ambitions springing in Nell's bosom.

When Nell faced, without warning, the half grown sylph fetched back from Cornwall by Old Anna, she had been pitched into a quandary. As the girl's dismay at meeting Nell attested, Rose had been raised in ignorance of her true family until that moment, unlike Joe and Dan and Gwyn who had been meshed into Nell's work from the moment they could lend a hand to help.

What to do with her, Nell had agonized. The secrecy surrounding the child had been for Rose's own protection but it had backfired badly. Nell could see from the Rose's indignation that the girl could not be trusted to take the family seriously or keep the dangerous secrets that must, of necessity, be confided to her. She was already too old, too untrained, too wayward to be a reliable part of Nell's enterprises in the street.

Besides, success and stability and had wrought changes in Nell. Now that money flowed through her hands in gushing streams, she was not proof against the parental ambitions of her time. She wanted Rose to have advantages. And she could now afford the unheard-of luxury of raising a daughter just for the sake of the exercise.

But how was it done?

Nell certainly couldn't have the girl living with her, a beacon to Teapot, in midst of her hive of thriving illicit activity. She looked hard about her and, as though she were the first mother ever to think of it, hit upon that venerable institution, the girls' boarding school.

Of course, at Nell's level, they couldn't be called schools exactly. They were more like houses of incarceration set up by enterprising, often desperate women hoping to parlay their few dubious qualifications into enough paying customers to keep bread on the table and the bailiff from the door.

Nell tried two before Mrs. Gresham's. Rose revolted in both. Mrs. Gresham's possessed what the others did not, stout iron grills on the windows, a vigilant keeper and a heavy piano with all its pedals working. After a several energetic rounds with Mrs. Gresham,

Rose abandoned her struggle and gave herself up to the distractions of the keyboard.

But if Mrs. Gresham was lulled over the years, Nell was not. She could feel in her bones the frustrated energy growing in the girl, the monumental impatience under the entrancing exterior. She allowed Rose out only under the escort of her brothers and she certainly didn't trust them as proof against Rose's charm. Joe hulked after her, awkward and adoring. Dan turned at once into a natural ally, ready to lead Rose into untold mischief but for fear of his mother.

Nell's fears had come true when, last month, Rose had absconded from the school and been found creating unholy pandemonium singing in a sailors' beer hall. Rose had been plucked from the joyously rioting men and clapped back into Gresham's so quickly her skull rattled. For all that Nell had blasted Mrs. Gresham, she knew it wasn't the keeper's fault. Rose was nearly nineteen, for blinking sake, far beyond the age any girl should be stuck cooling her toes in a coop like Gresham's. Nell knew more revolts were inevitable. What now, Nell asked herself, forced to face the results of her ambitious child rearing. She was a common barnyard hen who had hatched a bird of paradise and now hadn't the faintest idea what to do with it.

No idea until she remembered Amelia.

Nell's belated inspiration had come because of the newspapers. As she had struggled to hang onto her territory, Nell could not avoid being washed this way and that by the tides of change pouring through the city. She developed a thirst to know something of the larger world and made Dan read the newspapers to her out loud.

Dan bought only the most sensational and read what amused him. Through their florid accounts, Nell heard of visiting maharajas with jewels in their noses, cricket matches, private railway carriages, costume balls, royal garden parties, openings of Parliament, and rowing competitions until it all formed one lustrous, tantalizing whirl in her head.

All of it was punctuated with Dan's cracks and jokes and whoops of mock astonishment at world that wasn't real to him any more than it was real to Nell. After Rose had been extracted from the beer hall, Dan had snorted with laughter.

"Too bad Rose didn't get loose at one of them toff tea parties. She'd have laid a swathe there, by all hell's bells!"

What if she had?

At once, the fantasy world of the newspapers began to assume hard edges in Nell's mind. An idea stirred, murky, formless, but ponderously alive.

The next day, Nell had ordered Nips to drive her closed cab not on its usual rounds, but to fabled addresses from the society pages; Mayfair, Knightsbridge, Piccadilly, Pall Mall and the Strand. Wary as explorers, they made their way into the broad avenues Dan had so jokingly read about. Nell stared about her at tall white houses with uniformed maids scrubbing the front steps. She saw armfuls of parcels being delivered from smartly varnished delivery vans and footmen bowing haughty ladies from the door. Chancing on Hyde Park, Nell was practically run off the road by a stream of splendid equipages drawn by high-stepping matched pairs. Nell had been amazed at the horseflesh, and at the equally splendid top hats and silk cravats inside.

Out of many houses round the Park drifted the sound of piano music. Nell shouted Nips to a halt before one set of great bow windows. Inside, Nell glimpsed a whole flock of quality perched on velvet chairs, gathered in a circle around a vast grand piano. Every one gazed in admiration at the lady who stood next to it, singing her heart out while starched maids served punch in that high-ceilinged room.

The idea turned over, much like a whale heaving its huge bulk in black, swirling depths. Then it burst to the surface in a geyser of inspiration.

Rose should come here! Rose should be one of these!

The swoop of her own audacity made Nell stop breathing. Yet she knew that the escapade in the beer hall had only been the warning hiss before the complete exploding of the cork. Rose couldn't be contained any more than steam could be kept inside a boiling kettle. It was now only a matter of which direction the explosion was going to go. Without a guiding hand Rose would wreck herself even more spectacularly than Nell's own grandmother and all the other stunners who had made tragic legends of themselves before.

Very well, Nell decided grimly, if Rose has to explode, why not point her at the stars and let her go.

But how!

How to get her through those polished doors and past those vigilant footmen?

Even Nell knew that girls from the East End did not crash into the elegant rooms she had glimpsed unless it was to scrub or cook. Obscurely, Nell realized Rose needed some sort of respectability, some acceptable past if she were not to be sneered away. Someone had to open those doors. Someone Nell could tie a string on as firmly as a pup on a leash. Nell thought of only one such person within reach whose credentials rang sterling through and through. Amelia Radmore Corman. Ah yes, Nell knew exactly what sort of bait to dangle in front of that one.

Rose eyed Amelia eagerly, barely able to control the leaping in her breast. Despite being ignominiously pulled from the beer hall and hustled back to Gresham's, Rose regarded Amelia as a reward for her daring action, just as the wreck had been her reward, so long ago, for her trip across the Nose. She throbbed in expectation of some vast sea change in her life just as the wreck had brought. Oh please, please, let it be better than the one that had swept her out of the sweet sea air and into Gresham's jail.

Rose clasped her hands in her lap, hoping they weren't beginning to sweat. She must behave with such heroic restraint that the lady, so severe of figure, so stiffly upright of carriage, would never guess about the beer hall. If only Rose could impress this Mrs. Corman, perhaps her imprisonment was over. And Rose's gratitude would be boundless. Whatever Mrs. Corman wanted—help with her charity, fancy tales spun, hundreds of songs sung, anything so long as she could get Rose out, Rose was willing to do.

Warily, Rose glanced at Red Nell, some stubborn core still refusing to believe this impenetrable woman was her mother. Though Nell had slapped her into Gresham's, Rose knew it was only some kind of anteroom holding her back from the great excitement she felt was her destiny. Rose so passionately hungry to begin!

"Give us a song, colleen. Show Mrs. Corman what ye can do."

Best let the starchy Amelia see right away what she has to work with, Nell thought, before Rose has a chance to throw a fright into her with her tongue.

Immediately, Rose sat down at the piano in the corner broke into the first bars of the song chosen, the sentimental, innocuous and extremely popular ballad, Annie Laurie. If it hadn't been for music, Rose had no idea how she would have lived inside the walls of Gresham's for so long.

Rose's fingers flitted lightly over the keys, but her ability to play the piano was completely lost to Amelia as a voice suddenly rose up in liquid beauty and filled the stuffy room. It was Annie Laurie sung as Amelia had never heard it before and surely the only way the composer could have meant it sung. It soared, lilted, and carried the listener away. Amelia forgot all else but the sweet, enchanting sound.

Amelia herself was not musically inclined despite the hours of duty spent at her own piano lessons. She could play a waltz or minuet if she had to, with a mechanical rhythm, and even her teacher did not attempt to make her sing. Yet immediately, she recognized Rose as the treasure her mother insisted she was.

In satisfaction, Nell watched as Amelia sat enthralled after the last note fell away. But Nell was not going to stop at less than the full demonstration. Amelia must know the total value of what she was being offered.

"Sing one 'o those fancy ones, dearie, that the Eytalian fella taught ye."

To Amelia' astonishment, Rose threw back her head and broke into a florid operatic aria sung in its original Italian. Amelia vibrated with possibilities.

When Rose at last fell silent, Nell appeared to be actually beaming.

"Ach, all sortsa lessins she's had, and from a real grand master 'o the art, as usta live in the neighbourhood afore he came to his end of a purple apoplexy, bless his soul."

Red Nell believed in getting her services from those who fell directly under her thumb. With no discrimination in matters musical, Nell had hired as tutor a certain Signor Abruzzi, an ancient, broken down Italian opera singer stranded in one of her tenement attics. Signor Abruzzi had been chosen because of the impressive volume of noise he could still produce when in his cups and for his engaging braggadocio about his past successes, some of which was actually true.

To put matters simply, Signor Abruzzi drank, and Nell paid him enough to drink himself into bliss, so long as he sobered abruptly when Rose, escorted by Joe or Dan, came tapping at his door.

Signor Abruzzi was often only far enough along in the sobering process to be either in his maudlin, sentimental state or his comical, cynical state. When in his maudlin state, he taught Rose ballads sad enough to make a doorstop cry. Then he sat at window, weeping copious tears for his native Tuscany. He gazed at Rose with the eyes of an exiled spaniel and told her all of Tuscany would fall at her feet could they but glimpse her. Then he would fall to lamenting Melina, the divine, disdainful diva he had worshiped in his lost youth.

When in his comical, cynical state, Signor Abruzzi taught Rose how to waltz with a full goblet of grog balanced on her head and regaled her with the most shocking, scandalous and fantastical tales of his touring days. Rose learned to sing French, Italian and German songs so spiritedly no one would guess she hadn't a clue about their hair-raisingly ribald content.

However, when Signor Abruzzi was fully sober, he fell into his tyrannical state. He ranted and stomped and drove Rose up and down the scales with the persistence of a fiend. Nothing Rose did was right. It had to be better, better, better because Rose had a gift from the gods and if she didn't devote her every fibre to its service, she didn't deserve to hum a nursery rhyme. When this happened, Rose sent Dan out as quickly as possible for a large bottle of gin and personally helped Signor Abruzzi swallow it down.

Rose had loved the old roué dearly and consumed his tales as avidly as she had those of Jack Mabbin. It had been Signor Abruzzi's death that had triggered Rose's breakout to the beer hall where she had been sometimes, on the sly, with Dan. She felt she could not, would not endure the smothering of Gresham's a moment longer.

"There now," murmured Nell when silence fell, "ye see what I mean about me darlin'. She can't go on hidin' her light under a basket here. What's a poor mither to do with such a child?"

Amelia did indeed see. Thoughts of the sensation Rose would make, introduced at certain charity entertainments, flew into her head. Restlessly, she shifted in her chair while Rose ventured another swift, anxious peek at her mother.

"Rose," Nell rumbled, "why don't ye run in and see what's keepin' the tea?"

When Rose had tripped out, Nell sighed deeply within her black, rustling folds, partly for effect and partly because of the tortures of the corset.

"Me darlin' husband worked hard," she said at last, "and had his bit 'o luck. Luck enough to leave me with some bits 'o property and a tidy bit 'o brass for to live upon. Oh, I could do fair if I rented the place, but what's the gain of it worth beside the mither's ambition aburnin' in me bosom."

A sidelong glance saw spots of colour flagging Amelias cheeks. Amelia had her eyes fixed on the carpet, as though she were afraid to look anywhere else.

"I know I'm askin' ye ta fancy up a bit of a tale and I'm thruly beggin' yer pardon," Nell continued, actually managing to make her voice crack a little, "but I have to use me wee bit 'o wit to help the lass the best way I can. Surely, it's a wee fib to ask, that no one'll ever inquire into, you being the daughter of that famous Dr. Radmore and all. You've seen me child, how bloomin' she is and how she has it in her to go such a long long way with the gift the fairies gave her. It could," Nell paused significantly, "bring so much good for all."

"Good?" whispered Amelia, struggling with the ingrained conviction that a lie was the first of the devil's tools. "What sort of good?"

Nell closed one eye, then the other, calculating rapidly. Those that wanted things so badly, next to the breath of life itself as Amilia did, were the easiest to take in hand.

"Why Rose has a soft heart for wee orphans, too," Nell murmured, ever so careful not to startle her quarry. "And she'd have a debt o' gratitude she'd never finish paying. Why, your orphans'd be her orphans too, bless her heart. When she's singin' like the Queen o' May up among all them quality, why, shouldn't she make you famous too? And rake in tubs o' brass for the cause. After all, life's all a matter o' connections, is it not, now?"

"I...have few connections," Amelia replied helplessly.

"Ah, and no wonder, a fine hard-wurkin' lady such as yerself hidin' away, quiet as a mouse. Beggin' yer pardon, but a charity that's helpin' wee orphans needs to trumpet itself about right smartly. Folks need to feel it's goin' concern they're handin' their brass over to."

"We...my husband and I have only the most modest of operations..."

"Ach, now who's to know that," Nell broke in, "once ye puff yerself up with a fine, elegint name and ask yerself straight into all those gold-paved drawin' rooms!"

"But..."

That was all Amelia could say. In her shrewdness, Nell had struck upon a dream so deep Amelia had never so much as dared admit it to herself. Just as her eyes grew wide with the painful impossibility of it, Nell lifted both her square hands to her bombazine bosom and played the tantalizing hook into the shallows.

"You've seen me Rose. If ye lead her right, and give her the backin' o' yer name, why she could be yer golden key. And niver once would she leave off bein' yer handmaid in the matter of directin' cash into the wee orphan's coffers."

The dream unfurled in Amelia's head, vividly detailed, poundingly insistent. She saw herself standing, dark-gowned and severe, the orphans' champion, surrounded by people of wealth and substance anxious to aid the cause and anxious to have Rose grace their entertainments. For that was where Rose could be introduced respectably, an answer to Mrs. Fitzroy's demands. That was how Amelia might decently fulfill her part of the bargain!

In a mad extravagance of imagination, she saw a string of Refuges, hundreds of clean-faced children in schools, workshops, on great boats off to be settled on the healthy farms of Canada, all possible if only she could get the right connections, right sort of funds rolling in. Why, before the year was out, she could be scouring street after street, lifting child after child from wretchedness.

And somewhere, some place, she would find Katie and Mary.

The tantalizing vision evaporated. The great benefactors were out of Amelia's reach. She and Edwin couldn't even afford stationery fit to write such wealthy folk, never mind present an organization impressive enough to gain their smallest attention.

As clear to her as if Amelia had spoken aloud, Nell watched this interplay. The strength of Amelia's wanting caught Nell like a palpable heat and caused a new plan to burgeon. She had thought only to use Amelia to launch Rose into that shimmering, hitherto unreachable world beyond the warrens. Nell had done tidily out of Amelia and the Infant's Asylum, skimming her bit from Mr. Jenks with Amelia never the wiser. Now she saw that the scheme that could be as big as...well, as big as Nell and Amelia could push it to be! A nice fat thriving charity among the quality, with Amelia as the front, could bring Nell hundreds of pounds if skillfully milked as the Asylum had been milked.

A mine 'o gold looking me in the face, Amelia is, Nell thought, and me all this time too blind to see!

And in the middle of it all, nicely occupied, would be Rose!

Maternal relief flooded Nell's heart. Yes, Rose might be brought to heel at last, kept under Nell's powerful hand, the very siphon for the money soon to flow in gushes!

Now was time to sink the hook for good.

"To tell ye the truth, I've got more than me bit to launch Rose on. Me buildin' is yours, and clothes if ye need 'em, and a bit o' capital to do yerself up a gilded front. I've no doubt at all ye can get yerself hobnobbin' with duchesses if ye make up yer mind on it."

Amelia had but to stretch out her hand and grasp it what Providence was practically thrusting into her lap. She forced her mind back to Rose, trying to fathom why her own instincts, under the racing exhilaration, jangled with alarm. She did not know what any experienced person of the world could have told her. Taking on Rose was the same as accepting a keg of gunpowder with the fuses already lit and sparking.

The girl's talent is so obvious, so charming, so...enormous, Amelia thought, suddenly unable to blame Nell for trying, however crudely, to help her child along. And Rose doesn't seem Irish at all!

A bud of warmth opened for the struggling widow's efforts. What was Mrs. Fitzroy but one more mother, spiky carapace and all, trying to look after her young the best she knew how. Of course, Amelia ruminated, I'll have to take the girl in hand. Do something about her clothes and such. And do it in a hurry if I want to hit the start of the new London season...

Nell watched Amelia struggling, hopelessly impaled on the irresistible lure.

"I'd pay you back," Amelia heard herself saying, "the minute the donations made up the sum."

With great effort, Nell kept from grinning outwardly as broadly as she was grinning inside. That you will, she muttered silently to herself. That you surely will!

She extended a blunt palm.

"Here's me hand on it, Mrs. Corman, and ye'll have a mither's gratitude until me dyin' day."

Looking down at the hand, Amelia felt the heat rising up her throat, flaming around the scars on her cheeks.

I mustn't think about it, she told herself as a lifetime of rectitude rose up in her vitals and cried out. What harm can there be in helping a girl to sing!

Amelia's spine straightened in a manner James would have recognized. After all, wasn't she a Radmore? Hadn't her famous father been lionized by the wealthy and the great? James had adamantly forbidden any presumption on their father's memory. Now, perhaps, it was time to collect on a few debts of gratitude. Katie and Mary were wandering in the streets somewhere. How could Amelia not have a home to bring them to!

Just for the barest instant, as one empire builder facing another, the two women understood each other.

"Yes," Amelia said, recklessly committing herself as she grasped Nell's hand. "Yes, we have a bargain on it!"

Nell's fingers closed over Amelia's with a snap. Oh yes, Nell thought, with both a surging maternal triumph and a grim fatalism, we have a bargain. Rose is loose. The cat is truly set amongst the pigeons now!

CHAPTER TWENTY

They were penniless and Katie knew it. Gusts swirled her ragged skirt and attacked her exposed neck. There'd be no shelter tonight, no bread and scrape. They felt victims of some cosmic malice against which no amount of struggle could prevail.

"Oh Mary, what are we going to do?"

Mary's brow furrowed.

"Don't fret yourself. Tis that cold tonight I think I know where we can get in. Come."

They ended in a narrow lane strangely packed with people though the streets all around were deserted. A rusty sign, which neither Katie nor Mary could read, indicated that this was an asylum for houseless poor. Though the door was firmly shut, the shivering people waited expectantly. They were the poorest, their garments in cobwebby tatters, their bare feet purple as half-cooked meat from tramping in the cold.

"They lights the lamp above the door if they're agoin' ter open." Mary told Katie. "It's got ter freeze ice on the puddles afore they do."

Though those at the back stood dumbly, as if they lacked strength to do otherwise, there seemed to be jostling at the front. A surge went through the crowd when the lamp appeared. A stout officer blocked the door and began selecting who would go in, choosing those with tickets from various agencies entitling them to shelter. Mary and Katie pressed forward as eagerly as the rest but they were nowhere near when the officer raised his hand.

"Full up, full up now," he boomed, pulling the door shut behind him.

A groan swayed through those left in the street. Mary sighed and shuffled away. Something hard and sick knotted in Katie's stomach. With awful certainty, she knew they were walking towards the bridge. People with no place to sleep crawled under the arches for shelter.

People who were no good crawled into heaps of trash...

They couldn't have failed. Oh, they couldn't have failed as badly as that!

Tears started up at the back of her eyes, scalding to get out. Katie fought them, her throat as tight as if she were being strangled. To cry here, now, in front of Mary, would be unthinkable. A terrible conviction struck that this was all her fault for not attracting buyers. She didn't deserve to cry.

Mary grimaced at the apples left in the tray, apples so bruised and spoiled they could not be offered for sale tomorrow. Refuse whirled over the pavement, black-edged clouds billowed over the chimney pots. Mary twisted as if something inside her raged and strained, trying to free itself, trying, in one rebellious thrust of energy, to straighten her misshapen back. Her fused spine defeated her. She dropped back down, fingers brushing the dull skins of the apples.

"Well, we've got our supper here, lass. Regular picnic!"

Katie clutched Mary's skirt in a gesture she hadn't used since the nursery. Mary turned her flat cheekbones toward Katie and smiled—a smile so terrifying that the tears behind Katie's eyes sprang out onto her cheeks. Frantically, she scrubbed at her face to make them go away. Mary thrust and apple into Katie's hand.

"Here lass, have this."

Many and many a time Katie had longed for one of those apples but the rule was never to touch the stock. This one showed great brown blotches and roused Katie's ravenous stomach. She sank her teeth into it and drove into a mass of brown decay barely held together by the thin mottled skin. It frothed into her mouth and almost choked her.

"Yer got ter get it down!" Mary ground out. For two days neither of them had eaten anything except one saved up scrap of cheese.

With Mary's burning eye upon her, Katie swallowed the slippery flesh and felt it land in her stomach. Mary ate one too, the last of their poor stock. Hiking the tray up under her arm, she set out with Katie in search of a bed for the night.

They had rarely walked toward the river for the streets were worse there, a jumble of weary houses with the windows patched with oilcloth and pale haggard children nestling on broken stairs. They passed others like themselves, shapes drooping in the greyness without crust or shelter. Men in horrid overcoats dozed, openmouthed, against greasy walls, too far gone even to find a doorway. An old woman, sucking on a pipe, was using the last of the light to paw through a rubbish heap.

By the time Katie and Mary reached the river, a freezing sleet was beginning to fall, stinging their faces and spotting their clothes with ominous pinpricks. Mary hurried their steps. To get wet in those temperatures would be fatal. The river was heralded by a fishy, rank smell and the sudden, dark gleam of water bearing the shapes of barges moored together in shoals. They trudged to where a bridge arch sprang away and found it already packed with bodies trying to crouch above the tide line. These unfortunates rustled and murmured like a herd of despairing beasts at bay. Hideous, retching coughs racked the dimness. A large beggar with a stick defended the entrance.

"You, scarper. Get out!"

Mary's hand closed roughly on Katie's wrist.

"Come lass, we'll find another place."

Driven by fear along the blank, sealed faces of warehouses, they finally discovered an alley with a set of heavy wooden stairs down to the river wall. Under the stairs a ledge of stone ran back into a deep black space. A burst of frozen rain drove them scrambling up inside. Though the smell of the river bespoke the drains and sewers emptying into it, the niche was well above the water, likely to keep dry until morning.

Mary set up the heavy wooden tray at the entrance as a further barrier to the wind and turned round like a mother dog making a nest. Katie watched, half giddy from cold and hunger.

"You fit in here, you do," she said, hardly even aware that it was the first time she made mention of Mary's shape.

Mary stopped cold. Katie swallowed, afraid she had made Mary angry. Mary stared into the darkness where they would have to lay themselves down, then let out the queerest laugh that Katie had ever heard. A laugh that shivered with dark memories of the Yorkshire pits.

"Aye, I do fit in. A round back fer a round hole. Now come beside me. On the inside, away from the wind."

Automatically, they cuddled into a ball for warmth, Katie gathering her skirt together to make a pad against the stone. She drew her ankles up underneath and pillowed her head on Mary's thin side.

For a while, they remained silent with only the suck and wash of the river for company, the sound of the tide going out. The stone beneath them was like the very old stone of a crypt, its cold creeping up through their clothes into their joints. A question pushed and pushed at Katie's throat until, finally, it burst out.

"Mary, are...are we going to starve?"

"Oh now, what a daft thing ter say. Of course we ain't goin' ter starve."

But Mary's voice declared she thought it perfectly likely. A palpitation clutched Katie. They had no stock money for the morrow. Her hardy spirit looked into the face of utter destitution and struggled to hold ground.

The temperature outside was dropping rapidly. As a barrier, the apple tray was meagre. Under the scanty wrap of Mary's shawl, the two outcasts shivered steadily.

"Oh, I wish we were somewhere else!" Katie muttered vehemently.

"Where?"

"Anywhere!" She had no idea of any place outside the twisting streets of East End London, but it had seemed a fine, brave thing to say. "Where do you want to be, Mary?"

She thought Mary hadn't heard her until a harsh sigh fluttered in the gloom.

"Home," came Mary's voice, low and haunted. "I wish I was home!"

Confused, Katie thought Mary meant the Infant's Asylum. She, herself, often remembered, with longing, the regular bowls of thin oatmeal and the cramped, coffin like beds. Mary tried to tuck the shawl tighter around Katie, taking the numbing gusts herself along her ribs and neck.

"I wish I as back in Chorbury. We had a wee cottage there, me mam and da. We lived in the middle of some trees and there was green grass all round."

"G-grass all round?" Katie, through chattering teeth, was unable to conceive of such a thing. "Oh, where was it?"

"Why, outside the door, and in the fields and up in the hills and just everywhere, lass. When I was a wee lass like you."

Katie's eyes opened very wide. Never before had Mary ever spoken of her past or even hinted that one existed. Mary had always been there, the never-changing rock on which she anchored her life. She could not suppose that Mary had ever been a child like her.

"Oh Mary, t-t-tell me about when you were a little girl."

Mary grunted sharply, as if the idea hurt somewhere very deep. Freezing rain crackled above them while the wind rattled at the tray. Painfully, Mary opened the sealed vault of memory hoping to find some talisman against the looming despair.

"T'was a long time ago. We lived in a cottage with bracken growin' right up against the wall with plum trees blossomin' in the yard. The village was beyond the hill so that if yer looked out, yer'd think there wasn't a single house in the whole world but yer own, that wild it was."

Slowly, rustily, she began to talk as she had never talked before She spoke of sheep dotted on the hillsides like puffs of white cotton instead of the dirty bunches driven through the streets to Smithfield meat market. Of birds flying through clear air and nesting in hawthorn branches rather than in broken house gutters and chimney pots. As she spoke, her teeth stopped chattering and her voice became low and musical.

"Oh, lass, yer should hear the larks. Like regular music boxes they are, climbing up and up over the moors till yer can't even see 'em. And green linnets, too, singing their hearts out. Why on some days, lass, the sky is so blue yer'd think it was a piece 'o Stafford pottery. On those days, the hares play in the heather they do. I've seen 'em jumpin' and dodgin' as if there wasn't a fox left in the country."

"Heather?" breathed Katie. She'd never heard Mary speak as many words together before or talk about such things! She could not picture a pure blue sky for she had never seen one free of coal smoke. Birds to her were pigeons or starlings. Forgetting the cold too, she wondered passionately how a bird could sing.

"Aye, heather. It grows on the hills. It's brownish mostly when yer look at it by the mile. But once a year, oh, once a year when the summer's high, it blooms. Then yer ought ter see it, lass," Mary's voice grew softer than Katie had ever heard it. "It turns purple everywhere. It runs down the hollows and up the banks like they was afire with purple. On them days, when yer smell t'heather, why yer feel like a lark yerself. Yer half believe yer could hop right up off the moor and fly too!"

Katie imagined the heather as a carpet of violets from the market baskets and in bunches the whole length of Wheeble Lane. How heavenly it would be to run and jump into them. They'd be soft as soft and bear her up like a lovely, fragrant cloud so unlike the hard stones digging into her hip.

"Oh Mary, let's go there," she cried with a sudden, violent longing. "Let's go there tomorrow."

Mary stilled then dragged a breath from some depth far beyond Katie's experience.

"We c-can't, lass. It's miles and miles away and there'd be nowt ter eat anyhow. Nor no w-way ter get a livin'."

"But wouldn't your mother be there?"

Katie had seen a picture once, of a low white house springing out of painted yellow flowers. A woman stood in the door, offering a bowl of porridge, smiling and smiling.

"Me mam's dead. Just like me da. She died of a baby!"

"How can you die of a baby?" Katie wanted to know.

"Never yer mind. Just hope yer don't find out!"

Cold and hunger were distorting Katie's perceptions and the idea of dying of a baby gripped her powerfully. At the Asylum, so much had been said about herself as a baby, a baby nobody wanted. A dread conviction began to form.

"Mary, did my mother die of me?"

"What?"

"Did my mother die of me?"

"Mercy, lass, what a thing ter ask."

"Did she?"

Katie tried to struggle up in the dimness. Mary dragged her back into her encircling arms.

"Why that's summat only the Lord kin tell. Don't yer go worryin' yer head about it. Just go to sleep."

This did not squelch the horrid suspicion, but Katie burrowed closer. Mary had turned her body into a bent half moon with Katie curled up inside, her old shawl over them both. Their began to slide into that light-headed state that comes when the blood begins to forsake the extremities and runs deeper inside. Slowly, they drifted into a troubled sleep.

Katie was awakened by a prickling all over her body. She was so stiff with cold she couldn't move, so only her breath speeded up, leaving small white puffs in the air. Mustering much effort, she lifted her head from Mary's rising and falling ribs and opened her lashes.

The shafts from the cold moon above allowed her the shock of meeting two gleaming eyes set in a large head peering over the barrier of the apple tray. Mary! Oh Mary, wake up!

She was crying out silently, vainly inside her mind.

The eyes were like those of the shaggy brute kept at the back of Stiver's dolly shop, the one said once to have torn a man to pieces.

In horrid fascination, Katie watched the neck that protruded from the ragged collar stretch and stretch until the head was right inside the dimness under the stairs. The shoulders followed, showing they belonged to a huge, scraggly man who filled the entire entranceway. His face and neck and hair were the same colour as the tattered fabric clinging to his back as if he had been dipped in plaster then allowed to harden. His hair stood out in stiff, spiked clots.

Only his eyes, his awful eyes, shone vividly out of the caked mess. They glimmered and burned as they ran over the indistinct heap of female bodies secreted under the stairs. Katie felt their gaze palpably, as if one of the famished drainpipe rats were skittering across her skin.

The apparition paused. Ends of rags stood out from his body, refusing to flutter in the breeze. Now that he was closer, a rude animal smell that reeked of greasy, putrid tides and river mud mixed with some acrid musk tightened the roots of Katie's hair. Her small breath was whipped away entirely as a hideous grin crept across the man's face. He began to insinuate the rest of himself under the stairs with the ease and silence of an eel.

"M...M...Mary!" Katie croaked out as one knee pushed him forward.

In her exhausted sleep, Mary shifted groggily toward the plaintive call.

The man got the other knee up. The grin on his mud-coloured face was fixed, idiot-like. From the hips down, the man's flanks shone wetly, explaining why he was all of such a strange grey colour and why his rags had the rigidity of plaster. He belonged to the tribe of mud larks, waiting, day or night, for the tide to ebb so they could slide through the suck and ooze of the exposed banks to steal from grounded barges or pick through floating refuse for something worth a penny or two to supplement their begging. His body was encased in mud, both wet and dry. At the end of his legs, his bare feet dripped, like pale, bloated fishes. And now he had stumbled upon something of more interest than the other flotsam of the Thames.

"MARY!"

At this shriek, Mary whipped her crippled body around and sat up staring, with Katie pressed to her chest.

"Get away out o' here!" she hissed. "Git!"

The command only widened the gloating grin and drew those unblinking eyes. The man walked himself forward on his knees; his stare fixed on the hollow where was visible the faint swell of Mary's hunger-shrunken breasts. Mary scrambled up and thrust Katie violently into the evil-smelling, triangular hole behind her. Desperately, she made a grab for the apple tray. Lightning fast, the intruder grasped her wrist.

"Ha!" he rasped. "Ha!"

His other hand found Mary's hair and forced her down.

"Let go 'o me!" Mary ordered fiercely, her humped shape twisting. The man began to laugh silently in avid glee.

Mary flung up her other hand to slam at the fellow's face. His wrist glanced it away as if it were a gnat. With his hold on her hair, he bent Mary's head back.

"Uunnh...." she panted furiously, "Unh...uhn...."

With her free hand, she punched and scratched but it bounced off her attacker harmlessly, only dislodging showers of dried mud.

Katie's temple had glanced hard off a supporting timber, sending her down on her bottom. When she tried to move, she found all the blood in her had turned to icy sand. It filled her mouth so that she couldn't speak, ran out of her knees so that they collapsed, weak and empty, incapable of moving ever again.

Mary, Oh Mary, Mary MARY!

Mary was now fighting savagely, her teeth bared. Guttural grunts issued from her but no screams, as if it did not occur to her, even in extremity, to appeal to the world for help.

The sand inside Katie became crushed marble. She only saw Mary keeping her body, no matter what, between herself and the mud lark. As the creature knelt over her, Mary managed to grasp a chunk of rock from beside her and suddenly, with all the strength left in her, smash her attacker on the side of the head. He reeled back, bashing himself on the wood above him. Mary collapsed too, gasping for air.

For a long moment, the only thing heard under the stairs was horrible rasps for breath. Then the mud lark began to slither forward again.

Get up Mary, Katie pleaded silently. Get up now and fight. Now! Now is your chance!

The man, reared up on his knees, wheezing noisily. His eyes were rolled back in his head; his jaws hung open like a hinged trap that has just been sprung.

Get up, Mary, get up, get up!

Time seemed to stop when Mary did not move. The icy spell that had petrified Katie broke. She flung herself upon the beggar, kicking and biting and flailing with all her might. The surprise of her attack allowed her to gouge the fellow's cheeks and tear bloodily at his ear with her fingernails. Murderous rage sent her foot into his stomach and her fingers and into his spiky hair which she tried to rip away in chunks. The man grasped her dress front, tearing it at the shoulders as he lifted her away from himself and held her suspended, struggling and spitting, in the air before him.

Katie took the opportunity to draw both her knees up and slam the creature as hard as she could, both heels catching him hard in the throat. He let out a high-pitched, screech and dropped Katie. Choking horribly, he clutched at his neck and flung himself backward, slamming his shoulder against the stairs. With his eyes rolling back in his head, he tumbled outside and dragged himself back toward he river.

Faintness and nausea passed in waves over the child. Her head reeled, then blackness rushed in, blotting the whole world out.

When Katie came back to consciousness, she found herself supported in Mary's arms. Mary was feverishly searching all over her for signs of hurt. Suddenly, she clutched Katie to her breast swaying back and forth, not with the gentleness of a mother but with the fierceness of a disoriented, cornered animal.

"There yer sees, lass! Don't ever let them near. That's how yer gets a baby and that's how yer dies!"

Mary rocked even harder while Katie huddled deeply in the embrace that was the only true shelter she had ever known. She wanted to stay there forever, desperately drinking in the comfort of Mary's nearness. Gradually, Mary stilled. When she tried to heave herself up, she collapsed back, shaking. Jagged alarm raced through Katie.

"Mary..."

"Whist, lass, I'm just...I'm just tired. And...I've hit my head. Let's cuddle up in the corner now and see if we can get our rest."

Mary's voice had completely changed, now strangely faint and dreamy. Gratefully, Katie nestled deeper into the encircling arms. Mary slid down flat again, and groped about to find her shawl. Katie felt its familiar fold drop over her shoulder. When Katie stirred, Mary tucked her bony arm more tightly around the child.

For a while, Mary grew so still Katie thought she must be sleeping. Katie struggled with torpor herself, the release of tension drawing her weak body quickly toward sleep. She was jarred by Mary's hand which fumbling and slow, tucked something deep inside the bodice of Katie's dress.

"That's fer thee, lass. Never let it away from thee."

Mary's voice seemed frighteningly faint and far away.

"What...is it?"

"Why, a treasure. Yer must look after it sharp and see that... nothing happens to it."

The worn bit of cloth contained the money from Mr. Jenks' clock. For years, Mary had watched him furtively sliding the packets inside it and peering all around to make sure he wasn't seen. Mary knew it was money. Deep in her mind, she suspected it was the curate's money and that her brave stand was being somehow got round. When she finally took one of the packets, so thin and carefully wrapped in paper, she found it full of something she didn't even recognize. Having never seen more than one pound at a time in her life, she had no idea of the uses of the higher denominations before her. She only knew they were valuable. They had to be. Why else would Mr. Jenks be hiding them? And for sure they ought to belong to Katie.

So her thefts began, her own way of getting even each time Jenks caned Katie or made her scrub the flagstones by herself. Each packet was carefully replaced by one exactly like it, wrapped in brown paper, but filled with brown paper too. Mr. Jenks never looked beyond checking that the same number was squeezed into the narrow hiding place. Mary had bound the notes against her and kept them safe and never, in their hungriest times, had it occurred to her that they could be used. Now, Katie must have them.

Katie, though she felt as though she were lying deep under water, still felt a prick of alarm.

"You keep it, Mary. We're together so it's the same..."

Mary's hand stroked Katie's hair, slowly and jerkily.

"Hey, don't yer fret," Mary murmured dreamily into the frigid air. "Sure we're tergether. We'll stay tergether just as long as we can."

"But..."

"Listen, does yer want ter hear about the waterfall behind me mam's cottage and the harebells growin' in the ferns?"

Once again Mary led her into the summer mists of Yorkshire where, warmed and fed on beauty, Katie forgot about the packet and left behind the hostile night. When Katie finally drifted into sleep, Mary lay still for a moment, then, in an agony of pained muscles, she dragged the shawl loose from her shoulder, folded it double and put the entire bulk of it over Katie's head and body. She pulled her skirts loose from her knees and spread the fabric over Katie's legs so that the child was completely covered.

As much of her own body as she could, she wrapped around the child, willing what warmth she had left into Katie. Her own back, now covered by only a bit of thin dress, made a bulwark against the frigid blasts whipping over the apple tray. She couldn't actually feel where her hands and her feet were, for they seemed to have gone to sleep, just like she wanted to go to sleep herself. One thing though, she wasn't shivering any more. Wonderful it was, how the weather turned so warm. Why she didn't need the shawl anyway so Katie must have it.

Mary turned her head slightly to where ice pellets pelted down. She saw primroses falling out of an opal sky and heard a linnet singing.

"Why, Katie," she breathed in wonder. "We've got home after all. We'll just take a wee nap, then go up and ask me mam fer a nice cup o' tea."

Light woke Katie, the watery daylight of mid-morning reaching through the stairs, plucking at eyes sealed shut, lifting her from a strange dream of rabbits leaping over velvety carpets of blue flowers. She struggled to remember why she was there and why she was so cold. Even in her sleep, her teeth had chattered in her head. Her arms were numb, her body a brittle icicle.

Somehow she lifted her lids. The first thing she saw was streaks of frost outside and pellets of hail in the cracks between the stones. When she forced her knees to move, she was surprised to hear the faintest tinkle of ice falling from the folds of her skirt.

Was she frozen? Was that why she was colder than she had ever been in her life? The wind always bit one shoulder for all that she had the shawl doubled on her, but the side curled against dear Mary...

Katie's eyes flew wide. Mary, against whose side she had been sleeping, wasn't warm at all. She felt stone cold!

In a tearing fright, Katie sprang up.

"Mary," she screeched. "Mary, Mary!"

Grasping Mary by her poor humped shoulders, Katie shook her with all her might, only managing to dislodge bits of gravel. Mary's face, though still as river clay, bore such a queer smile that Katie stilled. How could Mary look so happy and yet be...yet be...

Katie grabbed one of Mary's hands, then dropped it with a gasp, for it was chill and rigid to her touch. Mary's bare legs protruded from her skirts which seemed to have their looseness all heaped up and piled over Katie too. There were dark marks on her neck from the mud lark's fingers. And a large stain of blood in her hair.

Mary had been killed! Mary was dead!

Katie swayed amidst a stunning blankness, afraid to touch Mary again, afraid to move. She crouched so long that a rat emerged from the stonework to peer at the tableau with bright, searching eyes. Cautiously it raised itself on it haunches, snuffling with its sharp nose at Mary's bare calf. Katie went mad.

"Get away! Get away! GET AWAY!"

She grabbed up the heavy apple tray and hurled it at the stone abutment behind Mary's knees. The rat squealed shrilly as a corner caught it on the side of the head. It fled in time to escape the hail of broken brick and handfuls of dirt Katie flung insanely at the crevice where it had disappeared.

She continued until Mary's skirt was covered with pebbles and debris. In the midst of it, she had begun to cry, small scraping sobs that had only begun to grasp the enormity of the catastrophe. Heavy footsteps crashed on the stairs.

"'Ere! Wot in blimey!"

One of the workmen from the warehouse was bending down, trying to see beneath the steps. His immense shadow, his reddened, kindly face, chapped from the wind, made Katie stumble back against Mary, but as soon as she felt the icy body, she sprang away again. The man was squatting on his haunches. Soon he would fill the entrance and trap her...

With a moan, Katie leaped for the open alley. As the startled workman put out his hand to help the frightened child, she slashed past him, fled up the stairs and into the street, running and running.

CHAPTER TWENTY-ONE

You die screaming through the opium. Aye, if you can afford opium. Nothing left of you but bones except where the horrid thing is growing.

Croom swilled from the tankard.

They flung you in the back of the charity ward so they don't have to listen to you rave. They clean up after you, if they clean up, loathing you with their faces.

Oh, he was used to people turning their noses up at a sweep. Gave them the wink right back, he did, even a bleeding earl. But in the ward, good Christ, he'd be on his back rolling his eyes at the rafters. And who'd be there to give a donkey's fart!

Croom banged on the counter for a refill, burping blearily.

Will might be there.

The tankard came back full. Croom nursed it unsteadily back to his bench by the fire. Will! Be just like the blighter to hang about, sopping bread so a sick man could eat, mopping up the bed if he were bid.

Croom burped again and peered over to where Will was minding the brushes, his knees tucked up cautiously under his chin. The lad hated pubs, that was sure, and wouldn't drink a drop. Yet he sat still as a pole whenever Croom wanted him to and without so much as a whine.

Will hated the chimney's too, Croom knew. Climbed into them shaking, even as he scraped, but he did what he was told. Now where would a fellow get another lad like that these days, Croom asked himself, growing maudlin. Eh! Bloody piece 'o gold, that boy. And you can't pass bugger all to him. Not even a brush!

Croom took another swallow, feeling the froth slide down his gullet. All his life, Croom had been a good pub companion but not a drunk. Today he was a drunk. Over the last month he'd been getting drunk with increasing frequency and not giving a good plucked damn about cleaning chimneys.

Why should he when the soot wart between his legs had blossomed into a painful, ulcerated sore and sprouted companions. The doctor said it was through him already, no use trying to cut out the growths. After a life of thinking himself immune, Croom was doomed by sweep's disease. The worst way he could imagine to go. Cancer of the scrotum.

Already the swelling had begun, and the never relenting pain snaked through his loins. He'd moved to the back of the lodging house, taken a crooked room just big enough for him and Will to sleep in. Now Croom worked only enough to keep himself in gin, aiming to spend as much of his life as possible fogged out on the pub's corner settle.

Only Will produced a stir of feeling. Ordinarily a shrewd, changeable, casual man, Croom had taken to mumbling "poor little blighter," in his sodden moments, seeing himself long ago committed to the life that led to his present torment. Despite the intermittent work, he kept the boy on, fed him sparsely and maundered on in a vague manner about different sorts of flues.

"Your trade, lad. Something to remember old Croom by!"

Croom shifted sideways and a sharper agony than any before knifed through him. Sweat broke out along his ribs. What would he have to do in a day or two? Stand up to drink at the christly bar?

He bit back one of the rages that had begun coming upon him this last month. Mute red rages spewing out what he could not tell in words. Once, when a cabman next to him had complained genially of boils, Croom had grabbed up a chair and sent it smashing against the wall. Twice he'd picked fistfights with strangers. When passersby tried to touch him for luck, he snarled savagely. Some evenings, he tramped home, reeking of booze and cursing at the sky, Will lugging the brushes warily behind him. The blackness of Croom's figure gave him the look of an outcast demon trailed by his own reluctant imp.

"Why don't you run off," he would suddenly roar at Will. "I ain't' got nothin' for you. Why don't you run off and do for yerself!"

Will only put his head down like a pup waiting for a blow. Croom would wheeze painfully and clench his fists. "All right, all right. Come and see if we can't find a crust somewheres in this God-cursed room."

He'd let Will eat the whole heel of bread himself. What did Croom want with food anyway, when he had to lie in bed with his legs sprawled like a shot duck just so the pain couldn't get the better of the gin.

Before he knew it, Croom's tankard was empty again. He staggered up for a refill as a dock worker slouched by. Knocked off balance, Croom dropped back to the bench, suffering such a stab that he leaped up with a bellow and took an ineffectual slam at the man with his fist.

"What's the matter wi' you!" the fellow growled. "Got a 'andful 'o burrs up yer arse! You mind I don't sock your lights out!"

A young smart aleck, leaning with his thumbs in his suspenders, grinned at the commotion.

"Aw, 'ave a 'eart, mate. Maybe old Croomy's got fruit rot from bein' a sweep. That's why he's so sweet-tempered lately!"

Nauseous fear lurched in Croom's innards. To have his trouble guessed at, joked about…

"Yer don't say," cried another voice. "'Ey, Croomy, got anything still 'anging on the vine?"

The jokes were jovial and not malicious, the banter of rough working men. Nevertheless, a restraint inside Croom broke, just as he knew it would, when the moment came. He dragged Will and the brushes outside and stood gulping the air until his brain cleared. Then he set out purposefully.

"Where are we going?" Will asked.

"You'll see."

Croom entered a dolly shop and pawned his brushes, his rope, his sacks and all his equipment save the ladder. This he took with him to the next pub he came to, a strange pub, and set about methodically drinking up the money.

Since Croom had already consumed much ale, he ought to have been reeling. This time, the he more drank the steadier he seemed to become, his eyes fixed on the grate, emptying one tankard after another. His face, despite the amounts of liquid, grew drier and tighter. At last, as if he could hold no more, he rose and made his way to the door, swaying like a man walking on glass. Will rushed to follow.

"Ge' away 'ome now. G'way, g'ome!" he slurred at Will as if shooing a stray mongrel.

He gave a surprisingly hard shove, then staggered. Will felt apprehension crawl over him.

"No. No. You can hardly walk. I got to take you back."

"I can walk well enough for what I want. Now get along 'ome wi' ye! Ye won't be seeing me no more."

Under the gaslight, Croom's eyes looked glassy as watch faces. Will knew how much the man had drunk and wondered how he kept weaving along. The raw wind bit at Croom's carelessly unbuttoned coat. To Will's amazement, Croom began to sing.

"Oh the sweep goes up and the sweep goes down
In among the chimneys
All soot 'e is and black as crows
In among the..."

He broke off, blurrily surprised to see Will still there.

"Tis a cold night, lad. I said get along back."

The roughness was gone, replaced by an almost apologetic kindness that echoed eerily in the empty street. When Will didn't move, Croom lurched back against a wall, supporting himself with one hand.

"Fergot your pay, din't I. Well, let's see what the old sot's got."

Croom fumbled through his pockets, coming up with an assortment of coins. These he stuffed into Will's hands. When he saw how few they were, he shrugged.

"All I can scrape, lad. Now get on with you. Sleep out o' the wind."

"But Mr. Croom, where will you..."

"Never you mind that. I'll find me a nice comfy couch this night. For sure I will."

The weird, burning gleam of Croom's gaze made Will back away. Why was Mr. Croom acting so queer? Why had he pawned their brushes and then given over the last money in his pockets? Why didn't he want to go home?"

All the boy could think of was that Croom was going to stop with Mrs. Frawley down the block, who sometimes took in men of nights. Mrs. Frawley always sent Croom back in a fine, lusty mood.

The street was dark and frightening for a lad alone, especially if he had pennies in his pockets, Will walked away very slowly, keeping to the shadows. Hard as he tried to convince himself that Croom as going to Mrs. Frawley, he couldn't believe it. Something dreadful clutched out from the midst of Croom's erratic merriment.

Will reached a corner where the street widened. There he stopped and turned, for in the stillness of the night, he thought he heard the familiar scrape of the ladder.

He had.

Croom, despite his extreme drunkenness, retained the agility of his trade. He was scrambling up the roof of the tallest house at hand. Groping, he found the small iron grips placed for the convenience of sweeps, using them to haul himself up to the peak. No London Bridge for me, he thought, with the cold, murky waters and who knew what down there. He wanted what he was sure of. In his trade he'd seen more than a few slip and take the tumble. Good trustworthy pavement would do the job.

Chimney sweep and his climbing boy.

Grasping the last grip, he dragged himself upright and looked out over the dim jumble of roofs about him. Far away he saw the great dome of St. Paul's floating serenely in the night. Behind him there was the dark slash of the Thames twinkled over with the riding lights of ships. Here and there, at the most improbable heights, flapped rows of laundry. Croom grinned. He'd stolen petticoats right off the lines when he was a lad. Snowing, it was called, and required nothing but the ability to run. Ah, them was the days and he'd like to say goodbye with a flourish.

The sulphurous yellow of the few street lamps was aided by gleams from the moon when the scudding clouds momentarily thinned. In one of these intervals, Will looked up and his blood congealed in his breast!

There, beside a cluster of chimneys, a man stood four storeys above the street! The man was Joshua Croom!

"Oh noooo!" Will gasped. "Nooo!"

Smoke curled up around the figure and moonlight brushed it to the colour of ancient pewter. Will stood rigid as the shape stretched itself, took off its top hat, and swept low in a great bow to all the chimney pots of London. Then, resolutely, it propelled itself backwards, down over the gable end, forever from Will's sight.

Will gaped upward like a stone boy until he heard shouting and a hullabaloo around the corner. The roots of Will's hair turned to needles of terror. He began to run, pounding through the streets.. He ran until he reached the lodging house, sped in through the back and slammed the door behind him.

Without candle or fire the room was frigid but Will threw himself down in Croom's creaky chair and sat staring into the darkness, his heart pumping and stuttering, his blood rushing heavily in his ears.

Presently, his breathing slowed to a ragged rasp. No matter how he screwed shut his eyes, he could not rid them of the image branded inside his lids. That grotesque, eloquent bow, that slow arching backward like a diver, like a man falling into bed.

Gone! Forever!

No Mr. Croom tossing down a load of salvaged coals for the fire. No Mr. Croom rooting out cooked potatoes to share or winking over some sly deal. Though Will had been worked hard at a trade he hated, he had gotten used to Croom, his only company other than snatched words with Katie in the street. In all Croom's final bouts of objectless fury, he had not struck Will. And he had given him the last pennies he owned.

He ain't coming back. I'm all alone!

A black abandonment welled up deep inside. Will, who hated taverns and feared men smelling of liquor, groped his way to the cupboard. He extracted a bottle of Croom's gin, three quarters full, and began to drink. The fiery spirit choked and revolted him, but he kept on, wanting it, needing it, sucking the raw spirit into his young body until the hot waves lifted him up and away. Then he stumbled to Croom's bed and dropped, blessedly dead, at last, to the events of the night.

CHAPTER TWENTY-TWO

"Oh, your arm!" Amelia cried as the shiny open vehicle swayed around a corner, barely missing a lamp post.

Amelia and Rose were speeding along toward their first public appearance together in a smart open carriage provided, as nearly all else had been provided, by cash from Red Nell. Rose flicked her elbow out of danger as the carriage clattered ahead, strewing mud right and left.

The vehicle was from a hire firm of the better class, quite unaccustomed to entering the sort of district where the Refuge was situated. The driver had arrived in purse-lipped disapproval and rattled off the moment he had loaded his passengers. A young blood, he was immensely proud of his equipage and he expected to spend his days flashing about fashionable neighbourhoods to the admiration of elegant ladies' maids out on errands. On top of this, the sight of Rose done up in rustling peach, quite turned his head. He was determined to show how quickly, how disdainfully, he could whisk her out of that seedy backwater, leaving a trail of curses in his wake.

Rose balanced adroitly, taking care not to crush her afternoon dress of pale silk under its matching cloak trimmed so stylishly with worked French braid. She was nothing but madly fizzing spirits inside. Today was the day! Surely today her adventure was really going to begin.

Amelia perched beside her, heart slowing and racing by turns. She struggled to conquer her nerves before they reached Crisp Court, one of London's grand new houses, for tea. Amelia had discovered that the prickling of an unquiet conscience was everything the religious tracts promised. The more she committed.

The irony was that, no sooner had they moved into the new quarters on Mrs. Fitzroy's largess than a Scottish reformer had fallen ill. Edwin sped off to fill in all the man's remaining lecture dates. The earnings would restore Edwin's confidence. They would also keep him away for weeks, leaving Amelia with the managing of everything on her hands.

"Shan't be surprised if you're running half of London when I come back," Edwin rumbled with a grin. "I'll miss you, my dear. My regards to Cousin Fitzroy when she appears."

Amelia remembered not to flinch. Already, she had been making secret expeditions to Gresham's. Rose couldn't be introduced to anybody until Amelia was certain she passed muster.

Clothes. That was the first concern. Rose couldn't possibly go out dressed in any of those unsightly things in the wardrobe at the Academy. Since Mrs. Fitzroy had made it clear no expense was to be spared, Amelia had at once scrounged up a clever dressmaker and set her to work.

Nervously, Amelia examined Rose again. Every time she was near the young woman, Amelia found herself so unsettled she could barely keep from twitching. Her own squirming scruples, she supposed.

Yet Rose was unsettling with high colour in her cheeks and her grey green eyes brilliant with anticipation. Was it the dress, Amelia wondered, scanning its folds again in nervous worry. In palest peach silk with cream lace ruching, tiny buttons and high neck, it was as maidenly and demure in style as Amelia had been able to wring from the dressmaker. A vestal virgin from old Rome wouldn't have been out of place wearing it. A vestal virgin would have felt armoured, for goodness sake. So why, then, did the very trim on the skirt hint of wayward dancing? Why did the sedate little hat, which had clung to Rose's temple with such reserve during the fitting, now snap its ribbons with pure impudence and frolic like some other hat altogether?

In the struggle to overpower Rose, the dress had been quite defeated and it was too late for Amelia to frantically analyze how else she could have clad the girl. She gave up and folded her hands tightly in her lap. Amelia herself wore her best maroon serge, plain and sturdy. Even though Mrs. Fitzroy clearly meant Amelia to order whatever she herself needed for the foray, it was here that Amelia baulked. Proudly Amelia made a point of taking not a penny of the money for her own personal use. Her own clothes, provided by Edwin, should do, she resolved, even if she were to encounter the queen.

Rose remained as much of an enigma now to Amelia as she had that first afternoon they'd met. Dealing with Rose was like dealing with a smooth stone, lovely to handle but supplying almost no grip. Rose had complied with all Amelia's instructions with an eager, almost suspect docility, yet Amelia could not shake the feeling of a pleasant surface with gunpowder underneath.

Amelia struggled hard not to fall under Rose's charm for then the possibility of all sorts of unthinkable adventures began to nibble at the brain. She began to understand why Mrs. Gresham maintained the dour standoffishness of a prison warden. How else to maintain order with such mischief in the nest? Amelia only grew more determined to make her venture pay off on the side of virtue.

Luckily, the girl spoke well, Amelia thought, unaware of how much she was tantalized by her inability to trace the accent to its roots. What tripped off so musically off Rose's tongue was an imitation of Mrs. Gresham tempered with enough robust Cornish to blot out the teeth-gritting affectation. A soft grace note of Irish, picked up from Maeve and Nell, added a final piquancy to the whole.

About Rose's other talent, that of an irrepressible mimic, Amelia had no suspicion even though Rose was, in Amelia's very presence, absorbing Amelia's graceful walk and way of sipping tea. Amelia did not know how often Rose had reduced her fellow inmates to hysterics with her devastating imitations of Mrs. Gresham passing out parsimonious rations or of Reverend Fowler droning on and on Sunday after Sunday.

Amelia's hopes were pinned on Rose getting to sing at Crisp Court. She wasn't blind to the fact that society's interest in her cause was bound to increase if some scintillating entertainment came along with the package. Competent performers were always in demand, if only to prevent the inept and the tone deaf from inflicting their own squawking efforts. Amelia was also intensely conscious of the huge debt she was piling up with Mrs. Fitzroy and anxious to keep her end of the bargain.

Beyond singing at Mrs. Crisp's—and that would depend upon the whim of the hostess—Amelia had little idea of what Mrs. Fitzroy expected about Rose's musical ambitions. However, if today were a success, Amelia had firm ideas of her own. Rose would be a labourer for the Refuge. She would entertain at teas and bazaars, help collect used clothing for the children, hand out tracts at lectures and lend a hand to Ida as the number of children began to grow. She meant to counter today's deception with bracing moral tonic.

The path to Crisp Court had been sudden and daring. Despite Mrs. Fitzroy's temporary largess, the ever-haunting spectre of destitution had given Amelia a lightness of head and a boldness of

action she wouldn't have dreamed of before. She had simply lifted
her pen and written a letter.

Such a letter!

Mrs. Fitzroy is right, Amelia decided, still queasy from her
brush with eviction. What's the use of begging donations from people as poor as ourselves? I have go where people are rich. I need a
scheme that's really...grand!

Rushing out before she lost her nerve, Amelia bought the
creamiest, most expensive stationery the neighbourhood had to offer and snatched up her pen. The Universal Hope Children's Refuge,
she wrote, her cloudy dreams forged at a pen-stroke into an emigration agency sending little ones to the very edges of the Empire
where fresh air, health and warm farm families waited to enfold
them. An agency meant to bring money rolling in from sources
copiously awash with the stuff. An agency with herself and Edwin
at its head.

Overcoming a lifetime of conditioning by James, Amelia in-
voked the one asset she had never dared use before, the name of
her famous father. Addressing the letter to the most prominent
Nonconformist lady the grapevine could supply, Amelia dropped
it into the post. Methodists must turn to Methodists, she decided.
And I might as well be hung for a sheep as for lamb.

To Amelia's astonishment, a reply swiftly appeared. Dr.
Radmore, it seemed, had been almost as illustrious among
Methodists as among Anglicans. Amelia was invited, as a repre-
sentative of her organization, to tea at a house called Crisp Court.
There she would be introduced to similarly minded ladies and per-
haps have the opportunity to speak on behalf of her cause.

Crisp Court! Never mind that Amelia had never heard of it;
she knew the address well enough, a precinct crammed with social
citadels she could never have stormed on her own. Amelia hugged
the formal note to her bosom. Providence was smiling indeed!

Amelia accepted at once, mentioning that she would be accompanied by her cousin and associate, Miss Rose Fitzroy, who would
be most pleased to entertain the ladies with a song during tea. Oh
please, just please let Rose behave herself until after the song.

A day later, Amelia felt her elation plummet. It was one thing
to be introduced, yet if she couldn't make an impression, if she let
herself be shouldered out, all would be lost. She wouldn't be invited
back. Then where would she be!

The streets fed from the wharves and were crammed with ship-related traffic impeding rapid progress. Obstructed by a dray, the driver sheared off into a side street which he hoped was a narrow shortcut to the thoroughfare leading on to Crisp Court. He bullied imperiously through until he found his way blocked only by a broad-backed man tramping along with a canvas duffle, such as common seamen carry, flung across his shoulder.

Unlike the rest of the thrust-aside pedestrians, the fellow's stride did not alter at the driver's shouts and the noise of the carriage behind. The man had been looking about with the air of a stranger in town and did not mean to be hurried by anyone.

"Hey, move aside there, dolt!" the driver bellowed, jerking at the horse. "Make way!"

A vendor of flypaper had dropped half his wares onto the cobbles to escape the carriage wheels. Furious, the vendor snatched up a stone and shied it at the horse to avenge the destruction of his stock-in-trade.

The animal was already confused by the noise, nettled by the driver and much irritated by the check rein the driver had shortened to force the animal's neck into a higher arch. The stone struck its sensitive inner thigh. This was the last straw. The horse reared, crashed into the side wall, then yanked the carriage forward in a horrid prelude to a bolt.

The driver promptly lost one rein and began dragging frantically at the other as the beast plunged toward the busier cross street where real calamity waited. It slammed a shoulder roundly into the man ahead, sending the duffle flying.

The fellow stumbled, the righted himself with catlike quickness out of reach of the hooves. The next instant, he had grabbed the horse's bridle and dragged it to a halt, giving the driver time to recover the slipped rein. The driver sawed at the horse's mouth and glared at the man who had stopped its flight

"Out of my way," the young hot-blood yelled as though he had been personally insulted. "Let go of that animal at once!"

He lashed out with his long carriage whip in a punitive whack at the horse for daring to assert its own ideas. The whip whistled wide, missing by fractions the cheek of the stranger. From the front, he displayed an immense dark beard, a battered sheepskin vest over an even rougher wool shirt, and a sunburnt complexion certainly not attained in smoggy London. He released the horse and grasped the end of the whip on its upswing. Gripping it tightly, the stranger advanced on the carriage. The driver would either have to let go of the whip handle or be twitched out of his box onto the street.

Amelia and Rose watched all this unfold in petrified slow motion. When the horse took advantage of its freedom to rear again. Rose was tossed against the door, which promptly flew open. She grabbed at the side too late to save herself. She would have pitched toward the cobbles had not the bearded man released the buggy whip, seized Rose by the arms and stopped her fall inches from his sheepskin chest.

For a moment, the two were suspended in peculiar stillness. Up close, the fellow was even rougher and wilder. His untrimmed beard, unlike the Vandykes and goatees of gentlemen or even the jolly side whiskers of sailors, wouldn't have been out of place on a shaggy hermit escaped from a cave. His hair, thick and dark as the pelt of an animal, looked as though it had been cut, not very recently, with a knife. Atop this head was jammed, not a common workman's cap, but a broad-brimmed foreign hat, weather-stained to the colour of an old saddle and sporting curious leather braiding round the crown.

In his face, ire at the driver warred with astonishment at suddenly finding himself with two hands full of silk and strawberry blonde pulchritude. He stared hard as though he hadn't seen a woman in years, certainly not one scented with jasmine, swathed in fashionable elegance and with skin as glowing as a new peach. Amelia half rose from her seat. The stranger hefted Rose back into the carriage and released her abruptly. He then swept the ladies an ironical bow containing his whole opinion of their driver and whatever urgent necessity required them to mow down other traffic in the street. The last they saw of him was an impudent grin in the forest of whiskers as he retrieved his sea bag.

"That brute didn't soil your clothing did he?" Amelia sputtered as the gained the main thoroughfare. Grubby hand prints on Rose's new gown were all they needed if and when they survived the rest of this carriage ride.

Rose shook her head. She only knew that, in her moment in his hands, he brought the smell of the sea with him. Not the dirty, tide-stained waters of the Thames, but the vast, clean ocean, echoing with the cries of gulls. For a thrilling moment, London vanished. Rose was transported back to a wind-whipped freedom she hadn't felt since Old Anna turned the gypsy wagon from the Cornish coast so long ago.

CHAPTER TWENTY-THREE

Amelia's nerves would not have been calmed by sight of her hostess pacing up and down like a large, taffeta whirlwind in her sprawling drawing room. Louisa Crisp was quite as unstrung as Amelia, though she expressed it by wringing her hands and harassing the maids about the silver. Her house, Crisp Court, was a raw, red, Neo-Gothick newcomer shattering the classical harmony of a posh and settled block. A block which had imagined itself immune to the assaults of the rude new money flooding into London.

Louisa, as new to the city as her house, had no concept of the local sensibilities she had upset when her gargoyle and battlement encrusted edifice shouldered uninvited into the high-toned neighbourhood. Only when the house was finished and she sent her card around did Louisa feel the frost emanating from her neighbours. Only then did Louisa realize the corner she had backed herself into and to take alarm.

The pinnacle of Louisa's ambition, the culmination of Milton Crisp's money getting, had been to come at last to London. On top of that, Louisa possessed that most fearsomely motivating of reasons for an assault on Society, a daughter almost ripe for the marriage market. Louisa Crisp had just one year to establish herself in acceptable circles before Camille, now away at school, would require a splashing London debut.

Louisa faced this daunting task alone. Milton had died just when the furnishings were being ordered. Fortunately, Milton left Louisa with a son to look after business and tubs of money to fund her campaign. The period of mourning, so hampering upon outside activities, had given Louisa time to cram the house with the latest in pseudo-medieval plush and faux Jacobite carved oak.

Louisa herself, though raised with all the pains her fond parents could muster, certainly hadn't earned by birth the dizzying heights she now hoped to conquer. The daughter of a prosperous forage merchant, she had been nurtured up diligently in the arts of shell gluing, tea giving and displaying complicated dresses to advantage.

Her reward had been Milton Crisp whose pride and joy was a row of thundering cotton mills producing cotton and profits in equally ample quantities. Her parents had gone to their graves thinking their daughter a resounding success.

That doting pair could not see Louisa twisting at her knuckles and grappling up the courage to plunge into the larger fray today. Louisa knew she was about to be tested in the fires that forge. Should she or her entertainment be found wanting, Crisp Court could turn into a shunned hulk and Camille might as well decamp to a popish nunnery.

"Mrs. Wharton, ma'am," the head parlour maid announced, startling Louisa into realizing the first of her guests had arrived.

Althea Wharton! Oh, thank the stars above!

Louisa bore down eagerly upon the small, plump form in the archway. Althea Wharton had the most comforting way of smoothing out frazzled beginnings. How like her to come early to help her new friend cope with the crowd.

"My dear Mrs. Wharton!" Louisa cried. "Oh, do come in and look at the peonies I've ordered for the sideboards."

It was the sort of thing one could say to Althea Wharton. Her knowing, twinkly look, her ready, conspiratorial laugh, made people feel instantly at home. Louisa had an even greater reason for overflowing gratitude. It had been a letter of introduction to Althea Wharton that was now providing Louisa with this first tenuous toehold on London's slippery social pyramid. Over tea, Mrs. Wharton had seen Louisa's problem at once. She had set down her cup and declared, "Charity, my dear. Charity can get you practically anywhere."

To Louisa, Althea Wharton was simply the kindest of souls, suggesting Louisa host a charity planning tea and using her own name to secure a prestigious list of guests. However, Althea Wharton was at Crisp Court for exactly the same reason that was bringing Amelia—the sweet, seductive scent of money.

Althea Wharton was a comfortably rounded, diminutive woman well into the most indeterminate regions of middle age. She had a knot of ashy brown hair worn with old-fashioned side curls and the face of a friendly lemur. Her wide, round eyes protruded slightly as though scarcely able to contain their happy interest in everything around her. It took a flinty heart indeed not to feel like a cherished old friend after five minutes in Althea's presence.

This disarming manner was Althea's greatest asset. Althea Wharton was, both by nature and profession, an arranger of human affairs. She combined, to pleasant advantage, multitudinous connections, piercingly shrewd powers of observation, and an otter's instinct for riding the turbulent social waves.

London contained, at every level, such arrangers. These persons, generally female, were, under their various guises, subtle and enterprising entrepreneurs. Lacking financial capital of their own, they made their way through expenditure of their other assets, often far more valuable than mere money, namely their wits, their influence and their very useful connections.

Captain Barnaby Wharton, since deceased, had kept Althea as a mistress for a number of years before making her his wife. Althea's route to her current position had been long and circuitous and, had they known of it, would have shocked the good Methodist ladies into swoons.

Child of a schoolmaster and a haberdasher's daughter, Althea had fallen madly in love as a girl and run off. Like many another such passionate fool, she soon found herself abandoned and penniless, an event that stamped her with a permanently jaundiced view of romance. She had fallen so low that she had had to resort to going with men at an inn. Her warm nature, however, soon made her a favourite in the tap room, jollying folks to come and drink the beer. The landlord put her on a stipend for the business she attracted and thought about marrying her himself for her advantage behind the bar.

Captain Barnaby Wharton, travelling through, had been felled at the inn by a nasty influenza. Althea nursed him so cheerfully through his three weeks of recovery that the captain sincerely regretted being able to walk upright again. He took such a fancy to Althea that he swept her straight off to London and set her up in a tidy little house in Maida Vale.

Barnaby was a man of enough position to have cronies among the influential of London and he introduced Althea among them. Of a gregarious disposition, Barnaby needed entertainment and needed company, neither of which could be provided by his chronically ailing wife. He turned to Althea, initiating her into the easy, pleasurable world rich gentlemen had created to play in, the world that existed, unseen and exciting, just below the glossy, respectable surface of polite society.

Althea proved such an agreeable companion that she was soon much in demand, especially for her way of smoothing blunders, mediating quarrels and untangling, to everyone's satisfaction, an increasingly interesting variety of complications.

When the first Mrs. Wharton died, the captain decided he wanted comfort in his house enough to marry Althea and damn the consequences. The transition proved smoother than even Barnaby could have anticipated. Althea's pleasant ways soon had his stuffy neighbours, his female relatives and his loyal servants all embracing her with never a suspicion of her scandalous past.

Barnaby's cronies, who would have frozen him out had it been any other such woman, also capitulated. After a suitable wait to see how Althea got on, they also received her into the respectable part of their lives. They let their families associate with her and their wives include her in their elaborate dinners, though always with amused exchange of glances with Barnaby and Althea.

Althea, now mistress of large old house and considerable social position, adjusted to life quite as well as she had on the reverse side of respectability. She was soon giving sought after parties, sorting out differences, arranging delicate matters and generally pouring sorely needed balm on the troubles around her.

But only after Barnaby died was Althea truly free to pursue her own inclinations and ambitions. She had to, since she found herself of very uncertain pocketbook in a world where ladies could make no visible effort toward their own support. Forced upon her own resources, Althea resorted to her ingenuity and formidable social skills in order to survive. To keep up her mossily corniced Georgian house, her servants, dear as old friends, her cherished aging cats and the lively social life of which she was so enamoured, Althea became what was discreetly known as a "social godmother." For the right consideration, Mrs. Wharton would take certain chosen protégés under her wing and steer them toward success in the fast-running, treacherous currents of London's social life.

Such a person as Althea might be sought out by foreigners, such as wealthy but hopelessly democratic Americans, bent on a toehold in notoriously insular British society. Or newcomers from rudely industrial cities at a loss as to how to establish themselves in the capital. Or minor aristocrats from the Continent bristling with tin penny titles and far too much swagger for the prejudiced British eye.

By far the most common function of the social godmother was that of tossing awkward daughters of ambitious families into the way of a good marriage, especially during the pressure cooker of the London Season, that gigantic marriage mart for all the girls who had "come out" that year. Because the Season was so short, lasting only the spring and summer months, a sense of driving urgency prevailed. Families often flung themselves into debt in frantic efforts to survive in the nerve-racking cattle drive of parties, balls, concerts, receptions, teas and picnics. Althea soon found herself much in demand as a guide for such girls, curbing their more glaring gaffs and stage-managing them into the paths of the men they set their eye upon.

Althea did so with aplomb and felt she could not be blamed for keeping her own interests to the fore. If a family was bent on snaring that supremely eligible young lord, Althea saw no need to mention the amount of debt attached to him, his affinity for drink or his collection of mistresses. The only thing Althea was adamant about was keeping all her protégés safe from the infection, the inconvenience, the fatal, impractical madness of actual romance.

Althea's connections on the other side of the social coin remained. Truth to tell, Althea found the arranging of marriages only mildly satisfying. Once the gulping bride and relieved relatives had rushed off to the church, Althea discovered herself embarrassingly superfluous. The bride would then vanish into boring domesticity, never to glow and laugh and dance as she had that one galloping Season of her husband hunt.

What a waste, Althea would think, then brighten as Barnaby's cronies continued to come to her with their difficulties and to introduce her discreetly to others like themselves. Though she glided, in perfect camouflage, through many circles, Althea secretly preferred her links to the demimonde where position was so much more fluid, the stakes so much more exciting and the profits so much more lucrative. More than one glittering *grande coquette* owed her start to Althea, more than one "ruined woman" found herself cleverly resurrected in another guise. And everyone, respectable or not, expressed gratitude satisfactorily, either in cash or favours worth more than gold in the bank.

What Althea loved was the feeling of being the secret mechanism behind the scenes played out around her. She loved to watch the chase of expressions across faces, the sudden invitation extended, the connection made. She loved to untangle the clumsy knots people bumbled themselves into. She loved to judge character at a glance then see it unfolding, exactly as she had predicted. She prided herself helping people to use their own resources, without their even being aware of it, for the mutual benefit of themselves and Althea Wharton.

This feeling was elevated into a glow by secret resort to the pocket Althea had stitched into all her garments. In that pocket, Althea carried a slim handsomely engraved silver flask. The flask contained not brandy, which would have left a ruinously identifiable scent, but a lethal mix of pure Russian vodka in which was dissolved a handful of Bantree's Premium Sugared Mints. Althea rationed herself to a careful number of sips every day. On the wings they provided, she soared through her best manoeuvring, each sleight of hand, each leap of her own nimble wit.

To remain serviceable, a fabric of connections had continually to be tended, expanded and kept up to date. Althea had spotted Louisa Crisp's vast potential at once. Potential mainly in the form of unlimited funds, a desperate hunger to succeed and no husband to interfere. Althea hadn't the faintest prejudice against provincial parvenus so long as they could splendidly pay their way. She made up her mind to get Louisa started.

"Charity," she had advised, tapping Louisa confidentially on the arm and dreaming of all the intriguing entertainments that could be held in such a cavernous new mansion. "There are ladies hoping to join forces and discuss their concerns. Why don't you offer to host a tea?"

Charity work, so long as one gave generously, was one place where classes could mix. Louisa had passionately embraced the suggestion, praying that the convergence of so many prominent ladies upon her brocaded couches would finally provide the entrée she longed for. She blessed Althea for the introductions and the invitations that made it possible for Louisa to begin.

For Althea, the tea was an experiment in Louisa's favour. Should it succeed, then infinite future arrangements were possible. Should the seed fail to germinate, Althea might shrug and go on her way. Or, if Louisa proved desperate enough, Althea might suggest, delicately, a more commercial arrangement for help storming the barricades. Althea was not above tweaking the tilted noses on Louisa's block.

As Althea admired the flower arrangements, Mrs. Stanhope-White arrived in company with Mrs. Smithing and Mrs. Hasler, giving Louisa someone to conduct into her vast drawing room. When she heard more activity at the front door, Louisa braced herself optimistically. With Althea at her side she could face the guests, even Lady Stackley whose grandmother had been the third cousin of an earl!

When the hired carriage finally drew up before Crisp Court, Amelia could not prevent herself from gaping. The facade was so worked over with turrets, battlements and arrow slits that the place could have held its own against an army of pikemen. Yet the structure was so new the red building stones were still uncoated by London's sooty smogs. Amelia alighted and mastered her quaking knees. She might not carry a pike but she was mounting an assault nonetheless.

The massive oak front door gave way to a foyer complete with marble floor, crested side chairs and a brass and crystal chandelier suspended from a moulded plaster rosette sporting heraldic creatures peering down. A grand staircase swept upward, guarded by suspiciously shiny jousting armour and enough dark paneling for a Tudor banqueting hall. Amelia could barely glimpse all this due to the surprise of suddenly confronting a gigantic stuffed bear around which all traffic had to swirl.

The creature, a good seven feet tall, reared furiously upright on its hind legs, frozen as it slashed the air, with paws as large as luncheon plates. Amelia nearly didn't hear the maid attempting to usher her into the presence of the chatelaine of all that splendour, Mrs. Louisa Crisp.

So many ladies, was Amelia's first thought as she and Rose were led through the wide archway. She was both taken aback by the numbers and relieved that she could take temporary refuge in anonymity. It was one thing to make a bargain with an Irish widow in a back street. It was quite another to be standing here, in the midst of this coffer-ceilinged drawing room, about to brazenly commence her subterfuge. Her stomach felt rigid as a plank and on her brow surely throbbed the brand of the devil. Oh please, please let Rose not do anything to give their pretence away!

Louisa was so nearly overcome by the abundance of social grace filling up her sofas that she resembled a ship heeling precariously under too much sail. Almost as an omen, the maid got Amelia's name wrong. Not only did Louisa not have the slightest concept of Dr. Radmore's fame, but her gaze flew straight to the scars running up the side of Amelia's cheek. When Amelia reddened, Louisa hastily diverted her gaze to Amelia's dress. Nonplussed by Amelia's starkly plain serge, Louisa seated the two behind some potted palms almost out of sight.

So long had Amelia been in pinched circumstances that the interior of Crisp Court overwhelmed her. Above all, Louisa had wanted Crisp Court to be solid. She felt she would be judged on the weight of her silver, the heaviness of her furniture and the ponderousness of the atmosphere

Louisa had swelled at the thought of the piano which had come all the way from Italy, and of the carpeting, enough, collectively, to do a small rugby field. She took pride in having personally chosen almost everything, including the fern stands in the guise of knights-at-arms sprouting green fronds from their casques and the waist-high palm trees of beaten silver metal that supported fruit bowls heaped with costly waxed fruit. The walls, all papered in dark reds and browns, sported massive, gilt-framed paintings of noble exploits or dead game. The draperies were all three layers deep, the mahogany sideboards pierced with Gothic tracery a perfect challenge to the maids to polish and clean. No spare corner or empty shelf, Louisa was satisfied, had escaped her.

As Amelia gazed around at the stained glass, the curving arches opening on space after space, a new revelation flooded over her.

Methodists, Amelia thought with dawning astonishment, were rich.

All her life Amelia had imagined Methodists as plain folk in plain meeting halls parting sparingly with pence while droning hymns devoid of musical ornament. Her forays to service with Edwin had done little to change that impression. Yet Crisp Court gave off such a vulgar, dizzying aura of money that Amelia felt quite drunken at the possibilities.

Where does all this wealth come from, she wondered in a fever. Who are these people?

Amelia was at last face to face the new money flooding London, money from industry, railways and trade, sweat-begotten riches that were the new lifeblood of England, vastly different, so much brasher, than the genteel agriculture-based incomes that had supported the titled aristocracy for the last thousand years. This money meant to breach the bristling defences of the entrenched establishment no matter how much derisive envy the upper classes heaped upon it.

Rose was in such a state of such rapt delight that she appeared to have gone into a trance. Amelia poked her surreptitiously in the ribs.

"Stop staring," she whispered under her breath. "People will think you've never been in a fine house before!"

Well, I haven't, Rose almost whispered back as she came back to herself with a start. But I want to be inside a lot more of them. Oh, I do!

Rose still felt the hands of bearded man on her arms. Stirred up by the scent of the sea carried with him, a hundred half-buried memories of bare feet in hot sand, of seabirds soaring up the cliff faces, of salt winds blowing from America flared in her bosom. He had been a sign, a confirmation that some great change was about to happen. The dusty layers of Gresham's were peeling away, a dried husk crumbling back to reveal this spellbinding new prospect.

Yes, Rose breathed, yes, yes, this is for me. At long last, her life was about to begin!

CHAPTER TWENTY-FOUR

Henry Crisp ought to have been long gone from the house, avoiding the aggressively female tea his mother was throwing. However, he'd taken refuge in his study with a floor, a grand staircase and a tapestried corridor between himself and the feminine event in the drawing room below. The messenger from the bank, instructed to bring the confidential communication to the house, had been late, trapping Henry until the ladies should depart.

Henry wasn't thinking about his mother's guests. He was eying the thick yellow envelope at last in his hand. Hundreds of miles the news had come, out of the creaking belly of a ship, passed from clerk to clerk until it lay on the polished surface of Henry's desk. Henry tore open the flap. When he read what was inside, he would know!

Henry Crisp, though not yet thirty, was too covertly intense to retain any aura of youth. Tall enough and compactly built, he favoured suits of a shade that so blended with his baby-fine brown hair as to give an impression of sleek monochrome. Yet to look at him, one might easily guess he was the direct descendent of a sallow, black clad, perpendicular industrialist got up to look like a steam engine and suspicious of anything that diverted from the desperate business of moneymaking. Though the money served Henry now, he retained the questing, restless look of the opportunistic species, lips thinning, gaze roving in continual speculation.

He had a sharp nose and curiously fleshy cheeks rough-grained from adolescent acne scars. These blemishes showed up in certain lights, vanished in others, giving a queerly corrupt look to his otherwise good-looking face. His lips, because of the way he pressed them together, did not ordinarily betray the sensuality they showed when caught at rest. A lifetime of watching and waiting had given him superb self-control except for his habit of flexing hands at his sides when agitated. Despite the blandness of his colours, which suggested some natural desire to blend into the surroundings, there was something coiled about Henry, a sense of some smooth, deceptive mechanism ready to spring.

When at work in his study, it was Henry's custom to flick his gaze periodically about the wealth of Crisp Court like a man reassuring himself they were firmly in his possession. Though he sometimes gave in to a pleasurable grunt, more often the two lines setting themselves on either side of his mouth would tense. Despite the blessings lavished upon him by circumstance, here was a man convinced, in some endlessly gnawing way, that he never had enough.

When finished a task, Henry often meditated upon the glass bell jars on display all around the room. The jars, flawlessly polished on ornate bases, contained in their sealed interiors, an assortment of monstrous beetles, striped reptiles, feathered raptors and sinuous mammals arranged in attitudes meant to be vignettes from real life. Not for Henry the leaping swordfish on walls or stag heads protruding over mantels. Anything in his collection had to be small enough to fit inside jars, captured dustless and immobile, for Henry's delectation.

Henry was not an enthusiast about zoology. He simply liked creatures in bell jars. The creatures he chose all had to have one quality in common, a sense of unexpected, elegant predation. Fanged, clawed, feathered they sat, with parted beaks, outstretched talons, sharpened teeth. Predation they exuded, but also an air, which Henry didn't seem to notice, of barely arrested decay and blank deadness in their staring glass eyes.

On Henry's desk, which would have suited a twelfth century chancellor snatching duchies for the crown, sat the favourite of Henry's collection, a shrike. The shrike especially pleased him. Though it looked like a songbird and sang like a songbird, its beak was hooked and it fell on its prey like a hawk. Insects, reptiles, mice, other small birds fell victim to this deceptive miniature predator with its smooth grey back and roguish black mask. The shrike in the jar sat with beak parted triumphantly and wings half open. At its feet, an exquisitely preserved field mouse lay impaled on a thorn.

Henry tossed the reports from the envelope aside, concentrating only on the bottom sheet, the summary statement, written on the bank's crackling stationery. His gaze narrowed while a breath hissed out of him of shamefully avid relief. Relief followed by a sliding smile such as he would never dare let his mother see. Still no word. And over four years since any of the bank drafts had been cashed.

Yes, perhaps he could sit easy now. Perhaps he was finally free. The smile hovered, then burst into a bark of laughter.

Just as quickly, the laughter faded. A new avidity leaped into his eyes. Yes, he was safe, everything was truly his. Now to go raiding in the vast treasure trove of risk and opportunity waiting in London for someone as shrewd and ready as himself.

Essential to Henry's conquest of London was his mother's tea downstairs. Though insulated from the event by his masculine cocoon, Henry was intensely aware of its importance. The ambition that had built Crisp Court burned hotly in Henry's bosom. He was the one who had shed the smoking, pounding, sweating mills and brought the Crisps to London. He had longed for London ever since he had learned to add and subtract. London, capital of the world, a city swept along on the most exhilarating, terrifying surge of commercial energy the world had ever seen.

Just as Henry violently longed to be part of that surge, he was also acutely aware that it was the approval of the ladies who could edge the Crisps into the sphere he aimed for. Above all, Henry needed connections if he were to make inroads among the men of capital and speculation in the city. His mother awash in charitable projects and Camille married off well would be an immeasurable advantage to a fellow itching to get his fingers into the tantalizing financial pies England had to offer.

The idea of Camille advantageously wed allowed Henry to imagine himself picking over the crop of pink, voluptuous daughters belonging to the men he would do business with. He had contained himself for years. Now the tightly wound desires within him pressed against the breaking point. He had taken to dreaming of bosoms and splayed arms and naked thighs, unable to realize it was his frustrated, stifled sexuality getting ready to explode.

Yes, let mother lavish tea and cakes and fat donations upon the charity ladies, Henry thought, fixing his faith in her ability to entertain. Louisa must establish them here, so that they could transform themselves and leave the grungy source of their wealth forever behind.

The buzz of feminine conversation, the scurry of parlour maids and the rustle of Henry's papers weren't the only activity at Crisp Court. Had Henry glanced out the mullioned window he would have spotted a figure loping up the street with a stride designed to eat up distances far beyond the cobblestones of London.The weight of his single piece of luggage, the rough canvas duffle over his shoulder, signified for little in the peculiar intentness of his motion. He proved the very man who had blocked the passage of Rose and Amelia's carriage earlier in the day. With his untamed beard, his much-worn hat and his air of an adventurer, he seemed as out of place as possible in that substantial neighbourhood.

Nevertheless, he tramped on until he arrived in front of Crisp Court where he stopped abruptly, dropped his bag to the cobbles, and stared up at the facade before him. His look missed not a flourish of the polychrome stonework, a leer of the gargoyles, or an angle of the crenelations defending the rooftop. A reaction stirred, so deeply buried in the beard that no observer could have told whether it was humour, derision or plain amazement at the ambition reaching for the sky.

If such a man, improbable as it seemed, had business at Crisp Court, he ought to have slipped round at once to the tradesman's entrance. Ignoring the side lane for the lower orders, the stranger hefted his luggage and strolled up to the massive front door. What's more, he did not pay so much as glance at the bell or the haughty brass knocker. He simply pulled the door open. The gaudily tiled foyer was examined with the same keen gaze and when it reached the bear, a flash of teeth appeared. The fellow was stepping completely inside when the butler appeared, bristling.

"You there! How dare you wander in. Get away..."

The rest died in thunderstruck silence as the intruder turned his head. With a laugh, the newcomer touched a finger to his lips.

"Not a word, Mellon." He jerked his head toward the roomful of women visible through the double doors. "You've waited ten years to announce me. We'll hold out now until the ladies decide to leave."

Mellon stood rooted. The new arrival paused to reconnoitre, spotted an unoccupied salon, and stepped softly into it, duffle and all, pulling the door to behind. Only then did Mellon twitch to life and bolt toward the sanctuary of the butler's pantry. Jehosepat, he thought, there'll be the devil to pay now. Mr. Adam is back!

In the drawing room things weren't going well for Amelia. She didn't know what she had expected, but it certainly hadn't been such a collection of women, each with such vital interests to promote. She wasn't accustomed to large gatherings and certainly not to competition with personages of such position, experience and self-possession. Personages confident in their purpose, urgent about their needs and familiar with each other. With no chance to get a word in edgewise, Amelia's mouth grew steadily drier and her stomach clenched.

Everything's depending on me, she thought in a panic. If I can't make myself heard, if I don't thrust my enterprise forward, how will the Refuge stay alive! How will we all eat!

The more such thoughts assaulted her, the more appallingly certain she became that her legs wouldn't hold her if she rose or her lips open for the words she must say. Her speech, on a piece of paper folded small, had plastered itself sweatily to her palm.. Her old tongue-tied shyness increased until she was almost paralyzed. Not now, she begged it vainly, oh not now!

The very opulence of Crisp Court began to mock Amelia. The thickness of the carpets caressed her feet. The tall gilt clocks, the massive tassels tying back heavy layers of drapery all taunted her as though they had their prices printed on their sides, for Amelia now knew, from her struggles with the pawn shops, almost to the penny what each item was worth. Just to own one of these items now seemed a gross self-indulgence, never mind this great house crammed from top to bottom with meals snatched away from the poor. Lost in the sea of beaded bosoms, feathered hats and assured poses, she blinked hard against the horrible sinking inside her.

What a fool I was to write that letter, she thought in despair. What fool to think I could trade on father's name and get some notice. All I'm likely to gain is a cup of tea and a slice of...of cream cake I won't even be able to swallow!

She was nothing here. Her cause was nothing. She had flung herself insanely in, far out of her depth. And now, not only would her failure put herself and Edwin out into the street, but they'd never be able to repay the impossible sum owed to that eccentric and frightening Mrs. Fitzroy.

Stop, she commanded herself, digging her fingernails into the palms of her hands. Stop!

The appeal she had agonized over and so painstakingly pre-pared, tumbled in disjointed fragments through her head. She must remember it. She must speak. She must! Biting her lip, she ven-tured a sidelong glance at Rose, who had remained so admirably still during the proceedings. Rose had strict orders to greet people politely, sit as quietly as she could and smile, smile, smile.

High colour touched Rose's cheeks, fading and returning in arcs of pink ever since the incident with the carriage. Only natural,

Amelia supposed, after being nearly pitched out by a runaway hired horse.

Perched on the edge of her chair, Rose had been gazing about her with open wonder, as though she had never seen a marble mantel shaped like a castle gate or life-sized, enamelled pairs of blue china goats before, which she hadn't. The impact of Crisp Court was as if the wall at Gresham's had suddenly collapsed, revealing a shining world of fable on the other side. The tumbling emotions roused by the carriage accident only increased their pitch, swirling round and round inside Rose, all mixed with the print of masculine hands on her shoulders and the dizzying, memory-filled scent of the sea.

At least she's behaving, Amelia noted amidst her fluster. Glances at the girl brought on a renewed attack of guilt in Amelia. Surely it must be obvious to everyone in the room that her introduction of Rose was a total fraud.

So preoccupied did Amelia become with these notions that only the low rattle of china jerked her out of her absorption. Horrors! The maids were appearing with the tea!

They've forgotten all about me! I'm never going to get to speak!

The discussions had stopped with a finality that could not be breached, realizing Amelia's worst fear. The hostess herself was stepping to the fore.

Louisa halted in the middle of the room and all the silk, taffeta and whalebone in which she was encased halted with her. A despairing groan escaped. Rose looked sharply round and come face to face with Amelia's panic.

"Thank you everyone," Louisa was saying in what she hoped were mellifluous tones. "We'll have refreshments now. And I'm sure some of your number will be kind enough to oblige us with some entertainment."

Rose popped out of her trance. Good grief, no wonder Amelia looked like that. She hadn't got to give a word of her speech and now here came the trolleys with tea!

Louisa had been supplied, thanks to Mrs. Wharton, with a mental list of ladies who would be pleased to demonstrate their musical skills. There would be time for one, perhaps two, before the tea broke up, so her choice was critical. Relying on Althea's advice, Louisa had settled on Mrs. Minnie Halverstone, known to entertain lavishly and possessing three unwed sons.

There was a pleased murmur as the maids, white aprons over best black and white uniforms, began to pass round cups of tea and plates of cake, all with the precision Louisa and Mellon had drilled into them for this great occasion.

With Louisa's announcement, Rose actually saw the pallor seep into Amelia's lips. She also saw Louisa's gaze fixed upon a portly woman at the opposite side of the room. When Louisa walked over to the massive pianoforte, Mrs. Halverstone was already setting her teacup aside in anticipation.

Rose suffered her own horrible plunge. If Amelia didn't succeed, if Amelia didn't get to make her speech, then...their chance would be gone. Rose's own chance would vanish, the new clothes and careful coaching all for nothing. After only one glimpse, she'd be banished forever from this splendour, shut up again at Gresham's.

She could not, would not let such a calamity occur!

"We have with us today, a lady who I'm sure will delight us with a song," Louisa announced. "Would you please welcome...."

"Thank you," Rose declared in a clear, carrying voice. "I'm very happy to oblige."

CHAPTER TWENTY-FIVE

Rose swooped to her feet and started forward, accompanied by a croak from Amelia. Louisa was caught with her mouth open and Mrs. Halverstone's name frozen on her tongue. Mrs. Halverstone stared. The other women twisted in their chairs to find out who had dared to snatch the initiative out of the very jaws of the hostess.

"Miss...ah....Miss.... "

Oh God, Louisa groped in crazed confusion, what's her name...I can't remember her name...

"Rose Fitzroy," Rose supplied, gliding past.

"Miss Rose...er, Rose Fitzroy," Louisa finished in a scramble, inwardly raging that some untried newcomer should usurp the piano at such a vital crux.

Coolly, as though she had been entertaining in great houses all her life, Rose seated herself on the polished bench. The room fell into goggle-eyed silence behind her. Rose lifted her hands with a flourish, laid them on the keys and began to sing.

Upstairs, Henry had pulled out the key to his desk from his waistcoat pocket and unlocked his most private drawer. He was just stuffing the bank envelope inside when he was struck into stillness by a sound that lifted up and pierced even the door behind which Henry was barricaded. Henry's head came up. A quiver ran through his body like a violin string sinuously raked.

"What the good Christ!"

He scrambled to look into the corridor. The sound swelled round him, exuberant and beckoning. He tried to pause, but his feet, almost of their own accord, made their way toward the drawing room, furtive because male dignity couldn't allow him to be observed peeping into a nest of behatted charity ladies sipping tea. On the stairs he hesitated but the mesmerizing sound drew him on, down into the empty foyer where he still could not see.

In a fever to peer into the drawing room, Henry siddled to the only cover available, the huge stuffed bear. From under the bear's armpit that Henry caught his first sight of Rose, hair aflame in the slanting sun, fingers caressing the gleaming keys.

As Rose sang, the last shred of maidenly modesty in the gown Amelia had so carefully chosen evaporated. Rose became a confection of pinks and peaches and pearl, like that moment when the sun peeps over the horizon, infusing everything with light. A lavish blossom, Rose unfolded in the room, vibrantly reflected in the dark polish of the piano.

Henry peered unbelievingly at the creature that had been in his house, his own house, all afternoon without him so much as suspecting. Things formerly heavy and immovable shifted inside him. A progression of dry fire raced up his limbs, as though the inside of his bones were crackling. As saliva dried up in his mouth, he licked his lips. His breath began to come in low, shallow pants as the tight spring suppressing his desires for so long snapped like rusted metal. He had found the first of his risk ventures in London. He had found something he became absolutely determined to own.

Althea Wharton had spared scarcely a glance for the pair behind the greenery, so when Rose openly hijacked Louisa's entertainment, Althea was as startled as the rest.

Well! Althea had breathed admiringly. Well, well!

The moment Rose Fitzroy began to sing, Mrs. Wharton felt the hairs prickle on her arms.

"That girl!" she whispered, knowing only that a life's ambition was coalescing before her eyes, "I must have that girl!"

The arranger, the manager, the artist in her leaped. Until now she hadn't realized how little challenge she had been finding in mediocre marriage mongering, pedestrian quarrels and charity teas.

In a split second, Althea grasped the impact of Rose's being, her alluring natural sensuality, her thrilling voice and the wildness that burst out from every stitch of the high necked dress Amelia had encased her in. She felt like a farmer, accidentally cracking a toe over one of the biggest rough diamonds on the veldt.

Bolt upright, Althea processed what scraps of information she could retrieve. Rose Fitzroy was a relative of some sort...a cousin of the starkly dressed Amelia Corman, who represented some child rescue scheme.

Amelia Corman was the daughter of Dr. Lionel Radmore. Yes, yes, Althea remembered spotting the half-discarded letter and insisting Amelia come to the tea. Excellent pedigree, Althea ruminated, blessing her own foresight about the invitation, but bound to be poor, a condition Althea could detect like an odour in the air. They'd need cartloads of money to launch an assault on the heights.

Wondering what it was she would arrange, Althea paused. I know nothing about Miss Fitzroy, she thought, except...

Except in the column of Rose's neck, the lilt of her voice and her outrageous piracy of the entertainment, Althea already knew everything it was necessary to know.

Such a girl, such a precious girl would be wasted in the marriage mart though Althea had no doubt a mob of infatuated fools would vie for her hand even were she penniless. Nor would Miss Fitzroy, judging from what she had just done, take kindly to the marriage bonds. She must have been mewed up indeed not to have been in all sorts of delicious trouble already.

Miss Fitzroy's connection with Dr. Radmore was a priceless asset and would give her a fine beginning. At once Althea knew Rose's future just as much as she recognized her own ambition. For how many years had she dreamed of lifting to the peak of fame one of those rare, sought after, extravagantly adored, and extremely profitable, comets who occasionally blazed across the London firmament. Personages who needed no other claim save their own entrancing existence. Never had Althea spotted a young woman of more perilous, breath-shaking promise than Rose Fitzroy!

Mrs. Wharton sat in such a turmoil of exciting, complicated, tortuous possibilities that she scarcely realized when the song was ended. With great effort, she managed to control her inner commotion about an opportunity so great it might be quite beyond her grasp.

The song Rose had chosen, Two Lilies Bright, was a wonderfully melancholy tale of two young maidens abandoned without a home. Even Amelia had been stilled. Only when the last, melting notes died away did she suffer renewed mortification at Rose's unspeakable boldness. Yet in the cascade of applause, Rose's piratical entry was already erased. Louisa jumped to her feet and sailed over. She had forgotten all about the musical Mrs. Halverstone.

"My dear, how absolutely touching! You must be the toast of the city with a voice like that," Louisa gushed nonsensically.

Intoxicated at having had command of the great pianoforte, the finest she had ever touched, Rose turned to her hostess.

"I've just come up to visit my cousin, Mrs. Corman," she announced, "and help her saving orphans from the streets. It's the least I can do after her getting nearly burned to a cinder snatching tattered basket girls from their horrid fate!"

Every eye picked out Amelia, who blushed furiously.

The blush threw into high relief the white lines of scarring that ran up out of Amelia's high collar and reached along one cheek. Louisa suddenly remembered that this unadorned Mrs. Corman was the daughter of some important somebody or other and she hadn't got a word in edgeways since the tea began. She descended upon her neglected guest.

"Mrs. Corman, you must tell us about your experience."

Amelia coloured even more hotly. Above all, she hated to speak of that devastating afternoon which had so shifted the centre of her life. Rose saw Amelia's mouth quiver and realized her mentor was going to freeze up just at this critical moment.

"Marched straight into a blazing inferno, she did. Plucked the children from the clutches of a brute that was incinerating them alive. That's what he did with the ones too weak to work any more. Burnt them up to ashes and kidnapped new children from the street. Amelia will be pleased to tell you all about her Refuge," Rose added promptingly.

"Oh!" was all the ladies could whisper, struck speechless.

Amelia's found herself the stunned focus of the entire room. Her tongue turned into a useless leaden instrument, her body remained glued to her chair. Alert now, everyone was taking in every stitch of Amelia's maroon serge, so stark among all the silks and laces and yards of cord. All of them were tracing the fire's brand on her neck and cheek. And all of them, surely, must guess she could bear no family relationship at all to the hoyden who had just told such a whopper of a tale!

I must speak! They're waiting for me to speak! This is my only chance!

Still Amelia could not move. Her accursed bashfulness swept up in a flood. Her deception about Rose, her own poor pretensions, must blaze upon her forehead.

I should never have done it! I should never have come here! I've ruined everything. Oh, who did I think I was that I could build a Refuge and get any credit with women such as these!

Suffocated by the opulence of Crisp Court, Amelia felt drowning in embarrassment and guilt and wished she could vanish away. Her cheeks burned redder and redder against the white scars. Even the fragments of Amelia's speech had disappeared, leaving an echoing cavity in their place. Bodies would soon begin to shift. Mrs. Crisp would speak to someone else. Her moment would be lost.

Amelia squeezed her eyes shut. Help, she whispered inwardly, oh please help!

Not a word of the speech returned. Instead, Amelia's head filled with images. Baby Katie, scrawny as a plucked chicken, rescued from stinking mud. Mary, the Infants' Asylum servant. Cully covered with vermin in the cellar, jerking mutely as that wet-eyed creature lashed her with his switch. Oh, what mattered a drawing room deception in this face of this?

Mary looked at her and Katie looked at her and strength flowed back into her limbs. Just as Mrs. Crisp was turning away, Amelia rose to her feet, head high in the best Radmore spirit, her being flung into revolt by the ostentation all around.

Forgetting she had even had a speech, Amelia began to speak straight from her earnest, unvarnished soul. She told the truth about the Refuge, how it struggled to exist, how she and her husband lived there, owning barely the clothes on their backs, every penny of their resources poured into maintaining desperately needy children.

Amelia could not have been aware of the arresting picture she made her spareness in such dramatic contrast to the earthiness that hung like a cloud about Rose. In her own way, she was making a move as bold as that Rose. Her words spellbound the listeners, momentarily transported by Amelia's vision of hundreds, perhaps thousands of destitute children rescued for useful lives, children who might have no one at all should the fledgeling Refuge be unable to take them in.

Her dark-clad figure, her lifted profile, the burning earnestness of her words, and, most of all, her battle scars showing white against her heated skin, gripped the hearts of all. Scarcely a listener could not imagine Amelia plunging bravely through the flames to save the weakest of the weak. Scarcely a listener was not breathless as Amelia spoke of Mary, broken in the mines, of Katie found in a gutter and now lost, of Cully, basket child rescued from slavery only to lie, abandoned in the workhouse, because a wounded, destitute Amelia had no bed to give her. When she finished, there wasn't a one in the room that didn't feel overfed, overdressed and far too inexcusably rich to get away without instant amends.

After a long moment of silence, a buzz started up, excited and eager. Louisa rushed to enfold Amelia and Rose with her expansive presence.

"I'll have that very basket girl," Louisa pledged as the ladies began to stand up, "to train in my kitchen. Send her at once!"

Outside, Henry remained, shielded by the great stuffed bear and perhaps, the only one oblivious to Amelia's words. His devouring gaze had never left Rose where she stood beside the piano. Even when the ladies clustered about Amelia with a flurry of questions, invitations and earnest promises as they pressed their cards into her hand, Henry failed to retreat. He could feel his palms burning, his feet rooted. Nothing like this had ever happened to him. He was immobile from the blow.

Finally, the guests began taking leave of Louisa who had stationed herself just inside the drawing room double doors. Rose and Amelia appeared with Althea Wharton behind them. Althea hovered, knowing this was not the time to accost either of them.

About to make a pleasant remark to a friend, Althea spied a male figure, lurking in the shadows behind the towering bear. At about the same instant, Henry realized his predicament. Caught between trying to slip away or brazen it out as though accidentally crossing the foyer, he found himself unable to move.

Ho! Althea thought. Here's a merry case. If she could believe her eyes, she could have sworn Henry Crisp was looking at Rose with utter besottment on his face. In a flash of glorious serendipity, Althea suddenly knew how everything was going to be paid for.

"Mr. Crisp," cried Althea, seizing her vast good luck, "let me introduce you to our singer, Miss Rose Fitzroy."

Henry had no choice but to step from his hiding place. Gentlemen stood outside in thunderstorms rather than be caught within a mile of a ladies' afternoon tea.

Rose looked up at Henry expectantly, then with puzzlement. Henry responded, slow as a sleepwalker, to Althea's words. Rose extended her hand politely but Henry remained motionless creating dawning amusement in the eyes of women around him. Perhaps affairs at this upstart Crisp Court were going prove more interesting than expected. A good many women who hadn't a clue was going on, would later claim to have been present the very moment Henry Crisp became scandalously obsessed with Rose Fitzroy.

Just when the situation threatened to become acute, the newcomer stepped out from the salon behind and grinned at Rose.

"Please excuse my brother, Miss Fitzroy. True beauty renders him speechless as a post. Allow me instead to see you and your charming cousin to the door."

The civilized voice issuing from the astonishing exterior caught everyone by surprise. Rose felt her eyes going wide. The stranger bowed.

"Yes, me. Adam Crisp at your service no matter where you decide to fall out of carriages."

Adam stood almost half a head taller than his brother, and considerably broader. The vest he wore, leather side out, was decorated with a painted pattern in some vegetable dye almost faded away from wear. The rest of his clothes showed equal evidence of hard use as did his rough boots which planted themselves, wildly incongruous, on the polished marble floor.

Before anyone else could react, Rose and Amelia found themselves skillfully manoeuvred out from under Henry's nose and down the steps to where their conveyance awaited. Adam handed Amelia in, then Rose, his large hand warm on her elbow. Up close, Rose saw he had hair the colour of bark, streaked from the sun. His eyes were of an amber brown, with the sort of creases at the corners only a life outdoors could give. His words, when he spoke, were overlaid by long flat vowels that had nothing whatever to do with England. The carriage door was halfway closed when Adam stopped it, rocking back on his heels.

"I'll be seeing you," he said to Rose with a conviction that left not the slightest doubt. Adam, too, had been listening to Rose's alluring song.

By the time he watched the carriage drive off, all of the other ladies had spilled out onto the steps to seek their own vehicles. They went quickly, dying to chatter the moment they were out of earshot.

Face settling into grimmer lines, Adam strode back inside where Henry was still standing, the colour induced by Rose now drained away to a cold grey-white. The visitor grinned at the sight.

"It's true. I'm not a ghost. I'm here in the flesh, arrived in London this very day."

Henry's chest heaved.

"What in blazes are you doing back here!" he exploded.

"This," Adam returned, drawing a battered envelope from an inside pocket. "No thanks to you, but a lawyer's letter. It might have taken me two years to get it but it says our father is dead. I came as fast as I could."

Further rejoinder was prevented by a gasp behind them. Louisa had just spotted her newly arrived son and fainted clean away!

CHAPTER TWENTY-SIX

"Oh Adam, where have you been," Louisa burst out, pushing away the pillows shoved behind her. "Ten years! Ten years without not a sign except the crate with that...that monstrous stuffed bear! We thought you were dead!"

They were in the blue salon with the furor dying down and the door just shut behind Mellon and two anxious maids. Louisa could not stop devouring Adam with her eyes. What had happened to the callow youth, all gangling limbs and defiance, who had gone away? How had he turned into this big-shouldered, shaggy barbarian? A man who had simply scooped her up from the floor and carried her, as though she were made of feathers, here to the sofa where there had been such a flap about getting her to revive.

Too agitated to sit, Henry stood with his back to the window, clenching and unclenching his hands. Adam had dragged out one of the chairs and straddled it backwards, his elbows resting atop the curving back, wool shirt, canvas trousers and scarred boots clashing wildly with the surroundings. The thickness of his whiskers spread like a beard of Joshua ready for battle. Louisa expected the chair to crack any moment under his weight.

"And if you were going to come back, did you have to march in looking like a...a damned sheepherder, right into the middle of mother's guests, scaring them half to death," Henry grimaced. "God knows what they'll be saying to each other over dinner tonight!"

Adam flicked his brother a complicated look.

"A few witnesses were best just to make sure you couldn't disclaim me. Besides, you needed rescuing when you fell tongue-tied and besotted before the lovely Rose Fitzroy."

Henry reddened violently. Miss Fitzroy had ignited a tumult in Henry's breast both visceral and unexplainable.

"Adam!"

Louisa was still shaken and pie-eyed. But emotion, now that the shock was wearing off, was gushing up in her, all the emotion she had suppressed so rigorously since the disaster that had sent Adam off.

His possible death had been like a blank spot she had carefully kept in her mind. Never to be spoken of, scarcely to be thought of but always aching there unseen.

How could she have expected the wait to be so long, or the silence so awful since that dreadful ago day when Adam had been bundled down to that ship? That day when fire and calamity and scandal had turned all the Crisp lives topsy turvy. Calamity that had flung Milton into such a frenzy he had shouted Adam out of his sight and banished him to the colonies. How young Adam had been, how full of stricken confusion when the father he adored thrust him furiously away.

With a mother's eyes, Louisa devoured Adam, noticing scars that hadn't been there before, seeing how deeply the tan had burnt into his skin, weathering it like a sea captain's, a look wholly at odds with Henry who was the normal pallid shade of an English gentleman. Adam moved with supple confidence now and snapped with quick decision. His eyes had the piercingly direct look only acquired by scanning distant horizons. His hands were long and powerful and hard with calluses. His thighs were thick with saddle muscles and he sat on chairs as though they were still objects alien to him.

Memories tumbled back. A sturdy toddler racing joyously across the nursery floor toward Louisa or working and working until he had conquered the steepest stairs. Adam riding back from the mills on Milton's shoulder, smeared with oily grime, chortling with the delight of discovering some machine's inner gears and cogs.

Her first-born son was there in the room and she had feared him perished!

Suddenly, Louisa was crying, all the pent-up, smothered longing of ten years rushing out of her. Adam was across and had her in a bear's embrace, the chair overturned behind him. He held his mother with the hunger of one bitterly cut off from home and finally returned. Then, a large cotton handkerchief appeared from Adam's pocket.

"There, blow hard mother," Adam husked roughly. "It'll clear your head."

Henry's hands flexed again at the happy tears spilling from his mother's eyes. The old black bile, the jealousy, rose up as if it had never gone away, the primal conviction, rooted beyond conscious memory, that his mother, his father or anyone given the chance, always preferred Adam to him.

"Are you planning to stay," Henry demanded, bite in his voice.

An invisible whirlwind seemed to start up in the room. Old history, old resentments, old furies, which lain like so many leaves disintegrating on a forest floor, were picked up and sent flying round and round, unseen, but getting in everyone's mouth and eyes and hair, striking in a hundred sharp assaults.

Like Louisa, Henry couldn't stop looking at Adam. Angry disquiet, almost fear, flickered through his face. Adam turned from their mother as though hearing Henry clearly for the first time.

"What kind of question is that to ask of a long-lost brother?"

Though Adam was only a little older than Henry, the weathered, hardened look of the outdoorsman gave him a maturity far beyond Henry's indoor smoothness. The flush on Henry's face darkened. His memory burned with the image of Adam deliberately spiriting Rose Fitzroy right from under his nose and out to her carriage.

"I hope you'll have the decency to stay out of trouble this time."

Adam scowled involuntarily before his teeth showed again in a tiger-like smile.

"Ten years banished to the wilderness makes that a tall order, Henry. I'm not even sure I remember what civilized behaviour is like. If there is such a thing, that is."

"Why did you come back anyway? And why now? It's...indecent to come back now!"

He couldn't squelch a note of petulance, a man whose well-laid plans were now gratuitously thrown into disarray.

"What you really mean is why now, why so long after father's death."

Adam righted the chair he had knocked over, then jammed his hands into his pockets.

"I was in the west. I didn't even get the news until I returned halfway across the continent. And then it was only a note from a bank lawyer dated almost three years previous. So warm, so full of family concern," Adam ground out in bitter irony. "I took a ship as soon as I could. A trip to see if anything has changed."

His words broke off, the words of a man who had missed the funeral of his father. A man full of unfinished business. A man with things sorely amiss between himself and his departed parent.

Adam's chest tightened with grief for Milton Crisp. Louisa crushed Adam's handkerchief into a ball and struggled determinedly to her feet.

"Adam, this is your home and of course you're going to stay. I'll have Mrs. Quincy get the Kenilworth suite ready for you at once."

This produced another burst of agitation in Henry.

"What in blazes have you been doing over there anyway? God knows, you were sent enough money over the years."

Money Louisa had forced Henry, much against his will, to send.

"I might ask the same thing of you, Henry. You appear to have jettisoned everything father cared about and set yourself up in this oversized mausoleum? I can't imagine him agreeing to it. He would have suffocated in here."

The lines on either side of Henry's mouth deepened.

"The mills were outdated. We sold off at a fantastic profit when the new dock expansion came in. Why struggle with machines when London is the place to be. There's more risk capital here..."

Henry clamped off the rest, sorry his mouth had run away with him even that far. Adam's face was a thundercloud.

"I can't see him selling, no matter how many new docks were planned. Certainly not just because you wanted to."

This dart, from an old quarrel, made Henry rush to strike a frontal blow. If Adam was back, the order of power had to be established at once.

"He didn't have to do it on my say so. I did it. He gave everything to me after he fell into apoplexy."

A vein pulsed at Adam's temple. He went very still.

"Apoplexy?"

"He took a fit not a year after you left. He wasn't much use to himself or anyone else ever afterward. That's when he handed the mills over to me," Henry rapped out, aware he was informing an elder son that he had no inheritance. "He gave them to me. He gave me everything, Adam. I was the one who decided we should make the move."

Louisa watched the pair with apprehension. As Adam rose slowly, jaggedly to his feet, Henry stepped away from the window.

"He gave them to me because he finally realized I was the one with some sense. I was the one who stuck with him. I was reliable. I wasn't the one who..."

"Stop!"

Louisa felt the room closing in, not big enough to contain the two men in it together. Her cry was the same that had echoed a thousand times during the turbulence of their youth. By reflex, both subsided. How, Louisa wondered, was she going to control two such sons without Milton around to lay down the law.

"I want peace in the house and peace between you," she told them sternly. "And peace in front of Camille when she comes back from school. Do you understand?"

Adam had been away too long, had been missed too sorely to have old wounds torn open the first hour he was back. Oh, what could ail Henry that he must prod his brother like that!

Henry continued to scowl. Adam made a visible effort to control himself. With that sure-footed step of his, he moved back to his mother.

"Peace follows me everywhere I go," he rumbled between a grin and a grimace. "Now mother, how about giving a grand tour of this monument you have built. And are there any of those tea cakes left over? I'm starved.

CHAPTER TWENTY-SEVEN

Some children are born at war with each other, Louisa thought sinkingly as she went with Adam out of the room. Adam and Henry were certainly two of them. Already, the old tensions flooded back like dark smoke filling the air.

Oh, why did Adam have to be so perverse with Henry? Why couldn't the two of them just get along!

As soon as the question reached her mind, Louisa squelched it, never wanting go down that track. They were men now, and it shocked her once again that these two large male creatures were hers. Yet Louisa was wrong about Adam's perversity. It was Henry, not Adam, who had entered the world in a state of combat with his older brother. The trouble began, though Louisa had failed to notice, when Henry had been born.

Born second.

How the infant had absorbed this fact remained a mystery, but from the earliest moment Henry had seemed aware of his diminished position and resentful of it. Perhaps the annoyance the colicky, demanding baby created in his nursemaids impressed upon him a feeling of rejection while seeing those same nursemaids dote on hardy little Adam, careening about the nursery on his fat toddler legs. Perhaps it was the sight of Milton Crisp, stopping in to watch Adam thrive that drove the indignation deeper, for it only took the sight of Milton's looming form to set Henry shrieking to be noticed too. Though Milton was a man who required sons, he was not a man with much tolerance or knowledge of children, certainly not red-faced ones who howled.

"Make him stop that infernal racket," Milton would bellow at the nurse, then stomp out carrying Adam away with him on his arm.

With the instinct of all children, Henry knew where the real power lay in that large, rich household and grew enraged when Adam got preference. Ever since Henry had been old enough to understand the crippling disadvantages of being a younger son, he had been eaten with a bone-deep anger at the injustice of his own junior, inferior status.

Young Adam had not minded Henry at all at first. In fact, he had been inordinately pleased when Louisa had magically produced a new brother. In his childish way, he had been fascinated by the baby until he realized that the baby cried more often than it gurgled and that the nursemaids constantly shooed him away to keep Henry from flying into a temper.

Frustrated, Adam lost interest until Henry grew large enough to dash about and be of use in a game. Henry used his mobility to fly at Adam, an activity Adam tolerated good-naturedly until, one day, he received a nasty bite.

He retaliated by biting Henry back, hard. Henry immediately screeched at the top of his lungs, displaying to all the teeth marks on his calf. Milton was drawn by the ruckus with gratifying results. Adam received a thorough whacking without a chance to show the bite marks of his own.

The incident might have remained a triviality of childhood had not Milton also insisted that Adam apologize. Adam had taken the whacking in stride. He refused to apologize for something he didn't consider his fault. The more Milton insisted, the more dog-stubborn Adam became, revealing a side of himself the autocratic paterfamilias had not seen before. Finally Milton was driven into a shouting rage and the household thrown into an uproar. A week of further resistance despite bread, water and more whacking established in Milton's head the idea of Adam as a recalcitrant, wayward boy who needed unrelenting discipline to break his truculence.

From this small seed grew the adversarial relationship between Adam and Milton that seemed to careen from bad to worse each year. Henry was delighted. With childish cunning, he quickly learned that if he were obediently compliant, he could take telling shots at Adam from behind perfect cover. Angry Adam hardly suspected the source when he blamed for yet another misdeed it did no good to cry innocence for.

In reaction, Adam really did become rebellious, plunging constantly into the trouble he saw little point trying to avoid. As the boys grew older, Henry's animosity toward his brother did not abate. Soon, even the battles between Milton and Adam began to infuriate Henry. He felt the very towering strength of Milton's displeasure with Adam was a measure of the industrialist's attachment to the boy. Milton drove Adam harder because he expected more and knew Adam was capable of more than Henry.

No matter how much Henry seethed, Milton remained unthinkingly oblivious to his younger son. And Henry, though unable to articulate it, sensed why. Under all the conflict, Milton was secretly pleased at having produced such a stubborn, robust specimen as Adam was turning out to be.

The gut sense that his father was discounting him because of preoccupation with Adam, preyed on the Henry, triggering the latent obsessiveness in him. His cheated outrage that Adam should also be the oldest grew into a permanent affront that Adam should exist at all.

Nor could Louisa rectify this troubled state. To make up for Milton's pyrotechnics, she tried to be scrupulously fair, loving both boys equally. She succeeded only making Henry feel more cheated. If his mother had to strain to be impartial, what did that say about whom she really preferred! He grew ever more skillful at sabotaging Adam without anyone guessing what was really going on.

Milton Crisp, neither a patient man nor observant about his family, was but one generation from Josiah Crisp, the hard-driving, shrewdly practical iron dealer who had invented an improvement on the flying shuttle, taken over a small cotton mill and built it into the behemoths Milton ran. Raised in an abrupt manner to control a rough industry, Milton had no time for excuses, explanations or investigations. He demanded the same discipline and order from his children he expected from his work force. If he got it, he thought no more about the matter. If he didn't, he swiftly taught the miscreants the error of their conduct, then stomped roaring from the house.

Milton's real life was in the mills. Though money flowed in rivers into his coffers, he never gave a thought to enjoying it or using any of it to take his ease. Morning to evening, his pleasure was to be in the set of dusty offices with clerks jumping to his command and the vibration of the looms throbbing through the floor. When Milton spent his money it was to buy hard assets in the form of more buildings, more machinery, more labourers. He was still close enough to a working man himself to want to see what he owned thump and whirl and visibly earn its keep. Though Louisa had all the funds she wanted, Milton would not hear of moving out of the big, dark, unfashionable old house his father had bought and had no interest in entertainments. Louisa countered by engaging the best tutors she could find for her boys, determined to drum some refinement into them before they slipped her hands altogether.

This situation lurched along until Adam was a gangling adolescent, clumping about the house, spending more and more time at the mills after school hours. Though the streak of rebellion in the boy irritated Milton like a stone in his boot, Milton often arrived home in the evenings looking pleased, Adam trudging behind. More proof, Henry thought bitterly, that his father would always swing round to Adam in the end.

Henry stewed and ruminated and went on the attack. He used Adam's scarf to tie some firecrackers to the back of Mr. Dalmage's carriage. Mr. Dalmage was one of Milton's largest customers and it was the man's habit to rumble up in his massive old coach to lunch with Milton and then place his orders. The firecrackers terrified the horses, the carriage turned over in a ditch and Mr. Dalmage barely escaped without a broken neck.

Milton's shouts had shaken the house and sent the servants scurrying for cover.

"Very well, then," he had bellowed, "since you can't behave here, we'll send you to some place that can deal with you!"

Milton shipped Adam off to Stokely Elms, a school that specialized in taking unruly boys in hand. In an era when the best of public schools required the hide of a crocodile to endure, Stokely Elms set out to genuinely pulverize the sinners delivered into its clutches.

A school, no matter how harsh, may be survived providing it is fair. However, Adam was large for his age, dogged by his story and looked naturally insubordinate. The masters set themselves to break him. The boy's intelligent mind coped with the punitive doses of classics forced down his throat. His hardy constitution stood up to the ice in the washbowls, the four a.m. roustings, and the stale bread cubes and boiled potatoes that was the staple diet.

His spirit, however, rebelled against public birching across bare buttocks for the smallest of crimes and the near starvation for greater. Food deprivation, the masters had found, was a very effective punishment with growing boys who would think of nothing but their stomachs if allowed. Hunger was excellent discipline for the soul and sure destroyer of low carnal impulses. Miscreants were routinely starved to the point where cowslip roots, nasturtiums, hyacinths and crocus bulbs were dug up and greedily eaten, not to mention acorns secretly collected and cooked over candles into some semblance of edibility. Sweets, fruit and tuck boxes were only a distant memory to those moulded under Stokely Elms' iron regime.

Adam stood it as long as he could. Then one famished afternoon, he decided to remedy his diet by shinnying down a drainpipe with three other boys. They slipped into the woods beyond to poach some dinner for themselves. Under the influence of a book of wilderness adventures, they meant to bag a rabbit or a pheasant. To their own astonishment, the boys brought down a half-grown roe deer. Thoughts of roasting venison overcame any terrors about the enormity of the crime. They built a fire in a hollow. Barely able to contain the saliva in their mouths, they set about grilling deer meat on wands of green willow.

Unfortunately, the forest belonged to a powerful sporting lord who, despite trip guns, man traps and gamekeepers, had been so tormented by poachers that he swore the next culprit would be lucky to escape with his miserable life. The boys' fire was spotted by a gamekeeper whose shouts brought the landowner himself along with his younger son. The boys scattered, all escaping save Adam, who fell into one of the pits laid about to catch poachers. With the evidence sizzling over the coals before him, the landowner had turned livid. A deer! One of his precious roe deer!

"Strip the thieving bastard. I'll teach him!

The landowner laid on with a split branch, beating Adam until the boy had collapsed, covered with bleeding welts, half senseless. Through the scarlet haze, Adam never forgot the hands of the gamekeeper holding him brutally, gleefully steady. Nor did he forget the pale-eyed grinning son, younger than Adam, who took in the beating with an almost lewd relish as he kicked the half-cooked deer meat into the dirt. Meat which, even in the midst of his agony, Adam hungered for.

Afterward, Adam had been tossed back into the trap, a deep hole with slick wet sides no lad could crawl out of.

"Rot and die, serve you right," the choleric landlord had shouted while his son sneered over the edge.

Of the day and two black nights Adam had spent there, imagining himself abandoned, he could not afterward think. His most maddened efforts to escape only tore his hands cruelly and left deep gouges in the slippery clay walls. Nor could he even slump to the bottom in exhaustion. Heavy rains began to fill the pit with water which had reached waist height before two furious schoolmasters arrived to yank him out.

The lord, when he discovered where the boys had come from, had taken further vengeance by promptly terminating the lease of Stokely Elms. In the uproar that ensued, several masters were all for leaving Adam right where the boy had been flung. When they finally did retrieve him, Adam was thrashed again in front of the whole school, then dragged before a magistrate on a charge of poaching. He escaped prison only by reason of the staggering ransom forked over by Milton Crisp.

Though Milton's wrath had been terrible, far worse for Adam was the sight of his father writhing in obsequious apology before the lord. Milton's automatic and fearful subservience to the upper class galled Adam deeply and planted a permanent distaste for the breed. Bewildered, Adam couldn't understand that even someone as strong as Milton was still close enough to his humble roots to have a superstitious dread of a title. Milton remembered, if the boy didn't, that only a few short years before, a whole family could be transported to Australia for seven years for the poaching of a single scrawny hare. After the apology, Milton had paced his office, white fury stretching the skin over the hinges of his jaws.

"Since school had done you no good, it's time you made your own way. Don't think you're going to grow up wasting my money and expecting to have the business handed over like a plum on a platter. You'll start in the mills, at the bottom, and earn your keep. You'll sweat for anything you get. And if you can't stomach it, get out and never bother me again!"

Over Louisa's wails, Adam had been bundled out of the house and handed over the toughest foreman. Adam started lower than the commonest working lad. He sweated bales of cotton off ships, shovelled coal for the mill boilers, swept horse dung out of the yards, worked the same brutal hours in the same heat and noise as the others did. Henry's smug self-contained pleasure knew no bounds when Adam was banished to the factory floor. No one who wasn't raised to it, Henry was convinced, could last there. When Adam came limping home he would be discredited for good.

Henry and Milton waited for Adam to beg forgiveness, beg admission back into the house. Adam did not. He slept in the sheds where the mill hands slept and took on the work with grim bloody-mindedness. His young body, which had always been muscular and large for his age, was applied to back-breaking tasks. When it was discovered that he was the owner's son out slumming, Adam also learned very quickly how to use his fists.

Adam stuck it out, initially because he had no choice, then, because he found dignity there. After he had gamely beaten his share of scoffers, sweat was how he earned respect. However hard the work, the system was not hopelessly tipped against him as it had been at the school. And the tasks gave him something to take out his boiling emotions upon. He thrived in the pounding five storey mills even though the gas lights fouled the atmosphere and the noise of the steam-driven looms was so confounding a person could not hear himself shout.

At first, out of sight was out of mind for Henry. He felt vindicated, in control, almost as though he were now the only son. While Adam, in rough clothes, became indistinguishable from the lads and men he laboured with, Henry was still being educated as a gentleman in readiness, as Henry saw it, for command. He was certain he only had to wait until Adam messed up and ruined himself forever in Milton's eyes. Never did Henry miss an opportunity to subtly plant in his father's mind how unreliable Adam was, how unsuitable for the business. For the first time, Henry felt he basked fully in Milton's favour and he thought Adam a fool.

As the first year passed, and then the second and the third, Adam found that hard labour could be not only be endured, it could be rewarded. Natural ability made him advance, first as a warehouse mule, then a mill hand, then a crew head, each position won with a double effort because of who he was.

He learned to be jolly in a pub yet keep most of his pay. To Louisa's chagrin, he bet on pigeon races and played football behind the mill with the carters' lads. His regular dress was a flat workman's cap, broken at the brim, hob-nailed boots and britches of battered fustian. He spat on his hands when he tackled a task and sang rude, lusty songs when he and his mates tramped off for a half-holiday.

Slowly, Henry realized that his father was watching Adam closely, had been watching him closely all along. Under the industrialist's beetling brows, approval began to show, then a pride his cryptic grunts couldn't suppress. When Adam reached a job that required a cravat, Milton suddenly ordered him back into the house to live.

"Time you found out what the mills are really about. Get yourself a decent coat and start at the office tomorrow."

Caught aback, Adam struggled with old hurts and confusions, then drowned them all in a great leap of eagerness, a son's desperate longing for his father's approval. Milton, still prickly and glowering, harumphed to cover his pleasure at Adam's dogged perseverance among the machines.

Adam came. But when he moved into the house again, he was rough, rock-muscled and brimming with the early manhood hard physical work engenders. He sat astraddle on chairs, joked with the maids, ate ravenously of the unaccustomed fine fare and thumped about alarmingly in the interior which Louisa had laboured so hard to refine. His walk had acquired the jaunty confidence of one ready at all times to put up his fists if he had to. He no longer fit comfortably into the coat and cravat necessary for the office and he looked all comers too directly in the eye. Louisa groaned at the ruination of her efforts to polish her son. Milton developed a pleased rumble and took Adam with him to the bowels of the powerhouse when the new steam engines were being installed.

Henry, now wearing a cravat himself and training in the business, regarded Adam as a stranger rudely trying to push into a place long forfeited. Henry watched as his mother tearfully welcomed the maverick back to the fold. Unaware of Henry's seething bosom, Louisa sped about, harrying tailors and bootmakers as she set about turning Adam into the gentleman she was determined he should be. Even little Camille was so thrilled with this newfound, boisterous big brother that she forgot that Henry existed at all.

Milton worked Adam relentlessly in the office, but his demands were the demands of expectation. The harder he drove Adam the harder he seemed to be testing him, secretly, desperately hoping that the rebellious boy he had battled would become a man worthy, one day, to take over the helm of all Milton's industries.

Silently, insidiously, Henry waited for the inevitable explosion between Milton and Adam. It did not come. Adam had gained enough assurance from his years in the rough to stand his ground calmly in the face of Milton's blustering temper. The wary, lurching, mutually mistrustful relationship between the two gradually mellowed. Adam was given a desk near Milton's and clerks of his own. Adam had become, once again, the firstborn, stamped as the son strong enough, shrewd enough to survive in the dog-eat-dog world of cotton manufacturing. One day, Henry realized sickly, Adam would be in complete control!

Henry found himself edged aside, never mind that it was his own distaste for noise, machinery and bellowing at mill hands that kept him from the thick of things. Henry didn't lack interest in business. On the contrary, he was fascinated by the permutations and possibilities of sales and trade. It was the money he was interested in and not the working mills. Indeed, the more he delved into the world of commerce, the more he felt stifled by the noisy, shuddering buildings. Mills, after all, contained only so many sly, grubby workers to squeeze labour from and they produced only a single product, vulnerable to the whims of the marketplace.

Couldn't his father see, he wondered irritably, that a new era had arrived? Why sweat to make things when the capital tied up could be invested in a thousand more interesting ways? Railways, shipping, coal mines, arms manufacture, why it was all just sitting there crying out for cash. Money, once invested, did the work all by itself, growing and multiplying while its owner enjoyed his leisure, never again needing to step inside some sweltering, roaring factory. When Henry dared suggest such ideas to his father, Milton swore vehemently and called Henry a fool, as if a man couldn't live without being attached through the navel to some idiotically clanking machine.

While Henry burned at the sums of money flowing under his fingers which he could not touch, he saw Adam being taught to love the deafening trade. If Adam got control, the Crisp capital would never be pried out of the smokestacks and the shuddering looms and freed to the ways Henry longed to use it. For Henry, money's ability to grow meant ability to accumulate power. Above all, Henry longed for power. Now, even if he were to be given half, he could never bear to be left in partnership with Adam, never bear to be subject to his brother's orders, never bear to have less than complete control.

Oh, the curse of being the younger son!

Henry racked his brain, going round and round the problem to see if he could find a chink to break the growing bond between Adam and his father.

He did find one. He discovered that Adam, during his stint with the working class, had picked up one of their vices. He had learned to enjoy his pint at the pub after all the sweaty work was done. Adam still liked to slip off to indulge in a drink with his old comrades even though Milton would have been livid had he known. Drink, according to Milton, was the ruin of the working man and the ruin of the working man was the ruin of the mills. Milton, virulently temperance, was intransigent on the matter of drink.

While Henry wondered obsessively how best to turn this fault to his own advantage, disaster fell upon the cotton industry because of the American Civil War. The American South had been the main supplier of cotton for the mills and the money from the cotton had been the very lifeblood of the South's economy. Going for the jugular, the North blockaded the Southern ports, strangling trade. Any cotton shipped had to run the blockade. Any money earned either sat uselessly in a British bank or took its chances with the blockade again in the form of luxury goods, arms or gold.

The Crisp mills were soon as famished for cotton as the rest of the industry. The mill hands faced dire privation, even starvation for lack of work. Adam and Milton greeted the situation with intense worry. Henry felt only rising glee. Didn't the Crisp mills sit on an enormously valuable piece of property at the end of the proposed new railway line. Perhaps now, Henry thought, Milton could be persuaded to sell the mills for a railway terminus and yards. These would bring, as a natural consequence, a vast dock development on what was then Crisp waterfront. They'd be out of the wretched cotton business altogether, Henry thought, and into the glorious, civilized, endlessly opportunistic world of capital speculation.

Henry's suggestions were swept aside in a string of curses. The mills were the mainstay of a mill town. Milton could not conceive of any other life than that of crashing looms, sweaty bodies and floating fibres. While the dock planners looked at other sites, Henry bit his tongue and waited for the crippled production to finally move his father. Just as Henry imagined his father about to crack, the mills had an enormous windfall. A string of ships laden with cotton had braved a howling storm to slip the blockade. Milton managed to beat out the other mill owners, securing almost the entire supply for his own. With the precious cargo stuffed into the dockside warehouses, jubilation raced through the town. There would be food on the tables and clothes on children's backs, at least until this supply of raw cotton was spun and sold.

"You'll look after the shipments, Adam," Milton had decreed. "Live at the warehouses if you have to, just don't let anything happen to those bales!"

Henry seethed as Adam shouldered this grave responsibility, the final stamp of Milton's increased esteem. Then Henry discovered that Adam, while doing his job, was fraternizing with his old working buddies, merrily sharing their pints of ale.

Ah, thought Henry, if only father could see him at it. Then what would he think of his favourite!

Henry had used the key stolen from his father's office to let himself into the warehouse, to leave the bottles of gin where the men watching with Adam wouldn't be able to resist them, to pour gin into the ale jug he guessed Adam would companionably sample.

That's all, Henry swore to himself ever after, that he had meant to do. Yet while he had been at the back of the cavernous building, lurking among the bales, an impulse, a stupendous idea, had swept over him, gripping him with such force that he had to sink down and be sick between his knees.

The compulsion became so strong he could not understand why it had not seized him before. It was so beautifully, terrifyingly simple. If the cotton burned, the mills would be useless and then his father would surely, surely see reason and sell. Sell before another site for the docks was chosen!

Still vomiting, Henry had flung down a handful of lighted matches and run and run and run.

The warehouses had burned. Not just the one Adam had been in, but all of them, for Henry had not thought about the wind. Despair swept the mill workers who had raced to the site, then rage. Word had gotten out that gin bottles had been found in the ashes in the very spot where the fire started and Adam Crisp had supposed to have been guarding the bales. The workers had gone on a rampage, smashing up the mill yard and yelling for Adam's blood.

Milton had dragged his soot-streaked older son before him, all the hope he had been nurturing now bitterly crushed.

"Get out of my sight," he had bellowed, not caring that Adam could barely stand on his feet, singed and battered from his frenzied efforts to contain the blaze. "Get out of the country. Go anywhere. Just so long as I never have to look at you again!"

Protest was useless. Adam had been slung onto a ship for Canada with nothing but the clothes on his back and one carpetbag jammed to bursting by a distraught Louisa. Adam had been tossed into the ranks of the remittance men, those disgraces paid by their families to stay far out of sight. Louisa had cried for days, greatly upsetting small Camille and galling Henry with this intensity of maternal grief.

One day, the winter after Adam's departure, Milton Crisp had collapsed on the mill floor, convulsed by an apoplectic fit. Crippled, then gradually speechless, Milton had no choice but to rely on his one remaining son. Years before his wildest imaginings, Henry got his hands on the full reins of power.

CHAPTER TWENTY-EIGHT

Will struggled toward consciousness. He felt flung down a well with a load of rocks crashing after him. Oh, how his head throbbed with brazen, hideous, clanging pain.

He gave himself to greyness again, slept, woke and slept until daylight forced itself under his lids. For a long time he couldn't remember who he was or where he was or why he ought to open his eyes. Gradually, he worked out that he was Will, the climbing boy, curled up on the pungent back room mattress. An unburned candle sat on the table. The tiny hearth yawned at him, vacant and cold.

Yet he wasn't cold. Not cold at all.

Slowly, this curious fact penetrated his alcoholic haze. Another fact followed. He wasn't alone in the bed. Somebody was in there with him!

He was not immediately alarmed. In his young life, he had slept in all manner of dosses, the poor huddling together of necessity to share body heat. Yet as Will's brain began to function, he understood that no one was supposed to be in this room but Mr. Croom. And Mr. Croom was...

Will shoved himself up hastily on his elbow.

The creature was scarcely as big as himself, curled up into a tight little wad, bony knees sticking into his side. Cautiously, Will lifted the grey blanket. A matted auburn braid tumbled away from small cheeks streaked with mud and tears.

Katie?" Will whispered incredulously. "Is it you?"

Indeed it was. Katie, his single friend. She lay like one dead though her ribs moved to show she was breathing. Carefully, Will replaced the cover and sank back into the shared warmth. The fresh wave of misery about to engulf him receded. He wasn't alone now. Not at all.

He did not trouble to fathom what Katie was doing there in such a state. He only feared she might wake and run off again, leaving him on his own. He must have forgotten to bolt the door last night, a dangerous thing in that part of London.

Katie slept, motionless, until far into the afternoon, her spent body sponging up rest as if it hadn't lain down for a dozen years. Finally, when her puffy eyes flickered open, she found Will sitting at the table looking down at her, a half loaf of bread in front of him and a mug of tea. The room swam dizzily. Only two things registered in her disoriented mind as they had with Will. She was warm and she wasn't alone.

Her eyelids felt so enormously heavy she could only hold them open for a moment at a time. Fragmented impressions reached her of two chairs, a shelf with some crockery, pegs on which a coat hung, blistered wainscotting, a floor of pitted planks. All of it floated in a circle around Will's face. Will who, with rain and lack of work had grown less sooty so that even the fairness of his hair was showing through. Whenever the awful void tried to clutch her again, she fixed herself fast on that face. Now the only familiar face in the whole world. A face in which wonder, concern and a new shyness mixed in equal, anxious parts.

"Does you want a bite to eat?" she heard him ask, sounding a great distance away.

She struggled to remember what food was. Something she had craved once upon a time, wanted so badly she could have eaten old boots raw. Now it held no interest. Her tongue was so parched that food would stick like sawdust. With the faintest of motions, she shook her head.

"A drink then. I've made tea."

Only the vast importance of having a guest had given Will the strength to get up at all and light a tiny fire. He'd reeled at every and had to clutch the wall. Hung over, of course. He'd seen his pa this way a hundred times and heard the all the heavy-footed jokes.

It ain't so funny. More like being run over by old Tovey's freight wagon.

He had to help Katie lift her head to drink from the teacup. Up close, she was the queerest colour Will had ever seen.

"How did you come here? Where's Mary?"

Katie winced as if Will had ground her eye with a burning cinder. In an instant, she was curled into a ball again, the covers dragged over her head. She would not answer any of Will's worried questions. When he peeped under the blanket, he saw she was as unconscious as when he had first found her.

Well!

Will settled down, with that inborn patience of his, to wait.

He could not have imagined Katie's flight from the riverbank, fear striking through her vitals, her mind shrieking, Mary, Mary, MARY!

Katie had pounded through the streets knowing only that Mary was cold and stiff, like that the dead beggar woman Katie had once seen. Mary would never wake up any more.

Katie skidded on the slippery pavement. Acrid patches of fog stung her cheeks, mixing with her tears. Her heart was a mauled thing, forcibly torn from its frame. Instinct pulled her in a circle, back toward the only source of love she had ever known.

Weak from exertion, she stopped at last. Panic stabbed as she realized she was lost. At once, a nameless terror drove her on again, a terror of knowing she was utterly alone in a city that let you die all stiff under some stairs if you didn't sell enough to get your dinner.

Head down, she hurtled past tenement houses, old clothing stores, a hurdy gurdy man playing doggedly under a porch. She bumped into a woman struggling with an armload of baskets, then out into an open space lined with wagons and stalls. The market! She was in the market! She knew where she was.

She swayed as fresh misery shook her. The market had been a place of hope, from which she and Mary had started out with fresh red apples and the conviction that today would be the day their luck would surely change.

Leaning against a dray, Katie stared sightlessly at the late customers bargaining for leftover goods. She had not a farthing with her and if old Davy Twiggins, who rented trays, should catch sight of her, she would have to tell him the tray was lost and Mary was... Mary was...

Tears welled in her throat. The dray owner walked around and gave her a shove away from his tailgate.

"Get on wi' ye. None 'o your light fingered tricks here"

Katie lurched into a side alley among several ash barrels, never more wretched in her life. It would be easy, oh so easy, just to crawl behind the barrels and lie down.

Despite all the running, the cold had seeped so completely into her body that her arms and legs no longer belonged to her. A heavy weight pressed on her chest. She began in insinuate herself into a small space between the barrels and the wall, uncaring that it was wet and fatally chill. She was deaf to the ancient, primal voice of survival that cried out, "Not here! You'll die here!"

She had sunk to her knees when she was dully distracted by a rattle of wheels parting the people in the market street. Katie glimpsed a stolid profile in the driver's seat and froze. She recognized Nip driving Red Nell's cab.

Red Nell looks over her domain.

A small, white-hot bubble of anger penetrated the paralyzing cold in Katie's bosom. The cab was held up in the street and Red Nell was opening the door to see what the obstacle was. Suddenly, Katie was flying at the vehicle, flying into the bulk of Nell's body, hitting and tearing, while a high animal shriek issued from her throat. The attack was so unexpected and so violent that everyone, including Red Nell, was immobilized. Nell did not react until Katie clamped her small, sharp teeth around Nell's finger. Nell let out a sudden roar and flung the child to the pavement.

"Get her," Nell bellowed, blood spurting onto her skirt. "Get the wee snipe and let me tear the gob offa her. Get her!"

Katie cannonaded among the crowd, sliding from the grasping hands, flying away, so filthy and indistinguishable from all the other swarming urchins that Nell's cohorts lost her at once.

How Katie found Mawton Alley, she never afterward remembered except that she had been drawn along by the memory of a blackened face, a friend's face, as pinched as her own. It was dark when Katie felt her way to the back door and tried the handle. From the overpowering smell of soot inside, she knew she had the right place. What she feared was meeting Croom.

Bitter gusts sent her tiptoeing over the sill. There seemed to be nobody inside. Tottering, she crept forward, intending just to sit down on a chair. She encountered the edge of a bed instead. Strangely, in all that icy room, the bed felt warm and she was desperate for heat. Her head was swelling atrociously, red and yellow lights burst behind her eyes. Soundlessly, she toppled onto the mattress and crawled in.

Katie slept far into the evening, twitching and tossing with such increasing frequency that Will was afraid to leave her. When she awoke, she bore no resemblance to the sturdy, exuberant fruit seller Will remembered. She was more like a hollow shape, a figure who had had all the substance blown out of her. Her skin, between the smudges, was so pale, so almost transparent, that Will felt he could look through her to the ticking if he tried. Will felt her forehead and found it fiery hot.

"Hey, you're sick, ain't you!"

Not knowing what to do he asked again, "Where's Mary?"

Katie shrank back.

"Gone," was all she could whisper. "Gone..."

Another boy, one with sense, would have immediately pawned as many of Croom's few belongings as he could lay hands on and lit out for unknown territory. Such an idea did not occur to Will. His stout, honest heart now fixed itself on Katie for wasn't she his friend, his only friend in all London. He would no more have left her than he would have left his pa when the man was sprawled under a hedge in the rain convulsed in the worst throes of drunkenness.

"You just have a nice sleep then. Room's paid up till Sunday."

That gave them three days during which Katie alternately shivered and sweated and moaned, incoherent in the grip of the fever that ravaged her emaciated form. Will never left her side except to spend his pennies recklessly on what he thought might restore her, mostly fried mackerel and current pudding, neither of which Katie could swallow.

Alternately, Will gave her mouthfuls of leftover gin from the bottle. When her teeth chattered, he dragged Croom's spare coat over her. When her head felt like a hot coal, Will thought it a good sign, since the lurid flush kept her from the cold. In mutual need, the two children clung together, never thinking to appeal for help beyond the room door. When he could, Will curled up beside Katie, both to keep himself warm and protect his companion when her chill exceeded anything the room could produce. Katie lived in an underwater cavern tumbling with apples and bruised feet and sleety rain, rooms full of pulsing bodies and greasy, ravenous rats. She would moan and cry out. Then Will's anxious face would swim into view and a restless calm would touch her.

Gradually, Will appeared more often while the other, nightmarish things receded. Inch by inch, Katie's badly shocked mind struggled to preserve itself. To this end it threw together jumbles of things and then jumbled them some more, then welded them into a solid mass deposited in a deep, plastered-over crypt from which the happenings under the river stairs were never again meant to escape.

On the third day, Katie sat up in bed and looked at Will. All the bones in her face seemed to be visible. Her expression was of one lost in a far country with no idea how to return.

"You'll want tea then?" Will asked in joy at her improvement.

Katie accepted cup shakily. Shelter, even in adank sweep's room, was a miracle to her.

Will didn't ask again what happened to Mary. If he had, Katie wouldn't have had words for it. Or understanding. She remembered about the Asylum and about selling apples. But the immediate past was only a foggy, threatening blankness from which she wrenched herself. It had become a dark, visceral layer of bedrock on which her future must construct itself, a weight her wavering spirit must struggle to bear.

On Sunday, a key turned in the unused hall door. There stood Biddy Mack, the landlady, flanked by two lugubrious fellows in black.

"Ye didn't tell me Mr. Croom was dead," she said scratchily, her eyes at the same time going to the thin girl propped up on the bed.

"Room's paid up till today," Will answered defensively.

With this Biddy had to agree. After all, the state of Mr. Croom's existence was none of her concern so long as she got her rent. She walked on in with the men behind her.

"These gentlemen have come to clear the place of what's to be had to pay for Mr. Croom's burying. They're from the undertakers."

"Mothby and Mothby," the leaner one said. "We'll sell what we can from here. Rest'll have to come from the parish."

Under Biddy's eye the two began to sift the room with practised, furtive speed.

"Not that!" said Biddy sharply, "or that!" as the men tried to lay their hands on the crockery and the coal scuttle. "All that's mine. Let furnished, this room is."

The men had to make do with Croom's spare jacket, his spare boots, his smoking apparatus and the remaining bottle of gin. The brushes, the most valuable part of Croom's property, were in pawn, for the ticket had been in the corpse's pocket. There were no spare shirts, for Croom simply waited till the one he was wearing fell apart from soot and dirt, then bought himself another. They began to eye Will's coat and boots.

"Anything 'e bought 'is 'prentice would rightly be..."

"Oh get out wi' you. Shame! Trying to thieve the clothes from a poor lad's back!"

Prudently, the pair fled with what booty they already had. Biddy closed the door behind them and turned back to the children.

"Can ye pay up any more for the room?"

Will shook his head mutely.

"And you, girl, who are you?"

Dimly, Katie saw that Will was going to come out with the truth. Weary cunning, born of the streets, came to her.

"I'm....I'm his sister."

"Oh indeed!"

The woman looked her up and down, noting the visible bones and unnaturally flushed cheeks. Couldn't be more than nine or ten, she was thinking. And not steady on her feet if she had to do any walking.

"Well, I tell you what, you can stay the night anyway, but you got to be gone when I'm renting the place tomorrow. Folks wouldn't want to think children can creep into their rooms."

Later, Biddy passed them a wedge of cheese and a scuttle of coal from her own limited supply. Croom had been a good lodger right up until the last when he'd turned to drink. Well, a good many turned to drink and had their reasons, no doubt. A good many did themselves in too. Sometimes best all round when you saw what life was leading to.

The lad would have a tough shift in the street but he could always take to holding horses or running messages. As for the girl, she didn't have a month left in her, Biddy calculated, not skinny as a twig like that and the fever burning in her eyes. Biddy spared a sigh for what she could not help, then turned her attention to deciding which new lodger represented the most profit and the least danger to the furnishings.

CHAPTER TWENTY-NINE

"Yer got to throw a fit convincin' like. 'Ere, watch this!"

Before the eyes of Katie and Will, Fank keeled suddenly over into the straw, a thready cry wobbling from his throat. The boy's body arched and flopped like a stranded fish. His eyes rolled back, his dark teeth chattered ferociously.

"Ah, aaaah, aaAAAHHHHH!" he wheezed, and fell limp, looking beyond all earthly help, glazed eyes fixed on a better world beyond.

Long seconds ticked by. Fank did not so much as blink or move his chest to breathe. Just as Will began to fear Fank has really croaked it, the pathetic corpse leaped up grinning

"Like that. Can yer do it?"

Fank was the leader of a gang, if it could be called that, of half a dozen urchins Katie's age. Fank himself was thirteen though so undersized he easily passed for ten. Katie and Will had literally fallen in with him when they had crept into an abandoned cellarway the previous night and found themselves in a tangle of bodies huddled in old packing straw. Katie and Will gladly added their body heat.

At daybreak, Fank looked over the newcomers and spotted that rare capital in the world of pint-sized pickpockets, the look of genuine innocence. What's more, the girl, for all she tottered like a churchyard spook, had the air of having come from something better. Skinny as she was, she stood straight and bore none of the brands of the gutter such as rickety limbs, crossed eyes, or weeping patches of scrofula. And the way she talked! Why folks would fall for that like ninepins! Not to mention that she had a face the rozzers didn't know.

Fank paced the cubbyhole den, deciding what to do with this windfall. Obviously they were green as cabbages and couldn't be trusted with light finger work. Therefore they'd have to be decoys. In his racketing way, he explained the rules of the gang. Stick together. Never rat. Bring back each day's take and share it round. Fank was the brains of the operation. He kicked out anybody that didn't earn his keep and had dibs on anything he took a fancy to. Privilege of rank.

Katie hadn't been fit to walk when they left the lodging house the previous morning but she walked anyway. Will supported her with his sturdy little shoulder under her. Penniless now, he gallantly hid his hunger when tormented by the fragrance of fried eels and hot pork pies. Every half block or so, Katie had had to sit down to keep from collapsing. Will sat with her and never once thought of running off to carry parcels for a coin. Now, miraculously, Fank and his friends were going to take them in.

"All right," Fank rapped out, "let's get agoin' if we wants somethin' in our gobs tonight."

Bad weather and bad luck had dogged the gang for a week and they were ravenous. Besides, the girl looked as though she'd be dead mutton any minute. Better use her while she could still get about on her pegs.

Katie felt the fever burning in her vitals and struggled to conceal it, knowing people wanted nothing to do with starvelings reeling on their feet. Out they went and crossed one of the borders Katie had never known existed, out of the warren of mean streets onto a wider thoroughfare where people in unpatched coats and flashy dresses were beginning to converge upon a music hall. The building was bigger and gaudier than any Katie had ever seen, with fluted pillars sprouting into lush stone foliage on top. Carved ladies, partly naked, peeped coyly out between. The tall doors now swinging open for the crowd gave a glimpse of blazing gaslights and numerous mirrors within.

The capacity audience contained a high percentage of racy looking men. Fank looked Katie over critically. Wetting the corner of his shirt tail in a puddle, he scrubbed her face until it shone white and damp in contrast to her smudged neck and matted hair.

"There. Now they can see yer fiz."

Even he was a little startled by what he had uncovered, a face gleaming with an unearthly paleness and dominated by those vivid green eyes. Having no idea how recently that face had been marked by deep experience, Fank rubbed his hands gleefully. What a corker the girl would be. Oh, let her bring the hungry lads some luck!

"Just walk into the mob and drop down sick-lookin' as yer can," he instructed her. "But if they starts liftin' yer about, just sit up, dizzy like, and say yer feels middlin' fine. Don't want any of 'em acarryin' yer off."

When next Katie looked, Fank and his confederates had melted away, pulling Will along with them. She swallowed hard at finding herself again alone.

"Come girl, out of the way," boomed a portly man with an equally portly woman on his arm. "Don't know why there's beggars everywhere a fellow steps."

The fever licked up again. Katie saw the purple capillaries on the man's cheeks, and his enormous nose, up close, as through a magnifying glass.

"I'm not a beggar," she declared in her clear, unbeggarly voice. "I'm..."

And doing vast credit to Fank, she swooned at the man's feet.

Katie, used to being avoided as she tried to sell apples, could not have reckoned on the effect of a small girl suddenly taken with a fit. There was a sudden milling of music hall goers, then the formation of an agitated knot. Some cried, "Oh! Oh!" Others peered at her face and prodded at her shoulders. Very dimly, Katie heard the portly man say to his companion, "Don't touch her, Liz. Likely diseased!"

Will, standing in an alley where Fank had put him, barely prevented himself from dashing out to Katie's aid. So preoccupied was he that he failed to notice the boys of the gang, about five of them, fading in and out among the distracted people like swift, busy wraiths.

Katie had genuinely fainted. She came back to reality finding a man trying to pry her jaws open so he could pour in brandy from his flask. The fiery drops made her cough and sputter. She recoiled violently.

"Leave me be!" she cried and staggered off through the forest of skirts and knees.

Her precipitous flight caused a panic among Fank's lads who scuttled hurriedly away in separate directions. When Katie and Will got back to the hideaway, Katie sank into the straw, shaking from her effort.

"There's nobody here," Will said slowly. "Do you think they was fooling us?"

He was now so hungry he felt he could eat a plate of shoe buckles. Since Katie was too weak to leave, they huddled. Eventually, Fank and the crew came tumbling back.

"Three foglers and a purse. Could have done better if yer hadn't hopped up so soon and scarpered off. Give us a bit o' warnin' next time."

Pleased nevertheless, Fank pulled out a handful of coins and distributed them round. His boys and Katie got fourpence each. Katie turned the money over in disbelief. A night's doss it would have bought when the cold winds started, or a meat pie when her sides had been rubbing together for very hunger behind the apple tray. Some days fourpence would have been a fabulous profit yet here it was it in her hand, magically, just for falling down in the street.

"How did you get this?" she asked weakly. The coins felt unnaturally heavy in her palm.

Fank and the boys burst into hoots.

"Told yer she was green," Fank grinned. Then, turning to Katie, "It's what was in the purse an' we got a cove what buys the foglers."

"Foglers?"

They all rolled their eyes at each other again.

"Andkerchiefs. Good brass for a flash kingsman, you know."

"Oh." Katie subsided into the straw, everything distorted in her slightly unhinged mind. "You mean you...stole all this?"

Her whisper sent the gang rolling about in the straw with yelps of mirth and derision.

"Yer might say that," Fank drawled," Yer just might!"

Fank himself had no definition of theft. Whatever he could get his hands on, by whatever method, he saw as rightly his. Katie despite her life in the streets, had little knowledge of theft for she and Mary had had nothing to steal save the few handfuls of berries sacrificed to Bert. In the Asylum there had been rare instances of pilfering—an older girl spooning up a toddler's meal, finished gloves furtively switched from one pile to another to make up a laggard's quota. Lack of opportunity and fear of Jenks rather than general virtue kept the crime level low. Mr. Willoughby, of course, had been convinced the Asylum children were brim full of criminality straining to break out. Original sin, he informed Jenks, must be beaten out of children on a daily basis.

For lack of other stimulation, Mr. Willoughby's rantings had penetrated deeply. The crackling of Willoughby's unfortunate burnt moth hissed in Katie's ears. They had STOLEN! The toasting devils were going to run them through with spits.

Yet the boys ran out and soon came back, not the least bit singed, stuffing their mouths with pigs-in-blankets obtained from the pasty stand. Since it was the first food they'd had in a day and a half, they devoured it like famished wolf cubs, crumbs flying, elbows keeping the reaching fingers of their fellows away. Only Fank controlled himself.

"I'll buy yer something with your share if you like," he said to Katie. "Yer look right fagged."

In truth, he was pleased beyond words at the effect Katie produced on the crowd. He meant to work her as judiciously as he could before she keeled over and didn't get up again. Katie looked round to find Will and spotted him biting his lip while he watched the others eat.

"Hey, Will hasn't got his share," she cried, rousing for her friend.

"He didn't do nothin' but stand about lookin' daft."

"He's hungry too."

"Well we don't want 'im. Just you."

Fank had decided this the moment he saw Will shifting uselessly, gaping at Katie on the ground instead of looking sharp and trying to learn from the lads. Will was just a clumsy lump. No amount of innocent face could make up for that. Katie immediately forgot about the devil.

"He stays!"

The sudden force brought Fank round in surprise. He started to bristle.

"Who says? You?"

"Yes, me!"

Unbelievably, this half dead snip was staring at Fank unwaveringly.

"Stuff it!" Fank spat. The rest of the boys stopped eating and closed ranks behind him, meaning to pitch Will from their den. Weak as she was, Katie began to struggle to her feet.

"I'm going too then."

She made her way resolutely toward Will. Fank saw his luck about to walk away.

"Sit down! It ain't you we're chuckin' out!"

For all his size, few ever challenged Fank, yet he felt he might burn up in Katie's fever-heated eyes.

"We're going."

"Yer'll starve out there. Neither of yer could find a farthin' if it was stuffed up yer nose."

Katie grasped Will's arm. Fank saw his orders were no use. Pride struggled sharply with practicality.

"Oh all right. He can stay then. But you feed 'im."

And we'll see how long that lasts, he snorted. Givin' away what she's scraped for herself!

To Fank's astonishment, Katie gave Will all her pennies. He went out and came back with some scrupulously purchased beef pudding. He swallowed his share in a single gulp then watched as Katie was unable to eat more than a bite. The rest of the gang swarmed about her in the unbelievable hope that she might give them her leftovers. Instead, she passed the heavy stuff to Will who dispatched it instantly.

Determined to regain his ascendancy, Fank went for a walk and eventually came back with a gaudy scarf which he tossed at Katie.

"Tie this over that tatty mop o' yours. Y' won't look so much like a beggar."

Katie struggled from a half conscious doze to find the cheap wool warming her cold ears.

"Where did you get it?"

Fank grinned. The boys let out a snide giggle.

"The canty stalls. I'm fast."

In fact, he had taken considerable risk to whip the thing into his pocket.

"Did you buy it?" Her life selling apples now made her mind revolve obsessively on economic matters.

"Don't be a clod!"

Stolen, thought Katie again, but the sting was drawn from the word. She was deep in the straw, teeth chattering from chill. Under the scarf the heat of the fever stoked itself again, radiating downward till the shivering stopped.

Throughout the next days, Katie existed mostly by force of stubborn will rapidly shredding toward the last of its resources. Fank, bent on profit and expecting Katie to expire any minute, took her out as often as he dared and watched her drop in the street while he and his lads buzzed among the crowd, picking pockets as fast as they could. When Will objected, Fank jerked his cap rudely at him.

"Earn yer own keep then, useless git. Then maybe she could have a decent kip in the straw."

The fever, like a malignant parasite, seemed to devour whatever nourishment Katie got into herself. Nor did drinking the unwholesome drinks the lads brought her help. The last time she went out, her mind was so blurred she followed Fank's instructions like a blind girl in the dark. Will, who had been feeding himself from her share of pennies, made up his mind to desperate action. He told Fank that he, too, meant to pick pockets.

"No! Yer stay outa the game. Yer'd give it away first try. Me an' the lads 'ud scarper. Leave yer to the rozzers. They'll put yer in the clinker till yer rot like a turd!"

Will looked at his feet mutely, burning with the contempt of the other boys.

I can do it if I want. I can!

He had watched with all his might as the lads slid among the crowd. Whipping hankies looked simple as pie once you got your eyes sharp for it.

They'd had a capricious run of sunshine with corresponding increase in music hall goers. This time the wind was back driving and cold. The more cautious lads didn't like the wind. Though it disguised touch of seeking fingers, it was just as likely to blow back a coat flap to reveal all. However, the gang was starving as usual so they hurried Katie off to where yellow light spilled out and cabs were starting to line up.

Katie, hanging onto Will, felt as if she were walking on felt cushions. The fever was making her sweat, so the wind felt wonderfully cool. Loosening the scarf, she exposed her neck.

"There," Fank hissed, pointing her to the steps where the crowd was converging. He and the rest spread out.

Katie drifted into the milling crowd, fragile as glass. Sometimes she experienced moments of exaggerated clarity and this was one. The music from inside the hall, sounding magical, tinkled around her mixed with the bursts of laughter. In slow motion, as from a distance, she watched herself turn around on the steps, her ragged skirt belling out from her. Dramatically, she crumpled to the ground.

She had more than the usual effect, owing to the grace of her fall and the sheen the gaslight cast upon the almost pellucid planes of her face.

"Make room, make room," came the immediate response. "A girl has fainted here."

The boisterous music hall goers, good-humoured in anticipation of the show, gathered about Katie, wanting to help, unsure what to do. Fank and his minions were among them like ghosts, relieving them of their portables.

And so was Will.

He slid up behind Fank who had chosen a burly man with a lot of coat. Fank was leaning close to the man, trying his trouser pocket. Against the shield of Fank's body, Will decided to go for that same fellow's tail pocket where there was sure to be a handkerchief. As he had seen Fank do, he tried to cover his motion with one hand while slipping the other into the pocket to make off with his handkerchief. His fingers caught on the fabric edge.

"Hey, what's this," the man growled, and in an instant had Will by the wrist and Fank too. "Little sneak thieves is it?"

Will was frozen with fear and could only see, out of the corner of his eye, the other lads taking to their heels around a corner. Fank went loose in the man's grip and clasped the burly arm with his free hand in appeal.

"Oh sir, I wasn't stealing nothin' I was trying to get to my sister, I was! Look how she'd taken sick!"

Fank tugged hard in Katie's direction, but the man's iron hold did not relax.

"Oh ho, I know what you were up to. You were sticking your filthy paw in my pocket."

Fank peered up his captor in wide-eyed indignation, his entire scrawny body thrust bravely straight.

"I'm no pickpocket, sir! No me. Me dear old mu'ver would tumble in 'er grave at the very idea. Yes, tumble she would, sir, 'er that was as godfearin' a Judy as ever was spawned..."

"Shut up, you nasty little robber. I caught you red-handed didn't I! And that 'sister' of yours is in on it, as far I can see. She isn't going to get away with it either."

The big man began hauling Will and Fank forcibly in Katie's direction. Will, seeing the danger, came to life.

"Katie, Katie, get up! This man is goin' t'get you!"

Katie, sunk to some netherworld, heard his cry. Heroically, she began to stir, a laboured sigh heaving her chest. The street swam before her eyes, a jumble of legs, cab wheels, lamp posts. The man had halted, yelling for a constable he spotted passing the end of the street. Seeing the blue suit approach, Will panicked and began to fight with all the strength of his bony, soot-grained body.

"Let go 'o me, Let go 'o me," he protested, twisting and leaping, perfectly blind to the ferocious warning grimaces from Fank.

Will's yells ballooned inside Katie's head. Somehow she got to her feet. Somehow she staggered through the crowd toward Will's panicky voice. There was something in the way though. A cab horse that had just pulled up.

Katie tried to crawl underneath. The scrape of her head on the animal's belly sent the animal into a curveting jump, knocking Katie down. Before anyone could pull her free, the horse twitched up a hind leg and struck Katie a glancing blow along the side of the head with one of its iron-shod hooves.

Katie fell bonelessly to the cobbles though only Will seemed to see what had happened to her. Appalled, Will then redoubled his efforts to get to her, half dragging his captor and Fank behind.

The policeman puffed up.

"What's the trouble here?"

"These lads were trying to pick my pocket," the burly man snarled.

"Were they now?" The policeman eyed Will and Fank as if they were a new species of cockroach. "Catch them with anything?"

Had his hand right in my pocket, the sneaking creep. No mistake about it."

Well then," rumbled the policeman, "I had just better take the two of them in to the..."

"Gracious, what's happening here," spluttered an authoritative female voice. A tall, limber woman with a lively face, towering plumes on her hat and a snake peeping from a wicker carrying case stepped over. Madame Zofta worked as a contortionist just before the intermissions. She could not bear to see children bullied by the police.

Half a dozen versions assaulted the woman's ears.

"Nonsense!" Madame Zofta scoffed to the burly man and the constable. "Picking pockets! I don't believe a word of it. How could such adorable lads be so dishonest!"

Madame Zofta knew perfectly well what the lads had been up to but that made no difference. Having grown up on the wrong side of the law herself, she stood automatically with its victims. The burly man launched into indignant protests, a brick shade mounting his neck. Fank clutched his heart with his free hand and screwed his face up into the most piteous of appeals.

"Oh bless yer 'heart, ma'am for noticin' a poor, simple lad wot is bein' 'ard done by. I was only 'ere ter earn a penny fer me old granny wot is sick in 'er bed. And 'elp me sister wot you can see 'as fainted from 'unger there and been stepped on by a 'orse. Me mu'ver up in heaven..,"

Madame Zofta silenced Fank with a penny from her purse and a wink earned for his performance. A fleeting grin rewarded her as Fank clapped the coin to his bosom and dropped to his knees, actual tears popping out from beneath his lashes. His weight tugged on the burly man and made Fank awkward to hold. Madam Zofta turned again to Fank's captor. The crowd that a few moments ago would have been glad to lynch a pickpocket, had begun to growl balefully in its throat. There were isolated cries of, "Let the boys go there, hey!" And, "They weren't doing any harm."

"There sir, surely you cannot continue to accuse such a poor, poor lad of picking your pockets," Madam Zofta declared.

Against the change in the crowd and Madame Zofta's hat plumes, the burly man lost conviction. His fingers loosened, releasing the boys. Madame Zofta chuckled softly and slipped away toward the stage door, all without noticing Katie prostrate beside the cab. The constable, thwarted of his arrest, glowered at Will and Fank.

"Get out here and stay out if you know what's good for you. And take that chit with the fainting fits out with you!"

The policeman trudged off the way he had come. The cabman, who hadn't moved from his seat, stared down at Katie.

"Ain't a fit. Another corpse for the wagon, if you ask me." Absolving his horse of all responsibility, he added, with melodrama, "Could even be the cholera!"

A fearful murmur rushed through the onlookers. No one had forgotten the great cholera epidemics of the fifties that killed thousands. With a hoarse cry, Will darted past and began to shake Katie.

"She ain't dead! She ain't!" Tears were starting up in his eyes. Katie felt far too hot to be dead.

Will tried valiantly to lift Katie but couldn't despite his sobs of frustration.

"Cholera!" somebody else repeated, and the crowd stepped away from the child who bore such a clear stamp of death. Oh, those bad, bad boys, bringing her out like that! Where was her mama? Who was looking out for her to let her on the street in such condition!

Suddenly, Fank was beside Will, yanking up on Katie's other arm. Together with Will, he dragged Katie at breakneck speed out of the open street and around corners until he found an empty alley. Without ceremony, he dumped Katie on the cobbles and snarled at Will.

"Yer two thick clots! Yer stay away from us from now on, almost gettin' me nicked! She's done for anyhow and we don't need no stiffs lyin' about trippin' us up."

Fank sped off, leaving Will crouching over insensible Katie at his feet.

CHAPTER THIRTY

The dress caught Amelia's eye, brown fabric so filthy and tattered. it evoked only a bare flick of memory. Amelia did not have time for flicks of memory. She was intent only upon getting out of the door of that grisly institution and into the open air as fast as her legs would carry her.

With her boost from Mrs. Fitzroy and her heady success at Crisp Court, Amelia had plunged headlong into expanding her operation. The spaces in the fine new building cried out to be filled up. Renewed faith in Providence buoyed Amelia up.

Because of Cully, the single child salvaged from that horrible cellar, Amelia made a momentous leap. She couldn't restrict herself, as others did, to the "respectable poor". No, she must search out the neediest, most pitiable cases, no matter where they were to be found. Lice-infested, spindle-ribbed, droop-lidded, or halt, they would be the penance whereby she paid her debt over the deception about Rose. Since she lacked the resolution to brave the nearby rookeries, teeming with crime and belligerent drunkards, she hit upon walking the hospital charity wards. But once she had crossed the grey, forbidding threshold, she unwittingly stepped into an encounter that left her fighting nausea against the wainscoting

"You'd better rest and come back another time," the matron suggested, hiding her impatience with these lily-faced do-gooders. "None of the need is going anywhere."

"No," gasped Amelia," I will...go on. Just let me get my breath."

Overpowering fumes of carbolic permeated the place, still not strong enough to hide the stench of wasting bodies, misery and death. Previously, in the streets, Amelia had seen poverty, beggars, drunkenness and hunger. In the female wards, she came face to shocking face with senile old women coughing their last, unwed slop workers screaming in childbirth, wives battered insensible and prostitutes horrible with knife wounds.

Amelia managed to get as far as the children's wards where tubercular ulcers, limbs mangled in factory accidents and babies burned black from falling into fireplaces finally drove her out. She was almost to the outer door when the twitch of memory compelled her to turn and stare the bundle lying in the shadows.

The girl had been hastily laid on a floor pallet, not yet undressed or washed, far too filthy to get near a bed. Her face was turned to the wall, a frowzy, greasy braid obscuring her face. Her breath came in the rapid, shallow pants of the very ill. Under the bits that clothed her, there seemed to be nothing left but bone.

It took all of Amelia's resolution to pull back the matted hair to see. The face was the face of a ghost, plastery white under the grime, bruised and sunken about the eyes. Amelia felt the floor tilt.

"Katie! Katie...is it you?"

Katie neither moved nor responded. Amelia ran to get the matron in charge. Matron sucked in her lips.

"Oh, don't expect anything. They get starved down like that then they get a fever and that's the end of them. That one's had a nasty crack on the head as well. You can talk to her brother. He's been hanging about the door since she came in. Pair of pickpockets from the look of them."

Pickpockets? Brother? Who could be masquerading as Katie's brother?

Will was huddled in what passed for a waiting room along with other relatives forbidden entry. A cup of tea and a bun got the story out of Will, straight and unvarnished, while his simple, distressed soul shone from his eyes.

"You've been a friend to Katie," Amelia said, not caring if he were a pickpocket or not. "Let's go and see how she is. Then I know a nice place where you can spend the night."

At that very moment Katie was being swabbed off by one of the rough women employed for the job. As she stripped off Katie's rags, her hand pulled out a tattered band which seemed to be but one more strip of Katie's ruined clothes until her fingers caught the faint crinkle inside it. Surreptitiously, the woman peeled the rags back and gaped. Money! Bloomin' fortune, it looked like. This scrawny sneak must've stolen it whole and stuck it down her dress so nobody'd find it.

What she held was Mr. Jenks' ill-gotten skimmings which Mary had stolen and stuffed into Katie's bodice. Katie never had an inkling what the bit of cloth contained.

The woman's hands trembled, for she thought in pittances. Fear welled up at the unexpected windfall. Such luck could only be put in her way by the devil. The hair pricked on her scalp as dread and greed battled within her. Then someone opened the door at the far end of the hall and greed won. Hastily, the woman shoved the packet into her own bosom and slapped water over Katie so vigorously as to puddle on the floor.

When Amelia and Will returned, they found Katie reeking of lice killer, and tucked into a coarse gown on a pallet. Hot and flushed, she was pitiably thin under the sheet. Her forehead bloomed with a swollen bruise curved like a horseshoe.

"She wasn't bad as that, even back in the room," Will muttered worriedly. Yet he'd feared she was dead in the alley after Fank dumped her. His cries had halted a wrinkled coster woman with a barrow. Laying Katie atop the potatoes, they had got her to this ward.

Oh why did Amelia suddenly remember a tiny, irrepressible baby waving its arms at her in the Infant's Asylum. A saucy, red-headed scrap thriving determinedly. To have journeyed so far and come to this!

Amelia sank down beside Katie and took up both small, limp hands.

"Katie dear," she pleaded. "Katie, wake up."

Hot pity swelled in Amelia's chest and a desperate desire that Katie should live. She hadn't realized, until now, how much she loved the child. As yet, none in Amelia's care had died.

Katie drifted in a deep muffled blackness pierced now and then by tongues of flame. The fever was recurring with full force, attacking a constitution finally too battered to resist. At her lowest ebb, Katie's body grew heavier and heavier in the darkness, sinking toward the fiery bottom where she would be immolated, burned away until there was nothing left of her, not even ash. She would feel nothing, know nothing. Everything would be over. Uncaring about devils with toasting forks, she drifted downward even as she felt someone rocking her and a voice trying to penetrate.

"Katie! Katie, can you hear?"

Not the most loved voice in the world. Not Mary's voice. But a lovely voice, a voice she knew. Slowly, Katie let out an exhausted sigh.

"Katie! You must not die!"

She was being shaken now, and that was uncomfortable. Her brow furrowed. She wanted to keep drifting towards oblivion, but there was so much urgency in the voice, a voice she had once so much wanted to please.

Like a weary sea bird caught in a dive, she stretched out crumpled wings and slowed the plunge. For a moment, she hovered uncertainly in the gloom, listening to the soft words, pleading and insistent. "Come back, come back," it implored. "We want you to stay."

She paused, puzzled, irritated, but unable to resist turning to the cool hands cradling her forehead. Her crumpled wings unfurled a little further and beat heavily back into the cold upper air.

It took forever to get her eyes open. All she could make out, at first, was a dim form bending over her. The form was familiar. She forced her lids wider. Fine, severe features swam into view, the dark hair, the cameo brooch at the throat. Katie's mind began to search. Her lips barely moved with the effort.

"Miss Radmore?"

"It's me, Katie darling. I've come to take care of you."

Hands touched her gently, the way Mary's used to. The voice wanted her, really wanted her to stay. Will, behind Amelia's shoulder, was twisting at his shirt as though he meant to twist the tail clean off.

Katie closed her eyes again and felt fingers pushing back the tangle of hair at her brow. A banging, metallic pain had started up on her forehead. Why had she not noticed it before?

"Katie, we're going to find a home for you. Away off in Canada where there's nothing but green fields and sweet warm sunshine and...and other children to be your friends. There's women there that want a little girl like you very badly. They bake plum pies every day and have...kittens in the barn..."

Oh, lass, yer should hear the larks. Like regular music boxes they are, climbing up and up over the moors till yer can't even see 'em. And green linnets, too, singing their hearts out.

Katie gasped in breath with a suddenness that startled Amelia. Fantastical pictures tumbled through her mind.

"Will...will there be...larks?" she whispered in a voice so thready Amelia could hardly hear it.

"Of course there'll be larks," cried Amelia, who would have promised kangaroos and hippogryphs.

"And...Will can come too?"

"Of course Will can come."

Katie ruminated on this pledge. Slowly, the black void began to recede, spread over with a vision of a place she had never been. She saw herself walking over acres of sweet scented purple where the birds sang and the hares jumped from the market cages and played games about her feet. She would never be cold again.

A spark, almost extinguished, rekindled. Hope took up residence once again in those green eyes. When Amelia, unable to speak for emotion, shifted the pillow, Katie even managed to turn her head. Larks! She was going where she could see larks!

"Well, can you beat that!" exclaimed a nurse walking by with duty rosters in her hand. One less they'd have to carry out in a box!

CHAPTER THIRTY-ONE

"Come, my dear. You must see the garden square at the back. The very spot where Black Rob shot Sir George Alcott dead in a duel!"

With sheepdog skill, Althea extracted Rose from the chattering guests gathered by the piano and herded her toward the stairs. Her palms tingled unbearably. The prize was so near. Now to secure it!

Althea realized that speed was of the essence. Like Nell, she sensed in the girl the frustrated forces ready to erupt. Rose had to be shifted, as soon as possible, under her wing. She arranged an intimate little musicale. Rose and Amelia were invited. Louisa Crisp was also asked, but not Henry. No use, Althea reasoned, to add that complication before practical arrangements could be made. About Louisa's other son, that, rough-hewn creature striding in out of nowhere, Althea could not spare the time to ruminate.

The musicale was a display of Althea's power for anyone with a grain of discernment to see. The guests, a selection of Althea's more influential friends, were lively, easy-going, speculative people steeped in a wry worldly knowledge quite lacking among the earnest ladies of Louisa's tea. They were people with impressive invitations to extend, but only at Althea's behest. People who definitely were not Methodists.

Althea's house with its Georgian front, graceful fanlights and ivy-mantled walls was as steeped in layers of living, as Louisa's was screaming with raw newness.

The well-used possessions of generations of Whartons mixed in comfortable familiarity. Sofas with curving backs and commodious arms were quite content to display their fading brocade. Dusky Aubusson rugs showed the traffic of half a century imprinted on their faces. A savour of Regency intrigue and dalliance hung about the ribbon-backed chairs and the marquetry tables worn at the edges by endless games of whist. The time-clouded, gilt-framed mirrors still seemed to reflect languid bucks making outrageous love to ladies in wispy, high-waisted Empire gowns. The graceful walnut writing desk held secret knowledge of flirtatious notes happily dashed off. One almost expected one of the dim, genial old portraits to wink as one walked by or the loveseat to sigh at the tales it had to tell. This house, with its reassuringly old, slightly tattered air and its rambling rooms, declared established legitimacy and was a major foundation of Althea's cachet.

Against this mellow atmosphere, Rose glowed like a bright splash of spring. Althea had observed Rose closely during the musicale. The girl was fresh and unjaded, that was for sure, Althea thought, seeing the pleasure with which Rose looked about her and the merriment she lavished on her songs. Rose also ate with gusto which Althea also approved. Ladies who ate with gusto did everything else with gusto too.

The impression Rose made on her guests, even those who wore their roué air like an amusing cloak, was everything Althea could have wished for. The gleams in their eyes told Althea how easily Rose could be launched, how handily managed into that fast-paced world awkward debutantes could only quake to think about.

Yet Rose, she was pleased to see, was not melting or fluttering before even the outrageous flattery coming from Sir Geoffrey White and usually blasé Lord Cedric Blake, both quite comically taken with her.

Rose gazed back as though they were some new species of biped and she couldn't wait to see what they might do next. Nearby, Louisa Crisp was containing a paroxysm of delight at being part of this select gathering. Althea smiled warmly at Louisa. She has no idea, Althea thought, how closely she's going to connected to the progress of Miss Fitzroy.

Yes, it was not from Rose's performance, but from the faces of her friends that Althea knew her instincts had been right. Though Rose's honey-drenched soprano might rival Jenny Lind, the Swedish Nightingale adored for a decade, Althea didn't base her judgment on talent. Rose, Althea suspected, lacked the depth of musical training, the knowledge, the experience of the true musician. Rose's appetite for life, her obvious eagerness to get to it, all of it, revealed her refusal to subordinate every other impulse to the austere demands of art. And thank goodness. Who but a madwoman would want to subordinate life to art? Thank goodness Rose was not possessed by that particular demon.

Nor for Rose the stodgy marriage market, the awful strictures of demure respectability. No, Rose had been designed by nature and circumstance to be, purely and brilliantly, a sensation. That was about as closely as Althea could define it. Every once in a while there appeared someone with a blazing inborn magnetism that made the trappings about it secondary. Such a woman might be a grande coquette, an admired songbird, a radiant personality, a goddess of the stage, a beacon of light or a, but a sensation was all of these rolled into one. Rose could be exactly *succès de scandale*, a piquant new taste to rouse jaded, feverish, ever-questing London Town. Oh yes, how very much, and how profitable, Rose Fitzroy could be with the right hand, the right vision to guide her.

Though Althea had paired Amelia with the garrulous Edith Balfour, she spotted Amelia's twitch of anxiety as Althea herded Rose away. Amelia had been sticking to Rose like a cockleburr, looking oddly horrified as Rose described her family home to Sir Geoffrey, evidently a hilltop Cornish manor with "two towers in the front and Moorish servants saved off a shipwreck. And cattle," Rose didn't hesitate to add, "so sleek the dragonflies slip off their hides when they land!"

Indeed!

Althea stifled a chuckle. The more she watched, the more fascinated she had become by the interplay between the severely proper Amelia Corman, who was trying so hard not to squirm in her chair, and the ebullient Rose. The more Althea searched for similarities of shape and feature that might proclaim them relatives, the fewer she found. If Mrs. Corman actually was a cousin to this frisky hoyden, Althea might just have to eat her bedcap.

Oh well, Althea dearly loved a mystery. Her most discreet inquiries had been unable to turn up information on the girl and her contacts didn't reach into distant Cornwall. What wouldn't she give to know how Rose had really come to be connected to the exceedingly respectable Mrs. Corman!

Stroking a grey tabby curled beside her, Althea smiled to herself. She would find it all out for Althea was a genius at winkling out confidences. There wasn't a person on earth who wouldn't, she had perfect confidence, sooner or later, unburden to her if encouraged enough.

The immediate question was whether Rose would want what Althea wanted. Could Rose be controlled? If the girl was worth anything at all, she couldn't. However, she could be managed, with scarcely an idea of whose hand was on the rein.

Amelia Corman might present more difficulty. Far too subtle to make Rose commercial, Althea knew there was nothing like a heart-tugging charity to provide cover. If the venture was to work, Rose and Amelia were inextricably bound together. The exemplary Mrs. Corman would keep Rose in the respectable mainstream. Rose, if handled right, would pour more money into Mrs. Corman's Refuge than the woman could beg in fifty years on her own. The way to control Amelia was to control the conduit through which donations, the lifeblood of the Refuge, flowed.

Stainless angels of charity, however, were not the folk to negotiate what Althea had in mind. When the refreshments were served, Althea deftly whisked Rose from the room.

Rose followed Althea up the curving stairs, along a wide corridor and into an unexpected sitting room at the back. The room was as gracefully worn as the rest of the house. A tall window looked out on the hidden park which made up the heart of the block, shared only by the householders abutting it. Fresh tea under a knitted cosy steamed on a side table. Iced cakes sat on a scalloped plate. A private domain away from curious ears, Althea had long ago discovered, was essential to anyone with the faintest interest in arrangements.

Rose immediately sailed over to the corner where a large, untidy parrot crouched on its metal stand blinking with sardonic yellow eyes.

"Oh!," Rose chortled. "What a disreputable fellow he is."

Althea laughed and sat down at one end of the sofa.

"That's Squib. I keep him to remind me of youthful folly."

This was quite true. Squib had been given to Althea by her first and only love, the sea-going fellow she had been so foolish to run off with. She had no idea how old Squib was. Parrots lived to be a hundred, people said and Squib was well past his salad days. Constantly shedding lime green feathers on the floor, Squib was a shabby, squawking, bad-tempered bird which all of Althea's servants longed to strangle. Althea dearly loved the troublesome old fowl whose hoarse remarks had followed her through all the changing circumstances of her life.

Squib was one more essential part of the comfortable, gracious house, a place old-fashioned and sentimental, where Althea found herself attached to timeworn furniture and cherishing aged cats. For all that the house gave the impression of old money, it was old insolvency that nibbled at Althea's heels. Althea hadn't the least intention of giving up the genial domicile where she fitted so well or the devoted staff who cared so lovingly for her every need.

So, to the game at hand! Althea hovered in a final, considering pause. Then the tingle of the adventurer moved through her.

"Sit down, my dear," she murmured, going for the tea tray and deciding on the gamble. "I've been dying to have a cosy little chat."

Bless the coming London Season, Althea exalted, chock full of balls, entertainments and private musicales, all them just waiting to be ignited by the firecracker that was Miss Rose Fitzroy!

CHAPTER THIRTY-TWO

"What you were thinking of, inventing that Cornish manor house? Don't you know people have connections all over the country!"

Rose hadn't said a word all the way back from Wharton House and said nothing now. Her hands were folded demurely in her lap and her attention fixed upon a spot on the upholstery, disturbed only when they drew up in front of Gresham's. Perhaps the girl had been properly awed by her invitation, Amelia reflected after seeing Rose safely inside, and finally been convinced to behave.

Had Amelia noticed the turbulence in Rose's grey-green eyes, she might have turned the carriage back on the spot. Rose had been sitting so still, breathing so carefully for very fear that she might burst into whoops in Amelia's presence. Her heart pattered, her thoughts threatened to fly loose in the whirl of possibilities Mrs. Wharton had put into her head.

"Change your dress, Rose," Mrs. Gresham ordered as Rose stepped inside. "We dine in half an hour. All of us look forward to hearing about your day."

Mrs. Gresham took the great front door key from her key ring and locked the door again just as she always did. The moment the lock clanked, Rose was overcome by an intense desire to rush outside again. Gresham's closed in like a suffocating blanket. The smell of cooking that always wafted from the kitchen, the air stagnating inside windows that were never opened, clogged in her lungs. Not since those first days after coming up from Cornwall had she felt so frantic to get out.

She knew better than to reveal the impulse. Now Rose found Mrs. Gresham eying her hat and her gown and the very flush Rose brought in on her cheeks with a famished interest that suddenly made Rose flinch.

Why, she's trapped in here herself, Rose suddenly thought. A leap of adult consciousness showed her how thin Mrs. Gresham's life really was. Like the other inmates, Mrs. Gresham also salivated over any speck of novelty that would enliven existence there.

I must get out of here, I must!

After Crisp Court and Wharton House, Rose now understood what a mingy, iron-grilled prison Gresham's really was and a fearful thought occurred. After those tall tales she had told about a family estate, what if she were traced to this place! What if Mrs. Wharton discovered how many years she had spent right here in a dingy, back street, monotonous jail!

Well, nobody was going to whip away this glorious chance, not if she had to squeeze out through the keyhole to make what that amazing Mrs. Wharton talked about come true.

Rose had drifted down from Althea's private sitting room in a daze at what had just taken place. She couldn't even remember the words. She only knew that Mrs. Wharton had quite calmly laid before her a proposition perfectly dizzying in its boldness.

Without being able to explain it, Rose was certain in her bones about its rightness. During all the years Signor Abruzzi had been filling her head with exaggerated tales of his divine Italian diva, Rose had longed for those same splendours. Now, straight out of nowhere, the means had dropped into her lap.

"My dear," Mrs. Wharton had smiled, looking ever so kind, "you've seen what a simple invitation to the right house can do. I can make you madly in demand if you will accept the guidance of my hand."

Rose had stopped in the midst of biting into a current cake and stared hard at the diminutive woman. Mrs. Wharton was calmly sipping from a flowery china teacup as though she made girls the toast of London every day.

"And why would I need guidance?" Rose asked, a flag of perversity raising itself as she remembered the admiration she had aroused in the salon. She couldn't swallow any of the current cake for fear that Mrs. Wharton was joking.

Althea laughed her warm, confidential laugh, not taking the least offense. She poured herself more tea and blinked her lemur eyes.

"It was I, you will notice, who arranged the invitation here, I who got you to Crisp Court and I who can manage every other invitation you'll need along the way. Oh I grant," she added comfortably," that you could become very much in demand by yourself. But should you choose the wrong houses, why the right houses won't have you. And, if the right houses wouldn't have you, why pretty soon the wrong houses wouldn't have you either. This is the Season, my dear. Nine day wonders come and go like fireflies. Sensations are managed."

What sort of sensation remained tantalizingly vague. Rose felt very inexperienced. She liked Althea's twinkling eyes. Above all, she passionately longed for the freedom dangled before her.

"Heave laddies," shrieked the parrot. "Hard awind! Awwk!"

With her next sip of tea, Althea had explained carefully to Rose, not cloaking the matter in any veils Rose might see through, the role of the social mentor and the necessity for one. She also conveyed, mainly by a comfortable, straightforward air of understanding, that she deserved to be well rewarded for any success by Rose. Amelia would have choked on the idea. And Althea had no concept of the watchful Red Nell.

Unable now to even taste the tea, Rose heard, once again, the roaring of the sea and felt the raucous wind teasing her as she scrambled up the Nose. When she looked at Althea, it might just as well have been Jack Mabbin looking out of her eyes.

Hard awind, indeed! Althea grinned, one privateer recognizing another. Oh yes, Rose Fitzroy would do just fine in London!

Feeling infinitely more worldly than the rest of the inmates, Rose dashed up the stairs at Gresham's. They were girls. Rose savoured the bloom of womanhood. Some of it had come to her when she met the eyes of Adam Crisp and read the distant horizons in them.

And she could hardly bear another minute caged up at the ladies' academy.

But how to escape? Gresham held the keys to every door. The windows were grilled. Even the skylight had been firmly nailed shut. And what about her mother catching her and shipping her back? Or coming up with some new scheme to ruin the prospects she had set her heart upon?

Mother!

Rose still baulked vehemently at the idea. It surely could not be true, the stubborn core of Rose insisted, that that blunt, terrifying woman in the queer clothes could be her mother. Not when Jack Mabbin had promised her a duchess or a least a woman who wouldn't scare Mrs. Gresham half to death whenever instructions had to be given.

The way to skip out of her mother's reach, Rose decided, was to skip out of Gresham's and straight to Althea Wharton.

Yet short of setting the house afire, Rose could imagine no way out until she heard the swish of a broom working its way along the hall. Rose pulled the wielder of the broom into the room and shut the door.

"Nan, will you sell me that dress you're wearing?"

Nan was a skinny, cowed creature who came in to do the heavy cleaning. She had been warned in grisly terms by Mrs. Gresham to have no doings with Miss Rose or any of the young ladies. Mrs. Gresham suspected, but could not prove, that Nan had been involved in Rose's infamous flit through the skylight. The idea of another encounter with Rose's tartar of a mother made the skin shrink on Mrs. Gresham's nape.

"Oh, I can't, Miss Rose, I can't," Nan protested in frightened tones. "Let me go. Mrs. Gresham'll skin me alive if she catches me in here talking to you."

"Nan, please. I really need it."

"What for?"

Nan looked down at the plain cotton dress that hung down around her ankles. Frayed about the hems, scrubbed to a faded blue, it had seen much hard use and was one of only two that Nan owned.

"Never you mind. Just sell it to me."

Nan held out valiantly until Rose pulled open the doors of her wardrobe. Inside glimmered the new dresses from Amelia.

"I'll trade one of these."

Nan's eyes grew huge.

"Oh, I couldn't, Miss. Oh no, not one of them!"

Rose pulled out a day dress such as Nan could not hope to own in her entire life, with yards of edging and a lacy fichu at the neck.

"Nan, you can wear this to a big house and apply for a post as a parlourmaid. See how fine you'd look if you just brushed your hair up nicely."

Between Rose and the amazing vision of herself in the looking glass, Nan gave in. She longed to escape Gresham's too. If the worst came to the worst, she could sell the dress for weeks of wages.

Clad in Nan's drab clothing, Rose crept downstairs early the next morning and slipped into the pantry, right beside the back door. Finally, she heard Mrs. Gresham coming to unlock the cupboards for the day's rations.

"Ma'am, I'm ready to go to Neally's for the milk now," Rose announced in a remarkably accurate imitation of Nan's reedy voice.

Mrs. Gresham, halted, surprised and suspicious.

You're early. Have you washed out the slop jars?"

"Yes, ma'am," Rose lied stoutly.

"And filled the coal box?"

"Yes, ma'am."

Mrs. Gresham, who had a great ear for a falsehood, came over and peered into the dimness of the pantry. Rose bent down and busied herself so that only the familiar blue of Nan's skirt was showing. Her pulse was racketing to match the pails which she rattled industriously. After an eon, Mrs. Gresham gave a grunt, selected a key, and opened the back door. Before the woman could blink, Rose was through and gone, racing down the alley to the street as fast as her legs could carry her, milk jug spinning on the flagstones behind her.

Rose ran until Mrs. Gresham's screeches died into the distance. Around corner after corner she dashed, down side streets and through alleys until she was certain no one could follow her. Then she smoothed her hair, straightened her back and set out jauntily for Wharton House.

Oh, how it felt good to walk! How long had it been since she had just been able to walk and walk and use up a fraction of the energy burning in her limbs.

Why, I could walk to Scotland if I wanted to, Rose decided, wishing she could embrace with her two arms the carters, the dray horses and the crossing sweepers as she passed them by. Her steps half danced, drawing looks and smiles from those she passed. She even forgot her superstitious fear that Red Nell might reach out and grasp her from any doorway she passed.

Rose was unsure exactly where Althea's house was but by asking regularly along the way, she was pointed toward the West End. The closer she got the more she found herself looked at in a peculiar way and, several times, she was accosted by men. However, she simply laughed and dodged nimbly away into the passing crowds.

As she reached the environs of the well-to-do, the people thinned and the streets widened. There were carriages now with smartly turned-out drivers and equally smart horses. Servants trotted by on errands, many giving Rose a cold and hostile stare which Rose scarcely noticed. She began to think with anticipation of the fine dinner Mrs. Wharton would provide.

The gentlemen in this neighbourhood wore coats of excellent broadcloth with velvet lapels. The canes they brandished gleamed with silver heads, their gloves were of thick kid and their large gold watches hung on Albert watch chains. A number gave Rose very direct looks. One of them, travelling in a cab, pulled up beside her.

"Hey, pretty maid, allow me to give you a lift to save those dainty feet of yours. I'll trade you a ride for a kiss."

A florid face under a rakish top hat leered out at her. Rose turned to stare back, one of Jack Mabbin's choice rejoinders on her lips, when a Peeler appeared around a corner swinging his stick. At once, the florid gentleman tapped on the roof and the cab sped off. The policeman, who had seen the exchange, blocked Rose's path.

"Well, well, what have we here. Bit out of your way, aren't you, Miss Doxy. Folks here don't fancy your sort cluttering the pavements. You'd best come down to the station. A taste of sweat labour the gaol might make you think twice about fouling decent streets..."

His hand had just gripped an incredulous Rose by the elbow when a voice boomed out behind them.

"Why Rose, there you are. I told you we should have taken the carriage. Officer, kindly unhand my sister."

CHAPTER THIRTY-THREE

Rose felt herself deftly plucked from the officer's grip and propelled
around the corner at the end of the block before she managed to drag her rescuer to a halt and peer into laughing amber eyes. Below those eyes, brash cheekbones and an indecently naked chin emerged, tempered by a grin. Part of Rose was confused by this looming stranger. Part of her recognized him instantly.

"You've shaved your beard," she cried, half in reproach. The only survival of the luxuriant facial hair was a large, villainous moustache which drooped at the corners of Adam's mouth. A new suit of good broadcloth had replaced the sheepskin vest and canvas trousers. It didn't succeed in smoothing him into a gentleman.

"We better stroll on," Adam advised as the thwarted policeman glared through the spikes of a wrought iron fence.

"If she's his sister, I'm a flyin' donkey," the policeman muttered angrily, disgruntled at the antics of the rich. How was he expected to keep the streets decent when impudent baggages like that got snatched from his clutches without a by your leave!

"Close call," Adam commented when they turned into a street of elegant shops. "He was all set to arrest you."

"Arrest me!"

Rose halted, too surprised for indignation. Adam's brows shot up.

"Well, what did you expect, on foot alone in this neighbourhood and without a hat."

"Is it a crime to walk about without a hat?"

"In this neighbourhood it likely is. Ladies of....um, a certain persuasion risk jail or, at the very least, reformers with bibles should they parade openly. We had better remedy the situation."

Adam stopped short of explaining that hatlessness was a certain sign of prostitution and possible prostitutes were swept instantly from streets where the wives and daughters of gentlemen might have their delicacy offended. Spotting a smart little hat shop, Adam lumbered in, Rose in tow, and ran a critical eye over the frippery on display.

"That one," Adam decreed for Rose. "In view of the rest of you."

So Rose was equipped with a flowery brimmed straw hat that tipped saucily to one side and fluttered festive yellow ribbons down her nape. The saleswoman, who clearly thought a scullery maid was embarking upon an adventure, picked out the best. The lass might as well have as fine a hat as possible while the getting was good.

"Now then," Adam said, relieved to be into the street again, "if you're rushing off to join the French Foreign Legion, perhaps I could escort you to the recruiting post."

Only then did it occur to Rose the picture she must present, tramping through the streets in Nan's frayed kitchen dress splotched with stains. Adam's eyes gleamed at the puzzle.

"Well, I can't just leave you standing on the pavement. If you won't tell me where you're going, perhaps I could interest you in lunch."

As if waiting to be asked, Rose's stomach issued a lusty growl. She'd left Gresham's without a bite. What's more, she didn't have a penny even to buy a bun.

"Hmmm, no breakfast either," commiserated Adam. "Better fix that."

Just the sight of Rose looking about as though she wanted crunch London up and devour it, revived him. Adam darted into a shop opposite with pies and loaves and pyramids of fruit in its window and shortly emerged with a wicker basket under his arm.

"Here's provisions. Let's go."

Adam couldn't stop glancing at Rose, could scarcely believe it was her. He'd been walking the streets, as he had much of the time since he'd returned to England. A man of action deprived of action, he'd taken it out in mileage on the cobblestones while he went round and round inside himself trying vainly to sort out the confusion there. He didn't know what he'd been expecting. The shock of his father's death had propelled him back over the Atlantic. In Canada, he had been waiting and waiting.

Waiting for words that now would never come.

And now everything was in Henry's hands. Everything!

Yet it wasn't even this that shook him so much. It was that his father had given it all away so easily. Had not called Adam back, or written to him.

Or forgiven him!

Or even acknowledged Adam still existed.

Hadn't even acknowledged an elder son still alive in the world.

This was the blow that tore at his foundations, sent him into black and disconnected moodiness. This final repudiation drove him tramping, unable to rest as he wrestled with the dark things that had lived at the back of his consciousness the whole time in Canada.

In London, his mind seemed unable to tell him what to do. The old torment pulled at him, confused memories dominated by Milton's bitterly disappointed face. Then he'd spotted the mass of strawberry curls and the policeman closing in. Seeking to rescue an unfortunate, he plucked the girl from the Peeler's grip. To his astonishment, he found it was Rose Fitzroy in a servant's old dress nothing like the creature in shimmering silk who had swept the day at his mother's tea.

Until he ran into Rose he hadn't realized how much the city grated on him, how much the new clothes irked him or the pushing crowds aggravated him. Rose in tow, he headed for open country, in this case Hyde Park.

The park, that splendid bit of countryside sealed up in the heart of London, embraced them in a haze of sunshine spilling through the branches of its huge plane trees. Dogs and children raced and shouted. Nannies congregated with perambulators. Tucked in a leafy nook an old woman set herself up in a folding chair, knitting on her lap and a bottle of stout, settled for a day of believing she was home in Kent.

Rose dropped her dignity and skipped at the novelty of being on grass again and hearing breezes in branches overhead. Adam couldn't stop glancing sideways at the novelty of a girl burning inside the faded dress like a glad spring bonfire.

I've been too long in the bush with the moose, he decided wryly.

Before them shimmered the Serpentine, that lovely, curving lake cradled in the heart of the park. Rose clapped her hands together.

"Oh, we must go out in a boat."

They hired a rowboat and pushed off. Rose hadn't been near water since Two Spar Cove. Adam pulled off his coat and rolled up his sleeves in the warm sun, fitting into the boat as naturally as any of the Mabbin brothers. Rose watched him take up the oars and row with a lazy, competent stroke to the centre where they bobbed gently. The great city around them receded, their only company the breeze that set the wavelets sparkling.

Adam opened the basket, attracting a family of ducks. Together, they devoured cold chicken, fresh buttered bread, plum pudding and Stilton cheese..

"I haven't been so hungry in years!" Rose declared, licking the crumbs from her fingers.

She looked Adam over again, digesting the radical change in him since she had seen him at Crisp Court. The gentleman's clothing only seemed to reveal, more indecently still, wrists roped with sinews, a body that had thrived on unsparing use, and an outdoorsman's alert, soft-footed air.

"Do I really look so odd?" Adam murmured. It had been a pleasure watching her eat.

"Not so odd as the last time I saw you. Oh, the looks on those ladies' faces when you introduced yourself."

They broke into a yelp of laughter.

"They were a sight."

"Well, you were shaggy as a thorn bush." Rose remembered the impudent grin inside all that facial hair. "Your own mother wouldn't have known you. I've heard even gentlemen in Canada know how to shave?"

"What makes you think I'm a gentleman?"

He was teasing, but also meant the question. The very manner in which he leaned back, sunlight on bare, tanned forearms separated him from the formal black-clad figures escorting ladies along the park paths.

"Not the faintest scrap of evidence, I suppose."

With food in her stomach and the street far away, Rose seized these stolen moments when she was free of Gresham's and had not yet flung herself upon Mrs. Wharton. She wanted to snatch as much as she could of this precious interlude where a woman, newly released from a cage, might do anything she pleased. She dared Adam with her grey-green eyes. Mrs. Wharton could wait.

The boat seemed to drift, but Rose could feel the deft, gentle oar flicks keeping them in open water. As they floated into the lee of some massive willows, the ducks followed, gabbling softly. Swallows dipped over the water, flashes of sheeny blue with pale undersides. The boat rocked almost imperceptibly under Rose flooding her with memories of afternoons aboard the Mabbin lugger as it butted its way through waves rolling all the way in from

America. Jack had told her of the fleets that went to fish there, to the Banks where codfish were so thick all a fisherman needed do was lower a bucket over the side. Flung down on her stomach atop the cliffs, Rose used to stare at that tantalizing horizon and wonder whether they had smugglers over there too.

The boat floated lazily near the shore.

"What did you see in Canada? Do they have villages? Does any of it look like London?"

She could not help intense curiosity about the mystery of this wild man transformed.

Well, not very transformed. From the way Adam spread himself at ease, he was a man who would always need room for himself, always look as though he longed to shuck off his civilized skin. Even wearing the suit, there seemed to be little of the British in him. He bore the stamp of another land. When he opened his mouth, a strange Canadian accent spiced his speech.

Adam shifted comfortably on the thwart.

"Wood, everything's built of wood. When my ship got into Halifax, I thought it the strangest town of skinny wooden houses that ever I could have imagined."

"What did you do when you got there?"

He spared only a blink for what his mother would think of the revelation and said, "I travelled on up the river until I got to Upper Canada. Then I went straight to a lumber camp."

Yes, he'd become a logger pretty quick when he'd found winter blasting in and himself with nothing in his pockets to spend. He'd taken to the logging camp, crammed in a bunkhouse with dozens of others and sweating logs from the bush every day, all because he'd been constitutionally unable to touch the meagre bank draft his mother managed to slip past Milton, stamping him as another shameful remittance man some family was trying to push out of sight. He'd handed the money to a woman half mad from melancholia and frantic to get back to England with her brood. Unable to forget the howl of the mill workers the night of the fire, Adam had given all subsequent drafts away, mostly to families fleeing the jobless English mill regions and cast up destitute upon that unfamiliar shore. Adam kept only his wages and whatever his own resourcefulness could bring.

For the first time since he'd arrived in England, Adam found himself wanting to talk about Canada. At Crisp Court, Henry refused to ask and his mother was afraid to know. Louisa had suffered enough from him working in the mills. She didn't need to know about fleas and bacon grease and metal that shattered with the cold. In Rose's sea-mist eyes he found frank interest that had nothing prying about it.

Adam told Rose about the babble of foreign tongues in the camps, the high kick contests at night, measured on the stovepipe, the log drives on the river when the ice went out, the bedlam in the rough lumbering towns the day the wages were paid.

"Were you only a woodcutter?" Rose asked. He was the kind of man she knew about, the kind she trusted.

Sunlight flashed lazily on the oar blades as Adam gave them another dip. A flotilla of silver water beetles scurried out of range.

"Oh no, that was only the start of it, merely the start. I wasn't a month out of the lumber camp when I was plucked out of the Welland Canal with a boathook by Harriet Quinn who kept me for her own."

Adam stroked his moustache, irrationally tickled at the sudden disquiet in Rose's eye. Harriet had been fifty if a day when she had hauled Adam, dripping, up onto the stern of her boat.

"Teach you to stay off the lock gates. Don'tcha know they're slippery as a eel's gizzard weather like this?"

Adam had been trying to walk across. Black ice of late spring and gloom of dusk had been his undoing. Since he'd fallen in on the lower side of the gates he might have been in a deal of trouble except for the boathook. His rescuer thrust him into the wheelhouse of the squat, blunt-bowed steamer to dry out.

Harriet was a bow-legged, brass-lunged scrap of a woman from whose swarthy face every race of the continent looked out. She had a potato of a nose from an accident during a storm and a habit of squinching one eye shut as she talked. Harriet not only owned the steamer, but sailed it herself. Her whole pride was the Widgeon, a raffish old tramp that carried any sort of cargo that could be got into the hold and tackled any bay or river or stretch of lakes where business might be had.

Discovering that Adam knew all about machinery from the mills, she had taken him on, his job to keep the cantankerous old engine steaming while Harriet navigated the tricky channels in search of work. Harriet had taken to Adam from the first and soon he was her right hand as they ploughed from port to rag-tail port.

In the American War Between the States, Harriet had done well. After the war ended, the undersized Widgeon had scramble harder for survival. For his skill at persuading cargoes aboard, Harriet started giving Adam a percentage. The two took the ups and downs together. Each time they steamed to home port, Adam would visit the bank, silently hoping for some communication from home. There would only be that scanty remittance, cold and blank, which Adam got rid of, to the endless tide of immigrants, as soon as he was able.

It was from the deck of the Widgeon, in the muddy infant metropolis of Toronto, that Adam and Harriet had watched the fireworks celebrating the birth of a new nation, Canada, four half-tamed provinces banding together for safety, a wary eye on the flexing muscles of their giant neighbour to the south.

"Got some future, this place," Harriet had commented over the much-gnawed stem of the pipe she was never without. "Them as got their wits'll keep an eye to it, and stop hankering back."

Friends that they were, Adam had never confided in Harriet about his real reasons for being in the country. Shortly after, Adam came across, in one of the jumbled trade lots they often had to deal with, the enormous stuffed bear, dearest trophy of an old hunter now anxious to unload it for portable cash. In a fit of bitterness,

Adam had bought it and shipped it to England, a sardonic messenger for what he could not find words to say.

No reply came. Adam and Harriet and a shifting population of hands continued on, braving half-navigable rivers, butting through Great Lake storms, shovelling coal into the Widgeon's hungry maw. Then, one day, Harriet had called Adam over to the rail and pointed at a larger boat moored nearby.

"The Iris is for sale. Twice the size of the Widgeon and just needs her steering gear rebuilt. I got money put by and I know you do too. This country's growing faster than a pumpkin in July. If we sold the Widgeon, we could get the Iris and double our trade. Partners. How about it?"

In a year or two, with the Iris working for them, there could be another steamer, and perhaps another. Yet even as Adam's blood leaped at the possibilities, the old, dark unrest had swept over him. The Iris meant binding himself when, he could not, would not, be bound.

Adam knew he would have to leave. He told Rose about Laroche, a wiry, French-speaking hand who fought seasickness constantly and couldn't stand the walls of spruce and pine as they bucked fast rivers to deliver their goods. A prairie man, his mother was one of the Métis who lived on the Red River since the first white trappers and whose roots ran far back into the Blood and Blackfoot Indians, hunters of buffalo as long as there had been buffalo to hunt. When Laroche had spotted Adam brooding on the deck he had poked him amiably in the shoulder.

"Let's get out of dis prison of trees. West, dat's where to go. Big hunts out dere now. Eh, what do you say?"

Adam had taken nearly all his accumulated funds, all his share of the trading, and left them in a large envelope for Harriet, propped against the steam gauge.

"Buy the Iris for yourself, "he had written, hoping it would compensate. "Good sailing and good luck!"

Adam and Laroche had gone down through the United States and out all the way by rail to Minneapolis and St. Paul. Out onto plains that had dumbfounded him with their openness, their dramatic skies, their endless, gargantuan space. It had been no trouble at all, with Laroche along, to hook into the waves of hunters who had been coming west since the end of the American Civil War. Adam had learned to handle a Winchester as though it were an extension of his arm, to ride hardy, leather-mouthed, plains mustangs, to gallop unswervingly alongside that thundering, dangerous river of flesh, the buffalo herd.

With a knack honed during countless nights around campfires and potbellied stoves, Adam told of massive horned beasts as far as the eye could see, their dust obscuring a scorching prairie sun. Laroche had hunted with the skill of his ancestors and Adam had galloped at his side, gripping the mustang between his knees, firing in a frenzied madness of heat and dust and shouts and the primal exhilaration of the hunt.

But the days ended in brown bodies strewn sometimes miles in their wake and then the job of skinning them. Gruesome, back-breaking work up to the elbows in gore. The hides had to be staked out to dry while the thousands of pounds of meat putrefied into a stench no prairie wind could blow out of the nostrils.

""Whyever such slaughter?" Rose demanded horrified.

"Hides. Tough buffalo hides. After the War Between the States was finished, everybody in the east started building factories. Every factory needs belts to run the machines. All those hides got sold east to make belts for the machines."

"Did you kill hundreds?"

Adam paused, then shook his head sharply. The endless travelling satisfied the fretful need inside Adam, the limitless space, the violent, towering sky helped suppress the gnawing thing inside him. But in the end, it had been all too much.

"Two thirds of the hides were going to waste, the carcasses rotting before the animal even got skinned. It was just...it was revolting after a while. I left."

He had sickened of the slaughter and the carelessness. Families he remembered, families in the workless mill towns, would have had a winter well fed with just one haunch of that meat. He turned east again, a bronzed, toughened man equally at ease with a rifle or a long, razory skinning knife. A man with a taste for freedom.

After three years of absence, he had returned to discover the news of his father's death. The ground might as well have vanished beneath him. He had walked straight onto the first ship heading for home.

Adam's tale trailed off as he came back to the present. He ran his hand uncomfortably over his naked chin. Dragonflies darted and hovered, iridescent slivers lighter than the air. A pair of grey herons stood by the shore, unperturbed by the human population. In the middle of the lake, two white swans stretched out their necks to each other.

"Your turn now," Adam broke in, deviltry restored to his cheeks. "So tell me, is it Mrs. Gresham's Academy you're running away from today?"

CHAPTER THIRTY-FOUR

Rose's mouth popped open.

"How...?"

For an awful moment, Rose supposed Adam might be in league with her mother. Adam laughed.

"Amazing what you can get out of a hire carriage driver. He was happy to tell me what he thought of the place where he collected you"

A small wave slapped the side. Adam took up the oars and propelled them toward shore where alder bushes bent down to the water and a stand of beech offered welcoming shade. The bow scraped softly onto the gravel. Adam hauled the boat easily up to safer grounding and offered Rose his hand.

Alarmed that her secret exposed, she let him help her over the gunnel. The callouses on his hand scraped her palm, sending a swift, unidentified arrow up her forearms. She hovered a breathless moment before he released her.

His approving speculation reassured her. The safety she felt with him crept back squelching the fear of losing what she had not yet even grasped. No point in labouring the charade now. Not with her sporting a servant's frayed dress and clearly a runaway. She dimpled at Adam's ingenuity.

"Well, I did live at Mrs. Gresham's, until this morning. This dress belongs to Nan who does the scrubbing. I...um, borrowed it to get past Mrs. Gresham at the door."

Against all the strictures of her mother, of Amelia, of her own future hopes, the truth flew out easily under such knowing eyes. Besides, a man who had tramped into Crisp Court wearing a hermit's beard and tattered sheepskin was hardly in a position to find fault.

"Might I ask where you're running off to?"

"To seek my fortune, of course," Rose grinned, brash as Dick Whittington's cat.

And that's exactly what I'm doing, Rose realized, lusty and hungry for life. On the brink of her life's adventure she regarded Adam steadily. Adam saw her resolution almost visibly, like the granite ribs of a riverbed revealed below the dashing current.

So how did a girl, bright as a new guinea, seek her fortune in smoky old London?

Rose supplied a rollicking account of her ruse to escape, mimicking Mrs. Gresham's squawk by the door.

"Doesn't bear much resemblance to a Cornish manor," Adam told her when he stopped laughing. "Oh yes, I heard all about that from my mother."

Adam discovered an untrampled patch filled with daisies, buttercups and purple clover. Rose flung herself down and spread her arms wide just as she used to do as a child and gazed up at wings of cloud adrift in a tender sky.

"In Cornwall," Rose began, dreamy with another time, "our house had ship's ribs for a ceiling and we sat about in captain's chairs salvaged from wrecks. Maeve had a comb of carved mother-of-pearl from a Spanisher gone down with the Armada. She used to let me wear it when Penn and I paraded about in the old green velvet cloak. When times got hard, we had to trade it for..."

She stopped short for she had actually been there in her mind, smelling the stew bubbling in the pot, teased by Dave and Mawky, dandling the baby in her arms. She hadn't let herself think of the snug Mabbin house, nestled into its hill, in years.

"I see," murmured Adam as though people confessed to living under roofs of ship's timbers every day. "Who was Maeve? Your sister?"

"My mo...,"

Rose almost said "mother," for that's what black-haired Irish Maeve had really been. It was Maeve's lap Rose had wriggled into, Maeve's bosom Rose had cried against, Maeve's hands that had plucked out the twigs and wind-tangles caught in Rose's flying hair.

"I lived with Maeve and Jack, and the rest of their children. Oh but it was jolly!"

She hoped they'd got to Ireland and were living high as twenty lords after the brandy was sold from the wreck. Oh Maeve...

"What about your real mother then?"

Rose blinked back to the park.

"A duchess who came to bad fortune in the wars."

Now why had she said that?

Rose thought of the mysterious, forceful figure who had taken her from the gypsy wagon and plunked her into Gresham's. Whose word did she have except old Anna's that Nell Fitzroy was her real mother? Rose didn't even know who the woman really was or what the woman did outside of Gresham's except that she was "in business". Dan and Joe, so unlike the straightforward, boisterous Mabbin boys, clammed up like misers' purses whenever Rose got inquisitive.

"I mean...I do know, but I don't..."

Rose came to a confused halt. This Adam who handled a boat like a Mabbin had drawn more out of her in an hour than anyone else in all her time in London. How was she to get along in Mrs. Wharton's world, Rose asked herself, if she had already given away this much her first day to a man she barely knew.

Ah, but she did know him, some buried part of herself seemed to say. She knew the face the seasons had lived in, she knew the way he sat easily, grounded on the earth, she knew the eyes that looked at her so directly.

"And the redoubtably upright Mrs. Corman? I don't think I see a family resemblance here." Adam was saying lazily, trying to cover his curiosity about this sunny creature.

Rose was tempted to tell him even about that although she knew she could not, would not. That thing earthy and strong about him tempted her potently. She fixed her eyes on the triangle of bronzed skin at the base of his throat and felt something happen to her lungs.

"This is getting a little one-sided, Mr. Crisp. You're full of tales about steamboats and buffalo but you've not said a word about your own family. And how did you end up in Canada anyway?"

She had meant merely to deflect further probes about Amelia and was astonished to see his mouth go tight and a jerking pulse flick at the corner of his jaw.

"I was sent to seek my fortune, too" he replied, his parody of Rose not hiding the bitter rawness underneath. Even Rose could see his dark inner turmoil.

"Did you find it? Your fortune, I mean?"

Rose asked so earnestly that a half laugh was teased from Adam's throat. He thought of the large Crisp fortune all in Henry's hands. He thought of the lumber camp where he had slogged through the snow, he thought of the sweltering plains where the heat had been like thick syrup permeated through and through with the reek of all the wantonly slaughtered bodies. Lastly, regretfully, he thought of Harriet Quinn leaning on the wheel of the old Widgeon while the labouring pistons shook the deck beneath their feet.

"Perhaps," he said slowly, "my fortune was meeting you today."

A charged silence fell between them. Looking up sharply, Rose saw a kind of mute shock as Adam realized the gallantry was utterly true. She found her heart in her throat and a primitive excitement beginning to throb at her core. In that moment, some old shell she hadn't even known she was wearing shattered and fell away leaving her in some new state she couldn't recognize, except that she felt so vibrantly alive her blood sang like stream waters dancing over bright stones.

This happiness combined with a panic that told her how perilous it was, on her first day of freedom, to sit near this man who was captivating her so.

"I can't sit still a moment longer," Rose declared as if fleeing something inevitable. "Let's go see the rest of the park."

Spring had flung itself over Hyde Park so enthusiastically as to make that trodden swatch of green forget it was a city park and imagine it was still a royal hunting ground, with kings hallooing after wild boar in the underbrush. Rose could hardly contain herself. She wanted to dance on the grass, tweak the ears of old gentlemen, sweep toddlers up and bite their delectable pink necks. Gresham's was leaving her like old dry dust blowing away in the wind.

Adam thought he would never again see such gambolling freedom like one of those wild prairie mustangs leaping a corral gate and kicking up its heels in exuberant abandon. Music drifted from the band shell where people sat in rows of canvas chairs and the sun glinted golden from the instruments. Rose automatically turned toward the melody, then spotted a whir of wings in the foliage.

"Look, there's a chough. King Arthur's bird. It's good luck to see one."

Adam could only watch the tendrils of fair hair that tumbled about her face. They should never be brushed back, he thought. On impulse, he broke off a blossom and tucked it into Rose's curls where it nestled as though it had come home. Rose touched the petals and felt the throb inside her again.

"I'm glad," grinned Adam about the bird. "I could use seeing a whole flock."

For the first time since he had arrived in London, the tumult driving him was soothed. How had she got inside of him, he asked himself, bemused, her brightness illuminating an inner landscape he hadn't known was so full of gloom.

They hurried to mingle with the crowds gathered to watch the afternoon parade of carriages on Rotten Row. The Row, its name a strange corruption of Route en Roi, or King's road, was an old royal road through Hyde Park parallel the busy street of Knightsbridge. If there was a single place in which society contrived to show itself off in all its luster, it was by the obligatory afternoon drive along the Row.

Rose pressed forward to gaze at the unbroken stream of brilliant equipages now speeding smartly by. Team of bays and greys and matched, oil-smooth blacks flashed along in the hands of drivers tricked out in elaborate livery. The occupants of open carriages displayed their froth of fine silks and flourished frilled parasols. Not to be outdone, heavy old family coaches rumbled by festooned with footmen resplendent in blue coats and immense brass buttons.

Under the shade of the chestnut trees, casually watching the parade, other members of society gossiped and laughed. Side-whiskered gentlemen in white top hats and silver-headed canes leaned over iron railings of the Row to chat with elegant, long-skirted equestriennes who laughed behind their veils and sat with ease in their sidesaddles. Still other gentlemen lolled on the fashionable grassy slope, supremely confident in their leisure, pleased to be with others of their kind. That some of the equestriennes, or "pretty horse breakers" were very elegant courtesans neither Rose nor Adam had any idea. Rose only marvelled at their jaunty hats and their riding habits that fitted like a second skin.

Adam felt Rose's fascination with the favoured beings enthroned above the carriage wheels. While the crowd craned their necks, Adam had a sudden memory of a split branch laid viciously into his boyish flesh and of his father reduced to abject scraping for Adam's sin of hunting a young deer. Adam glared at the shimmering demigods bestowing their presence on the park.

"They're only flesh and blood like the rest of us," Adam muttered, hackles rising.

Rose barely heard him. She gave little hops to see over the heads of those in front of her, using Adam's arm for balance.

"I'm going to mix with them and sing for them," Rose confided in a rush. "I'm on my way to live at Wharton House with Mrs. Althea Wharton!"

Adam's eyebrows shot up so far that the rest of his scalp moved back.

"You mean, you're going to be an adventuress?"

"Why yes, I'm going to be an adventuress,"

Rose missed his meaning entirely and thought no one could have put her intentions more aptly. The flash of her eyes would have done credit to Red Nell. She was practically dancing now, the slim flame of her in Nan's worn blue dress receiving looks as was Adam who had put his coat slung over his shoulder and now no cravat. Rose could hardly wait to get on with life.

"I'm going see about me as much as I can. I'm never going to be trapped in a place like Gresham's ever again!"

"When you fling yourself into a maelstrom, you might find the current stronger than you imagine."

Rose was the girl who had climbed the Nose and captured a wreck single-handed. She began to laugh. The pair of dimples she had discovered beside Adam's moustache had turned divertingly stern.

"You'll make a wonderful fierce old man, passing out grim warnings to young ladies you meet in parks."

Such high adventure shone in her that Adam suddenly did feel old. Had he ever been like her, he asked himself. Had he ever, in his whole life had such hope?

"Yes! On the day his father had taken him back from the mill yard. Or certain mornings with Harriet when the old Widgeon nosed out into the lake, bulging with cargo and glee after a feisty scramble with the competition. Or with the first dip of the bow up a new river so clear the boat seemed to float upon transparent air.

No use to argue here, he saw. Rose would fight free of anyone who tried to grasp her.

And how could he blame her when she made him think of that first morning he had stepped off the ship in Canada and suddenly smelt the invigorating air of freedom and space. He remembered the sharp longing for far reaches that had sent him off with Laroche. He'd put civilization behind him, shunning even the half-formed towns and villages of the new continent.

Rose, on the other hand, was determined to plunge straight into the heart of this teeming, pulsing society that made him feel as though his collar was slowly choking off his breath. She was setting out upon a path he could not follow, this brave, newly-coined woman of the world who had no concept of its boundaries.

Besides, Adam asked himself, what did he really know about London when his youth had been spent in the mills and his manhood in Canada. For all he could fathom, there might be a perfectly respectable institute for young ladies seeking adventures in this prodigal town. The parade of carriages thinned, reminding them that the afternoon was wearing late. The mood had changed. It was time they were on their way.

"Let me row," she insisted as they climbed back into the boat and with skill took them back to the hire dock. They joined the other park-goers streaming toward the gates and home.

And home, Rose tremulously hoped, would be Wharton House.

Adam hailed a cab. Wordlessly, they sat together as the horse clopped along, both oppressed by a sense of parting, of coming to a fork in the road.

"There it is," Rose called out as Wharton House hove into view. The rosy glow of evening gilded the west facades all along the street. The inside of the cab trembled with intimacy.

Adam tapped the roof to get the driver to stop. He and Rose sat motionless, caught in a moment which took an eon to pass. When Adam shifted to get out, Rose laid a restraining hand upon his arm.

"No, I'll go to the door alone."

Her eyes were wide and serious. She could not let him get out with her or she might not be able to go on through that door at all. While her fingers rested ever so lightly on Adam's wrist, the horse had time to stamp the cobbles with one hind foot and shake its bridle lazily. Then Rose's hair tumbled softly away from her face, revealing to Adam the tenderness, the utter vulnerability of her neck. Adam groaned, unable to help himself.

"Before you go," he whispered hoarsely, and put one of his arms around her.

Rose didn't move. At the light, questioning touch of Adam's lips, she sighed. Then Adam was kissing her, making her shudder with that emotion she did not understand. When he drew away, he caressed her curls and traced her temple with his lips. Rose raised her face to him, seeming to invite a kiss in good earnest. His fingers slipped into her hair to stop her.

"Don't," he murmured, but she kissed him anyway in a spurt of happiness, quick as a hummingbird.

"I have to go now."

"Are you sure?"

Rose tried to subdue the beating in her throat. If she lingered a moment longer, she would be lost. She could not be lost, not before she had even begun.

"I am!"

Before her stood the graceful portal of Althea Wharton's house, a gateway to magical possibilities.

Sighing, Adam opened the door of the cab. What could he say to a dazzling girl with such anticipation blazing in her eye? He could only watch as Rose tripped up to Althea's gently worn doorstep. Over the tumult in her breast, Rose grasped the knocker the way she had reached out to grasp her liberty. And if that liberty already had a price, that only made it more precious.

"Yes", she whispered ardently to herself, "yes!" And sent the knocker crashing down.

Althea was roused from a doze by a flustered maid informing her she had a visitor. She found Rose seated on the foyer bench with nose sunburnt, a scrub girl's dress gathered about her knees and new staw hat shaking its yellow ribbons at her.

"I've come to live with you," Rose announced. "And to begin!"

Indeed! thought Althea admiringly after she had gotten over her astonishment. Good for you, Rose. You couldn't make a better start than this!

Down the street, after the cab had been dismissed, Adam swore softly under his breath. Somehow, in an afternoon, Rose Fitzroy had nested in heart. He barely prevented himself from slamming his fist into a wall.

CHAPTER THIRTY-FIVE

She was not to open the curtains to look out. She was not to make any noise or ring for Maddie or ask another time for that fat, spoiled dog of hers. She was to sit still in her room and do nothing at all until further orders came.

Laura had been quite speechless that this Faxon Atworth, whom she had scarcely even heard of, should sail into the house and start spouting commands. She had forgotten about keeping her gaze lowered like a proper young lady and stared openly at the stiff, long-nosed pipe-legged fellow with his belly, like a melon, sticking out from under his black coat. As he spoke, he hadn't used her name or looked at Laura once. His gaze veered as if Laura wasn't actually there at all.

"Lady Atworth passed away in Bedford Tuesday morning," he announced by way of explanation. "I am master here now."

These words made no sense to Laura, though their pleased smugness brought an unpleasant plunge to her stomach.

"I'll be back in two shakes of a lamb's tail," Gran had promised, patting Laura briskly on the head. And she had rattled off to Bedford to shop, as she did twice a year, staying two or even three days if there were a great many things to buy.

This man could have nothing to do with reality, especially since he added nothing more to this extraordinary speech, but walked out abruptly, leaving Laura standing gape-mouthed on the mellow old carpet of her room.

It couldn't possibly be true, she told herself indignantly, secure in the knowledge that Gran would never act in such a disorganized manner. Any minute now Gran would come sailing back, making an uproar in the hall with all her packages. Maybe Gran was back right now and resting in her room. Driving such a distance always made her want to take a nap.

Laura almost sped Gran's room to see if Gran were there. Yet she knew Gran never came in the door without immediately sending to see what Laura was doing. No, Laura decided to wait, trained as she was in obedience. With Gran gone the house was without a head and Faxon Atworth carried authority. Laura would bear any amount of waiting rather than have to confront him again alone. The unease of his presence filled all the corridors and all the rooms save this one haven that was Laura's domain.

Laura wrenched her mind to the drawn curtains. Who ever heard of not being able to look out the window? That was silly. One of Laura's chief pleasures was looking out over the gentle Bedfordshire hills she had loved since birth. She had watched the sheep drift down the slopes and pass beneath the froth of wild crab apple bloom. She knew when Mullens raked the drive and trimmed the lopsided topiary bird started way back in the seventeen hundreds when such curious green creatures were the fashion. She needed to look out now and see the comforting, unchanging stability of the beech woods and the sundial. She needed it now, especially when her chest was starting into a topsy-turvy turmoil that frightened her so.

Somehow she could not, dared not touch the curtains.

And after Faxon Atworth left, shutting the door firmly behind himself, Laura found his orders enforced by Miss Tate.

"Grandmother never made me stay in my room. And I want to see her!" Laura cried in a sudden panic. "I do!"

"Well, you can't," Miss Tate replied in an odd, scratchy voice. "Now you just go and play with your dolls."

This admonition alarmed Laura even more. This was not the time of day for dolls, it was the time of day for lessons. And afterwards, before high tea in state, there would be her cherished walk with her grandmother see how the foals were doing.

Laura sat obediently in her armchair until tea time, then marched to the door, meaning to have the familiar ritual. In the corridor, Laura all but collided with Miss Tate who actually looked as if she'd been lying in wait. Laura tried to march on but found, to her astonishment, that Miss Tate had her by the elbow and was propelling her back into her room toward the squat chintz chair by the fire. Miss Tate had never laid a forcible hand on her before. Laura began to protest indignantly.

"Grandmother...."

"Lady Atworth is dead," Miss Tate answered firmly. "You must do what Mr. Atworth from Durbury wishes now. We all must!"

Laura paled and fought the constriction in her throat. What was confusing was not this preposterous, patently untrue statement about her grandmother but the queer behaviour of Miss Tate. After a lifetime of being the centre around which everything revolved, Laura sensed, with a child's infallible sense, that Miss Tate had somehow changed sides. She was now, inexplicably and hurtfully, in league with this intruding Faxon Atworth and that was why one couldn't trust a single word she said.

Yet why would Miss Tate, hitherto kind, if stuffy, suddenly want to side with such an objectionable man?

As for her grandmother, Laura did not believe for a minute that that formidable lady was not rumbling briskly along toward Atworth House in the coach, her purchases piled high at the back and Tom, the coachman, singing at the top of his lungs.

"Why do we have to do what Mr. Atworth says," demanded Laura, pretending her ears hadn't heard the terrible words.

"Because he is Lady Atworth's cousin and her heir. Atworth House is his now to do with as he pleases."

"It's not! I'm her heir!" cried Laura who knew this the same way she knew her foot had five toes. She could not conceive of strangers at Atworth any more than she could conceive of her grandmother dead.

"Well, he has the running of the place," Miss Tate returned hastily. She had no intention of going into the tangle of events that had come upon the house with Faxon Atworth's precipitous arrival. Let him do his own explaining.

Laura remained silent for some moments, then tried a different tack. She had seen Faxon's carriage, loaded with Faxon and family, arrive.

"Is that lady in the black dress his wife?"

"Certainly. And the young gentleman and the young lady in black are his children."

Your cousins, Miss Tate was about to add, then shut her lips. Something was wrong here, very wrong. Faxon Atworth had not yet once used Laura's name and had given immediate and severe instructions to everyone.

"That...child is to stay in her room until I order otherwise and no one is to speak to her except Miss Tate. Is that understood!"

Pindling had actually opened his mouth to protest but had been silenced by a glare. The staff was in shock, of course, at Lady Atworth just dropping in the street like that, stone dead with no warning of any kind. And her so hearty and not old either. Went to show how a person couldn't trust the finest of health. The Durbury Atworths had been sent for straight from Bedford and, thanks to the new railroad line, they arrived at Atworth house before the body was brought home. The servants, like the crew of a rudderless ship, accepted a new captain uneasily, but with relief. Servants, no matter how favoured in the household, must have someone to obey.

"Mrs. Atworth has two chins and looks like an old black rain cloud in that dress."

"We never make comments upon the appearance of our elders and our betters," Miss Tate admonished, ever the governess.

"They're not our betters," Laura shot back mutinously, wanting to vent the seething, nameless emotion eating at her insides. "Nobody is better than Gran!"

"Was," insisted Miss Tate, making another attempt to impress reality on this bewildered child. She could not imagine why Faxon Atworth was acting so harshly but she had worked in other houses where inexplicable feuds had hissed and boiled like lava under a treacherous crust. Faxon Atworth no sooner had his hat off than he'd given Miss Tate her notice. The sooner she packed her trunks and was gone, she decided, the better.

"Was! How many times must you be told, Laura! Your grandmother is dead!"

Laura swallowed back real fear.

"Then...why haven't I got a mourning dress," she asked in sudden triumph. "If Gran were dead, I'd be dressed all in black with a veil down to my knees. And...and I'd sit with a lamp by her coffin every minute of the day and night. Gran wouldn't want anybody else, wouldn't let anybody else..."

Her voice clogged up in her throat at the queer look coming over the governess.

Miss Tate," called an alien voice from the depths of the hall, "Miss Tate, you are required. Please come at once."

The young woman hesitated, then turned her back, sped out and shut the door behind her. Laura stood frozen as she heard an unbelievable sound, the sound of the key turning in the lock of her room.

A day and a half later, Laura was still in the same state of shock. She hadn't flung herself against the door as a more direct child might have done; she hadn't torn back the shrouded drapes and shouted for help from the window. Instead, she'd clutched the pride Lady Atworth had ingrained and scarcely moved across the floor.

If she didn't pound on the door, she'd never know for sure that she was locked in. If she didn't shout from the window, she'd never discover that no one, not even the staff who had cosseted her since infancy, would come to her aid. All this was just temporary. Incomprehensible, very upsetting, but just temporary because of Faxon Atworth pushing in and playing mean tricks. Any time now, Gran would sweep through and take Mr. Faxon down several dozen pegs, thank you!

Food appeared and was taken away barely touched. That Cook had crowded the tray with raspberry tarts and Laura's favourite breaded chops only served to increase the fear vibrating beneath Laura's skin. Maddie, who brought the trays, murmured in embarrassment, tended the fire, and kept her eyes down, always locking the door as she went.

The size of the house could not conceal the hushed activity going on in its depths. From time to time vehicles came up the drive, more traffic than the lime trees had seen in years. The door knocker rapped discreetly and Laura imagined Pindling rushing to bow each caller in with the special gravity of his. There were footsteps in the halls, rustlings and murmurs and now and then, a sharp word of distress. Once, far away, Laura had picked out the disconsolate barking of Bollo and knew she was confined to the potting shed. The barking stopped with a yelp and hadn't been heard since. All about was a suppressed excitement and restless stir exactly as if some dangerous fever were trying to take the house in its grip.

By the afternoon of that third day since the news had been brought to her, Laura sat straight-backed and stiff, fighting a terrible but nameless premonition. Lady Atworth had given Laura the south bedroom because it was the child's favourite, peopled as it was with its previous tenants, among them Lady Edith and Lady Joan who had climbed down the very ivy vine growing outside.

Except for the new pink wallpaper and the matching counterpane, everything in the room was as old and angular as the house. The bed was a four-poster with spare, uncarved lines. The mantle was tall and severe, the window seat worn down from generations of occupants curling there. At the foot of the bed was an ancient dower chest, the bride's initials still carved on the lid. Laura's chest of drawers stood as high as the ceiling and had its mouldings carved from the solid oak instead of merely appliqued as in later, laxer times. Laura suddenly wanted to run her fingers over these things again, to feel the touch of other hands, dead long ago, but her family nevertheless, reaching out to her assuring her she was one of them and everything was going to be all right.

Her dolls sat silently on their shelves and tried to keep her company. Old dolls mostly, with porcelain or wooden faces who, refurbished anew in smocked dresses and jaunty hats, had survived generations of Atworth children. They formed another complicated family headed by Laura and did their best to substitute for other little girls to play with.

Laura even thought of her own clothes hanging in the wardrobes. The cambric petticoats, the underskirts of fine batiste, the winter dresses of blue faille and velvet trimmed with embossed velvet and fringe, the summer dresses of mandarin silk and white muslin edged with Valenciennes, the leghorn hats and rice straw bonnets, the patent leather shoes lined with cream, the neat kid gloves, the fine cotton stockings with dainty openwork up the sides.

Each outfit whispered to her of Gran's love since clothing was Gran's one extravagance to her, all made by a seamstress moved down from London. The smooth feel of them, the reassuring slide of them over her body she now remembered as a hug from Gran and she fought a tear at the back of her eye.

In the midst of wishing passionately that she had Bollo to cuddle, Laura became aware that something was going on outside. Hooves and carriage wheels, a great many of them it seemed, had crunched up the drive and become still. Voices, low and subdued, drifted up but did not move toward the portals. Laura, lifting her head to listen, felt an unbearable pressure building up inside her. At last, in a fit of anxious rebellion, she pushed the forbidden drapes aside and swallowed hard at what she saw.

A number of carriages which Laura recognized as belonging to their scattered neighbours were drawn up discreetly back along the drive. In front of them, directly before the wide stone steps of the entrance, stood a vehicle such as Laura had only seen in books. It resembled an enormous glass box on wheels, bearing round its top a cornice of ornate black acanthus leaves above equally ornate scrollwork around its pediment. Inside the cornice, out of a thing that looked like a tall black crown, a mass of black metal plumes rose, unnaturally refusing to move in wind. A pair of black horses were hitched to this conveyance, each also bearing black plumes, real ones this time that dipped and waved eerily each time the animals tossed their heads. A driver and a footman, identically dressed in long black coats and tall black hats, sat at attention as if they made of metal too.

The servants took places at the very back of the steps, all of them dressed in grimmest mourning, even Maddie whom Laura had never seen out of her striped print. Other people began to come out, including Mrs. Atworth and the young Atworths who looked tightly smug in their black. Laura recognized Reverend Cass, the vicar, Mr. and Mrs. Connley from Withes, the property bordering the Atworth estate on the west, Colonel and Mrs. Stamerton, from Bothwell on the east, a few people of consequence from the village and others Laura didn't recognize. All of them left a wide path to the black conveyance as if contagion would touch them should they step near it.

Finally, six men came out. Laura didn't notice the men, only what they were carrying—a great polished wooden thing.

A coffin!

In growing horror, Laura watched as they slid the coffin into the plush interior and shut the door on it so that it gleamed inside the glass, like something in a ghastly display case.

"Gran! Gran! Gran," came the ragged howl inside Laura's throat. The thing was a coffin, the vehicle a hearse. It couldn't be. No, no! What they had been telling her couldn't be true. Gran would never leave her. Gran would never go away without saying goodbye. Gran wasn't in there. She couldn't be. She couldn't!

Petrified, Laura watched as the hearse began to proceed along the drive at a stately, nerve-tearing funereal pace. The crowd broke and climbed into their separate carriages and began to follow. The whole procession moved further and further away, slowly going out of sight under the ancient limes. Laura felt a cold wind, an icy wind go over her as her heart begin to thud and thud. She raced to the door of her bedroom and tried to pull it open. When the locked handle refused to move, she began to pound on the wood, then throw herself against it, screaming to get out. But even though Laura sank down on the carpet, sobbing, neither nor Pindling, nor Maddie or even Miss Tate dared come to her aid.

CHAPTER THIRTY-SIX

"You pick out a dress to wear, miss. Any dress you want."

Maddie, the upstairs maid, stood where Laura's wardrobe was kept, the sunlight falling through the mullions in long bars across the floor. Maddie's sturdy form looked so rigid it could barely move and her dear, honest face was swollen and red in a most alarming manner. Her orders were that "the child" be dressed in the plainest manner possible. Her offer of a choice to Laura amounted to a raging act of defiance.

"What's happening, Maddie?" Laura begged. "Where's Miss Tate? Why have they locked me up?"

"I'm not supposed to discuss anything with you, Miss Laura. Anyway, I can't. I don't know."

Like the other servants, Maddie was shaken through and through with the scandal of Mr. Faxon not allowing Miss Laura to go to her own grandmother's funeral, not allowing her even one last look when the coffin stood in state downstairs. A bleeding shame it was, not that she, Maddie, a simple housemaid, could fathom the whys and wherefores among the gentry. A bleeding shame it was nevertheless, with Miss Laura white as a bed sheet with big dark blotches under her eyes. All of them had heard her screaming as the funeral cortege pulled away and wouldn't, on any account, care to repeat the experience.

Miss Tate has gone to Ipswich," Maddie added, offering the one scrap of information she knew. "Got a new position there right away, she did."

"But she's my..."

"Now please miss, do get dressed. Mr. Atworth can get terribly cross if anyone keeps him waiting."

Silently, Laura picked out a cherry-coloured velvet dress with deep puffs and much cording around the shoulder pleats. White guipure lace with deep points edged the collar and the same lace was folded back for the cuffs. A sash of paler cherry also had lace ends and tied into an immense, rustling bow.

"Oh miss, I don't think..."

"It was my grandmother's favourite!"

It was the dress Lady Atworth had ordered for Christmas, rich and dashing so that Laura should feel festive during the season.

Quickly, her hands shaking, Maddie slipped the thing over Laura's head, saw to shoes and stockings and hooks and sashes, then buttoned Laura into her coat which was worked silk velveteen quite fine enough to go with the dress. As they went into the hall, Laura saw empty boxes piled up and two strange servants.

"Everything," one was saying to the other, "every scrap that even hints of the girl"

They stopped speaking when Laura appeared and stared at her as she walked past, as if she had grown two heads. Laura could hear other voices in the house, movement, even a high youthful laugh that must have belonged to one of Faxon's children. Someone plinked carelessly on the pianoforte downstairs but Maddie led Laura down the back stairs into the passage by the kitchen to emerge at the servants' door. Faxon Atworth waited there with a large gentleman wearing a tobacco sprinkled waistcoat. Again he did not look at Laura as he dismissed Maddie firmly.

"This is the child, Mr. Whalley," Faxon said to the man, "that Lady Atworth has been harboring. An imposter. I made investigations so as to be completely certain of my facts against such a day as today." Faxon cleared his throat and Mr. Whalley eyed Laura with the same curiosity as the new maids. "The child's real name is Basing. She's illegitimate bastard of one Maisie Basing, a creature of loose morals, now deceased, who worked in a teashop in Cambridge. Here are all the documents of proof."

Faxon drew from his pocket a thick yellow envelope which he handed over. Mr. Whalley perused the contents. "Hummm," he grunted. "Hemmm...I see. Yes."

He glanced sharply at Laura and back again. Laura, who comprehended nothing of what was going on except that a bad word had been used, strained her ears to see if Cook was in the kitchen and might rescue her.

"The child rightfully belongs in the workhouse," Faxon continued, still not looking down, "but she would very soon be old enough to perhaps come back here on her own, making scandalous claims. Therefore, Mr. Whalley, I want you to put her into the hands of one of those charities dealing in child emigration. Let her go into service somewhere overseas. She'll get a living better than she deserves and Atworth House will be free from harassment. It would be unthinkable, absolutely unthinkable, that anyone cast aspersion on the character of the late, much esteemed Mr. Charles!"

Faxon seemed to swell up at the very thought, then gave himself a shake.

"Remove her, Mr. Whalley. I'll see your trouble is made well worth your while."

This promise galvanized Whalley who was a minor solicitor glad of a shilling wherever it was to be found. Pocketing the papers, he took Laura by the wrist.

"I'll see to it at once. All proper and legal. Come along, Basing. Look smart!"

Even as Laura peeped over her shoulder to see who Basing was, she felt herself propelled out the scullery entrance into the wind. A shabby open chaise awaited into which the man heaved her as if she were a sack of discarded rags. Only when he climbed up beside her and the horse began to move did Laura realize the man meant to take her with him down the back lane to the road.

"Stop! Stop!" she cried and when he didn't, she tried to jump out. The man's hand shot out and held her fast by the elbow, struggle as she might against his strength. The chaise jogged on past the boxwood hedges, a glimpse of the distant, cherished rose garden, the great limes that seemed to rustle and clack their branches in dismay. As the vehicle turned out the final gate, a horrible smothering sense of finality overcame Laura. It really was true! Gran was dead! Gran couldn't help her. This awful man was taking her away!

Sobs, then shrieks tore at her throat as she twisted on the seat, watching the gabled roof and tall, beloved chimneys of Atworth House sink behind the greenery irrevocably from her sight.

CHAPTER THIRTY-SEVEN

Strawberry Rose, as she was instantly, happily christened, became popular so quickly even Althea felt flung along by events.

London, that splendid old city, far older than Madrid or Vienna or Amsterdam, had seen a tumult of changes since the time the Romans had picked that precise spot in the gravel, the earliest where low tide let the great river be forded, to build their imperial outpost. After the retreating Caesars, centuries tumbled past with the city constantly renewing itself, constantly growing until, in that glorious decade of the eighteen-seventies, it reigned as the greatest city in the world, capital of the greatest empire ever assembled, imperial red mapped into the farthest corners of the world.

With the Pax Britannica enforced by the Royal Navy and based on its mighty lead in industrial productivity, Britain basked at the very peak of its world supremacy. London was its major port, largest consumer market, centre of its government and seat of the royal court. This leviathan metropolis lying under its dense canopy of smoke, this gilded city, centre of the civilized world, had become the focal point for conspicuous consumption and the luxury trades. Ravenous for novelty and sensation, the profits of the Empire burned in its vast pockets to be spent in frivolous ways. This fevered extravagance, this exhilarated gaiety, reached its height during the whirlwind weeks of the London Season.

London, that glorious spring, was a thrilling oasis where life did not stop at eleven p.m. as it did in the rest of the country. The Season was an orgy of entertainment in which ivory cards of invitation fell like snowflakes. A girl with her mother, in from the dull old hinterlands, suddenly found herself two or three deep every evening in balls. No matter the hour, there was always more dinners, more parties, more dances to go to. She might waltz until dawn, rush home for a hurried breakfast and start all over again with a picnic or a row on the Serpentine before the sleepy maids had laid the table for lunch.

Under Althea's nimble guidance, Rose performed at a select musicale. Instantly, she was in demand for a party, then a musical picnic in support of the ragged schools. Then, so quickly Althea's head swam, Rose became the rage.

Some Seasons, an icy, high-born beauty caught on, humbly worshipped from afar. Others, a drooping sloe-eyed damsel would capture the imagination. This year, hungry for a gust of bracing air, the dashing circles embraced the novelty of Rose Fitzroy with unabashed delight.

The eligible bachelors of the circle, who were the big game, the quarry of the Season, shyer than mountain stags, wilier than ancient, hook-scarred trout, flocked after Rose. The married men, with barely a guilty glance at their wives, capered on the heels of the bachelors, delighted to make fools of themselves.

Florid romantic posturing was the language of the day, a splendid sport for all, under cover of which married or single could rhapsodize the object of favour to ridiculous lengths. Adoring Rose became an instant fad, the giddy infection leaping from man to man scrambling to join the spirited frolic.

It helped a great deal that Rose had arrived without a label. Clearly, she was not a debutante, not one of those white clad, husband hungry creatures who appeared each spring, ephemeral as Mayflies and lasting in the sunlight about as long. Nor was Rose a hardened adventuress, a dampeningly solemn, high-minded artiste, or even an obvious climber.

She was more like some dollop of spontaneous joy who had mysteriously appeared to enchant them with her voice, her eyes, her laugh and, above all, her scandalously abundant energy. She was there so that everyone could have more fun.

So many flowers arrived at Wharton House that the old walls might have been forgiven for wondering if the heady days of the Regency were back. Bad poetry by the yard accompanied vast boxes of Danish caramels, Turkish delights or decadent French bons bons. At dinners, Rose might discover a gold bracelet or an inlaid ivory fan concealed in her napkin.

Sometimes admirers quite lost their heads as did young Elroy Wilton who tore the peonies from in front of his sister's house, where Rose was leaving a party, and flung them in front of her carriage in a frenzy of adoration. Old Sir Alex Maggers actually got down on his knees to beg Rose to be his mistress. One of Rose's slippers was stolen and spotted, the next day, in state atop a flagpole.

A garlanded chestnut riding hack was found one morning tied to Wharton House front door. Lord Cedric Blake, so amusingly taken by Rose at Althea's first experimental musicale, ground up a pearl on a dare and swallowed it in Rose's honour.

There seemed no end to the follies they egged each other on to in Rose's name. But follies, flowers and slippers atop flag poles don't pay the bills, Althea thought, drawing steadily and relentlessly upon Henry's Crisp's money. Money without which Rose's deceptively butterfly-like progress could not have been accomplished. Thank goodness Henry Crisp was so nicely rich and so obsessed.

When Henry Crisp had begged a private interview, Althea had instantly banished Rose to the dressmaker and emitted a relieved sigh, saved from making the first advance herself.

"I won't beat about the pond, Mrs. Wharton." Henry hadn't even waited until his teacup was filled. "I've heard from...certain sources, that you are a woman who makes arrangements. I wish to make an arrangement about Miss Rose Fitzroy."

Even as he sat, Henry was eaten by the image of Adam sweeping Rose off to her carriage and of Rose's laughing eyes alive with interest in the hairy ox. Well, Henry refused to waste time competing like a schoolboy with Adam's unspeakable brashness. He disdained to cavort like Rose's other admirers. The moment he discovered that Rose was living with Mrs. Wharton, he knew what he must do. He would buy Mrs. Wharton's services no matter what the cost before someone else beat him to the transaction. He would buy Rose Fitzroy for himself!

Wharton house and Althea in her natural setting told Henry volumes about her sources of income. For the first time, he felt certain he could win.

Letting Henry stew, Althea assessed him over the silver of her guest tea set. His combination of fevered avidity for Rose and his direct business manner were perfect. Althea appreciated the lack of sidling about. She could feel the heat in Henry. That heat was necessary to get the money but it also made Henry Crisp a dangerous man if crossed. She was very careful about her commitments. In return for the money Henry practically shoved upon her, she made sure Henry knew the gamble he was taking.

"A gamble you will see that I win," Henry returned tightly. "I expect Miss Fitzroy's favour at the appropriate time."

Checking her stab of unease, Althea worked out an arrangement guaranteeing Henry invitations, involvement in Rose's activities and enough time at her side to warn the rest of her admirers that Henry was her patron. In this game of skill and daring, Althea was betting on her own ability to keep the upper hand. Althea remembered the fever flash at Crisp Court, the lust Henry thought he was concealing so well. The trick was how to keep him under control. Unfortunately, Henry Crisp did not appear to have a sporting instinct in him. He expected a genuine payoff and could make a deal of trouble if he didn't get his money's worth.

Althea sighed. If life were fair, every woman would be entitled to a wealthy patron instead of the uncertain prospects scrambled after wherever they were found. She would let Rose wreak delightful havoc on the male hearts of London while keeping her from the pitfall of actual romance. Rose, fortunate girl, could have no idea of her immense good luck at tumbling into Althea Wharton's hands, saved from the disaster she was bound to fall into on her own. Properly managed, Althea saw years of happy profit ahead. Besides, what she was giving to the Crisps, a place in the social firmament, was more valuable that the whole Crisp fortune, something no money could buy should society slam its doors.

Details of business were never mentioned to Rose who was taking so spiritedly to the fray. Such dash, such splendid verve, Althea thought, quite unaware that Rose had been trained up by the boldest set of smugglers on the Cornish coast.

Rose had, Althea wryly had to admit, played an excellent game of keeping her past to herself. Rose had proved so resistant to probes about her background that Althea knew something large was being hidden. Fascinated, she pryed no further. What woman worth a brass farthing didn't have a mystery to defend?

So, with silken fingers, Althea absorbed quantities of Henry's money to finance Rose's meteoric rise. Subtly, she promoted Louisa and Henry as patrons of the girl, preparing for the time when Rose's other admirers must be put on notice that Henry had her favour.

Althea steered Rose away from any hint of tainting commercialism, keeping her much-in-demand talents to the round of parties, musicales, high teas and picnics given in the name of charity. Rose joined other gifted, often highly connected amateurs in fund-raising concerts her adorers flocked to see.

Not since the advent of Jenny Lind, the Swedish Nightengale, had there been such a flurry. Yet Rose was always, in the eyes of the public, shadowed and protected by the austere, impeccably respectable image of her cousin, the former Amelia Radmore, that angel of mercy lifting waifs from the gutters. Regardless of how outrageously Rose behaved she could not, unsettled matrons believed, be as wild as all that if she were Amelia Corman's cousin and the famous Dr. Lionel Radmore's niece.

The appeal of Amelia's spartan sincerity, complete with battle scars, coupled with Rose's extravagance of colour, could not be underestimated. Through it all, Rose stuck staunchly to her bargain to support Amelia's cause. She could never repay what Amelia had done for her. The smuggler's code declared that bounty be shared with all who aided in the enterprise.

Because of Rose, the story of Amelia and the basket cellar fire spread rapidly, turning her into a dauntless heroine. People wanted to look at the scars and hear the tale. Once Amelia got over her shock at Rose's defection to Mrs. Wharton, she discovered in her ersatz cousin a resource beyond her most extravagant dreams, especially regarding the contributions of sundry besotted gentlemen who relieved their consciences by pouring money on a noble cause.

So Rose sallied forth armed with lace and laughter, longing to gobble up life whole. If she could have gotten away with it, she would have turned cartwheels in the street. In short, Rose learned to play.

The modest wardrobe Amelia had organized, now abandoned at Gresham's, was replaced by costumes of clever, ingenuous simplicity as to be the most fetching. The very restraint of their lines turned Rose into a beguiling confection no other girl could imitate. As men fought to dance with her and schemed to be introduced, Rose displayed a nimble gift for badinage, that necessary skill to counter the aggressive flattery flying at her from all sides. Very quickly, she discovered the value of arch banter, a charming gulp, a mysterious chuckle behind her fan.

Rose learned to play cards with skill and to cheat with a shameless boldness that made it a delight to lose to her. When asked, she could tell fortunes with such conviction the recipients found themselves believing, until the next morning at least, her outrageous predictions. Her admirers adored her every caprice.

The heart of Rose's appeal remained her gift of song. For all her versatility, she soon discovered she was best at the old favourites. She could melt hearts to waxy puddles with her soulful rendition of Home Sweet Home, a melody almost as popular as the national anthem. She made familiar songs fresh and alive again. Music welled up from inside of her, sweet sustenance from some inner, invisible spring.

Althea was both enchanted and appalled by Rose's bright, questing eyes that seemed to have no concept of limits. Despite Mrs. Gresham's most rigorous efforts, Rose had never lost her conviction that rules didn't apply to her. Jack's promise of marvelous things years ago, among the salvaged brandy kegs seemed to be coming true. Rose was only grasping her birthright. Althea wasn't sure who was propelling who as she scrambled to steer Rose around dangers the songstress was too blithe, too inexperienced to see.

As it was, rumours scooted about in all directions. Had Rose really played at whist all night and egged her opponents into gambling away a whole month of dance cards, people asked each other as they bit into jam-drenched scones. Had she really walked a second floor parapet on a dare? Had she really gotten a tiny tattoo of ship on her shoulder blade? And what about the rumour that she had slipped on a footman's uniform and ridden all the way through London on the back of the Killan's coach before they discovered the prank. It was a wonder Amelia Corman's hair wasn't curling at the roots!

Amelia, too, could scarcely believe what was happening and was far too unworldly to realize how it was fuelled. Her admonitions had no effect on Rose, her anxious questions were skilfully soothed by Mrs. Wharton. Hiding her terror that her masquerade would be discovered, Amelia could not help being dazzled by Rose's successes. And Mrs. Wharton, that experienced woman of the world, Amelia told herself, would surely exert the strong hand that Amelia could not. Althea thought of her commitments and kept Rose's future conveniently blurry lest it turn out a fearful surprise.

In the midst of it all was Henry Crisp whom Rose treated with the same cavalier good humour she extended to the rest of her admirers. If he was at her side more often than the others, if he appeared to have more privileges, Rose supposed it was because of Mrs. Wharton's odd partiality for the fellow and Louisa Crisp's energetic involvement in Refuge support.

As for Henry, he bided his time and smouldered with acquisitive desire. Laissez-faire capitalism, in which heaps of cash were a sign of divine favour, had created a world in which God blessed the shrewd. Henry salivated over the cornucopia of investments, propositions and money-making schemes London had to offer. He meant to take advantage of as many as he could. And Rose would be the best part of his reward for shucking off the mills and coming here.

The more Rose grew in popularity, the more obsessed with her Henry became. He was like a field of dry, dead grass suddenly aflame. When alone, he would find himself staring, with glassy, unfocussed eyes, toward a medallion on the wall or a clinker in the fireplace. Sometimes, right in the middle of a conversation, his colour would change from pale to heated to pale again for no apparent reason save that he had been thinking about Rose's dimpled elbows or all the little buttons down the back of her dress he longed to tear away.

Henry's obsession was inextricably mixed up with a secret rage. Rage at every glance Rose did not give him, every laugh she shared that was not his, every song she sang that was not exclusively for him. He covered this rage with a barely controlled mask and kept himself in check. Let those other men make fools of themselves as much as they wished, he told himself. He would have the last laugh in the end.

CHAPTER THIRTY-EIGHT

Under Althea's guidance, Louisa plunged into charity work, adopting Amelia's cause like a shipwrecked sailor clutching a life-saving spar. Now that Adam had sauntered in, looking like a wild man of the Antipodes, she felt she had to work doubly hard to make up for his presence. Besides, after being inundated with appalling information about destitute children, her heart had gushed with generous impulse. She acted firmly upon her resolve, uttered impulsively at the tea, to take three of the orphans into her home to train.

Henry, who might have objected, now didn't care who his mother brought into the house. Orphans or dancing monkeys, it was all one to him so long as it strengthened the connection to Rose. The housekeeper was of a different mind.

"Street arabs, ma'am!" Mrs. Quincy spluttered, aghast." Why, they'll be off with the silver the minute our back is turned!"

Mrs. Quincy had once run the home of a minor member of Parliament and had been persuaded to Crisp Court with great difficulty. Louisa put up a firm front.

"Now Mrs. Quincy, Mrs. Corman assured me that these three are quite trustworthy, not like the ones that sleep in barrels and steal umbrellas for a living. We must do our honest Christian duty."

Mrs. Quincy distrusted talk of Christian duty. It meant those plaguey reformers wanted a run at a person's pocketbook.

"The poor rates are something staggering already. Urchins ought to be provided for without having to take them into your kitchen."

But Louisa had had her emotions stirred. Enough of the forage merchant's daughter was left in her to make her aware of her own good fortune washing around her, in waves of break front cabinets, sumptuous draperies and the Neo-Gothick pile of Crisp Court itself. What this house needed, the muted fleck throwing into contrast all the splendour, was three little paupers gratefully nourished by its beneficence.

"The refuges are overflowing Mrs Corman says and it's harder for girls. If we train three here as domestics, they'll never be at a loss for an honest occupation."

"How long will they be here, ma'am?"

"Only until transport is arranged to Canada. It's all matter of funds."

Mrs. Quincy heartily approved of shipping paupers to Canada as soon as possible. She saw gold cufflinks and silver teaspoons vanishing into the dust cloth of some light-fingered chit but argument was useless. The mistress had made up her mind and didn't mean to be troubled with the practicalities of training feral street waifs. Perhaps Mrs. Crisp was like those Mohammedans who must weave a mistake into every carpet to deflect the jealousy of their god.

"I see."

Mrs. Quincy retreated in starchy disapproval to brace for the invasion.

"You must all be good girls and behave your very best at Crisp Court," Amelia admonished the three children preparing to follow Amelia from the Refuge. "You are all very lucky to be going there. The house a regular mansion with ever so many servants. You'll learn all sorts of things that will help you when you get to Canada."

Louisa had insisted on receiving the charity girls as soon as possible, so Amelia spoke as she helped tug Katie into the plain cloth coat that went over the equally plain dress and pinafore the Refuge issued. Though still exceedingly thin from her illness, Katie was now well enough to go to Crisp Court with the other two. Katie should not miss this chance. Good food was what Katie needed, the rich, nourishing food of a wealthy house, not the spartan fare the Refuge had to offer.

Katie's resilience at getting back on her feet pleased Amelia whose heart was wrung by what a scrap of hope and a scrap of care could do. Amelia hoped Crisp Court might revive the bright-eyed child she remembered, changing this silent girl with the anxious face and wooden movements as though some inner spring hung broken.

The worst had been when Amelia tried to discover what had happened to Mary. Katie had begun to shudder. The more Amelia asked, the more violent the shudders became, mute terror in Katie's eyes voicing everything her tongue would not. Finally, Amelia gathered the child into a blind embrace end held her the age it took for the shaking to stop. Later, she elicited some garbled words about selling fruit and freezing, and some fantastic character called Red Nell. But if Amelia tried to speak of Mary, the shudders would begin again and stricken horror slide into Katie's eyes.

Things were worse with Katie than even Amelia imagined. Her faith in safety, her faith in life had been demolished the way no abuse from Jenks could ever have done. Her young mind could not cope with it and might yet decide to die to escape it. All Katie could do was stand mutely while Amelia buttoned the cheap coat and dropped maxims for a life Katie could not comprehend.

"Don't get attached to them," Mrs. Dwyer of the Charity Organization Society had warned Amelia years ago. "You can't be impartial and it's too hard on you when they don't live."

Blast impartial! When Mrs. Crisp had requested three orphans to train in her kitchen, of course Katie had to have the chance. After an enormous battle with the mats, Katie's hair had been restored to a wiry, coppery braid. Amelia gave Katie a reassuring pat and a wary flicker responded in Katie's eyes.

"Is it far?" Katie asked, anxious about leaving this island of safety. "Is it as far as Canada?"

Amelia laughed. One thing Katie could do was ask questions about Canada as though Canada were some promised land of healing and safety no British bulwark could offer. Amelia answered as best she could but Katie still could not conceive of an ocean.

"No, it's right in the middle of London where the rich people live with carriages of their own and real silver teapots for their tea."

Katie could not conceive of these things either so she remained still while Ethel, a general help hired by the refuge, closed the small tin trunk assigned each girl. Two dresses and aprons, two night shifts, two pair of stockings, a change of underclothes. Very generous, Ethel thought, for a verminous child who'd arrived without a shred to her name.

"The three of you will be like sisters," Amelia continued, encompassing the others in her gaze, "so you must be friends and look out for each other."

"What about Will?" Katie asked, wishing him with her on this frightening journey.

"I told you, he's gone to the House of Industry. He's got a cot of his own to sleep in and meals every day. Soon he'll be put out to work at a useful trade for a boy."

"They won't make him climb the chimneys, will they?" Katie demanded in alarm. "He hates it so."

Amelia patted Katie's cheek, thinking what a loyal soul she was. As for that chimney sweep, Croom, oh the things she'd like to have done to him, forcing a little lad up those dreadful holes! They'd washed Will, and scrubbed him, but nothing would ever get the soot from his elbows and knees. Snaking black scars set in by brine, like a savage's tattoos, he'd carry for the rest of his life because of Croom.

"Of course not. I believe he'll learn to make boots. Now let's hurry. We don't want to be late and irritate the housekeeper."

Recently graduated from the sick room, Katie had had little time to inspect her companions. Amelia hustled her charges outside into the waiting cab. She took cabs with reckless impunity now, discovering that her status as married woman and head of a charity had freed her from the censure she and Mabel had so feared in the past.

When the iron-rimmed wheels started up, panic began to engulf Katie as they moved away from the Refuge. Amelia spotted the queasy shade of Katie's face.

Perhaps the poor child's never been on a moving vehicle before, never mind a closed cab going smartly down the street!

"Don't watch the outside. Look at me."

Amelia winked at Katie. Then, astonishingly, made a funny face.

Katie's mouth fell open. The clenched knot in her stomach began to subside.

"Here, have one of these."

Amelia pulled a paper sack from her pocket and handed Katie a sweet. Kate gazed curiously at the red and white striped peppermint until Amelia indicated she was to put it in her mouth.

Amelia certainly did not approve of bribing children with candy but found, as her mission spread, people had begun pressing bags of sweets, "for the little orphans, ma'am", upon her. The peppermints in her pocket had been shoved there absent-mindedly after the greengrocer came by.

Katie's expressive features sprang to life. Amelia could actually see the taste of sugar and mint burst in the child's mouth, feel the surprise wiping out the terror of the closed in cab.

I'll have to stop being such a tartar about plain food, Amelia decided. Poor little beggars have hardly ever tasted a treat.

Amelia handed a peppermint to the second child in their compartment, Cully. Seeing the candy was to eat, Cully grabbed it with the speed of a spider monkey and stuffed it into her jaws. Amelia sighed, wondering how the Crisps were going to cope with this one.

Cully was none other than the very basket child Mabel had snatched from the stampede out of the burning cellar. Hundreds of such children had been discovered in attics and cubbyholes all over the city. In fact, it was an encounter with one such exploited group, crouching under the rafters, that had moved Annie Macpherson to start the child emigration movement.

After the fire, Cully had been deposited in the workhouse where she lay for ages, ill and coughing, in the infirmary. Then she was passed to the casual ward, neglected among the human flotsam passing through. Amelia and Edward had scooped her up the moment their first small house was set up.

The festering cuts on Cully's face had healed into a fan of thin white lines, giving her a look of having just pushed her way through a thicket. Despite an improvement of diet, she was quite undersized for her age which could have been anywhere from eight to twelve. One of her eyes wandered, discomfiting those who couldn't tell where she was looking. Her stick-like legs were bent from rickets, giving a strange bounce to her gait. At the moment, she was also quite short of hair. The mats had been chopped off at the workhouse, leaving the array of dark bristles poking from underneath her hat. Cully was as undomesticated as a bush savage and a more unsuitable candidate to work in opulent Crisp Court Amelia couldn't imagine. If Louisa hadn't insisted, indeed demanded, over all Amelia's protests, the very child from the cellar fire, Amelia would never have let Cully go.

"You mustn't snatch things, Cully. And you must remember to say thank you afterward."

Cully merely clamped her mouth tightly as if afraid Amelia might try to pry the peppermint out again. Then the new taste burst. Cully's eyes became unfocused and a sort of ecstasy took possession. While she sucked the peppermint, she looked as if one could have shot her over the moon and she wouldn't have noticed.

Amelia offered a peppermint to the fourth occupant of the compartment, Laura Basing, who shook her head and went back to staring sightlessly out at the grimy buildings passing by.

Katie found her panic diminished and ventured to peep out the window again. The cab turned into a fine neighbourhood such as Katie had never suspected existed. Ornate lamp posts had lovely lamps atop them. Tall house fronts rose up with stately windows, fancy iron grilling and not a single beggar in front. Goodness, there were even trees!

Absorbed in the spectacle Katie was unaware of Amelia watching her quizzically. Katie had seemed such a pallid little thing, lying on her sick bed. She was pallid now, yet, should Katie's real animation return, Amelia supposed, it would put the other two to shame.

Cully, oblivious to the novel sights, had crammed herself in the corner, intent on making the peppermint last an unbelievable amount of time. Her one straight eye was fixed unwaveringly on Amelia's pocket where she knew the rest of the sweets to be.

The other child, Laura, drooped against the upholstery, numb and silent. Laura had been dropped at the Refuge by a corpulent man who had clutched the child roughly by the collar the whole time he had been making sure Amelia understood the girl must be shipped to Canada with the first party Amelia managed to organize.

"A tea shop bastard that's been trying to worm in above her place," he had sneered, shaking the child. "There'll be no more of that, I can tell you. Not for the likes of her no matter what kind of tales she tries to tell!"

Shocked through, Amelia thought. Casualty of the class war. And damn to hot Hades all rakes who callously tossed aside the products of their philandering.

Cully swallowed with a gulp, making sure Amelia knew the mint was finished. Cully was, Amelia saw, the sort of child a dress would never fit no matter how carefully chosen. Her new outfit, exactly the same as Katie's, sagged about the hem as Katie's did not and the coat seemed to have developed great pockets of air between the fabric and the scrawny body beneath.

Each time Amelia's fingers twitched, Cully's eyes widened eagerly, waiting for another mint. The child had a short nose and broad, slightly protruding mouth that gave her the look of a good-humoured post box. Despite her appalling background, an illogical optimism seemed to have lodged itself inside her, giving her an expression of perpetual hope. For sure, the sweet bag would be empty before the end of the trip.

Unlike Cully, Laura had nothing about her of the starving pauper. She was a lovely child aglow with that translucent, unmistakably country-bred skin known as English roses. The dress and coat she had arrived in, though sadly crushed from enforced sitting, had been a wonder of tucks and velvet and delicately pointed lace. She had sobbed bitterly when they had been taken away from her in favour of the sturdy institutional outfit.

"They are far too costly for any child here to own," Amelia had explained kindly but firmly. "We will sell them and put the money toward your passage."

Laura's protests had died back into the daze still paralyzing the girl. Well, she ought to shake out of it at Crisp Court, Amelia decided. Going there was a stroke of luck half the orphans in London would kill for. Of the group, Katie ought to be the natural leader, Cully the enthusiastic volunteer, Laura the unhappy conscript dragged against her will from a far far better life.

At Crisp Court the little party stood a moment staring at the gargoyles. Then Amelia mounted the wide front steps and rang the bell. Mellon glanced at the charity dresses and motioned the party toward a pair of tall, carved doors.

"Mrs. Corman and the orphans," he announced in a sepulchral voice as he pushed the doors open.

Ordinarily, Louisa would not have been in the large drawing room but she had been inspecting the new print of a dying Gaul on suspicion that it might not be as fashionably pathetic as she had led to believe by the dealer. She eagerly received her guests.

Once inside, Katie's turmoil in the cab was replaced by confused bedazzlement. The room was the hugest room she had ever seen, sweeping away to curved bay windows fitted with a rainbow of stained glass. The ceiling flowed with flowery plaster work, the fireplace was immense, the walls covered with flocked wallpaper of a red such Katie had never before imagined. Couches overstuffed as the bodies of dead dinosaurs sat about while high-backed chairs sported clusters of carved fruit on their crested backs. Ottomans, armchairs, occasional tables, a monstrous Chinese vase overspilling with artificial flowers, took up all the extra room. The walls were dominated by paintings, in heavy gilt frames, of noble stags and expiring heroes. The scent of money and furniture polish permeated the room where no speck of dust dared penetrate. Oh, it was so...so beyond all words that Katie had barely felt Amelia prod her.

"Say good day to your benefactor, Katie."

Katie's attention turned to a figure by the window, a substantial woman in magnolia silk sitting in one of the balloon back chairs. The woman was so of a piece with the rest of the room that Katie had missed her altogether.

Mrs. Crisp rose to inspect them. Her bosom glittered with passementarie beading and her train followed her scratchily across the carpet pile.

"Mrs. Corman," she greeted warmly, delighted that her newest novelties had arrived. "I'll just send for Mrs. Quincy who's to take charge."

Mrs. Quincy appeared and looked hard at Amelia's protégés.

"Are these the orphans for Crisp Court?"

When Amelia averred that they were, Mrs. Quincy drew her brows together.

"This one doesn't look like a pauper," the housekeeper declared, eying Laura as though she were a fraudulent grocery order. "Too well fed, if you ask me. Mrs. Crisp wanted genuine paupers for her charitable aid."

Amelia stiffened.

"I assure you they're genuine paupers. This letter tells heir histories.

Amelia drew a long envelope from her handbag. Mrs. Crisp had demanded the backgrounds of each orphan, set out in the most affecting terms possible. The housekeeper turned the missive over suspiciously before handing it to her mistress.

By now, Louisa had also noticed that Laura appeared surprisingly plump and smooth for a pauper. The one in the middle, all bones and staring green eyes, certainly looked the part, but the one at the end, goodness! Cully's wandering eye and tilting stance unsettled Louisa. The fan of healed switch marks across the child's face threw her into outright agitation. What could Amelia be thinking of, bringing such a diseased looking specimen into Crisp Court!

"And this is Cully, who is the basket child you especially requested, Mrs. Crisp, "Amelia declared, recognizing the expression on Louisa's face. "I'm sure you'll take special care of her here."

"Oh."

Louisa could hardly object after the fuss she had made. When would she learn to examine goods before she had them delivered!

Louisa tried not to stare at Cully while Amelia gave the awe-struck children a brave speech about gratitude, obedience and hard work. Only when Amelia turned to go did they come to life. Clinging like chicks to their mother, they sped after her back to the foyer where she could only hug each one and leave them to their fate.

"Come along," Mrs. Quincy commanded briskly. "And don't let me catch any of you in this front foyer again."

Mrs. Quincy had progressed not a dozen steps before she realized she had only Laura in her wake. A high, keening cry, like a rabbit in a snare, wavered up behind her. Cully was clutching Katie so tightly the seams of Katie's coat looked about to pop. Cully had just caught sight of the huge stuffed bear.

"Good gracious! What's the matter here?"

Cully emitted strangled squawk at the huge teeth of the monster. When Mrs. Quincy gave Katie a shake, Katie bolted to one of the side pillars and stood with her back against it, unnerved by all the gleaming floors, dark panelling and impossibly high ceilings.

Cully flung herself at Mrs. Quincy, grasping the woman's knees for protection from bear. She nearly sent the housekeeper backwards onto the tiles.

"You, child. Let go, I say. Let go!" Mrs. Quincy ordered furiously, attempting to pry Cully loose. Every horrid thing Mrs. Quincy had ever heard about crazed, homicidal paupers rushed into her head.

Her undignified shriek brought Mellon. The butler pulled Cully loose only to have her clamp herself violently to the butler's own well-starched middle.

"Whatever is the matter with the creature?" Mrs. Quincy snapped, "You'd think she was being eaten alive!"

Mellon peered down at the cropped, burrowing head. There had been talk in the servant's hall of the charity orphans, but this was worse than anybody expected.

"Why, Mrs. Quincy, she must be from those rookeries. Never been in a grand house before, I wager. And that bear is enough to thrust any child half out of its wits."

Mellon hauled Cully bodily toward the servants' door. Mrs. Quincy turned back for Katie who was still pressed against the pillar.

"Come along now," she ordered shortly. "You're not afraid of stuffed bears too are you?"

Katie wasn't afraid, she was overwhelmed. The walls, the dirty, looming bricken walls that had closed around her since he first moment of consciousness, had fallen away. She felt as if she were about to float off her feet. Her eyes were huge because there was so much to fill them.

Even Laura was roused. The scent of polish, the sight of a butler, the echoing halls reminded her so much of Atworth House that
a stream of mingled hope and confusion dared assert itself inside
her benumbed breast.

CHAPTER THIRTY-NINE

"Lordy, where'd you get that chemise! Rich people shouldn't give such things to charity children. Only makes them give themselves airs!"

Fran, an upper housemaid, pointed disapprovingly at the befrilled undergarment which Amelia had allowed Laura to keep.

"It's my own, " Laura replied hotly from where she stood by her cot. "Made especially for me."

"Oh was it now," exclaimed the housemaid, startled, as everyone else had been startled, by Laura's gilded accent. "A chemise like that would cost nearly as much as one of Miss Camille's. How come you're living on charity?"

It wasn't yet six in the morning and Fran had been sent to get the three girls up for their first working day at Crisp Court. The children slept on cots hastily arranged in an attic under the eaves of the servants' wing. To Laura, the room was dreadful. To Katie and Cully, since it had a roof and warmth, it was pure luxury.

Laura's mouth quivered. Many strangers had looked her over nastily but this one was openly grilling her.

"My grandmother died and some bad people sent me away. Any time now, they're going to see the awful mistake and come for me," she countered, voicing the fantasy which was the only defence in her traumatized mind.

Fran raised both her eyebrows satirically. She was a square, salty woman with muscular arms from shifting furniture and turning mattresses. She had clawed up to her current position and detested those harbouring uppity notions about their place.

"Well now. I heard you was a young gentleman's bastard that was brought up on the sly and then chucked out. I can't see anybody wanting you back."

Amelia's letter, presenting a brief, honest history of each child, had been read by Louisa and passed on to Mrs. Quincy. Now the whole household knew the tale.

"I wasn't brought up on the sly," Laura cried. "My grandmother..."

"Enough of this! What's going on here?"

Marion, the head parlour maid, loomed in the doorway. All the female help save Mrs. Quincy and Cook, who had their own quarters, slept up here in the cluster of gable rooms and were bustling to get on about their jobs.

In short order, Katie, Cully and Laura, arrayed in their charity dresses, were lined up in the kitchen where they were given a cup of tea and fitted with aprons and dust caps in order to be suitably uniformed as staff.

The kitchen in the basement was a vast room centred around an enormous cooking range. Every conceivable sort of cooking utensil equipped the place as well as sinks of zinc, cake safes, vegetable bins, meat larders and great scrubbed wooden tables for the work. It was here that Cully had crouched, recovering from her fit of hysterics. It was here that she had caught the scent of roasting beef and baking pies in the ovens nearby. It was here, like a small, blotched hedgehog, she suddenly sat up, nose twitching in amazed speculation about this monster infested pile. Could it possibly be that it was also crammed with food?

This paradise was presided over by Mrs. Wunkle, known to the whole house simply as Cook. A wispy, high-strung woman, her tendency to anxiety under pressure was far outweighed by her abilities in the kitchen. Louisa had stood fast in her defence even when Althea had hinted that splendid French émigré chefs, fleeing the collapse of the Second Empire, were to be had for the picking.

"Now then," Mrs. Quincy rapped out, "you're to work for your keep here and learn to be of use. All of the rough work is to be done before the family rises for breakfast. Have any of you ever cleaned a grate?"

The children looked at her blankly.

"Answer me properly!"

"No ma'am," said Katie, well prompted by her Asylum training and nervous from memories of Croom and the Asylum chimney. Cully, who had already taken to copying Katie, repeated this, parrot-like. Laura's tone meant certainly not!

The housekeeper pursed her lips thoughtfully. Mrs. Crisp, with her usual disregard for practicalities, had demanded that the children be taught immediately to clean a grate, a skill she imagined to be the first necessity for charity urchins who, one day, were to be thrown upon their own resources.

"Take them to the library and show them, Lucy and watch them closely. We have to know what we can trust them to do."

Ordinarily, Mrs. Quincy would never have allowed the children into such a fine room but the library, at the moment, possessed the only grate in need of attention.

Lucy was one of the under housemaids, much younger than Marion but with snap to her nonetheless. She marched the children out of the plain, white-painted halls and into the luxury on the other side. Puffing up with unaccustomed authority, Lucy warned the three severely never to use the main staircase.

"Back stairs is what servants use. And don't you go making clomping noises on them either or have any shoes that squeak. Nothing drives Mrs. Crisp to distraction more than a servant that squeaks. You got to do your work quiet like, just as if you wasn't really there at all."

They stepped into a large, oak-panelled room with arched windows and wine-coloured drapes. Katie inhaled the unimaginably exotic aroma of good leather, new rugs, and the lingering trace of expensive cigars. Lucy ordered them to spread a great cloth to protect the floor then opened her housemaid's box.

"You got to rub up every part of the grates every day, especially in winter when they're used. Mrs. Crisp is ever so particular about the shine."

The fire irons alone might have armed a medieval crusader. Watching hawkishly, Lucy showed the children how to set the irons aside, sweep up the ashes and dump them carefully into a pail. Katie could scarcely work for looking around her. There were shelves everywhere, floor to ceiling with a little ladder on a track so one could reach the top. The shelves were lined with books, all new and stiff in red Morocco leather. Katie had seen books in stalls but never dreamed of so mny together. They remained a tantalizing mystery since she could not read.

The door whispered open and Louisa herself, clad in a draped linen morning dress, came in. Lucy immediately dropped into a curtsy, very surprised. Mrs. Crisp, rarely abroad this early, considered it a breach of taste to see a housemaid at her tasks.

"Ah, they're at work, I see," Louisa murmured, betraying the reason for her visit. These children were, in an odd way, one of the keys that would bring her success and she had felt compelled to look at them again. She was pleased to see them already benefiting from the ash buckets of Crisp Court.

"Yes, ma'am, they are," Lucy affirmed. "You, children, curtsy to your betters!"

Louisa Crisp was such an overwhelming sight that nothing happened except that Katie let a scoop of ashes trickle back onto the hearth. Louisa stepped closer, noticing the short, bristly fringe sticking out all around under Cully's cap.

"Mercy, what happened to child's hair?"

Cully, who had no distinction of ranks in her cramped mind, immediately burst into a grin and whipped off the cap to reveal hair chopped to within of inches of her skull.

"All cutted off," she supplied helpfully, "because of the louses... and the tats."

A rattling intake of breath meant to Cully that she had cornered everyone's attention. Since meeting Amelia, Cully loved attention.

"BIG louses! Bitin' like...."

"That's enough!" Lucy gasped. "Lice indeed! The creature ought to be chased out with a broom!"

Louisa herself had paled. Mr. Dickens, even describing Oliver Twist, had never, she thought, mentioned lice.

Yet this was the very basket child she had so publically insisted upon having, the one that Amelia had rescued at the cost of grave burns to herself and of her brother's life. Louisa struggled for control, telling herself that ladies did not, could not know about...about vermin. Bravely she addressed Lucy.

"Are they clean now?"

"Oh yes, ma'am. Mrs. Quincy made special sure of that. Everything was inspected, even their drawers."

Cully, unaware of the undesirability of lice, went back contentedly to scraping ashes. Katie, who knew all about vermin herself, also began to work, but Laura remained staring at Cully. Had she really spent the night in a room with a girl who had had lice!

"Are they going to clean all the grates?" Louisa asked.

"Yes ma'am, and scrub the back stairs and wash the pots after the servants have had their meals. They are shedding idle ways and learning to labour for their keep." A searing heat mounted Laura's neck as she realized she was wearing a servant's cap and a servant's apron and was actually down on her knees brushing up cinders. Gran would have had apoplexy!

"What are their names?" Louisa wanted to know, unable to remember whether Amelia had actually told her yesterday.

"Mucker, Basing and...well, this one here's just Cully."

Cully favoured them with her perpetual grin. Laura put down the blacking brush she had been handed and stood up. In short, furious strokes, she wiped her hands on her apron. The numbed, stunned state that had possessed her since Mr. Whalley's chaise, fell away. Anger and confusion exploded to the surface.

"My name is Miss Atworth, if you please. And I don't clean grates. That's a job for housemaids!"

Her stance did justice to the Queen of Denmark. Her polished, imperious tones took everyone aback. Louisa blinked hard. Even Lucy went into a half curtsy before she came to her senses, furious at being so caught.

"Basing, get back to work before I call Mrs. Quincy!"

"Go ahead and call her!" challenged Laura, swinging round. After all, just who were these people, and how dare they try to order her about!

Louisa had never seen the help rebellious before. Lucy's gaze flew to her mistress, fearing to be thought incompetent.

"Fetch Mrs. Quincy at once!" Louisa ordered.

In a wink, Lucy was back with the housekeeper. Mrs. Quincy firmly shut the door and advanced upon Laura.

"Basing, you are ordered to clean out the grate."

"No!"

Laura regarded Mrs. Quincy with the all the assurance of her Atworth ancestors and her upbringing. Mrs. Quincy, like Lucy, was nonplussed. Louisa remained still, conveying clearly that it was up to the housekeeper to discipline her staff. Mrs. Quincy repeated her order. Laura tossed her brush into the fireplace.

"I said, it's a job for servants."

"And just what do you think you are then, Basing?"

"I'm not a servant! I'm Laura Atworth of Atworth House, Bedfordshire. I lived with my grandmother and we had servants of our own. Atworth House was built in the time of old Queen Elizabeth. It's a thousand times finer than this place all stuffed full of ugly things bought yesterday out of shops!"

What young Laura meant was that Crisp Court was laughably and unforgivably nouveau. In her innocence, she could not have slashed closer to Louisa's vanity. Louisa's ribs heaved against her stays. Mrs. Quincy, whose domain was also being sneered at, flew to the attack.

"Basing," she said ominously,"do you know what a bastard is?"

Unspeaking, Laura knotted her hands under her apron to stop their shaking.

"A bastard is a child who has no father and therefore no proper name and no one feed her and look after her. Where is your father, Basing?"

The terrible things Faxon Atworth had said roared in Laura's ears like a conflagration. She stiffened her back.

"My father was Charles Atworth. He died when I was a baby."

"Well now, if he was your father, he would have married your mother, wouldn't he? But he didn't. Your mother was just a tramp tea shop waitress who left you with nothing. If the people of this Atworth House took you in, they did so only out of charity and not because you were any sort of obligation."

One part of Laura devoured the awful facts. The other part spewed them up again.

"Lady Atworth was my grandmother!" Laura shouted, beginning to tremble. "Do you hear! My grandmother! She would have sent the stablemen after anybody who tried to make me clean a grate!"

Mrs. Quincy grabbed Laura's shoulder and gave her a violent shake.

"You won't shout that way! Ever!"

Words rose up in Laura's throat but she was too distraught to utter them. This thing had been like a terrible sore, growing and growing since the moment Faxon first confined her to her room. Now this woman was slashing at the wound.

Louisa Crisp stared at the tableau before her. So this was what they meant, she thought, by orphans being difficult to handle. Oh why did Mrs. Corman send her this misbegotten Laura Basing and that rickety Cully? Respectable children were what she had expected, Louisa lamented, cursing the fact that she could not now send them back.

"Lady Atworth is dead," Mrs. Quincy grated, going in for the kill. "Her heir wants no part of you. Therefore you depend on charity. Crisp Court is giving you charity. You better be grateful for that charity, Basing, and start cleaning that grate!"

A series of hot little breaths caught at Laura's throat. Her eyes automatically flew to Louisa for help, Louisa, the mistress here, who must sure understand she wasn't a servant, didn't grovel, didn't... couldn't...

But Louisa was looking as though she had just discovered beetles inside her corset. Laura had been cast truly adrift.

"I won't clean grates. I won't, I won't. I'm..."

Mrs. Quincy cuffed Laura hard on the ear. Gasping, Laura clapped her hand to her head and backed up, knocking over the andirons. No one had ever struck her before. Gran would have killed them.

"Are you ready to go to work?"

"No!"

Laura struggled frantically to hold onto who she was. If she had to clea grates, if she became a servant, then Atworth House was nothing and she was nothing and she'd rather be dead.

"Lucy, pick up that blacking brush she threw. Basing, hold out your hands."

Laura shut her hands into fists and clenched them against her sides. Mrs. Quincy nodded to Lucy. In concert, they took hold of Laura's wrists and twisted them upward. The first crack of the brush across Laura's knuckles drew a rough yelp of disbelief. At the second blow, she began to twist violently.

"Let me go! You let me go!"

The grip of the two women was inflexible. In a very few moments, Laura was reduced to a howling little girl who crumpled down on the floor in a heap and rubbed her hands against her chest trying to wipe out the hideous burning.

"Now, Basing, are your ready to clean the grate?"

Laura only sobbed louder. When Mrs. Quincy stepped toward her, Laura cringed away. Shaking, she picked up the blacking brush and set to work on the smoke-stained metal assigned her.

Embarrassed at having witnessed such a distressing scene, Louisa sped away. Dear, dear, so intransigent! Then she brightened at the thought of seeing to the placing of the new jardinières, just delivered that morning, for the conservatory.

When the children went to bed that night, Laura lay with her face to the wall, a very different child than when she had arrived. Within the space of minutes, the solid underpinnings of her identity, so patiently constructed by Lady Atworth, had been torn from under her. She had been flung into a bitter, drowning sea of humiliation. No matter how she flailed and thrashed, there was no support, not a thing to hold onto as the icy waves tossed her helplessly with their force.

Cully was fast asleep, her stomach ecstatically digesting the chicken pie they had been given for dinner. Katie lay in the moonlight seeping in the gable window and watched Laura. Laura was the only other person she had met who spoke as beautifully as Katie's adored Mrs. Corman.

The three of you will be like sisters. You must make friends and look out for each other.

"Huh!" Katie murmured aloud, "That wasn't even a hard drubbing you got today." She had weathered much worse regularly from old Jenksy.

Laura didn't move though Katie thought she saw the girl's shoulder heaving.

"What do you know about it!" Laura retorted.

"Lots."

Laura pulled the sheet over her head as if she wished the rest of the house would go to China. Katie could see that Laura hadn't the faintest idea about places like the Infant's Asylum. Piqued, she pushed herself up on her elbow. The good dinner and the wonders of Crisp Court were making her feel more energetic than she had in many weeks.

"I'm a bastard too!"

So there! Let her swallow that!

Slowly, Laura's face reappeared.

"You are?"

"Sure I am."

If this lovely girl who spoke in such royal tones could be a bastard, perhaps the condition wasn't so bad. Katie told Laura about Jenksy and how he came at her all the time with a switch, spouting that word.

"Didn't you want to just...just kill him!"

Jenks' face, that last time, flashed into her mind. A sharp, hot burst inside showed her how much she wanted to make him pay. She couldn't articulate such a thing to Laura so she related how she'd got back by throwing the bucket of soot.

"No! Oh, wouldn't Mrs. Quincy have...squealed!"

Katie gave way to a muffled giggle. Laura's mouth twitched. Why, Laura's just a simpleton about getting along, Katie realized, feeling oddly protective toward this girl whose grace she was starting to admire.

Katie herself had had a good day, an amazing day, as a matter of fact. The work, all new and interesting, was nothing at all beside apple selling. Time and again, she basked in the heat while staring out at the wind which lashed the windows but couldn't get in. After the library grate, she had been confined to scrubbing pots in the scullery, but her mind remained agog with the marvels just beyond the servants' door.

"I'd like to throw soot at Mrs. Quincy," Laura muttered savagely. "Throw it at them all!"

"Well you'd better not. I don't see what's wrong with cleaning a grate anyway."

"Because...because...."

And since Laura was so alone with no else to tell, she opened her former life to Katie, spilling the horror of being torn away.

"And now I'm....now Gran's dead and I've got nobody!'

"Well I'm here," said Katie. Her own lost Mary stirred cloudily at the back of her mind, telling her that a person couldn't be left alone. A person had to have somebody.

When Laura didn't answer, Katie sat up and tucked her knees under her, remembering her friend, Will. It was grand to have a friend. The grandest thing in the world. Katie longed for someone, anyone, who would help keep her from the dark, formless dreams that tormented her each night.

"Look," she proposed, "why don't you and me stick together. You know, look out for each other and that."

Laura peered at her skinny companion in the dimness, grasping at the warmth flowing from such an unlikely source. Friendship was new to Laura also.

"All right."

"And me," Cully chimed, bouncing up like a released jack-in-the-box. "Me! I'm a bastard too!"

She had been listening to the whole thing. Katie and Laura looked at each other, already taking Cully under their protection.

"All right," they vowed again together.

Salvaged, at least temporarily, from their respective heartaches, the three managed a grin in the silvery gloom.

CHAPTER FORTY

"She's coming! Hats in the air, fellows. Haggerty, stop imitating a seasick sheep!"

Rose's admirers had galloped to the edge of the crowd and were now engaged in constructing, by branishing their top hats, an impromptu triumphal arch under which Rose would have to dash. They were young bloods, following Rose about with a lusty boisterousness they wouldn't have dared show any of the official debs.

Rose, appreciating the arch, chucked some of the human pillars under their chins with her fan.

"You boys will all get sunstruck without your hats," she sallied as they leaned forward hoping to inhale the spicy fragrance that always trailed behind her.

"We're sunstruck already," the smitten Haggerty cried, "from being caught in your own dazzling rays."

Rose laughed and teased young Haggerty as extravagantly back. She adored all her followers and treated them with good-natured indulgence that kept them flocking at her heels. When Haggerty dropped his hat, overcome by her sheer proximity, Rose darted away toward the pair of chambers hastily converted into dressing rooms for her.

Light as a bird, she flitted inside, never before carried so high on a crest of success. Officially, the event was the St. Aidan's Bazaar and Recital in Aid of the Distressed. Unofficially, it was a paen to Rose Fitzroy and the wave that lifted her up to heady celebrity amongst the cheering crowd.

The event was held mostly outdoors in a summer bower called Kelsey Gardens, spread with booths and games and refreshment stands for the occasion. Kelsey Gardens had once surrounded a mansion built by one of the merry nobles returned with Charles II after the Restoration. The estate and the mansion had long ago been gobbled up in the sprawling urban expansion. Yet enough of the gardens remained to be used for the Bazaar as well as two wings of the old house now all but absorbed in a later building reaching to the street behind.

Rose had sung raised above the crowd in an airy half-crumbling garden structure which copied a miniature temple of Diana, the slim columns almost lost in a mist of rambling wisteria set against ancient cedars and tall, clipped yew.

The crowd, swelling up in a holiday mood, had bought up nearly everything in the booths, a bonanza for the causes, including Amelia's Refuge, sharing the proceeds.

Rose sang to more people than she'd ever seen before, every ledge, gate arch, tree and lamp post base possessed by some eager listener. The remaining windows of the old mansion peered down with interest. And if shapes moved behind their panes, Althea could have told Rose that two hundred years of intrigue had provided many a vantage point unseen by common folk outside.

As cheering roars echoed, Rose truly tasted mass adoration. She felt herself soaring above the booths and the crowd, Signor Abruzzi's tales tumbling through her mind like multi-coloured stars.

How could Rose not soar when she gave off such an air of sweet youth, innocent naughtiness and a carefree delight that epitomized the mood of the city right then. A look at her might make the most cynical believe, at least for a moment, that never was anyone so fortunate as to be alive at such a time, in such a country, on such a fine summer's day.

"Daisy," Rose called out to the maid Althea had equipped her with. "Daisy, where are you?" They did not have a great deal of time to linger. Tonight, Crisp Court was exerting itself with a reception at which she was practically guest of honour.

The very idea of a dressing room tickled Rose enormously. Dressing rooms had figured large in the tales of Signor Abruzzi. A dressing room was, by nature, a place of assignations and secrecy where tribute flooded in and fair divas broke hearts by the bucketful.

Rose was all the more light-hearted because she was without Mrs. Wharton hovering, ever watchful, somewhere in the background. From the moment Rose had moved into Wharton House, Althea Wharton had always been there, keeping an invisible hand on everything Rose did. Yet that afternoon, when they had been getting ready to leave for the Bazaar, Althea had suddenly gone a cheesy white and sat down hard on a sofa, her hand pressed over her eyes.

"What is it?" Rose had asked anxiously. She had never seen anyone that colour before.

"My head hurts. Oh, of all the perverse times!" Pulsating stars exploded on the insides of Althea's eyelids. Her stomach turned over with engulfing nausea. "Tonight...the reception. Oh...."

With great effort, Althea managed to lift her face and regard Rose through slits of lids.

"You'll have to go alone. I...must...go to bed. You behave yourself. You...oh, don't go getting into trouble with me not there to... to..."

The words died out as Althea shut her eyes again. All her careful plans skittered madly in her head. Tonight at Crisp Court was important, so important. Tonight was the night when debts would have to be paid off, when Rose would have to...

"Henry..." was all Althea could groan before the whiteness engulfed her. After that, she wouldn't have cared if the whole of England got up and sailed to Fiji so long as she could lie down and not be bothered by knowing about it.

Althea's maid philosophically assured Rose that it was only one of the mistress's sick headaches.

"She'll be right as a pin this time tomorrow, Miss, unless its one of her three-day wallopers. You run along now and let me take care of it."

Unacquainted with the tortures reserved for migraine sufferers, Rose had ceased to worry as soon as she heard the word "headache", associated in her mind with Mrs. Gresham's transparently fake complaints when the girls grew too obstreperous. High spirits restored, Rose had set out with only Daisy to escort her. Althea, tottering, tackled the immense journey to her bed.

Now Rose bubbled with the giddy sense of liberty. Each day was still a gift package that she had only to tear open to find fresh treasures. After the long greyness of Gresham's, Rose was determined never to let a single pleasure escape.

The room had once been a lady's chamber and still had a tall old clothes press and the panelling fashionable in Charles' time. Rose peeped out the window at the people beginning to stream away. Each day might be an exciting gift package, but it usually failed to contain the prize Rose thought about most—Adam Crisp. She had scanned the audience for him. The departing crowd did not yield up his wide shoulders or that villanous moustache.

She was always glancing around for him even in all the places he couldn't possibly be. Now her heart pattered eagerly at the idea of going to the reception and seeing him at home, for surely he must attend his mother's entertainment.

No doubt about it, Adam Crisp had lodged himself inside Rose. When she danced, she could not help wondering what that particular waltz or quadrille would be like in Adam's arms. Whenever she had pulled some outrageous caper at cards or got almost choked up on a sentimental song, or made merry until first light of dawn, she longed to chatter about with Adam. With no other person did she share that easy intimacy acquired that day in Hyde Park when they had worn the hours away with talk. And no one else knew as much about her as she had shared with Adam Crisp.

Now that Rose regarded the entire male population as her private fief, there had been stolen kisses, yet never another like that first one in the cab. Perhaps the reason Rose felt so free to sample so many men, like a hummingbird helping itself to an endless meadow of flowers, was her effort to recapture that one slow, questing kiss that had set her afire.

She saw Adam only rarely after she moved in with Mrs. Wharton. Adam did not frequent such circles and seemed often away on mysterious errands. Nevertheless, she hungered to know where he was and what he was doing. She asked Henry Crisp rather more often than she should, considering that she only got a growl for an answer. She learned not to mention Adam to Althea, for the name conjured up the frown of someone wanting no unpredictables in her careful plans.

The strange condition Rose was in regarding Adam grew stronger and stronger, all the more confusing because she flitted through a world in which flirtation was everything and serious emotion the height of awkwardness.

An irrational worry filled her that Adam might leave for Canada and she wouldn't see him again. How ironic that, with all the males in pursuit of her, the first man she had met had moved into her mind and settled there. The stories he had told her had settled there too. Sometimes she would wake up at night and find she had been dreaming of wind in long grasses, trees tall as church towers, dances in barns, cold air that nipped and braced, northern lights sprawled in glittering swathes across the sky.

Sometimes she longed to breathe that wild clean air.

When Adam did appear, usually from nowhere, he kept his distance, exempt from the obligation to flirt imposed upon the rest of the male mob. When they talked it was as if they were taking up their conversation exactly where they had broken off the time before. Rose, who felt she could tease every other man in the universe, found she could not tease Adam. Her heart always gave an irrepressable jump at the sight of him. Sometimes, in the midst of dandyish bucks or fluttering ladies, Rose longed to share a knowing look or a droll, ironical glance with him.

Rose half guessed that Adam found himself in a world in which he no longer fitted. The niceties of etiquette his mother had laboured so valiantly to instill had pretty well gone by the boards in lumber camps and prairie tents. Such a man could never take seriously ten-course meals, engraved visiting cards or even the proper attitude to servants. With great difficulty, he prevented himself from swearing aloud at his mother's side.

"Where have you been?" Rose would demand after Adam had dropped from sight for yet another troubling age.

"Why looking about me as any good lad just home should do," he would quip, rubbing his chin and giving her a raffish grin that almost fooled her about the restlessness underneath. His watchful air mingled curiously with an impatience held rigidly in check, an almost visible desire to get on with things.

Adam had been looking about. Disliking to be in the house with Henry, Adam spent as much time as he could away, poking about shipyards, visiting foundries, even looking into farms to see whether there was any possible way he could fit back into this old land. Each time he returned to Crisp Court, he became more oppressed by the feeling that the very earth under his feet had been trodden over, layered with soot and worn stale by others living on it for a thousand years.

One day he'll simply take a notion and be off, a small voice at the back of Rose's mind warned her. How long can he stand not putting himself to use?

She could not explain the spurt of panic this idea induced. Not when she was flying from picnic to party to musicale with Althea, not when the sweet, joyous frolic of her own liberty was bringing so much delight. Rose only knew that when she lay awake and thought of him, invisible, honeyed arrows pierced her flesh. In her airy bedroom, she relived the kiss in the cab but could not tell that Adam was committing larceny on her heart.

CHAPTER FORTY-ONE

Rose shook herself from her reverie. She was excited about the reception for she dearly loved a party. Not only was she to be a guest of honour but her concert was to be announced, the one that was to be hers alone. She imagined herself arriving at Crisp Court, the glow of her garden performance trailing after her, a sparkling tail of light.

"Daisy," Rose called out slipping into the chair before the mirror, "have you got my..."

Her hand froze halfway to tucking back wisps of hair. Behind her stood a painted dressing screen behind which Daisy was supposed to be gathering Rose's things. Instead a square, commanding personage stepped out, bringing Rose scrambling to her feet.

"M...mother!" she stammered, unable to believe her eyes. "Where's Daisy?"

To gain entry, Red Nell had crammed herself into the garb of a flower seller. A wicker basket sat on the floor, fragrant cargo spilling over the rim. A vast knitted shawl enveloped Nell's shoulders. A straw hat flopped its broad brim downward, all but concealing the grim face underneath. A good thing too. No flower seller ought to look that intimidating.

"Gone out," Nell returned laconically.

Panic gripped Rose. She had not seen her mother since their last meeting at Gresham's. She had made her bolt for freedom and only begun to stop looking over her shoulder for the looming figure. Now she shrank, irrationally filled with a fear that she was going to be snatched out of this dream just the way she'd been plucked from the gypsy wagon and slapped into Gresham's.

"Have ye fergotten yer family, girl?" Nell s demanded. "Do ye mean to shuck us off like old tea leaves from a cup?"

The older woman's presence swelled into all the corners. The room became much smaller.

"I have not," Rose parried gamely. "Haven't I stuck by Amelia Corman like the bargain was! Haven't I been pouring money into her lap by the tubful!"

"And didn't ye skip out of Mrs. Gresham's without leavin' so much as a wink behind ye!"

Nell had been in a ferment ever since Rose had vanished from Gresham's and turned up inside the elevated confines of Wharton House. Being cut off from the action wasn't at all what Nell had envisioned when she had launched Rose into the scintillating stream. Her inability to reach into Althea's domain as she had into Gresham's only increased her frustration. Despite her secret approval of the boldness of the girl, she had no intention of allowing Rose out of her grasp.

Truth to tell, Nell was suffering a roil of mixed feelings unprecedented in her life. Nell had not expected to feel this panic even as she was amazed at Rose's success. Powerful maternal emotions churned up in her bosom. Over and over she kept thinking of Gwyn, turned rebellious too, and murdered in a coal bin.

None of this had been helped by Dan, who read the newspapers to his mother, dwelling on the articles in which Rose was mentioned at this party or that. Dan was at his mother day and night to take advantage of Rose's luck. Steadily, he hatched schemes for the purpose while Joe brooded, mastiff-like, missing the sister he adored.

Down a quick slide to a nasty landin', Rose might be goin' if she's not taken in hand, Nell had been thinking, full of worry. Nell had gone to all the trouble of bluffing her way in so that she could order Rose back to the path originally plotted. Live with Amelia, work with Amelia so that, in good time, the skimming of all those tempting funds could begin. Miss no opportunity was Nell's credo. Time Rose quit playing and started earning her keep.

Rose struggled to hang onto her nerve for she could see some unyielding purpose in her mother's eye.

"I couldn't bear Gresham's, not one moment longer. I was only following our plan."

"Oh ye were! Then might I ask where all the money's comin' from that's buyin' them dresses and payin' fer the parties?"

If Nell wasn't the source of brass for Rose, then who was? And what were they getting in return?

"Don't be daft," Rose exclaimed, to whom the question of financing had not occurred.

"Daft! Listen, me girl..."

Nell's eruption was cut short by a firm but discreet rap on the door behind them connecting to a side corridor. Before Rose could respond, the door opened. In stepped a plump gentleman of middling height, with a soft dark, impeccably groomed beard and even more impeccable tailoring. Receding hair above a smooth forehead was brushed back carefully and his hands gleamed with care. He stood solidly, exuding the prime of life, taking in every detail of Rose in one smiling, practised glance.

"Ah, Miss Fitzroy," he beamed, tilting his head, "I knew I would find you here. You're even lovelier in person than seen across a crowd. I've come to personally convey my admiration."

Rose straightened sharply at this invasion. By now she was used to male hijinks but they didn't usually pursue her through feminine doors. This visitor acted as though all rooms were his own. Even his eyes twinkled as though he were hoarding some stupendous secret behind his expectant smile.

Nell stepped abruptly between her daughter and the intruder.

"And just who might ye be, boyo?"

Her broad, rough Irish would have knocked down a dockside thug. This ordinary seeming fellow, though much startled, gazed back with private amusement.

"Only an ardent admirer of Miss Fitzroy who couldn't wait to congratulate her on her performance."

This statement was combined with an animated interest in the grace of Rose's neck and the high colour aroused by the arrival of her mother. Nell didn't like the cast of the fellow's eye, especially not when it was roving over her daughter. This gentleman, she saw, had lechery on his mind in spades.

"Well, don't ye know not ter come bargin' in where ye've not been asked," Nell ground out, advancing, "so take your sheep's eyes and yer slick tongue out 'o here before I do the removin' meself. Hurry up now, out, out!"

Next thing, Nell had the side door open and him by the shoulder. One sturdy thrust propelled him out they way he had come with the door slammed behind.

Rose had time to collect herself. Such a well-turned out admirer, pushy though he was, brought back to her the splendid success of her day.

"He was my visitor," Rose spluttered, seizing upon the fellow as the pivot to do battle with her mother. Her breath came hard as she screwed up her nerve.

"Well he's nobody's visitor now. The cheek of him, pushin' in when I'm having a talk. Ye've glimpsed the back 'o that one fer good."

"Oh, we'll see!"

"And what d'ye mean by that?"

Silly though it might be, Rose clung hard to her proprietorship of the bearded intruder. With her mother watching, she reached into dressing table drawer for the notepaper kept there and the pen and ink.

"I mean this."

Rose snatched up the pen and scribbled a hasty impudent note which she folded swiftly. Writing was one act that could stymie illiterate Nell. On impulse, Rose pulled a rosebud from one of her many bouquets and tucked it into the paper. As defiantly as if she were skipping past massed cannon, Rose stuck her head out into the corridor.

"You lad," she called to one of the boys who hung about for errands. "There's a gentleman with whiskers who'd just left out the side door. Please run this note to him before he's gone completely."

Winking, Rose pressed a coin into the lad's fingers and was rewarded with a worshipful blush as crimson as his waistcoat. Cherishing the brush of Rose's hand far more than the generous tip, he flew off to do her bidding.

"What have ye gone and done now?" Nell demanded, bristling at Rose's temerity. She distrusted all writing, especially folded notes passed about under her nose.

"Only invited the poor soul to the reception. Least I could do after having him pitched out by the scruff!"

The act, impulsive and unladylike, filled Rose with a sense of her own power. After all, she asked herself about Nell, what can she really do? Carry me off in her basket? The very idea provoked a renegade giggle that didn't dare pop out. Signor Abruzzi would have been proud.

Yes, she was free! Her chains fell away. No one could make her do a thing she didn't wish to do, not even this formidable woman who called herself mother. Her wide eyes challenged Nell directly. Nell halted at this open mutiny. She was already too late. Rose could no more be diverted from her course than any of the other headstrong beauties scattered among her ancestors.

Sligo, Mayo and Donegal and no rest anywhere, they kept after her that fierce.

An intense, mystical conviction came over Nell that Rose flirted with a tragic end. Daisy dashed back in followed by two others who had shared the stage with Rose, and came up short before Nell.

"It's all right, Daisy, this lady was just leaving. Look at the lovely roses she delivered."

Nell could only drop back into her flower seller guise. Shooting Rose a baleful look, she hoisted her basket and marched out, leaving a trail of dropped petals on the floor behind her.

CHAPTER FORTY-TWO

"Amy, I had no idea!"

Edwin gaped from the carriage Louisa had insisted on sending for them. Crisp Court blazed light from its many mullioned windows. Music floated out from the musicians behind screens of feathery palms. Footmen in livery flung open the embossed doors. The occupants of other carriages jamming the kerb were handed up the broad steps.

"Mrs. Crisp has been very kind to our cause, darling. We must do everything we can to repay her," Amelia told him, her neck throbbing from anxiety.

Edwin had returned from Scotland only that morning. Amelia was wrung out from the task of introducing him to all the startling advances she had wrought in his absence, not the least of which were her new connections with wealthy Crisp Court. Edwin was dumbfounded at discovering himself titular head of an organization operating in the black and already inquiring about distribution homes in Canada. Please, Amelia begged, addressing the inscrutable Providence raining such difficult bounty, just let us get safely through the evening. Just let Edwin survive meeting Rose!

"But your letters..."

Edwin couldn't connect the "providential associations" Amelia had described to this red Gothick pile plopped on such a prime London corner. He wouldn't have got near this amount of money if he'd thumped on his lectern for twenty years.

"I'm afraid I'm a poor correspondent," Amelia kept her eyes averted. "I did try to explain. I had to move quickly when this wonderful opportunity appeared. It's such a relief to have you back at my side."

She hugged Edwin's elbow tighter but Edwin's head was still swivelling to take in the gargoyles as they went in.

"Amelia, dear!" Louisa trilled, instantly swooping down. "This must be that errant husband of yours come back in time for Derby

Week. Mr. Corman, you must be bursting with amazement about Miss Fitzroy. Oh, I've such a horde of introductions to make!"

England, that jolly sporting nation, regarded the annual Derby at Epsom Downs, as one of the very pinnacles of the London Season. Since Epsom racecourse was only twelve miles from London, all Londoners, high and low, claimed Derby Day enthusiastically as their own. The days leading up to the horse race provided excuse for revels of every description, culminating in the riotous orgy at Epsom on race day itself.

Louisa Crisp, like a salmon flinging itself into the raging stream, chose Derby week to launch her first major entertainment. The reception, naturally, had been Althea Wharton's idea.

"With Rose as a special guest," Althea had exclaimed, blinking her protruding eyes as though just struck with the lucky inspiration. "We'll announce Rose's concert in support of the Refuge. The tickets will be sold out in a day!"

Opportunities were to be snatched where one found them. Louisa pounced on this one. To count for anything at all, she scarcely needed Althea to remind her, she had to give entertainments to which people of significance would come. Now, thanks to her link with Amelia Corman's Refuge and the runaway success of Rose Fitzroy, London's stubborn social barriers were beginning to come down.

Divine intervention was the only way Louisa could describe the indispensable Mrs. Wharton. She fervently thanked whatever celestial whim had provided this guide through the treacherous, unfamiliar quicksands all about. Nor did Louisa dare baulk at the price. If there was but one path to success, Louisa meant to take it, even if it meant being whirled away on the tail of the comet known as Rose Fitzroy!

Althea congratulated herself for her own clever management. The connection between Rose and Amelia Corman's emigration scheme would have been a brilliant idea even had Rose not so staunchly insisted upon it herself. The respectable ladies of the charitable committees, whatever their private opinions, would be pressed far before they would relinquish such a valuable gusher of cash. Wasn't life delightful, Althea thought, licking secret minty savour from her lips, when one had some genuine material to work with.

Louisa latched onto Edwin and Amelia all the more tightly for having just learned that Althea Wharton was indisposed. The note had arrived as the first of the guests began pouring in. Sir Herbert Bentley and his wife had accepted the invitation. And Dean Wickham, for mercy sakes! And Mr. and Mrs. Dunstan, the Ballthorpes and that influential, indefatigable dowager, Lady Bliggs. Without Althea, Louisa was on her own. Her forage merchant antecedents rose up and made her weak at what she was attempting.

Amelia's Refuge would need funds raised for the next fifty years if Louisa were lucky. And how would Louisa ever have guessed, without Althea's nudging, that this austere, impoverished charity toiler in the atrocious dresses should have a father famous to half of London and enough impeccable respectability to lend even Louisa priceless cachet.

And even more priceless than Dr. Radmore, the Refuge and respectability, was Amelia's intimate affiliation with Rose Fitzroy, the dynamo powering it all.

Louisa pressed Amelia's hand warmly, not letting herself wonder why Amelia looked as though she had a thistle down her back. Amelia's husband, Louisa was pleased to notice, was peeping about with a most gratifying wonder and was heartily bluff with the host of people Louisa presented him to.

"Well, you have been busy, my dear," he commented to Amelia over a large gulp of the fruit punch. "If you can make progress like this, I'll have to go away more often."

Amelia scanned her husband for signs of wounded self-esteem but only saw him expand and turn an anticipatory eye toward the refreshment tables. Oh, how good it was to have him back, to touch his curly beard and inhale the warm, woolly smell of his jackets. How she looked forward to shifting much of the burden to his shoulders.

Louisa found herself steadily asked, especially by the men, about when Rose was expected to arrive.

"Soon," Louisa told them all, "soon."

But not too soon, she hoped, trying to calculate just when this unsettling creature might appear. As late as decently possible because of the unpredictable uproar she created in her wake.

Yet as time ticked by Louisa had reason to wish otherwise. People sat about in groups, the ladies toying with their fans, the gentlemen leaning their elbows on pieces of furniture and looking as if they would like to pull out their watches. In a spurt of alarm, Louisa realized she didn't know what to say to these people without Althea Wharton's easy chatter at her side.

The awful stamp of boredom and dullness, once fallen upon Crisp Court, would be almost as bad as outright ostracism in the intensely competitive round of the Season. People would think of every excuse in the future to avoid coming and would squirm like worms on hooks if forced.

The reception must succeed! It must!

Louisa patted at the dampness developing along her hairline and tried not to think of the letter she had received only that morning. A letter boldly dashed across rough yellow writing paper that would have done better credit to a packing firm than a young lady schooled for years in the art of charming penmanship.

The trouble had begun when Camille had rejected the new spring dresses Louisa had forwarded, determined her daughter should hold her own amongst all the exalted principessas and honorables she was quartered with.

"Dear Mama," Camille had written from that horrendously expensive Swiss finishing school Louisa had sent her to, "please don't order any more new gowns for me. The clothes I have are perfectly serviceable and will do me for many years to come. Miss Haplein, whom we all adore, has shown us the folly of vainly pursuing fashion when there are so many nobler matters to occupy our minds. Plain sturdy covering is all the human body needs, Miss Haplein says. I've unstitched the ribbons and laces from the dresses I have and given all such impractical frippery to the poor to vend in the street."

Louisa had read on in growing horror. Instead of being "finished", as Louisa was paying so exorbitantly to have done, Camille had fallen under influence of a deranged school mistress who had not only forbidden corsets, but had been taking the girls in her care on hair-raising hiking expeditions and telling them women ought to vote and sit in Parliament!

Louisa had written back recounting the heady social circles into which she was making entry and dangling the tantalizing prospects being assembled for Camille's debut the following year. A trunkload of heavy books had arrived along with a letter dismissing Louisa's labours airily.

"You needn't go to the bother, Mummy. I'll have no time for parties when I come home and I've made up my mind never to marry. By the time next year is out, I expect either to be at work reclaiming fallen seamstresses in London rookeries or on my way to India to snatch widows from blazing funeral pyres. Miss Haplein..."

Phoebe had had to snatch the letter away and help Louisa put her head between her knees. The moment she could trust herself to hold a pen, Louisa had written back ordering her daughter out of that nest of foreign subversives immediately. And Louisa meant to fire a scorching rebuke at Mrs. Schipley who had recommended the infernal, unnatural idea of education abroad.

Meantime she must quickly establish herself among these people Althea had been so kind as to introduce her to. Camille must have a proper coming out. Goodness, they had better get a husband on the hook before the girl could blurt out Miss Haplein's insane ideas and ruin her prospects altogether.

Missing Althea acutely, Louisa rustled off to greet some stragglers. Adam had chosen to go off on some mysterious journey or other, which was a relief, considering the effect he had created at the tea. But, goodness, why wasn't Henry busy here lending a hand!

But Henry was utterly preoccupied with keeping a constant, heated watch toward the door.

"Spend what you need, don't spare it," was all he'd said when Louisa had proposed this reception. His eyes had flickered with covetous sparks.

His obsession had progressed to the point where the reception had only one meaning for him—Rose! His whole measure of success in London had become caught up his ability to control, to possess, Rose. Just as the size of a man's bank account was considered, in that free-rolling era of laissez-faire capitalism, commensurate with his favour in heaven, so Henry saw in proprietorship of the singer so many admired, his signal to the world of potency, of a man to respect, a man to deal with.

Pink punch untouched, Henry thought how Rose had already been well worth the investment. His connection with her was affording entry to the world of London capital and big speculation he so longed for. After months of cold-shouldering, he found himself introduced to a group of investors only too pleased to accept a large chunk of Henry's money for their project.

His lips were sealed over it, of course, for it involved a lightning slash into the heart of London as other consortiums had done with such huge success. The trick was to buy, with no hint of the scheme, in the poorest neighbourhoods where property was the cheapest. The lower the cost, the bigger the profits. Profits gave Henry a tremulous, all-over pleasure just under his skin.

That pleasure had become enmeshed with Rose. Dry heat licked over Henry at the thought of having her under his roof. It was time for his expenditure of cash to pay off. The Wharton woman surely knew exactly what the return must be.

Oh yes, she knew all right, Henry thought to himself, for wasn't this reception only a way of delivering Rose over into his power? Too feverish to care how Mrs. Wharton did things, Henry only expected Rose to be prepared. Throughout her rise in popularity, he had watched all the other men making fools of themselves at her heels while secretly hoarding the knowledge that he, Henry Crisp, held the trump card.

Tonight he meant to play that card. Press his claim, publicly stamp himself upon Rose, advertise to all that he was in possession. Even Althea Wharton's absence was a sign. Henry didn't believe for a moment she was ill. She was absenting herself to leave the field to him.

What's more, by some fortunate turn of fate, Adam wasn't there to complicate things. Adam would come back to find Henry had stolen several marches right under Adam's nose. Henry couldn't wait to see Adam's brash brown face collapse when he found Rose obediently on Henry's arm. In his mind, as clearly as if it were actually before him, he saw the hollow at the base Rose's throat where her collarbones met, a hollow where he meant to...

He felt his eyes closing into slits and popped them open again. Win Rose and somehow get rid of Adam again. Be done fending off curious conjecture and probing

questions as to why a younger brother had inherited everything. The questions made Henry sweat. While Adam was around, Henry lived with the gut-clutching fear that it all might somehow slip away as things had done when he was young.

Then there was an uproar at the door. Rose sailed in, afloat, invincible after her triumph of the afternoon, her daring, victorious skirmish with Red Nell.

The arrival of Rose was like a burst of fizzing bubbles into a flat, dull drink. The subdued chatter turned into a merry hubbub. The men shoved themselves away from the furniture; the women craned their necks to see. In a trice, Crisp Court was in a party mood.

"Hello, cousin dear," Rose warbled as she kissed Amelia, laughing inwardly at the pinkness shooting up Amelia's cheek as Amelia introduced Edwin. "So this is the fearsome husband."

Edwin, like a myriad other men, found himself caught in grey-green eyes that made him feel instantly fascinating.

"Not fearsome to you, I hope," Edwin mumbled, feeling warm as a midsummer bonfire.

"Oh I adore fearsome men. Such a pity all the best ones were taken while I was stuck away in Cornwall. Trust dear cousin Amelia to choose the pick of the lot before the rest of us had our poor little chance, you fortunate fellow."

Grinning with mischief, Rose rendered Edwin speechless.

"For goodness sake," Amelia snapped as Rose glided off, "close your mouth before the whole room sees your tonsils!"

Edwin could hardly be blamed for his bedazzlement. The success of her recital, reinforced by her defiance of her mother, filled Rose with reckless animation. She appeared impossibly fetching in butter satin touched all over with pools of gold from the gaslights. Words like "whipped cream" and "mother-of-pearl" and "witch-craft" suggested themselves in the minds of her besotted admirers as they followed each maddening swish of her dress and glimpsed the beribboned kid slippers peeping from under her hems.

Spurts of laughter and a travelling knot of people always indicated her spot. Louisa could look over her guests with relief, then a bounding satisfaction. Dean Wickham told amusing anecdotes about his early years in the missionary service. Mrs. Ballthorpe complimented Louisa on the profusion and heaviness of floral arrangements and the colour of the punch. Lady Bliggs, who had come on the arm of her nephew up from his commission in the army, looked everywhere with shrewd, wrinkle encased eyes, making Louisa imagine how favourably Crisp Court would be described at breakfasts and teas in so many families that mattered.

As Rose drifted off through at least two sets of double doors, drawing a flock of men after her, Henry controlled himself, waiting until the moment was right. Mrs. Wharton would have her well primed he expected. Rose could not turn from him now without grave insult. Saliva thickened in his mouth at the thought of Rose holding tightly to his elbow, showing the rest who the real favourite was, feeling her move only as he directed. He waited until Rose had ensconced herself at a distance with men ranged around her pleased as schoolboys, then pushed himself away from the mantel.

He had taken only a step toward claiming that flame of strawberry hair when Mellon appeared before Louisa with a note on a silver tray. Distractedly, Louisa opened it, read it, then read it again.

Her heart tottered against her corset stays before she realized it was only someone playing a wicked joke. Oh, of all times to have to deal with foolery like this!

"There's a military gentleman awaiting a reply, madam," Mellon said in his usual lugubrious tone. Mellon was an old retainer, trained up by Milton Crisp. Unlike the rest of the staff, he was not impressed with this new building or the shenanigans of London gentlemen.

"Tell him," Louisa sputtered shortly," that the Prince of Wales and party is more than welcome at any entertainment I provide. And if he appears with gilded wings and a cherub perched on his head, all the better for the diversion of the guests, I say!"

Mellon retreated, pleased, for he shared Louisa's opinion of the tasteless prank.

Louisa had just turned back to Mrs. Ballthorpe, when there was a commotion near the entrance. Mellon reappeared, now barely able to keep his eyes in his head.

"Ladies and gentlemen," he quavered, piercing even that merry hubbub, "His Royal Highness, the Prince of Wales, and p-p-party!"

CHAPTER FORTY-THREE

Conversation perished. All gazes swung to the entrance. There, unbelievably, stood the familiar, stocky figure of the Prince himself, his crowd of ever-present cronies at his heels.

Louisa gaped at a sight that could not possibly exist even though it persisted before her eyes. Her corset seemed to contract until no air reached her lungs. Both of her feet glued themselves to the floor.

The doings of the Prince were always of paramount fascination in London. Even Louisa had heard how he moved, with indefatigable energy, from party to party during the Season. Since all doors stood automatically open, awaiting his choice, no one ever had the temerity to issue an invitation. Never in hundred years could Louisa once have dreamed HE might come to Crisp Court!

Through the dots dancing before her eyes, Louisa watched as the Prince approached, good-humouredly taking in her state.

"Thank you for including a few last minute guests," he murmured with charming ease. "I'm here at the behest of the matchless Miss Fitzroy. I'm afraid I really can't do much about the gilded wings or a cherub perching on my head."

By the time Louisa recovered from imminent collapse, the Prince was circulating about, indicating to the flabbergasted guests that this was an informal visit, protocol set aside. Everyone, the twinkling royal eyes indicated, was to go on enjoying themselves as thoroughly as His Highness's own party intended to.

After the first reeling shock, a blinding excitement engulfed Louisa, swiftly followed by terror. Would her buffet be suitable for him to eat? Which chair would he sit upon? How long would he stay? Louisa had heard that the Prince's favourite dish was plainly broiled truffles served up in a silver dish. Clammy chills broke out along her shoulder blades. Crisp Court did not contain a single truffle. Mellon, oh where was Mellon! She had a hundred frantic orders for the servants.

Far off, through the sets of double doors, Rose missed the commotion. A thickset, military individual bowed before her. A newly arrived gentleman, he said, wished to speak with her. Looking up. Rose saw the fellow who had been summarily ousted from her dressing room.

"Oh, so you did come," she laughed, pleased. "Perhaps this time we'll be able to get the introductions without a flower seller bundling you into the hall like a packet of bad cheese!"

Choking sounds stuck in throats all round. Failing to notice, Rose thought only what a friendly, pompous gent this newcomer looked. She leaned forward, another quip on her lips. The military individual cut sharply in.

"Allow me. May I present His Royal Highness, the Prince of Wales!"

The Prince enjoyed nothing so much as the sensation his presence caused when not expected. He stood before Rose, a plump five foot six, his much imitated royal beard concealing a receding chin, beaming to see Rose's reaction.

Rose reared back humorously, imagining she was being teased. There were so many duplications of the Prince strolling about London that one couldn't be expected to recognize the real thing if one tripped over it.

"Queen of Daffodils, pleased to meet you, too," she grinned, dipping in an elaborate mock curtsy. Only when she heard gasps punctuating a petrified silence did Rose realize this was no imitation and said, "Oh!"

Edward, Prince of Wales, heir to throne, when he was introduced to Rose, had reached his thirties and stood in the full tide of his manhood. His late father, the earnest, hard-working, all-too-Germanic Prince Albert had been far too virtuous for the British people to fix their affections upon. His widowed mother, Queen Victoria, kept herself in austere seclusion at Windsor out of public sight. Edward, known familiarly as Bertie, filled up his parent's place in the public eye and made up for every interesting frivolity his solemn progenitors lacked.

Sober and industrious, Victoria and Albert set out to live lives utterly different from their reprobate ancestors who ranged from Albert's "wicked, rakish uncles" to the dandyish old King, "swollen, gouty, bewigged and bedaubed", whom Victoria had succeeded. Their eldest son, future king of the greatest empire the world had ever seen, was the gravest responsibility of all.

Bertie was a result of Victoria and Albert's efforts to raise "the most perfect man". This scientific process subjected the boy to such a restricted, chaperoned, joyless childhood devoted to so many improving pursuits as to practically guarantee that he would be fascinated with frivolity for the rest of his life. Even when allowed to study at Oxford, Bertie had an old general in constant attendance keeping at bay any young who might lead him into folly. Bertie was also kept apart from the opposite sex, assuring his obsession with their mysterious, tantalizing charms. Naturally, he was hideously frustrated.

Indifferent scholarship landed him in Curragh Camp in Ireland to be a soldier. The officers, taking pity on the young Prince's condition, smuggled Nellie Clifden, a pretty actress, into the Prince's quarters to relieve him, at last, of his burdensome virginity. Unfortunately, Nellie boasted. Rumour reached Prince Albert who rushed by train to berate his fallen son. Returning to Windsor, he took typhoid and subsequently died, but not before his delirious ravings revealed Bertie's sin to the Queen who was tenderly nursing her husband. Victoria blamed Bertie for her beloved Albert's illness and death, unable to even look upon her heir without a shudder.

Having once tasted the pleasures of the flesh, Bertie soon fell into error again, for he had inherited all the energy, vigour and gargantuan appetites of his Hanoverian forebears. Hurried consultations decided that if Bertie couldn't control himself, it was better for him to marry than to burn, especially if he were in danger of burning up the royal reputation. The Prince quickly found himself wed to the beautiful, innocent Princess Alexandra of Denmark.

Alexandra, only eighteen, had absolutely no suspicion of what she was taking on in this pink-faced, charming cherub of a husband. Instead of checking Bertie, marriage gave him his full freedom. In charge of his own affairs at last, he promptly moved into newly renovated Marlborough House with its countless bedrooms, well-stocked cellar, magnificent garden adjoining the Mall and the loveliest ballroom in the city. After a youth of being the most scrupulously fussed over, guarded and supervised young man in England, Bertie became, overnight, the most sought after, lavishly endowed, loved and envied prince in Europe.

Bertie at once fell in with the sort of rich, idle, decadent aristocrats that the industrious, essentially middle class Victoria and Albert had so despised. Just as predicted, they led Bertie merrily astray. In turn, Bertie helped them beggar themselves, one after another, for the honour of entertaining him. Alexandra, after a valiant effort at the start of their married life, gave up trying to keep up with her husband's impetuous pace. Retiring to Sandringham, she absorbed herself in her children and left Bertie to his hedonistic pursuits. When forced to come to town, she developed chronic lateness as a defence against her husband's relentless energy and appetite for glittering events.

Under other circumstances, Bertie might have become an effective man of action. He possessed vigour, bravery and, under his rakishness, a kindly, sentimental heart. However the Queen, unable to forgive him for her dear Albert's death and scarcely able to contemplate the failure of all their efforts to raise the ideal prince, refused to give her son anything serious to do. Consequently, Bertie's enormous energies were devoted entirely to the pursuit of pleasure. He lived his life as though perpetually famished for every delight denied him as a youth. He went from party to theatre to racecourse, seemingly determined to gorge himself until the day he died.

Starved for royalty in that most patriotic of eras the public took to Bertie instantly. Bertie had the stage all to himself. His formidable mother remained a sombre figure shut up in Windsor Castle. Although her dear Albert had been dead over a decade, she grieved inconsolably, swathed in black silk mourning. Victoria still had Albert's clothes laid out every night on his bed and ordered a fresh basin of water put in his room every morning. Over her bed, she kept a photo of her husband taken after he was dead. She slept with his red dressing gown thrown over her. This seclusion was broken by only a few public appearances and dull receptions. Receptions finished very promptly, Victoria discovered, if no refreshments were served and no one allowed to sit down in the presence of the monarch.

As for Bertie, Marlborough House became the very heart of fashionable London. He and his family decreed behaviour and decreed fashion. Men copied the Prince's hats, suits, beard and even his gait. When a touch of arthritis gave Alexandra a slight hitch in her step, society women had a shoe heel shortened so that they, too, could walk with the stylish Alexandra limp.

Bertie held supreme authority over social life and death. A casual word from the royal lips could mean hopeless banishment. His favour opened all doors. An invitation to a private dinner party at Marlborough House or, better, Sandringham, allowed all else to follow. One would be in demand, touched with the princely glamour of being one of his "special set". He extended his favour democratically to anyone who pleased him; jockeys as well as financiers, sailors as well as chocolate merchants were invited along. Only intellectuals were excluded due Bertie's fear of being bored by their talk.

In return for providing unsurpassable prestige, Bertie had no need to expend money of his own. Life had little more to offer a citizen than a visit from the Prince. And the Prince might very well visit for days at a time if a person's house was comfortable enough, the table first class, the shooting decent, a racecourse nearby and the conversation cheerful.

The Prince had a public life and a private life, both of which he enjoyed tremendously. He adored uniforms, ceremony, formal balls and grand occasions. He also hosted wild parties at Marlborough House in which guests sailed down stair railings and staged slap-stick battles with soda siphons. Disguised as an ordinary gentleman in a hansom cab, he drove out to observe life in districts of London where princes did not go. He loved to fling on old clothes and rush out to watch a fire. Hushed rumour had it that he had worked his way, incognito, through the temptations the worst dives in the city had to offer.

His friends remained the "bad set" his father had warned him against, friends who were flamboyant and immensely rich, who lived on the leading edge of fashion, or who were the free-living old nobility. The people Victoria described as those "wretched, ignorant, high-born beings who live only to kill time".

Tutored by such associates, Bertie had no difficulty killing time. There was horse racing, shooting and hunting. There was playing cards for money until early in the morning or gambling at casinos when abroad. There were billiards and cock fighting and ratting matches. There were music halls and theatre. After the theatre, Rules or the Cafe Royal or Kittner's which provided not only superb meals but private rooms with settees for post prandial sex.

Above all, there were women. The Prince had a very keen eye for the ladies, and by the time he was introduced to Rose, he was a proficient rake. After Nellie Clifden, Bertie came to regard the female population as one gigantic smorgasbord. He had learned from such sybarites as the former Emperor of France, Napoleon III, who insisted that he had to have a woman after every meal just as he had to have a good cigar.

Bertie was abetted in his womanizing by a certain Major Hoggett who performed many best unmentioned duties for his master. Hoggett, the same who had just introduced the Prince to

Rose, was a thick-bodied ramrod of a man who managed to jingle and creak with the military accoutrements he dearly loved to wear. He had straw-pale hair cut very short and even paler, stubbier lashes. His role with the Prince was not apparent to outsiders who assumed him simply another boon companion helping the riot along. Hoggett could laugh with the loudest and carouse with the best. Yet a ruthless watchfulness also resided in the pale blue eyes. What passed as drink-induced ruddiness really indicated a thinly concealed choleric nature. His capacity for immediate, efficient and drastic action made him an ideal guardian-companion for a prince who must be gratified fully while kept, at all costs, from open public scandal.

Above all, Hoggett loved to flex his control by choosing the women himself to feed his master's appetites. Through the Prince, Hoggett lived out his own lascivious fantasies. While his master satisfied himself, Hoggett burned with shiny-eyed, vicarious lust.

In pursuit of a new fancy, the Prince could prove amazingly persistent, but it had been Hoggett who had sniffed out the rumours of Miss Rose Fitzroy and slipped his master to see her. Bertie had been quite enthralled as Rose sang in the vine-hung little temple. Thwarted in his attempt to astonish her by a visit to her dressing room, he had pursued her to Crisp Court. Hoggett, as much as the Prince, had fixed his appetite upon Rose. Rose, he decided, should not get away.

Any party naturally revolved around the Prince the way rapids revolved around the deceptively smooth centre of a whirlpool. Full of amiability, the Prince kept Rose at his side, drawing her along as he circulated, insisting she sit beside him when he sat, treating her to the full battery of his personable charm as he nodded and joked and was gracious to the company.

Up until then, in her brief but spectacular weeks of freedom, Rose had seen her relations with men as a game at which, invisibly coached by Althea, she easily excelled. She had not met the sort of men who accompanied the Prince. These cronies or "heavy swells", were as wealthy, reckless and pleasure-seeking as they were self indulgent. They were acquainted with places and pursuits that would have made Louisa's hair stand on end. And they were used to getting what they wanted.

Nor did Rose guess that she faced, in this genial, gregarious fellow, one of the most accomplished roués in the realm. To those who knew the Prince, it soon became obvious why he was at the party. Though Bertie didn't deviate from proper, easy, royal etiquette, he was after Rose as certainly as any stag after a doe in heat.

The Prince's followers did not take well to Crisp Court. Veterans of the hard-drinking sprees at Marlborough House, they were appalled to find themselves at a temperance event offering nothing stronger than fruit punch. Now they stood about with pink filled cups in their hand, restless with the cravings of aroused but unsatisfied thirst.

Precluded by the Prince's interest from pursuing Rose, they amused themselves for a while by eying the screechingly nouveau furnishings filling up Crisp Court and exchanging derisive glances. When that sport palled, they scanned the temperance ladies and decided there was no game there.

Finally, a young viscount, seeing yet another bowl of innocuous pink stuff ferried in, tossed the contents of his cup into potted palm and clapped it down on the sideboard beside him.

"Hell's bells, I can't stomach any more of this wash water. I need a drink!"

His voice cut keenly across the hubbub.

"Right! If it's drink you want, it's drink you shall have. All you have to do is tell our butler your pleasure!"

Adam was standing there, sudden as a thunderclap, his evening clothes incongruous on his workman's frame. Rose spun and saw him framed in an arch across the room. He looked as she had never seen him before, scraped and dangerous. Even from the distance, Rose felt the impact of some bruised fury tightening his face.

Why does he look like that, Rose wondered, pierced with alarm.

For a moment the only presence in the crowded rooms was Adam's. His eyes met hers and the evening changed. There was no drawing back this time. His gaze hungrily sought her. Rose responded with a spontaneous impulse toward him. Before she could even take a step, Bertie moved on again, carrying her off. Ever alert, Major Hoggett had caught the interplay and it brought a quick, predatory twitch to his mouth. So that's the game, is it, he thought. We'll soon put an end to that!

Rivals to the Prince was concerned, could not be tolerated. Hoggett ferreted them out and smashed them, loving the hot surge their destruction gave. Adam Crisp was targeted.

"Champagne!" the thirsty viscount cried, seizing the opportunity. "Champagne all round. Champagne is His Highness' favourite drink!"

A rousing chorus arose from his companions. There would be no choice now but to rush to find supplies.

CHAPTER FORTY-FOUR

The arrival of alcohol, frantically procured from a pub by the servants, sent disquiet racing through Louisa's original guests, almost all teetotalers. Once the Prince accepted an alcoholic beverage, no one dared voice objection. Acutely conscious of pinched nostrils all around her, Louisa glared at Adam and saw the tearingly reckless mood he was in.

Why, oh why could Adam never stay away from trouble!

When the ferment caused by the Prince died down, the party did not coalesce into something more splendid than before. Like an imperfect recipe, it separated into its elements. The Prince gave his attention to Rose. The men previously surrounding Rose now also surrounded the Prince and Rose. The good charity ladies remained grouped exactly as they had been when abandoned by their spouses after Rose arrived. Many of Louisa's lesser guests found themselves barely able to speak or eat due to the presence of royalty. Those strongly temperance pointedly divided themselves from those depraved enough to consort with Demon Rum.

To make matters worse, more of the Prince's cronies converged upon Crisp Court. A group of dissolute young lords who dogged him infiltrated the assemblage, even wilder with the application of champagne. Louisa's original guests shrank as this new clique spread noisy merriment into the over-warm crowd.

Many who had been at Louisa's first tea craned their necks to peer at Adam, the renegade encouraging this havoc. His extraordinary arrival, shaggy as Robinson Crusoe, on his mother's doorstep. engendered fantastical speculation about his life in the colonies. They remembered how he had spirited the newly discovered Rose Fitzroy out from under Henry's nose while Henry gaped like a moonstruck pup. And now this prank of introducing liquor into the house...

Well!

Louisa knew perfectly well that gossip flew around about her wayward elder son. Why on earth had he come to the reception when he knew how out of place he'd be? Goodness, he was tanned as a Hindoo against that white shirt. Next thing, he'd be telling people how he'd done manual labour at the mills!

Adam wasn't helping matters by remaining inside the drawing room arch, his elbow on a tall sideboard, a glass in hand that most certainly did not contain fruit punch. The crowd, the heat, the onslaught of faces and voices struck him forcefully after the solitary, racketing ride in the train pursued by his own demons. Cut off from getting at Henry, cut off from Rose, he concentrated on not crushing into splinters the heavy crystal in his hand.

Patience, oh damn and bloody patience!

He didn't know why he had opened the way to liquor except that he badly wanted a drink himself. The lumber camps had long since sunk any temperance teachings. The red haze of his rage against Henry had boiled over to include these restless, thirsty lordlings overrunning his mother's home. Let them pickle themselves to their roving eyeballs if that's what they desired. Anything to bedevil Henry's unspeakable, conniving, thin-lipped hypocrisy that had cost him so dear!

The thirsty lords drank all the more heartily to make up for the drought, moving steadily back through the spaces created by previous all the double doors Louisa had had flung open. They bore Rose along with them, a rolling wave carrying scintillating foam on its crest.

Rose, agitated by Adam's savage look, could barely see over the melee of elegantly clad bodies that hedged her round. A fizzing goblet was thrust into her hand. She shone as the jewel in the charmed circle of deference around the Prince who exuded such smooth pleasantness it amounted to treason not to be at ease.

"A song, a song," the Prince's companions were soon calling out. How could they have champagne without music to go with it? A pink-nosed baronet whispered to Rose the kind of music His Highness favoured.

"Something with a tune a fellow can make out. None of that blasted weepy, moping stuff!"

Bertie dearly loved a catchy tune. The only music worth listening to, in his opinion, was martial music. A rollicking ditty combined with a pretty singer was the apex of felicity. Wrenching her attention back, Rose swept to her feet, launching into an old favourite, "The Lady and the Hawthorn Tree."

Singing, combined with champagne, worked its customary magic. Her spirits shot up, the exhilaration of her afternoon floated back to her. She could not speak to Adam, so she drowned her misgivings in a burst of melody. Merrily, she slipped from one popular song to the next. The evening grew ever more boisterous, fuelled not least by Rose herself. Glasses of weightless champagne, tossed off between choruses, rendered her tipsy and increased her radiance. She held the eye of every man around her and the attention, willing or not, of everyone at the reception.

Lightness filled her, not the least because Althea was not hovering nearby, a brown wren among peacocks, subjecting Rose to the constraints of her wise, humorous, ever interested gaze. Rose had not understood the power of Althea's presence until she was free of it.

And hadn't she slipped her mother's grip in the dressing room! If she could manage that, there wasn't a thing she couldn't do! Wasn't the admiration of the grand Prince of Wales himself proof of it? She felt herself the pivot of the party around which everything else took orbit.

Yes, even more than the Prince himself.

As she sang, Rose found it impossible to be in awe. She had never thought about royalty except in the abstract. Princes wore enchanted cloaks and fought battles from the prows of silk-sailed ships. This prince, with his conventional evening dress, his plump cheeks, genially smiling eyes had certainly never been near an enchanted cloak in his life.

Why, he just like any other fellow, Rose thought. She matched his grins and leaned toward him in that playful, saucy, intimate manner she had acquired to deal with her many followers. Oddly, the whole thing reminded her of sitting at Jack Mabbin's feet, with everyone singing their hearts out in the village pub.

On the periphery Major Hoggett watched with his chilly, calculating eyes. Above all, he watched Adam.

The Prince was surely enjoying himself. The hour approached, then passed, when upstanding citizens, replete with prawns in butter, would have headed sleepily home to bed. Tonight, since it would have been the height of rudeness to depart before the royal personage, this was impossible. So the older and staider sat, prisoners of etiquette, their eyes growing heavier, while the revelry continued around Rose.

Rose galloped through all the engaging repertoire which Althea had armed her with. She moved on to the immensely popular songs of Mr. Gilbert and Mr. Sullivan, helped out by assorted well-lubricated baritones. Crowding ever closer, the men's eyes shinily perusing Rose's lithe throat and expressive arms. The heavy swells, breathing brandy fumes, exuded the conviction that the world, Rose included, existed only to give them pleasure.

One of them, paunchy gentleman with dyed whiskers and a tiger's tooth on his watch chain, broke into what he insisted was a Mogul hunting chant picked up from his beaters in India.

"Top that, Miss Fitzroy," he flung out jokingly. "How about a ditty in Swahili, or Chinese!"

Well, Rose knew songs in foreign languages even if she didn't understand what they meant. She broke into one of the merry songs in Italian that Signor Abruzzi taught her when most comically inebriated. When Rose had tried it during the serious lessons, her teacher had stopped her sternly and told her such a song could only be sung "when a king is at your feet".

Rose had no idea Signor Abruzzi placed this unlikely condition on the song simply to stop her singing it ever. The extreme naughtiness of the lyrics made even reprobate Abruzzi recoil when he was sober.

Given the level of scholarship among her listeners, Rose would have gotten away with it had not been for a couple of escapees from Oxford just back from their Grand Tour. Enamoured with Boccaccio, they had spent a whole winter soaking themselves in that golden tongue. They goggled through the wine fumes at Rose and at each other, scarcely able to believe their ears.

"Gad!"

A whispered translation raced round the Prince's followers and, inevitably, into the ear of Bertie himself. The Prince's face changed as the faces of his cronies changed. His look became heavy and charged. Hoggett gave a hard smirk. The ribald song was as good as a signal. Why else would the baggage sing such a thing! With one mischievous impulse, Rose unknowingly set herself outside the bounds of respectability, clearing the way for whatever methods necessary. His instincts had been right, thought Hoggett. This flamboyant nightingale would find the net dropping over her very shortly indeed!

Among the ladies, Louisa was giving a good imitation of a woman stuck through with a spit and pretending mightily nothing was amiss. Would could possess Adam, she asked herself over the knot growing in her stomach. What!

Louisa could have throttled her son for starting such a revel. As for Henry, all she saw of him was a glimpse of silhouette so rigid he might have been having his toes gnawed by ferrets instead of entertaining royalty.

Or perhaps this was how royalty was entertained, Louisa thought, trying to ignore the sounds coming through the archways. Her worshipful concepts of the aristocracy were rapidly being shot to pieces as yelps of laughter and a tinkle betraying the breakage of her best crystal floated through the smoky air. Old names and unassailable titles, she was rapidly discovering, only gave their owners license to be a loud and as riotous as they pleased. And the crowd had carried Rose back now almost as far as the billiard room, a place no lady ever set foot. Beyond that lay the conservatory and door to the garden.

Louisa also suffered the mute, violent, stiff-necked disapproval radiating from Mellon, perhaps the most unfortunately affected of the servants. Trained up in the rigorously temperance household of Milton Crisp, Mellon was that rarity of rarities, a butler utterly unfamiliar with handling spirituous drinks. "Woe to him that putteth the bottle to his neighbours' lips," echoed the Scriptures in his ears. He might just as well have been sending out trays festooned with poisonous adders. Had it not been for one of the hired footmen, who had worked in a pub, strange permutations indeed might have reached the exalted guests.

Standing next to a stained oak fireplace, Henry turned hot eyes on the Prince. Once he had gotten over the astonishment of the royal presence, Henry soon saw it had nothing to do with Crisp Court and everything to do with Rose.

This was the evening Althea Wharton had been supposed to make good on the large investment Henry had ploughed in. Whatever the wretched woman did, she was to have schooled Rose to show her favour to Henry tonight, attaching herself publicly and clearly.

And now...and now...

The royal boar had come out of nowhere, displacing all others. Instead of awe, impotent rage churned in Henry's breast. Thwarted, pushed aside, he became horribly tortured by every advance on Rose by the glossy new crowd.

As Henry seethed, the change in pack energy telegraphed it-self even to the far periphery of the revels. People could not fail to notice the different quality of the laughter, the increased boldness in the court paid to Rose. Murmurs spread, uneasy speculations formed in the minds of even the staidest of monarchists, for the Prince had not diverted his attention from Rose since his arrival. A number of husbands exchanged significant glances. Mrs. Ballthorpe leaned precariously. Her daughter-in-law almost fell off the sofa in her effort to see what Miss Fitzroy was doing to create such sudden whispering through the crowd.

Nearby, Amelia sat in even worse condition than Louisa. As Rose's nearest relative in the eyes of the world, Amelia steeled her-self against the glances of Mrs. Stanhope-White and Lady Bliggs. Lips bitten and nape aflame, philosophy had deserted her. She was not pricing each useless vase or superfluous armchair and trans-lating their cost into meals and overcoats or passages to Canada.

All she could think of was that Edwin, goggle-eyed with plea-sure, was in there with those same men who were turning Crisp Court into a noisy riot. He was part of the riot.

And he was drinking champagne!

Outside, fuming with the deepest frustration of all, sat Red Nell, shadowed in her closed cab, watching the lighted windows that shut her out from the brilliant, unreachable world inside.

CHAPTER FORTY-FIVE

Katie, Cully and Laura had worked since before dawn in the fevered preparations. The servants' quarters had been abuzz with chatter about Miss Rose for weeks, so the three knew quite a lot about this fascinating personage who was, amazingly, Miss Amelia's cousin. She was from a place called Cornwall, which Laura explained was at the very end of England and full of pirates. She had first sung at a tea Mrs. Crisp had given for charity ladies. Now everyone wanted to hear her and listeners got shivers all the way up their spines, she was so enchanting.

Best of all, she sang so that rich people would send money to Amelia's Refuge to help other abandoned children like themselves. Louisa Crisp meant to announce a concert by Rose in support of the Refuge. The servants expected the tickets would be sold out in an hour.

Laura, soaked in horse lore, knew that the Derby was the most famous of all horse races and the occasion of parties of every kind. "It's called the Season," she told her two fast friends. "Everyone travels down to London and young ladies who have just come out catch husbands."

Her voice trailed off, remembering how Gran had promised her a Season of splendours when her time came. Katie and Cully did not grasp the concept but listened with riveted interest nevertheless. Katie was proud that such a sensation as Miss Rose should belong to her own Mrs. Corman. Cully merely grinned wider with her post box mouth.

For days, the three children had been caught up in the storm of dusting and polishing that roared through the house, followed by Amazonian labours in the kitchen under the sweating countenance of Cook. Extra footmen had been hired and outfitted with medieval tabards. Mellon, the dour, ancient butler, stalked about snapping orders.

When the day arrived, the formal uniforms of the staff quivered with nervous anticipation. The excitement animated Katie into a semblance of her old green-eyed self. Good food was filling her out so that she now looked more like a little girl and less like a fever-racked skeleton teetering on the brink of death. Laura, who now had work-reddened hands and callouses on her knees from scrubbing floors, lapsed into wooden silence. Cully, no matter how much work she had to do, remained in a state of bliss ever since she discovered there would be food every single day and she didn't have to sleep on a wet, cold cellar floor.

The three slaved in the kitchen and scullery where there were pots to be scoured, vegetables peeled, coal lugged for the immense black kitchen range gulping it hungrily. Katie carried plates, wiped tables, mopped up spills and dodged Cook's wooden spoon as the woman grew more agitated about her tasks.

"They're starting to come," whispered Fran who had been in the upper region. Katie managed a dash to a forbidden side window to glimpse carriages disgorging graceful shapes in evening cloaks. Who wore the grandest gown, the entire staff had no doubt. Louisa had been a masterpiece in purple striped ivory faille in the newest princess style. Her massive overskirt was square and long behind, trimmed with heavy netted fringe. Two broad swathes of silk crossed in front then knotted behind and fell over the train, each tied with an enormous fringed bow. A piece of Boiteuse drapery, caught at the shoulder, swept round the neck and down the front diagonally where it was fastened with yet another bow.

At her throat, ears and wrists, Louisa wore amethysts that had cost the price of a small villa and winked their value each time she shifted. She sallied forth as very embodiment of Crisp wealth, Crisp solitity, Crisp pride.

Activity behind the baize doors to the service regions grew more frenetic. Immediately there was a demand for great bowls of pink punch continually made up and lugged out.

"Sir Herbert Bentley is out there, and Dean Wickham,"Fran told them as she sped by. "Mr and Mrs. Dunstan are talking to Ballthorpes and Lady Bliggs certainly has never seen such grand flower arrangements before."

Katie had boggled earlier at the great vases it took two maids to carry, overflowing with roses while she followed behind with a whisk and dustpan to sweep up fallen petals. Now backstairs help like the children and the kitchen staff depended for the news on servants like Fran, Lucy, Milly and the footmen who actually got to serve out front. They would see the guests and hear Miss Rose sing, as she was bound to when asked. Excited voices and merry laughter told them Rose had arrived.

"She's wearing the most elegant butter cream satin," Lucy gushed, "with rosebuds in those masses of curls. Even the married gentlemen are following her about. "The looks on the faces of their wives, oh, they're a treat."

Katie devoured these reports. She wished she could discuss them with Laura, but Laura had only grown more stolidly blank as the evening wore on. And Cully was confined to the scullery with enough soapy water and sticky jelly moulds to keep her out of mischief's way. Just when Katie was contemplating a daring, renegade effort to peep at the party herself, Fran came barrelling back, her eyes practically popping out of her head.

"You can't imagine what's happened," she panted. "Himself is here! Nearly caused old Mellon to faint on the doorstep. And now he's talking to Miss Rose too!"

"Who," they all pressed. Who?"

"Why his Royalness himself. The Prince of Wales!"

A mass infusion of smelling salts wouldn't have been out of place. Cook turned the colour of a cauliflower and dropped her ladle with a crash.

"Did Mrs. Crisp invite him?" Milly asked in wonder.

"Oh don't be silly," cried Fran. "The Prince can go anywhere he likes. But to choose Crisp Court..."

She shook her head as though some diety from Olympus had alighted in their abode. John, one of the footmen and veteran of several establishments, let out a snort.

"Everybody knows the Prince has a fine eye for the ladies. If you ask me, it's Miss Rose that's brought him through our doors."

"Back to work the lot of you," Mrs. Quincy cried, bearing down at full speed. "Didn't you hear the news!"

Cook had to have cold towels applied to her forehead before she could face the stove again. She flew at the cooking as though possessed. Ivy, the scullery maid, sat down hard at the thought of the Prince eating prawns boiled in a pot she herself had scoured. The maids and footmen with access to the front regions had everyone hanging on their every harried word as they rushed about.

"Thank goodness, Mr. Adam has just come back," breathed Marion. "He can help Mr. Henry and his mother hold the ramparts."

Katie's ears pricked up at the mention of Mr. Adam.

If she had a hero in the house, it was Mr. Adam, not only because he had actually been to that magical place called Canada, but he had taken time out, now and then, to tell her about it.

Not long after her arrival she had been struggling with a bucket of water up the stairs for the wash jugs, ever so careful not to spill any on the carpet. Mr. Adam, with his quiet tread, had appeared from nowhere. His large hand relieved her of her burden.

"Where are those lazy footmen? Haven't they anything better to than let little girls lug water for them!"

Katie was so surprised she couldn't reply. None of the family were supposed to be upstairs this time of the day. Mr. Adam gave her wink and, himself, poured the water into the china jugs standing beside their blue and white washbowls. He was big and brown and had muscles standing out all over him, unlike the soft shape of Mr. Henry.

"What's your name?" he asked.

"Mucker, sir."

She dipped in the automatic curtsy Marion had drilled into her.

"Ah, one of the urchins drafted into hard labour in the kitchen. Tell me, what sin put you into Mrs. Quincy's clutches?"

This good-humoured question flung Katie into tongue-tied silence. A bruised look seized her face as it always did when anyone tried to inquire into her past.

"None of my beeswax, I see." Adam took in the frightful thinness Cook's rations had only begun to remedy and wondered what had befallen the poor little blighter before Amelia Corman got her.

Katie hesitated, knowing she should take her bucket and go. Yet...Mr. Adam had been to Canada. Canada was the haven she had been promised when Miss Amelia had lured her back from the darkness. She burned to know about Canada.

"I'm going to Canada when I'm done here," Katie blurted out. "Do they really have larks? Is it true all the hills turn purple and the hares dance and there's a woman there that wants a wee girl like me?"

Hunger her eyes stood out in a little maid who would have nothing but drudgery ahead of her if she stayed in England.

"Oh there's larks," Adam told her generously. "Meadowlarks. And rabbits that play in the snow when the moon is really bright. There's women too, I'm sure would have room for a little lass like you. Look!" He suddenly reached under his collar and came up with a thin leather thong threaded with small coloured beads. "This is from Canada. I got it for luck from a fellow who was almost a Red Indian. It's for you. As long as you wear it why, it'll be almost as if you're already there yourself."

The hope in the child's eyes was almost painful to see. Reverently, Katie slipped the bit of leather around her own neck and hid it inside her uniform.

Thereafter Adam always spared Katie a wink and sometimes paused to tell her about icebergs with rainbows frozen inside them and summer hillsides with berries so sweet you could almost hear them singing on the bushes. He became a hero of mythic proportions, a direct link to the land Katie had fixed her heart upon.

And now he was here talking to a genuine prince. She wished with all her heart she could see it. She had no opportunity because, impossible as it seemed, a second shock wave topped the first. Not only had Mr. Adam spoken to His Royal Highness, he had told the Prince he and his party could drink alcohol if they wished.

"What can he be thinking," cried Fran, "letting that evil stuff into this house."

Supplies appeared from somewhere best not spoken of. Soon the devil's brew brought on the loudness and rowdiness. And even in the distant kitchen regions they picked up the trill of Miss Rose singing. When Katie heard that the drinking lords had moved Mr. Adam's great stuffed bear into the main reception room so that Rose could sing from its encircling arms, she just had to have a glimpse.

CHAPTER FORTY-SIX

Adam watched Rose borne out of sight the way a man watches desert water drain away into the sand. The laceration inside held him immobile, the writhing, grinding fury, the silent howl that had possessed him throughout the day.

That morning, Adam had set off on a journey he could no longer avoid. Now he was back, a hot sear in his eyes as he scanned the crowd for Henry. Tonight, Henry would have much to answer for. Adam didn't give a damn if a dozen princes stirred the dust at his mother's party.

Adam had just returned from standing where he'd known he'd have to stand ever since he'd arrived in England—the site of the warehouses that had so disastrously burned down that long ago night. This journey had lain in his consciousness all the years in exile. Finally, he had stepped into the railway station and bought his ticket.

He had no idea why he'd expected to see the black rubble still lying there with the stubs of walls sticking up along with the overpowering burnt-cloth stench of consumed cotton. Instead, there was only a stretch of fresh paving ending at a wall and a set of handsome iron gates. The gates stood open to more paving, new buildings and an impressive wharf outside.

It was gone, really all gone. Not just the warehouse, but the mill buildings, the belching chimneys, the brick yards alive with wagons and men clomping about in heavy boots.

He looked to where his father's offices used to be, the place he had glanced toward so often when banished in the yard, the place he had finally achieved. All he saw was the gable of a strange ships' chandler store and more gates pointing their iron spikes at the sky.

He had already been to the place where the dark, commodious old house of his boyhood had stood, the familiar approaches making him expect, against all logic, that it might be still waiting and welcoming. It, too, had vanished, cleared away for the access road to the expanded dock facilities. Beyond a brick wall, he could hear the chuffing and clanging on the new railway lines carrying freight from the wharves.

When he stepped to where the warehouse had stood, he had to turn until he spotted the church steeple visible from the warehouse door where he used to sit.

Fury and despair flooded over him.

Memory surged in a scalding wave—the screaming shouts, the frantic racing about, the roaring, swaying columns of fire pouring sparks into the black night sky. Back again came the awful clutch in his chest as he saw the precious store of baled cotton devoured. Back came the twisted horror on the face of his father as he had lurched up, his shirt unbuttoned, hair flying in unkempt spikes about his head. Back came the white-faced crowd of mill workers, roused from their beds by the lurid glare. Back came the despairing wail as they realized the mills wouldn't run, starvation looked their children in the face.

Adam had swayed in the bitter storm of images. This was what he had been avoiding for so many years, this abscess inside him, throbbing just below awareness. It had driven him back here to lean into this lashing pain on the spot where the charred earth lay hidden under new paving stones.

An hour later, Adam stalked into the offices of Clayvers and Clayvers, the solicitors who had always handled the business of Milton Crisp. Jeremiah Clayvers was a long-jawed, grizzled, abrupt old man much of a piece of Milton Crisp himself. He rose in surprise when Adam was ushered in, a frown knotting his brushy brows. Another one who thought Adam responsible for the fire.

"Your father has been dead for over three years. To what do I owe this unexpected visit?"

His tone declared that he never expected Adam to show his face in England and especially not there. Adam told him where he'd just been, and saw the twitch of surprise on lawyer's face. Sitting tautly in Clayvers' stiff leather visitor's chair, Adam learned how Milton had changed after Adam's banishment, turning gloomy and hard. How it hadn't been long before Milton had had the disabling fit.

"Took the heart clean out of him," Clayvers accused Adam with his eyes. "Signed off more and more to Henry. Made them put his invalid chair at the window upstairs where he could look out at the mills. Hour after hour, he just stared at the empty smokestacks. Finally, he quit even trying to struggle. Just shrank down in that chair when Henry sold the property off fast as he could for the new dock improvements.

Clayvers let that information sink in then ground on.

"Henry said it was only a sensible business thing to do when the mills were worth a fortune just for the land they were standing on and nothing at all sitting idle. Henry didn't want to run them."

Clayvers was a hard, practical man used to making hard, practical decisions with an eye to profit. Nevertheless, his voice rasped acidly. He seemed to be seeing, as Adam was seeing, a helpless Milton, trapped inside a ruin of a body, fretting himself into a wasted hulk. Clayvers had been Milton's friend as well as his solicitor.

"He didn't take to London," Clayvers finished bitingly. "Snapped his roots off. Died when they got him there."

Adam shuddered. Only here, from Clayvers, was he learning the real extent of Milton's collapse. He could not imagine his father in London, torn from the smoke-blackened soil that had nurtured him and made him rich. How could those large hands lie idle? How could the impatient force of him have languished about Crisp Court with nothing but flocked wallpaper to look at while Henry, gloating Henry, jumped into the game of paper profits.

Clayvers saw the ropes of muscle outlining themselves along Adam's jaw. Surprise warred with the grim disapproval that had informed him since Adam walked in. He took in the well-used hands, so like Milton's, and the pain crying out from the set of his shoulders. Clayvers had liked Adam, and treated him as the heir apparent back in the halcyon days when Milton had taken the difficult youth into the office. Letting out something like a sigh, he flexed his arms.

"Why didn't you come back?" he asked slowly, in a baffled voice. "None of it would have happened if you had come back. Milton wanted you to have it all."

Adam went still, a dark heat rising through his face. Clayvers shook his head.

"He thought about you, you know. He got me to help him write, before he got too bad, that is, asking you to come home, giving the letters to Henry to put into the bank communications. When he didn't hear anything, he gave up. Next thing, Henry was running it all."

There was regret, but also a note that said Adam deserved the loss for ignoring his father. When Adam emerged from the office, the heat had roared into a seething fury that precluded speech. No letter had come to him in Canada. And if nothing had got through to him, it was Henry who had stopped it. Henry, now lording it over Crisp Court and sniffing after Rose!

He had waited for that word. In the lumber camps, on the lakes, on the prairie, he had waited, losing hope, imagining his father implacably disgusted with him. And now, to find out it had been Henry who had stopped the messages!

Back in the train station, Adam dropped down on one of the benches to wait, alone save for a woman mopping the floor.

The woman was old, too old for the heavy mop which she dragged back and forth over the stone flags, thrusting the handle with a laboured grunt each time the sodden mop head moved. The expanse of wet floor widened as though pursuing her until it had put her right back against Adam's bench. She pressed a hand wearily into the small of her back, then bent to lug the bucket further on. When she backed into Adam's foot, Adam roused himself to move. He found her staring at him.

"Adam Crisp!"

Adam looked up, startled. The woman's eyes were wide and her mouth was tight just from uttering his name. Her hair was white now and the flesh that used to make up a comfortable double chin hung in an empty wattle, but the same large nose and emphatic brows were there as of old.

"Mrs. Duggan?"

"Aye, it's me. And I never expected to see you walking the streets of this town again," she spat vehemently.

"I came back to....er, look. How's Billy?"

Billy Duggan had been one of the lads on the crew when Adam had first been put to work in the mills. Billy had helped him out when Adam had no idea what to do. Billy had no family except this doting grandmother who baked massive current buns for Adam's and Billy's dinner sacks. Adam had boarded for a while in their small, tidy home. What was she doing mopping up in the station?

The old woman's bosom heaved thinly.

"Billy's dead. With no work in the mills, he went to be a soldier. Got hisself shot in one of them foreign places. Now there's just me to look out for myself."

The muscles on her old arms stood out in thin cords. The way she supported herself with the mop handle told Adam more than all the frays on her dress and the cracked boots sticking out under her hems.

Ten years might have passed but she was one who had not forgotten. Before Adam could find anything to say, she turned her back on him and began mopping again, slowly, labouriously, with that pained grunt before each thrust of the handle. She would keep mopping as long as one stringy sinew held to another. For when she stopped mopping, the workhouse awaited.

The slap of water on flagstones echoed more deafeningly in Adam's ears than the roar of the train he jumped up to meet.

CHAPTER FORTY-SEVEN

Champagne, which Rose had never drunk in such quantities, was having its effect. She felt cut loose, like a hot air balloon breaking through into giddy ether in which she could only to ride out the runaway flight.

Several men had begun to freely smoke. Loud male laughter boomed out. The Prince's cronies crowded ever closer to Rose, their cheeks flushed with brandy, eyes overheated at the soft swell of Rose's bosom.

Though she still felt the merry centre of thing, unease plucked at Rose, some instinct trying to warn of wolf pack energy building up. Boldly as she laughed and bantered, Rose had no experience dealing with determined privileged men who skillfully got their way. The Prince's eyes were shiny as he wetted his red lips periodically in the depths of his beautifully trimmed beard. He bore the air of a man supremely confident of getting what he wanted. It was clear that he intended to have Rose.

"How about another song from sunny Italy," the paunchy lord with the dyed whiskers called out again. "We DO enjoy it so!"

Guffaws burst out. Bertie's cronies exchanged knowing glances.

"Goodness, if you crowd so, I won't have room," Rose exclaimed. The men would soon be seriously crushing the hems of her dress. At once, a party of champagne-inspired young Turks broke away and stumbled into the corridor.

"A savage protector for Miss Fitzroy," Adam heard behind him moments later, thickly smothered in mirth.

"And won't she need it, the luscious morsel!"

"'Luscious' is hardly the word Halimand was using."

Adam caught the bawdy laughter just as the drunken young bloods staggered back toward the Prince lugging, of all things, the huge stuffed bear from the foyer.

"Hoopa! Up into the arms of nature you go, fair kidnapper of helpless hearts!

Thanks to the beast's abductors, Rose soon stood on a fat hassock encircled by the massive forearms of the bear. Grasping the thick fur, Rose could now see over the heads around her. As a compass turns toward a magnetic pole, she searched out Adam who now moved abruptly forward. When he reached the crowd around the Prince, he felt he had stumbled into a pack of large, sleek hounds closing in on their prey.

Rose saw his hard impatience, like a visible disturbance in the room. Other revellers faded. What it is it? What's wrong, her eyes asked as she felt him pulling her from her champagne haze.

Must be the bubbly playing tricks, she thought. Yet, she knew liquor had nothing to do with how she became conscious of every Adam's every detail, from slashed look on his face down to the bands of white where his cuffs showed at his wrists. A silent, charged dialogue had been flitting between them since the moment Adam arrived.

Someone laughed lightly and Rose was back with Adam on the sunny Serpentine, feeling the boat handled easily, seeing Adam his collar open, his sleeves rolled up over brown, competent arms. Unbidden, dark rivers began to shift and flow within her, intimations of a passion none of her myriad pursuers had been able to ignite.

"Oooops, by gad, bad shot!"

A fat lord with a protruding upper lip had attempted to drink to Rose and sloshed wine down his shirt front. He thought this highly amusing.

Rose glanced down at men crowding her, pressing in with their laughter and their loud jokes. Too many were eying her, too many making her unsettled, smothered. Somehow, when she hadn't been paying attention, things had got out of control.

What was wrong with them, Rose asked herself. For some unfathomable reason, she was now on the wrong end of the laughs. Adam began to wade decisively forward.

Several men had already turned round to see who was attracting so much of Rose's attention. Major Hoggett spotted Adam's advance and knew it meant trouble. Attuned to the heavy wash of sexual currents, he had not missed Henry Crisp's furious fixation with Rose. Henry he did not trouble about. Adam Crisp was a different matter. Hoggett had caught the silent interchanges with Rose.

Hoggett's features, curiously small and pushed together in the large moon of his face, grew tighter. He had been awaiting just this opportunity. Hoggett's job was to smooth the path for his royal master and he loved to crush rivals. Only when they were smashed could Hoggett find some relief for the damnable burning frustration at always having to pass the prizes on to Bertie.

In the short time he had been in the house, Hoggett had investigated the Crisps, absorbing information from introductions, the buzz of conversation, the interplay of cross currents in a room. Adam Crisp, he knew had recently come back from the hinterlands of Canada which must account for the rough cast of the fellow evening dress could not polish over.

A hothead, Hoggett decided, easily made a buffoon. From the look of him, a mere prod would do it. Then they'd see how Miss Fitzroy took to a man laughed out of the presence of the Prince.

"Mr. Crisp," he boomed out in a jocular, mocking tone, "I hear you sent this bear back from the wilderness as a souvenir. Tell me, did you shoot it yourself or did it just look at you and drop dead from fright!"

Adam did not even pause. When the laughter at Hoggett's witticism died, he was among them with one foot up on one of Louisa's Moroccan leather footstools, an elbow resting on his knee. The hubbub died down as guests strained surreptitiously to hear what the refugee from the colonies would say.

"Grizzlies don't drop dead for anything but a bullet in a spot very dear to them as you can plainly guess. A big boar grizzly, now, is an unpredictable beast. A fellow like this," Adam's free hand circled toward the rearing giant, "why he swaggers about, thinking he owns the whole mountain, just as far as the eye can see. He brings along his own fleas and ticks who glut themselves feeding off the bear's rump. Then come the scavenger birds and the foxes and such living high off scraps from his kills. And there'd be smaller bears, of course, having their dinners snatched away."

Adam proceeded to outline, in unflattering detail, the personal habits of the boar grizzly, his gaze ticking steadily all around the circle, making sure Bertie was included. A number of guests were so foolish as to laugh at the saltier bits. Those at the front did not doubt what kind of allegory was contained in the tale.

Bertie, with deliberate royal obtuseness, leaned back as though he failed to see what the bear had to do with him. Hoggett had furious bulges all up the back of his neck and into the base of his skull. A number of royal cronies looked nonplussed. Louisa clutched the arm of the sofa as though it were a sinking log in a quicksand bog.

"So you see," Adam finished, addressing Hoggett, "the bear didn't die of fright."

Adam pushed himself away from the footstool and stood up. The evening jacket looked even more out of place on his work-hardened shoulders. The brand of sun and weather on his face was a living reproach to the idle lives around him.

Goodness, Rose thought, the bear itself might as well have come to life. She saw that none of them knew how to cope with Adam. He had done this for her, tweaked the noses of even his royal bigness, the Prince. Why else would Adam have done such a thing except...except...

Her heart took another swoop, wild as an engine racing down a hill. He's not getting away to Canada, she suddenly decided. Not before I have my chance!

The arrival of the late supper required by the Season broke the tension. Bertie, famous for the dinners he put away, indicated his interest. Everyone around him rose to their feet, the crowd stretching and stirring. Rose slipped down from her perch with one thing on her mind. She must see Adam.

She met his eye only for a moment before Hoggett and a whole phalanx of tipsy cronies crowded between. Uncertainly, she paused, then felt a slip of paper thrust into her palm. She turned but no one was there save the same shifting bodies as before.

"The garden," read the slanting lines in the note. "Come now.

CHAPTER FORTY-EIGHT

"Oh, Mr. Adam's telling about bears," Fran told her breathless audience in the kitchen. "Leaning over His Highness himself with a tale fit to make their hair stand up!"

Katie left off sweeping vegetable peels and knew she just had to hear Mr. Adam telling about the foyer bear. But how?

"Is there nobody to get these tarts up the stairs before they go all cool! Mucker, drop that broom and get a move on."

Cook, sweating and frazzled before the hot black range, commandeered Katie to run up to the long table behind the service doors where items were set in readiness for the maids and footmen. Unable to believe it, Katie sped away. When she deposited the tray, she gazed down the corridor where she been grimly ordered not to go. Yet...she positively must hear Mr. Adam even if Cook made her scrub tiles for a month. And she longed to glimpse her dear Mrs. Corman whom she hadn't seen since the day she had been brought to Crisp Court.

She slipped around the corner and, for one vivid moment, as Milly, bearing a cushion heavily splotched with punch, pushed the swinging door open, was afforded a glorious, panoramic view of the nearest reception room.

Miss Rose was indeed in the midst of a crowd of gentlemen and raised above them as though she were standing on one of the leather hassocks. Directly behind her was the huge stuffed bear, protecting her with its hairy arms. The gaslights cast pools of gold on her shimmering satin skirts. Her eyes sparkled as she laughed at something one of the gentlemen had said. Everyone seemed to looking at Rose, the ladies in the distance in splendid dresses, the plump gentlemen and Mr. Adam most fiercely of all.

"Mucker! Get back to the kitchen. Mrs. Quincy is coming and she'll have your hide!"

Katie dashed back toward the table but found her retreat cut off by the formidable Mrs. Quincy herself. Before the housekeeper should notice her, Katie stepped sideways into another a forbidden room, the green pantry.

A single dim light was burning inside. To her astonishment, Katie bumped into Laura, who was also in the taboo space. Behind them stood the reason the pantry was off limits, the row of ornate cakes it had taken the hired pastry chef ages to construct. Now they awaited their moment of glory.

"What are you doing here?" Katie whispered.

Laura pointed over her shoulder. Katie's innards twisted.

"Oh no! Oh Cully, how could you!"

Cully failed to answer. She was sprawled on a stool, her stomach hard and round as a football, a smile of glazed ecstasy illuminating her face. Icing smeared her cheeks. In front of her lay a scene of carnage. One of the cakes displayed a gaping hole with the middle eaten out. Cully lay transported to some region of bliss beyond earthly recall, chunks of cakey interior smearing her fists.

"Aaaaah," Cully sighed, her head lolling slightly, "soooo good!"

The cakes had exerted an irresistible force on Cully since the chef arrived. She had watched the icing arabesques and multi-coloured roses take shape to ornament the baked delights. The saliva glands in her mouth began to work until her mouth was filled with a longing to taste, merely to taste, one of the tantalizing creations.

Mustn't touch! Mustn't touch! Mustn't touch!

Cully had siddled into the pantry when no one was looking and gazed at a single rosebud on the corner. Surely no one would miss a rosebud. Her hand snaked out, her post box mouth closed on a joy of sweetness. Again her fingers darted. A trance took her and she was lost.

"Cully!"

No amount of jabbing would rouse her. The hole in the back of the cake looked like a badger's burrow. How could such small person could have devoured so much without being hollow to her ankles.

"It's RUINED!" choked Laura. "Mrs. Quincy will KILL us. Whatever will we do?"

Laura could only stand with both hands clapped across her mouth, but Katie began swiftly looking around.

"Look, it's not so bad if we can get all the crumbs off and fill the hole. Go get the icing sugar from the other pantry. I'll see what I can do."

She shoved Laura off on her larcenous errand and spotted the top shelf where servants kept their private provisions. Fran's mother had sent her a Dundee cake. Half of it remained, carefully wrapped in waxed paper. Katie grabbed it down and cut pieces to fit the gap. By the time Laura was back, the icing sugar in a bowl hidden under her apron, Katie was smoothing off the roughened edges of her work.

"How clever," cried Laura, admiringly.

Adding some water, Katie turned the icing sugar into a paste and began slathering it on the damaged side, terrified they'd be discovered any minute. The repair looked plain but passable in the dim light. Perhaps no one would notice on the crowded refreshment tables out front. Now to get rid of the evidence.

"Brush Cully off and get her up to bed. We'll tell Cook she was taken sick. I've got to hide this mess."

Katie wrapped the crumpled waxed paper and remains of the Dundee cake in the large handkerchief Mrs. Quincy made them carry and jammed the bulge under her apron. In the kitchen, Katie encountered Milly carrying a cleaning bucket filled with glass shards.

"One of the Prince's gentlemen knocked the Waterford fruit bowl down and broke it all to bits."

"Well, don't just stand there," Cook sputtered. "Put it in the dust bin. And remember to tell Mrs. Quincy what happened."

Katie darted between Milly and the door.

"I can put it out. Let me."

Milly handed over the pail. Katie slipped out into the service alley where the great dust bins stood. Quick as she could, Katie dumped in the damning cake remains and then the shards to hide them.

From outside, Crisp Court blazed with light while music and laughter floated out. In the street fine equipages waited with liveried coachmen and matched carriage horses shaking their groomed heads. Alone in the alley, Katie seized her chance to see more of the party. If she couldn't view the main event, at least she could peep into the garden which twinkled with fairy lights and had a real fountain. Finding toeholds between the bricks, Katie grasped the ivy to hoist herself high enough to peer over the garden wall.

CHAPTER FORTY-NINE

A flutter caught in Rose's breast. Yes, the garden. How clever of Adam. The champagne throbbed in her temples and she longed for fresh air. And she must see Adam, find out what was so blackly driving him.

To her surprise, she found no trouble escaping. Not a single hand reached for her or voice demanded attention. The royal mob let her vanish as easily as if she had turned invisible. Well, she thought wryly, so much for being more interesting than the food!

One set of eyes was not diverted. Henry watched Rose to see who she'd go off with, hoping his vain, furious hope that now she'd come to him. He resembled, more than ever, the shrike under glass in his study.

Rose wore a necklace of fine Malaya moonstones that seemed to glimmer in their milky depths with light taken from the smooth skin and beating heart under them. I paid for those moonstones, Henry was thinking savagely. Whether she knows it or not, she owes me! He was becoming that most dangerous creature, the controlled man verging on loss of control. Henry saw Rose lift her head, caught her sudden stealthy purpose as she moved away. With a surge of bile he realized he could not see Adam either.

The garden was a shadowed, mysterious, fragrant expanse opening from the conservatory. Louisa had brought to the city her love of growing things, filling the garden as soon as possible with shrubs, overflowing blossoms and even large plane trees dragged in with difficulty and dropped into holes dug by swearing work crews. For the reception, she had fairy lanterns strung in their branches in case any of her guests should wander out into the warmth of the evening. The coloured paper globes floated like captive moons, giving a faint, misty illumination to the dimness.

At the back rose Louisa's pride and joy, her garden folly. The folly, more appropriately named than even Louisa suspected, was a bit of architectural whimsy usually scattered near country houses in the form of a tiny, pseudo-classical temple, grotesque statuary or some bizarre formation of rocks never seen in nature. Louisa's folly consisted of an artificial gothic ruin that pretended some old monastery had tumbled down among the gardenias. Carved stone arches formed a grotto in which a small stream of water cascaded down a wall and a pair of clever entrances gave the delightful suggestion of a crypt. Tonight it looked as haunted and romantic as Louisa could have wished.

Rose slipped into the garden and looked swiftly around her. Seeing no one in the open, she glided toward the folly and stepped under the artfully broken arches. It was dark inside but also cool, and the burble of running water attracted her. Closing her eyes, she tilted her head back, listening to the sound of crickets and the faint chatter of the breeze in the leaves overhead.

Half hidden, Rose was but a dimly perceived cloud of glimmering satin. A prickly feeling of being watched made her open her lids again. A dark shape moved over near the gleam of falling water.

Rose took two steps of glad approach then paused.

"Who is it? Who's there?"

Wordlessly, the shape inclined toward her, barely visible against the gloom. Then a male voice murmured something very indistinct. The voice wasn't Adam's.

Perhaps because she had been thinking so intensely about Adam, Althea's words about Henry Crisp flashed into Rose's head. "Special consideration," was all she remembered. Henry had been watching her all evening. It would be just like him to follow her out here.

"Henry?"

The shape did not speak again, but came forward, taking one of Rose's hands, then the other, kissing her knuckles warmly. While Rose was immobile with surprise, it slipped an arm around her and bent closer. Brandied breath on her neck caused Rose to give a yelp of surprise.

"Henry Crisp, is that you?" she demanded as she struggled involuntarily backward. "Stop this at once!"

A footstep crunched on the gravel. Adam heard Henry's name and saw Rose twisting away. All the compacted rage of the day detonated in Adam's head. Before he knew what he was doing, his large hardened fist connected oh-so-satisfyingly with the skull of Rose's companion.

The shadowed head snapped back, then the dark bulk crumpled forward, out of the folly, uttering an astonished groan as it fell. The conservatory door swung open, allowing a shaft of light to illuminate the darkness.

There, in front of Adam, instead of Henry, lay the sprawled, semi-conscious body of Bertie, Prince of Wales!

The jolt of the blow throbbed up Adam's elbow and into his shoulder. His lips curled back in a snarl containing all the emotions driving him since his visit to Clayvers. He couldn't seem to get a breath or drop his arm back down to his side. He could hear only the sound of his own pulse thundering in his ears.

The ensuing moment stretched into an eon. Then barely audible, an indrawn gasp from Rose brought the night alive again. Rose and Adam stood staring at each other, the thud of the punch, the collapsing body fading away, leaving a silence in which the yearning essence in each leaped up and recognized the other.

The naked shock, the ragged, open passion looking out of Adam's face made the night shift on its axis. Rose stared dazedly into some new reality she never before been able to perceive, as if she had stumbled into a different garden, a different moonlight, a different world. Her breath caught deep inside and stayed there as the moment flowed around them. The endless, wordless moment in which everything was understood, a moment in which nothing else existed except this depth of knowing, this ache of wanting.

A strangled intake of air broke the moment. Sound came rushing back. Henry stood in the doorway, showing the whites of his horrified eyes. A tongue of light spilled across Rose's half-turned form, Adam's hovering fist and the royal body sprawled unmoving on the gravel.

A heartbeat later, Hoggett thrust violently past, followed by two cohorts who sent Henry stumbling by their rush. The night erupted into action. Hoggett barked staccato commands while his companions, faces aghast, bent over to the fallen Prince. A third man wedged himself firmly in the door, sealing off the garden from the rest of the reception. From an inner pocket, Hoggett drew a small but lethal-looking pistol which he trained both on Adam and the horrified Henry. All hint of tipsy riot gone, Hoggett crouched over the prostrate form at his feet.

"Your Highness, are you all right? Are you wounded?"

A faint groan finally issued from the royal bulk. Hoggett gestured to the two aides. Between them, they took the Prince's arms over their shoulders and hauled him limply upright. Snapped his fingers, Hoggett pointed a door set obscurely into the garden wall.

Staggering a little, the aides wrenched the gate open and disappeared into the darkness beyond. Hoggett spun back to the figures frozen in the dappled gloom.

Hoggett and his royal master had developed a well-oiled routine smoothing the Prince's pursuit of women. Hoggett had been the one who had the note slipped to Rose. Hoggett had been the one to shift the knowing cronies into a screen allowing the Prince to vanish, unremarked, into the garden, bent on wooing.

Hoggett cursed himself for noticing too late that Adam Crisp had gone outside too, blundering after Rose like an elk in rut. Unforgivably careless, Hoggett told himself. Now this disaster! Well, Crisp would rue the day he ever heard of Rose Fitzroy!

It took only moments for the containment machinery to spring into operation, closing the princely ranks against outsiders and lesser mortals. Hoggett lowered his head bullishly.

"You two," he hissed to Henry and Adam, will come with me. Gorsline, make sure Miss Fitzroy remains here and speaks to no one until I say."

Before either Adam or Henry could recover speech, they were marched straight upstairs into Henry's study, the heavy oaken door slammed behind them and guarded outside by another suddenly untipsy blueblood. Henry fled behind his desk, Adam stood against the unlit fireplace, a bell jar displaying its predatory contents by his shoulders. Hoggett fixed both brothers with frigid eyes.

"First," he grated, addressing himself to Henry, "no mention of this incident, no whisper, no breath will get out or you will be ruined. Ruined so badly that you won't even be able to get a chimney sweep to visit. No one will do business with you. More likely, they'll spit at you in the street. You and all the bloated pretensions of this house will be finished in London. Do you understand!"

Henry opened his mouth in a fish-like gape. Hoggett turned on Adam. Violent menace reddened his face, shot through with an ugly gloating.

"And you, Adam Crisp, will get out of England by the first means you can find, if you value your uncouth hide. And don't try to creep back until after our present prince has become a sovereign and passed away himself!"

The gloating tore at something buried in Adam. He had spent a day battered, rocked, raked by memories. The round, boiled face of a boy red with that same gloating swam up, gloating as the torn-off branch slashed into Adam's back and head for the dead roe deer.

The branch whipping him in a white haze of pain. Adam held by the hair, by the neck, by the ear. That'll teach you, you thieving lickspittle, that'll teach you to kill our deer...

"I'll be damned," Adam exploded, "if I'll be run off by a...."

Hoggett slammed his fist so hard on Henry's baronial desk that the shrike in its case jumped on the shining surface.

"Do you know what happens to people who attack royalty in this country?" Hoggett spat with cutting softness. "They are considered dangerous lunatics. There is no question of courts of law or recourse or publicity. They are simply swept up and put where they can do no more harm—into lunatic asylums. And generally never thought of again! I would advise you to comply with my orders."

Hoggett watched Adam whiten around the lips. Smelling a primal dread, he stepped closer, until he was breathing in Adam's face.

"Yes, in the madhouse, in with the gibbering idiots that have to have their own filth sloshed off with buckets. Oh, you can shout all you want in there and they'll only put you in irons for your trouble. So make a run for it, lout! And never," Hoggett relished the threat as though he could taste it, "ever be found near Miss Fitzroy again!"

The branch lashing and lashing, meaning to maim, meaning to kill. All the while the boy stood watching, fascinated, excited, puffing his lips. The blood of the slain roe deer mixed with Adam's own blood from the gashes in the side of his face, his shoulder, his buttocks, the bare calves of his legs...

Hoggett!

Hoggett had been that boy!

Hoggett stood with his feet wide in a strut, eyes boring into Adam's, daring him to move, daring him with the threat of the aides waiting outside ready whisk Adam out the garden gate to oblivion that very moment.

Adam knew that Hoggett didn't recognize him, but Adam would never forget that glee-glutted young face taking a final look over the rim of the man-trap as Adam lay sprawled at the bottom. Now Hoggett, over his fury, stared at Adam with the same look. When Adam remained motionless, Hoggett released his breath in a grunt, turned on his heel and stalked out. The study door slammed with a thud that made fire irons rattle. Henry lurched up with an uneven stagger.

"You fool!" he choked out, barely able to speak. "You...you, asinine bag of dog vomit! You bring nothing but trouble, nosing after Rose Fitzroy. Of all the stupid, stupid..."

Fury choked him. His hand came up to jab Adam in the chest. Adam grabbed his brother's wrist in one lightning thrust and squeezed until Henry thought the bone would crack. Scowling, Adam flung Henry aside and stormed from the study.

In the reception rooms, Louisa stood by the door stricken through with consternation. What was happening to her party, she asked herself as she pasted a smile on and accepted yet another hasty farewell. Why was everything coming to this screeching end?

One minute she had been watching an inebriated young lord flicking a cigar butt into one of her paired Scottish urns. The next, Sir Cedric Walsing was in front of her thanking her elaborately for her hospitality to the Prince. As soon as the words were out, the man bowed and vanished, leaving Louisa to slowly grasp the knowledge that the Prince himself had already departed without a word to his hostess, without even being seen.

Was this customary, she wondered, a horrid chill clutching in the region of her liver. Was it a snub? Had she committed some awful gaffe that had caused him to get up and leave, branding Crisp Court inadequate forever?

And where were Henry and Adam, who ought to have been beside her, helping to see the guests to the door?

"Goodbye, goodbye," Louisa nodded as more people rustled past. Was it her imagination or were sharp-eyed looks being exchanged and lips pressed together. Althea Wharton would have known what to make of it. Oh why tonight, of all nights, did Althea have to fall ill!

Rose had been the first to be carried off, ostensibly to be escorted home by a party of hearty male followers. Louisa didn't even dare consider the proprieties of that or why Rose had looked so queer.

As if at a signal, the rest of the guests leaped up and decided they must go, first those who had come with the Prince, then those Louisa had invited, streaming toward the door. The exodus happened so quickly the maids could hardly keep up with the retrieval of wraps. Louisa would have wrung her hands if she could. Even Amelia Corman stormed past her, Edwin, who smelled of liquor, sheepishly in tow. Dear, dear, Louisa remembered thinking, I wouldn't want to be that man when Amelia gets him home!

Soon the vast rooms were as empty as if some chill gust had swept the brilliant company away. Something had gone wrong, dreadfully wrong!

But what?

Louisa couldn't imagine it. Didn't want to imagine it. Didn't want to see signs among the servants. Avoiding Mellon's much affronted face, Louisa fled up the stairs to the sanctuary of her bedroom.

She did not see Adam striding from the house nor Henry swaying beside his desk. Unable to find expression for the paroxysm tearing his chest, Henry snatched up the bell jar nearest at hand. As hard as he could, he flung it against the fireplace where it smashed into splintered glass around the stiff, dry corpse of the shrike.

CHAPTER FIFTY

"Out of the sack with you! Sleepin' like drainpipes when whole house is crammed with glasses and slops and gentlemen's cigar butts that's got to be cleared away before the family stirs!"

Lucy gave the girls a yank on the leg that tumbled them out of their cots. Lucy was groggy herself and rushing anxiously. What with His Highness flipping in, setting the whole house thunderstruck, Lucy didn't know if her nerves would ever be put back to rights.

Of one thing Lucy was sure—there was something awfully queer about they way the reception had ended, the Prince just disappearing and everyone else streaming out as though a trumpet had sounded.

"Like rats off a barge," Fran had whispered as she and Lucy dashed about hunting up ladies' cloaks. "What do you suppose happened?"

Speculation among the servants would be something fervent when they finally got some breakfast in the kitchen. Lucy, herself, had seen the mistress flee to her rooms, mouth like a clothes pin, when she ought to have been tripping on the air. Mr. Henry, she'd got one glimpse of him looking white as pudding paste. And Mr. Adam, goodness, no one had seen him around at all!

They'd certainly have to spend the morning trying to smooth down Cook who believed all the upsets had something to do with the food!

Katie emerged from her slumbers with a pop, blinking in surprise at Lucy's departing rump. She was still sprawled, exactly where she'd flung herself waiting breathlessly for Laura and Cully to come in. Now here they were wriggling out of their nightshirts to start another day. At the sight of her friends the stupendous thing roared up in her mind, her incredible, hoarded, overwhelming jolt of news.

What was it?

She rubbed at one eye then leaped onto the bare floorboards. Laura poured water from the jug into the washbowl. Katie grabbed her arm.

"There was such a fight, Laura! Mr. Adam hit the Prince! Knocked him out on the gravel, cold as a cabbage! I saw it myself from over the garden wall!"

Katie had clung to the wall, peering though the foliage of the plane tree next to the eerie fake Gothic ruin. She had been closer to the folly than she liked. By way of keeping the three children out of the garden, Lucy had told them that the folly had a ghost in it, a murdered Jesuit with a dripping dagger sticking in his gullet. Cully couldn't grasp what a Jesuit was, even when Lucy explained in gory detail. Katie recognized him as a near relative of Mr. Willoughby's fearful Jesuschrist bleeding his buckets of blood. Laura insisted there could be no real ghosts in a puffed up house just built yesterday

Jesuit or no Jesuit, Katie had hung on, trying to glimpse through the windows the ladies in their dresses, like magnificent butterflies. Above all, she wanted to see the Prince who had been astounded by Mr. Adam's story about the bear. As someone opened the conservatory door Katie had flattened herself, obscured by the leaves.

The swish of fabric and light steps approached. Katie made out the cloudy shimmer of satin under the fairy lanterns and heard a languorous sigh. After that there had been more steps, some scuffling, then the sudden curse as Mr. Adam's fist flashed out and a rotund shape toppled to the gravel.

In the heated confusion that followed, Katie stayed still as a carving, watching as the man with the boiled eyes rushed out past Mr. Henry gawking in the doorway, hauled the fallen shape from the ground and summoned minions to help. "Your Highness," they had called him in alarmed voices as they whisked him away.

The man hustled Mr. Adam and Mr. Henry roughly out of sight and then took Miss Fitzroy by the arm. All the while talking in fierce low tones, he thrust her into the conservatory, leaving the garden empty and Katie skittering back to the servant's door.

Though Katie had no idea what the punch had been about, anything Adam did acquired heroic proportions in her eyes. Her excited whisper as she told the tale carried out into the corridor and halted Phoebe, Louisa's personal maid, dead in her tracks. Katie might just as well have loosed a volley of shrapnel. Each work struck with its own appalling slash.

Not true! Can't be!

Even though Louisa, last night, had been so agitated Phoebe had barely been able to unbutton her from her gown.

Yet....if it were...it just might explain...

Phoebe's heartbeat lurched as she remembered what Jeremy, the footman, had been telling in the kitchen passage. His royal nibs himself, weaving like a hooked eel. Three of them it took to get him to his carriage and one to hold this ruddy great handkerchief to his head!

Ardently temperance Phoebe hadn't been surprised about the weaving. Any gentleman, even a prince, who let liquor touch his lips, was bound to weave. And footmen told the most exaggerated tales.

But just suppose....

Oh, impossible! Too dreadful to contemplate!

Phoebe's pulse did another frantic somersault, unnerved as a foot soldier thrust into possession of some dreadful secret of state. In a minute, those three goggle-eyed chits would be down in the kitchen blatting their heads off to all who cared to hear.

"You!" Phoebe cracked out, looming ominously in the doorway. "All three of you, come with me!"

The children jumped. They were afraid of Phoebe as was most of the other lower staff. Phoebe had come with Louisa from the mills and been her maid before Louisa was even married. She was intensely loyal to her mistress. Without so much as letting them tie their apron strings, Phoebe marched the startled three off towards the stairs.

Ivy, the kitchen maid, relieved at not being caught eating purloined chocolates behind the attic clothes press, slipped off toward breakfast. A fever of excitement glinted in her eye. Who would ever believe her, she chortled, hugging a new secret far more scrumptious than the sweets.

Phoebe was so scandalized that she completely forgot the hour. The silence of Louisa's bedroom was shattered by the spectacle of the maid prodding her three charges toward Louisa's bed. Hoisting herself from the tangle of sheets where she had tossed through the night, Louisa gaped at the intruders. Her hair was up in rags and the residue of Abbott's Turkish Restorative Cream glistened on her face. No one but Phoebe ever saw her in such condition.

"What on earth...?"

"These children have a shocking tale to tell, ma'am. You'd better hear it straight from their own mouths."

Louisa looked even more bewildered. Phoebe gave Katie a jab in the shoulder blade.

"Tell the mistress what you just said in the attic!"

Katie had had time speak of only one thing in the attic and, from the looks of Phoebe, it had been the wrong thing. She clamped her mouth shut. Phoebe's knuckle ground sharply into her ribs.

"Tell the mistress!"

Katie drew in her shoulders, fearing to incriminate herself for spying on the garden. Years with Jenks made her automatically resist bullying demands. Phoebe turned her outraged eye to Laura.

"Basing!"

But Laura was already deathly pale. Striking a prince was a ticket straight to the execution block. She was petrified to be in a household that had anything to do with such a crime.

A little desperate, Phoebe turned to Cully. Cully had not been raised on tales of highborn bloodshed and vengeful broadaxes. When Phoebe took her by the scruff, her slot of a mouth popped wide open.

"Mr. Adam socked Mr. Prince in the choppers and conked 'im flat. Sack 'o dead mackerels 'e was like when they lugged 'im to 'is coach!" Cully added, starting to grin. She had little idea of what a prince was, but thought a good scrap entertaining at any time.

As Louisa deciphered this devastating tidbit, her face blanched to match the bed linen.

"Struck...His Royal Highness...!"

"That's right, ma'am," Phoebe burst out. "Jeremy said he saw His Highness practically carried to his coach, though he supposed it was on account of drinking all that wicked champagne!"

The bed, the floor, the house reeled under Louisa.

"Are you sure?" she whispered. "They're not just making it up?"

"Wouldn't say so, ma'am," Phoebe advised with unswerving faith in her ability to spot a whopper. "You, Mucker, tell us just what you saw!"

Katie had no choice but to confess how she had climbed up the wall and seen the Prince laid low. Louisa's mouth quivered with increasing horror.

"Oh..," she moaned, ashen at the great fist of ruin looming over her home. Dots appeared before her eyes. She swooned weakly back into her heap of pillows.

"You three," Phoebe ordered sharply, "go stand in the dressing room and don't you stir a foot out of there till you're told or you'll end up out in the gutter inside of a minute living with the rats!"

The efficient application of cold cloths and smelling salts revived Louisa into a dawn jagged with anxiety. When the sensation of having taken a stunning blow receded enough for Louisa to move, she flung off the covers. Her mother's heart twisted within her.

Why, why, WHY did Adam have to bring disaster down with everything he touched!

She thought of Camille, innocently unstitching the ribbons from her latest gowns, all unaware that everything built up for her was teetering on the verge of a crash. And Henry! Henry had known of this last night and left her to cope with the exodus of guests all on her own!

Henry!

Another spurt of fear, mixed with anger now, volleyed through her. Without pausing to tear the rags from her hair, Louisa fumbled into her wrapper and rushed down the corridor into Henry's rooms. She found them empty, his bed unslept in, his night clothes still laid out and waiting. Speeding out, Louisa followed instinct straight to Henry's study.

He sat in the dark leather swivel chair, staring, like the stuffed birds and animals around him, hollow-eyed into the street. He still wore his evening clothes, though he had ripped off his cravat and torn open the collar of his shirt. Obviously, he had been hunched there all night.

"Henry?"

The maroon leather creaked as he turned. His look shook her. He was a ravaged man to whom sleep was a wasteland.

"It's true then, it is true about the Prince!" Icy coldness clawed at Louisa's throat. "Oh, we're ruined."

The chair thudded against the desk.

"Jumping Christ, who told you?"

"One of those charity children was peeping over the wall. She saw it all!"

The news seemed one more boulder striking a man already staggering in a landslide. Henry slumped further. Fresh panic assaulted Louisa.

"Where," she demanded, "is...Adam?"

And what did they do to people who struck down royalty?

A vision of her son up against a wall before a firing squad of grenadiers flared luridly into Louisa's imagination. Through red-rimmed eyes, Henry read her blind concern. The ancient acid seeped up.

"Gone to the devil, I hope! Stowed in the guts of some stinking scow bound for Tasmania! Gone before the sun came up!"

Louisa's fingers flew to her cheek, encountering the remains of her night cream. The first intimations of loss and hope were sinking in.

"I...but...he...he struck the heir to the throne?"

Henry turned bitterly from his mother's anxious eyes. Anxious, as always, for Adam.

"Look," he gritted, "the last thing Marlborough House wants is public scandal. The incident will be completely hushed up. No action will be taken provided Adam has got his carcass out of the country as fast as he can, never to come back so long as the Prince is alive!"

It's happening all over again, Louisa thought against a surge of tears. The family torn apart over Adam's hot-headed action. Her son, her firstborn, whom she had been almost convinced was dead, had been returned to her, only to be snatched by another disaster.

Against all odds, she grasped at hope.

"But if...if Marlborough House isn't going to do anything and Adam swore never to say a word..."

"Oh he won't say a word. If he hasn't gone by the next ship out, they'll drag him off and throw him into an insane asylum. He can rave his head off, chained up with the other screaming lunatics, for the rest of his life!"

Because the powdery horror on his mother's face was so gratifying, Henry plunged on, assaulting her graphically with their interview with Hoggett, leaving out no detail that would excoriate her quavering devotion to Adam, merciless as fright grew by leaps in her eyes.

When Louisa had been reduced to a bleached form on the sofa opposite, Henry found the effort had done nothing at all to purge the boil festering inside him. His mother's very terror, ratcheted up and up as he spewed Hoggett's threats at her, had only made the thing burn until he ground his teeth together and swung his chair back toward the window so that Louisa should not see his face.

Louisa worked at getting air back into her lungs. To have a child torn away, no matter how grown up, was like having a piece of flesh ripped out and tossed into the sea. It had been bad enough when Milton's rage had sent Adam off to Canada but she had believed he would travel about the colony, write to her, and when Milton cooled, surely come back.

When he hadn't written, when he had done nothing but ship that atrocious stuffed bear, she had been confused. Still later, when he hadn't written and hadn't collected his money, the loss had been like the final bleeding from a wound she could never have imagined would be lethal.

This time, just when her mother's heart had begun to be restored, he was gone forever, unable even to say goodbye.

She fought uselessly against the renewed tearing. Her perceptions had turned into raw nerve ends. Yet even their rawness was overwhelmed by the blackness radiating from her other son. Louisa stretched out a hand toward him.

"Henry?"

This time her voice was laced with a distraught awareness that Henry was in misery too. Henry slewed around and fixed his mother with a glare full of a fury that bewildered Louisa. Her eyes suddenly widened.

"Henry, why did Adam strike the Prince?"

Henry's cheekbones turned white. Louisa's mind raced back to the tale wrung from the stammering children.

"Mr. Henry was just staring and staring but Miss Fitzroy never looked at him at all."

Louisa now noticed the lines scored harshly down on either side of Henry's mouth. His shoulders looked rigid enough to snap. His nails were sunk into leather on the arms of the chair. In a room filled only with the tick of the clock and the early morning rumble of wheels on the cobbles, Louisa grew very still. Through Henry's torment a smell came to her. A smell she hadn't sensed for so many years it had been all but forgotten.

The smell of passion, of obsession.

It wasn't Adam or even the disaster with the Prince that had kept Henry gaunt and sleepless in that chair all night. It was torment over Rose Fitzroy!

"Rose!" Louisa breathed, scarcely aware of uttering the name aloud on the air. Oh didn't Rose Fitzroy cause upsets wherever she set her wayward little foot!

A mere whisper.

Henry twitched as though pierced through the body. He'd got rid of Adam but could suck no pleasure from it. All that had been cancelled the instant Rose turned to Adam in the garden. The instant Henry had felt the leap of desire between them just as surely as if he had reached out and grasped a tongue of lightning. That loss and betrayal ate into Henry's vitals with relentless, imperishable teeth.

CHAPTER FIFTY-ONE

A veil inside Louisa was rent. She was transported backward to another time, galloping along the river track, Fletcher at her heels on that rangy black he had taken out to exercise. Her upcoming wedding to Milton Crisp was scarcely a week away. She wore Milton's engagement ring proudly on her hand, everyone in her family, including herself, enormously pleased at the wealthy match. Several times, she had caught Fletcher gazing at the big emerald and pearl bauble. Half mesmerized by the long curl of his lip, Louisa always pulled on her gloves, exasperated that a groom, this groom, should have an opinion. Therefore, what had happened with Fletcher that day she could only attribute to the most frenzied prenuptial insanity.

Fletcher's air of natural insubordination would have made the man unfit for employ save that he could handle horses like no other. Louisa's father, a substantial forage merchant, indulged himself keeping a number of blooded horses, both to play the squire himself and trade for handsome profits. Fletcher had come to them from the army, though under what circumstance he had gained his discharge, no one had been able to ascertain. He had never walked like a groom nor tugged his forelock like a groom. When Louisa, fond of riding, discovered he had been in Egypt and in India, Fletcher became, despite his status, a figure of exotic fascination inside her circumscribed world.

Ordinarily, Louisa would have had no communication with grooms save that, whenever she went riding, a groom was assigned to accompany her to tend her horse when she visited and see no accidents befell. Louisa soon learned to request a mount when no one but Fletcher was available for the job. On these rides, Louisa would talk to him, trying casually to draw out of him the adventures of his army life. He had been with the artillery, riding the gunnery horses, harnessed four and six, as they hauled field pieces behind. Louisa had dreamed of the glossy, sweating bodies beneath him. Dreamed of him galloping through exploding shells while the iron gun jounced over the battlefield amidst streaming flags and victory cries.

Fletcher's tanned face would only close up tight.

"Bloody crime what happens to horses in a war, miss," was all he would say. "I'm done with all that. Will you be needing the mare any more today?"

The more Fletcher kept the tantalizing fabric of his life to himself, the more Louisa became intrigued with the dark, large-boned man who walked with a natural swagger and rode with an ease not one of Louisa's male acquaintances could match. Certainly not Milton, who sat stiffly on a horse, out of his natural element of factory floor and trading hall. Milton came riding only because Louisa insisted on it, tolerating the exercise as some necessary part of the courting ritual, much like the musical evenings impatiently sat through and the red-faced, flowery letters laboriously penned while a smirking messenger waited to carry them off.

Milton did not like Fletcher following them and told the groom to keep his distance even though the man was necessary to carry picnic baskets and plucked wildflowers and hold the horses whenever Milton and Louisa chose to dismount. With Milton beside her, Louisa felt even more intensely Fletcher regarding her from under those heavy lids. Even as Milton talked to her about their honeymoon journey and how long he could spare from his mills, Louisa found herself thinking about the strand of dark hair that fell across Fletcher's forehead or his strong fingers running across the coat of her chestnut mare. She was no help at all in planning the wedding trip.

As Louisa's wedding day approached, these confused feelings only increased. She was proud, very proud to be marrying Milton Crisp. After all, wasn't he rich, hadn't he picked her out right away from the mob of other girls vying for his attention. She was having eight bridesmaids, for gracious sakes and all eight of them giggled and teased, sharing Louisa's delight.

Yet, sucked into the whirlwind of preparations, Louisa had begun to experience an overwhelming feeling of suffocation and irrational nerves, a sense of all possibilities closing off save this one. What did she expect, she asked herself indignantly in her efforts to clear her head. Did she want to be an old biddy of twenty-three or four settling for a clergyman or a pot-bellied widower with five children nearly as old as herself? Couldn't she appreciate her own vast good luck?

Apparently not.

Even a determined plunge into menu consultation and bridal wreath choices couldn't obliterate the thought of all the young men she had not danced with, all the places she had not seen. Egypt, she kept thinking, India—and longed desperately to inhale their spicy winds. She tried to shake the feeling away, knowing it was Fletcher, a mere groom, who had caused her to yearn. Fletcher with his swinging military stride and the brand of the tropic sun still burnt into his face and his lips closed over all the tantalizing hints and scraps that might inform her of the vast unobtainable world beyond her gates.

In a house happily awhirl, Louisa had just spent the morning in one of the final fittings of her wedding gown. The dress was love-ly—white satin embroidered with seed pearls nestling amongst a silken tracery of vines. Delicate scalloped flounces of pleated chiffon descended in graduated tiers from her shoulders to the floor and a collar of costly handmade lace lay at the neck. The veil swept to the floor as well, also caught with pearls, and there would be a crown of blossoms to hold it in place. The white kid gloves she would wear lay in their box on the dresser. Hairpins studded with pearls would hold her hair in a shining knot under the veil. Her white satin slippers had pearls sewn into their bows and looked fit to dance atop the very dew.

"Oh miss, won't you look a treat, floating down that aisle just like a misty angel out of a cloud. Mr. Crisp will bust when he sees you," crooned Mrs. Potts, the dressmaker, as she tacked up the last endless hem.

The dress was the very one Louisa had been dreaming of since she was a girl. Suddenly she couldn't wait to pull it off and get away from the dressmaker's fluttering. Hoping a ride might clear these incomprehensible bridal nerves, Louisa fled to the stable. She absolutely must, she said, carry a sample of lace up to Sally Granger who was to be her maid of honour. With on one else about, Fletcher was assigned to accompany her.

Sally, provokingly, was not at home. Louisa, instead of returning on the usual, populated trail through the village, had galloped perversely off across the common and down the twisting, isolated river track, the long way home,

Impassively, Fletcher galloped after, keeping the right distance and saying nothing even as Louisa kicked her mare into a mad tear along the springy path, heedless of dangerous low branches and thorny briars snatching at her habit.

Louisa dashed past the stepping stones that were ancient when the Romans arrived, past an old boat lying in the reeds, past wild cherry and plum, pink with blossoms humming with bees. Down the track into the deeper woods she went, reckless and headlong until a sudden burst of quail in the mare's face caused the animal to jam her hooves into the earth and rear sideways in fright. Louisa was flung out of the precarious sidesaddle and into a bank of ferns. Instantly, Fletcher was down from his horse and running toward her. He found her struggling to rise, a bramble grasping her fast by the skirt. For the merest moment he paused, framed by the oaks, then knelt to untangle her.

The fall had knocked the wind from her lungs. Perhaps because she had been so jolted, her senses leaped furiously alive as Fletcher bent, the closest he had ever been. Every thrilling, illicit thought Louisa had ever harboured about Fletcher's muscled shoulders, his tangled hair, his tantalizingly stubbled jaw tumbled loose from their obscurity and rushed to the forefront of her mind. She caught the smell of him—sun-heated cotton, light sweat, leather, combining into a man-musk that made her giddy. She looked up, seeing only the line of a scar hidden in his eyebrow, the springing, tousled dark hairs of his head, hearing the soft scrape of his sleeve sliding past his side. Unable to move, she found all of it incredibly, alarmingly hypnotic.

Louisa could feel the marsh marigolds blooming in a wash of orange. Her blood ran riot along with the white evening campion, the field daisies, the buttercups and the yellow irises starring the tall grass at the water's edge. Lying so still, Louisa seemed to know all about the emerald mosses clustered on forest earth so cool and dark.

Then sunlight flashed on Milton's ring. Louisa had been overcome with that choking sense of all doors closing save the ordinary one she had chosen. Why, she might never be able even to ride her chestnut mare again, for she was going to live in town with Milton in his big dark house surrounded by cobblestones and brick streets. A surging started in her blood, an uncontrollable longing for just one sweet, unimaginable thing, one glorious mouthful of forbidden fruit before the wall of marriage forever shut her in.

As Fletcher worked at freeing her riding habit, each twitch of fabric felt as though he were touching her naked skin. Soft grasses thrust up between the ferns and the sound of running water vibrated in the air. Fletcher handled the bay stallion Louisa's father was so proud of. A stallion kept far away, as was proper, from maidenly Louisa. Louisa remembered the stallion's screams of challenge from his distant paddock and felt quite unable to lift her head.

Fletcher had stopped unplucking her skirt and was looking down at her, lips parted. Louisa had no idea how long she had been staring back, her mouth hungry, the fever burning openly in her eyes. Sunlight and shadow dappling Fletcher made him seem like another part of the forest. Louisa's hand lifted to touch that beard shadow. Lightly, her fingers trailed along until they rested in the very cleft at the tip of his chin.

Fletcher remained motionless, the tail of her skirt still in his hands. A quiver shuddered through him. With a swift release of breath, he let go of the brambles and bent to kiss Louisa.

It had been fiery and urgent and totally wordless. The whirring of the quail's flight expanded into a roar that swept her into a blazing vortex in which she tried to consume Fletcher, to grasp enough for a whole lifetime out of their thrashing among the ferns. When, at last, Fletcher lay half across her, spent in the ruins of her riding habit, Louisa had turned her face up to the sun in blind triumph.

Yes! she'd panted exultingly. Yes! Oh yes!

The next morning Louisa woke up as an invalid wakes, cold and horribly lucid after a raging sickness which has burned itself off in the night. Her throat was rigid with fright at what she had done, terrified that Fletcher had bragged it all over the stables before the horses were fed.

But Fletcher was gone, no one knew where. America, Louisa guessed, after she began breathing again. He had only ever spoken a couple of words about the place but Louisa knew. She pictured him, dressed in buckskin, pursuing wild horses over windswept plains. In trepidation and profound relief Louisa had rushed to the altar. On her wedding night she had dreamed of Fletcher. Throughout her pregnancy, she shut out the images. When Adam had been born, she had looked at his dark thatch and knew, as only a mother could, that this was Fletcher's child.

Milton never had a ghost of a suspicion. Rather, he had been delighted beyond words with the lusty, screeching boy, a suitable heir to his industries! Louisa stopped quaking and buried the adventure under layers of grateful complacency at her fine life with her husband. Even after Henry came along, looking so different, even after Adam and Milton began their struggles, even after the awful upheaval that drove Adam off to Canada, Louisa chose not to remember his origins. No trace remained save that the scent of lathered horses could still make her weak.

Louisa fumbled a blind hand to her forehead. Why did it all come flooding back now? Why were the pictures so graphic she could feel the scrape of Fletcher's jaw against her own, smell the ferns they had crushed...

Nothing but today's disaster! Nothing but the rank, thwarted smell of passion rising from Henry!

Helplessly, Louisa went toward Henry and tried to touch his shoulder.

"Henry, my dear..."

Henry read the bumbling, pitying compassion in his mother's face and shrank away as though scalded. The metallic throbbing in him touched Louisa as if it were in her own body. How could she not have been overcome with memories of Fletcher in such an atmosphere of frustrated, agonized, tormented lust!

Louisa had never suffered much from turning over the past. If she ever spared a speculation for how different her life might have been had she not been able to wed quickly, she immediately regarded her marriage as God's providence and a way to provide her with all the wealth of Milton Crisp.

Now a horrible notion struck her. Was she being punished because of her transgression? Had she been punished all along and hadn't even had the sense to see it? The struggles between Adam and Milton stood out in a stark light. Had Milton been unable to be at peace with the boy because Adam was not a true heir? The warehouse fire, Adam's banishment, Milton's crippling fit. Yes, and Milton finally dying rather than live in London!

And now this...this debacle with the Prince!

A myriad religious tracts inundated her mind. Had she brought all these plagues upon her house? Had the mills of retribution been grinding away as the years slipped by? Would they go on grinding until she made it right?

"I'm...sorry," she groaned, struggling in her tide of belated, superstitious guilt.

Her queerly disjointed pitch made Henry turn his head sharply. "What?"

"I'm...I'm sorry!"

Louisa's eyes were squeezed shut. She was lost somewhere inside herself, a thing Henry had never seen before. A twisting instinct drove Henry to his feet. Whatever she was blundering on about, it had to do with Adam and Henry violently wanted to know.

"What? What are you sorry for?"

Louisa clutched a handful of her wrapper in her fist. Her unfocussed eyes didn't even see Henry, only Milton's face, rigid with indrawn pain, the day after Adam had left.

"Milton loved Adam like his own and never guessed..."

Henry had her by the shoulders and Louisa shut her mouth like a trap. Henry's brain raced through the months from the wedding to Adam's birth, suddenly convulsed by an unthinkable possibility.

"Guessed what, mother? Guessed what?"

Louisa's lips turned bloodless. She was badly frightened by what she saw in Henry's eyes. Henry's fingers bit deeply into her shoulders.

"Mother! Guessed what?"

He began to shake Louisa so forcefully her head jerked back and forth and the sleeve tore on her wrapper. The ripping cloth made Henry stop. He stared savagely into his mother's face.

He did not need to wring the words out of her. She turned hot and pale and scarlet again in such a fervid, uncharacteristic conflagration that she might as well have had her guilt set in burning letters on her brow. Henry walked on numb feet over to the window frame where he leaned, heart beating heavily. He couldn't look anywhere in the room, only at the window pane where a fly walked aimlessly on the outside of the glass.

Adam wasn't even Milton Crisp's son!

The revelation filled Henry's mind in a blinding fireball. Then, as that faded, a kind of awful, sick relief spilled through him that whatever he did to Adam had been justified. After the relief, galloped anger. Not just anger, but a slashing, acrid rage at all he had been cheated out of because of Adam. Yes, cheated of his mother's adoration, his father's regard by a usurper who had no right to be there. Some stranger, like the progeny of the cuckoo, a bird that lays eggs in the nests of other birds and laughs while its ungainly offspring push the true hatchlings over the edge and out.

Gulping air, Henry struggled to regain control. For an age, he stood against the window frame watching the fly. When, at last, he turned to face his mother again, his eyes were shuttered, the seething turmoil around this new fact hidden deep in his bosom.

Louisa had not moved. She could scarcely remember what she had said; only that she had groaned aloud and Henry had gone mad.

She was panting in quick, scratchy gulps while she blinked at her sleeve where Henry had torn it. When she looked up, she saw that Henry had contained himself.

With an almost an audible clank, a shutter came down over the previous scene, a scene that had not, could not possibly have taken place. Henry eased himself down into the leather chair again. Louisa pulled her wrapper tight along with her dignity. In the crucible of that awful morning, Louisa at last realized that both her sons were men, capable of passions she shuddered to think about, infected by the same infernos that had once burned hotly in her own upholstered depths.

In the charged silence, it was Louisa who began to think how they were to salvage things. If she thought steadfastly about the practical present, the dangerous past might be quickly buried.

"We must go on as if...as if nothing happened at the reception," she whispered out of depths of courage she didn't know she had. "We must...for the sake of Camille."

Camille, Louisa was determined, should not be cheated out of her chance no matter what. Henry wasn't thinking of his sister. He had found a new weapon, massive and deadly. His paralysis was gone.

Patience, he told himself. He must have patience in the midst of this calamity. Had he not had patience all his life and won in the end! His mother was right. They must go on as if nothing had happened. Go on until he saw whose bluff was called.

"Yes, for the sake of Camille".

Louisa sank back until a frightful thought galvanized her.

"Those children! We can't let them back into the kitchen! The tale would be through the servants before noon."

Louisa quaked at the consequences. The girls couldn't stay. But neither could they go back to the Refuge where they'd only spill everything to Edwin and Amelia.

Henry scraped one hand distractedly through his hair.

"I shall take care of the matter."

"But Mrs. Corman..."

"We'll send them off for training, at our own expense, of course. She left them in our hands. Have their boxes ready within the hour."

Louisa fled to ring for Phoebe who would see to the packing at once.

CHAPTER FIFTY-TWO

Across town, Althea Wharton was coming face to face with the same events which had rocked Louisa. She had awakened early. Weak and wrung out, but without, thank all merciful deities, the sick white throbbing that meant another day of drawn blinds and clammy wash cloths. Memory flooded back. What had Rose Fitzroy, that unsupervised hellion, been up to at Crisp Court while Althea had been hors de combat? Althea groped for her flask, sampled its contents, then rang for Daisy to bring tea.

Five minutes after Daisy's arrival, Althea was sitting bolt upright against her pillows. The tea cooled untasted, the teacup trembled for its life in one white-knuckled hand even though Daisy hadn't, as yet, touched upon the reception. The pop-eyed maid had only got as far as the Prince of Wales—the Prince of Wales, no less—being driven out of Rose's dressing room by some dreadful, orange-haired creature who had got in while everyone was busy with the bazaar.

"Why no, ma'am," Daisy was saying to Althea's croak, "he did keep in good spirit about it even though nobody had a notion who he was. Miss Rose didn't when she sent that note after him, asking him on the Crisps'."

The cup tipped toward the bed, saved by Daisy who nimbly set it on the bedside table. Daisy was a plain, efficient, observant girl and an excellent conduit of information, which was why Althea had assigned her as maid-cum-warder to Rose. Unfortunately, Daisy had a weakness for melodrama. Oblivious to the look on Althea's face, Daisy breathlessly described how the Prince had actually followed Rose to Crisp Court and swept into the reception with his horde of followers.

"Mrs. Crisp was fit to swoon in a bun basket when His Highness walked in," Daisy exclaimed all too accurately. "Oh, their faces! The whole house started buzzing like a monstrous great swarm of bees."

Daisy's knowledge of the actual reception was maddeningly limited due to her confinement, with the rest of the ladies' maids, in the guest bedrooms. Maids were expected to remain out of sight, needles at the ready in case of a loosened hem or lace torn from a bodice during an enthusiastic waltz. Visiting maids also tidied curls, kept track of wraps and knowledgeably sponged whisker marks from bare shoulders before sharp-eyed mamas noticed. Their information about the event itself had to be gleaned through peeps down staircases and wrung from the harried house staff. Nevertheless, Daisy did know all about the sudden appearance of alcohol in that fortress of high temperance and its effect upon the gentlemen pursuing Rose.

By the time Daisy had finished her narrative, Althea's mind was reeling. The rocketing impact of knowing the Prince had actually followed Rose to Crisp Court, the scandal of her subsequent behaviour, rushed by, completely swallowed up in the final, cataclysmic part of Daisy's tale. From the disappearance of the Prince and the swift decampment of his set, Althea knew instantly that something had gone dreadfully awry. Icy pricks broke out along her scalp. Rose, she wagered grimly, could tell her exactly what that something was!

Within minutes, Althea's resurrection was complete. Cursing sick headaches in general, and yesterday's headache in particular, Althea was making her resolute way, via the support of consecutive pieces of furniture, toward Rose's room.

She found Rose motionless in the window seat, the morning sun turning her loosened curls into a tangle of strawberry fire down the back of the thin wrapper Rose had pulled around her shoulders. Rose in disarray proved even more fetching than Rose carefully dressed. Yet Rose was still as a marble girl and likely had been sitting that way for hours. Her face, softly gilded in the morning light, had the battered, stricken look of one plunged into hard affliction for the first time in her life.

Althea dropped a hand upon Rose's shoulder. "Tell me," she commanded, "what happened with the Prince."

Rose started up, her blanched cheeks informing Althea of the worst. In the reddened lids and drawn, pale mouth, Althea read the unmistakable traces of high revelry. Sleeplessness in the face of a hangover spelled big trouble indeed. Rose bit her lower lip but Althea would have no intransigence.

"No use looking at me like that. Daisy told me all about Crisp Court."

The tremour under Althea's hand made Althea's consternation climb by notches. She planted herself on the other end of the window seat.

"There was liquor, I hear. Champagne to be exact. His Royal Highness is known to be especially fond of champagne."

Deftly, Althea squeezed out an account of the shenanigans during the singing. Deplorable, but certainly not unexpected when gentlemen and spirits came together. Althea squelched a twinkle at what Louisa Crisp, Amelia Corman and all those other temperance dragons must have suffered.

Rose lapsed into silence without, Althea could see, getting to the nub of the matter. Scandalous behaviour was one thing. But if Rose had truly offended the Prince, they might as well all consign themselves to the rubbish heap immediately.

"Rose, you have to tell me. There are consequences."

Yes, consequences. Rose felt illness rise inside her and she turned even chalkier. Over and over in her head she kept hearing Hoggett's voice.

"If Adam Crisp so much as shows a hair in England after to-night, he'll be seized. He'll never see free light of day again!"

Never would she forget Hoggett's stubby-lashed eyes boring into her in the carriage as his features flared and dimmed in passing street lamps. Never would she forget his damp hand on her elbow and his even damper breath upon her neck. How could she have thought him such a bluff, jolly fellow at the reception? How was it that she hadn't seen below the mask to the horrid sliminess underneath?

She had been held in the garden after everyone else had disappeared, then jerked bodily though the conservatory door and into a passageway, face to face again with Hoggett. His coarse pale hair had seemed to bristle over his reddening scalp beneath. His mouth was livid.

"You will give no hint of what you have seen," he ground out. "You will go back to the reception with me and you will smile and smile and you'll say goodnight to your hostess. You will get into your carriage for an escort home. Do you understand?"

The skin of Hoggett's face had a mottled sheen. Menace glittered from his small, deep-set eyes.

"You will be leaving immediately. You will be taken straight home. If you fail to do exactly as you are told, you will be subject to arrest for aiding an attack upon our future sovereign."

He had thrust her back into the lights and the laughter, his fingers leaving a vicious warning dig in her arm. After the gloom of the garden, the noise and the brightness struck at Rose like a blow. All the champagne she had drunk filled her head with a thick buzzing sensation. Confused, disoriented by the rush of events, Rose longed to flee for sanctuary. Her heart began to beat with a steadily escalating panic. What had they done with Adam!

All around, some powerful, invisible machine had kicked into action. The royal retinue, that pack of languid, careless pleasure seekers, straightened up and took final gulps from their glasses. Casually, but with unmistakable purpose, they began streaming toward the door.

Rose found herself in the carriage clattering away. Instead of the leisurely, riotous parade such an exit might have occasioned on another night, the vehicle headed swiftly toward Wharton House. Instead of Daisy, Major Hoggett sat in the shadows across from her.

"Where is Adam Crisp?" she had demanded gamely despite the bullying blows rained upon her. "You wouldn't dare push me about like this if he were here!"

"I would," Hoggett returned, leering, "and I shall, for you'll never see Adam Crisp again!"

Time became warped as Hoggett told her that Adam was almost certainly, at that very moment, scuttling aboard the first tramp ship he could find. Calcutta or Tierra del Fuego, it didn't matter where it was bound, so long as it was swiftly away from the docks.

"And you, my troublesome canary, will be lucky to sing in a dock-side gin cavern if you go telling any tales. What's more, another word with Adam Crisp, supposing he hasn't had the sense to run for it, and you shouldn't forget about arrest for conspiracy yourself!"

Hoggett's eyes glittered. His knees imprisoned Rose firmly in the corner where she sat. His heated gaze ravaged her up and down.

He's enjoying this! He enjoys having me at his mercy!

Despite her previous escapades, Rose received, for the first time in her life, the sense of a man's lust crawling all over her. She felt hunted. Her stomach knotted in painful instinctive revulsion.

All night, Hoggett's words had throbbed in Rose's mind, flinging her between towering, blazing anger and mouth-parching dread. A pallor crept up her cheeks and into the skin around her eyes. Althea saw something she had never seen in Rose before. She saw fear.

"Tell me," Althea repeated over inner palpitations.

In mute misery, Rose shook her head.

"I was ordered never to..."

"Who ordered you?"

The satinwood clock ticked the agonized moments away. A tumbled curtain of hair obscured Rose's face.

"Who?" Althea pressed.

"Major...Hoggett."

Queasiness spiraled in Althea's innards. She already knew from Daisy that Hoggett had ridden back with Rose after the reception. Hoggett was the Prince's panderer, a dangerous worm in a splendid coat.

All her hopes collapsed around her.

"Rose," Althea said finally in her voice of most serious authority, "you know there can't be secrets between us. You must tell me what happened. You must have someone to guide you though this."

Oddly, Rose thought of her own mother who could make strong men flinch with a glower of her eye. Could her mother have made Hoggett take his bullying knees and his horrid gloat away?

Rose felt alone, cast loose as she had not felt since she stood on the shore watching the Mabbin lugger heel into the wind for Cork.

Slowly, she turned to Althea. Did she dare?

The friendly lemur eyes were fixed on her with intense concern from under a floppy house cap. The morning sunshine made Hoggett weirdly unreal.

But he was real, all too real. Rose couldn't hold the secret any longer.

"The Prince was punched in the garden," she burst out. "Cold at my feet. They carried him off as fast as they could through the back gate. Then that horrible Major Hoggett dragged me away and told me I wasn't to breathe a word or I'd be lucky to sing at a dockside dive!"

Althea's protruding eyes seemed to grow and grow until they truly looked as though they would pop from her head and dangle by their strings. For the first time since her sailor had deserted, Althea was speechless.

An attack on the Prince's person! Awful! Impossible! Treasonous!

"Goodness," Rose reached into Althea's pocket for the flask, "you had better have a bracer!"

Althea gulped a pungent mouthful and waited for the bite. Black ruin swirled about her head. She felt like a sword thrust victim just before the knees began to buckle.

Think! For pity's sake, think!

Another swallow sent fumes of vodka to her brain. Out of the ruins, two enormous facts reared up. First, with flinging off the restraints of propriety at the reception, Rose's future was decided. Just as Althea predicted, Rose had proven too spirited to stick to convention. Therefore she was destined to be unconventional, a figure of daring and fascination, cut free, increasingly surrounded by one scandal after another. Rose had swerved onto the glamorous, dangerous path.

The other fact was that the Prince of Wales himself, the indefatigable, womanizing Bertie, had, on the strength of a glimpse at a charity bazaar, been inflamed enough pursue Rose to the point of getting knocked down over the girl.

The idea of the Prince being struck flung Althea into another dizzy spell. Yet if, she managed to think of him as not a prince, but a man, why, didn't the episode bear all the signs of a swift, besotted infatuation!

The Prince was well known for his prodigious appetites where the fair sex was involved, from experiments in the darkest dens of vice to afternoon visits to the wives of his friends when the friends weren't home. How very easily Rose could become just another of the actresses and singers toyed with and left behind in his wake.

The huddle of Rose's shoulders moved Althea strongly.

Well, Bertie wouldn't be allowed to! Not with Rose. If he wanted Rose, he should only have her in the exalted manner possible!

Althea's heart began to racket unevenly against her ribs.

Oh did she dare even think of it!

Did she dare even try!

She had woken this morning to find herself clinging by her fingernails to a mountain cliff. She could either hang there in fright and fall to her doom. Or she could try to scale the peak which hung to tantalizingly, so perilously in sight.

Althea applied recklessly to the flask again. In for a penny, in for a crown. If she didn't try, they might be as good as finished anyway. Her fortitude began to rush back. Her very flesh acquired goose bumps at the possibilities.

First of all, Rose would not be a disposable pleasure, a bagatelle for His Highness. Certainly not, Althea resolved. If anything, Rose had the makings of a grand royal mistress. One of the most powerful women in England.

Or in the Empire!

All with Althea Wharton at her shoulder to show her what to do!

Althea's insides took another plunge at even thinking the thought. Oh, the intrigues, the connections, the influence she could have. Mesmerized, Althea imagined decreeing fashion, shaping trends, why, even touching the politics of a nation. And why not, she asked herself. It wasn't as though she couldn't do a better job than those already blundering about in power.

The temptation of political influence danced before Althea, for was this not the tradition of great mistresses! Had they not, throughout history, affected the fate of nation after nation, and much for the better too, Althea did not hesitate to add!

But could she do it? Could she grasp power undreamed of in a simple social godmother?

Oh yes! If only she and Rose were bold enough.

Only the boldest of action would save them now. Althea would be risking her all on Rose. If she tried and failed, they'd both be ruined.

But if they won...

The gambler in Althea began to thrill. Jumping to her feet, she began to pace up and down, her mind racing at a feverish pace.

"We must go ahead with the concert," Althea announced in a burst of inspiration. "We must make it the most coveted event of the Season. Everyone will be dying to see you after what happened at Crisp Court. They'll fight for tickets. We'll...why, we'll put the tickets up for auction!"

Rose must go fearlessly forth. The people who mattered must dare to see her. They must be made to compete for the privilege.

"No one is supposed to know about what happened at Crisp Court," Rose cried, fingers flying to her throat

"Nonsense. With a houseful of people and servants everywhere, it can't help but be all over town by evening. Every drawing room will be mad with speculation and we must use it to our own advantage."

The girl didn't understand that there were secrets and there were secrets.

Among the aristocracy, the unwritten rules let one indulge in whatever vices one liked so long as no scandal reached the common public. Or, as one wit put it, one didn't frighten the horses. To break the rule was to be drummed smartly from the ranks. Among the elite, delicious gossip circulated freely. The servants who served tea to randy visitors, carried notes and changed the sheets, knew everything and were the most highly entertained of all.

Rumour of a royal brouhaha over Rose would make the girl an object of fascination. That notoriety could be transformed into poison or to gold. They must seize the moment or be finished for good. Mrs. Corman and her Refuge became, as a shining shield, more vital than ever before.

Althea snapped her fingers in the air.

"An all-Canadian theme, I think, since that's where Amelia plans to ship the little paupers. The Prince always supports charities."

Then a sickening thought occurred. What if the Prince were more seriously injured than any of them imagined? He had been carried off barely staggering, Rose said. He could have a fractured jaw, or smashed cheekbone or be enraged from a brutally aching head. God's knees, people died from blows to the head!

Knowing that way insanity lay, Althea squelched the thought.

"We'll make it into a masquerade," she affirmed, plunging on along the path she had committed herself to. "Everyone must come in costume. Everyone! There'll be a costume ball afterwards at Crisp Court. Louisa and Henry will gladly pay and pay just to remain..."

"No!" Rose's voice was a frayed thread. "No, it can't be all over town. It can't. They'll catch him. They...they'll...oh he won't even have a chance to get away!"

Rose clutched the edge of the window seat. Althea peered at her sharply then sat down beside her again.

"Rose," she said very quietly, "You had better tell me exactly why you were out in that garden and who you were to meet. And who they're going catch if the story gets around."

The fairy lights swam before Rose's eyes again, and Adam, bent on desperate action.

"He...the Prince, followed me out," Rose murmured shakily. Scarlet seared through her cheeks, as good, to Althea, as signal flags.

With horror, Rose had heard the awful crunch when the Adam's fist connected to the head of the Prince. She had watched, petrified, as the Prince's face took on a look of extreme astonishment while his bulk wavered, tilted and crashed to the earth.

Then the door had opened, spilling light across the scene. Her eyes had locked with Adam's, in those mere seconds forging between them an understanding, primal, visceral, permanent.

"Who hit His Highness?" Althea demanded in a voice that would brook no evasions as error washed into Rose's eyes. "Who?"

"Adam Crisp!"

The name leaped out in a release of unbearable pressure.

Adam Crisp hit him," Rose whispered in a cracked voice. "And Major Hoggett said they'd send him to a...a lunatic asylum if they ever caught him. With...rats. Adam couldn't stand it there. He'd die!"

In a cold, relishing voice, Hoggett had explained exactly what happened to those who dared attack royalty.

"No trial, no appeal for blackguards like that. He'll just be locked up, chained if need be, and left to rave with the madmen until he rots."

No threat he could have picked was worse than this one.

"And....if I ever spoke to Adam Crisp again, I'd...I could be arrested too for...for conspiracy to harm the Prince!"

Her desolation made Althea see, with a sudden shattering flash, what had happened. Oh, disaster of disasters, Rose had fallen in love with that renegade. This catastrophe had to be extinguished, stamped out, erased at once before it ruined them all!

CHAPTER FIFTY-THREE

Crisp Court remained in the grip of frantic cleaning and tidying. The mess of wine bottles, cigar butts, sticky glasses and alcohol-smelling stains left by the frolicking gentlemen was unaccustomed and shocking. Mellon regarded the goblets as though they were burnt cinders left by infernal orgy. Mrs. Wunkle tasted leftovers anxiously, certain she would discover something ominously amiss. Ivy, dragooned from the kitchen, sped about trying all the chairs on which the Prince had sat.

While Henry might brood in his study, Louisa could afford no such luxury. The captain of a storm-tossed ship must appear on the bridge, assuring the crew that all is well. Agitated as she was, Louisa descended for breakfast determined to act as though the reception had been a resounding success.

After keeping composure before the staff, Louisa donned her grandest visiting dress and set off for luncheon at the Ballthorpes. Despite sick waves churning through her stomach, she must appear unquestioningly confident. If she were coldly received at the Ballthorpes'...

With Louisa gone and the cleaning done, a sepulchral hush fell over the Crisp Court. Rain pelted the windows, adding to the gloom. Worn out from their labours, the staff was only too glad to slip away for some well-earned rest. The rain turned into a thunderstorm, a clap of thunder covering the sound of a door slamming and boots upon the stair.

Adam got no further than the second landing before he was confronted by Henry who yanked open his study door. He greeted Adam with red-tinged, disbelieving eyes.

"How dare you come back here! How dare you set foot in this house after the damage you've done!"

Water ran in runnels from Adam's thick dark hair and his moustache. He shook himself like a soaked beast.

"I came to speak to mother, if that's all right with you," Adam growled sarcastically through his teeth.

Rose's passionate look in the garden burned like an acid in Henry's bones.

"It's not! Get out of here! Get away before anybody sees you! Mother's not home."

Adam continued to the top of the stairs.

"Get of this house I say!" Henry half shouted, backing up involuntarily.

"If mother isn't here, then I'll have to see you, won't I."

Adam looked frighteningly queer and very large in the storm-streaked evening clothes he still wore. He swept Henry before him into the study and slammed the door. Henry began to breathe heavily as Adam squinched on the polished floor.

"I went to look at where the mills used to be yesterday. I saw Clayvers. I found out about father and how I never got any of his messages. I could kill you for that!"

Through the torn-open collar of Adam's shirt a heavy pulse accelerated, the rage of man deliberately deprived of family he had desperately longed for.

This was the last thing Henry expected. His face quivered like that of a pilfering boy found out. He stepped backward unti he thudded up against the hard edge of his desk. The stuffed shrike still lay among the broken glass shards where it had smashed against the fireplace, no maid having dared the room. The other creatures studied the scene with their dead glass eyes.

"Father took a fit. He wasn't right in his mind. We had no need of a troublemaker such as you."

"I guess not. I might have kept him from being stripped of everything he held dear. I might have stopped the vulture in the nest from picking him clean!"

White ringed Henry's lips. The rest of his face grew purplish and mottled.

"It was about time somebody did something with the property. I took it over, I took care of it, I dragged it into modern times. Here we are in London, aren't we, not in some backwater dead from a foreign war. I'm going to multiply the Crisp fortune into something to reckon with!"

"By doing what? Selling any silverware that's left?"

"By buying. There's plenty to buy into in London and I've bought in already. I'm going to own part of..."

"Of a sweatshop turning out hats? Or perhaps a line of cabs? Or..."

"Or a railway line," Henry fired back, completely forgetting the heavy bond of secrecy required of all investors. "A new track into the city, a new station. Hundreds of passengers every day and Henry Crisp getting a profit from each!"

Greed glowed on Henry's face. The more money he could make, the deeper he could bury away the match in the warehouse that set him on this road. To grasp and grasp was the only way he could stamp out the memory. Even Adam was taken aback by the reach of Henry's ambition. In his many London tramps he had seen what the new railways did to the districts they punched through.

"And where is there room for another new station?"

Belatedly, Henry's mouth clamped shut.

"I am not at liberty to say. No need to be held up for ransom because a bunch of squalid speculators have discovered our plans."

Flinty hardness caught Adam's cheek.

"Some part of the city where property is cheapest, no doubt, with hundreds of poor sods turfed out of their hovels into the street. Never let human misery interfere with stuffing your pockets!"

Even dishevelled and sleepless and under terrible threat, Adam still loomed as the older brother who cut off the light to his sibling. Henry was provoked beyond endurance.

"At least I'm not an incompetent. I didn't let a year's supply of raw material go up in flames!"

The attack speareded straight into the abscess of pain, of guilt that lived at Adam's core. Henry pushed himself away from his desk, head jutted forward.

"The whole future of the mills was in your hands. Father trusted you with it. And what did you do? You sat drinking gin and let it all go up in smoke. You didn't deserve to hear from father ever again!"

The long ago night roared through Adam's memory again, so lurid it might have happened yesterday. He knew he hadn't been drinking gin. He had been watching, patrolling with all the gravity of the responsibility pressing on his shoulders. Through a hundred nights he had agonized about how the fire had started.

Henry took another step, crunching shards of glass underfoot. He was now so livid he didn't care that he was shouting about the very thing he had been loathe to think about all these years.

"That fire turned the mills into idle hulks. What was the use of them without cotton to spin. Father would have hung onto them like a fool. I was the one who pried the mills out of his grip and got rid of them for the docks. Hadn't I been telling him to do that since I first went to work in his office?"

Henry's avidity triggered an ancient wisp of memory. Lightning from the window illuminated Henry's face. The old acne pits resembled a ruined landscape.

"You took advantage of a sick man who couldn't defend himself from you."

"Advantage is taken where advantage is to be had," Henry flung back savagely. "Advantage is to be made wherever one can. I made mine right under your nose."

The ancient wisp of memory grew stronger, the image of a shape skittering from the back of a warehouse. It had flitted at the back of Adam's brain for years. Now, as though lit by its own needle of lightning, it suddenly stood out in hard-edged clarity.

Adam's mouth slowly opened. Then his pulse exploded with incendiary force in his forehead.

"It was you! You who started that fire!"

However Adam knew this, he knew it gut-deep. The shape had been but a shadow, faceless, insubstantial, but the very way it had melted into blacker darkness now told Adam whose shadow it had been. Henry himself was telling him now. Adam had not guessed the extent of his brother's greed.

"You burned those warehouses and you broke father's heart. Why didn't you just pick up a brick and kill him yourself!"

All the years of restless aching, all the blame Adam had staggered under, all the grief at Milton's loss detonated outward at Henry. In two steps he had flung Henry against the desk again and had him by the throat. The fabric of Henry's shirt made a high, tearing sound ripping under Adam's grip. Frantically, Henry's hands scrabbled behind him on the desk for something to use against Adam, but the shrike was already smashed. His eyes whitened with fright. He struck back with the cruelest weapon he could find.

"Let go of me! You don't deserve anything. You're...you're not even Milton Crisp's real son. He wasn't your father at all!"

The ripping abruptly halted. Adam could not possibly have heard the words right.

"You...low, vindictive bastard...you call yourself a brother..."

With a furtive twist, Henry freed himself and lurched over to the mantel. More glass splintered under his feet and his collar hung askew.

"I don't call myself a brother. I am not your brother. I found out from mother this morning that you are not Milton Crisp's son!"

Gloating flooded Henry's face. Adam felt a great throb inside himself, like a strike on a hollow, muffled drum.

"You take that filthy lie back."

"I will not!"

Only now did Henry understand how much he had been longing to fling these very words at Adam. They justified everything he had ever done, even to burning the warehouses. Even if he had burned down the whole town, it was no longer any of Adam's business. No wonder there had always been trouble between them. Dealing with Adam had been like trying to deal with a badly bred horse that ought to have been turned off as soon as it was foaled. Triumph burgeoned at the papery bleakness gripping Adam's face.

"Ask mother if you don't believe me," Henry taunted. "Go ahead, ask her."

Adam did not move. They both knew he couldn't do it. Couldn't because Adam knew it must be true. Even Henry would not dare such an utterance without rock-hard belief. All Henry's words migrated to Adam's stomach and lodged in a kind of nausea that made him unsure whether his legs would still work.

"Now, get out of the house, get away from here to the godforsaken wilderness you came from," Henry hammered out. "Go and use that loutish brawn to get your living. Go! And never darken this door again!"

Thunder cracked overhead, sounding like a section of the sky tearing itself across, tearing Adam inside where he could bleed. Very slowly, with the stunned concentration of an accident victim, Adam felt his way down the stairs and out.

CHAPTER FIFTY-FOUR

Derby Day dawned splendidly. Jaunty shreds of cloud made the blue more vivid while an impudent breeze snapped flags and made off with caps in a very embodiment of the levity ahead for all.

There had been racing on the spot ever since the twelfth Earl of Derby began to entertain his friends with races at his country estate fifteen miles from the heart of London. The Oakes, a race for fillies, had been started in seventeen seventy-nine, The Derby, for colts and fillies, had been going since seventeen-eighty. Despite these elevated beginnings, Derby Day had evolved into one of the most democratic days England had to offer. Derby Day belonged to all.

Everyone who could find transport made their way to Epsom Downs. Parliament would not sit on Derby Day so that its members might cheer their favourites on. Bankers, merchants, squires and army officers brought their families in finery-filled carriages. The Cockney region under the Bow bells emptied to drink stout out of sloshing jugs and shout their wares at Epsom. Every shell game artist, street hawker and acrobat who could manage hied to Epsom to try their luck. While actually watching the races might be a pleasant bonus, the real purpose was to see and be seen, to picnic and laugh, to turn a profit, to relish as much of the hijinks as possible. And for everyone, the highlight of the day would be a cherished glimpse of their own beloved Bertie, their sporting Prince of Wales.

In a nation more addicted to sport than any other on earth, Bertie was enormously popular for his love of racing which he backed up with entries from the royal stables. Like everyone else, he bet on his favourites, endearing himself all the more to the tolerant British public. Who could fail to feel that all was well when royalty was visibly enjoying itself with the rest of the population? Bertie attended in a grand style, driving onto the course in a glittering carriage procession with his friends. Derby Day, that most important of all days in British racing, was unthinkable without his presence.

From before dawn, the road had been jammed with carriages, horse-drawn omnibuses sagging with passengers, hired cabs and mobs of the lower orders making their way on foot. The entire racecourse seemed one uproarious fair, a marvellously chaotic holiday playground in which the English, high and low, reasserted their inborn love of liberty, reclaiming the freedoms squelched by the dreary grip of industry. Striped tents had sprung up selling drink and food. Booths and sideshows displayed giants, dwarves, painted minstrels and performing dogs. Choruses of recently scrubbed working men drowned out lads with fiddles and accordions. Young women with tambourines made unblushing advances to grinning strangers. Old parties guzzled ale and shouted ribald jests at one another. There were betting pools, games of chance, wrestling contests and fortune tellers. For those that liked their entertainment more rough-edged, cockfighting and "purring matches" or kick fighting in clogs, could be found in certain tents at the back of the course.

Interspersed in this merry melee were the carriages of the affluent classes drawn up on the grass to get the best views of the track, the ladies in them afroth with summer silks, saucy parasols and whimsical confections masquerading as hats.

Through this vast, spontaneous carnival, one figure strode bluntly across the grass, paying no heed to the milling masses, deflecting revellers from his path.

With knotted brow, Adam Crisp lumbered along. Stiff beard stubble shadowed his jaw. Springing hair had been raked and pulled entirely beyond the discipline of a comb. All hint of the gentleman vanished. Adam had reverted to the clothes he had stepped off the ship in. Canvas trousers, rough cotton shirt and the sheepskin vest had reappeared, fitting him as naturally as a pelt fits a wolf. On his head sat the weather-stained, broad-brimmed hat, maverick amidst the sea of flat workman's caps. He looked as though he had not rested since his clash with Henry at Crisp Court and resembled a harried beast driven by relentless burning in its gut.

Adam felt every bit as stormy as he looked. Where he had been and what he had done since he had stomped out of his brother's study he could not completely say, except that it was better not mentioned in the light of day.

And here he was at the Derby.

Why?

To gulp some clean air, for one thing. To pound some of the frenzy out of his limbs by walking here, devouring the miles with his loping stride. Oh how he needed to use his body again. He longed for windswept prairie grasses beneath his feet or the forest scent of pine.

Waves of claustrophobia struck. Nightmares about the muddy poacher's trap which turned into a lunatic asylum and woke him clammy with perspiration. He didn't doubt for a moment that Hoggett would do exactly as he had said. And do it in a way that would leave no chance to fight, no way to defend himself.

A runaway log boom, a pain-maddened buffalo, rapids roaring under the bow of the Widgeon he could face. A windowless cell with no exit filled him with a sick dread. He'd snatched Derby Day to escape the city, to walk and to seethe in the safety of the mob.

So if he wanted safety, why was he here instead of on the deck of one of the myriad ships continually slipping down the Thames and away?

The sizzle of roasting roe deer returned and the lash of the branch across his back and legs. Mixed inextricably were the light eyes fixed upon him in thick, slow-breathing pleasure. He hadn't left London because some stubborn core couldn't let Hoggett beat him.

No! Rot that excuse! He'd come because he couldn't stay away. He'd come in hopes of seeing, even just once from afar, Rose Fitzroy!

So I do see her? Then what?

He couldn't tell. Adam was a man who had just had the axis of his life wrenched askew by Henry's revelations.

Milton Crisp not his father! Milton Crisp, that hard, impatient, energetic figure who had raised Adam, driven him, punished him, demanded of him, trained him, banished him and, ultimately, loved him. Only now, when this central pivot had been smashed, did Adam see how he had spent all his life revolving around it, trying to please his father, unable to settle even in the fastnesses of Canada for waiting for his father's call.

He had come back to England to lay old ghosts. Instead, the ghosts had reared up to gobble him up alive. His father...

No, not his father, but Milton Crisp!

The broken axis inside him yawed again.

Who was his father? Had Milton known? Known all along and that was why he had been so harsh?

And his mother? Who had she really been in love with? What had happened to her those years ago as her wedding approached?

Adam shook his head hard, unable to fling the unthinkable from his mind. He reeled and floundered in such shifting perplexity that he drove himself blindly through the crowd, wishing mightily for a lumberjack's axe in his hands or a hammer-headed mustang between his knees so that he might drown everything in straining physical exertion.

Above all, he longed for a glimpse of Rose the way a man longs for a draught of restoring spring water. He shouldered his way in the ever more dangerous direction of the stands where the cream of society was packed, the overflow lolling in their carriages at the sides. When he thrust to the brow of a small knoll, he halted, able to see over the heads of the milling race goers.

At first, he saw only more chaos. His trained eyes finally picked out a swatch of ivory and blue and under the hat, a mass of strawberry curls that could have only one owner. His heart gave a mighty kick against his ribs. Rose was indeed at the Derby, seated at the side of Althea in the Wharton carriage.

"Of course, we must go," Althea had insisted, picking out a dress both outrageous in its wealth of flounces, and coolly reserved in its narrow blue stripes. "Anybody who's anybody goes to the Derby along with hordes who are not. Imagine how it would look if we stayed home. Chin up, my girl. Nobody is going to imagine Althea Wharton or Rose Fitzroy on the run!"

Althea had outdone herself in her own hat of raspberry silk adorned with rooster tails dyed to match, her best brave front to cover her gnawing anxiety about the Prince's injuries. Only when she could see him with her own eyes would she be able to take whole breaths again. They would watch the races from the open carriage, Althea decided, displaying Rose to view but keeping her away from the crowds in the stands.

Rose's arrival had caused a gratifying flurry. However, Rose's former admirers were more polite and more wary. Was this simply the deference of lesser beings to Bertie's interest, Althea wondered, or because Rose was already touched by social blight.

Smiling at those around her, Rose managed to return remarks, even a little banter. Yet she barely moved in the carriage or turned around where she sat. Ever since her talk with Althea on the window seat, Rose had found herself in a most peculiarly inanimate condition.

After Althea had swished out, Rose had felt numb in her face, her lips, her fingertips. Now the numbness had slowly penetrated until it settled all the way through her flesh into her bones like some poison tipping a dart she hadn't felt until it was too late. Althea had been doubly kind and solicitous, buzzing about so busily that Rose had had scarcely a moment to dwell on the hollow feeling inside. She let herself be carried along. And here she was, dressed in her jaunty blue-striped flounces, smiling over the side of the open vehicle.

Althea was breathing easier at Rose's compliance, yet knew that her very success with Rose was but another sign of Rose's attachment to Adam Crisp.

Far away on the knoll, Adam could not see Rose's face, stiffly brittle or her hands clutching her parasol as if it were the last solid handhold on earth. He only saw the extravagant froth of her dress, the impudent bob of her hat plumes as she apparently joked with the inevitable knot of men around her carriage.

All about her, lacquer on the other vehicles gleamed in the sun while liveried servants hurried to unpack sumptuous picnic lunches and fend off the nosegay sellers. Once again Adam saw the Prince toppling, relived again the depth of her look, felt that conflagration that burst, without warning, into a fiery tongue enveloping them both.

Adam wanted nothing so much as to pluck Rose from the carriage and bound away on hundred league boots. Locked in that privileged circle, Rose might as well have been on some other continent.

I'm going see about me. Grasp what I can with my hands and hold on tight.

She'd vowed that on the Serpentine. Amidst all the gaiety was she having her day? Did she still want the path that diverged so sharply from his own?

Caught in his own doubts and conflicts, Adam was unaware that another interested party had set up amongst the vast throng ripe for the plucking. Derby Day was always one of Red Nell's biggest money-makers and she supervised activities from her closed cab stationed only yards away on the very same knoll. Nell was always preternaturally alert at the Derby. The easy booty had to be grabbed under the very noses of a constabulary beefed up for the occasion. Such a crowd might also provide cover for Teapot, Nell's ever-menacing nemesis. Nell never knew when, or how, he might try to strike.

Today, Nell was hard put to think about her crack corps of pickpockets, her shrewdly rigged games of chance and the troops of busy vendors owing her a cut. She could only think about Rose. The showdown in the dressing room had shaken Nell. Rose, headstrong creature, had genuinely leaped the wall. Like Gwyn, Nell thought in gloomy foreboding about Rose's future.

Outside Crisp Court, Nell had kept a troubled, frustrated watch on the festivities, catching only distant glimpses of the gilded scenes inside. Her vigil was upset by a reeling figure assisted from the alley into the finest carriage which sped urgently off, followed shortly by a stream of companion carriages. The coachmen and footmen had turned tight-faced and silent as they hurried to leave. As if this wasn't enough to alarm Nell, she had seen Rose pushed by the arm into the Wharton carriage by a strange, red-faced man who looked furious and who, Nell knew instantly, was a bully.

And, instead of the maid, the man climbed inside with Rose!

Nell had followed as swiftly as she could, relieved to see Rose returned to Mrs. Wharton's and not to some more sinister place. When the man roughly escorted Rose to the Wharton door Nell's hackles rose. Any fool could see that something was nastily wrong. How provoking not to understand what that something was.

Now, from behind the half-drawn blinds of her cab Nell had an excellent view of the activity all around. She had chosen the knoll for exactly the same reason Adam had; its view of the Wharton vehicle. The crowd split around an obstacle that drew Nell's eye.

Pricked by the unerring memory that was her most formidable weapon, Nell stared hard. One of those fancy Crisp Court people but dressed like a cattle herder and with every atom of his attention fixed on the carriage where Rose sat!

Nell had left Crisp Court too quickly to have seen Adam striding from the house, but the young horse-holder she had paid to hang about had certainly spotted him.

"Proper blazin', 'e was," the observant lad had informed Nell. "And slippin' out by the servants' alley too!"

That information, coupled with the sight of the man shed of his gentleman's garb and looking so murkily desperate filled Nell with alarm. The signs written all over him. Danger! Nothing but danger for Rose!

Fearing the man intended to wade straight for Rose's carriage, Nell rapped on the cab window for the young ruffian lounging nearby.

"Patchy, quick now, get me Joe and Dan."

CHAPTER FIFTY-FIVE

The jolt from the left sent Adam sideways, almost knocking into a woman with a baby in her arms.

"Hey," Adam sputtered, "look where you're going, mate."

He found himself nose to nose with a man as big as himself. A man with heavy scowling features and black hair tumbling down over his eyes. The man shoved closer, breathing in Adam's face.

"Who's going to make me? Not some jackass standing in my way!"

Already much agitated, Adam thrust his boots into the trampled grass.

"Jackasses kick bloody hard...."

Another man insinuated himself between two, decked in a flashy striped waistcoat and a top hat cocked over one eye.

"Hey, this here's our champion. You want to fight him, you put your money up or keep your blathering to yourself. From the look of you, you wouldn't have the stomach."

Sparley Dan could bait with the best. The big man was Joe Varden. Both had been sent by Nell.

Adam felt a red heat pounding up toward his head. Joe's chin jutted aggressively. Dan's brows rose mockingly. He tucked one thumb in his suspenders and poked the other into Adam's chest.

"Wotcher, wotcher, put up yer dukes and fight our champion." Dan chanted, half to Adam, half to the people around. "You goes home rich if you beat our champion!"

Behind Dan, being erected at breakneck speed, was Nell's portable boxing ring. In crowds like this, her stable of fighters brought in tidy profits by challenging all comers.

"Our Joe'll smear you," another of Nell's touts began to shout, dancing about Adam. " Witless sod, go ahead and try 'im!"

Wrenched from his concentration on Rose, Adam breathed hard, trying to control the hotness inside him. Joe blocked his path away, arms crossed over his heavily muscled chest. Knots of people began to gather, watching to see what Adam would do. A taunting circle formed, trained by Nell at goading marks into a fight.

"Aw, this one's scared. Lookit 'im turn lily white."

"Give 'im a biff, Joe. Pull 'is nose and see if it falls off."

"Hey, ain't ya got the stuffin' to make a little bet!"

Impudent, jibing cockerels hemmed Adam in making comic faces around the toothpicks hanging from their mouths. Adam remembered other challenges, in the mills and the lumber camps, when the only recourse was to fight.

The idea, once in his head, slashed the hot bubble inside him, spilling the rage and chaos churning in his gut. A fight! Oh yes, a fight where he could take out with his fists the blackness fermenting inside him against Hoggett and Henry and the shameful stupidity of circumstance.

The need was terrible yet Adam forced himself sideways to walk away if he could. Joe stepped in front of him again, immovable as a horned bull. When Adam moved to thrust Joe aside. Dan stuck his face in, breathing beery fumes.

"Oh now, you don't touch our champion unless we sees the colour of your money. Put it here, man. We're the ones that hold it while you fight!"

Money! That was a laugh! He'd worked his passage over from Canada. What he had left was the remains of his share from trading raw buffalo hides. Dan rocked back on his heels.

"Aw, poor fatherless bastard ain't got the stuffin'. All puff and no guts..."

That common insult was too much. In one mad moment, Adam whipped out his purse and waved it, only wanting to plow his fists into this towering, arrogant lout.

An avid crowd coalesced around the makeshift ring, thirst for blood in their eyes. "Fight, fight, fight!" some lads began to chant. Bets began to fly, quickly taken by Nell's nimble touts used to staging such battles then vanishing, along with the ring, with ghostly speed.

The odds shot up in favour of Joe. Adam barely noticed. In bloody-minded determination, he stepped though the ropes. Joe was already stripped to the waist and strutting insolent challenge. His fans hooted derisively at Adam.

"Corners all and come out scrappin'," Dan bellowed.

Joe launched himself at Adam and the fight was on, bare-fisted and brutal after the manner of the day. The two lunged at each other, Joe with brute confidence in his own strength, Adam driven by the seething inside him. The shouts of the onlookers faded away as he slugged and dodged, slipped on grass, rebounded from the ropes, took telling blows on his chest and ribs and temple.

The fight raged on in the blazing sun, a fight that would end only when one of the opponents dropped. Some famous fighters had been known to last as long as sixty rounds before being able to down their adversaries. Adam, after his first reckless charge, began to recover his wits and resort to knowledge hard won on mill floors and in the lumber camps.

Joe, despite his conviction that he was fighting to defend his sister, realized he had taken on an adversary who wasn't going to topple before brute strength.

Nell saw this too and signalled from behind the blind of her cab. The jug containing the water which the fighters gulped and sloshed across their faces between rounds was subtly changed with another. When next Adam sprang at Joe, he suddenly felt everything around him slow, including his own limbs. When his own arm was only halfway up from his side, he saw a punch coming at him from across the ring, the face behind it grinning. Oddly, though he looked at the knuckles for a long time, he was unable to move from their path. The fist connected to the side of his head like a crack of thunder, spinning him sideways off his feet.

How could I let that happen, he asked himself gravely as he tumbled to the ground. Then his eyes rolled back in his head and the world went white.

The whiteness, the paralysis, lasted only until he heard the referee finishing up with the count.

"....seven...eight....nine...," the referee was saying in a maddeningly stretched drawl.

As the man spoke, Adam was rowing the air with hands and feet, determined spring up. Only when the referee said, "Ten!" with emphasis, did the Adam realize that his limbs hadn't been moving at all. The frantic action had been all in his head.

When he did manage to raise himself to one elbow, the crushed grass stems beneath him loomed unnaturally large, each blade looking like a long green sword. Whistles and cheers and shouts assaulted his ears. Through distorted, but curiously crystal gaze, he saw the referee parading Joe in a circle, brandishing the raised arm of victory.

Violently, Adam tried to stagger up, bent on going for his ring mate and damn any rules. However, the makeshift boxing ring was already being dismantled around him and touts were making good to the crowd on bets. Adam found his legs still would not obey him and the force of Joe's punch reverberated inside his brain, booming like some giant cannon. Veteran of numerous wilderness altercations, he had never experienced anything like this. As from a great distance, the obvious began to penetrate. Getting one leg under him, he rose swaying to his feet.

"The fight was rigged," he shouted stupidly. "There was dope in that water I drank,"

Hoots and jeers bombarded him.

"You took a punch and you went down. Don't make excuses," the referee admonished.

There was now no trace of jug or water. Adam stood upright with the dizziness rapidly receding.

"Now," Sparley Dan vaunted, "time you paid up."

Sparley Dan was waving the purse that, Adam realized, must have been extracted from his trousers when he was down. Sparley Dan opened it and turned it upside down. Nothing came out. It was empty. All Adam's money was gone.

"You've done us," Dan accused, ruffling up.

Two Dan's separated fuzzily before coming back together. They had already cleaned every farthing from his purse.

I've been had, straight up the arse and over the steeple!

Some other time Adam could have laughed at himself for falling into such a trap. Only now Dan was advancing, backed by several large toughs.

"Looks like we'll have to wring it out of your hide," Dan said from behind a boyish grin. "Have at him, lads!"

Instructions were to throw such a scare into Adam that he'd take to his heels over the horizon and never dare stick his snout near Rose again.

Adam shook his head hard, trying to clear it, while his large fists bunched up again. Skullduggery had its price. Just let them try...

Then, over the shoulders of his immediate attackers, Adam caught sight of other men, well-dressed men, pushing purposefully toward him. This contingent, unlike the boxing rowdies, was cool, swift and inconspicuous, with no intention of making a fuss in public.

Hoggett's men!

Blinking slowly Adam watched them approach. Only when they actually lunged did he have sense enough to scramble for escape.

Down near the stands, where the carriages were drawn up, the distant commotion attracted attention. Althea craned her neck. When she heard the cheers and shout of victory Althea could not resist standing up, as a number of other carriage occupants did, to see the outcome.

For a brief fraction, the mob of onlookers parted, allowing Althea to glimpse a certain pair of shoulders. Her side curls jerked in alarm.

"What is it?" Rose wanted to know, rousing herself from her stillness.

"Nothing...ah, just some kind of fracas."

Rose half rose, trying to look. Althea plopped back down into her seat, taking Rose with her. She had been seeing things, of course she had, Althea assured herself. A trick of the eye, the glare of the sun. Imagine, thinking some reeling racecourse brawler resembled Adam Crisp.

A huge, joyous roar drowned out further thought, for it heralded the arrival of the royal parade. Althea clutched the upholstery hard as she waited for the royal landau to roll into view. Then, oh glory, there he was, the sturdy figure of Bertie leaning back on the cushions, waving with his immense geniality to cheering crowds.

He was alive, he was fine!

Yes, oh yes," Althea chortled to herself. We are going to have one spectacular concert, my girl. We surely will!

CHAPTER FIFTY-SIX

Adam skidded to the low stone wall, took a plunge over and flattened himself in the corner where some old boards shored up a broken gap. His breath whistled out in scorching rasps as he found a slit to peer through. An athletic man in a sporting coat raced across the hummocky meadow, looking this way and that in search of his quarry. Two more pounded out of an orchard and met the first. All were winded and dishevelled from the chase across the farms beside the racecourse.

"Where'd the bastard get to? Hoggett wants him bad."

The others couldn't answer, scanning the landscape. For a moment, all three seemed to stare directly at Adam's hiding place. Sweat broke out in globules as Adam thought about a barred room with no air and no window. Every muscle tensed for combat.

Touch me, you misbegotten dungheads and I'll tie your guts around your necks for neckties.

They hesitated, then started over to investigate the wall. Adam ground his toes into the earth, ready to spring. Before he could, a furious squeal rent the air, a massive white body hurtled past at the approaching men.

"Christ!"

They halted and backed away, stumbling as the monster flung half its bulk over the wall in and effort to get at them.

"He can't be in there. Look!"

They spotted the jagged, splashing trail Adam smashed through the grasses by the brook and went haring off through the water themselves, unaware of how their target had doubled back, flinging himself out of sight when his hunters appeared.

Adam sagged against the rough stones. He'd jumped into a pigsty and been saved by an enormous white sow roaring out of the low hutch behind him. The sow ran along the wall until she was satisfied the threat had retreated, then noticed the other intruder inside her pen. She trotted in a half circle, eying Adam suspiciously out of her little pink-rimmed eyes. In the hutch door swarmed the pearly offspring she was defending.

Adam remained motionless while the shouts of Hoggett's men faded into the distance. The thugs from the boxing racket, he wagered, wouldn't leave their protecting crowds.

Trying to decide whether to charge, the sow's sides heaved. A cracked laugh plucked at Adam's throat.

"It's me they wanted for the spit, piggy, not your tykes."

Adam flung himself over the boards and rolled flat into the grass on the other side. Face down, Adam felt his own sweating terror of the lunatic asylum hanging about him, fetid as a stench. He had dodged through the people and the trees still fighting dizziness. With his purse robbed, there was nothing in his pockets to get him back to the docks, never mind pay for passage. And now Hoggett knew he was still in the country in direct defiance of the banishment order. Adam had seen the bullying relish in Hoggett's face. Hoggett would not rest until Adam was trapped and broken.

Hunted, woozy and smeared with pig mire, Adam lay about as low as he had ever been.

"So toss that nonsense!" he rumbled and sat up.

The massive bruises from Joe Varden's fists began to throb. Lunatic laughter caught at his throat. What a fool to let racecourse crooks trick him. He deserved to be broke.

He lurched down to the brook to let the sunlit water wash away the muck from the sty and the wobbliness from his legs. His face tipped skyward. God, he'd forgotten what real air tasted like after all that acrid yellow fog choking him in London.

To his amazement, the rage that had possessed him about Henry and Crisp Court, the convoluted, twisting thing that driven him, tormented him, unsettled him all these years was gone. The clash of fists in that makeshift ring, the pounding race afterwards had somehow cleansed him as though he had just expelled some black, clogging mass from his chest.

He splashed up more cold water and shook himself like a large, wet wolf. Even the staggering information that Milton Crisp might not be his father failed to bedevil him. Whatever ancient folly his mother had committed, he couldn't judge her now. Only the future counted.

Ghosts dogging him lost their hold. He knew he must get out of London, out of England, back to Canada. No longer could he bear the cramped and teeming crowds, this land that felt old and trodden down by centuries of weary feet. He needed the fresh free space. He needed to be where he belonged.

"Yes, I'm going home," he announced to a passing sparrow.

He he felt crazily free to do exactly as he wished. At last, he fitted comfortably within his own skin.

So why did he not leap up and bound away?

Because of a look exchanged in a garden under the fairy lights. He and Rose had spoken wordlessly and made an unbreakable pact.

In Hyde Park she had been a glowing torch of a girl, so full of rapture at being footloose that surely a circle of light must have shone about her as she skipped along. Had Hoggett done anything to her? What was she hiding in her heart as she sat over there in by the stands, looking so gay under her frivolity of a parasol?

Adam understood now that he had lived flooded by memories of her, that they had seeped into his thoughts, bloomed in his dreams, murmured endlessly into his ears with the breeze.

Was she happy over on the racecourse? Was she still pursuing the dream that had propelled her? Or did she remember how they had surrounded her, that sleek, deliberate pack with her as prey? Did she want to escape it all just as much as he?

A new resolution formed though of what outcome he couldn't say. Only that the stirring felt like old skin, old debris breaking up and sloughing away from fresh tissue underneath.

On the narrow road snaking on the other side of the pig pen, a group of men came tramping along, fortified by ale, no doubt as they had passed the Derby. Their flat caps and earth-stained clothes marked them as one of the itinerant work crews who followed new railway construction laying tracks across the land.

Adam scrambled up the stream bank toward them. Here was work, here was food, here was perfect cover should the search for him go on. As he reached the road, Adam paused. On impulse, he pulled off his sheepskin vest, rolled it into a tight parcel and tied it with twine from his pocket.

"Boy," he called to a brisk, tidy lad head heading down the road on the opposite side, "I have a job for you."

He felt around in his pockets and found he had only one item of wealth remaining, the gold watch belonging to Milton Crisp that his mother had passed on to him. Past attachment warred briefly with present urgency. Adam held out the parcel.

"Take this to London, to Wharton House, and deliver it to Miss Rose Fitzroy."

Awed by the watch, the lad nodded eagerly, unable to believe his luck.

"And remember, not a word where it came from no matter who tries to ask."

The boy nodded again, very earnestly, and set off. The vest went with him, a wordless message to Rose, though of what, Adam could not at that moment say. He only knew that, at all costs, he had to dispatch it.

With a sigh, he fell into step with the tramping crew.

CHAPTER FIFTY-SEVEN

"Lazy scut! Wake up there! Try workin' for a livin' for a change!"

Laura had been nodding sideways, the heavy jacket slipping from her fingers to the littered floor. The wooden barrel slat Buller always carried slammed hard across her shoulders, jerking from her exhausted doze with a cry. The narrow bench teetered, causing weary protests as its other occupants pricked themselves with needles and lost their places on seams. After twelve or fourteen hours of enforced immobility, aching spines screamed at the slightest shift.

Buller was the foreman, a short, sly, pot-bellied fellow with wide, toad-grey lips which he licked again and again as though driven by some marshy necessity to keep them wet. Wherever he was in the stifling, overcrowded room, he seemed to know what Laura was doing and whether she was flagging at the mountain of slop tailoring that passed through her hands.

Had the floor dropped out of Crisp Court beneath their feet and plummeted the children into some nether chamber of hell, the effect could not have been more powerful upon Katie and Laura than Bardle's Men's Tailoring Company. Cully, veteran of the basket cellars, had seen much worse.

After remaining in Mrs. Crisp's dressing room, surrounded by vast dresses all around like so many headless Louisa's hemming them in, their swift transfer by Phoebe to the errand carriage with their trunks had been a shock. A shock that only grew as they discovered they were not being taken to Mrs. Corman's Refuge but toward the waterfront.

With all speed, they had been conveyed into a region of narrow streets, jumbled warehouses and gaunt workers trudging to and fro, eyes averted from the cook stalls. Boot manufacturers, cabinet makers, ship's chandlers were jammed in, shoulder to shoulder, with blank windowed buildings whose function hinted at the considerably more sinister.

The thin animation Katie had acquired at Crisp Court instantly faded. The moment she caught the odour and the glimmer of the river a black, nameless dread engulfed her. When they were bundled out of the errand carriage and left inside the clanging iron gates of Bardle's, she knew she had truly fallen out of Miss Amelia's hands. She was banished again, lost and she'd never get back!

Henry Crisp had hastily arranged the transfer. Working conditions didn't concern him. All that mattered was that the place had connections with workhouses which supplied child labour and that it kept those being "trained" locked up within its confines. Henry wanted no disgruntled runaways squealing back to Crisp Court or Mrs. Corman with tales of garden catastrophes.

Bardle's differed from the myriad other slop tailoring operations only in the scope of Silas Bardle's greed and his shrewd measure of the almost bottomless market for rough work clothes. Clothes which could be sold in great wholesale lots wherever labouring men needed garments for their backs. High volume at the lowest possible cost was the key, the very recipe for hideously sweated labour.

A great many industries had a voracious appetite for youthful workers. The young were easily intimidated, usually defenceless and, above all, cheap. Bardle employed children whenever he could. They sewed nearly as fast as adults yet didn't cost as much to feed. Like other establishments in the neighbourhood, he received, under the guise of "apprenticeships", a steady supply from the workhouse and assorted gullible, overloaded charitable operations. He maintained connections with the ragged schools which gathered poor children from the street and sent them to Bardle's "to earn their keep and learn the habits of sober, steady employment." Charity children were the best. Without family or freedom, they could be worked at his mercy. And if one or two should squeeze out of a window and disappear, no hue and cry was raised. Defectors were replaced before the afternoon was gone.

Bardle's occupied the various floors and cellars of some old brick buildings built haphazardly around a courtyard sealed with an iron gate beyond which the live-in labour could not pass. Bardle's kept its junior work force from fleeing by incarcerating them in a long, bar-windowed dormitory furnished with straw pallets upon which the exhausted workers collapsed at the end of their shifts. The cost of this accommodation, as well as that of the indefinable substances boiled up in iron pots as food, was deducted from the children's wages. Such exercise as could be snatched was taken in the yard behind the tall, spiked gate.

Bardle had equipped one floor with rows of that recently invented marvel, the sewing machine. Awkward and primitive, these machines were aconnected together and powered by a whirling belt from a central engine. Women operated them standing up over a trough from which fabric was endlessly fed into the machines' clanking jaws.

Child factory workers started very young.

Katie, Cully and Laura were certainly not among those strong enough or skilled enough to run the newfangled contraptions. Consigned to an airless, infernally hot room directly below, they stitched linings into coats by hand, hemmed cuffs and sewed on button after button after button. When a rush order was in, they were often expected to sit as many as eighteen or twenty hours in the day while the sewing machines clattered overhead. Legs went numb and Buller circled, always waiting for his chance to strike.

Today, the girls were stitching facings onto jackets made from a rough material called shoddy. Old wool, shredded by a toothed machine called a "devil", had been rewoven with enough new wool to create this cheap, sturdy fabric for men's work garments. Laura scrambled to pick up the fallen coat, beyond even thinking about her swollen fingers which had been irritated raw by the shoddy within a day. She could sense Buller behind her, fondling his stick, looking for a new place to whack her. Buller frightened Laura more than any human being she had ever met. His attention seemed to be fixed on her, endless and relentless, even when he wasn't there. When he stared her up and down, his gaze felt like the trailing of a hot wet hand.

From the first, Buller had noticed the three newcomers in whom, despite everything, the superior nutrition and cleanly habits enforced by Crisp Court lingered on. Laura stood out glaringly, her Atworth upbringing surrounded her like a blinking halo. It showed in the grace with which she moved, the shrinking she felt from her poorer fellows and, above all, the lifetime of good food which had produced a beautiful, healthy child in the midst of all the pinched, undernourished bodies around her. From the moment she entered, the eye of the foreman was upon her covetously.

"A fine for nodding off, Lady Lump," Buller sniggered, licking his toadish lips again. "Costs brass when the quality goes off to sleep."

The fines were another profitable innovation of Silas Bardle, fines backed up by physical punishment. A slick foreman could see most of a girl's meagre wages clawed back in penalties. Quite a few actually found themselves owing Bardle. Buller was expert at eliciting the maximum.

A bench away, Katie saw Laura cringe back to work. If Laura had at least been able to understand Crisp Court, Bardle's was an incomprehensible nether cosmos into which the blackest, most malignant of fates flung her. The worst was the awful, gruelling monotony of the work, the excruciating boredom that devoured her with teeth of acid and no escape from the tyranny of the needle. At day's end, she had to fling herself down onto a straw pallet in a sweat-smelling room full of other bodies lying in an equally ex-hausted trance. Her trunk had been rifled the very first night. The embroidered chemise, her last vestige of Atworth house, vanished without a trace.

The first thing Laura learned at Bardle's was not to speak. Her gilded accent invariably produced gapes of astonishment, then a barrage of dreadful, prying questions. It was awful enough to be regarded as some kind of two-headed freak. It was even worse to be ragged mercilessly by all these rough, dirty people just because she'd once had a happy life with enough to eat and pretty clothes on her back.

The worst nemesis was the foreman, whose harassment passed into some frightening realm Laura could not understand. Buller not only liked to hit her, he liked to touch her, all the while breathing noisily. He'd run his hands all over her face that first day, snickering about her "butter-pat skin, wot looked good enough to lick right off!" He'd suddenly be behind her, jerking her straight on the bench, his fingers wandering down her neck and under her collar like damp, seeking heads of snakes. He'd stare at her with a peculiar wet glaze in his eyes until the other workers stared at her too.

"Buller's got the fancies fer you, dearie," a woman machine operator warned darkly. "Don't want to let 'im get you alone."

More desperately than ever, Laura clung to her two friends, though of course the first thing Buller did was see that they didn't sit together. Cully was pushed into a corner where she got her own share of whacks for making clumsy seams. She didn't seem to mind. Working with the doggedness she had learned in the basket cellar she kept her eye on Katie and Laura lest they disappear.

Katie, hair scraped into a frowzy braid, was in the worst state of all. She was the one responsible for all of them ending up at Bardle's.

My fault, my fault, Katie's mind screamed at her when she saw Laura whacked by Buller until she was too frightened even to sink down on the floor and howl. They were here in this horrid place because Katie had been somewhere she shouldn't, seen something she shouldn't and she had told! In a flick, the easy work and good food of Crisp Court had been whipped away.

Yes, it's my fault, Katie told herself again, for no one had given them a word of explanation for the move. It had to be because she had failed Mrs. Corman. Katie didn't believe for a minute that anyone could have sent her here without Mrs. Corman permitting it.

Mrs. Corman must hate her for the awful thing she had done. Mrs. Corman must have been the one to send her away!

Whatever uncertain recovery had begun in Katie after she had been found by Amelia, now swiftly reversed itself. Mr Willoughby used to thunder that all children were bad, especially girls. The crushing guilt of bringing her friends here connected Katie to something even more unspeakable buried so deep she couldn't even guess what it was.

What windows the room had were so begrimed light could hardly penetrate and they had so many broken panes that there were more rags in the frames than glass. The sound and smell of the river, unseen yet close, made this claustrophobia worse. The dank odour, the wash of the waves was even stronger when the children were curled up, attempting to sleep. The insidious, shifting rush of tides outside filled Katie with a creeping horror which she could not put a name to. Something black and horrible, which she had sealed away inside, was heaving and rattling behind its wall. If it ever got out, Katie felt she would die.

"And what are you starin' at, Carroty," Buller yelled out over the many bent heads. "You're askin' for a fine lick too, you idle squit!"

Katie's needle flew into the facing she was stitching. If she got Buller angry enough, he'd hit Laura again. Katie knew how Laura feared and hated the man. The cheap, starchy fare of the factory had already gone far to turn Katie pinched and nervous. She jabbed her finger with her needle but dared not flinch. Dragging the heavy coat further into her lap she clutched tight the one miracle that had occurred.

She had seen Will!

On a drizzly afternoon, when the children were being allowed to stretch their legs in the yard during the brief supper break, Katie, Laura and Cully had been leaning against the gate, staring into the street outside. As they did so, a careful file of boys had come marching along, Will's familiar figure near the rear. Scarcely able to believe her eyes, Katie had flung herself against the grille.

"Will! Will! Over here!"

Equally astonished, Will had broken rank to run to her.

"Katie! What are you doin' 'ere."

"We got sent down to sew coats. And you?"

Will puffed up proudly, for he had on a whole shirt, a whole vest and trousers that didn't need hacking off at the bottom.

"I'm with the lads here trainin' to make boots. There's a whole factory for boots just past the pub there. Mr. Corman fixed it up so's we'd know something useful. We all sleep in the shed behind the factory with the bully picture of the boot n the door. We've just been to chapel."

The man in charge of the line noticed Will was missing.

"You, boy, get back in line."

Katie thrust out a frantic arm, trying to reach out to him.

"Will, when'll I see you again?"

Will couldn't say, for the man hustled him away.

Will went looking back over his shoulder at Katie's pale face behind the gate bars. Katie watched for him whenever she could thereafter and got to wave, at least, when the bootmaker boys marched past.

"He's my friend," Katie insisted to Laura and Cully, glad they had seen him and knew he wasn't a figment of her imagination.

The three girls clung together all the more tightly, strengthened, just a little, from knowing another one of Mrs. Corman's charges was nearby.

CHAPTER FIFTY-EIGHT

The last whistle of the day snapped the tension holding the workers in place. They stumbled up and streamed toward their greyish dinners and snatched hours of rest. Laura found a hand gripping her shoulder.

"Not so fast, Madame Rubbish! You ain't finished! Got a job for you back here!"

Buller was staring queerly at Laura with that slippery gaze of his. Laura shrank, desperate to get out with the rest. Buller held her still until the crowd had vanished.

"Pick up them coats there and come with me."

Buller pointed to a mound of finished work, his eyes glittering damply. When Laura didn't move, he gave her a prod that sent her lurching forward.

"Pick 'em up, I say."

Buller flung a heap of coats into Laura's arms so that she staggered under the weight. Another prod set her tottering toward the door which opened on the stairs to the cellar.

There was a boy, Cluff, whose job was to load the finished coats on his cart and take them down a ramp to the cellar from the outside. Laura had never been down there but she knew it was here the coats were bundled for shipping and where new bolts of shoddy waited until they were needed. Since the shift was ended, there wouldn't be anybody down there.

Hating each step, Laura made her way down. The cellar was a cavernous space lit only by a dim gas jet and heaped to the ceiling with piles of goods. As Laura hesitated, there was a quick patter on the stairs behind her. Katie appeared, also bearing an armload of coats.

"Come to help," Katie mumbled from behind her load.

Laura let out a shaky breath. Good old Katie, loyally sticking beside her.

Buller glowered briefly, then switched to a nasty grin.

"Two for the price of one then. Ain't bad. Get along here."

Buller pushed them into the narrow, maze-like passages between the piled goods and they were instantly lost. The musty air, almost suffocating with particles of dust and wool, clogged in their nostrils. Unable to halt, the girls suffered stronger and stronger pricklings of alarm. Soon, they were at the far end of the cellar, the floor sloping beneath their feet as they went. At the furthest, most deserted point, Buller peered furtively behind him then pushed open a low door half-hidden behind a stack of old boxes. The next instant, he relieved the girls of the coats, shoved them through and slammed the door behind him. Another cellar lay before them, disused and heaped with mouldering rubbish.

"Get steppin'. Hurry it up!"

His face was now very mottled. He seemed in a tremendous rush. Katie baulked in her tracks.

"I said, move it!"

Buller grasped Laura by one arm and herself by the other. He propelled them both bodily through another door and down a set of wooden steps onto a damp dirt floor. They could barely see where to put their feet.

"I don't want to go here..."

Buller jerked the breath out of Laura, pulling the girls up more steps, stealthily across an alley and down into yet another cellar. Katie glimpsed the greyness of the river and the salt-stained sides of ships rising up like wall. There was no way to tell where they were going. The warehouses and manufactories had grown like devouring shells over the older buildings along the waterfront, creating an incomprehensible warren.

The second cellar gave onto a third, then to with steps down into an even lower level. There were dank puddles on the floor and a rusty metal door at one end. Buller pulled this door open and all but flung the two girls through. He was panting hard now, far beyond what the exertion should have cost him, his face broken out in a sheen of sly excitement. He licked his lips until they glistened even more wetly than his face and slammed the door on the two girls.

Katie and Laura found themselves in low, cramped room lit only by a tiny, heavily barred window above their heads, opening directly onto the river. Katie could hear the water slapping underneath and the sound made her queasy. When their eyes adjusted, they saw that the very mortar was crumbling with damp from between the stones. The puddle that occupied most of the floor had already soaked their feet. Laura looked fearfully about.

"I don't see any...."

The door flew open again and Cully was tossed inside. Behind her, Buller cursed violently under his breath.

"Damned crawlin' sneak. You'll wish you'd kept your ugly gob where it belongs when you find out what you've got yourself into!"

Oblivious, Cully flung herself joyfully at her two friends. She had never once been separated from them since they had met at Crisp Court. If she couldn't actually stand next to Katie or Laura, she always had her eye on them, always knew exactly where they were. When Buller had taken them, she had doubled back, slipping frantically through all the forbidden cellars in her efforts to stay close. Buller had grabbed her when her rickety legs had sent her tripping over a heap of bricks scarcely a yard behind the man.

Cully hopped with from one foot to the other. She was in the midst of hugging her friends tightly when they heard the unmistakable slam of a heavy bar dropping into place. Laura flew over and twisted at the handle.

"He's...he's locked us in?" she cried incredulously. "Why is he locking us up in a cellar?"

A nameless, awful fear crawled up her spine. There was nothing in the narrow room, absolutely nothing except cobwebs hanging lifelessly from the ceiling and dirt all around. The thickness of the beams supporting the blackened planking attested that this was another warehouse, built to stand the heavy loads of the Thames-side shipping trade. The dank stone walls only offered one patch of relief – a splotch of equally dank brick mortared up a very long time ago.

Silence gripped the children who became too frightened even to speculate about why they might be there. An age crawled by. Cully, boosted up by Laura, peeped out the window.

"Ain't nothin' but water, close enough to poke a stick in."

This led to another fearful speculation.

"You don't think the water will get high enough to come in the window do you?" Laura ventured. "I mean...with the tides?"

She wished she hadn't said it, from the way Katie looked. Cully's stomach rumbled. They'd had no food since the bread and tea wolfed down hours ago at the noon break. Hungry and tired, they crouched down along the wall, longing for the bright kitchen at Crisp Court, longing even more desperately for Mrs. Corman.

Despite the traffic on the river, the room was peculiarly quiet. In the watery light, no information filtered in save the monotonous slap, slap, slap of the Thames. The three huddled in each other's meagre warmth in the least muddy of the corners, unmoving until the scree of the door jolted them upright. Buller pushed in accompanied by a massive, hook-jawed companion swathed, neck to toe, in a dark greatcoat. In the fading light Buller carried a lantern which he thrust into the children's faces.

"That's her," Buller pointed to Laura. "The treat I was tellin' you about."

Buller was bobbing obsequiously in the presence of the other man who, Laura saw, had a nose smashed all to one side of his face and eyes like rough pebbles stuck into his flesh. She pressed her back flat against the sharp edges of stone behind her. All over again, she felt Mr. Whalley dragging her from Atworth House to his chaise cart. This man, her frightened instincts screeched, was a thousand times worse.

Her forebodings were perfectly right. Mr. Slagge kept an office not far away as a ship's purchasing agent. Under this facade, Slagge controlled a tangle of murky connections that led straight back to Teapot. Ships involved with Slagge often slipped away from the dock carrying, secretly locked in their holds, cargoes of hapless girls which Slagge sold outright to interested parties on the Continent. White slaving was Slagge's game and children his specialty. He assessed each of the three before him.

When he saw Laura, a hot greed shot into his eyes and his breath whistled in his misshaped nostrils.

"Ain't bad by half, Buller. I won't argue the goin' rate."

"Goin' rate!" Buller croaked, outraged out of his subservience. "Why just look at her. Ain't a mark on her, got all her teeth and talks like a toff to boot. Raised on cakes and cream in the country, she was, and ain't been spoiled either. You know what gents'll pay for them that ain't been spoiled."

"How do I know you ain't spoiled her yourself?"

Buller licked his lips all around again. The lantern rattled in his hand.

"Don't think I ain't been through the fires thinkin' about it, but I kept her for you. You won't find another like her unless you kidnap out of a countess's carriage. Worth a fortune, she is, and you know it."

Slagge knew it all too well. In the notorious child brothels he dealt with, customers placed an enormous premium on virgins, especially pretty child virgins like this one. Why in London itself there were streets in which every bed held an old man fondling two children. So much molestation went on amongst the poor that genuine virginity was almost unknown. Hence real virgins, or those that could be successfully faked as virgins, were valuable indeed.

Determined to make good on his rare find, Buller held out even in the face of Slagge's fearful demeanour. He squirmed and bobbed and wheedled to get his price. All the while this haggling was going on, Slagge's breath whistled heavily and his eyes never left Laura, devouring her country bred loveliness still shining through, still only a little muddied by London smog and the scant starch diet.

They settled on triple what Buller usually got when he spirited a likely prospect out of Bardle's. Slagge paid up, knowing it was a pittance to the sums that would be his when he himself cashed in on the girl. A ship was waiting and the further he shipped his find south the more her English freshness would fetch.

"She can go out a dawn," Slagge said, clicking his teeth in satisfaction and jerking thumb at Laura. "The Dragoman sails for Marseilles. Certain Turkish gentlemen take profitable interest in what I send to Marseilles."

He had a special customer down there who serviced the more peculiar bordellos of Istanbul. These bordellos devoured girls at an enormous rate and would pay an untold sum for such as Laura. Buller grinned ingratiatingly and set himself to wring yet more from Slagge.

"This one?" he pointed to Katie, hoping to pass her off as another prize. "She can go too?"

Slagge had been so occupied with Laura that he had barely noticed the other two. He inspected Katie closely, taking in the thinness of her face and the dark bruises of exhaustion under her eyes. A half-contemptuous snort expanded his ruined nostrils even though he saw that Katie was decently formed underneath it all.

"Got the streets written all over her. Ain't hardly worth the cross-Channel trade unless she's a scrapper. Redheads generally is. Tell you what, Buller, half rate for you if I ship her to Brussels."

"She ain't been tampered with neither!" Buller protested "Straight from the same big house as the other. "Half rate is highway robbery!"

"She ain't worth brass like the other one so you take what I offer and count yourself lucky."

Slagge's light moved to Cully. He let out a snarl.

"What do you mean bringin' me a useless bit of trash like this! You must be soft in the head!"

Even Buller knew Cully was worthless.

"Sneaking little stoat followed me. What could I do but stick her in with the others?"

"Followed you! You fool, she didn't..."

"No, it was just her," Buller assured hastily. "I took care. I always do."

"But, now she's seen us."

Buller flinched in the face of Slagge's fury, his amphibian mouth sucking wordlessly in.

"You know what's got to be done," Slagge grated harshly. "The river, so she's just some mud lark as copped it in the tide."

Buller shifted cravenly until Slagge grimaced in contempt.

"I'll take care of it. Now get out of my sight and don't be so careless again or it'll be you that's in the river!"

Buller scuttled out, bumping into the bony, shambling henchman summoned by Slagge's gesture. Slagge stabbed a finger at the children.

"I want those two delivered to the ships at first light and that runt disposed of. The quicker you get to it, the farther the carcass goes down river with the current."

"Right," mumbled the thug, making no move to step into the room. The crack in his voice caused Slagge to peer at him sharply.

"Look, I took you because Teapot thrust you on me. Teapot won't take it kindly if you ain't got the stomach for your job!"

"I'll do it, no fear," the figure asserted hurriedly. "I'll not get in wrong with Teapot."

Slagge emitted a menacing growl, ran a last gloating glance over Laura and strode out, leaving the lantern on a hook. The thug took it down, the better to see, for the children were doing their best to crawl into the blackest corner shadows. As the light illuminated the man, Katie's eyes grew huge and her chest turned to ice.

Jenksy! Jenksy was here! He had her cornered!

Yes, Morton Jenks stood there, bent over in that cellar, because he was in Teapot's clutches just as surely as the children before him. He might rail, he might seethe, he might curse, but escape was impossible.

Jenks looked like a scarecrow now, with his old frock coat buttoned high over his shirtless body and his bare feet jammed into broken boots. Starvation had driven him to this extremity. Starvation, a bit of grit and a wretched scrap of a girl who had chosen the wrong moment to blot his life by flinging a bucket of soot.

His rage at the Asylum, when he'd done throwing things after fleeing Katie and Mary, had boiled back into a single fiery centre—his left eye. The fragment of grit from the soot Katie had flung had not come out. Jenks had clawed at it the whole time Julius's man of business strutted about the Asylum, listing all the articles of furnishing Jenks would have been able, could he have seen, to appropriate for himself. All night he'd rinsed and plucked and probed and Ida had done the same but the grit refused to come free. By morning, in a paroxysm of aggravation, he had ordered Ida to sell everything she could find and hand over the money. The dealer Ida called practically stole the stuff as soon as he saw Jenks was unable to bargain.

With stabs of misery pulsing through his head, Jenks had had to listen to the children hauled off, howling, to the workhouse while Ida trotted about mumbling like the sodding lunatic she was. Jenks had snatched the money from her, all there was from the furniture, the bits of housekeeping money unearthed from Ida's pockets, the coins from selling Ida's and Mary's clothes to the rag and bone man. Jenks had just started running. Yes, just left Ida standing there in front of the stripped Asylum, her mouth dropped open into a fat round hole.

"Morty," she had shrieked in a high-pitched, unbelieving voice, "MOOORTY! COME BAAACK!"

He took to his heels, and if it hadn't been for the damned piece of grit, he'd have hied off to the furthest city he could and found some way to start up anew.

The running had turned his eye to fire. He'd stumbled and crashed and cursed and finally had to take a room, the first room he came across, never mind that it was in a screevers' lurk and did nothing for his safety. There he'd writhed until a sharp lad showed up with a fellow who claimed to have learned from a famous eye doctor.

"Camphaliptum of Arabia u'd clean that right up, guv. Draw the pain out sweet as a mu'ver's kiss. Only got a bit left, saved up from when I was doctorin' the Sultan 'o Turkey. Worth its weight in gold, me mixture. Couldn't part wi' me last drop fer less."

"Give it to me," Jenks had bellowed, brain swimming in molten lava. "I'll pay, I'll pay. Here!"

So the quack had got the furniture money, the housekeeping money and the shirt Jenks had torn off and flung on the floor. The drops did nothing but fill his eye with sticky, viscous oil, leaving Jenks to rock back and forth on the straw mattress, until the infection burned itself out on its own. Before it was finished, he was tossed out, destitute, into the street.

About what followed, he could scarcely bear to think about, save that, eventually, he wandered into an alley and found an arm about his throat, dragging him into a doorway. Staggering like a drunken spider, he was forced inside. The room was tiny and badly lit. The arm choked Jenks. Something pointed and very sharp was half buried in the flesh under his chin.

A knife! Oh God, a knife!

Imagining his throat cut, he all but passed out. Jenks found himself pushed up against the wall, face ground into the plaster, shivering and shaking.

"Now Mr. Jenks," hissed a sibilant voice, "you ain't goin' to make a sop o' yourself screeching' and kickin' if I lets you go?"

Jenks tried to nod. Slowly, the arm relaxed and the knife fell away. Jenks slumped against the wall. When he managed to turn around, he was face to face with a man he hadn't seen since his baby-farming days.

Teapot was still as yellow skinned and eely as ever. He grinned out of the midst of a scraggly streaked beard at Jenks' dismayed recognition.

"Well, well, Jenks, been some time, ain't it. Hear you're workin' for that thievin' Irish slopbag, Red Nell."

The room reeled a second time. Jenks cringed back from the knife he expected in the gut. That was Teapot's way. Teapot hated Red Nell. A grin on Teapot's face was the most frightening sign of all.

Teapot, half a head shorter than Jenks, merely scratched at the ever-present fleas and lice of such neighbourhoods. Jenks' terror tickled him no end.

"Quite a shiner you got there, Jenks. Can't imagine you in a fight."

A great patch all round Jenks' left eye had a sunken blackened appearance where it once swelled hideously. The eyelid was nastily purple and drooped lower than its mate. Despite his fear, Jenks' mouth twisted into bitter fury, pleasing Teapot further.

"Got the worst of it, eh? And blimey if you ain't out of a job!"

Quaking, Jenks had expected Teapot to slice him through with the unpredictable viciousness for which he was renowned. Teapot had been vicious enough, after he was done laughing, but instead of knifing Jenks, he only dragged him back into his clutches. Jenks grovelled and fell on a heel of bread, his first remuneration as one of Slagge's thugs. Jenks would live on mouse turds and whey, as Teapot well knew, just to get in off the merciless street.

The work, scuttling about on unmentionable errands and packing brats into ship's holds, was the dirtiest, especially since Slagge didn't like him, didn't want him and would use the first slip to get rid of him. Yet Teapot had Slagge by the throat as much as he had Jenks. Jenks couldn't afford slips. Whenever his stomach started to fail him, he remembered the stench of Teapot's fetid breath in his face and found his nerve in a hurry.

"I knows you'll do good, Jenksy, 'cause if you don't, it'll be your guts I'm stringing up for sausage skins."

Teapot had made an extremely graphic slash with the knife he carried, as if he were gutting a fish. Jenks' whole body twitched convulsively.

"Understood?"

Jenks had opened his mouth but, since nothing came out of it, he contrived to nod. The ferocity vanished from Teapot's face as quickly as it had come. He laughed heartily.

"Oh, ain't you a precious one. Now best get away from me, Mr. Jenks. I do believe you've wet your trousers."

Now Jenks struggled to screw himself up to the task that Slagge had flung at him. Sooner or later he had known it would some to this, that he'd have to do the dirty work Ida had always done, he'd have to do the snuffing out with his own hands. Waves of cowardice churned through his stomach, bitterness churned up. He saw what he had fallen to—a cringing, crawling wretch, licking Teapot's boots for mouldy crumbs.

And still a warder of brats!

He lifted his lantern high and the light fell upon the three forms shivering in the corner. He had to squint hard with his good eye, certain he was hallucinating.

Katie Mucker, the whelp that had caused all his troubles!

Katie in Teapot's grasp!

Violent rage welled up in Jenks, twice as furious for the loss of his good life, his savings and his eye!

Katie cringed against the back wall, her eyes enormous. Only fear of Teapot prevented Jenks from picking her up and smashing her to pulp against the jagged foundations. He loomed up, his features contorted in the yellow flicker of light.

"So here you are, you snivelling bit of rat vomit. Got yourself in a real dung pot this time, ain't you."

The fate in store for Katie suddenly filled Jenks with a savage glee. What's more, he could see from her eyes she'd finally learned real fright. All that was missing now was that sneaking hunchback, Mary. Oh, what wouldn't Jenks give to have her cornered too and marked for the river.

Jenks grabbed Katie by the front of her dress.

"Where's Mary? Where is she?"

A superstitious fear that Mary might be lurking somewhere about drove Jenks. He shook Katie hard.

"Tell me? Where is that twisted bag of witlessness? Where?"

Black dread bloomed in Katie's eyes, blotting out Jenks, blotting out everything save the roar of the river, the stink of river mud. She went limp as a rag in his grip. When Jenks flung her down, Katie crouched in a fetal ball, hands crammed over her ears to shut out the horrible words. Jenks swore, knowing he could kill Katie and he wouldn't get an answer. Well something had taught the whelp a few proper lessons in terror. In that he could take satisfaction. Anyway, she wouldn't last a week where Teapot was sending her. Yeah, Teapot was giving her what she deserved.

Teapot!

Jenks remembered he still had a job to do. And do fast if he valued his skin. Jenks snatched up Cully and jammed her under his arm, her cries stifled by his big palm over her mouth. Laura, then Katie, flung themselves at Jenks but they might as well have been moths bouncing off a boulder. A kick sent them crumpling into the puddle behind them.

The last thing Katie and Laura heard behind the slamming door was Cully's heels hitting the other side as she struggled madly in Jenks' grasp. The thuds died with the fading crunch of Jenks' footsteps. The girls knew, with a horrible intuition, that Jenks was heading straight toward the river stairs.

CHAPTER FIFTY-NINE

"I won't draw an easy breath until that all that money is safe in the bank," Amelia was saying as the carriage Louisa had sent for them clattered though the streets. "To have a mountain of...of cash in a glass box for everyone to view! I can't imagine what Louisa and Mrs. Wharton are thinking of!"

Her hands were already clammy inside her gloves at being responsible for that unbelievable heap of revenue from the concert ticket auction just lying loose in notes. Althea Wharton and Louisa Crisp had come up with the idea of putting the money into a large coffer with glass sides, so that everyone could see the rapidly growing proceeds. Nothing gratified benefactors more, they insisted, than a touch of visible drama.

Stupendous wonder alternated with spurts of stage fright at the very public role she and Edwin would play tonight as official representatives of the Refuge. They were speeding back to the Refuge so they could dress for the concert and ball.

Amelia could never have imagined, when she began, how much her great venture would throw her into the public eye, nor how Rose Fitzroy would burst out of her hands within a week of being introduced to society. No one ever guessed the writhings Amelia suppressed as Rose, Cousin Rose, merrily appropriated the virtuous, protecting cloak of the Radmore name. Stoically she endured the fascinated gazes flicking between her and Rose. The children, she thought. The money!

Most certainly, Amelia was sure Rose failed utterly to grasp the moral gravity of the deception. Why else would Rose tease her so impishly? Why else would Rose persist in sending Amelia silk paisley shawls, impudent hats with egret feathers and, once, pink pantaloons frothing with hand-made lace?

Uncorrupted, Amelia sold the items and added the proceeds to the cause. She then appeared as severely dressed as before, sartorial honour intact. She dared not consider a fearful suspicion that Rose might be relaying gifts from men!

"You'll do fine, my dear. Mrs. Wharton has organized everything so splendidly."

Edwin would have liked to reach over and give his wife a bracing pat, yet didn't dare. Truth to tell, marital relations remained severely strained between Edwin and Amelia. After the pre-Derby reception, Edwin had been effectively sent to Coventry, as the phrase went, and greatly feared he might never be allowed to return. His clumsy efforts at reconciliation at been rebuffed by a wall of painful disillusion, a grim new knowledge of the perfidious natures of men, even Edwin, when exposed to frivolous aristocrats, bewitching females and freely flowing champagne.

Amelia did nothing overt, of course. The silent reproach in her eyes was a thousand times worse than any shrewish scolding. Amidst the simplest discussion of kitchen drains or children's shoes, a sigh from Amelia's bosom conveyed her sad new knowledge that all men were gullible wretches behind their smiles and there was little help for them.

Am I a wretch, Edwin had been asking himself since the reception.

Edwin had never experienced anything like Rose Fitzroy. Captivated from the first moment,, his tongue had taken to schoolboyish stumbling while damning scarlet rushed through his beard. Dumbfounded, Amelia had watched the progress of his enthralment all the way to his rushing off, with barely a mumble, to stand gaping at the edge of the Prince's party.

Edwin's warm-blooded nature had been overwhelmed by the cachet of occupying the same room as the Prince of Wales. His ruddiness turned florid, his eyes had grown shiny as his connection to this improbable relative of his wife went straight to his head. After Rose's first songs, Edwin had lost his head entirely and taken to quaffing champagne.

It had been bad enough for Amelia, seated on a circular bench around a pillar, to overhear Mrs. Watson muttering to Lady Gillis that Rose Fitzroy was "a baggage" no matter how divinely she sang. Or to see Mrs. Smithing raise her eyebrows meaningly at her sister and watch Mrs. Stanhope-White's mouth contract into a rigid line. But to know that Edwin, the very head of the Refuge, was in full view guzzling alcohol and gaping, Edwin, who was supposed to be proof against such low lures, was too much. How could she ever, Amelia asked herself, forgive him for such a debacle!

Oh, he can hang his head now, Amelia sniffed to herself. He hadn't the least idea what it had been like for her to have to extract her husband, quite visibly tipsy, from the reception and march with him to the door past all those appalled gazes. He might claim he barely remembered a thing, but Amelia had caught him that very morning, an inane smile on his lips, as surely as anything daydreaming about Crisp Court.

Amelia suppressed a pained sigh, her hands folded firmly, untouchably, together in her lap. Edwin dropped back against the horsehair seat, remembering how he used to hold those slender fingers, the scars on them familiar and dear. Oh how, he'd like to know, was a fellow to get through marriage with a relative like Rose Fitzroy and a wife who was a card-carrying angel of mercy without a vice to her name.

More and more of that evening was coming back in uncomfortably vivid flashes.

After the first glass of champagne, which did not taste in least like the poison of vipers as he had been led to believe, Edwin had developed the most peculiar floating sensation. Rose herself had unfurled into a sort of roseate being with light caught in her hair and those moonstones nesting so warmly against her neck. Edwin had become utterly engrossed by the way the folds of her satin skirt changed every time she moved.

"She is a goddess of the air," he remembered saying giddily to the person plucking at his arm, then discovering that person was his wife. There had been two of Amelia, even though there seemed to be only one Rose. Then Rose was gone and the Prince was gone and Amelia's fingers had been delicate rods of iron hauling him away.

In the morning there had been dark marks inside his elbow. Since neither Edwin nor Amelia had any idea how to conduct a good, four square marital battle, Amelia spent her days with her mouth set in that telltale way that had nothing to do with worry about the money. Crisp Court hovered between the two like a large, invisible bee deafening them with its hum. Now Amelia bristled with unspoken reservations about how Edwin would behave at the ball.

The carriage swung into their street and the horse pulled up sharp. Some enormous uproar was going on right in front of the Refuge.

"What on earth...?"

Amelia leaned out of the window, then her tongue froze. She literally couldn't believe what she was seeing. The carriage had been jerked to a halt by a street half-blocked by piled-up cots, a sprawling heap of mattresses and a jumble of furniture, trunks and even kitchen pots all over the cobblestones.

On the opposite side of the street huddled all the children, staring, whimpering, howling. Also howling was Ida Jenks. A half dozen tough-looking men were in the act of nailing boards over the doors and windows of the Refuge from which every warm body and possession seemed to have been unceremoniously flung.

"What the devil's going on here," Edwin shouted, leaping from the carriage and wading headlong through the confusion. Amelia followed, appalled to see her green parlour chair lying on its side, her petticoats slung over it. The children rushed toward her in a terrified flock.

The largest of the men, with eczema on his nose and hammy shoulders sticking out of a torn waistcoat, ignored Edwin until Edwin actually grasped him by the arm. The fellow twisted hard, sending Edwin staggering. Another man faced down Edwin's outrage.

"You lot don't live 'ere no more. Not you, not the brats! If you know what's good for you, you get this rubbish out of sight before we chucks it all in the drink!"

The fellow had blunted, eel-like features and eyes that didn't seem to have any lids. The greasy shine on his pocked, yellowish skin and a string of straggling whiskers only heightened the impression of some vicious sea creature slipping out of ambush to attack.

Amelia sped over, impeded by frightened children clinging to her skirts.

"I don't know what you think you're doing, but you had better stop this instant. We rent this building from Mrs. Fitzroy and she'll..."

A bark of eely laughter cut Amelia short.

"Get your brats and your fancy twat out of 'ere before you end up sliced in teeny pieces. This 'ere buildin' belongs to somebody else now and we ain't got time for Red Nell's toadies," Teapot snarled. He had a wicked knife stuck into his waistband. His fingers flickered over it menacingly.

Amelia faltered but did not retreat.

"This is our...home!" she spluttered. "We shall call the...the constabulary. We won't tolerate this...this...."

The knife flicked from its resting place, the long sharp blade of it glittering in the light.

"Go and call the Peelers," Teapot grinned, "if you can find any with the nerve to come. We're runnin' off rats tonight. All Red Nell's rats! You might say there's been a change o' bosses in the neighbourhood!"

At the sight of the knife, the children began to screech. Edwin hastily pulled Amelia and the young ones out of reach.

"Look here you, blackguard..."

Teapot's laugh snaked through the air, loaded with slithering threat.

"Red Nell's finished here for good, so stick your tails between your legs and scarper with the rest of the scuts. Come on lads, there's lots more work to do."

Teapot was leaving the building nailed up tighter than a turtle's ass. He could hardly contain his paroxysm of delight at his lightning coup which had just swallowed up Red Nell's territory. The old trot had got careless, not noticing how Teapot's forces had begun to swarm. Years of lying in wait, of arcane plotting and insidious strikes, had paid off, especially with backing from tough new allies on the waterfront. Teapot had, in one swift, treacherous operation, overran every cobblestone the Irish bloat face thought she had her stamp on. Now all that remained was to run her and her whelps to ground and exterminate them. Every thug Teapot had was on the hunt. He'd have them, he swore, before the night was out!

"And don't you go tryin' to break back in," Teapot advised Edwin and Amelia cheerfully as he and his crew set out, "or you'll end up with your hamstrings cut neat as sliced bacon. Push chairs for the both o' you till your dyin' day!"

With a final sneer, he vanished, leaving Edwin and Amelia up to their armpits in chaos and wailing children. They stared at each other with jagged eyes. Neither could muster enough saliva to speak about the threat. Both of them feared it was real.

Instinctively, Amelia peered around in search of help only to discover more eerie evidence of calamity. Not a trace of the traffic usual for that time of day was visible. The street was deserted and so was the neighbourhood. Every house was closed and barred and shuttered. Not a single window showed a sign of life.

A race of cloud and distant rumble of thunder finally galvanized the Cormans. Edwin pulled out his pocket watch. The hour of the concert was swiftly approaching. The concert could not possibly be missed. They exchanged a stunned, stricken look.

"You'll have to go alone, Amy," Edwin told her, blustering into action. "I'll see what I can do about the children and get our things in somewhere out of the rain. I'll just...I'll try and get there as soon as I can."

Amelia could scarcely take in the calamity, but she knew that the money in the glass chest was now their only salvation.

"My dress!"

In panic, Amelia surveyed the mess, finally spotting the cloth bag containing her concert attire sticking out from under a heap of bedding. Clutching it to her bosom, she stood on the cobbles, wondering how she was going to change.

Like all the other establishments on the street, Mrs. Frum's cubbyhole of a junk shop was shuttered tight. Amelia sped over and hammered on the door. Just as she despaired of life inside, the bolt crept back.

"Mrs. Frum, as you can see, the most extraordinary trouble has fallen upon us and I have nowhere to change my dress. If I could please come in?"

The old woman hesitated for another age then jerked Amelia inside by the elbow. Mrs. Frum bore the huddled, white-eyed look of civilians trapped in the middle of a war that is not their own.

"Dearie, dearie, much as me shop's worth, they catch me 'elping you. Change your dress, quick as you can. And come to the back 'ere, case they're apeepin' in me windows."

Mrs. Frum acted as though there were eyes in the walls and the rafters too. She hurried Amelia through the crooked picture frames and cracked shoes and third-hand kitchen wares that made up her pitiable stock to the bare little room where she lived.

"Who?" Amelia cried in exasperated frustration as she struggled with the tiny buttons down her back.

"Teapot, Teapot, Teapot," Mrs. Frum rocked on her heels. "He's grabbed it all. Everything all around. Oh, tain't 'ealthy to be one of Red Nell's pets like you. I'd get out of these streets quick as quick. And take the kiddies too."

"Red Nell? Who is Red Nell? And whoever she is, I'm not one of her pets," Amelia ground out from under a spill of fabric. "Oh could you help me get the rest of this over my head?"

Since the event was a masquerade, Amelia's costume was a plain dark brown gown with the high neck she always wore because of her scars. Wide white cuffs and a large, square white collar were meant to suggest some brave colonial matron in charge of the poor, the lost and the needy. In honour of the grandeur of the occasion, Amelia had allowed both collar and cuffs a narrow edging of lace as well as the simple cap that went with the outfit.

Mrs. Frum smacked her toothless gums as she tugged at the fabric.

"Course you are, dearie. In her buildin' you are...were. Teapot's buildin' now, gawdamercy. Oh, oh, Teapot'll squeeze my wee shop till it's dead. At least Nell was regular. Now I'll go distracted never knowin' what I have to pay."

All this came to Amelia in spurts through her attempts to dress her hair without a glass. Mrs. Frum, everyone knew, was well on her way to her dotage.

"Don't be ridiculous," Amelia said firmly, pulling the cap tight and making for the door. "The building belongs to Mrs. Fitzroy! I'll get to the bottom of this in a wink just as soon as I can see her."

CHAPTER SIXTY

"Mad for you, Miss Rose, mad for you, the whole house and His Highness as well. Why, the roof' will be down before the night's over. Hold still while I set this hook!"

It was happening just as Althea had insisted it would!

Rose stood being prepared for the tableau the curtain would rise upon after intermission ended. She was poised on the small, raised platform that would centre the tableau. Daisy and two theatrical dressers fluttered about her fixing on the long gauzy veil that was to fall away dramatically after the curtain opened.

Not long before, Rose had hovered in the footlights, arms outstretched, as waves of applause surged around her and flowers fell at her feet. Since the beginning of the concert she had floated in the midst of a multi-coloured blizzard. Her admirers had crowded lustily in, laden with armloads of roses until the stage was inundated, lush blooms lying in drifts, their scent overpowering even the gas lights.

Althea had gone all out, hiring the newly built Gryphon Theatre, with seats of scarlet plush and a domed ceiling painted with rosy nymphs and cherubs smiling down. The crowded balconies were pale cream edged with gilt leaf. The whole was an intimate private theatre dedicated to this one spelllbinding evening.

Rose had been tossed so thoroughly by Althea into the preparations that she had barely had time to sleep, never mind think where all this was leading her. She felt quite disembodied as she looked out over a theatre crammed with people madly clapping, their upturned faces shimmering. In the royal box, Rose could just make out the Prince himself, bending toward her. Open pleasure suffused his face. Even from a distance, his eyes seemed to gleam warmly. The crowd surreptitiously peeped from Bertie to Rose and back again, fascination more than a little at war with good manners.

And how could he not be pleased, Althea Wharton thought as she re her seat in an inconspicuous box opposite. How could he not, with Rose creating sorcery upon the stage, a crown of coral and cream roses pinned into her heaps of luxuriant red gold hair. Roses that mysteriously emitted flashes of green and scarlet fire whenever Rose moved her head.

Althea tried very hard not to get goose bumps thinking of the value of the emerald and ruby necklace so cleverly entwined inside the flowery wreath. She tried not to grow faint at the idea of it falling off by accident and getting lost in the drifts of flowers on stage.

If Rose knew how I sweated to get that necklace, Althea grimaced, remembering the cramps in her stomach during the negotiations with Hoggett. Numerous secret gulps from her flask had been needed to maintain her unruffled demeanour. Dangerously bold though it was, Althea had held firm in her demands, determined that Rose should have the highest possible value. Only when the price matched the prize, Althea knew, would she truly hold the attention of that indulged and fickle prince. Hoggett had delivered the necklace himself, laying the leather case on the tea table, staring at Althea with his pale, bullying eyes.

"The Valnoor Rope. A gift from a maharaja to the Crown."

Althea had been unable to stare back. She had been too busy gaping at the necklace, the token she had demanded upon the arrangement with the Prince. Pour cement upon a deal, had always been her credo. These jewels were the biggest dollop of cement Althea had ever seen. For one awful moment, as she wondered whether Hoggett had brazenly rifled Princess Alexandra's own store of jewels. Her nerve almost failed her for what she had undertaken.

"On loan only," Hoggett had warned, his pupils glinting above the immensely valuable stones. "Never to be displayed in any way in which they could be publicly recognized. They are to be a private token only between His Highness and Miss Fitzroy. "You understand the importance of such a gesture on His Highness's part!"

Althea had nodded, fingers locked around her fan. During the negotiations, Hoggett had spoken bluntly, as one handler dealing with another. The Prince, Hoggett's manner bristled, was more in the habit of receiving than giving. Mrs. Wharton and Miss Fitzroy had better be impressed with the high favour being extended.

"Keep your bargain and we will keep ours!" he glowered as he turned on his heel and was gone.

Yes, the bargain was a wedding for Rose with a possible speed!

Althea controlled her dislike of Hoggett and fixed her mind on the glorious prospects ahead. They had weathered the punching disaster well so far. But triumph could turn to ash in a minute if

Rose weren't managed right. Rose, who had been like a sleepwalker, docile and blankly compliant. Naturally the girl had to recover from her shock and come to grips with the hard practicalities. Rose, Althea saw, needed a firm push into her own great good fortune. Althea was providing it.

So for the concert, Althea had cleverly entwined the jewels into the garland where they could wink and flash surreptitiously, a continuous private conversation between the singer and the Prince. Mrs. Smithing, got up as a wealthy milkmaid, had touched Althea's arm at the door.

"Althea dear, the idea for this concert was inspired. You can't imagine how much fun it was, putting our costumes together!"

Of course the woman was bursting with questions about Rose which she didn't dare ask.

Althea's decision to forge ahead with the concert had been nothing short of genius. She had been perfectly right about the speed of the rumour, helped on by what a sharp-eared maid had overheard that fateful day at the reception. The tale of an altercation at Crisp Court had leaped from kitchen to butler's pantry to drawing room and salon until every family that mattered was whispering avidly, except into royal ears. Details remained so safely, deliciously vague as to have people even speculating about a duel. The Prince was certainly drawn to the concert by interest in Rose. Perhaps there might be another the thrilling brouhaha before the evening was out.

The spectacle of the Prince's pursuit, rarely so public, was heightened by the rich and ridiculously nouveau Henry Crisp's obvious fixation on Rose which had provided amusing gossip for weeks. Poor Henry would have to step very far aside tonight at Crisp Court. And that brother of his, exaggerated into a veritable Robinson Crusoe, had disappeared right off the map. Both Henry and his mother turned such an interesting shade of puce when asked about the fellow. The final bit of icing was Rose's connection to the excruciatingly respectable Amelia Corman who had been visibly squirming ever since Louisa's Derby week reception.

Possession of a concert ticket had escalated into one of the best social coups of the Season. A very expensive one. With a limited number of seats but apparently unlimited amounts of money washing about, Althea had put the tickets up for auction. Bidders had almost fallen to fisticuffs in their eagerness to trade fat sums for entry to the event, all for the benefit of the children's Refuge, of course. Althea had had to sit down, dizzy from the magnitude of her success.

With the ticket came an invitation to the ball planned immediately afterward at Crisp Court. Even the all-Canadian fancy dress theme, sprung without the usual weeks of notice proved an entertaining challenge to everyone's powers of improvisation, a change from classical, medieval or Louis XIV motifs that were the usual fare.

Many must have rifled the attics of their grandparents, for the crowd was sprinkled with a proliferation of brocaded waistcoats, velvet suits or dresses spreading into panniers at the side. The men perceived themselves as colonial governors, chief traders or military guardians of the vast frontiers. The ladies tended more to a romantic salute to untamed nature by means of bits of fur and leather, sprays of feathers and bunches of artificial fruit attached to their gowns. Fantastic headdresses tried to evoke the native Indian dress. One lady even had bars of colour painted onto her cheeks to match the beaded finery in her hair.

The crowd buzzed with excitement.

All of this motley crowd found itself in great high spirits. All except Amelia Corman. What on earth could be the matter with Amelia, Althea wondered worriedly, looking across at the box where Amelia had, on the very cusp of being inexcusably late, rushed in and sank down. Amelia, who ought to have been ecstatic, appeared the very picture of distraction as she sat like wooden figure in her seat. Althea could have sworn some of the buttons on

Amelia's costume were not quite hooked. As it was, a long wisp of hair trailed out of one side of the cap Amelia wore and she had on no ear bobs whatsoever. The seat beside her, reserved for Edwin Corman, was empty altogether, driving Althea to surmise about a domestic altercation. She might at least spare a smile for the money, Althea thought tartly. Her Refuge is going to be rich as ten gold monkeys the moment the ball is over!

Althea glanced over to where Henry Crisp sat with his mother. Althea had had a difficult, trying time taming him back into her scheme. Henry had been jagged with outrage, for which Althea could not blame him one bit.

"So," Althea had murmured mildly, as some dark inner storm drove Henry pacing up and down her sitting room. "I pass on fondest compliments from Miss Fitzroy. I presume you return the same."

The swathe of red inflaming Henry's face and the bulge in the veins there told Althea how grim the situation was. Patiently she had listened him seethe, patiently she had worked him round until he was sitting opposite, his hands on his knees, fingers jabbin sharply into the fabric of his trousers.

Althea dared not give the slightest hint that she knew of the events in Crisp Court garden. When she saw Henry ready to withdraw the money he had been pouring into Rose's advancement, she did not lose her head.

"You have a large investment already in Miss Fitzroy. Perhaps," she advised when she judged the moment right, "you ought to consider making it permanent."

Henry had spent the first half of the concert watching the light ripple along Rose's slender arms and gathering himself around the intention hardening inside him. After the garden, her name had been ash in his mouth, yet his body had continued to burn. How odd that it had been Althea Wharton who had rescued him from the tormenting fires of jealousy. After a black outburst at the very idea, the plan Althea offered seemed right and just. Yes, let Adam choke on that one if he ever got the news. Oh yes indeed!

"In my own good time," Henry had warned Althea dourly, determined make her sweat. "It's up to you to see to it, do you understand!"

"Of course," Althea conceded with all the humble grace of an opponent who had won the game. Let Henry gloat. He would find out, too late, there was one lion he could not drive away.

"Get those children lined up. Everyone find your places," the stage director called out. "The Prince has finishing dining. He'll in his box any moment."

Since it was Bertie's custom to demolish a substantial meal during theatre intermissions, especially if he needed to be fortified for a ball, everyone else had been waiting. The flurry around Rose intensified. Costumed figures began to rush hurriedly about.

Tableaux were popular at amateur entertainment and even Rose's concert could not be complete without one. A tableau consisted of exactly that, a number of figures dressed in costumes and revealed in fixed poses, usually to illustrate some noble allegorical meaning such as Britannia conquering the Romans, or Virtue instructing the Sages. Tableaux provided a fine opportunity for participants to show themselves off to advantage without actually having to display any talent.

In this tableau, Rose was to be surrounded by a crowd of children dressed as paupers but actually recruited from the families of the very well-to-do eager to support Amelia's Refuge. The children would stand in a circle, beseeching little hands outstretched to Rose's mysterious figure. A veil of palest green and gold, draped Rose head to toe. Underneath it, Rose struggled to balance a sheaf of wheat under one arm and a basket artfully heaped with waxed fruit under the other. At the appropriate moment the veil was to fall away, revealing to the imploring youth, the hope and the abundance of the New World, symbolized, of course, by Rose. Althea wagered there wouldn't be a heart unmoved.

Ever since Althea had taken her in hand the morning after the incident at Crisp Court, Rose had been in a strange, half disembodied state. Numbness lingered like the after effects of some paralyzing drug. All her turbulent feelings for Adam Crisp had got buried under the barrage of Althea's firmness, Althea's warm, determined reasoning that brooked no argument. When Rose suffered a pang, Althea told her the spasm was some mere hitch of indigestion a sensible person would ignore. Through out all the hurried preparations for the concert, Althea herded Rose with a terrier's persistence, never giving Rose time to think.

And Althea must have been right, Rose thought over and over again to herself, lost in the maze of her mentor's logic. Wasn't it all coming true, just as Althea had promised? Wasn't it all as Signor Abruzzi had described? Back at Gresham's could she have imagined this? Didn't she wish heartily that the old Italian reprobate could have seen her as the hall shook with applause? Wouldn't he have had told her this was what she was meant for and she must snatch it all as quickly as she could?

Yet at Wharton House, hidden under the bed, Rose had the sheepskin vest. When Rose returned from the Derby, it had been waiting for her, a rough parcel amongst the usual overflowing bunches of flowers.

"A caution what people send," Daisy had been muttering, the vest held by two fingers heading for the dustbin.

Rose, brushing her hair, glimpsed it in the mirror and started up.

"Give that to me, Daisy. Who sent it? How did it get here?"

Nothing was known save that a boy had dropped it off at the door. Rose knew who had sent it. Gladness and fearful turmoil spurted up. The old vest had all the adventures of ten years in the wilderness worked into its battered folds. When Daisy left, Rose pressed it to her face, inhaling the tang of untainted air, the smell of pine, the scent of Adam.

For a long time, she clung to it, trying to calm herself. What did he mean by this? Was he gone from England already? Surely, she told herself swallowing back icy dread, surely he must be, had to be, safe from Hoggett's grasping claws.

Then a new anguish struck. Though her heart had leaped toward him in the garden, Adam had never once, since she had met him, tried to invite her into his life. Perhaps, fooled by the flirtations of so many men, she had assumed Adam cherished her too. The vest might be only a sort of ironical farewell gift. Perhaps she had everything completely wrong!

She had hidden the vest away, a message she couldn't interpret. She was glad, she told herself, that Adam had gotten away. There was a price to be paid for everything, Althea was fond of saying. If little shards of glass floated inside Rose, cutting and piercing, maybe they were the dues she had to pay to gain her ambition's peak.

"Places, places!" the manager cried out hurriedly. "His Highness has just entered the royal box."

With nervous giggles, the children spread into their circle while Rose took tighter hold of her props. The lights dimmed. The last of the scurrying amateurs bumped into each other in the half dark as they struggled to get into position.

Around Rose the players had been turned into misty shadows by the veil thrown over her. She did not see the hulking figure, obscured from head to heels in a heavy hooded cloak, which lumbered from the backstage gloom. Before Rose could realize that the tableau had acquired an extra member, the hooded shape had stepped up behind her and slipped large hands about her waist.

"Don't move!" Adam breathed into her ear. "I couldn't think of any other way to get this close!

CHAPTER SIXTY-ONE

The platform under Rose's feet tilted. Only the warmth of Adam's hands held her upright.

"I had to see you," Adam husked, voice laced with urgency.

The railway navies had accepted him without comment. Within half a day, Adam had been so covered with sweat and grime that Hoggett might have stood a yard away and never recognized him. Adam had flung himself into the toil and, at night, lay outside with the crew staring hard at the stars.

Rose had haunted him like a never-ending melody until he knew he was saturated with her, saturated to his bones, that the haunting would go on to the end of his life if he did not act upon its call. Finally, he had taken his pay and veered back to London determined to try his lot with her once and for all. Slipping along the waterfront, he had made his bargain for passage then gone in search of Rose. He had but one evening to reach her and he discovered it was the evening of her concert.

No fool about the traps Hoggett might have laid around her, he had followed the throng to the theatre. He would have cursed his luck had he not realized that the cover of crowds and confusion was the safest cover of all. He hit upon a perilous plan to get in.

Luckily for him, the Gryphon had a choice of back entrances, none of them locked. Once inside, Adam found the whole backstage in hectic disarray, peopled as it was by Rose's supporting cast, amateurs all, in varying sorts of bizarre dress. From behind a large painted backdrop, Adam waited while she sang and almost turned away. Who was he to be here, he asked himself as Rose lifted her arms to the roars of applause. Who was he to ask her to leave such success, such adulation behind?

Then he remembered her look under the vines of the folly, the leap he had felt from her, palpable and ringing. Even a caged bird sings. She must have her offer of freedom too, however chancy.

Beside him Adam spotted a row of floor-length brown hooded cloaks hung from pegs, from an opera of the previous week.

Snatching one, he pulled its hood far down over his head, turning him into a monk or a wizard, face deep in shadow. He would have but a moment for his say.

"You...you shouldn't be here," Rose gasped through unmoving lips as renegade gladness flooded through her. She had never expected to see him again. She thought he had abandoned her to Henry.

"I can't stay," Adam whispered urgently. "I'm leaving for Canada tonight. I couldn't go without coming here, without saying that...saying I love you, without asking if you want to come away with me."

Rose could not speak for her tongue cleaved to the roof of her mouth. The orchestra was swinging up into a crescendo. Before Adam could move, the curtain rippled back and he found himself bathed in light and exposed to the gaze of the entire hall. Flowers lay strewn like a just gathered garden all around. He froze into the immobility learned hunting with Laroche.

A bevy of dancers had crossed before the tableau. Now the children, from their trailing, theatrical tatters, were lifting their hands. The music changed again, the violins pleading. Adam's bent hood was almost against Rose's neck, the veil shrouding her scraping his cheek. He could not see any part of her face.

"After the concert, slip out the back. There'll be a cab and passage on a ship that's leaving with the tide. We'll race up some river and find Harriet Quinn and be damned all the Hoggetts in the world!"

Sweet fragrance filled Adam's nostrils. The garland on Rose's head glittered inexplicably with bits of starfire through the thin veil. On cue, the veil was released. In slow, gratifying billows, it fluttered down into a pool around Rose's feet.

The audience uttered a low, admiring gasp. Rose wore a dress of spring green maple leaves appliqued on top of each other, each leaf individually edged with seed pearls that might very well have been drops of dew. The leaves swept diagonally from shoulder to hems, making the tender flesh of Rose's shoulders and arms appear to be freshly budding from some living green sheath. The whole was brilliantly conceived without other ornament save the circlet of roses. Rose looked like the very spirit of a New World, a fresh-minted woman, luminous and vital.

Caught in Adam's grip, time vanished. Rose seemed to forget where she was or why she was there. She could feel herself floating high above the crowd, looking down at the rising of their bosoms, the bobbing of their heads together as they peered at the stage.

Though the spectators had no way of knowing an unplanned figure had joined the tableau, Adam's rough, dark look, so at odds with the bright grace of Rose and the children, began to cause an uneasy stir. Audiences liked their allegory obvious and clear. So who was that hooded character towering over the Hope of the New World and what could he stand for? What's more, he appeared to be whispering urgently into Hope's pearly ear instead of evincing the statue-like stillness required for a tableau.

In her box, Louisa Crisp took a frightened gulp. Something about the set of those shoulders, the way the cloaked man stood...

Henry, too, stared hard at the stage. He stiffened, a nauseating flame licking at his gut.

Hoggett, coldly vigilant ever since Adam had been sighted at the Derby, lounged at the side. Though he frowned at the incongruous addition, it was the sudden scarlet in Rose's cheeks that alerted him. A glance at the Crisp box told him both occupants were taut and distracted. Henry turned slightly, his eyes meeting those of Hoggett before flicking urgently back to the tableau. For the merest fraction, Hoggett looked puzzled, then his eyes narrowed. He nodded behind him. A silent movement began toward the wings.

Adam caught the movement.

"The back," he whispered again to Rose, and then he was gone.

His departure was like a part of herself breaking away, leaving a ragged hole. Her mind could not work, her throat closed tight as a whole universe inside her flew apart in splintered confusion. Desperate signals from musicians were trying to tell her it was time to break the tableau and begin a song.

Adam flitted through the backstage disorder into the twisting passage he had entered by, and finally, out one of the rear doors. The small street behind the Gryphon thankfully remained deserted. Adam slipped over to an alley where a hidden dogleg gave him cover from which to watch for Rose.

No sooner had he settled than a large arm reached from behind and locked around his neck.

"You forget about botherin' 'er, mate, ever again!"

CHAPTER SIXTY-TWO

The struggling cries of Cully were cut off by the slam of the door leaving Katie and Laura swamped in a silence that petrified their vitals.

Laura pressed flat against the stone behind her, heedless of the dirty, seepwater staining her back. Her flagellated mind could not grasp what was happening, or why. She whimpered soundlessly, riven by a premonition of unspeakable fate.

Katie had sunk down until she was nothing but a narrow, distorted shape dissolving in the shadows. She could not remember what Jenks had said, only that his words had been boulders crashing down until she was smashed open, pulverized, until he had done what he had been trying to do since she was a baby. Until he had broken her. Then he had ground his heels in the ruins and dragged Cully off to die!

My fault! My fault!

Oh Cully, he'll take his big hands, he'll crush your neck, he'll stick you down in the water, he'll...

A wet shape reared up in her memory, all the same colour as the river mud, grinning and grinning. A strangled sound wormed out. Katie crouched even harder into the corner. Outside the barred window, the tide was turning, bumping the moored boats against the river wall.

Mary, Katie thought, Mary!

The shape in her memory pushed itself up from the river. A glistening leg slid over the stone lip of the wall.

Mary...Cully...

My fault!

Madly, she struggled to blot out the pictures. Outside, the relentless water lapped and sucked. The smells assaulted her of slimy stone, noxious sludge, rotting wood and the oily, indescribable rankness of the river up close.

The other leg heaved up. The dripping, mud-slimed torso slipped toward them. Katie was backed up, as far as she could get, under the stairs...

Fists jammed into convulsive balls, Katie tried to ward off the hideous thing.

Jenksy's done it by now! Oh Cully...Mary...noooooo!

Jenks had cracked the sealed place in Katie's mind. She became swallowed in terror of what was leaking out of it, a person clamping a hand over some mortal wound, unable to keep lifeblood from spilling out no matter how hard the fingers pressed.

My fault! My fault...

The accusation roared into the most horrible fear of childhood, the fear of being abandoned. Now Katie was truly, utterly forsaken. Mary would not come for her. Mrs. Corman would not come for her as she had once, miraculously, come at the hospital.

And she deserved to be left! Deserved it! She hadn't been able to look after Mary. Then she'd told about the punch and got them sent to Bardle's and now Cully was being...being...

All my fault!

The mud-slicked, grinning creature slithered closer. An anguished, keening tore out of Katie's throat and rent the air.

"D....don't Katie. Oh...don't," Laura begged, terribly frightened by the sound.

Katie struggled even harder to block the writhing memories which would surely kill her if they got out. Back they had to go, back into their Stygian crypt, under the leaden weight that crushed at Katie, would crush her for the rest of her life to keep the pictures shut in.

The two friends clung together, as tightly as if they were trying to fuse themselves. If their their arms grasped violently enough, they might make it so they could not be torn away from each other as Cully had been torn away, not dragged outside where the river waited and sinister ships, their holds full of stinking water from the bilge.

Time passed, though how much they could not tell. They huddled motionless, through what were probably their last hours, perhaps their last minutes together. They had not known how much they loved each other until now when they were sunk in a pit of horror, knowing how useless it was to cry for help.

Only the faintest illumination penetrated the cell from lights reflected off the water. Time crawled horribly. The tide rushed on, tugging all the moored craft in its direction, filling the dimness with its relentless burbling. Then, in the midst of the darkness they heard something else. Something that began high and descended unevenly toward them. A horrid, inexplicable scrabbling.

Saliva dried in their throats. Could it be Jenks coming back for them, reeking of Cully's death?

The scrabble became louder. They couldn't tell its source.

"R...rats," Laura quavered. She used to be more afraid of rats than anything. Oh please, let it be rats!

A lurid rocket went off in Katie's mind.

Greasy rat nosing under Mary's hem, sniffing at her leg...

Katie began to feel blindly for pebbles, gravel, anything to throw, her eyes unseeing saucers in the gloom.

The scrabbling grew louder in the wall, right behind their heads. A rat as big as a coach dog! Laura began to shiver, unable to move. The scrabbling halted, punctuated by grunting then a shower of hard fragments rained down on the girls. With a screech, they bolted to the far side of the cramped enclosure, hearts banging in their throats.

Petrified, they heard more fragments fall. Half a brick cracked, rocked and fell out, leaving a black patch of emptiness. The patch seemed, incredibly, to gleam.

An eye! It was an eye!

Laura began to hyperventilate, her breath hucking in tiny, scraping gasps that would soon make her pass out. The other half of the brick tumbled from its place. Katie's limbs turned to empty sacks.

The rat that had been after Mary...coming to get her!

"Sssssttt!" the rat whispered. "Katie? Is that you?"

She couldn't be hearing this! She couldn't!

"Katie?"

Katie's mouth would not open, then it did.

"Will? Is...are you..."

"It's me. Are you locked up?"

He was real, he was!

"I...yes! Laura too. Oh....what are you doing in the wall?"

"It's a chimney. They covered up an old fireplace here. Help me get the bricks out."

Laura struggled out of her faintness and lunged at hope.

"Come on, Katie! Come on!"

Laura dragged at Katie's arm until Katie came to life. The two girls attacked the bricks from one side while Will pushed from the other. Into the cracks they shoved their fingers, working out one maddening piece of mortar after another, not caring how it cut or tore. When another brick fell out Katie got her hands in and pulled with all her might. Crumbly as the ancient mortar seemed, the other bricks would not give.

Renewed hysteria clawed at Katie's gut. To be so close and yet not be able to get through the wall!

"They're going to sell us and send us away in a boat," Laura panted. "We've got to get out. We've got to!"

A third brick cracked audibly but would not budge. Laura burst into tears. Katie yanked fruitlessly at the edges of the hole. The dash of hope now withdrawn was far crueler than any despair.

"Pull," begged Will urgently. "You've got to pull!"

But Katie had already begun to sink down into a defeated ball. Struggle was no use. She didn't deserve to get away.

She was halfway to the slimy floor when blunt, ghostly hand seemed to jerk at her shoulder and a thread of a ghostly voice, long unheard, struggled into her mind.

Tha's not lyin' down on me now, are yer, lass! Yer can't. Oh yer can't. Yer got to rage, lass. Oh who's ter be ragin' fer me if yer just lie down...

"Katie...." Laura moaned, "Katie help us...."

Will's faint shape receded and Laura thought he was abandoning them. She could not see that Will was only thrusting his shoulders against the back of the old fireplace to brace himself, his feet on the stubborn brick.

"Now," he whispered from inside the hollow gloom.

With all his might, he strained with his legs and grunted. Then Katie was on her knees again beside Laura, pulling frantically. Without warning, the entire centre gave way, collapsing at Katie's feet with a clatter of tumbling bricks and a smother of soot.

All three children stiffened, sure the racket warned the whole waterfront. In the beating silence that followed a faint thud penetrated, the slam of a distant door. Laura's eyes seemed to start in her head.

"They're...c..c.coming!"

"Then come on," Will urged. "You got to get away."

Falling over each other, Laura and Katie scrambled through the ragged gap in the bricks, only to find themselves jammed into a tiny, exitless space against Will's body.

"Oh...."

"Up the chimney, quick as you can!" Will ordered.

Unable to perceive anything but a black trap, Laura began to whimper. Will jerked at her elbow.

"Hurry up. It's all right. I climbed down it, didn't I?"

The three young bodies flailed blindly about, striking each other with knees and elbows. Finally, Will succeeded in hoisting Katie up into the pitchy space above their heads. When he let go, she found herself suspended only by means of knees jammed against gritty vertical walls. Her muscles strained madly to prevent herself from slipping back down. Will prodded at her ankle.

"Get goin', Katie. I got to get Laura in."

Eyes tightly shut, Katie managed to shinny further up the cramped passage. The Asylum came back to her, the lit newspaper singeing past, Will's screams above her head. Laura's head bumped her toes.

Keep movin'! Got to keep movin'!

Inch by inch, Katie wormed her way along, supported by tiny toeholds and ledges. The flue twisted and narrowed alarmingly. Below her, Laura seemed to be gibbering incoherently.

"I'm right behind you," Will was trying to tell them. "You can't fall."

Oh but they could, Katie knew. If she slipped, she would take them all back down into old firepit. Jenksy's huge hand would pluck them out. Her tendons stretched until they seemed like threads that must snap at any moment.

"I can't go up any more," Laura moaned as if infected by the thought. "It hurts. I...can't hang on...."

Katie forced her head up and saw above her a metallic square of sky. A sharp frenzy caught her.

"You've got to," Katie told Laura hoarsely. "Do you want to end up on a stinking old boat!"

"Shinny out when you get to the top," Will instructed, panting now himself, "and lie flat on the roof in case anybody sees you. "I'm right behind you pushin'."

The scree of the door to the room below acted like a lightning prod. The three fugitives propelled themselves up the rough interior with no care as to how much they cut and bruised themselves.

A terrified spurt sent them squeezing out of the chimney top and sprawling onto the unkempt slates where they lay panting, filthy and unrecognizable as trolls dug up from a mine.

So relieved were they to be out of the chimney that it took them a moment to realize they were clinging to the narrow ridge of a very steep roof which promised, with the slightest slip of the foot, to send them barrelling straight into the Thames. Will slithered past their legs.

"Follow me. You're all right as long as you don't start to slip."

Flat on their stomachs, they crawled over the roof ridge and down the other side, the slates rattling under them. Will led them to rusty iron grips installed for the use of sweeps. They tumbled to a lower roof, then onto a shed and finally, fell in a heap to the ground. A bundle of wet rags popped out from behind a cart. Cully cannonballed into their arms.

They clutched her tight, uttering cries of joy. When they could separate themselves, they found Cully dripping wet, her thin hair in spikes, her dress sticking to her matchstick legs and smeared with ooze. She shook all over. Her little slot mouth was stretched and thin as though awful reality had finally wiped out its eternally optimistic grin.

"Cully," the girls croaked simultaneously, "how...?"

"It was her that brought me here," Will told them. "Didn't I tell you."

There had been no time to wonder how or why Will had found them.

"Jenksy didn't drown you," Katie cried, then stopped at Cully's soaked condition. "But...he must have tried."

Cully flinched as none of them had ever seen her do and her lips closed up tight. Jenksy had tried very hard.

Jenks had carried Cully out to the river as ordered, riding on the satisfaction of Katie's predicament, relying on it to get him through drowning the scrawny brat and shoving the body into the undertow. Scuttling to the stone steps leading down to the water, he found the river rising and dangerous. In filthy whorls it swirled at his feet, its cargo of rubbish bobbing about looking for something to stick to. Distastefully, Jenks had edged down, Cully squirming in his grip.

What if he were seen, he thought! The idea sent him to his knees in an effort to get below the river wall. Snatching Cully, he thrust her head into the sucking water. A job for Ida, he cursed bitterly. Ida always took care of snuffing the brats.

He supposed it would be like drowning a cat, but Cully bucked in his grip with hysterical force, twisting and kicking. Jenks swore again, gripping her as hard as he could, forcing her even further under. Casual laughter from an anchored ship sent the blood pounding in his eyes.

Drown, you filthy squirming whelp! Hurry up and drown!

In her manic flailing, both Cully's feet flew out, catching Jenks below the shin, knocking him off balance on the treacherously slippery steps. He tried to hold onto Cully and save himself at the same time, flopping to his seat with a splash. Cully slipped from his grip and vanished into the water out of reach.

Soaked to the waist, Jenks clawed upright again. Frantically, he felt around under the water but only encountered a hunk of waterlogged wood thick with slime. Cold water sucked at his knees, threatening to pull him down into the current himself. He stumbled backward up the steps and ran along the wall, staring down.

No trace. He must have finished off the brat after all. He let the air halfway out of his lungs before he caught sight of something clinging to the side of the barge tied up just ahead. Something that had a white face and streaming clothes.

By the time Jenks ran over to the barge, the thing had shimmied away but not into the river. All of his straining searches could not spot her in the murk. Oh blazes, if she got away and told, it would be a knife in the back from Teapot before a day was out!

Icy sweat broke out under Jenks' collar. When he found himself running from trash heap to mooring rope to a heap of abandoned boxes, he forced himself to stop.

Think! Think! Where would the skittering whelp go?

Cully had crawled up between the stern of the barge and the wall and collapsed behind the very boxes Jenks had been flinging around to find her. She sucked air into her lungs in horrible, watery gasps costing an agony to keep silent. Yet even in this extremity her valiant little heart would not surrender. The moment the sparks of life rekindled, she pivoted back toward the single lodestone that sustained her day by day.

Help Katie, help Laura! Help Katie, help Laura! Got to!

The refrain pounded inside Cully's abused little skull. Cully was loyal, even above life itself, to the only friends she had ever possessed in her brief, battered existence. She huddled until Jenks had stumbled off, her head reeling. Resourcefulness was not one of Cully's strong points. Her own desperate determination struggled long and hard until an idea came to her. That boy that was Katie's friend. She had to get him. He was the only help she knew.

Drenched and bruised, she had crawled along the side of a building away from Jenks, sprung to her feet and run until she found the door with the boot on it Katie had described. Afraid to waken any adults, she squeezed through a narrow window gap and tiptoed among the sleeping boys until she found Will. And now...oh, now here were Katie and Laura, black as sweeps but alive and free.

"Oh Katie!" she blubbered, so transported she could barely talk, "Oh Katie..."

A gaunt, hulking ogre loomed up at the end of the alley.

"Jesus Christ in a handcart!" spluttered Jenks. "Here's the lot you are loose. How in Hades..."

Unable to find Cully, Jenks had racked his brains trying to think where she might go. Years of herding brats hadn't been wasted. She'd try and sneak back to where the other ones were.

Jenks had scuttled into the building and, tore open the heavy prison door. He found the room empty, an old fireplace punched open and a scrabbling far up what must have been the old chimney. Incredulous, he raced back outside, skittered along the wall until he spotted Cully as well as the other two standing free as birds as well. Teapot's profits on the hoof. If they all did a flit, Jenks might as well drown himself immediately and save Teapot the trouble.

Jenks lunged, actually getting a handful of Laura's skirt, but his hesitation had given his quarry time to leap. They were off at a sprint, leaving Jenks with a shred of tattered calico dangling from his fingers. Swearing, he started after them, but the children driven by terror, turned fleet as hunted hares.

"Run!" Katie shrieked to her friends pounding beside her, "Run!

Twice, Jenks nearly caught one of them as he galloped clumsily in their wake. Will had the presence of mind to duck Jenks' swooping grasp. Katie actually felt Jenksy's hot hand upon her shoulder and shot round a lamp post that smashed into his wrist, knocking it away.

The children ran until their lungs fried and their legs cramped. They bumped into people, dodged cab horses, darted under wagons, skidded around corner after corner, always hearing Jenks' feet thundering just behind. And when they could run no more, collapsing into each other, they discovered that the sound of Jenks in pursuit was pounding only in their heads. They must have lost him blocks ago amongst the labyrinthine streets. They gasped against walls only enough to restore themselves then floundered on.

"Whe...where are we going," Laura rasped when she found enough voice to speak.

There was no need to answer. Without even consciously knowing it, they had been running hard toward the Refuge and Amelia.

The Refuge, the Refuge, was the one refrain on their minds never mind the rain starting to pelt down. Oh, to get to shelter and safety and Mrs. Corman's protecting arms.

By the time they rounded the familiar corner, the hearts in their bosoms laboured unbearably. They tottered together up to the Refuge door only to find it boarded up so stoutly the door behind couldn't even be seen.

After groping unbelievingly for a door handle sealed from their reach, the children fell back. In the watery illumination from a streetlamp an inconceivable prospect greeted them. All the windows were boarded up as tightly as the door. The glass behind was black.

Exchanging a wild look, the children peered through the cracks at a horrifying sight. The rooms inside were stripped of all furniture. All trace of human life obliterated. All the busy, crowded activity of the Refuge was vanished. The place was empty as a looted tomb.

For a crazy moment they supposed they must have come to the wrong place.. Another place with a second hand shop across the street and a butcher's on the corner. They raced around to the side entrance in the alley. This door was boarded up as firmly as the front. Beside it, they tripped over Amelia's proud, carefully painted sign lying against the wall, smashed into splinters. It was like finding the body of a loved one gruesomely murdered in the gutter.

Renewed gusts of rain struck, washing away the last bits of flotsam left from the carts hastily hired by Edwin to save the furnishings strewn on the pavement. Black despair swelled in the children's throats. The street around them was eerily devoid of life. The few shops were shuttered tight. The other buildings crouched like abandoned hulks, no hint of movement within.

"Somebody's coming," Laura whispered as a rough tapping broke the stillness.

It was Mumby Mack, a local beggar who half-hopped on a peg leg and was frighteningly crazy to boot. Nevertheless, the children braved him.

"Gone, gone," he hissed to their importuning questions, "swept away by t'broom 'o t'devil. Haaa!" He leered sideways as rain turned his beard into growths of yellow seaweed.

"But where? Where have they gone?" Laura demanded.

"Into t'devil's handbag! Haaaa! That he keeps at 'is hip, full 'o whirlwinds. They don't come back, them as gets swept up by t' devil's broom. No, never!"

Mumby lurched off, launched on a tearing rant as was his custom. The children huddled wetly, chilled through and through. Even in the cellar, even in the dread grip of Slagge there had always been Amelia, always the Refuge.

Now the centre of the known world collapsed. For all they knew, the devil really had come, or some silent plague had struck, leaving the children the only hapless survivors in a pitiless desert of stone.

CHAPTER SIXTY-THREE

"Now!" Henry insisted vehemently, "I will have everyone's attention now."

Yes, in the midst of the music, the crowd pouring through Crisp Court, and the royal proprieties, he was going to do it. Before this throng of witnesses, he was going to have Rose. Not a moment longer would he wait. He paid for her, earned her. Now she was going to be his!

The hooded figure in the tableau had set him off. Like everyone else, he had no way of supposing it wasn't a planned part of the picture. Yet the way it hovered over Rose, the eerily familiar way it stood, filled Henry with alarm and a racing urgency to clinch his hold.

Here, at Crisp Court, he watched Rose blooming so brightly amidst the crowd swirling around her. He saw the looks on men's faces. Most of all, he remembered Adam's face, its ardour revealed, etched out in the light from the conservatory door that night in the garden. The music faded, movement halted, every face turned to Henry Crisp who had mounted the steps of the curving staircase, all the better to be seen. Rose stopped below him, realization dawning. Her lips parted in a soundless plea he refused to acknowledge. He turned to the people.

"Today, I am the happiest man on earth. I would like to announce the engagement between myself and Miss Rose Fitzroy!"

The costumed assembly was struck dumb. Cavaliers, voyageurs, governors and Indian matrons, stood agape as they digested this bombshell. As Henry grasped Rose's hand and drew her up the steps to stand beside him, a scattering of stricken groans issued from the younger bloods. Other men, worldly and long married, smiled to themselves. They understood perfectly well the reason for the engagement and now looked forward to joining the chase in merry earnest.

Henry's words reached Rose as sound might reach someone deep under water. Motion slowed absurdly as she saw Henry come toward her, felt him take her hand, felt him pull her up to his side. Her toe stubbed cruelly against one of the steps but she could not notice it. With every eye upon her, she turned, resistlessly accepting Henry's proprietorship. Only then, only when Rose herself showed them that the extravagant announcement was true, did the crowd burst into a hubbub of cries, exclamations and, finally, congratulating applause.

Knowing approval, followed by pleasurable expectancy, lit up the face of the Prince from his place of honour at the top of the ballroom.

Standing next to Rose, in public ownership at last, the tension eating at Henry since the tableau was broken. The hardness inside him burst into a flood of satisfaction, a decisive victory such as he had been seeking all his life. He had triumphed over Adam. And even the very starkness of Rose's face was pleasing.

No more slipping into gardens for you, he thought adamantly, for the interchange between Rose and Adam remained a burning stone under his heart. He, not Adam, possessed Rose, would possess her for a lifetime and Adam could never do a thing about it.

As for Rose, he had years and years in which to get his revenge upon her for that look. He could punish her, at his leisure, for her misbegotten passion whenever he chose. He could watch her knowing that the very beating power of Adam's existence, the knowledge of his unattainable, exiled being would torment her for the rest of her days.

Rose, taking Henry's arm, felt the waves of astonishment washing through the crowds, saw the race of whispers, the startled inquiring looks.

Why him, demanded the agonized expression on young Haggerty's face, for he had expended nearly half his yearly allowance for the concert ticket. Why!

And why did Rose, even in that marvelous leafy dress, look as though all the colour had been drained out of her, leaving a paper figure inside?

Rose herself had no idea how she had lived through the last endless portion of the concert. Afterward, after the curtain had rung down and the backstage had dissolved into a rush of bodies, Rose had snatched another of the cloaks from the peg and nimbly dodged into one of the deserted back passages. The chaos in the theatre was matched by chaos inside her. The success of the show, all mixed with the shock of Adam's nearness, set her heart plunging madly between excitement and terror and rushing anarchy. She only knew she had to see Adam, to know he was still free, to know he had actually been real. All the conflicting messages galloping through her would be resolved by one sight of him, one touch. Oh, just let him be still waiting out there!

Shrouded, Rose slipped to the same scarcely used back door Adam had found. Chest tight, she had peered into the night. Outside, there was nothing, only an expanse of deserted cobbles with no Adam, no cab.

"Adam?" she whispered, struggling with disappointment, fear and confused hope. "Are you there?"

A thick body blocked her way.

"We have him," Hoggett informed her coolly. "So if you've any thoughts of rebellion, put them clean out of your mind!"

Rose stared at Hoggett in appalled dismay. Icy sleet poured over the glory of her evening.

"Before you open your mouth to beg,"Hoggett said, "let me dangle some hope. If you be a sensible woman and accept the right invitations, if you give up this foolishness and are properly amenable to dear, lovestruck Henry Crisp, I might find it in me to relent. When all is done and settled, Adam Crisp could very well be kindly set on a ship bound for Hudson's Bay or the China Sea."

"How do I know you'll keep your word?"

"You don't. However my word is all you've got. Make your choice!"

Events took on a phantasmagoric quality as Hoggett returned her to the noisy mob waiting to escort her to Crisp Court. She had moved through the festiveness of the ball as through thick syrup. Now, on Henry's arm, she glided from one group to another, seeing their lips move, hearing their words break into fragments, all of them meaningless.

The engagement plan had been hovering over Rose ever since her fateful talk with Althea Wharton, a scheme that been almost invisibly but inexorably taking shape without Rose giving it any of her attention. Without notice, without warning, it had been sprung upon her, catching her helpless against Henry's pouncing strike.

Althea appeared at Rose's side and took possession of the circulating couple lest the bride-to-be do something impulsive that might be dearly regretted later.

"Congratulations, my dear," Althea crooned, leaning on tiptoe to kiss Rose's cheek. "Now the world is yours!"

Unlike Rose, Althea had been expecting the announcement, though certainly not in the precipitous manner Henry had chosen. Annoyed as she might be at Henry's impetuous action, she could not disagree with his method. Surprise was the quickest way to snap the trap, quick, clean and painless.

Rose, Althea was pleased to see, appeared to be sensibly acquiescing, even though she looked too dazed for Althea's liking. Althea peeped over to where Henry was being congratulated, enviously, by a knot of men and squeezed Rose's hand.

"Don't worry. He's a great asset and only a minor inconvenience. Between us, we'll keep him in his place."

Althea had no qualms about hoodwinking Henry. The rewards of his cuckolding would be many and ample, all the investments, all the prestige he could cope with. One day, when he regained perspective, he would thank Althea heartily though gratitude in the immediate future might be too much to expect.

Rose blinked at her smiling mentor. Did Althea know, could she have any idea of the jagged breakage inside Rose's bosom? Rose half opened her mouth to speak when Hoggett appeared, bowing and clicking his heels with military satisfaction.

"His Royal Highness wishes to extend his personal felicitations. Please follow me."

Hoggett was ramrod straight and perfectly correct, yet never had he exuded so strongly the rampant fleshiness that filled Rose with revulsion. He has Adam, she thought. He can order him chained to a wall for the rest of his life!

With Althea for escort, Rose walked slowly behind Hoggett over to the Prince, who took her hand and squeezed it knowingly, his eyes never lifting from hers. All his appetites gleamed in their depths.

"Warmest congratulations, Miss Fitzroy. A wise move." He inclined his head closer. "I look forward to complimenting you even more warmly in private."

His glance flicked to the circlet of roses which glimmered with a maharaja's tribute. Hoggett appeared just behind his master.

"Naturally, you are invited to join the party at Frayne Manor, in company with Mrs. Wharton, of course. His Royal Highness will be most pleased with your attendance there."

Frayne Manor was a country estate. Rose was invited to one of those long weekends when the elite played secure in the privacy of their own broad acres. Hoggett nibbled his lower lip while Althea

all but swooned at the honour. Rose realized they were all looking at her in a most peculiar manner—the Prince, Hoggett, even
Althea upon whose face fluttered a dazzled, flushed, half worldly
sad expression. Rose thought of herself in a large house away from
the city, with no one there but Hoggett's people and the Prince's
people.

For Henry had not been invited!

The Prince under the arches of the folly, waiting for her, reaching for her...

They intend to hand me over to him there, pass me on to the
Prince like a gift package with not a thing I can do about it!

Beside her, Hoggett was congratulating himself on the treat he
had lined up for his master. A rare extraordinary treat for a jaded
prince, a beauty who was safely engaged but not yet soiled. Henry
Crisp would have his wedding night snatched away from him as
deftly as a magpie snatches a shiny penny. How pleasantly grateful
Bertie would be, how more indispensable Hoggett would become,
how much deeper into royal favour would he insinuate himself.

Rose hurried back to Henry, only to find he had been watching her every move, exaltation blazing from his face. In Henry's
clenched fists and the flush under his acne scars, Rose read her
future. Henry Crisp would not be the easy-to-control fool Althea
had promised, a convenient ticket to freedom. No wife of his would
flit as she pleased. Henry would strangle her first.

Oh why, oh why didn't I just say yes to Adam right there on the
stage, Rose asked herself in anguish. Why didn't I just leave with
him, right in the middle of the tableau!

A terrible hunger rose in her to be near Adam, to see, to touch
him, a terrible regret at rescue and safety which had been so near
and was now so hopelessly far.

I can't let them do this to me! I won't!

Now, finally, she was horrifyingly aware of the enormous sticky
web she had fallen into. All the glamour had been an illusion, fake,
fatal. She had put out both hands to grasp life and ended up with
this armful of calamity. The bone-bitter knowledge made Rose gather herself and lift her head. Althea, still in a gleeful paroxysm over
the royal invitation, missed this perilous change.

Althea was trying to get a hold of herself enough to find Amelia
for it was time to make ceremonial presentation of all the funds
collected by the concert. Proudly, Althea glanced at the ornate glass
receptacle on a draped pedestal at the front of the ballroom and

congratulated herself on her bright idea. The case, about the size of a small sea chest, had originally contained one of Henry Crisp's unpleasant stuffed bird scenes before Althea had extracted the loan of it. Althea had filled the case to the brim with the donation money, all in cash, success for all to see. Atop the glass lid a model ship tilted at full sail, a scarlet maple leaf painted on each miniature canvas. The ship's name, hastily painted over the original, was now The Orphan's Hope, a telling touch, Althea decided, for this, too, had been her inspiration.

"Is that wise?" Amelia asked timidly when Althea proposed putting the money on view.

Althea had regarded Amelia pityingly. Really, if Amelia meant to go after large sums of money, she must learn how to extract them with the kind of drama that left the happy donors ready to give more. Surely Amelia could see how pleased the guests were with this delightfully vulgar amount of cash as evidence of their own generosity.

No sooner had Althea found Amelia and gotten her into position beside the chest when Rose came striding toward them. Rose might not be able to revolt against her chain but she could make her captors pay.

"In honour of my engagement," she announced, in tones that rang to the very back of the crowd, "I wish to add my own token to the children's cause.

With that, she tore the circlet of roses from her hair and dropped it, rubies, emeralds and all, into the chest. The thing had burned, like a ring of embers, atop her head. The horror on the faces of Althea, Hoggett and the Prince at the royal ransom she had just thrown away was almost worth the gesture.

CHAPTER SIXTY-FOUR

A blunt hand shot out from behind a rubber tree and scooped three lobster pastries from the tray Lucy was carrying past. Before Lucy could see who, the shadowy figure faded behind the shrubbery, presumably to devour booty without recourse to napkin, fork or plate.

"Lordawmighty!" Lucy muttered, hurrying on to the refreshment tables, "some you'd think hadn't eaten for a week!"

If Lucy had said two days, she would have been just about right. Red Nell had been battered from one skirmish to the next, barely escaping with her neck, never mind snatching a bite on the way. She swallowed the pastries in a couple of ravenous gulps. Her legs still ached from the urgency of her flight, her mind reeled and staggered under the realization that Teapot had actually done it. After all these years, he had clobbered her with such a single, treacherous, devastating blow that she didn't have so much as a strip of cobbles left to her name, never mind houses and streets and bully boys to command. Teapot's toughs were even now scouring the streets for her. If she so much as stepped out of Crisp Court in her current state, she'd end up dead in an alley before an hour was out!

Rose! She'd let herself get so distracted with Rose she'd forgotten she had territory to run. Forgotten about Teapot's threat, never believed the slimy, insidious scum could ever have mounted such a grab. But mount it he had, backed by sinister newcomers suddenly interested in Nell's assets. Disaster had come crashing in from all directions, with a splintering of doors, with fists and knives and such a swarming of vicious rats that Nell had barely escaped with her life in her hands, never mind any of the treasure she had worked so hard to build.

Fool! she ranted at herself. And how long was she safe for now? Only a few more hours. Only until this packed affair ended. Then... oh then, she would have to take her thin chance with Teapot in the streets.

When Nell saw all had collapsed, the ancient mother instinct erupted in her, the same as when she had haunted the famine coast, tottering against the wind, struggling to protect her young no matter what the cost.

Rose! she was thinking. Teapot won't get my Rose! Not the way he bashed Flan! Not the way he took me darlin' Gwyn and the poor bairn born among the coal!

The blow of Teapot's attack had brought back all of Nell's losses; hunger, Flan crashing to the cobbles, the waxy, birth-dishevelled corpse of Gwyn flung, like rubbish, for her mother to find. In desperate times, the clan closed to protect itself. They now raced to find Rose, to shield her, Joe to the concert hall, Dan to Wharton House, Nell, toward Crisp Court. She meant to get inside even if she had to cosh one of those high-nosed footmen to do it. With her own power shattered, Rose's glittering success became, to Nell, an insubstantial illusion, a flashy, silly sham that would fly to tatters when Teapot struck.

Nell had come to snatch Rose bodily if there was no other way. There was nothing for it but a boat to Ireland for the lot of them, nameless and unnoticed amidst a similar deported mob. They'd take to the tinkers' wagons again if they had to. And not a bad life either, Nell was thinking as she longed for a gulp of salty, wind-scoured air. What was mud in the wheels and a slow plod in the Irish rain if you kept your hide intact.

How Nell had slipped in past the footmen at the door would have boggled Louisa. Nell's luck was that the affair was a costume ball, for Nell had fled Teapot in her ordinary dress of scarlet military jacket, multi-coloured layers of skirt and garishly hennaed curls streaming loose from their pins. In the shadows, Nell had draped her own pocket bandana down over her forehead to all but cover her eyes then snatched a cockaded hat from a hapless postillion to jam down over it all.

Thus attired, she had marched in with the crowd, the tabarded footman tabarded backing away at Nell's stare. Inside, Nell almost gave herself away by gaping about her at the elaborate plaster work, the vaulting ceilings, the chandeliers alight with a twinkling glow—a glow that was revealing the mud on Nell's hems and the battle-torn state of her coat. Drawing about her the formidable cloak of her own presence, she joined the stream flowing toward the ballroom. Despite the many questioning brows, none jostling Nell could find the nerve to question her.

Mercifully soon, the crowd eddied Nell out into a deserted alcove set behind two pillars. She collapsed on a bench to watch and wait. From the dimness behind the rubber plant she had a fragmented view of ballroom, now alive with people. Her mind was only on one thing—her first sight of Rose.

Eventually, a commotion rearranged the crowd around a bright centre. As Nell adjusted gritty eyes to the blur of colour and bodies, she could make out her distant daughter but not hear what was going on. She glimpsed Rose at the side of Henry Crisp and heard the sudden clamour among the guests. One more tribute to Rose's talent Nell supposed. She only sought a way to whisk Rose out.

Hoggett swaggered along in Rose's wake, mightily pleased with himself. Even her defiant gesture with her circlet of flowers caused only a moment of ire at the headstrong little fool. When he saw her safely surrounded with buzzing people, he snapped his fingers at two footmen.

"The donations to the Refuge have been displayed long enough," he said to Louisa. "The dancing is about to begin. Please show me a private room where they can be safely locked until they are claimed by the Cormans. I myself will keep the key."

He would, slip back and reclaim the necklace before anyone realized it was more than a wreath of glowing blooms.

Louise led the way to the only suitable room she could think of, her own blue salon. She did not hear the clunk of a bench falling over in the alcove as she and the footmen passed. Nell had seen the one thing that could wrench her attention from Rose—a glass chest stuffed to the lid with an unbelievable fortune in cash!

CHAPTER SIXTY-FIVE

"My gracious, how sly you've all been, Mrs. Corman, keeping Miss Fitzroy's engagement such a secret. You can hear masculine hearts breaking all the way to Greenwich!"

Mrs. Ballthorpe, Mrs. Halverstone and Mrs. Smithing, had descended upon Amelia with avidly inquisitive eyes. But they found Amelia flummoxed as the rest about the thunderbolt dropped amongst them. And she was already so distracted about the children that not even a wedding on the spot could have upset her universe more. The sudden engagement was a message from another planet. Rose had so long flown out of Amelia's control that nothing Rose did could surprise.

From the moment she arrived, Amelia had been thrust into the limelight. She had had to tell a whopping lie about why Edwin wasn't there, give speeches of thanks, chat to ticket holders and, above all, take formal presentation of that glass chest stuffed to the lid with money. She could hardly confess to all the smiling benefactors that even as the violins tuned up for a waltz, the children were homeless and might still be shivering in a rain-soaked, deserted street.

What's more, Amelia hadn't discovered the magnitude of the profits until actually confronted with the chest, overflowing an astronomical sum that made her dizzy. Her head swam at all the uses it must go to. Each farthing became precious. That money could rescue them from their disaster, quell the panic and terror roiling so violently inside her.

How soon can I take possession, was all Amelia was thinking. How soon I can get it to Edwin and the children?

So Hoggett's sudden decision to move the chest filled her with trepidation. She watched anxiously as footmen lifted their burden and proceeded out of sight. Despite assurance it was safely under lock and key, Amelia could not smother the bursts of anxiety making her stomach clench. She would only be able to breathe while the money was in her sight. She excused herself and slipped off down the corridor.

Just to look. Just to make sure.

The hall was quite deserted with only a soft gas jet burning. Amelia caught sight of the doors of the blue salon, double doors, polished and solid. Feeling foolish, Amelia was about to turn away when she noticed just a sliver of door edge, ever so slightly ajar. A prickle ran down her neck. Hadn't Major Hoggett assured her it was firmly locked.

Tiptoeing closer, she gave the door a testing push. Soundlessly, it swung open. As soundlessly, Amelia stepped through and stopped, unable to believe her eyes. A lunatic soldier in a skirt was bent over the chest stuffing the contents as quickly as possible into her bulging jacket.

Someone was helping themselves to the money!

Exhaustion fell away from Nell as she had gaped after Hoggett and the chest. That much money was safety and escape.

Bleedin' hell, that much money was revenge!

With such resources, Nell could smash Teapot back into the gutters he had crawled from. No haring off to Ireland to plod the back roads in the cold and the damp. With that money and the wits that she had left, Nell could come at Teapot from behind, strike her blow when he was all puffed up with conquest.

Wipe him out for good!

Money sitting there for the taking.

No longer was Nell a wounded animal seeking survival for herself and hers. Savage hope resurrected itself along with a thirst for retribution. And wasn't the money practically hers. How else could such a sum have got there if Rose hadn't attracted it? Nell had followed the footmen and waited behind some ferns until the hall was clear.

The lock was nothing to Nell who had it open with a hairpin before a baby could wink. Lacking a carrier for so much money, Nell had simply tied a cord from one of the drapes tightly around her waist to prevent anything falling past it. She then began stuffing the money down her neck and inside her jacket as quickly as she could, swelling her stout form into a top-heavy balloon. She intended to march brazenly straight past the servants into the street.

A soft gasp made Nell pivot. Amelia Corman was standing there, gaping at the plundered glass case, the model ship lying on its side, and the grotesque female figure caught with fist full of notes.

The two stared at each other. As Amelia's mouth twitched open, preparing to scream, Nell lunged. In an instant, she had one arm around Amelia's waist and the other clamped over Amelia's mouth.

Amelia, who had never been manhandled in her life, went rigid, too astonished even for outrage. Nell cursed under her breath. What was she to do now—stand and hold the silly woman until someone else walked in and found them locked together?

Amelia recovered enough to struggle, only to find herself held immobile. She tried harder and the blunt hand ground more heavily into her jaw. A red flood passed through Amelia's brain. This creature had been robbing the chest! Stealing the safety of the Refuge, perhaps the lives of the children.

Stealing the very future away!

Cots and clothes and shelter and ships and all the things she needed to buy tumbled through Amelia's head. She couldn't, wouldn't let anyone plunder it.

Amelia began to twist and kick, ineffectually at first, then with more desperate force, lashing into Nell's shins with her heeled shoes and digging crookedly with her elbows.

"Achhh!" Nell yelped as Amelia jabbed her on the kneecap.

The crackle of bank notes under Nell's coat drove up Amelia's frenzy. She twisted again and Nell bumped into the sharp corner of a table. In a minute, she'd knock something over with a crash and attract some meddling servant.

Nell's fingers crept up from Amelia's mouth to also cover her nose.

The deprivation of air was abrupt and terrifying. She means to make me pass out, Amelia thought incredulously as she clawed at the arms gripping her. And I'm not! I'm not going to!

She kicked harder. Nell lurched and her grip tightened. Amelia began to see great yellow blotches before her eyes. She was going to faint. And if she fainted, this thief would make off with everything. Gritting her teeth heroically, Amelia struggled for air, lashing and corkscrewing as she tried to pry the iron fingers away.

Dimly, she felt another force slam into her, a small body, with small fists pummelling and flailing. It made not the slightest difference to the hand clamped across her face.

The yellow splotches turned into explosions, fire sucked at her starving lungs. Amelia felt herself reeling, felt all the money slipping away, all her work, all the deception, the children shivering....crying...on the street ....

Amelia collapsed onto the blue carpet and lay in a tangle of skirts. Just before blackness engulfed her, Amelia dimly imagined the small body biting, kicking and punching, belonged to Katie Mucker.

CHAPTER SIXTY-SIX

Amelia was right about seeing Katie. As darkness thickened outside the abandoned Refuge, the children fled the frightening disaster. Only when they reached Crisp Court did they realize where blind instinct had led them.

Soaked though, they crouched in the lane behind, relief at the familiar building battling fear of being captured again, sent back to Bardle's. Yet there were carriages, lights and music drifting out. If there was a party, Mrs. Corman might be inside. Shivering like a motherless pup, Katie insisted she be the one to try to find her. Squeezing through the coal shute, she began her quest.

Because the building was so crammed with people, Katie's progress was excruciatingly slow. Along back passages, up servants' stairs, Katie crept, hiding each time she heard a human step. A dozen times, flattened into the shadows, she thought her heart was going to hammer right out of her chest. She left damp footprints and a trail of drips behind her until, at last, she could peep through a service door at the ball going on.

In that milling, costumed, extravagantly dressed mob she couldn't see Mrs. Corman anywhere. Katie frantically scanned the crowd until she heard servants coming and scuttled behind a stack of chairs. Fran chattered to a strange maid hired for the occasion.

"...I don't know how they expect to dance," Fran was saying. "Wonder the place doesn't burst at the seams."

"Must be why they carried off that chest full of cash. Thought my jaw would pop off at the sight!"

Fran laughed. "Oh, Mrs. Corman's money for that Refuge, lucky her. They put it in the blue salon but didn't bother with the pedestal it sat on. Listen, can you beat that match between Rose Fitzroy and Mr. Henry..."

Fran and her companion marched out of earshot. Katie stood up. If Mrs. Corman's money was in the blue salon, then maybe Mrs. Corman was there too. Katie reversed her direction for another perilous journey. The salon door was half open. Quick as a mouse, Katie flitted inside and shut the door behind her.

She met a sight so strange she could not, at first, make head or tail of it. The shape was Mrs. Corman's. Yet that shape was locked in what appeared to be mortal combat with another shape, both of them struggling and grunting.

Then the smell struck Katie like no other in London, a smell she still didn't understand was peat. Katie only knew it as the smell that seeped out when the cab door opened and out stepped...her!

Red Nell!

Red Nell was hurting Miss Amelia!

Katie flew at the figure, kicking and flailing, a small, sooty exclamation mark of fury in that opulent room. Nell swore violently under her breath, but did not lessen her grip on Amelia. Her small assailant tore and hit with a demented energy, all the while emitting anguished, stuttering sobs. The pipe stem arms and skinny knees could do little against Nell's smothering hold on Amelia who now swayed weakly on her feet.

When Amelia collapsed to the floor, Nell turned to her new assailant. Enraged, she snatched the child by the back of the neck and lifted her into the air by the scruff like a bedraggled alley cat. She had just begun to violently shake her catch when a brawny hand shot out grabbed her from behind. Weakened by two days of hunger, sleeplessness and headlong flight, Nell tripped against the table leg, fell backward against this new aggressor and lost the fight.

At their feet, with gasps and wheezes, Amelia came to again. For a couple of uncomprehending seconds, she blinked at the ceiling then scrambled woozily to her knees, amazed that no hard arm squeezed her throat. As she opened her mouth to screech for help, the grimmest of male voices said, "Don't make a sound, Mrs. Corman, or I'm done for!"

"Mr. Crisp," Amelia croaked incredulously, as her rescuer swam into focus. And beside him, a small, soaked, blackened figure that was...Katie.

Adam, contrary to what Rose had been told, had not been captured by Hoggett. As he waited, hidden within sight of the Gryphon's back door, cab nearby to spirit Rose off, he had been seized by Joe Varden. His struggle with what he first imagined to be a common footpad turned to astonishment as he recognized the prize fighter who had beaten him so underhandedly. This time, Adam settled his difference in a narrow alley without benefit of ring, referee or dubious water to drink. When he finally thrust

Joe Varden to the cobbles and got back to the theatre, everyone, including his waiting cab, was gone.

Cursing, he sped on to Crisp Court and, stymied by the crowds, managed to slip into the blue salon to hide out while he sought some safe way to reach his mother. She would speak to Rose for him. He knew she would. So he almost jumped out when Louisa herself had opened the door with Hoggett and the footmen behind her. He had sweated behind the draperies until they left again. Then Adam found himself locked in.

Amelia knew nothing of Adam's difficulties save that he hadn't been seen some time. Still holding tightly to Red Nell, Adam looked like a man clutching a red-hot poker with nowhere to drop it. Katie flew to Amelia and clamped herself around her waist. Amelia dragged herself to her feet, Katie and all.

"This...this creature was stealing the money," Amelia choked out. "We must get..."

Nell struggled sideways. Her hat and bandana, which had clung gamely on all through the battle, tumbled away. Amelia's eyes goggled.

"You!"

Nell glowered from under her garish locks. Amelia stared back at the original engineer of all her good luck. Her impulse to scream died away.

"Mr. Crisp. I know her. There must be some explanation!"

Adam prudently retained his hold.

"I came to see Rose," he said in a rush. "Could you please go and fetch her, Mrs. Corman. And see that no one knows about me but her."

"But..."

"Mrs. Corman, please. I beg of you. I must speak to your cousin."

His voice was raw and cracked. Amelia peered at the lines of tension etched into his face and saw how it was with him.

"But my dear Mr. Crisp," she murmured with compassion, "Rose became formally engaged this evening to your brother."

Something crucial ripped asunder inside Adam. Nothing mattered now, not his own hide, not a hundred years on the end of a chain. Nothing mattered but Rose who could not know what grief, what misery she bought with Henry.

"Impossible!"

Dropping Nell in a heap, Adam went tearing off toward the ballroom.

CHAPTER SIXTY-SEVEN

The dancers were finishing a quadrille when Adam pushed in from the back. The room was so crowded, so filled with strange costumes, that he wasn't, at first, noticed. He shouldered recklessly through the crush, small exclamations peppering the air as he was recognized by those he bumped aside. Henry stood with Rose not far from the Prince. The last violin strain died. Henry turned and felt his every pore contract.

What was that misbegotten wretch doing here! Why was he still in England? Was this some insane, spiteful effort to ruin them all just at the peak of success!

Rose followed Henry's stare.

Adam!

Hoggett hadn't captured him! Hoggett had been lying!

Bounding, irrational joy flooded through her before her stomach seized. What madness was he committing! If he hadn't been captured at the theatre, he was as good as trapped now. Why was he doing this?

The burning inside Adam carried him all the way to Rose standing beside Henry near the royal party. His feet would go no further.

At close range, his rough woollen shirt and work-stained moleskin trousers stood out starkly. Hard labour had added new creases at the corners of his eyes and toughened his hands into leather. His hair sprang up, dishevelled. His face bore the marks of Joe Varden's fists, partly obscured by his beard beginning to grow back to glossy darkness. He stood defiantly, earthy and raw.

Hoggett eeled from the knot of royal cronies to insert himself between Adam and the Prince. His disbelief gave way to a choleric surge that pinkened the scalp visible under his pale hair, swiftly mixed with nasty gloating at the man's foolhardiness. The minute Adam stepped from the ballroom the clown was finished.

But there must be no public incident!

Slowly, Hoggett pivoted on his heel toward Rose, silently warning to her, menace glittering from under his colourless spikes of lashes.

A frisson rippled through the people nearby, a low buzz among those who had heard the rumour about Adam Crisp and the abrupt ending of Louisa's last reception. Adam had rushed in blindly. Now, with so many fascinated gazes riveted upon him, he remembered his danger. The awful, fatal danger he had flung himself into.

Rose's eyes were very wide. She had been caught with one hand half lifted and tendrils drifting loose from where she had pulled the circlet from her hair.

Never brush them back, never, never, Adam thought, just as he had that day in the park when he had broken off white blossoms and nested them there.

Rose's look met Adam's and locked. She dared not move. Though she did not so much as glance at Hoggett, she could feel his intimidation as strongly as if he had been wrenching her elbow. Hoggett might have fooled her about capturing Adam but the rest of his threats were not lies. Move, his scowl declared, and Adam Crisp is done.

Already a darkening purple bruise slashed across Adam's cheek and up toward his temple. One corner of his lip had a split in it. His right eye in a day or two it would be black with a throbbing shiner. Maybe Hoggett really did catch Adam, Rose thought, her stomach clenching. Maybe Adam got away somehow, all to rush straight here into the trap again.

For me!

Adam could only hover there, offering himself. What else was there to do when he found his heart stained through and through with the essence of another? The pulse at the base of Rose's throat began to leap and tremble. Black alarm invaded the pupils of her eyes, so strong that, for one excruciating moment, Adam wondered whether he had misjudged her completely and made the worst mistake of his life.

He felt again the poacher pit trap, filling up with cold seep-water while his hands dug helplessly at the mud-slick sides. Hoggett's moon face became once again the face of the lashless boy casting a final, relishing stare over the edge before bounding away.

Well, damn them all!

No more dodging, no more running. He had passage booked on a ship, the *Peregrine*, due to sail with tonight's tide. If they meant to grab him, drown him in the pit, then let them do it! He was damned if he'd live under any more bans, prohibitions or terrors. A crazy lightness took him. A leaden breastplate fell away. Now he could breathe.

Time to see just what this Prince, this imperial potentate-in-waiting, was made of!

That Prince in question had first looked astonished at Adam's arrival. He remained unmoving in the great, gilt-encrusted chair Louisa had provided for him, but his back no longer touched the velvet behind him. If there was one thing Bertie cared about, it was keeping himself from open public scandal. His easy geniality had vanished, his every muscle was alert to the danger here of a scene.

Hoggett, furiously aware of the same danger, dared not take open action on the dance floor. However, a signal had already put his minions in place. Let this lout step from the sight of the crowd and he'd be gibbering with the lunatics before the night was out.

Hoggett had now edged far enough over so that he was not only between Adam and Bertie but between Adam and Rose. All of them, like figures on a chess board, seemed caught in an impasse. This impasse steadily worsened as more and more of the crowd craned their necks and stepped on each other's feet in an effort to see.

Althea and Louisa had watched Adam's approach in a kind of horrible slow motion. In her head, Althea heard the sound of ninepins, the clatter of her life collapsing into ruin around her. Every survival instinct in her shrieked for action but the only idea that came to her was that of grasping Rose by the back of her dress and holding fast until Adam was removed.

Rose felt herself drowning in a tumult of fear and longing. Get away, her brain shouted to Adam. Run, escape while Hoggett doesn't yet have his hands on you!

Her heart drummed a different message. *I love you!* it cried. *Stay!*

I must do something, I must!

Adam silently demanded his answer, a man too harassed for anything but this driving directness. Until she saw Adam, Rose had been growing steadily colder and colder. She'd had an ache in every bone like a toothache and been too numb to feel it until now.

Adam was the only warmth in the room.

Beside her, Henry's stomach churned and lurched. He fought a sick weakness about the kneecaps.

The match, he saw himself dropping the lighted match, saw the flames licking tentatively at the side of the cotton bales, spiralling around the wooden pillar, pouring upward, exploding from the roof...

His hand shot out to grip Rose by the wrist, fingers digging into her flesh in dire warning. Rose felt the fear and violence streaming off him as if some awful, revealing fissure in him had opened. Revulsion overwhelmed her. With a single twist, Rose wrenched free. Unable to stop herself, any more than a rock could stop the tide, she bolted away from Henry and straight into Adam's arms.

"Yes, oh yes!" she breathed as Adam enfolded her as if he would never again let her go.

Enough questing in search of she knew not what. She had found what she wanted. She must have it, if only for a moment.

Now the whole room was halted by the spectacle of Rose Fitzroy flying precipitously into another man's arms.

Hoggett prevented himself from from pouncing on Adam Crisp then and there. Vindictive victory infused his look. Adam Crisp was his anyway. As for Rose, she was one songbird who was shortly going to be very sorry indeed for embarrassing the Prince in such a manner.

Behind Hoggett, Henry's face had turned into a Chinese mask of pure rage. His fists opened and clenched, opened and clenched against the sides of his legs. The stares of the ball guests burned his very skin.

Adam had received Rose with a deep groan, embracing her with something beyond joy, shuddering with the shock of two matched pieces flying together.

When he came back to his senses, Adam caught the avid intent on Hoggett's face.

What have I done! What have I brought upon Rose, he asked himself, beginning to grasp the disaster his impulsive rush was creating. He made a movement to disengage himself. Rose stopped him.

"No," she whispered fiercely. "I don't want it any other way."

Some rose petals still lay in her hair, opulently scented. Adam wanted to press his face into them. This might be the last time, the last he'd ever hold her. Hoggett waited for his prey to move.

"We can't stand here forever," Adam murmured to Rose without an alternative in mind.

It was Rose who lifted herself away and turned to draw Adam after her, willing to take the chance. Hoggett glanced at the side doors behind which his trap lay. A slow smile crept along his lips as he waited for the two to step into their own ruin. They had only gone half a step when quiet voice cut in.

"Major Hoggett, would you please step this way. His Highness would like a word."

They had forgotten the Prince who had not stirred as he watched the drama with a still, wary face. Rose and Adam halted. They saw Hoggett bend close to Bertie, saw a low, rapid conversation made up of questions on the Prince's part, ever tighter answers from Hoggett.

"Major Hoggett," they finally overheard Bertie say, an edge to his voice, "I fear you have been overextending yourself. I suggest you return to your regiment to take up less onerous duties."

Hoggett's face collapsed upon itself. Rose wondered why they didn't hear the squealing of his joints as he bowed and backed away.

What now, Rose asked herself anxiously. Then, to her astonishment, who should she glimpse, hovering in the obscurity just behind the Prince but Althea Wharton. Althea had the glazed, half-incredulous look of having just dodged a cannonball and bracing lest there be another.

What is she doing there? What on earth did she say?

The truth, Althea could have answered had she been able. The last play in direst extremity, the very last, was to resort to the truth. Swift as a ghost, Althea had flitted through the transfixed crowd and thrust herself behind the Prince's chair. She'd spilled it all as fast as she could into the Prince's ear, especially the part about Hoggett and the lunatic asylum. She'd startled Bertie right out of his royal complacency just as surely as if she had planted a thorn in his seat cushion. Public catatrophe could explode at any moment.

The interplay with Hoggett had been so subtle that only those very near to the Prince were aware of it. Hoggett left the Prince face to face with the man who had punched him senseless in the garden.

Cannonball number two, hissing though the air.

Althea bent close to the Prince again. She had heard that, underneath all the philandering, Bertie had a kindly, decent heart. Another rule in direst extremity was never gamble on sentiment.

"Your Highness," she murmured, "such a public misfortune for poor Henry Crisp!"

She continued to speak until finally, Bertie rose to his feet. Rose and Adam, suffered a moment of dreadful suspense. The Prince's look met Rose's in wry recognition of what could have been. Then, slowly, he nodded to Rose, nodded to Adam. Not congratulations exactly, but a sort of blessing. And a way to dissociate himself from the snickers that would afflict Henry Crisp as it became the joke of the Season how Henry had been jilted within an hour of becoming engaged, right in the midst of his own costume ball.

Behind the Prince, Althea sought Rose's attention and made tiny, urgent flicks with her ivory-handled fan. Get going while the getting is good, the fan said. Princes were notoriously fickle.

Adam and Rose bowed deeply to Bertie in a jumble of gratitude and disbelief amidst the excited ripple in the crowd.

"Let's go. Let's go now!" Rose whispered urgently,

Adam pivoted with Rose and strode toward one of the arched doorways. Only when they were through it did he suddenly remember how he had come to be in the ballroom in the first place.

"Good Christ, Mrs. Corman! I've left Mrs. Corman trapped with a...a madwoman. Come on!"

CHAPTER SIXTY-EIGHT

Hand in hand, Adam and Rose fled past the guests, past the staring footmen, away down the corridors to where Adam had abandoned Amelia.

Inside the blue salon, the scene exactly as Adam had left it. The thief, the woman Amelia claimed she knew, remained at bay behind the half emptied glass chest, her scarlet jacket stuffed to bulges, her cockaded hat upside down on the floor. Amelia stood rigidly between the chest and the door. The threat of a scream on Amelia's lips held Nell in her place, as dangerous as a hissing bomb. Rose and Adam hurtled in to break the frozen impass.

Amelia dropped her shoulders in relief.

"It's...it's Mrs. Fitzroy." She still could not grasp what she was seeing. "I just can't..."

Rose crashed into Adam's shoulder and stopped cold.

"Oh," she gasped, "...oh!"

Adam flung a protective arm around her. He'd abandoned Mrs. Corman with a brazen, violent thief.

"This woman was trying to steal the Refuge money." He realized he could now resort to the law. "We have to call..."

"No! You can't. She's...she's my mother!"

That startled everyone, most of all, Rose.

"It's true," Amelia put in after Adam's brows climbed his forehead. "She..she rescued Edwin and me when we were next to penniless on the street. She thought up the whole idea of...of coming to Crisp Court, gave us our building, hired that carriage that almost ran over you. I can't believe..." Amelia shook her head hard. "She's a respectable widow..."

"She's not! She's not!" burst out a stormy vehemence at her side. "She's Red Nell and she cheats everybody! And...and," Katie's voice scraped with anguish, "she's the one that made us starve, me and Mary!"

No one had dared move a muscle during the interminable standoff while Adam was gone. Amelia's nerves had become thin wires so she had been scarcely aware of Katie burrowing into her skirts. Now she dared glance down.

"Katie...you're soaked. Why aren't you in the kitchen helping?"

"They don't want us to help. Mr. Crisp sent us to an awful place by the river. We...ran away." Her finger jabbed at Red Nell. "She took our pennies. She's tricking you now. She makes everybody starve."

"Oh child, that can't be so," Amelia cried, recoiling from the name Teapot had flung at her as he wrecked the Refuge. "I've met her myself. She's a widow who..."

"She rides in an old brown cab and she grabs money from everybody. If you don't give it to her, she sends bullies. Everybody's scared of her, for streets and streets..."

Between hooking sobs, hardly understanding what she said, Katie spilled Nell's criminal empire into shocked, incredulous ears.

"And she was even taking money from old Jenksy, out of the money he was keeping for himself. M...Mary told me so!"

Nell remained unspeaking, crumpled banknotes sticking out of her jacket. She did not need to speak. Her forceful personality was seeping into every corner of the room, slowly gripping the others. She denied nothing. Luckily, she did not recognize in soot-streaked Katie the crazed imp that had bitten her in the market.

Rose and Amelia were most bewildered. Amelia could not square the eccentric but respectable Mrs. Fitzroy with the dishevelled gorgon before her. Rose's head swarmed dizzily with childhood fantasies about the duchess with a trumpeter and Jack's tales of finding her among the seaweed, singing in a foreign tongue. And of the woman, intimidating and iron-gripped, who had loomed up inside the gypsy wagon. Never could she have imagined anything such as this child was telling.

Katie's teeth chattered in spurts. She shivered against Amelia, leaving wet black smudges wherever she touched. The fury, fear and despair pouring out of her were almost palpable.

"But...why are you here, Mrs. Fitzroy," Amelia demanded, crazily civil despite the marks of Nell's fingers throbbing on her face. "Why are you stealing the money?"

"Yes, why?" Rose wanted to know. Of all of them, she was the one who saw how desperately Red Nell was a bay.

"To stay alive," Nell returned bluntly. "And to keep you alive. Teapot's overrun all me territory."

"Teapot?"

"Me mortal enemy, girl. He killed your da over a sack of rubbish, he killed your sister and her baby. For years he's been lyin' in wait, and now he's flattened me."

A tremor through Nell's jowls gave away her exhaustion, but the rest of her bulk did not budge. Rose felt her own eyes stretching.

"Father? Sister? Killed?"

Oddly, Rose hadn't the faintest doubt about Nell's words, only a sense of great boulders dropped into her universe, flinging her upside down in the backwash.

"Aye, certainly girl. Why d'ye think I sent ye all the way down to Cornwall. That little and helpless ye were that Teapot would've gulped ye up in a bite!"

Nell lifted both palms in a gesture of frustration, then dropped them to her sides again.

"Isn't it for you I've battered me way here tonight, to whisk ye away from Teapot's reach, for he'd get ye as surely as he got me darlin' Gwyn if I left ye on yer own. Tis only by accident I spotted this great pot of money that's givin' me a chance of gettin' back what I've lost."

Primal mother love stood naked under Nell's hooded lids. A scent came back to Rose, the earthy scent of peat which Rose had never paid attention to before. Ancient, foggy memories swam up and splashed to the surface of her mind. From before Cornwall. Memories of nestling in a warm, broad lap. Of two brothers teasing her, one of them holding out molasses treacle. Of someone singing a rhyme, dandling her before a window full of sun.

"We're going tonight, Adam and I, to Canada. We must. There's a ship leaving with the tide. This...Teapot can never get me."

Mother, she kept saying over and over again in her head, mother!

"Canada?" Nell scowled at Adam, all dark suspicion, a mother facing the kidnapper of her child. "And what are ye proposin' to do in such a wild place as that?"

"We'll have boats of our own, and run a trade all up and down the waters there. Why the country's a new as a queen's penny. We can't help but get on grandly. There are no Teapots there," Rose cried, grasping what a vast change of life she was flinging herself into.

Nell doubted that there were no Teapots, but at least there wouldn't be the one plaguing her in London. The mention of trade now, that was something else, something Nell and hers had always thrived at.

"It is a partner then, you're to be in all this trade along the waters?" Nell demanded, scrutinizing the pair.

"Of course," Rose and Adam said as one, then looked at each other in a tumbling astonishment. For the first time, the excitement of taking up an enterprise together touched them. There were oh so many possibilities, ahead.

Nell read Rose's resolution, saw there was no stopping this headlong flight. She'll be out of harm's way and on her own knock, Nell thought, and no hounds after her with knives in their belts. And certainly better than a tinker's life on rutted Irish tracks.

Nell said no more. A daughter out of harm's way left the road open for truly punishing run at Teapot.

If only she could get the cash!

CHAPTER SIXTY-NINE

Silence fell. Nell, bulging with bank notes, faced Amelia desperate to keep the money for the Refuge. Rose could not leave her mother in such straits.

"She...might die if she goes back into the streets without money. And," a dark blaze flashed in Rose's eyes, "somebody needs to avenge my sister and my father."

The ancient bonds of family gripped Rose as surely as if she had grown up in Red Nell's bosom. My sister! I had a sister, she thought in a rage of loss. How they could have sung together, laughed together. And how could a man walk free who had struck their father dead over a sack of rubbish!

She hungered to know so much that only this woman could tell her. Here was the answer to that gap inside her that all the Mabbins in Cornwall hadn't been able to fill. Here was the woman who had given her life and saved her life and sent her far away so she could grow up wild as a bird without a thought of lurking enemies.

Adam saw that he would not get Rose away even when Hoggett might burst in any minute because the Prince had changed his mind. He paced, then stopped abruptly in his tracks.

"Then she shall have the money. All of it, every last pound!"

Incredulous at his own idea, he laughed aloud. In what looked like a fit of lunatic extravagance, he grabbed up the remaining banknotes from the bottom of the chest and shoved them at Nell. Amelia emitted a high mewling sound.

"Don't worry, Mrs. Corman. Just watch."

Adam sprang over to his mother's rosewood writing desk and scrabbled around until he came up with sheets of paper and a pot of ink. He began to write as rapidly, pausing only to grin before scribbling even faster. He signed with a flourish, large and bold. With great ceremony, he handed the finished product to Amelia whose brows flew into a knot.

"But...it's a confession to stealing the money yourself," she got out, wondering which one of them had gone mad.

"Yes. And guaranteeing that Henry will make full restitution. Believe me, Henry will have the money replaced by noon tomorrow rather than have his brother known as a common thief, not to mention one who robs destitute orphans and charity ladies." he handed the finished product to Amelia whose brows flew into a knot.

"But...it's a confession to stealing the money yourself," she got out, wondering which one of them had gone mad.

"Yes. And guaranteeing that Henry will make full restitution. Believe me, Henry will have the money replaced by noon tomorrow rather than have his brother known as a common thief, not to mention one who robs destitute orphans and charity ladies."

Oh the pure ingenuity of it! It was one thing for a brother to vanish into a lunatic asylum with everyone supposing he had gone to overseas. It was quite another to have him publicly confessed as a wicked criminal, smearing everyone around with the same black brush. Adam chortled at holding Henry up for ransom.

"Read on. Finish the letter."

"It contains things about...a warehouse fire and a grab for railway land." Amelia looked up, baffled. "I don't understand."

"You don't have to. All you have to know is that Henry will cough up any amount to avoid the public scandal of a robber in the family and his own black schemes. It will work as long as you have the courage to use the letter, Mrs. Corman. You must hold onto it as surety for Henry's good conduct in the future."

Admiration flitted into Red Nell's beleaguered eyes. Awful foreboding about Rose taking up with this man receded. Perhaps, between the brains of the two of them, they'd kick up storms over in that distant Canada, so handily outside Teapot's reach.

"But..." Amelia still couldn't grapple with it.

"And you may leave with the money," Adam turned gravely to Nell who was clutching the lapels of her jacket together over the loot within, "on condition that Mrs. Corman and her Refuge are under your protection. For always. You don't skim her profits, she skims yours!"

Nell glowered fiercely but could crack no whips.

"You must give your solemn word, Mrs. Fitzroy. You must shake hands upon it with Mrs. Corman."

Nell fixed them both with eyes like ancient emeralds. It was a hard bargain, but not a bad one if it gave you back your life. She loosened one square palm from her lapel, spat upon it and advanced upon a horrified Amelia.

"Tis spit that seals a promise," Nell forcibly grasped Amelia's hand with her own. There might have been no charity for herself and her own tottering on the famine shores, but by the hairs on the devil's rump, charity was going to get her out of her trouble now.

Amelia clutched at the air and tried to pull away. Adam was beside her in two steps.

"Don't you see, Mrs Corman? That whole region is the one my brother and his friends are planning to rip apart with their railway syndicate. This raid in the neighbourhood that... ah, Mrs. Fitzroy is talking about smells to high heaven. I'd bet Pall Mall that somebody is making sure they're in the right spot when those properties start getting bought up for demolition."

"Demolition! Another railway cut! Oh no!"

Amelia forgot about the state of her right palm. She remembered the chaos from the last project, hundreds of living places pulled down, the alleys choked with poor thrust into the streets, the surrounding warrens crammed as the newly homeless clawed for some place to stay.

"And this lady," Adam indicated Nell with a flourish, "is probably the only one equipped to reverse the tide, providing she's properly financed to get back into the fray."

"Not with my money!"

"Yes, your money. You just shook on it. Besides, didn't I just guarantee that Henry will have it all replaced by tomorrow?"

Amelia still baulked at such open blackmail. Her arms dropped back around Katie huddled against her.

"Mrs. Fitzroy will...um, get all her businesses going again," Adam assured her, "and your cut will come in. Don't you see? Much surer than hanging upon the whims of the rich. If the Prince blinks the wrong way, you're finished. But with Mrs. Fitzroy, you and your Refuge will be safe for years."

A raffish grin appeared under Adam's moustache.

"I think Mrs. Fitzroy, from the look of her, can be trusted to put paid to the railway scheme. If Henry tries it, Mrs. Corman, I'm trusting you to threaten to make the letter public. You must be brave and face him down."

The letter, dangling from Amelia's fingers, turned into a ten pound weight as she began to understand that all this was serious and that it really would be up to her to face down Henry Crisp. She shuddered. Rose must have thrown Henry's engagement back in his face.

"Your brother will not back down easily."

"Oh I don't know. Henry might already be a bit of a bad smell to the railway investors now that's he's made a jilted laughingstock of himself in front of the Prince."

That was the best revenge, to leave Henry stewing in his own juices, bereft of dignity, bereft of Rose who was worth more than everything Henry had scavenged from Milton Crisp.

Yet outer darkness for Henry might include the rest of the family too.

Abruptly, Adam sobered.

"I want you always to maintain your links with my mother," he told Amelia. "If she works with you, she'll always have a worthwhile pursuit no matter what judgment society passes upon her. My mother and, pretty soon, my sister, Camille."

What an excited letter he'd had from Camille, the sister he hadn't seen since she was a bouncing little girl. A letter brimming all over with fervent, hair-raising radical ideals. Camille would be saved from the horrors of the squirming, clawing marriage mart out there. Camille would find herself a man all on her own, certainly one guaranteed to give their mother palpitations. They would be anchored in the stern purpose of Amelia Corman and the shrewd ferocity of this bizarre Irishwoman who was Rose's mother, as a closer look made clear. If the worst came to the worst, why let the lot of them come to Canada and to try their luck there.

Nell buttoned her military jacket firmly over the booty acquired at such cost. The proximity of money next to her body infused strength. She fixed Adam with all the concentrated force she could muster.

"And you, Adam Crisp, will keep yer part 'o the bargain by takin' fine care 'o me Rose off in that land 'o man eatin' beasts and mile thick ice yer settin' off to. I'll track ye down meself to see ye do!"

Adam's eyes said he would, giving his bond. His mouth was about to add a sworn oath only the salon door flew open, steps pattered inside and screeched to a halt. Althea Wharton was staring at them, here protruding eyes growing larger and larger.

"Rose, you're still here!"

Rose whipped around. Althea noticed the plundered chest and grasped a sideboard for support.

"Don't ask," Rose warned in a voice that would have done justice to her mother. "It'll all be back in the coffers tomorrow."

Althea didn't intend to ask. She had a more urgent mission.

"The wreath, where's that wreath you tossed into the chest. I came to get it back."

Rose had forgotten about the wreath and the necklace, which she feared was now somewhere deep in the money-stuffed bosom of her mother. Then she spotted the circlet on the floor behind a table leg where Nell, having no interest in flowers, had tossed it. Rose hurried to pick it up and hand it to Althea, whose fist closed round it with immense relief.

"Oh Althea, I'm...I'm sorry about...everything," Rose began to realize what ruin her action brought down upon Althea. In spite of events gone awry, she remembered all Althea's kindness, all the effort Althea had expended to make her a success. "I wish..."

"You wish things could have been different?" Althea supplied, with a shake of her side curls. "Well they already are. Look!"

From the pocket where she kept her flask, Althea drew out the key to the blue salon.

"The Prince made Hoggett give it to me. Now that I've recovered the necklace, I believe he's discovering my usefulness."

Only up close did Rose notice how large Althea's lemur eyes were, how the flesh under her chin quivered. Althea looked like a woman who had just been granted the Valnoor Rope herself instead of one about to wither in the blast.

"It was you who made the Prince dismiss Hoggett! It was you who let Adam and myself get away!"

"Strictly self interest, my dear, strictly self-interest," Althea lifted fingers against suspicion of nobler motives. "I had to do something."

"But why did the Prince allow us go? Why should he be kind like that?" After all the trouble that had gone into trapping her, Rose couldn't fathom why the door had suddenly been flung upon, why she and Adam had been set free.

Althea slipped the salon key back into her pocket where it clicked softly against the flask.

"Ah, Rose, you are still such an innocent. Kindness had nothing to do with it, or at least not too much." Althea had not missed Bertie's twitch of regret at the way Rose clutched Adam and defied the room like a young Amazon at bay. "It was because of tossing away the circlet, cause of Adam storming into the ballroom like a lumberjack, for goodness sakes. Neither of you could be trusted to obey the rules. The Prince cannot afford folks like you. In a word, dears," Althea twinkled at the pair, "you were turned loose because you cannot be tamed!"

Rose only knew they were free so long as they got themselves out of the Prince's sight as soon as possible. As Althea started to pluck the wreath away from the necklace, Rose rescued a single perfect rosebud and entwined it in the clasp in thanks for their escape. Nell saw what she had discarded and gaped.

Althea's face became more monkey-like than ever in its struggle of mixed emotions. She could feel the drama in the room as palpably as if she had interrupted swordplay in action. The filthy child, she supposed, was natural for Amelia, but that frightening woman with the purple-orange hair and bulging coat!

Reliable instincts warned Althea to leave well enough alone. Wasn't she ecstatic enough at being of use to the Prince now that Hoggett wasn't there? Hadn't a world of new possibilities just fallen into her lap?

"I couldn't marry Henry," Rose said. "Never!"

Althea looked wryly at the young woman, still enfolded in the leafy sheath of her ball dress.

"Not even to save Adam Crisp?"

Rose half opened her mouth but could not answer. Althea smiled with gentle mockery. They both knew she would have wedded Henry if she had to.

"Never mind, my dear. Alas, the folly of love is inevitable. Some cannot be saved. Come and give me hug."

Rose flew to Althea and embraced the small woman, all their skirmishes expressed in that single gesture. When they pulled apart, they were both damp-eyed. Too bad Rose had turned out to be a bird that would beat herself to death against the bars instead of enjoying the gilded life inside. Ah well, Bertie would very grateful for the return of the necklace. Bertie's gratitude would provide endless new fields to reap.

The cast bronze mantel clock began to chime.

"The ship!" Adam cried with urgency.

Their own life called out to them, compelling them away from old tangles just shucked off. Adam had done the best he could here, leaving Mrs. Corman with a weapon, leaving his mother and Camille to join that vast legion of women who inexorably, with gloved, determined hands, would change the fabric of society.

"Go quickly, my dears," Althea urged. "Even I can't vouch for your safety until everything cools down."

Rose grasped Adam's arm and looked at Amelia and Red Nell. There were a thousand things to say but she couldn't think of a single one of them. She hugged Amelia and then flitted over to Red Nell.

"Goodbye...Mother."

With a rush, she grasped Red Nell to her and inhaled the peat-smelling warmth that had surrounded her as a child.

"Win for us, Mother. Beat Teapot."

"That I will, girl, now that yer out of me way for the worryin'. Don't forget yer kin when yer over there in that barbarous place. Don't think you've seen the last of us yet!"

"Of that I have no doubt," Rose returned between a laugh and a sob.

And, with that, they were gone.

Edwin huffed up to Crisp Court very late, long after the royal carriage had departed and the last few guests were trailing out. The ball had only grown more lively due to the excitement infused by the drama of Rose's departure and because Bertie had wanted no one to imagine him other than a disinterested patron of charity. A pose best served, Althea had managed to suggest, by his staying until the regular departure time. The maharaja's necklace, stowed in a royal pocket, had gone a long way to restoring Bertie's composure. Louisa spent the intervening time simply concentrating on breathing in and breathing out. Henry, nerve broken by such open humiliation, had long ago fled the public scene.

Up the front stairs and through the last straggle of people Edwin rushed until he spotted Amelia. His suit was streaked with mud and bagged from physical effort. Exhaustion made him completely forget the niceties of the Crisp Court occasion.

"My dear, the children are housed at last though I had to go all the way over to Wand Lane. Three carters are hauling our furnishings and...oooff!"

The wind was knocked out of him by Amelia, who had dropped the wrap she was holding and flung herself into his arms.

"My goodness, what's this in aid of?" Edwin exclaimed in delighted astonishment.

Amelia buried her face in his neck where she could smell rain and wool and the inevitable soot of the street. Inexpressible comfort shot through her.

"You, my darling husband. Oh Edwin, you may drink all the champagne you wish just so long as you never let me forget my luck again!"

Oh the pure ingenuity of it! It was one thing for a brother to vanish into a lunatic asylum with everyone supposing he had gone to overseas. It was quite another to have him publicly confessed as a wicked criminal, smearing everyone around with the same black brush. Adam chortled at holding Henry up for ransom.

"Read on. Finish the letter."

"It contains things about...a warehouse fire and a grab for railway land." Amelia looked up, baffled. "I don't understand."

"You don't have to. All you have to know is that Henry will cough up any amount to avoid the public scandal of a robber in the family and his own black schemes. It will work as long as you have the courage to use the letter, Mrs. Corman. You must hold onto it as surety for Henry's good conduct in the future."

Admiration flitted into Red Nell's beleaguered eyes. Awful foreboding about Rose taking up with this man receded. Perhaps, between the brains of the two of them, they'd kick up storms over in that distant Canada, so handily outside Teapot's reach.

"But..." Amelia still couldn't grapple with it.

"And you may leave with the money," Adam turned gravely to Nell who was clutching the lapels of her jacket together over the loot within, "on condition that Mrs. Corman and her Refuge are under your protection. For always. You don't skim her profits, she skims yours!"

Nell glowered fiercely but could crack no whips.

"You must give your solemn word, Mrs. Fitzroy. You must shake hands upon it with Mrs. Corman."

Nell fixed them both with eyes like ancient emeralds. It was a hard bargain, but not a bad one if it gave you back your life. She loosened one square palm from her lapel, spat upon it and advanced upon a horrified Amelia.

"Tis spit that seals a promise," Nell forcibly grasped Amelia's hand with her own. There might have been no charity for herself and her own tottering on the famine shores, but by the hairs on the devil's rump, charity was going to get her out of her trouble now.

Amelia clutched at the air and tried to pull away. Adam was beside her in two steps.

"Don't you see, Mrs Corman? That whole region is the one my brother and his friends are planning to rip apart with their railway syndicate. This raid in the neighbourhood that... ah, Mrs. Fitzroy is talking about smells to high heaven. I'd bet Pall Mall that somebody is making sure they're in the right spot when those properties start getting bought up for demolition."

"Demolition! Another railway cut! Oh no!"

Amelia forgot about the state of her right palm. She remembered the chaos from the last project, hundreds of living places pulled down, the alleys choked with poor thrust into the streets, the surrounding warrens crammed as the newly homeless clawed for some place to stay.

"And this lady," Adam indicated Nell with a flourish, "is probably the only one equipped to reverse the tide, providing she's properly financed to get back into the fray."

"Not with my money!"

"Yes, your money. You just shook on it. Besides, didn't I just guarantee that Henry will have it all replaced by tomorrow?"

Amelia still baulked at such open blackmail. Her arms dropped back around Katie huddled against her.

"Mrs. Fitzroy will...um, get all her businesses going again," Adam assured her, "and your cut will come in. Don't you see? Much surer than hanging upon the whims of the rich. If the Prince blinks the wrong way, you're finished. But with Mrs. Fitzroy, you and your Refuge will be safe for years."

A raffish grin appeared under Adam's moustache.

"I think Mrs. Fitzroy, from the look of her, can be trusted to put paid to the railway scheme. If Henry tries it, Mrs. Corman, I'm trusting you to threaten to make the letter public. You must be brave and face him down."

The letter, dangling from Amelia's fingers, turned into a ten pound weight as she began to understand that all this was serious and that it really would be up to her to face down Henry Crisp. She shuddered. Rose must have thrown Henry's engagement back in his face.

"Your brother will not back down easily."

"Oh I don't know. Henry might already be a bit of a bad smell to the railway investors now that's he's made a jilted laughingstock of himself in front of the Prince."

That was the best revenge, to leave Henry stewing in his own juices, bereft of dignity, bereft of Rose who was worth more than everything Henry had scavenged from Milton Crisp.

Yet outer darkness for Henry might include the rest of the family too.

Abruptly, Adam sobered.

"I want you always to maintain your links with my mother," he told Amelia. "If she works with you, she'll always have a worthwhile pursuit no matter what judgment society passes upon her. My mother and, pretty soon, my sister, Camille."

What an excited letter he'd had from Camille, the sister he hadn't seen since she was a bouncing little girl. A letter brimming all over with fervent, hair-raising radical ideals. Camille would be saved from the horrors of the squirming, clawing marriage mart out there. Camille would find herself a man all on her own, certainly one guaranteed to give their mother palpitations. They would be anchored in the stern purpose of Amelia Corman and the shrewd ferocity of this bizarre Irishwoman who was Rose's mother, as a closer look made clear. If the worst came to the worst, why let the lot of them come to Canada and to try their luck there.

Nell buttoned her military jacket firmly over the booty acquired at such cost. The proximity of money next to her body infused strength. She fixed Adam with all the concentrated force she could muster.

"And you, Adam Crisp, will keep yer part 'o the bargain by takin' fine care 'o me Rose off in that land 'o man eatin' beasts and mile thick ice yer settin' off to. I'll track ye down meself to see ye do!"

Adam's eyes said he would, giving his bond. His mouth was about to add a sworn oath only the salon door flew open, steps pattered inside and screeched to a halt. Althea Wharton was staring at them, here protruding eyes growing larger and larger.

"Rose, you're still here!"

Rose whipped around. Althea noticed the plundered chest and grasped a sideboard for support.

"Don't ask," Rose warned in a voice that would have done justice to her mother. "It'll all be back in the coffers tomorrow."

Althea didn't intend to ask. She had a more urgent mission.

"The wreath, where's that wreath you tossed into the chest. I came to get it back."

Rose had forgotten about the wreath and the necklace, which she feared was now somewhere deep in the money-stuffed bosom of her mother. Then she spotted the circlet on the floor behind a table leg where Nell, having no interest in flowers, had tossed it.

Rose hurried to pick it up and hand it to Althea, whose fist closed round it with immense relief.

"Oh Althea, I'm...I'm sorry about...everything," Rose began to realize what ruin her action brought down upon Althea. In spite of events gone awry, she remembered all Althea's kindness, all the effort Althea had expended to make her a success. "I wish..."

"You wish things could have been different?" Althea supplied, with a shake of her side curls. "Well they already are. Look!"

From the pocket where she kept her flask, Althea drew out the key to the blue salon.

"The Prince made Hoggett give it to me. Now that I've recovered the necklace, I believe he's discovering my usefulness."

Only up close did Rose notice how large Althea's lemur eyes were, how the flesh under her chin quivered. Althea looked like a woman who had just been granted the Valnoor Rope herself instead of one about to wither in the blast.

"It was you who made the Prince dismiss Hoggett! It was you who let Adam and myself get away!"

"Strictly self interest, my dear, strictly self-interest," Althea lifted fingers against suspicion of nobler motives. "I had to do something."

"But why did the Prince allow us go? Why should he be kind like that?" After all the trouble that had gone into trapping her, Rose couldn't fathom why the door had suddenly been flung upon, why she and Adam had been set free.

Althea slipped the salon key back into her pocket where it clicked softly against the flask.

"Ah, Rose, you are still such an innocent. Kindness had nothing to do with it, or at least not too much." Althea had not missed Bertie's twitch of regret at the way Rose clutched Adam and defied the room like a young Amazon at bay. "It was because of tossing away the circlet, because of Adam storming into the ballroom like a lumberjack, for goodness sakes. Neither of you could be trusted to obey the rules. The Prince cannot afford folks like you. In a word, dears," Althea twinkled at the pair, "you were turned loose because you cannot be tamed!"

Rose only knew they were free so long as they got themselves out of the Prince's sight as soon as possible. As Althea started to pluck the wreath away from the necklace, Rose rescued a single perfect rosebud and entwined it in the clasp in thanks for their escape. Nell saw what she had discarded and gaped.

Althea's face became more monkey-like than ever in its struggle of mixed emotions. She could feel the drama in the room as palpably as if she had interrupted swordplay in action. The filthy child, she supposed, was natural for Amelia, but that frightening woman with the purple-orange hair and bulging coat!

Reliable instincts warned Althea to leave well enough alone. Wasn't she ecstatic enough at being of use to the Prince now that Hoggett wasn't there? Hadn't a world of new possibilities just fallen into her lap?

"I couldn't marry Henry," Rose said. "Never!"

Althea looked wryly at the young woman, still enfolded in the leafy sheath of her ball dress.

"Not even to save Adam Crisp?"

Rose half opened her mouth but could not answer. Althea smiled with gentle mockery. They both knew she would have wedded Henry if she had to.

"Never mind, my dear. Alas, the folly of love is inevitable. Some cannot be saved. Come and give me hug."

Rose flew to Althea and embraced the small woman, all their skirmishes expressed in that single gesture. When they pulled apart, they were both damp-eyed. Too bad Rose had turned out to be a bird that would beat herself to death against the bars instead of enjoying the gilded life inside. Ah well, Bertie would very grateful for the return of the necklace. Bertie's gratitude would provide endless new fields to reap.

The cast bronze mantel clock began to chime.

"The ship!" Adam cried with urgency.

Their own life called out to them, compelling them away from old tangles just shucked off. Adam had done the best he could here, leaving Mrs. Corman with a weapon, leaving his mother and Camille to join that vast legion of women who inexorably, with gloved, determined hands, would change the fabric of society.

"Go quickly, my dears," Althea urged. "Even I can't vouch for your safety until everything cools down."

Rose grasped Adam's arm and looked at Amelia and Red Nell. There were a thousand things to say but she couldn't think of a single one of them. She hugged Amelia and then flitted over to Red Nell.

"Goodbye...Mother."

With a rush, she grasped Red Nell to her and inhaled the peat-smelling warmth that had surrounded her as a child.

"Win for us, Mother. Beat Teapot."

"That I will, girl, now that yer out of me way for the worryin'. Don't forget yer kin when yer over there in that barbarous place. Don't think you've seen the last of us yet!"

"Of that I have no doubt," Rose returned between a laugh and a sob.

And, with that, they were gone.

Edwin huffed up to Crisp Court very late, long after the royal carriage had departed and the last few guests were trailing out. The ball had only grown more lively due to the excitement infused by the drama of Rose's departure and because Bertie had wanted no one to imagine him other than a disinterested patron of charity. A pose best served, Althea had managed to suggest, by his staying until the regular departure time. The maharaja's necklace, stowed in a royal pocket, had gone a long way to restoring Bertie's composure. Louisa spent the intervening time simply concentrating on breathing in and breathing out. Henry, nerve broken by such open humiliation, had long ago fled the public scene.

Up the front stairs and through the last straggle of people Edwin rushed until he spotted Amelia. His suit was streaked with mud and bagged from physical effort. Exhaustion made him completely forget the niceties of the Crisp Court occasion.

"My dear, the children are housed at last though I had to go all the way over to Wand Lane. Three carters are hauling our furnishings and...ooooff!"

The wind was knocked out of him by Amelia, who had dropped the wrap she was holding and flung herself into his arms.

"My goodness, what's this in aid of?" Edwin exclaimed in delighted astonishment.

Amelia buried her face in his neck where she could smell rain and wool and the inevitable soot of the street. Inexpressible comfort shot through her.

"You, my darling husband. Oh Edwin, you may drink all the champagne you wish just so long as you never let me forget my luck again!"

CHAPTER SEVENTY

Canada! I'm going to Canada today!

The burnished promise, hoarded to Katie's bosom since waking in the hospital in Mrs. Corman's arms, was coming to pass. Her heart stuttered madly against her ribs as she marched to join the rows of other children walking toward the Mersey. Laura trudged on one side of her. Cully, dear Cully, hopped along at the other. Cully's slot of a mouth and scrubbed face bore an optimistic grin, regained the moment Mrs. Corman had scooped them up from behind the garden wall. Cully had no conception of Canada nor did she care. She would have boarded a dragon's back for moon so long as she was with her two friends on their journey.

Sunshine poured prodigally down on all of England that fine day. Even here, among the busy docks of Liverpool, scrubby trees sprang up at the sides of buildings and green grass fought up between the paving stones. An impudent wind carried a stirring scent to Katie, the sharp salt tang of the sea.

Mrs. Corman hurried behind, worrying about trunks and berths and whether they had eaten enough on the train. Only when she saw the grey shape of the ship lying up against the wharf, gangplanks leading into its bowels, did practical concerns flee her brain.

"This is it," she told Katie and the others. "This is what we've been working so hard for. And now...you are going as my first emigration party off to Canada!"

Mrs. Corman had been so happy about organizing them that Katie couldn't understand why tears were now springing into her idol's eyes.

"Oh, I wish Mr. Corman were here," she told them passionately. "He would be so proud of all of you. But someone had look after the Refuge while we see you onto the ship."

After Mrs. Corman had got over the surprise of finding not only Katie at Crisp Court, but Cully, Laura and Will huddling outside, she had gathered them up. Within a week, they all moved back into the Refuge building the children had found boarded up that fateful evening. And there seemed to be money for meals and clothes and getting this emigration party together much sooner than Mrs. Corman ever expected.

Now Katie found Mrs. Corman looking at her queerly, almost as though she didn't want to part with her into the vast unknown. Though still so thin as to be almost transparent, Katie was now transparent in such a luminous way that Mrs. Corman almost swore light shone right out of her. Pink touched Katie's pale cheeks and the wiry spring was tentatively back in her step. Bony as the child was, Mrs. Corman felt confident about sending her, sure she would do well.

How Katie has clung, grubby paws buried deep in Mrs. Corman's skirt as if she never meant to let go. Katie would not bear any truce with Red Nell. The mention of the woman evoked a desolate, sobbing wail.

"M..Mary's....Mary's killed because of her. Mary's dead!"

That's all it had taken, those dread words. The seams that had been splitting inside Katie, the plastered tomb she had been frantically trying to hold together in the cellar under the warehouse, had broken apart, the awful thing welling up and up...the awful thing...

"What so you mean, Mary's killed," Mrs. Corman had demanded in consternation. "Tell me."

Into Mrs. Corman's horrified ears, Katie spilled the whole, fearful story, the cold, the hunger and finally the horror under the stairs by the river. Curled into a fetal ball in Mrs. Corman's lap, barely audible, Katie had told of the last night, and the morning when Katie had stoned the rat from Mary's icy body. The dreadful, tearing sounds out of Katie's throat turned had into sobs and the sobs pounded themselves into silence. Katie had lain so limply in Mrs. Corman's arms that Amelia had been afraid that the very spirit might have leaked out of the child along with the tale.

At the story of the rough clothes factory and why they had all run away, Mrs. Corman frowned darkly.

"They didn"t tell me they sent you away, dear," Mrs. Corman said. "I would never leave you in such a place." With a grim look, she added, "Mr. Henry Crisp is going to make it up to the Refuge many times over. I promise."

With the black, vile poison at last purged, Katie had slept two nights and a day. When she woke, it had been with pale face, thin limbs and an emptiness in her ready to be filled up again with life. The crushing responsibility she had been carrying for Mary's death, for the banishment to the factory, for the abduction, for the near drowning of Cully rolled from her shoulders. Healing flowed back in. Once again, her hair sprang red and bushy, once again her eyes began to gleam like the first new shoots of spring. Filled with hops and anticipation, she was healthy enough to go to Canada.

Passage to a hope-filled new world begins.

Now they would join children drawn from different emigration homes, each with her name pinned to her shoulder and each furnished with a small tin trunk containing all her worldly possessions. The train ride to Liverpool had been exciting, but now the ship loomed up beside the dock. A sudden apprehension gripped Katie. They actually were going away. The parting was real!

Katie had only begun to digest this impact when a line of boys drew up beside her. She spotted a thatch of tow hair and everything else vanished in a whoop of joy.

"Will! Will! You're coming too, just like Mrs. Corman promised."

"That I am. Oh, but it's good to see you, Katie." Will lit from his top to his boots and grasped her hands. "Don't you look grand."

"You look grand yourself, Will. What a smashing suit."

She had nothing but admiration for the outfit of rough, cheap wool that was nevertheless without holes and, miracle of miracles, actually fitted. It was the first time she had ever seen Will so clean. Big-jointed and sturdy, he too had the spark of health.

Katie dashed back to Laura.

"Will's really coming too, just like Mrs. Corman said. Oh, I'm so glad!

Laura remembered Will's hand pushing her up that black, precipitous chimney and how he had led them along the roof peak as though it were a grassy path. Once she would have thought Will awkward and common. Now she didn't care. He was brave as Sir Ranald and Lady Joan and he would have stood firm beside Sir Geoffrey at Stanway Bridge no matter how many pikemen tried to batter through.

Yet...his grin was only for Katie.

A pang stabbed Laura that her dearest friend should have another friend who could so fill her with delight. Laura felt horribly alone. A funereal beat flooded her mind.

I am going away from Atworth House. When will I ever see it again?

As though it stood before her, Laura saw again the time-kissed Tudor brick, heard the whisper of the lime trees, the cry of the nesting rooks, the playful thunder of the foals galloping up to their knees in wildflowers. Gran squeezed her hand...

Laura gulped the melancholy back. In truth, she could not conceive of the distance to Canada any more than Katie could, though her lessons let her tell Katie about the prairies and the buffalo as they sometimes lay awake. Laura had grown alarmed to see how seriously Katie drank up every word.

"Katie, it's wild there. And big. They don't have houses for miles and miles and miles. We might have to live in tepees and melt snow for our tea."

"I don't mind," exclaimed Katie who ate, slept, breathed the dream, fully expecting Canada to change her into an entirely different girl altogether.

The line shuffled out onto the dock proper. They'd already been examined by a doctor who'd mostly looked down their throats and winked them past. Now a tall, brisk woman in a cloak appeared, patrolling the milling group, one of the ladies going with them on the boat.

"Come along girls, up the gangplank. Don't keep everybody waiting."

Laura's face was white and rigid. The gangplank over the strip of water between the ship and the dock might have been over a bottomless void. The few steps across it were steps into some other life. Gran, Gran, she wailed inside as tears began to seep from the corners of her eyes.

Mrs. Corman stopped at this last inch of England and gathered the children around her. All the noble admonitions fixed in her mind quite fled. She could not tell them to behave, or say their prayers or any of the other useless things grownups said to children upon parting. All around were wrenching scenes as other passengers, many also emigrating, were torn from relatives, never to return.

For a frantic moment, Amelia wanted to keep them all with her. Where are they going, she asked herself in a panic, as if she had never thought of it before. What am I sending them to? How can I be doing such a thing!

Her face quivered under a tidal wave of doubt at the sight of the ship and of the broad water washing beyond. Bravely, all Mrs. Corman was able to say was, "Goodbye, my darlings, goodbye, goodbye," as she hugged Katie the hardest.

She stood watching as they trundled up the gangplank, a row of diminutive figures vanishing into the ship's maw. Sailors moved about the decks. The gangplanks were drawn back, the big ship nudged away from the dock and set its nose down the Mersey. The children had been allowed out on deck to see the departure. Nearly all the passengers crowded to the stern, watching the bricken mass of Liverpool recede, scanning the dock where a mother or sister might be waving.

Katie wasn't among them. Almost by herself, she stood away up in the bow. She cared not at all for the old world dropping away behind her. She was straining her eyes far up ahead, trying to look out to sea, fully expecting to see Canada lying on the horizon, beckoning her home.

Aye, lass, Mary's voice whispered softly into her ear, *tis yer day to feel like a lark, to hop right up from t'heather and fly yerself!*

The End

Want to know how much scandalous trouble Katie gets into battling to come of age on a hardscrabble Canadian farm?

Here's a Sneak Peek at Katie's Ongoing Story

In

The Accidental Bootlegger

Chapter One

The day Katie's world started to crumble dawned hot as August. Too hot for September when autumn was trying to give notice. Leaves drooped. Dry roadside grass only stirred when Katie sped by, driving the aged buckboard as fast as it would stand, swirling pale dust behind.

Lean and wiry as a young hawk, Katie perched on a seat permanently sagged from the weight of the Motts for both Mildred and Grover Mott resembled squat barrels of pork. Since Katie was alone today, the seat swayed happily on its springs and the rangy sorrel between the shafts tried to turn her raking trot into a jolly canter just for the fun.

"Buckshot, no!"

Katie eased her up in time for the hill down to the village and the battle at the bridge.

A great wooden flour mill reared up beside the creek that plunged on down over the limestone escarpment. This rush of water was the reason the village founder, Guillaume Demorest, hot-footing it away from the American rebellion after carrying provisions to the British, buried his axe in the nearest oak and declared, "Here will I settle."

The first thing he did was build a mill. Now a successor provided a wooden bridge over the foaming stream that fed the water wheel.

The water hissed, the planks echoed and groaned. Buckshot either baulked stubbornly or shot across with a clatter that put the green frights into anyone who didn't know she would halt halfway down the village street.

Today, her burst of speed took the buckboard flying past the turn down to the Marsh Front, the village well and the hotel with Katie crying "Whoa", and hauling on the reins with all her might. Buckshot ignored the sawing bit, bent on bolting, it seemed, straight through into Coolidge's hop field on the other side.

The village street was deserted save for some dogs too hot to bark and the startling sight of a large piebald saddle horse in front of Bulford's general store. A man in black was tacking something to the outside notice board. Rattling wheels and Katie's exasperation caused him to whip around.

Wolf-quick, he shot into the street, grabbed Buckshot by the head and dragged her to a halt. Buckshot half reared and gave up the caper. A moment later, she stood docilely in her accustomed place before Bulford's.

"Nearly got away on you, didn't she, Miss."

Katie exhaled sharply.

"Oh, she was showing off. Never goes past here."

"Could have fooled me. Is this where you're stopping?"

Nodding, Katie started to climb down and found herself lifted lightly to the ground.

Unused to gallantry from any direction, she muttered a surprised thanks.

"You're welcome."

He lifted his broad-brimmed hat with a flourish that made Katie wonder if he was laughing at her.

As a British home girl, a charity child placed with the Motts since age ten to earn her keep, Katie had known her share of that. Now, at seventeen, she could spot and squelch a sideways remark almost before it fell off a speaker's tongue.

Perhaps the flash in Katie's eye quelled any move to introduce himself. Instead, the fellow's scrutiny sharpened, taking her in from listing straw hat to the hem of her sun-faded cotton dress and scarred boots sticking out underneath.

Katie assessed him back with a wariness picked up long ago in the warrens of East End London where she had begun her days.

The fellow wore a sharply cut suit complete with snowy shirt, black string tie, which no local man would possess, tall boots and a jaunty angle to his hat. At once, Katie suspected recklessness about him, an impression only strengthened by the fellow's sweeping moustache and pointed beard of the sort sported by stage villains and traveling hypnotists. A thin forked scar threaded one cheek, His nose looked as though it had seen a fight or two. The tooled saddle on the showy horse put him even more out of place.

From his drawl, he was likely an American.

Katie stopped staring when the man's grin came back. He gave Buckshot an approving slap on the neck and returned to tacking up his notice.

What's more, he hadn't said, "That animal is going kill somebody some day," as about everyone else in the village had managed to declare.

Buckshot, in her younger days, had been a notorious road horse. That is, she could out-trot any challenger when buggy drew alongside buggy on the way to church or town. Trouble was, Buckshot developed a taste for competition and an iron mouth no bit could hold until she was satisfied she had won. After his third dump in the ditch and the wreck of a nearly new buggy, Buckshot's furious owner swore he would either shoot the devilish beast or give her to the first fool idiot who came along.

That is how placid Grover Mott acquired, at very little cost, a mare that could eat up miles and do all sorts of jobs around the farm so long as one dodged the tricks she pulled when backs were turned. Katie got on with Buckshot so well that Grover allowed her to drive the horse out alone whenever needed.

Hot sun on Katie's shoulders reminded her why she had been rushing. She hurried to the back of the buckboard and started lifting down crates carefully packed with straw. They contained eggs and butter from the Mott farm and needed to be shifted to the cool of Bulford's cellar as quickly as possible.

Behind her, she heard the man finish with his poster. She turned to see him swing onto the back of his mount, which was being regarded with much suspicion by Buckshot. With a final lift of his hat, he suddenly winked at Katie, grinning as he left her with her mouth open and ambled off in the direction of town.

Well!

Katie grabbed up the butter crate. Money was scarce. Butter, eggs and all sorts of other farm stuffs were the currency here between farmers and storekeepers, traded for store goods or ticked off against credit owed.

The Mott hens had been busy as had Katie and Mildred Mott at the butter churn. Mildred hated hauling her bulk from the farm when she could help it. She gladly handed to Katie the job of getting the best she could for their labours from close-dealing Levi Bulford.

Katie's mouth set, her eyes began to snap. Even her red hair, the densely curly sort that required a tussle to subdue, seemed to glow brighter as flyaway wisps caught the light.

Her face, dashed with freckles from the sun, could not be called pretty. Rather it was keenly boned and most arresting when her green eyes were roused. Her straight, firm mouth looked capable of sudden humour but also a stubborn line. Nor had she ever lost the watchfulness acquired from a childhood most villagers could not imagine. A watchfulness that led to Mrs. Bulford's not entirely groundless opinion that the Mott's home girl was far too sharp for her own good. To Katie's annoyance, she knew Mrs. Bulford, president of the Ladies Aid, still kept a jaundiced eye on her whenever the woman tended the store.

Katie had passed other establishments on the way to Bulford's which she knew to be friendlier and likely more generous. But the Motts patronized Bulford's. In villages such as this, ties to a general store, once an account was opened, were as fixed as a plighted troth.

Pushing open the door, which set the bell tinkling, Katie, lugged in first one crate then the second. As she did so, a skinny young man strolled from the back of the store and stood behind the counter, watching but not helping.

Under her breath, Katie uttered an unladylike cuss.

She had expected to deal with the gaunt, lugubrious Levi Bulford or his oldest son, Bram, who was pretty well a copy of his father except that his Adam's apple hadn't yet achieved the heroic proportions of his pa's.

Instead here stood Newton, the younger son.

Katie's particular nemesis.

Unlike his towering brother and father, Newt was slight, ferret-nosed, and animated by a fidgety energy that sent his spying gaze here, there and everywhere. At school, he had been unable to sit still no matter how vigorously the strap was applied.

Seated in front of him in that same schoolhouse, for the brief time she had attended, Katie had suffered much from Newt's irrepressible inability to leave anything alone. Besides never letting her forget she was a charity girl, Newt was deadly with spitballs, put snakes in her desk, caterpillars in her hair, earthworms down her neck. The last straw was when Newt had got at a loose thread in the warm wool top Mildred had knitted. He pulled it with such stealth, Katie didn't notice until the back was unraveled, her thin chemise and bare, knobby spine exposed and the schoolroom rocking with smothered laughter.

The fight that broke out had been epic with bloodied noses, ripped sleeves and spectacular purple strap welts after the two had been broken up and punished.

Katie still suffered an instant neck-wringing urge whenever Newt came in sight...

Find out what happens next!
Get your copy of
The Accidental Bootlegger
Amazon.com or other booksellers

Visit the author's website:

gailhamiltonwriter.com

Follow Gail on X (formerly Twitter)

https://x.com/GHamilton9

Follow Katie on X (formerly Twitter)

https://x.com/KatieMucker

Follow Gail on Instagram

https://www.instagram.com/gailhamiltonwriter/

Post a Review

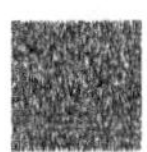

Please support the author by posting a review of this book on amazon.com, amazon.ca and elsewhere. Reviews not only help this book but all books and all authors by encouraging reading and describing enjoyment in the many diverse stories waiting to transport folks to fascinating other worlds.

Your participation is much appreciated.

ABOUT THE AUTHOR

Gail went straight from the farm to the University of Toronto, an expedition to Timbuctu and a varied career of teaching, copywriting, short stories and adaptation of the popular Road to Avonlea TV series for HarperCollins. A member of The Writer's Union of Canada she had great fun writing high-spirited romance novels for Harlequin and other publishers. Fascination with history's little known tales led to the **Tomorrow Country** and its action-packed sequel, **The Accidental Bootlegger**. Gail is now back in rural Ontario overlooking a pasture full of opinionated cattle and wild cranes nesting in her pond.